Introduction

An Unexpected Surprise by Rosey Dow
Angie McDonald has placed an ad for a mail-order bride—for her widowed brother-in-law and his motherless daughter. But when the beautiful Saundra arrives, Angie wonders if she's made a mistake and woven a very tangled web. When will Angie learn to leave matters in the hands of God?

Ribbon of Gold by Cathy Marie Hake
Carter Steadman tours the lucrative cotton mill he just inherited. Appalled by the intolerable working conditions, he resolves to institute sweeping changes. He meets a gentle-hearted weaver whose generosity to orphans humbles him. For Carter, it's love at first sight. For Isabel, it's impossible. Socially and spiritually, they are worlds apart. Can they both open their hearts and minds to God's will?

Light Beckons the Dawn by Susannah Hayden
Percy Morgan has hidden her past and stifled her future with a gruff exterior and immersed herself in work at a remote lumber camp. Faced with friendships offered by the few women in camp and the attentions of the camp doctor, Percy must decide if she can take a risk and reopen the pain of the past so that healing can begin.

The Reluctant Schoolmarm by Yvonne Lehman
When Christa Walsh steps off a train in the backwoods of North Carolina's Blue Ridge Mountains and reluctantly into the role of teacher, she finds the job more rewarding than she expected, winning the hearts of the children—and along the way, warming the heart of the man whose deception landed her the position.

School Bells and Wedding Bells by Colleen L. Reece
Freshly jilted and ready to take on the world, Meredith Rose Macrae enters an isolated Idaho hamlet with the force of a tornado. Neither she nor the town of Last Chance will ever be the same. And Brit Farley, rugged head of the local school board, faces the challenge of exchanging the new teacher's school bells for wedding bells.

Rose Kelly by Janet Spaeth
Rose believes a woman can do any job just as well as a man. But moving to Dakota Territory for six months to write articles on the homesteaders, she suddenly realizes that she may have taken on more than she can handle when trampling upon Eric Johansen's private past.

6 Historical Stories of Love that Takes Persuasion

The Reluctant BRIDES COLLECTION

Rosey Dow, Cathy Marie Hake,

Susannah Hayden, Yvonne Lehman, Colleen L. Reece, Janet Spaeth

BARBOUR BOOKS
An Imprint of Barbour Publishing, Inc.

Published by Barbour Books, an imprint of Barbour Publishing, Inc., 1810 Barbour Drive,
Uhrichsville, Ohio 44683, www.barbourbooks.com

Our mission is to inspire the world with the life-changing message of the Bible.

 Member of the
Evangelical Christian
Publishers Association

Printed in the United States of America.

AN
UNEXPECTED
SURPRISE

by Rosey Dow

Chapter 1

Long and low, the sound of the train's whistle reached the depot well ahead of Engine 826. Angie McDonald shaded her eyes against the glare of sun on snow to peer across the South Dakota prairie. The winter of 1872 promised to be a cold one, though it was still a month away.

"There it is!" twelve-year-old Judy Phillips cried, pointing at a growing black plume parallel to the horizon.

"Calm down," Angie told her blond niece, who was bouncing beside her under the eaves of the station house. "It'll be ten minutes before she gets here."

Judy stared at the tintype photograph in her gloved hand. Her head came just above Angie's shoulder. "I hope she's as nice as she looks in her picture." She rose up on her toes, anxiously watching her aunt's face. "What if she's mean? What if we don't like her? What if she doesn't like Papa?"

Angie pushed several strands of dark hair from her cheeks back under her bonnet. She put an arm around Judy and gave a gentle squeeze. "If things don't work out, we'll send dear Mrs. Dryden on her way."

"But what if Papa likes her, and we don't? I'm so scared." She tilted her freckled face toward the sky and squeezed her eyes shut. "Why did we do this?"

Angie gave the child a little shake. "Because we're desperate, that's why. Don't go weak-kneed on me now. We've been planning this for months. We've got to see it through."

"What if she talks to Papa about the love letters she thinks he wrote her?"

"She won't. Not if we handle it right."

Sparks flying, the iron horse screeched to a halt next to the tiny clapboard station. Angie and her charge stepped away from the building, shivering inside their wool coats and shawls—partly from the piercing breeze and partly from sheer nervousness. It was one thing to devise a scheme and quite another to meet it at the station.

The anxious pair watched five people step down to the platform before they spotted their guest. Saundra Dryden looked just like her picture. A blond, buxom German immigrant in black cape and bonnet, she stood two inches taller than Judy. Her clothes were not expensive; yet she had an elegance about her that was hard to define.

The woman turned expectantly when Angie said, "Mrs. Dryden? We're from the Flying P ranch. Lane had some things to do so we came to meet you. I'm Angie McDonald, Lane's sister-in-law, and this is his daughter, Judy."

Mrs. Dryden's right cheek dimpled when she smiled. "How nice to meet you!" She spoke clearly, but her words held the German dip and sway. She leaned toward the girl. "I've heard so much about you from your father's letters. You're more charming than I imagined." She gazed toward the end of the train. "I have two trunks."

7

"Give me your tickets." Angie held out her hand. "I'll have a porter bring them to our buggy. Judy, show Mrs. Dryden where the buggy is. I'll meet you there."

"Please call me Saundra." She beamed at the child. "You can tell me all about the ranch while we're waiting. I have never been on a real ranch before."

Angie hustled toward the baggage car. Who would have dreamed that she'd stoop to finding a mail-order bride for her backward brother-in-law? But what else could she do? She couldn't stay around the Flying P until she had gray hair and wrinkles.

She twisted the gold signet ring on her left hand, her engagement ring until Barry could afford a better one. She deserved a life of her own, didn't she? If she waited for Lane to find a replacement housekeeper, she'd be standing at the altar smelling of liniment instead of lavender.

A tiny thread of conscience skimmed across her thoughts. Maybe she should have waited for God to answer her prayers instead of rushing ahead with a scheme.

She shoved the thought to the back of her mind. She had waited two months. That was long enough. Besides, Christmas had become a dreaded chore since Lane's wife, Charlotte, died three years ago. Maybe Saundra would bring some light into the holidays this year.

Saundra's trunks thunked into the back of the box-shaped buggy under the muscle power of two teenage boys. Standing nearby, Angie heard Judy chattering about the stand of timber that Lane was harvesting this winter on his new quarter-section grant. He was hoping to pay off the bank loan on the ranch with what he would make on that timber.

Angie swung inside and picked up the reins. "Get up, Sheba...Dan." Impatient to be out of the biting cold, the gray and the black lurched ahead. Sheba was Angie's mare and trained to both the carriage and saddle, though she rarely rode her anymore.

Five miles to the south lay the Flying P. At the edge of town, the road stretched straight ahead of them, parallel ruts in a field of white. Last week's snow lay in drifted mounds for miles in every direction.

"What's he like, your father?" Saundra asked Judy, her blue eyes dancing. "He never described himself in his letters."

Angie answered first. "He's six feet three, with wide shoulders and long legs."

"He has dark hair and light blue eyes," Judy added.

"He's also terribly shy." Angie glanced at the newcomer. "If I were you, Saundra, I wouldn't mention his letters. He can be very eloquent when he's putting thoughts on paper, but in person he's painfully shy. You'll have to draw him out."

"The silent cowboy type?" Saundra nodded. "I have read about them."

"That's right," Judy said, sending Angie a wide-eyed look, "the strong, silent type."

"Tell us about yourself, Saundra," Angie said, as if she didn't already know the woman's statistics by heart.

"While I was growing up, my father was a theology professor in Heidelberg. My mother died two months before I turned eighteen, so when my father got an offer for a position at Harvard, we came to America. There was nothing to keep us in Germany any longer."

"You speak wonderful English," Angie said.

"My father made me practice until I wanted to scream." She smiled at Judy. "That's the way with fathers, no?"

"Yes!" Judy giggled.

Angie swallowed a smile. So far, so good.

"When my father died four years ago, I married Joseph Dryden. He owned a hotel. I cooked for the guests and managed the cleaning service for him.

"Joseph had a heart attack last year. The staff problems and those mountains of paperwork were too much for me. I sold the hotel with the understanding that I could keep my job as manager."

Her shoulders lifted. So did her shapely eyebrows. "But the new owner was impossible to please. The past six months have been nothing but misery for me. Your father's advertisement came at just the right time."

Beneath a sky full of wispy clouds, the thirty-year-old ranch house appeared on the horizon, a small two-story structure with a wide front porch and massive chimneys on each end. The house was twice as wide as it was deep. Rough lumber stained with dark oil covered the outer walls. The window frames and doors had last felt paint bristles five years ago. The white paint had chipped and peeled, but much of it remained to brave another harsh South Dakota winter.

The windows gleamed in the sunlight. Churned-up snow covered the yard with bits of brown grass poking through here and there. A shaggy collie barked a greeting.

"Quiet, Tip!" Angie called, pulling the horses to a halt near the back porch. She turned to Saundra. "Lane is working in the woods. He'll be home for supper."

"Good! I'll have time to comb my hair and press a clean dress." Lifting her skirts, she stepped daintily to the ground. Tip came around to sniff the stranger. Saundra tried to pat him, but he shied away.

"Tip doesn't like anyone to touch him," Judy told her. "He's a cattle dog."

Saundra bent to talk to the watchful animal. "We shall be great friends. You'll see."

Tip sat down and lifted his nose.

Angie hopped out and opened the buggy's back door. "Saundra, could you unpack some things out here to lighten the trunks? Then Judy and I could lift them."

"Why don't I take out what I need and wait for a man's strong arms to do the rest?"

"That's a great idea," Angie said, smiling. "Need a hand?"

Saundra produced some keys and reached for the closest piece of humpbacked luggage. "I'll be fine. I only want a dress and my hairbrush."

Leaving Judy to keep Saundra company, Angie walked across the porch and stepped inside the house to check the beans she had left simmering on the potbelly stove in the living room. In winter the potbelly served for both heating and cooking when she had to go out, because the kitchen range would go stone-cold with no one to feed it every few minutes.

The smoky scent of salted pork met her the moment she opened the door. Crossing the narrow kitchen to the wood box, she carried two split pieces down the hall and into the living room where the cast-iron pot bubbled. Grabbing a thick pad kept there for the purpose, she clanked open the door of the potbelly stove and shoved the logs inside, brushing bits of bark from her coat afterward.

Lane Phillips's presence filled this room as much as if he were sitting here. Everywhere Angie's eye strayed, his handiwork spoke of him. Even the thick-bottomed rocker had been born under his skillful hand.

What wasn't Lane's belonged to Charlotte: the hand-plaited rug, the curtains, the doilies.

Stirring beans, Angie drew in a slow breath. Stale, painful memories smothered her. She simply had to get away.

Chapter 2

The creak of the back door, then voices, reached Angie. "Your room is upstairs, next to mine and Angie's," Judy said. "I'll show you where."

Angie met them near the narrow stairs. "You can rest awhile if you'd like, Saundra. You must be exhausted. We won't have supper for another two hours."

"Once I freshen up, I'll feel fine. I'll help you put supper on the table." She smoothed the mound of green fabric hanging over her arm. "Could I use an iron perhaps?" She winked. "I must put my best foot forward, you know."

"Of course." Angie lifted her bonnet and pushed at her flyaway brown hair. Pulled back into a single braid, it would never behave. "I'll put the iron on the stove for you right away."

Judy followed Saundra up the steep steps. Angie bustled toward the kitchen for the iron. Cold as it was outside, she wanted to get the horses into the barn as soon as possible.

Lane didn't arrive until an hour after dark. Boots thunking on the bare wood floor, he strode into the kitchen. Behind him came Barry Kimball, Angie's stocky fiancé, Lane's only permanent hand. Barry had quarters in the barn and took his meals with the family.

Both men looked haggard with cold and exhaustion.

Barry's gaze sought Angie's, and Angie responded with a warm smile. She'd known the smooth-faced Kimball boy since they played with empty spools under their mothers' quilting tables. He was two years older than she, but she was the taller until they were teenagers. She could still outrun him.

He took off his hat and flipped calloused fingers through sandy hair that brushed his ears and collar. Twenty-six last August, he looked eighteen.

Lane lifted his ten-gallon hat and dropped it on a peg. His short, brown hair had a widow's peak in front and a hat crease around the back. When he spoke, his voice sounded weary beyond physical fatigue. "That stand of oak in the lower corner is full of wood ants."

Angie's heart sank. "How will we make this year's payment to the bank?"

Lane's sagging shoulders lifted then sank. "I'll have to go into town and talk to Crouse. Maybe he'll let things ride until next year."

Using two dish towels to pad her hands, Angie lifted a pot of boiling water off the stove and poured some into a metal basin on the stand near the door. She added a healthy amount of cold water to it. "This is the third year running that you've had to ask for more time. What if he can't help us?"

"We'll cross that bridge when we come to it, Angie."

She sighed and dropped the dish towel to the counter. Untying her apron, she avoided Lane's eyes. "She's here, Lane."

"Who?" He sent her a blank stare.

"My pen pal from the East. We've been planning her visit for weeks."

Lane frowned, a question in his eyes. Then he nodded. "Oh, yeah. I forgot all about her."

"Supper's in the dining room tonight in honor of our guest. After we eat, you'll need to carry in her trunks. They're still in the buggy."

"What's she like?" Barry asked, grinning and moving closer to his intended. "Does she have warts and a hook nose?"

Angie sent him an exasperated look. "Can't you ever be serious? Wait 'til you see her. You'll be surprised. Believe me."

Lane dipped into the water and rubbed his face. He reached blindly for the towel hanging on the stand in front of him. "We tramped all over those woods this afternoon and got nowhere," he said when he finished. "I'm bushed. And I could eat the house, floorboards and all."

"We're having beans and corn bread. Saundra made the corn bread."

"You mean she can cook, too?" Barry asked, raising his eyebrows.

Angie shook her head at him, a warning in her eyes. "Don't you embarrass me with your foolish talk, Barry Kimball. Saundra Dryden is a lady."

Lane moved aside for his ranch hand to use the washbasin. He reached for the comb on the windowsill and flicked it straight back through his hair without looking in the mirror put there for that purpose.

When Angie and the two men reached the dining room, Saundra stood behind the oak table, radiant in an emerald gown with white lace brushing her throat and wrists. Her pale tresses lay in perfect waves over her ears, high on top with a wide French twist in back.

Lane hugged his daughter then acknowledged Saundra's presence with a brief handshake. The woman stretched out her hand—what else could he do? He stepped to his chair at the head of the table.

Barry drew up short in the narrow doorway, face still, eyes wide. Flushing, he clasped the woman's hand as if it were made of blown glass. Angie saw his Adam's apple bob just before they took their seats.

As always, Barry prayed before the meal. Lane hadn't prayed or led in family worship since Charlotte died. He wasn't sullen. He was sad, the kind of deep sadness that went all the way to the soul. Tonight he wore a black expression that made even Judy take a second look at him.

When they started to pass the food, Angie spoke. "Lane, Saundra tells me she's from Germany. Isn't that interesting? Her father was a professor at Harvard."

The big man filled his plate. He scarcely seemed to hear.

Barry leaned forward. "You must have had some interesting experiences at a place like that." Angie nudged him with the bowl of beans. He took it, still watching the woman across from him.

Saundra smiled, her dimple in full display. "I was only in my teens at the time so I didn't get to many of the functions. My father made me stay at home to practice English and mathematics." Her lovely lips twisted provocatively. "Would you like to hear the logarithm tables recited?"

He let out a delighted chuckle. "Maybe on Sunday afternoon when there's more time."

"What's Harvard like?" Angie asked.

Saundra smiled and laid down her fork. "It was a place like any other place," she said. "At first I thought that America would be a fairyland with a gigantic mansion and handsome carriages for everyone."

Judy giggled.

Saundra beamed at her. "But when I arrived, I found stern-looking men wearing black gowns over their clothing and carrying fat books under their arms. The only ones who smiled were the freshmen boys. They hadn't learned what it meant to be a Harvard man yet."

Her eyes twinkled. "One of my favorite hobbies was playing tricks on them to see if I could make them human again." She tilted her head toward Judy. "I was just a little older than you then, my dear."

Judy leaned toward her, eyes big as her dinner plate. "What did you do?"

Saundra laughed in her throat. "I'll tell you about the very first one I ever did. You see, there was a smooth stone patio outside the dining hall. One time I grated a bar of soap and put it into a bottle of warm water. I shook it up very well then added some oil to it. While the men were eating, I emptied that bottle over the patio floor. When they burst out the door on the way to their next class, they started skating as if they were on a pond in January instead of at college in May."

She laughed again. "You should have heard them calling out and shouting. They grabbed each other and slid into the grass." She chuckled. "My father made me stay in the house for a month after that."

"Did anyone fall down?" Judy asked.

"Oh, lots of them did." She turned to Angie and said, "I was too young to realize how dangerous a slippery floor could be. It was all in fun, but I'm glad no one was hurt." She turned back to Judy. "My father had Maria, our housekeeper, lock up the soap for a couple of years after that."

Gasping, she remembered another story. "Speaking of soap, one time I shook Maria's grated soap through a strainer and got a fine powder. I sneaked into the college dining room one morning and mixed the powder into the sugar bowls where they sat on the sideboard ready for breakfast." She laughed and covered her mouth with slim fingers. "You should have seen the suds coming out of the coffee cups at breakfast."

"Did your father catch you that time?" Judy asked.

Saundra sobered. "That was two years after we came to Harvard, Judy. By then whenever anyone pulled a prank, he automatically looked at me." She picked up her fork. "I had to scrub floors for Maria for the entire month of February for that one."

Saundra kept Barry and Judy entertained for the rest of the meal. As soon as she finished one story, they'd coax her into another. Twice Angie tried to draw Lane into the conversation, but he focused on his meal—not rude, but not interested in chitchat either. Not once did he look at Saundra.

After the second round of coffee, Angie stood to clear the table. Judy gathered the cups and silverware.

Barry lurched to his feet. "Let me help you with that, Mrs. Dryden." He took a single plate from Saundra's hands and stacked it on his own.

"Call me Saundra. Please."

He gulped. "Of course—Saundra." Fumbling to get around his chair, he strode toward the kitchen.

Angie sent an irritated glance after her fiancé. What on earth had gotten into Barry?

Chapter 3

That night, tucked between snowy flannel sheets, Angie and Judy had a conference. Judy had given her room to Saundra—a small sacrifice, since icy winter nights were much cozier with two bodies under the eiderdown instead of one. Most nights Judy used to creep into her aunt's bed in the wee cold hours anyway. The upstairs had no heat.

"Papa hardly looked at her," Judy said, her face close to Angie's ear in the darkness. "She's beautiful, and he didn't even notice."

Angie let out a slow breath. She didn't want to worry Judy with the news about the spoiled timber. "He was tired and half-frozen when he got home tonight. Maybe when he's feeling better, he'll pay more attention to Saundra."

"We've got to *make* him pay attention to her." Judy threw her arm over her aunt. "What am I going to do if we can't find Papa a nice wife before you get married? I'll be all alone."

Angie returned the hug. "Don't worry, Hon. I'm not going anywhere until we find just the right woman."

Hot, flannel-wrapped bricks warmed their feet and relaxed taut nerves. The passage she'd read to Judy for that evening's devotions replayed through Angie's mind: Rebekah and Jacob and their deception. *This situation,* she told herself, *was different.*

With Judy's warm, sleep-quiet form next to her, Angie eased her neck onto the pillow and stared into the blackness.

As far back as she could remember, Angie had idolized Charlotte. Ten years older, Charlotte always seemed grown up to her sister. Angie wanted to be like her more than anything in the world.

But she couldn't.

Charlotte had the face of a princess. Angie was plain. Charlotte could make a feed sack look like a ball gown. Angie looked like a scarecrow in her Sunday best. Charlotte was dainty. Angie had a boyish heart tucked inside a gangly body.

Charlotte had married Prince Charming. Angie would settle for Barry Kimball, friend and fellow tree climber.

"You shouldn't feel so bad about your appearance," her mother had told Angie. "You are just as attractive as Charlotte in your own way."

Angie tossed her frizzy braids, certain her mother was only trying to make her feel better.

When Mom and Dad died of cholera, Angie came to live with Lane and Charlotte. Judy was four years old at the time. Angie had watched Lane's adoring eyes follow his wife's movements. Charlotte had a slim figure and glistening black hair that always looked fresh. No wonder Lane never tired of looking at her.

Angie had heard their laughter, had seen their delight in their tiny daughter. She had believed in their dream of a long life together.

When Charlotte died in childbirth with her second child, Angie felt betrayed. Where was God when Charlotte needed Him? Where was God when Charlotte's family needed Him?

Lane hadn't smiled since.

For weeks Angie didn't smile either. But nine-year-old Judy still had life in her, the boundless energy of a healthy child. Judy's fun-loving heart joined with Angie's until they became comrades, confidantes, conspirators.

The thought of leaving Judy brought a catch to Angie's breath. Turning, she pulled the quilt higher until it covered her ears and blocked out her doubts.

✶

The next morning Lane and Barry had gone outside to do the chores before Saundra came down for breakfast. Wearing a dark blue dress that made her eyes glow, she appeared in the kitchen looking eager and well rested.

"What can I do to help?" she asked as soon as she finished a pancake and two eggs. "I didn't come to be waited on like a queen."

Angie lifted the egg basket. "You could gather the eggs, if you don't mind. I usually do it this time of morning." She took her to the window and pointed. "That's the chicken coop there. Next to the barn."

Throwing Angie's long, heavy shawl about her head and shoulders, Saundra slipped the basket handle over her arm and picked her way across the snowy ranch yard. The day had dawned clear and calm. Angie hoped today would be a little warmer than yesterday.

The moment Saundra stepped off the porch, Judy pressed her nose against the windowpane.

"Get away from the window!" Angie scolded her. "She'll see you. Or worse, your father will see you."

"He can't see. He's inside the barn hitching the horses to the buggy." She snickered. "I wish I could sneak out there and spy."

Overcome by her own curiosity, Angie stayed a few feet from the window and peered over the girl's head.

Tail waving, Tip stayed at Saundra's heels. The tiny lady gripped the door handle of the chicken house, a lean-to attached to the sprawling barn. She tugged and twisted, but the door wouldn't budge.

Judy giggled and looked back at Angie. They shared a secret smile. Things were going exactly as planned.

At that moment the barn doors eased open. Dan and Sheba trotted out, the black buggy's iron wheels rumbling behind them. The horses stopped in the yard, heads bobbing, noses blowing out twin blasts of steam. The next instant a man wearing a sheepskin coat came into view from the other side of the buggy.

Barry.

Saundra turned toward him. He spoke with her a moment, pulled on the brim of his Stetson, then ambled over to the chicken house. He gave the door a fierce yank. It popped open.

Angie's teeth clamped her lower lip. "Why didn't Lane hitch the horses this morning?" she wailed. "One morning out of fifty he has Barry do it. Why today?"

"Look!" Judy said.

Barry entered the chicken house with their German guest. A few moments later they reappeared with Barry carrying the basket, a smiling Saundra at his side.

Angie yanked Judy away from the window and pulled her to the dish drainer. She shoved a cup and a dish towel into the girl's hands as the back door swung in.

Saundra stepped through the door then turned back. "Thank you, Barry. You are a real gentleman." She leaned down. "You, too, Tip!"

The dog barked once.

Chuckling softly, Saundra closed the door and set the basket on the table. She carefully lifted the shawl from her hair. "A full dozen. Is that what you usually get?"

Judy lifted the cup into the cupboard. "Give or take a few." She watched Saundra a moment. "Did you know Barry and Angie are engaged?"

Elbow deep in the dishpan, Angie had an urge to pinch her niece.

"How nice," Saundra said, smiling broadly. "He's a fine man, Angie. You're a lucky girl."

"Thanks," Angie said, her cheeks burning.

Saundra grew serious. "Do you think Lane is pleased that I'm here? He's hardly spoken to me." She picked up a damp cloth from the counter and wiped the table with smooth, wide swipes.

Angie dipped her hands in the rinsing basin and grabbed a towel. "That's what I was talking about on the way home from the depot. Lane's painfully shy. He takes awhile to warm up to anyone new.

"He's probably a little embarrassed to meet you face to face," she added. "You're very beautiful, you know. He may be overwhelmed."

Angie pulled up an encouraging smile and took a step toward Saundra. "Don't worry. He'll come around in time. Use your feminine charms on him."

The German woman studied Angie's face. "From his letters I expected that I would be fending him off, not chasing him. I am not sure I like the idea."

"Give him some time," Angie coaxed. "He needs you, Saundra. He's been desperately lonely since my sister died. Please give him a chance."

"Well, I came all this way. The least I can do is stay awhile." She smiled softly. "He is very good looking."

Angie grinned. "That's the spirit."

Saundra drew in a breath and smoothed the wave covering her ear. "I will finish ironing my things this morning, and then I'll wash my hair."

Judy opened a cupboard. "Here's the iron."

Filling the hot water reservoir in back of the stove, Angie suddenly cried, "Hurry, Judy! You'll be late for school."

Judy raced upstairs for her books, her feet thumping on every step. Angie set down the bucket to pull on her wool coat and flannel-lined bonnet. She was in the buggy, reins ready, when Judy burst out the door with her coat half on and her bonnet swinging.

Sheba and Dan set off at a brisk trot, trace chains rattling. Angie handled the team with habitual movements, her mind on the problem that haunted her. There had to be a way to wake Lane up. If she thought long and hard, she knew she could come up with something.

Chapter 4

Two days later, Angie got the chance she'd hoped for. That afternoon Barry left for a short visit with his folks, and Lane came in early for supper. They ate beef stew and rolls at the kitchen table—special treatment couldn't last forever—and Saundra was at her most charming. Best of all, Lane listened to her. He even grinned a few times.

The meal finished, Lane left the kitchen to fetch wood for the potbelly stove and to build a fire in the fireplace. Two fires in the living room were necessary on a night as bitter as this. Angie reached for her sweater that was hanging on a peg beside the door, hoping that Barry had chosen to stay overnight with his parents. It was too cold for a body to be outside.

"Don't worry about the dishes, Saundra," Angie said, when the woman began to clear the table. "Join Lane in the living room. You may be able to talk him into a game of checkers."

Saundra's eyes sparkled. "Does he like chess? My father and I played almost every night once I learned how. I haven't had a good game in years."

Judy's face creased into a toothy grin. "That's his favorite game. He has a marble chess set that Mama gave him on her last Christmas."

"Say a prayer," Saundra said, beaming. She smoothed down her skirt and floated through the door.

A curious twelve-year-old tiptoed after her.

"Judy!" Angie's whisper drew her back. "Don't make a nuisance of yourself." She handed the girl a bowl of food scraps. "Here. Feed Tip."

Half an hour later, Judy scooted upstairs to fetch the mittens she was knitting for her father's Christmas present. She sat by the kitchen stove, needles in hand, while Angie washed out the dishcloth and swept the floor.

"What should we get Saundra for Christmas, Judy? I've been thinking and thinking, and I haven't come up with a single idea. She seems to have everything she needs."

"We must think of something nice for her first Christmas with us." The knitting needles clicked half a dozen times. "I like Saundra. She makes me laugh."

"I like her, too." Angie propped the broom behind the door and lifted a small cloth sack of beans from the counter. "One thing we did right in all of this was to pick her." She dumped the dried limas on the table, sat down, and sorted out the bad ones.

"Papa seems in a good mood tonight."

"He took this month's quota of lumber to the yard today. So he can relax for a few days." She reached for a pot and scooped a pile of beans into it. Moving to the bucket on the counter, she washed the beans and set them soaking for tomorrow's lunch.

"Miss Hodgkins says we have to know our times tables by next Friday." Judy sighed. "I'll never get them all memorized. Especially the sixes."

"Why don't you ask Saundra for help? From what she says, she knows lots of math."

The girl brightened. "That's a good idea. I'll ask her tomorrow."

Angie added flour and milk to her sourdough starter and set it near the stove. A little after eight o'clock, she and Judy walked softly down the hall toward the stairs. Angie carried a wide candle on a saucer.

Lane and Saundra sat on either side of a small table in front of the fireplace, studying a chessboard. Dancing flames formed a backdrop behind them. A glass-shaded lamp added a bit of brightness to the room, but most of the light came from the fire.

Neither player spoke a word.

Angie and Judy crept up the stairs, afraid their very presence would spoil the players' concentration.

"Is it working?" Judy asked when Angie eased the door closed behind them. "Does he like her yet?"

Angie held tight arms across her fluttery middle. "These things take time, love. People have to get to know one another."

"Like you and Barry?"

Angie turned her head away. "Well, not quite as long as that. Most married couples don't grow up together, you know. Your parents didn't."

"They met at church, didn't they?"

"Yes, a revival meeting outside of Darby." It was an old story, one the girl still loved to hear. "We went to one of those come-and-camp affairs that lasted a week or more. Pa drove our buckboard half a day to get there." Angie gazed at the puffed biscuit quilt on the wide iron bedstead, reliving happier days. "Charlotte knocked over Lane's dinner plate while we were waiting in line for a glass of tea."

She looked into Judy's eager blue eyes. "From then on, your father hung around our family like a bee buzzing over a clover field. I was only eight at the time. I didn't understand what was going on until later, when he started riding ten miles just to take supper with us."

"You think a fellow would ride ten miles to see me?"

Angie tugged Judy's tawny braid. "I think he would. If he were the right one." She leaned down and made a funny face. "It's a little early for getting yourself wrought up over that kind of foolishness. Turn around so I can unbutton you. Time for bed."

After their Bible reading, Judy said a special prayer for her father. Angie swallowed hard. How could she bear to leave this dear child?

Angie took her time changing into her nightgown and brushing out her corkscrew curls. Her dark hair made a thick, wide mound that ended at her waist. She stared at the mirror image of the bush-like mass about her head and wished for shiny waves like a rippling waterfall.

Wrinkling her nose at her reflection, she formed a braid, blew out the candle, and gently slid between the sheets. Judy instinctively moved closer to her.

Half asleep, Angie felt a nudge in her ribs. "I'm awful thirsty, Angie."

"Must be that salty stew we had for supper." Shivering, she slid bare feet to the icy floor and lifted the pitcher from the dresser. "Empty. Wouldn't you know it? I'll have to go down and fill it."

She pulled on her heavy robe and shoved cold feet into cold shoes. Lighting the candle, she headed out the door. If possible, the hall seemed icier than the bedroom.

From the stairs she saw the dull orange glow of the fireplace. Two shadowy forms sat across from each other at the small table. Angie's lips twitched into a satisfied smile. Congratulating herself, she glided past the door.

Barry's voice made her jump. The candle rocked on the saucer.

"You win again! If that don't beat all."

Saundra chuckled. "I warned you, Barry. I've had lots of practice." She yawned. "That's enough for me. I must get my beauty sleep."

"I'll put the game away," he said. "Thanks for a fun evening, Saundra. We'll have to do it again."

"Good night." Her soft steps sounded on the stairs.

Angie waited in the kitchen until she heard a door close overhead. Eyes glinting, breast heaving, she marched into the living room.

Barry was placing each marble piece into a felt-lined section of a wide wooden box. Suddenly he jerked around. "Oh, hello, Angie. You startled me."

"What are you doing here, pray tell?"

He looked surprised. "What's got you so het up? My brother, Benji, didn't want to play checkers after supper, so I rode back. I came inside to see what Lane wanted done in the morning. He was in the middle of a game with Saundra. The game had gone on too long for him. He wanted to turn in, so he asked me to take his place." He peered at her from floor to crown.

She suddenly became aware of her tousled hair, her moth-eaten robe. Her cheeks burned but not totally from embarrassment. She set the pitcher and candle on the table and swept her hair out of her face. "I wanted him to spend the evening with Saundra." She gazed at him, face to face. "You spoiled it. You're always getting in the way, trying to get close to her."

He pushed away from the table and stood to his full five feet nine. "I'm not trying to get close to her. She and I just sort of stumble into each other. That's natural, living in the same place."

His boyish face grew still. "Say, what are you gettin' at? You jealous or something?" He laughed softly, that teasing look in his eyes.

"I've never been jealous in my life!"

He gave her his lopsided grin. "You sure look jealous. Your eyes are flashing fire."

He reached for her. "Come here, Angie girl. I'll prove you don't have nothing to worry about." He pulled her to him.

She twisted away. "Stop it, Barry! What if someone comes downstairs?"

His face grew still. "You never want to kiss me, Angie. No matter when or where."

She put her hand on his flannel sleeve. "I'm sorry, Barry. I don't want you to get the wrong idea. I trust you. It's just that—" She didn't know how to explain without telling all about her plans for Lane and Saundra. Barry was famous for blurting out secrets at the worst possible moment.

He touched her chin. "How's about setting a wedding date? You ready yet?"

She looked down. "Not until Lane finds a—housekeeper. I can't leave Judy here with only men around. A girl needs a woman."

He pursed his lips. "I reckon you're right, honey, but I sure hope we don't have to wait too much longer. Our cabin's ready, and Dad's holding a job for me. All you have to do is speak the word, and we'll tie the knot when Lane's spring crew gets here."

"If you want to hurry things up, stay away from Saundra," she pleaded softly. "Give Lane a chance to get acquainted with her."

"Say." His face showed keen interest. "I think I get it. You're matchmaking for Lane." He hooted. "What a belly buster! That hombre'll never get rehitched. You're barking up the wrong tree this time, Angie."

"Just keep out of Saundra's way. That's all I ask."

He watched her, a wary look in his eyes. "I'm not avoiding the lady if that's what you mean." His chin came up. "You can say what you want about it. I'll not be rude to her."

"That's not what I meant."

"Angie?" A wee voice called from upstairs. "Angie, I'm thirsty."

Shuffling to the door, she called softly, "Coming, honey. I got held up. I'll be right there." She returned to Barry. "Please, Barry, do what I ask. Will you?"

"I'll study on it." He picked up his hat. "Good night—sweetheart." Without looking at her again, he strode out the back door and into the night.

Feeling deflated, Angie retrieved the pitcher and candle from the middle of the chessboard and hurried to the kitchen.

Why had Barry suddenly turned stubborn? This was the first time he'd point-blank refused to do what she asked. And at such a crucial moment.

She poured water into the pitcher. Men! Who could understand them?

Chapter 5

The next morning Lane pushed his scrambled eggs around on his plate, eating little. Since the men had few chores that day, Barry drove Judy to school. As soon as Saundra finished her meal, she picked up the egg basket and headed for the chicken house.

"Are you feeling well?" Angie asked Lane while she cleared the table.

"My head feels heavy." He pushed back his plate. "Maybe I'd best take it easy today." He stood and reached for his coat. "I'll see to the stock." The door banged behind him.

Delighted that Lane had chosen that moment to go to the barn, Angie peered through the window and saw light snow drifting down. Across the yard Saundra yanked and pried at the chicken house door. Lane veered off course to help.

Angie grinned. Maybe he'd talk to her as Barry did yesterday.

But the moment the door snapped open, Lane strode to the barn without a second glance at Saundra.

Angie sighed. Besides the chess game, Lane had hardly noticed the lovely lady since she arrived almost a week ago. He could be so exasperating.

Finishing the few dishes, Angie started the laundry. In cold weather she always arranged two chairs facing each other to hold her washtub in the kitchen, a nice setup, so handy to the hot water reservoir. The kitchen stayed too hot for heavy work inside during the summer.

She was elbow-deep in suds when Saundra returned, scowling. "Two hens didn't want to get off their nests. They pecked me."

"Did you get their eggs?"

"Nein," she said abruptly, her lips pressed together. "Only six." She hung her black cape on a peg by the door.

Not wanting to push her, Angie said, "I'll go out later and take care of those biddies."

Saundra stepped closer to the washtub. "When you finish your clothes, may I wash some of mine?"

"Why, surely. You don't have to ask." Angie smiled. "We want you to feel at home, Saundra."

The German woman's face softened. "You have been very kind." She rolled up her sleeves. "What is for lunch? I can start preparing, no?"

Saundra stood at the counter peeling potatoes when Lane returned. Wringing out a stiff petticoat skirt, Angie noticed a lag in Lane's footsteps as he crossed the porch. She turned to see his haggard face in the doorway. A worn bridle hung limply in his hand.

"Lane, you look ill," Angie said.

"I'm just tired." He laid the bridle on a chair while he shrugged out of his sheepskin coat. "I'll stoke the fire in the living room and stitch this bridle back together. Tell Barry I want to see him when he comes in." His boots sounded loud in the hall.

Angie wanted to go after him and tell him he should be in bed, but she held her tongue. Lane Phillips hadn't spent a day in bed all the years she'd known him.

Saundra filled the teapot with water. "I'll make him a cup of tea."

"Better make him coffee," Angie told her. "He can't abide tea. He says it's a woman's drink."

An hour later Barry returned with Judy. "The snow's getting worse, so they canceled school," he said, pulling off his gloves and rubbing his chapped hands together.

Judy hugged Angie's middle, jostling her arm and spraying suds across the floor. "Yippee!"

Angie laughed at the girl's enthusiasm. "Change your clothes, girlie. You can shoo those old biddies off their nests. They gave Saundra a bad time this morning."

Stepping nearer the hot cookstove, his hands outstretched, Barry looked at Saundra, concerned. "You'd best let me give you a hand with the eggs in the mornings."

"Judy can help before she goes to school," Angie told him firmly. He'd never worried about Angie getting her hand pecked by a feisty hen. What had gotten into him? She splattered a wet skirt across her washboard. "Barry, Lane wants to see you in the living room," she said tightly.

Barry's expression stiffened. He hesitated, watching Angie with a strange light in his eyes. They made eye contact for a lingering moment, sizing each other up as though they'd just seen each other clearly for the first time.

Barry was the first to break away. He turned and marched out of the kitchen without a backward glance toward his beloved. Angie slapped the skirt with vengeance.

Saundra's lilting voice broke the silence. "Judy," she said brightly, "I'll come with you to the henhouse so you can give me some lessons on dealing with those hens."

They slipped into shawls and hurried outside into a yard filling quickly with fat, sticky flakes. A few minutes later Barry hurried through the kitchen after them. Without breaking stride, he told Angie as he passed her, "I'd best string a rope from the barn to the house in case the snow gets bad. We had a blizzard this time last year."

The snow lasted until midafternoon. When the sky cleared, Judy, Barry, and Angie wrapped themselves in triple layers of wool and scrambled into the yard.

While Judy made a snow angel near the front steps, Barry chased Angie around the yard with a mound of snow in his glove. She laughed and dodged his attempts to reach her face. Suddenly she whirled on him, a snowball in her hand. He ducked, and the missile landed on Judy's leg.

In one movement Judy was on her feet, packing snowballs and throwing them at two-second intervals.

"So that's the way you want to play, eh?" Barry yelled. He picked up a fat mound of snow and bore down on Judy.

Squealing, she turned and ran around the corner of the house.

Wearing her cape and an extra shawl, Saundra came out on the back porch to stand near the edge.

"Hi, Saundra!" Angie called. "Want to join us?"

"No, thanks," she replied, holding her shawl close to her body. "Getting cold and wet isn't my idea of a good time." She smiled. "I like to watch, though."

The next instant Judy dashed into the yard, a puffing Barry on her heels. He grabbed her and pulled her struggling form backward into the snow. Their laughter filled the yard.

Drawing apart, Barry and Judy lay still for a moment to catch their breath. Then Barry helped Judy to her feet.

The moment she regained her balance, Judy reached for more snow. "Here! Catch!" she called to Saundra as she flung a snowball at her. It hit Saundra's neck and dusted her front.

"Oh!" the little woman squealed, brushing at the frosty cold dripping down her collar. A disgusted expression came over her face, and she dashed inside the house.

Unaware of their guest's discomfort, Judy guffawed and aimed for Angie's face. A direct hit.

"Judy, you shouldn't have hit Saundra!" Barry said, huffing. "She's not used to playing rough like you are."

"Wake up, Barry!" Angie said, her temper boiling over. "She's *not* a china doll. And she's not *your* responsibility."

He stared at her, face still, his gloved hands holding a snowball. "What has gotten into you, Angie? I never knew you could be so mean. Saundra is our guest. We should be nice to her."

Angie turned away from him as though she wanted to brush the snow from her face. She was ashamed of herself and still furious at the same time.

"Wahoo!" Judy shrieked, heaving two missiles at once. They both hit Barry's chest.

He stared at Judy, his brow down and his chin up. "Want to play that way, do you?" He chuckled and pulled his neck further down into his collar.

Judy squealed and dove for cover behind Angie the moment Barry let his snowball fly. It hit the edge of Angie's wool scarf and splattered on her cheek.

He gave a triumphant holler and scooped up more ammunition.

Angie played a few minutes longer, but her heart had gone out of the game. Twilight was minutes away when Judy complained that her feet hurt from the cold, so the girls hurried to the house. Barry went to do the evening chores before supper.

"I'm sorry, Saundra," Judy said when they reached the kitchen and found her at the table peeling potatoes. "I didn't mean to hit your skin. I was aiming for your coat."

Saundra dropped a peeled spud into a pot of water and rubbed her chin with the back of her hand. "I feel silly for making such a fuss. I've never liked being in snowball fights since I was a girl."

"You were laughing at us," Judy said. "I thought you wanted to join in."

"I was acting as a spectator," she said, smiling at Judy to soften her words, "the same as at a horse race." She looked at Angie. "Lane just came in to say he's going up to bed now."

"He is? It's only five o'clock."

Saundra looked at Angie, concern in her eyes. "He kept rubbing his brow as if his head hurt."

Angie pulled a knife from a drawer and sat down to help Saundra. "I hope he's better by morning."

Saturday Lane moped about the house and fell asleep on the sofa after lunch. When the family gathered for Sunday breakfast, Lane's head drooped onto his hand. His cheeks were unusually red, and his eyes had a dull, glazed look.

"Lane Phillips," Angie said, "you're not going anywhere this morning except back to bed."

He looked at her as though she were far away. "I reckon the cold drive to church won't do me any good," he admitted. He scooted his chair back. "Barry, while you're at the church, tell Jake Sutton I've got a yearling I want to sell him, will you? Ask him to come by to look at it next week."

"Sure, Lane," Barry said. He shoveled fried potatoes and bacon into his wide mouth while Saundra refilled his coffee cup.

Lane plodded toward the stairs. Angie resisted the urge to go after him and lend him her strength. She knew he wouldn't take it kindly. He hated to be fussed over.

Sipping his coffee, his plate empty, Barry suddenly noticed Saundra's silk dress. High at the neck with a mass of tiny pleats across the front, it was the color of ripe cranberries. "I can't wait to see the look on the ladies' faces when you walk into church this morning," he told her. "Chancyville ain't never seen anything as pretty as you."

Angie had a sudden inspiration. "Lane shouldn't be left alone, Saundra. Would you mind looking after him while we're gone?"

Barry gave a puzzled frown.

Saundra said, "Of course not." She sent Angie a meaningful look, punctuated by a secret smile. "I'll have lunch ready when you get home."

Judy bounced out of her chair. "I want to get there early so I can talk to Molly before the opening session."

Barry chuckled and took a last sip of coffee. "The boss has spoken. Let's get going." He hustled outside to fetch the horses that were already hitched to the buggy.

Angie pulled off her apron and smoothed her brown wool dress—the only Sunday dress she'd owned for three years. She suddenly noticed a smooth spot on her right sleeve. This brown dress was made from the same pattern as her work dresses, only from finer fabric. Funny. Until this morning she'd never thought of needing anything else.

Tying on her navy bonnet, Angie slipped into her ankle-length coat and stepped outside. She ought to be pleased with herself for thinking of a way to force Lane and Saundra together. There was no way Lane could ignore Saundra when they were the only two in the house. She could hear Saundra's tinkling laugh and see her sparkling blue eyes, her hair neatly rolled into that gorgeous French twist. How could Lane resist her?

As the buggy headed down the long lane, a strange sinking feeling hit the pit of Angie's stomach. She pressed a hand against her waist and wondered if she were coming down with something.

Chapter 6

On the rear buggy seat, Judy tucked her small hand beneath Angie's elbow and leaned her head on her shoulder. Angie and Judy always sat in the back of the buggy. The cold wind seemed more brutal in the front. In spite of their sheltered seat, they shivered together under the thick buffalo robe all the way to church.

Barry hunched inside his jacket and concentrated on the road ahead of them. He didn't utter a word for the entire half-hour ride.

West of town, the tiny, whitewashed church stayed chilly in spite of padded foot warmers for every oak pew and a smoking coal stove near the pulpit. Angie clenched her hands inside a fur muff and snuggled close to Judy during the message. Brilliant light streaming through six glazed windowpanes seemed to add to the chill instead of relieving it.

Despite his raspy voice, the preacher's message rang clear. He told the story of Jacob and Rebekah, a classic tale of deceit, lies, and an unhappy ending. Angie studied the oak wood grain on the back of the next pew and tried to close her ears. Why did that story come up at every turn? She was getting tired of it.

At the church door, she shook the pastor's hand without stopping to talk. She spotted Judy in a group of children playing tag in the churchyard. "Judy!" she called. "It's time to go."

"Already?" Judy asked, her cheeks ruddy from the cold and exercise. "We just got outside."

"See? Barry's standing beside the buggy already." Angie nodded toward the row of black, box-shaped vehicles.

Judy cocked her head to get a better look at the wide man with a heavy gray beard standing next to Barry. "He's still talking to Mr. Sutton. Can't I play until he's through?" Judy begged.

"Sorry." Angie grasped the girl's hand. "Your father's sick, and I want to get home to him. Let's go."

Barry broke off his conversation when they arrived, and the little group set off. "Get along home, Cindy, Cindy," Barry sang when they were out of earshot of the church. Judy added her soprano to his baritone until the horses pricked up their ears. Angie stared at the snow-covered distance and wondered what was wrong with her today. Maybe she was catching something too.

A worried frown on her face, Saundra met them at the door. "I went up a few minutes ago, and Lane's got a fever. I think you ought to look at him, Angie."

Angie didn't stop to take off her coat. Rushing down the hall, she tugged her bonnet loose. Behind her, Barry asked Saundra more questions about Lane's condition. Judy trotted to catch up with Angie.

"What's wrong with him?" Judy asked, fear in her voice.

"I hope it's just a bad cold." Angie tapped on the bedroom door and opened it a crack. "Lane? Are you asleep?"

"Come in." His voice sounded so weak that Angie could hardly hear him.

Judy pushed through the door and ran to the brass bed. She threw herself across her father's chest. "Papa!"

Giving a muffled grunt under the impact, he weakly patted her back. Angie gently pulled the child off her father.

"Are you hurting anywhere?" Angie asked, touching his hot brow. His breath came in shallow, loose-lipped gasps.

"Everywhere. My joints especially."

She asked him a few more questions then touched Judy's shoulder. "He needs to rest, Judy. We'd best go out." To Lane she said, "I'll send up some sassafras and willow tea."

He grimaced.

"I know you don't like it, but it'll help you sleep." She pulled the covers close about his neck and resisted the impulse to touch his cheek. Standing, she whispered, "C'mon, Judy."

Outside the door his daughter said, "He looks so sick, Angie."

"I know." She hugged Judy close and tried to quiet her own fears. A heartfelt prayer winged upward.

When they reached the kitchen, in the center of the table lay a dried-apple pie beside a bowl of thick stew. Barry looked over the food. "You've been in the house all morning, Saundra. How about a walk to the pond after—?" Catching sight of Angie, he broke off.

Ignoring Barry, Angie said, "Lane has a fever all right." She pulled at her wide coat buttons. "I wish there were a doctor in Chancyville. Since old Doc Taylor died, we've all been praying for a new man to come in, but so far no one has." She hung up her coat. "I have some dried tea leaves in a tin somewhere. I'll make him a strong pot."

"I thought you said he doesn't like tea," Saundra said.

"He hates it." Angie reached for her gray apron. "Sometimes a person has to swallow things he doesn't like." She opened a cabinet door. "Now where did I put that tin?"

Fifteen minutes later she held a tray out to Saundra. "Here. Take this up to him."

Saundra peered into the mug full of dark tea. "What if he doesn't want it?"

"If he won't take it, let me know. I'll come up and make him drink it," Angie said.

Saundra looked uncertain. "I used to care for my father when he was sick, but he never gave me any trouble."

"Lane barks a lot, but he never bites." Angie watched her go and muttered under her breath, "Well, almost never."

"When can we eat?" Barry asked, sniffing the pie.

"No reason why you can't dig in," Angie told him, turning away. "Judy! Stop fidgeting and sit down." Angie joined them for the blessing. She spooned tiny portions onto her own plate but ate only a few bites. Nothing tasted good today.

Monday and Tuesday Lane lay in fevered semiconsciousness. The entire household felt the strain. Saundra made endless trips up and down the stairs. Angie fretted in the kitchen, keeping the teapot going, baking extra bread for freezing now that the weather had turned cold for good. She prayed for Lane with every movement.

Every afternoon after school, Judy rushed up the stairs then trudged back down to the kitchen fighting tears. "What if he doesn't get better, Angie?" she whimpered on Tuesday. "What if he dies like Mama did?"

Angie wrapped her arms around the girl and held her pigtailed head close to her heart. "Don't even think that way, Judy. Your father will get better in a few days. We have to keep up hope." She gave her an extra squeeze. "How about taking care of Tip and the chickens and then get out your quilting scraps after supper? We'll have a quiet evening in the kitchen."

Dashing the tears from her face, Judy plodded out to do the chores. She came in with Barry an hour later, both of them looking glum.

"I'm having a hard time getting the last of that wood split and stacked," Barry admitted, hanging up his hat. "We have about two cords left to do, and it's getting colder by the day. Lane wanted it all split before Thanksgiving in case we have a spell of bad weather."

"I'll try to help you stack some tomorrow," Angie promised, wondering where she'd get the strength to make good her promise.

Saundra took a tray of tea and toast up to Lane while Angie put supper on the table: creamed chip beef over biscuits. The only one who ate normal portions that evening was Barry.

The windows shone black when Barry sat with his chair pushed back, his feet straight out ahead of him, relaxing with a hand-whittled toothpick in his mouth. Angie and Judy were clearing the table when someone knocked lightly on the back door.

The sound made Angie jump. "Who could that be?" she asked. "I hope none of our neighbors is sick and needs help."

Barry stood to his feet and opened the door a crack. A moment later his face showed concern. He pulled the thick wooden door wider to reveal a thin man with a straggling gray beard. He stood propped against the doorjamb. He had sagging cheeks and hollow blue eyes. His ragged clothes hung on him as if they were made for someone much larger. His mouth drooped open, and his breath came in gasps.

Barry hesitated, staring as though he wondered if the person before him were a ghost or maybe a dream.

Angie hurried forward. "Come in," she said. "You look frozen."

"Thank you," the stranger rasped. "You are very kind." He spoke with a heavy German accent. His breathy voice formed the words slowly as though his face were frozen. "I've been walking for three days without food. All I had is *chust* some coffee." He set down a bundle of rags with a dented coffeepot tied to its side.

"Sit here," Angie said, pulling out a chair. She turned toward the door. "You're letting in the cold, Barry."

Her fiancé quickly closed the door. He returned to his seat, still watching the newcomer.

"I'll have you a plate of hot food in just a moment," Angie went on. She knew the frontier drill well. Any stranger in this kind of trouble needed tending to. A person never knew when he would be the one in need himself.

"I'm looking for work," the old fellow gasped. He rubbed bony chapped hands across a thick overcoat that had crude patches over its elbows. "Do you need a farm hand or someone to help in the house?"

Angie looked at Barry, eyebrows raised. When he didn't answer, she said, "We'll talk about that later, Mr.—"

"My name is Hans Grobner," he said, "and thank you kindly."

Judy sidled up to Angie while she ladled creamed beef onto a plate. "He talks like Saundra," the girl whispered.

Angie nodded, then sent her a warning look when the child would have continued talking.

Setting the brimming plate, a knife and fork, and a bowl full of biscuits in front of Hans, Angie asked, "Would you like some tea?"

He beamed at her. "That would be wonderful!" One hand reached for his fork while the other scooped up two fat biscuits.

Judy hustled out of the room and came back with Saundra a few minutes later. "This is Saundra," she proudly told Hans. "She's from Germany."

Immediately the old man was transformed. He came erect and looked at the blond woman before him. A gush of German came from him like water out of a newly primed pump. Saundra replied, and they shook hands.

For ten minutes Angie, Barry, and Judy listened to the guttural tones of a language they couldn't understand. Finally Saundra turned to Angie. "He has no family and no place to stay. His summer job ended more than a month ago. He's desperate for a place to wait out the winter. He wants to know if you need a man to help around the ranch. He said he'd even cook or scrub floors in exchange for a place to stay."

Angie looked at Barry. "We do need help until Lane gets back on his feet, but I'll have to talk it over with Lane before we commit ourselves." She spoke directly to Hans. "You are welcome to stay here for the night. There's no place close enough for you to reach tonight anyway. You can stay with Barry in the bunk room behind the barn. Come with him to breakfast in the morning, too."

Barry stood. "That's right, Hans. It's warm out there in the bunk room once I get the fire going." He reached for his coat. "I'll go out and stoke the potbelly stove now." He disappeared into the darkness.

Hans turned his attention back to his empty plate as if he'd forgotten that he'd already cleared it.

"Would you like some more?" Angie offered. "There's plenty."

"Thank you kindly, ma'am," he said. "I know God led me here to you fine people. If you had turned me away, I don't know what would have become of me."

"I'll get some blankets," Angie said. She set another full plate before him and hurried to the linen closet at the back of the pantry.

After he finished his meal, Hans didn't stay long to chat. He again thanked Angie and Saundra then clumped out to the barn, his bedding under one scrawny arm, his pack under the other.

Angie looked at Saundra. "What do you make of him?" she asked.

Saundra replied, "He's a very lonely man who has come into hard times. I'm glad you welcomed him in, Angie."

Angie shrugged. "I could never turn away someone in that kind of shape. It would be heartless to do that."

Chapter 7

Angie pulled off her apron. "I'm going up to see if Lane's still awake. I need to ask him what we can do for poor Hans."

She found Lane plucking at his quilt, with one leg in red woolen underwear lying halfway out from under the covers. When she reached the bed, he turned to give her a blank stare.

"Water," he gasped. "I'm so thirsty."

"It's the fever," she said, reaching for the glass and pitcher beside his bed. She helped him sit up and handed him the full glass.

When he lay back, she said, "We have a guest. He's a German man who stopped by looking for work."

Lane licked chapped lips. "A tramp, you mean."

"He's thin as a scarecrow, but I don't think he's a tramp, Lane. He acts too respectable. He even shook Saundra's hand when she spoke to him in German."

Lane peered at her. "You think tramps don't know how to shake hands?"

She grimaced. "That's not what I meant." She leaned closer. "Listen. Barry is worn out. He's doing the work of two men. If we could keep Hans on until you can go back to work, it would take a real strain off the rest of us."

"There's no money, Angie," he gasped.

"We could let him work for room and board," she said. "I think he'll be willing to do that. We have plenty of food in the root cellar and enough beef and venison in the smokehouse to last until next August."

"Keep an eye on him," Lane told her. "I don't like the idea of a strange man hanging around my ladies."

She chuckled. "Why, Lane, I didn't know you were so protective."

He reached for her hand. "I take care of things that belong to me, Angie. You know that."

A jolt went through her, and she jerked her hand away. "I'll talk to Hans and Barry in the morning," she murmured and stepped back from the bed. "Get some sleep now. I'll check on you later." She hurried from the room, her heart thumping, her hand tingling. Pausing in the hall, she pressed a dry palm against her brow.

"Are you sick, too, Angie?" Judy asked, eyeing her from the top of the stairs.

"No, hon," she said, stepping toward her. "I'm not sick, just tired. I guess we all are. Let's put out the lamps and go to bed soon."

"Can we have some warm milk first?" Judy asked. "I'm cold."

"We'll get out the last of Saundra's sugar cookies too," Angie added, putting her arm around the girl.

The next morning, Hans came to breakfast with his steel-gray hair slicked down and his beard neatly trimmed. His cheeks curved just beneath his eyes, and he had full red lips.

When he smiled at Angie, his whole face lit up. Amazing what a good night's sleep and warm, nourishing food could do for a person in just a few hours.

"Good morning, madam," Hans said, shaking her hand. "I must apologize for my rudeness last night. I was so cold and hungry that I forgot my manners."

Angie smiled up at him. "There's no need to apologize. I've been cold and hungry myself before." She looked toward the table. "Have a seat, and I'll serve up the hotcakes."

Barry moved around to his chair near the wall. "You don't have to tell me that twice, Angie girl. We've already split a sight of wood out there. I could eat a wagon load of these things." He nodded toward Hans. "We've got us a good hand here. I hope we get to keep him."

Angie spoke to Hans. "I talked with Lane, and he said you could stay on, but we can only give you room and board as wages. The farm's had some hard times lately, and there's no cash." She smiled. "But there's plenty of food and lots of wood to keep us warm."

Hans smiled broadly. His teeth were square-shaped. "What more can a man ask besides a full stomach and a nice fire?" He bent his head toward her. "Please, tell Mr. Lane that I'm very grateful."

Barry handed him the platter of hotcakes. "Help yourself, Hans, while they're still warm."

Soon afterward Judy came bounding down the stairs with her books in hand, and Angie left the kitchen to drive her to school.

As the buggy rumbled back into the yard an hour later, she waved at Barry and Hans standing beside the barn and surrounded by a thick pile of split logs. Barry leaned on a wide ax handle, and Hans had his arms piled high with wood. Both wore huge grins as though they shared a joke. They nodded at Angie, and Barry hefted the ax over his head, intent on an upright log positioned on a stump before him. With a sharp crack the wood split neatly in two and fell to the ground.

By this time Angie had pulled Dan to a halt beside the barn door. Barry dropped his ax and came to unhitch the horse for her. His face was flushed, his hair bristling.

He drew close to her when she climbed down. They were hidden from view between the buggy and the barn wall. Without warning, he pulled her into his arms and tried to kiss her.

With an irritated gasp, Angie pulled away. "Barry, why are you constantly embarrassing me? What if Hans came around the building?"

Hands on her upper arms, Barry twisted his mouth. "Whatsa matter with you, Angie? Lately you act like you don't want me around."

She stepped back. "I've got a lot on my mind, Barry. Lane's sick. Saundra's here," her voice choked, "and I already miss Judy."

"Miss her? We're only moving ten miles away, not to the next state. You'll see her plenty."

Angie stared at the ground. "It won't be the same, though, Barry." She drew in a breath and tilted her head back to look into his face. "I'm sorry. I know I haven't been much fun lately." She stood on tiptoe to peck his cheek. "I've got to help Saundra. She's getting worn out taking care of Lane."

Barry brightened. "She's been great, hasn't she? What a trooper."

Angie allowed him a quick nod and headed across the yard, skirts held above her ankles, her feet stretching out. Saundra was a trooper for carrying a few trays up the stairs? How about

Angie who had managed the entire house for years? Barry had never even noticed that.

Inside the warm kitchen, Angie pulled off her coat and attacked the breakfast dishes. She felt a tiredness inside that had nothing to do with chores or lack of sleep.

When Barry and Hans arrived for lunch, a pot of stew and a pan of biscuits sat ready on the stove. Hundreds of wood chips speckled their dark coats. Their faces shone with sweat despite the cold weather. Hans's rosy face creased into a grin when he saw Saundra. Immediately a rush of German filled the kitchen.

Unable to understand, Angie still enjoyed listening to the flow of conversation between them. She filled bowls and coffee cups while the men shed their coats and washed their hands. Gone from Hans's face was the desperation of the night before. In less than twenty-four hours, he'd changed from a hollow-eyed tramp into a gentleman with rosy cheeks and a ready laugh.

"Forgive me," Hans told Angie as he sank into his chair. "I can't help talking to Saundra in my own language." He smiled at the blond woman beside the stove. "It's been so long since I've been able to speak German." His words had a strange sort of singsong that made him nice to listen to.

Saundra picked up a small wooden tray holding a full porcelain teacup and some toasted bread. "It's a pleasure talking to you, too, Hans. Let's have a game of chess after supper, *ya?*"

"Ya!" their visitor said, his blue eyes twinkling. His gaze followed her until she disappeared down the hall; then he picked up two biscuits from the plate before him and lifted his spoon, a look of bliss on his face.

After three bowls of stew and four biscuits, Hans stayed behind when Barry went outside. "Miss Angie, Barry won't need me for at least two hours. May I help you with the dishes? I'm a good cook if you could use some help. Or maybe you have a floor for me to scrub?"

Angie stared at him, shocked. She'd never heard a man offer to help with housework before. "Why, thank you, Hans," she stammered. "You don't have to do that."

"Please." Genuine pleading appeared in his eyes. "You saved my life. I want to help. Chust tell me what to do."

Lifting two empty bowls from the table, she paused a moment longer. Finally she said, "As a matter of fact, things have been difficult with Lane sick." She considered. "Maybe you could do the floors in the downstairs. Not all of them today but between now and Thanksgiving."

"Thank you." He stood and grabbed his own bowl and cup then set them on the counter near the washbasin. "Show me the bucket and the soap, and I'll get started."

Trying not to stare at his delighted expression, Angie found the bucket, a rag, and a brush. "The crock of soap is behind the cellar door," she told him and returned to her washbasin in the kitchen. *What an unusual man.*

Angie finished the dishes and put a fat hen in the oven for supper. Thinking she would check on Lane, she hurried toward the stairs and drew up short.

Kneeling on the second step, Hans leaned forward until his nose almost touched the back corner of the fourth step. He seemed to be pulling on something. Suddenly he stiffened, and his brush swished along the length of the step.

"I'm sorry to bother you," Angie murmured, "but I need to get by you."

"Oh, Miss Angie!" he said, leaning until his shoulder touched the wall. "I didn't hear you there. Go right on up. Chust be careful. The wood is wet."

When Angie opened the door of the master bedroom, Saundra sat in the oak rocking chair beside Lane's bed. As Angie eased the door wider, Saundra's eyelids drooped then opened wide. Lane lay on the goose-down pillow with his head cocked toward his left shoulder, eyes closed, breathing softly.

"How is he?" Angie whispered.

Saundra shrugged. "The same. He's too weak to talk much, and he took only a little sip of tea."

Angie touched her shoulder. "Get some rest. I'll sit with him for a while."

Saundra stood to her feet and touched her hair at the back. "Thank you, Angie. I am a little tired." She padded out, and Angie sank into the chair.

Watching Lane's haggard features, Angie had an urge to sweep his black hair off his broad forehead, to rest her hand against his cheek. *Please, Lord, let him get well.* She repeated the sentence again and again in her mind. After awhile, her eyes drifted toward the gauzy curtain that let in a feeble light.

A deep sigh from the bed brought her to full awareness.

"Water," Lane muttered. "Gotta have water."

She picked up the glass on the bedside table and stood to help him lean forward and drink. Plucking the glass from his hand, she started to set it down but paused when he breathed, "Angie!"

"Yes, Lane? Do you need something?"

He reached out his thin fingers to clasp her hand, and his eyes drifted closed.

Tears welled up. What would happen to her if he didn't get well? What would happen to Judy?

Please, Lord, help him get better. She couldn't stop saying it.

An hour later Saundra came back to sit with Lane, and Angie returned to the kitchen. The polished wood on the stairs reflected the light from a nearby window in a honeyed gleam. On the way down Angie paused to peer into the corner that had captured Hans's interest. The corner shone—like all the other corners on the staircase. She straightened, pleased. Hans was a diligent worker. His cleaning supplies stood beside the back door, rinsed and ready for the next use.

With a smile Angie returned to her supper preparations. Hans was going to be a blessing to have around.

Thursday was Thanksgiving Day. Angie and Saundra planned a special menu, but as the days wore on, they wondered if they'd have anything to be thankful for.

The holiday spirit was squelched by the smell of sickness in the house. At Angie's prodding, Judy made half-moon pies with scraps of dough from Saundra's schnitzel and leftover dried-apple filling. A worried frown on her young face, Judy tasted one of her creations, declared it delicious, then left most of it on the saucer. She hadn't eaten a single full meal since her father became sick.

For most of Tuesday Judy sat on the top step outside her father's door, chin on hand. Her knitting lay in a tangle on her bed.

Wednesday Lane awoke with a clear head, but he still felt as weak as a newborn. Angie cooked a rich chicken broth, and Saundra fed it to him. When Saundra brought Lane's empty dishes to the kitchen, she sank into a chair, her delicate features drooping from fatigue, but she managed a pleased smile. "You were right. He's very nice."

"Is he better?" Angie asked, instantly alert.

Saundra nodded. "He thanked me kindly for looking after him." She stood and carried the tray toward the dishpan. "He wants to see you."

"Why don't you take a nap, Saundra?" Angie suggested. "I'll see to Lane today. You'll need your strength to cook the turkey tomorrow." Angie rinsed dishpan suds from her hands and hurried up the stairs.

When Angie stepped into his room, Lane lay on his side with his arm folded under his head, staring at the door. In silence he watched her progress toward him. His face looked worn and tired.

Angie sank into the rocking chair. The seat suddenly seemed so close to him. "You wanted to see me?" she asked.

"What are you up to?" His voice had gained strength since she last heard it.

"Up to?" Angie tried to look puzzled. "What do you mean?"

"Why do you keep sending Saundra here to look after me?"

Angie answered quickly. "She wants to help, Lane."

"That's mighty nice of her. But I'd rather have you." He studied the edge of his quilt. "Of course, if you're too busy—"

"It's not that. I just thought. . . ." Her voice trailed off. She couldn't think of a good ending for the sentence.

Lane's features relaxed, and he closed his eyes. "I'm sorry. I guess I'm being hard to live with." He rolled over onto his back.

She stood to lean over him. "I'm the one who should be sorry." She adjusted the quilt, trying not to look into his eyes, afraid and not sure why. Her heart rate stepped up a notch.

He touched her hand. "I've put a lot on you, Angie, these past years. I want you to know I appreciate everything you've done, how you've taken Judy under your wing and all."

"I was glad to do it." Wanting to pull away, yet enjoying his nearness, she drew in her lower lip. He released her hand, and she rubbed it on her skirt. "You'd best get some rest now," she murmured.

He nodded weakly, eyes closed. "When I wake up, I want to see Judy."

Angie tiptoed out and eased the door shut behind her. She crossed the hall to her room and closed the door, leaning on it. What was wrong with her? He hadn't scolded her, so why did she feel like crying?

Chapter 8

On Thanksgiving Day, Lane felt strong enough to join the family at a dining-room table filled with German delicacies as well as traditional American fare. Now that the crisis had passed, a sparkling energy filled the house. This would be a Thanksgiving to remember. Saundra and Angie had done themselves proud.

Beside the stuffed turkey sat a wide dish of hot potato salad sprinkled with tiny bits of bacon, a bowl of fresh noodles, and a plate holding dozens of cheese-filled pastries. Roast sweet potatoes and corn rounded out the feast with apple schnitzel and cheese strudel for dessert. The expression on Hans's face when he saw the table would have made a perfect portrait of a man entering the pearly gates.

While Lane ate tiny portions—his first complete meal in almost a week—Barry finished the potato salad almost single-handedly.

Hans beamed at Saundra and repeated at thirty-second intervals, "This is the best cheese strudel I've ever eaten, Saundra," sometimes in English and sometimes in German.

Angie sat near Lane, watching him eat, ready to run for anything he might need.

An hour later she walked with him up the stairs. He spoke little, and his hands trembled as he pulled off his shoes. Pausing to tidy the top of his wide bureau, she stayed until he dozed, tucked under the quilt.

When she returned to the kitchen, the family had slid chairs away from the table a few inches, relaxing against the backs of their chairs and sipping coffee.

"That was my last year in Frankfurt," Hans was saying. He squinted toward the ceiling. "Thirty—no, thirty-five years ago." He beamed at Judy, who was sitting beside him, staring and fascinated. "After that I went to Berlin and got a job with five hundred people under me."

"Wow," Judy breathed.

Saundra smiled, and Barry looked duly impressed.

Hans chuckled, his blue eyes twinkling. "It was a very important position." His glance included Angie in the conversation. "I mowed the city graveyard."

Barry guffawed. Saundra let out a light laugh, and Judy shared a smile with Angie.

Judy glanced at Saundra. "What was Christmas like in Germany? Did you do anything special there that we don't do here?"

"Oh, yes," Saundra said. "We always filled the Christmas tree with short white candles so it glowed like the sun."

"And don't forget the Christmas pickle," Hans added.

Judy's nose wrinkled. "Pickle?"

Saundra nodded. "Every Christmas Eve my mother would hide a pickle deep in the branches of the tree. The first one to find it would get a special present."

"Did you ever find it?" Judy asked her.

Saundra's eyes twinkled. "Not every year, but sometimes I did."

Hans said, "My brother, Johann, was always the winner in our family. I used to get mad at him. Especially when the present was fudge or a fat piece of fruitcake." He patted his thin stomach.

Judy giggled.

Hans looked at Saundra then. "Would you like to play chess after the dishes are put away, Frau Dryden?"

Saundra's lips curved upward. "Please call me Saundra," she said. "We're all friends here." Then she shook her head. "I'm sorry. I can't play with you tonight. I promised Barry a game."

Hans held up a wide palm. "Don't apologize. I'll make a reservation for tomorrow night then, *ya?*"

"Of course." She stood and began gathering plates.

"Don't, Saundra," Angie said. "Judy, Hans, and I will finish these. You need a rest. You're a guest here, remember?"

Saundra continued gathering plates. "I don't want to be a guest, Angie. Please. I'll help you." She moved toward the washbasin. "It's more fun that way."

Saundra started washing dishes while Judy and Angie finished clearing the table. Hans picked up a dish towel to dry the clean ones.

When there was nothing more for her to do, Judy called out to Barry where he leaned his chair back against the kitchen wall, idly watching the others work. "Barry, how about playing me a game of checkers while you wait for Saundra?" Judy asked him.

Barry brought his chair down on four legs. "You're on."

Judy set off for the living room at a trot. "I get the red ones," she called over her shoulder.

A few minutes later Saundra's lilting voice made Angie look at her. "You were right, Angie. Lane's a dear. Just like his letters."

"Has he said anything to you?" Angie asked. She tried to act casual, but her throat tightened, and she felt a familiar flutter in her middle.

"He hasn't spoken directly." Saundra smiled into the dishpan. "He calls me 'ma'am' at the end of every sentence."

"You like that?" Angie set the last plate in the cabinet.

"It's—quaint." Saundra reached for a serving bowl and placed it in the dishpan.

Her hands still moving across a glistening cup, Angie wondered about Saundra's definition of the word. Angie knew what *quaint* meant, but she'd never heard anyone actually use it before. She decided to change the subject.

"Saundra, I'm glad you're here to help us through the holidays." She glanced at Hans quietly wiping the table beside her. "You, too, Hans. We haven't had a happy Christmas since Charlotte died three years ago."

"It's been years for me, too," Saundra said. "At the hotel Christmas was a working day like any other."

"It was the same for me," Hans said, handing Saundra the dishcloth. "Since I came to America, I've always worked on a farm. Chores have to be done on the holidays the same as any other day." His expression grew sober. "I hope I can stay long enough to enjoy Christmas with your family."

Angie nodded. She couldn't stand the thought of turning Hans out into the cold again.

He was so helpful and entertaining, and Judy was getting attached to him. "I'd like that, too, Hans. I'll speak to Lane about it."

She set a cup on a shelf. "Let's make this the best Christmas ever. We can gather pine boughs to decorate the house. I saved some red velvet ribbon from one of Mother's party dresses. We can use it for the tree. We can string popcorn and cranberries, too."

Saundra's eyes sparkled. "I brought twenty-five white candles with me in case you'd like to put them on your tree this year."

"How lovely!" Angie exclaimed. "Judy will be beside herself when she sees them." She paused to retie her apron strings. "We'll have hot apple cider and sing carols by the fireplace."

"It sounds wonderful," Hans said wistfully.

Saundra plunged the roasting pan into sudsy water. "We must make a list soon."

When the last dish was put away, Saundra said, "After I beat Barry at the chessboard, we can work on that list."

Angie laughed. "It shouldn't take too long."

Hanging his dish towel neatly on the rack beside the kitchen window, Hans followed the ladies into the living room.

"He's got me!" Judy exclaimed when she saw them. "I've only got one man left, and Barry has three kings."

They gathered around the playing board to see Barry's black checker men surrounding Judy's lone red soldier. While they watched, Barry lifted the king on the far right and made a swift end to Judy's trooper.

"My turn," Saundra said, lifting the box of chessmen.

Angie drew open the top drawer on the maple secretary desk in the corner of the living room and pulled out a blank sheet of paper. "Let's plan what we'll bake for Christmas, Judy," she said. "Saundra can add her favorites when she finishes playing Barry."

"When I finish beating Barry, you mean," Saundra added, a gleam in her eye.

"Set 'em up," Barry said, a firm slant to his stubbled jaw.

Hans perched on the hearth near the crackling fire. He held his hands toward the flames for a while then moved to a low stool nearby.

Angie and Judy huddled together over their list.

"Gingerbread men," Judy said. "I'll decorate them with currants, and we can hang some of them on the tree." She looked at Angie. "We will have a tree this year, won't we? A big one?"

Angie smiled, her eyes wide, her face tilted sideways. "We'll see what we can work out." She glanced at her fiancé. "Barry will help us—won't you, Barry?"

He drew up and looked at her. "What are you getting me into now?"

"We want a big Christmas tree," Judy answered. "Will you help us get one?"

Barry grinned. "What do you think?"

Judy reached into Angie's darning basket standing beside her chair, picked up a ball of yarn, and threw it at him. Barry ducked, laughing. The ball rolled along the floor toward the hearth.

Suddenly Angie noticed Hans sitting close to the fireplace. He leaned forward, staring at the stones so intently that he seemed to be reading some message printed there. He leaned forward to touch a stone nearby.

The yarn ball touched the German man's brown work shoe and stopped. Hans reached down to pick it up and hand it to Judy. Then he returned to his stool and stared into the fire.

Angie turned back to her list, but Judy's chattering voice next to her sounded far away. What was Hans looking at?

A moment later Hans moved closer to the chess table to watch Saundra's contest with Barry, and Angie wondered if she had imagined the newcomer's strange behavior. At seven-thirty Hans said good night and trudged out to his room.

"Angie, the list is finished," Judy said, after Hans left. "Let's start making some ornaments for the tree. As big as it's going to be, we'll need lots of them."

Excited, they hurried upstairs to look in Angie's trunk. On the way past Lane's room, Angie paused to open the door a crack. Lane lay in the dim light of a coal-oil lamp, fast asleep.

The trunk was a treasure chest of fabric scraps, bits of ribbon and lace, mismatched mother-of-pearl buttons, embroidery thread, scarves, and outdated clothes. Armed with fabric scraps and lace, Angie and Judy returned to the kitchen table to sort and plan. Angie lit a lamp and two candles and set them in the middle of the table. The heat of the flames lent some warmth to a cold evening.

Saundra's game with Barry finished, the players arrived in the kitchen laughing. "See, I told you I'd win," Saundra told him. "Why should tonight be different from any other night?"

Barry grinned at her. "You'll have to teach me some of your tricks, Saundra, so's I can at least give you a run for your money."

"After Christmas," Saundra promised.

"Thanks for the game. Good night," he spoke softly to Saundra. "Good night, Angie," he said abruptly and headed out the door.

Angie didn't have time to return the good-bye. She looked up, startled, as the door closed.

"I suppose he's tired," Saundra said, taking a seat at the table. "He kept yawning while we were playing."

Angie chose not to comment on Barry's rudeness. Instead she picked up a scrap of red gingham. "You're full of ideas, Saundra. What could we make with this? To decorate the tree, I mean."

Saundra's eyes narrowed. She stroked the fabric. "We could starch it and make some snowflakes." She took the material in her hand. "Maybe we could make some cones to put candies in." She beamed at Judy. "That would be fun, wouldn't it?"

They talked until Judy's eyes began to droop.

"Let's wait until tomorrow afternoon to start any projects," Angie told the girl. "We'll set these things in my sewing basket until we're ready." She patted Judy's back. "Off to bed with you now. It's been an exciting day, and you're tired." Angie yawned. "So am I."

Saundra stood. "I'll go up with you, Judy," she said, lifting a lit candle and saucer from the table. "Good night, Angie."

"Good night," Angie said gently. "I'll be up in a few minutes." She picked up the fabric scraps and stacked them in a neat pile.

Despite Barry's fascination with Saundra, Angie couldn't help but like her. Saundra was a real lady all the way to the core. She was hardworking but with a lively sense of humor. Add beauty to that combination and what man could resist her?

Angie's lips quirked. What man besides Lane? He seemed to resist Saundra just fine. She paused, staring at the dark window across from her. Maybe she was wrong, though. Maybe

Lane had fallen to Saundra's charms since he became sick. Sighing, Angie stood and blew out the lamp. She lifted the last candle and saucer from the table and walked softly down the hall to the living room to place the fabric in her sewing basket.

The house creaked overhead, something that happened on every cold night. Setting the candle on the chess table, Angie looked at the fireplace. She stepped closer and sat on the low stool before the hearth where the banked fire smoldered in a black-and-orange glow.

What was Hans studying so hard when he'd sat there that evening? It must have been something on the stones. She turned her head one way and then the other, squinting hard. Finally she shrugged. Nothing was there that she could see except brown stones and gray mortar. She'd have to look again in daylight. Maybe she was missing something. But what?

It didn't make sense. Hans must have a habit of staring when he was lost in thought. She must be misreading him. Weary, she picked up the candle and trudged up the stairs.

Chapter 9

The next morning after breakfast, Saundra boiled some starch paste and taught Angie and Judy how to fashion a six-pointed star from fabric cones edged with lace. By noon they had six perfectly formed specimens. Angie laid them on the mantelpiece to dry while Judy set the table for lunch and Saundra took steaming meat pies from the oven.

Bending over at the waist, Angie again searched the fireplace stones for some pattern, some odd formation that might have caught Hans's eye last evening. Nothing was there but smooth creek stones the original builder had hauled to this site so many years before. Angie had polished these stones hundreds of times. Surely if something were unusual about them, she'd have seen it before now.

The back door banged, and she hurried toward the kitchen to help Saundra. The men had been splitting wood again that morning, and they'd be starving. On her way out, she met Lane at the bottom of the stairs. Still thin and pale, he had on his work clothes.

"Where do you think you're going?" she asked him, taking his arm.

He grinned, and her heart felt a sweet ache. She'd been so afraid she'd never again see him smile in that casual, easy way again.

"I'm going to get some lunch." He covered her hand where it lay on his arm.

She swallowed a lump in her throat. "And then back to bed, right?" She plucked at his sleeve. "These clothes don't give you permission to step outside, Mr. Phillips."

He nodded, amused. "Seriously, Angie, I'm doing much better. I ate a full breakfast, and I'm already hungry again. In a few days I'll be splitting wood with Barry again." They reached the kitchen door, and Barry looked up.

"Sorry, Lane, but you won't be splitting wood with me for months to come."

Lane's face formed a mock scowl. "Says who?"

"I do," Barry said, enjoying the moment. "We finished splitting the whole pile this morning."

Lane sank slowly into the head chair at the table. "You don't say." He glanced at Hans to his right. "I've got you to thank for that, don't I?"

Hans's fair cheeks turned pink. "It was nothing, Mr. Lane. I just helped Barry stack the wood. He did all the hard work."

"He's a good hand, Lane," Barry said. "Even though you're on the mend, I'd hate to give him his walking papers in the dead of winter like this."

At the stove Angie waited. She knew what Barry was hinting at. Would Lane get the message?

"You're right," Lane said, some spirit coming into his voice. "How would you like to stay on until spring?" he asked Hans. "The same arrangements as we have now: You help with chores and whatever else needs doing in exchange for room and board."

Angie turned to catch sight of Hans's head bobbing. "Thank you, Mr. Lane. Thank you again and again."

Lane glanced at Angie, the only one still standing. "Angie, are you ready to start? We need to ask the blessing."

Angie slid into her chair, and Barry prayed, "Thank You, dear Lord, for the food we are about to enjoy and for Your bounty. Amen."

Saundra gave Hans a wide smile. His full red lips spread outward and upward. "I know God led me here," he said. "It had to be God."

"Do you believe in God?" Judy asked.

"Ya"—his head bobbed again—"my mother was a God-fearing woman, and she always took me to church with her."

"That's good, Hans," Angie said gently, "but have you ever trusted Christ to forgive your sins and make you a new person in Him?"

Hans's cheeks grew pink. He slurped his coffee. "I'm not sure about that," he stammered.

Angie handed him the meat-pie dish. "We'll talk about it later," she told him, smiling. "Have some of Saundra's good cooking."

His expression relaxed, and he grasped the porcelain pan. "Thank you very much," he said and dug in.

That evening Saundra found a yellowed, handwritten pattern she had brought with her. Using it, she taught Judy to crochet a lace angel to top the tree. Angie watched the child's progress from the living room sofa while she darned socks. Worn out from a hard day at the woodpile, Barry and Hans had already gone to their room.

Lane took a seat near the fire in the living room. "I ought to go upstairs," he said, "but I can't face crawling into that bed yet." He leaned back and stretched out his legs. "That bedroom feels like a jail cell. I've been in it too much since I've been sick."

"Lane," Angie said, looking up from her work, "is there anything unusual about the fireplace?"

He squinted at her. "What's that?"

"I thought I saw Hans staring at the stones on the fireplace as though he were looking for something in the mortar—or something." She glanced at Saundra then back to Lane. "Do you have any idea what he may have been doing? This morning I looked at it myself, but I can't figure it out."

Lane shrugged. "You must have been imagining things, Angie." He chuckled. "You do have a wild imagination sometimes, you know."

Judy giggled.

Angie quirked in one corner of her mouth. "I'm beginning to wonder if I *was* imagining things."

Saundra looked up. "I wasn't sure how to tell you this, Angie, but I think you ought to know." She paused, her hands restless against the crochet instruction page. "Whenever we're alone, Hans starts speaking German. He asks me question after question about the house. It's happened three or four times." She laid down the crackling page. "I've wondered if he speaks German so no one else will understand what he's saying."

"What does he say?" Angie asked.

"He wants to know how long you've lived here. He asked if anyone has changed the house in the last twenty years—added rooms on or anything, I mean." Her perfect eyebrows arched upward. "He even asked me if I'd find out the answers for him."

"What did you tell him?" Judy asked. Her bright eyes told that she was enjoying this discussion more every minute.

Saundra's expression grew indignant. "I told him that I wouldn't trouble you good people with unnecessary questions."

Angie drew her elbows close to her middle. "Hans is such a nice man. I can't understand why he's so interested in this place. Do you think he came here for a reason?"

Saundra lifted her shoulders. "I have no idea, Angie. He may be German, but that doesn't mean he's automatically a special friend of mine." She sighed then went on. "I've been around hundreds of people in my life, and I've always thought I could judge a man's character from the moment I meet him."

Saundra's smooth face creased between her brows. "Hans has me puzzled, Angie. He's friendly, and he seems so kind. But sometimes he says things that seem peculiar."

Lane turned in his chair so that he faced Angie. "Do you think I should let him go? I don't want to take any chances. He may be a thief or worse."

"No, Daddy!" Judy cried. "Don't send Hans away. He's not a bad man. I know he's not."

Lane's expression grew tense. "Judy, I have to think of what's best for the family even if it's hard to do."

"Don't send him away," Angie said softly. "I don't think he'd hurt us."

Saundra nodded. "I don't think he's dangerous, Lane. I think he has some kind of secret." She glanced at Angie with an impish smile. "My feminine curiosity wants to know what it is."

Angie chuckled. "So does mine, Saundra. I never could stand it when I knew that I didn't know something."

"Me, too!" Judy added.

Suddenly Lane tilted his head back and laughed. "With you ladies on his trail, Hans will have to cry 'Uncle' and admit to whatever he's up to or get worried to distraction. I almost feel sorry for him."

"See this, Daddy?" Judy held up a flattened white crocheted ball with half a body hanging beneath it. "Wait 'til I get the wings finished. Then Saundra will soak it in starch so it'll hold its shape."

Lane took stock of Judy's progress. "That's beautiful already, honey."

"How nice of you to take time with Judy," Lane told Saundra, his smiling eyes on her face.

"It is my pleasure." She glowed.

He seemed confused and fumbled to get his feet beneath him. "I'm still a little weak. I'd best get myself off to bed while I can still climb those stairs." He laid his palm on Judy's head. "See you in the morning, chipmunk." He turned toward the sofa but didn't meet any one person's eyes. "Good night, ladies."

Angie dropped her sewing. "Do you need anything, Lane? Should I come up with you?"

"No, no." He waved her back. "I'll be fine. Maybe I'll light the lamp and read awhile."

A chorus of good nights followed him out of the living room.

Angie watched his back until he disappeared up the staircase.

Judy immediately forgot her crocheting. "Shall I follow Hans around and see what he does?"

she asked. She leaned toward Angie, tense excitement in her voice, her eyes dancing.

Angie reached forward to clasp the child's arm. "Don't you dare, Judy. You leave him alone." She glanced at Saundra then back at the girl beside her. "I don't want you to make him feel like he's being spied on. If there's anything going on, we'll catch on to it sooner or later." She gave Judy a pat. "Now off to bed with you. Scoot."

With a reluctant sigh Judy wrapped her cotton thread around the incomplete angel and carefully laid it in Angie's sewing basket. The tilt of her head told that she knew better than to argue when Angie gave her a direct command, but tonight she had a very hard time obeying. Her steps lagged, and she paused at the door.

"What could he be looking for?" Judy turned back to ask. "Do you think there's buried treasure on the farm—or maybe gold?" Her eyes grew round as saucers.

"Judy!" Angie made a move as though to rise from her seat.

With a loud giggle, the girl dashed up the stairs. An instant later the door slammed overhead.

Angie winced at the noise. "I hope Lane wasn't sleeping," she said. "That child is unstoppable sometimes."

"Like her aunt?" Saundra said in a teasing tone.

When Angie looked at her, surprised, Saundra let out a short laugh. "You have a wonderful quality, Angie—an indomitable spirit."

"Indomitable?" Angie asked.

Saundra nodded. "Right. You just said it. Unstoppable." She picked up a sock that Angie had laid on the sofa between them. "You should be thankful. I wish I had more of it myself."

Snipping off a thread, Angie folded another finished sock and laid it in the pile at her side. "Can you remember exactly what Hans asked you? His exact words?"

Saundra considered. "As I said, he asked me how long you had lived here." She drew in a slow breath, thinking hard. "He wanted to know if there were any hiding places where a child might play."

"Hiding places?" Angie thought about that. "Judy and I used to romp through this house by the hour. We know every inch of it, and I never saw anything like a hidey-hole." She shrugged and let her shoulders sag. "I'm tired, too. I guess I'll go up to bed."

She stood and looked back at Saundra. "I'm afraid we're all borrowing trouble. Hans probably has a habit of staring whenever he's thinking about anything serious. Maybe he misses his mother or something like that."

Saundra nodded. "Good night, Angie. Don't let it worry you. I'm sure our Hans isn't a bad man. I'd have spotted him right away if he was." She turned toward the smoldering fireplace. "I'll sit here alone for a few more minutes before I come upstairs. I enjoy the quiet."

"Good night," Angie said and climbed the cold stairs.

When she crawled into bed beside sleeping Judy, Angie tried to picture Hans's posture and the expression on his face when she'd seen him beside the hearth, but the image had already faded. Tired of thinking about it, she turned over and went promptly to sleep.

Chapter 10

Lane's strength grew with each new dawn. Sunday morning he said good-bye to the family at the back door when they set off for church. "I'm going to eat another biscuit and read a book by the fire," he told Angie as she tied on her bonnet.

"If you get tired, go up to bed," she told him, scanning his thin face. "I don't like leaving you here alone."

He grinned. "Hans is in his room in the barn. I can call him if I need something. Besides, I'm not an invalid, Angie. I'll be fine." He drew in a deep breath. "Tomorrow I'm going to start doing the chores with Barry and Hans."

At her raised eyebrow, he took a step back and chuckled.

Angie pulled her wool cape over her coat and fastened the frogs. Her shoes clumped on the wooden porch and down the steps to the buggy. She was the last one aboard.

Saundra sat in front with Barry, and Angie huddled under a thick robe with Judy.

Inside the church doors Saundra let Barry help her off with her coat in spite of the chill. Angie kept her wrap on. Her Sunday best was a brown wool dress with a deep yoke. Next to Saundra's cranberry gown, she felt like a frontier sparrow lighting beside a cardinal.

Barry had been right. Every lady's eye traced the seams on Saundra's silk dress. Every man under eighty nodded toward her with that special expression reserved only for the beautiful. Shoulders back, head high, Barry introduced her to anyone who would listen. Angie watched him, irritated. He never wore that look when *she* was on his arm.

"Good morning, Angie," willowy Mrs. Coldwell murmured at Angie's side. "How's Lane?"

Summoning a smile, Angie turned and said polite words she couldn't remember ten seconds later. She kept herself from looking at Barry until the service began, and then she glanced at him only once. What had gotten into him? He hadn't been the same since Saundra came to Chancyville.

Outside the church two hours later, Saundra put an arm around Angie's waist for a quick hug as they walked to their buggy where Barry was untying the horse.

From behind them came Judy's shrill scream: "You didn't tag me!"

"Yes, I did!" a boy's voice shouted back.

"What a wonderful congregation you have here, Angie," Saundra said with a bright smile. "And what a wonderful sermon!" Her eyes sparkled. "I'm so glad I could come here. You can't know what it's meant to me to get away from Chicago."

A second later the sparkle vanished. "If only Lane wasn't so shy." She glanced at Angie. "I thought he'd start talking to me by now. Even after spending so much time with him while he was sick, he still keeps a distance between us." She sighed. "What am I doing wrong?"

"Nothing," Angie said. "You're very charming, Saundra." She squeezed the German lady's hand. "Lane will come to his senses soon. I'm sure of it."

They reached the buggy, and Barry dashed forward to help Saundra climb up. When she had reached her seat, he turned to give Angie a hand then drew back, puzzled, at the arched look he received from his beloved. He shrugged and climbed into his seat, leaving Angie to board on her own.

"Judy!" Angie called as the horse backed away from the hitching post. "Judy!"

Her bonnet bouncing on her back, its strings around her neck, her braids loosened and hair sweeping her face, Judy vaulted into the buggy. "Do we have to go already?" she asked, panting. "We're playing freeze tag."

Angie held up the robe for Judy to slip under it. Laughing, she said, "We can freeze together right here, love."

Judy threw herself to the seat. "Oh, Angie. You know what I meant."

"We have to go," Angie told her, tucking the robe around them. "Your daddy is waiting for us."

Barry clucked to the horses, and the buggy rattled out of the churchyard. Quieting down at the rhythm and sway of the buggy on the dirt road, Judy laid her head on Angie's shoulder and seemed to doze. Barry chatted with Saundra about the church services, and Angie stared at the passing landscape.

Her carefully laid plans hadn't turned out anything as she'd imagined. Now that things had been set into play, she felt like a small child on a toboggan skidding down a slippery slope and unable to steer. Who knew where she would land?

Finally Barry pulled the buggy to a stop in front of the kitchen door. Angie was the first to reach the house. When she stepped inside the kitchen, she drew up at the edge of the open door, shocked. A pair of short legs covered by overalls seemed to be sprouting from under the kitchen cabinet. Hans lay on his back, his upper body completely inside the cupboard next to the stove.

Judy pushed in beside her. "What are you doing, Hans?" she cried, stooping down beside him to look inside the cupboard.

"Judy! You startled me!" he said, a laugh in his voice. He scooted out and sat up on the floor. His white hair stuck out in five directions. His chin had a dust smudge. "I was checking to see if I could make Angie a drain going from the basin in here and emptying outside. Then she wouldn't have to carry her dishwater outside in the cold."

Angie turned to glance at Saundra's flushed face beside her. They shared a meaningful look. What was Hans up to?

"A drain?" Angie asked, stepping inside so that Barry could shut the door.

"Sure." Hans's head bobbed. He turned to rest on his hands and knees and pushed himself upward to stand. Using his hands, he framed a space on the counter. "We could put a metal bowl with a hole in the bottom here and attach a hollow pipe to it. The pipe would go from here," he pointed, "to the outside wall and down to the ground."

"If the bowl has a hole in it, it's no good," Judy said.

"We'd make a cork stopper," Hans replied, as though it were no problem. He turned to Barry. "I saw it done in Rapid City."

Angie pulled at her bonnet strings. "It sounds wonderful, Hans, but right now I've got to get dinner on the table. We can talk about it later, all right?"

He nodded, eager to please. "I'll put these pots back," he said. "Maybe next week we can work on this."

Angie hung up her cape and headed for the stairs. She wanted to change out of her Sunday dress before she started cooking. Three strides later she paused in front of the living room's double doors, surprised to see them closed. She tried the handle. Locked.

She knocked lightly. "Lane? Are you all right?" she called.

"Are you back already?" came his reply.

Judy pressed close to Angie. "What are you doing, Daddy?"

Lane chuckled. "Didn't I ever teach you not to ask questions at Christmastime?" He paused. "I'll be out in a few minutes."

Angie grasped Judy's shoulders and turned her toward the stairs. "Let's change clothes. I've got to put those roast chickens on the table, and I could use your help."

Saundra swished past, and Judy fell into step with her. A few seconds later, Saundra's amused voice drifted down from the staircase. "Slow down, child," she said. "When you chatter so fast, I can't understand you."

At Angie's call for lunch, Lane emerged from the living room, a pleased grin on his face. He smiled into Angie's eyes, and her heart lurched. She hadn't seen that look since Charlotte died. Suddenly she felt like singing. Maybe things would turn out all right after all.

A moment later she realized she was staring at him and turned away, confused. "Judy," she said, "come and sit down—we're ready to eat."

When everyone was settled, Barry asked the blessing, and the meal began. Angie kept her attention on her plate. Something was happening to her, and she couldn't understand it. She wanted to be alone to sort it out. The trouble was, she couldn't decide if she was glad or sorry about it.

The moment her plate was clear, she excused herself and rushed upstairs. Saundra had already offered to finish the dishes, and Angie had to have a few minutes of quiet. By the time Judy came up to their room, Angie had drifted into a light doze, one arm curled under her pillow. She had a deliciously warm feeling way down deep.

Afternoon shadows grew long on that short winter day when Angie knocked on Saundra's door. The German lady opened it a crack. "Why, Angie, come in." She pulled the door wider. "This is the first time you've paid me a visit." She wore a flannel wrapper over a nightgown, her hair about her shoulders.

Feeling timid, Angie entered the room and glanced around. The thick eiderdown quilt was Saundra's. Six cut-glass bottles sat on the dresser scarf beside a silver brush and mirror set. "I hope I'm not disturbing you," Angie said. "Were you resting?"

"Not sleeping, dear—just relaxing. I wanted to get out of those stiff clothes for a few hours and rest."

Angie brushed at the flyaway strands around her face. "I was wondering—" she hesitated, embarrassed, then rushed ahead. "I wondered if you could give me some help with my hair."

Saundra laughed softly, a rich musical sound. "You have beautiful hair, Angie. You could do a hundred things with it."

"I've tried a bun, but it always falls out."

"Here—sit in this chair, and I'll help you." With a quick movement she snapped the thread holding the braid together at the bottom. "Would you like a twist like mine or a pompadour?" When Angie shrugged, Saundra came in front and put her hand on Angie's chin, turning her head. "A pompadour, I think."

"Whatever you say." Her voice turned wistful. "You always look so nice."

Saundra lifted the wide brush. "When I was a teenager, I looked like a plucked chicken, all legs and beak."

Angie chuckled, not believing her.

"Oh, it's true. My mother always told me I was beautiful, but I thought she was only trying to cheer me up."

"What happened?"

"I went to a girls' school the summer after my mother died. They had classes in etiquette and appearance." She brushed from Angie's crown to her waist with rhythmic strokes. "Who knows how I would have turned out if not for that summer?"

"I wish I could go to something like that."

"Now that I'm here, I'll teach you. Then you can teach your daughters." She turned away and picked up the mirror. Handing it to Angie, she said, "When I tell you, watch me so you'll know what to do." She put a dozen long hairpins between her lips and tried to talk around them. "Bend upside down."

"What?"

"Bend over!"

Wondering, Angie leaned forward until the tips of her hair touched the floor. Saundra brushed it downward then loosely gathered the whole mass a few inches behind Angie's forehead.

"Sit up now and look in the mirror." She twisted a loose rope of hair and coiled it neatly on top of the girl's head, tucking in pins as she went. "There now. How does that look?"

Angie held up the mirror. "It looks nice now, but in two minutes all kinds of strands will spring loose."

"It will look charming," Saundra said, smiling. "You need to learn something, Angie."

"What?"

"You are Angie McDonald."

She wrinkled her forehead. "So?"

"So don't try to be Saundra Dryden. God gave you lots of curly dark hair. It falls around your face sometimes. Is that so bad?" Using a hairpin, she gently pulled tiny ringlets from the edge of Angie's hairline. "They soften the angles on your face." She backed off to eye the effect. "Lovely."

Angie stared at herself in the mirror. She had to admit she'd never looked better. She laid the mirror on the dresser. "I have some dark green wool I've been saving for a new dress. Would you mind helping me make it? There's still time to finish it before Christmas."

"That's a marvelous idea." Saundra sat on the edge of the bed. "Can you get it now?"

Angie skipped to her room to fetch the fabric. Face alive with curiosity, Judy followed Angie back to Saundra's room and leaned against the bedpost. A few minutes later the girl scooted back onto the quilt and drew her half-finished angel and a crochet hook from her pocket.

The ladies spent the rest of the afternoon snipping and fitting, chatting and laughing. Like a butterfly turning inside its chrysalis, Angie felt her spirit move and change. It was exhilarating—and a little frightening.

The next morning Lane came to breakfast dressed in overalls for chores. He stopped dead in the kitchen door, his gaze on Angie for a full ten seconds. Blushing, she turned away from him.

Pouring coffee, she glanced up to find his gaze on her again and ran the hot brew over into the saucer.

"Judy!" she scolded her niece. "Why are you taking so long packing your school bag?" Immediately she regretted the words, born of her own agitation and not anything Judy had done.

Barry opened the door, letting in an icy gust. Hans came in at his heels. Shedding their coats, the men slid into seats.

"Gud morning!" Hans said, beaming. His cheeks had filled out, and his coat no longer hung like a loose feed sack. His twinkling eyes paused at Angie's flushed expression. "Very nice, Angie," he said, glancing at her hair. "Very pretty."

"Thank you, Hans." She poured his coffee without spilling a drop.

Saundra set a pitcher of warm sorghum on the table in front of Hans.

"Thank you kindly." Hans's blue eyes lost some of their twinkle as he looked up at Saundra. Instead a slow warmth kindled there. Angie glanced up in time to see it and to see Saundra's cheeks turn pink as the German lady turned away from him.

Barry picked up the platter of hotcakes and looked at Angie. His jaw sagged. "Say, where are you going so slicked up?"

"No place," she said, blushing. "I decided to do my hair different—that's all."

"Why? I liked it the other way."

"Don't tease her, Barry," Judy said wisely. "She'll get mad."

"I will not!"

Judy sent Barry a look that said I-told-you, and Angie struggled to get her nerves under control. Lane forked hotcakes into his mouth. He kept his gaze on his plate and took a wide path around Angie to fetch his coat and wool hat before he ducked out the door. Barry darted frequent glances at his fiancée while he finished breakfast.

When Judy had drained her cup of the last drop of milk, Saundra handed the egg basket to the girl. "Ten minutes 'til time to go."

"Don't let's be late for school this morning," Angie added, jabbing a fork into her last bit of pancake. "I'll be ready in two shakes."

Grabbing the basket's handle, the girl reached for her wrap and scooted outside as her father appeared at the barn door. "Wait for me!" she cried out to him from the open door. "Daddy!"

With a murmur of thanks to Angie and Saundra for the meal, Hans caught the door as Judy swung it closed and stepped outside behind her.

Still tugging on his coat, Barry paused by Angie's chair after Hans stepped outside. "Your hair looks good, Angie," he said, awkwardly patting her shoulder. "Maybe Saundra can tell you how to keep those strands from falling down like that."

"Barry, please." She moved away from him. He shrugged and clumped out the door.

Angie sighed and picked up her coffee cup. "Why does Barry always make a scene?" she asked no one in particular.

Saundra rattled the dishes in the wash pan and didn't answer her.

After dropping Judy at school, Angie slowed Dan and Sheba to a steady trot. The wind had a brisk feel this morning that made the air a combination of pleasure and pain. She enjoyed the steady rhythm of the horses' movements, the grating of metal wheels on sand and gravel, and the utter stillness of a winter's morning. Gazing over the horses' heads, Angie's thoughts swooped and swayed.

Why had Lane looked at her that way this morning? Why, he acted as though he'd never seen her before. Her cheeks tingled, and she pulled the scarf from her neck up over her nose.

The buggy rolled into the lane. Out of habit Angie looked across the stubbled fields on both sides. Everything was brown now. Not a blade of grass or a single leaf in sight. The only green came from the pines and firs among the trees in the hollow.

As the buggy drew near the house, a flick of blue caught her eye. Had someone ducked behind the corner of the house? She squinted at the weathered siding, straining to remember what she had seen. Her heart doubled its pace. For the first time in years, Angie felt afraid.

Saundra wasn't in the kitchen when Angie stepped inside. The dishpan sat empty and gleaming on the counter; the damp towel hung on its rod.

"Saundra?" Angie called. "Saundra? Where are you?"

No reply.

She stepped toward the back of the house. "Saundra?" Angie hurried to the back door and lifted the curtain to peer out the window. No one was there, not even any footprints. Maybe she was imagining things again.

"I'm up here," a lilting voice called from upstairs. "I'm collecting sheets to start the washing." Saundra appeared at the top of the stairs, her arms full of white linen. Her expression stiffened when she saw Angie's face. "Angie, what's the matter? You're pale."

"I thought I saw someone running out of the back of the house just now. How long have you been upstairs?" She pulled off her cape and scarf.

Saundra walked down a half dozen steps and stopped, thinking. "I finished the dishes shortly after you took Judy to school. Then I came up here." Moving deliberately with her bundle, she reached the bottom of the stairs. "I must have been upstairs about half an hour or maybe more."

With Angie beside her, they returned to the kitchen. Saundra dropped the sheets to the table. Angie hung up her wraps and lifted the washtub from its hook behind the door.

"Did you see who it was? Maybe it was Barry or Lane."

Angie shook her head. "Neither Barry nor Lane moves that fast. This was a kind of scared jerking motion, like a child who's playing hide and seek." She shrugged. "All I saw was a patch of blue near the ground like a pants leg or something. I didn't see the top half of whoever it was." She rubbed her chin. "Maybe I was dreaming. Maybe no one was really there."

Grating a bar of soap over the basin, Saundra straightened to look at her doubtfully. "Practical Angie? Dreaming? You are the last person in the world I'd expect that from."

"Don't count on it," Angie said ruefully. "I seem to be doing more than my share of dreaming these days."

Saundra paused, soap in one hand and the flat grater in the other. "Speaking of dreaming, I have to tell you something."

"What is it?"

Saundra avoided meeting her gaze. "I'm afraid—no, that's not what I want to say." She rubbed the soap slowly across rough metal, and flecks of tan fell to the washtub floor. "What I want to say is that I'm very confused. I know that I came here with an understanding between me and Lane"—her chin lifted—"and I mean to keep my word, but—" She sighed and searched for the right words. "I mean, the last couple of days I've been wondering—"

Suddenly she turned a shoulder toward Angie and leaned over the tub, grating furiously. "Forgive me. I shouldn't have said anything. It was stupid of me." In seconds she finished the soap and stood back.

Angie lifted a steaming kettle from the stove and poured it into the washtub. Billows of steam rose in the faces of both women. Suds rose like a tidal wave. Angie added some cool water from the bucket on the counter, and washday began.

The kitchen was unusually silent that morning. Questions flitted through Angie's mind like butterflies through a clover field. Who had been around the house that morning? Had he been inside? And what had Saundra nearly told her just now?

Chapter 11

At noon, Angie grabbed her cape and scarf and followed Lane outside after lunch. Barry and Hans were still at the table with Saundra, lingering over coffee and fat slices of walnut cake.

"Can I talk to you for a second?" Angie asked Lane, flinging the wool cape around her shoulders.

His head lifted, alert. "What's the matter?" White puffs came from his lips with every word.

"Let's walk. I don't want to be overheard." She draped the scarf around her hair.

They stepped off the porch and naturally headed toward the lane, their steps brisk in the cold. Tip came to join them. He looked twice his normal size with his thick fur coat now fully in.

Angie didn't waste time getting to the point. "When I came home from taking Judy this morning, I thought I saw someone around the back of the house. He seemed to be running away."

Lane scowled. "Who was it?"

"I didn't see his face, only some blue cloth like a pants leg or something."

"We're all wearing blue overalls," he said, "so that doesn't help any."

"Were you or Barry working up by the house today?" she asked.

"No. We were fixing a leak in the water trough behind the barn."

"Was Hans helping you?"

Lane's expression turned cold. "I'm going to have to let him go, Angie. Like it or not."

"Was he helping you?" Angie persisted.

"He was cleaning the stalls. We were out back, so we didn't see him much."

"Don't send him away," Angie said. "I may have been imagining things." She touched his sleeve. "Besides, nothing showed that someone had been inside the house. Whoever it was probably didn't come inside."

They turned back toward the house. "I'm going to keep a closer eye on him from here on out," Lane said.

She hated to ask the next question, but she had to. "Have you ever thought of putting locks on the outside doors?" Shivering, she pulled the cape tighter across her middle. "I had a creepy feeling this morning when I thought about a stranger lurking around our place."

Lane shook his head sadly. "We've never needed to lock up anything around here. It'll be a sorry day when we have to stoop to that."

At the edge of the yard, Angie stopped. Lane turned to face her. "I'm sure I probably imagined it," she said. "As a matter of fact, I'm almost sorry I mentioned it to you. I don't want to upset you over nothing."

His expression softened. "You're worried. I can tell." He touched her hand. "Are you sure about Hans? I could take him in to town and try to find him another job."

"Please don't do that. Judy would be so disappointed. She's getting attached to him. So is—" Suddenly she clamped her jaw tight. What was she doing? She'd almost spoken aloud the suspicion that was slowly growing inside her. The suspicion that would surely wreck Angie's carefully laid plans.

Instead of finishing her sentence, she said, "I'm cold. I'd best go back inside." Without another word she hurried away from Lane and didn't look back. With each new day she felt more uncertain about herself and everyone else. At this rate where would any of them end up? *Angie,* she told herself, *you're the only one who can end a game with everyone being the loser.*

✹

The first week of December Angie began to feel an excited expectancy. She chuckled with Saundra when they sat down to make their Christmas cooking list. She giggled with Judy while they planned special surprises for Lane. She smiled as she wrapped small presents in bits of colorful gingham and tied them with ribbon.

Soon after dawn on a Saturday morning, Lane and Angie, with Barry and Judy, wrapped themselves in triple layers of wool and headed for a stand of evergreens in the south pasture to find a Christmas tree. Judy chose the tallest tree in the grove, but Lane convinced her to change to one half that size. When the tree was loaded in the wagon, Angie and Barry climbed onto the back to sit on either side of the tree's narrow trunk. Lane perched on the front seat and handled the reins. Too excited to sit down, Judy followed the wagon, dancing around like a clown acrobat toy on a bouncing stick until she grew tired. Then she climbed up to join her father.

Cutting a wide swath through ten inches of snow, Sheba circled around to the front of the house.

"Whoa, Sheba," Lane called, leaning back on the reins.

The horse drew up near the little-used front door, and Lane jumped down to join Barry at the back of the wagon.

When Barry and Lane heaved the tree onto the porch, it landed quivering, full of wet, white clumps.

"This one's still too big," Lane said, panting. "We won't be able to get it around the corner of the hall into the living room." He gazed at the moving mound of branches and needles. "Funny how small it looked in the woods, and how huge it looks now."

"Don't cut it, Papa," Judy begged. She whirled around, her mittens wide apart. "We haven't had a tree in so long. I want a giant one."

Lane raised his eyebrows and looked at Barry.

"I'm game if you are," the younger man said.

"Let's get a hot drink before we start," Lane said, heading around the house toward the back door since the massive tree blocked the front door.

Saundra had hot coffee and cookies waiting for them. Hans had stayed behind to help her when the party set out to find a tree. When Lane had invited him to come along, Hans had said, "I've seen enough cold and snow to last me a lifetime. I'll keep Saundra company." He beamed at Saundra, and Angie stared. Was that a twinkle she'd glimpsed in Saundra's eye?

Pulling her cape around her coat, Angie had stepped outside into the cold stillness of the porch. Why had she tried to interfere with the course of their lives? Things were becoming complicated beyond anything she had ever imagined.

Back in the kitchen after their excursion, the tree hunters drank the steaming black brew at the kitchen table, soaking in the warmth of the room, enjoying the smell of roasting beef wafting from the oven, and munching warm molasses cookies.

Unable to sit still for more than thirty seconds, Judy rubbed a chilly wet mitten across the back of Barry's neck as she passed him. He sputtered coffee, set down the mug, and lunged for her. "You just wait, little missy," he cried when she squealed and dodged away from him. "I may not get you today, but tomorrow's coming mighty quick."

Standing beside the counter with his back near the washbasin, Hans laughed. He shared a warm look with Saundra. "It feels so good to be with a family again," he said. He lifted his own coffee mug. "To the Phillips family. May they prosper in this new year."

Angie's cold face crinkled when she smiled. "Why, thank you, Hans."

Lane scooted back his chair. "Let's get this job finished, Barry."

The men moved a table and an upholstered chair to make room for the tree in front of a tall front-facing window. Angie rescued doilies and china figurines standing near the route they'd have to take to bring the giant fir inside.

She threw on her cape and took a broom outside to brush snow off the boughs. Shivering, her ears burning, she hurried inside to stand beside the crackling fireplace while Lane threw wide the front door. In seconds a frigid wind sucked every bit of warmth out of the house.

With leather-gloved hands the men tugged at the rough tree trunk until the widest branches scraped across the threshold. Pine needles brushed both walls down the hall, making a whisking noise and leaving wet streaks on the plaster.

As Lane predicted, at the corner into the living room, the tree caught in a bind. It wouldn't move another inch.

"Push it your way," Lane said between breaths, jerking the trunk up and down to dislodge it.

"Can't," Barry said, diving underneath for a look. "Ow! This thing has sharp needles."

Saundra and Hans appeared in the kitchen door intent on the trouble in the hallway.

"What do you see?" Lane asked Barry, who lay under the tree.

"The doorjamb is holding some branches so they can't move." Barry pressed up on an armful of pine boughs. No good. He crawled out from under, his coat covered with clinging flecks of green.

"We'll have to cut it," Lane said.

Judy stood nearby, a small, freckled hand over her mouth and an anxious expression about her eyes. Lane glanced at her then gazed into Angie's hopeful face. A determined tightness came into his jaw. He backed away to look over the situation. "Say, Barry, how about if we raise the bottom more?"

"More? You know how heavy this thing is?"

Lane took the cut end of the trunk in both hands. "When I say so, heave." He drew in a breath. "One...two...three...heave!"

The tree lurched and lunged like a living thing. It sprang through the door and landed in a rustling heap on the hooked rug, scattering pine needles from hallway to hearth and knocking a tintype of Lane's parents off the wall.

"Yippee!" Judy hopped about, hugging a surprised Saundra, wrapping her arms around Barry, and bouncing away. She flew right back to throw her arms around Hans for a quick, breath-stopping hug then dashed through the room chanting, "We did it! We did it!"

"We did what?" Barry demanded, touching his scratched face. "I didn't see you lift anything." He grinned widely and pretended to punch her chin.

Lifting the tree upright, the men slid the trunk into a wide bucket filled with dirt they'd chopped loose from the frozen garden. Lane nailed three wooden slats to the trunk for bracing. The top spire brushed the ten-foot ceiling.

Standing back to admire his work, Lane dusted his clothes. "Well, that wasn't so bad." He grinned at Angie. "It sure looks nice."

Moving close enough to Lane to sense his presence, she wrapped her arms across her middle and filled her lungs with a pungent pine aroma. A hundred memories washed over her.

While they stood there lost in another time, another life, Barry and Saundra left the room to bring water for the tree and a broom to tidy the floor. Hans bustled after them.

After a long moment, Lane said, "Why didn't we do this before? I'd forgotten what it was like."

Judy snuggled against her father's side. "We're going to make popcorn and drink cocoa and sing carols, too."

Lane smiled down into her happy face.

"I'll get the decorations!" she said, dashing up the stairs.

Angie moved toward the door. "I guess I'd better find the popcorn."

All afternoon they sang and teased while transforming the living room into a Christmas haven. Angie found a box of her mother's china ornaments in a back cupboard and brought them out: a sled, a sleigh, and a golden harp.

"Saundra, you didn't!" Hans exclaimed when Saundra opened a box of white candles. He looked almost as excited as Judy. "I haven't seen candles on a tree since I was a *libeling* in Germany."

"I had to bring them," Saundra said. "It wouldn't seem like Christmas to me without candles." She pulled a roll of fine wire from her pocket. "Would you care to help me put them on the tree?"

"Mit pleasure," Hans said. He smiled into Saundra's eyes, and something passed between them, something intangible but very real.

Saundra's creamy cheeks turned a light shade of pink. She picked up two candles and busied herself at the tree. Hans followed suit.

Judy picked up a candle. "How do you fasten it to the tree, Saundra?" she asked, peering at the bottom of the wax.

"Here." Saundra handed her a fine silver wire about ten inches long. "Twist the wire around the bottom of the candle and fasten it to a branch." She stepped back and lifted a branch beside her. "Like this one. It's easy."

Judy's mouth puckered as she concentrated. When she stepped back, the candle sagged and slowly pointed toward the floorboards.

Hans chuckled. "Let me help you," he said. Though calloused, his short fingers moved with deft speed. "There. See how I did it?"

Judy bent down until her nose almost touched the wax. "Oh, yeah. Now I see." She reached for another candle. "Let me try again."

Even unlit, Saundra's white candles shone against dark green boughs.

"Can't we light them right away?" Judy begged.

"Let's wait," Angie told her. "If we light them now, we won't have any left for Christmas Eve." She shook the bowl of popcorn in her lap. "As big as this tree is, I'll be stringing popcorn until Christmas Day."

Angie found needles for everyone while Hans fetched a large bowl of fresh cranberries from the kitchen, and they started stringing in earnest. They ate more popcorn than they skewered. Their hands turned crimson with cranberry juice, and their fingers suffered countless needle pricks; yet their homemade garlands grew long enough to wrap the broad giant five times around.

With shining eyes Judy brought out her crocheted angel, now stiffly starched and majestic. Lane placed a step stool on a tabletop then climbed up to trim down the topmost branch and fasten the angel on top.

A few minutes later Saundra carried in a tray filled with steaming mugs of honeyed milk and a plate of golden cookies. While the others helped themselves to refreshments, she ran lightly up the stairs and came back with a shoe box in her hands. "My father bought this in Heidelberg just before we came to America. Would you mind if I set it on the mantle shelf?"

She moved to the sofa where Barry and Angie sat together. Hans stood at her elbow. Judy knelt on the rug beside Saundra so she could watch as Saundra lifted the lid.

Chapter 12

In a bed of yellow straw lay a ceramic crèche with a golden star on a fine wire beside it.

"Saundra, how lovely!" Angie exclaimed. "It's kind of you to share it with us." She moved two lanterns from the center of the mantel shelf to the sides to make room.

Saundra placed the tiny stable in the center of the thick oak shelf and covered the stable floor using straw from the box. With reverent care she placed the figures of Joseph, Mary, and the baby Jesus within the brown walls and positioned shepherds and animals outside. Last she hooked the fine wire into a hole at the back of the roof. The star glowed in lantern light radiating from both sides.

Eyes glistening, she looked around at each member of the family gathered there. "When my father was living, he always used to recite a special prayer after I set out the crèche. Would you mind if I say it?"

Lane cleared his throat. "Please do."

They all bowed their heads except Angie. She couldn't stop watching the tall man before her, his face bent low as Saundra prayed, his intent expression revealing emotions that ran as deep as a mountain spring.

"Dear Father," Saundra prayed, "I thank You for bringing us to this new land, to a new life. I thank You for sending Your Son to a new land one day long ago. We came here to find a better living. He came here to bear our sorrows, our suffering, our sin. Help us to remember always His greatest gift. Amen." She pulled a handkerchief from her sleeve and touched her cheeks.

Weeping openly, Hans mopped his face with a blue bandanna. He sniffed loudly and blew with a honking noise.

Lane turned away and stared at the tree. Or was it the dark window that had his attention? From the side Angie saw him swallow hard. She pulled in her lower lip and blinked twice, squeezing her eyelids tight each time.

Barry broke the mood. "How about a game of charades?"

"Goody! Goody!" Judy cried, jumping on tiptoe.

Smiling through her tears, Saundra nodded. "We used to play it at Harvard."

"I've got Angie on my team!" Judy cried.

Lane stood, stretched, and ambled toward the kitchen. A moment later the back door thumped.

Angie heard it. Her heart went with him.

The games continued until half past eight. Barry teamed with Saundra while Hans cheered them all on from his seat by the fire. Finally Saundra held up her hands. "No more for me, please. I'm too tired to think."

"Me, too," Barry said, reaching his arms high and arching his back.

Hans stood and set empty mugs on the tray. Saundra stepped over to help him.

"Don't bother clearing away the dishes," Angie told them. "You're both tired. I'll take care of them." She poked Judy's ribs. "It's half an hour past your bedtime. School tomorrow, remember?"

Judy groaned. "A whole week until vacation." Following Saundra, she stopped on the stairs to lean over the banister and admire the tree from a new vantage point.

"Judy," Angie called, a warning in her voice.

The girl skipped up the stairs, and a door banged shut.

Hans paused at the door and looked back toward Angie. He spoke softly, his words humble and sincere. "I want to thank you for letting me join the family tonight. Most people would have sent me to the bunkhouse so the family could have time alone."

"Hans!" Angie murmured. "We're happy the Lord led you here. We're enjoying your company."

Hans's expression took on a look of uncertainty. His gaze shifted away from Angie's. "Good night," he blurted out, then hurried away.

Angie continued gazing at the space where he'd stood. Why had his manner changed so abruptly? The longer she was around Hans the more she felt that something was wrong. Yet he was so open and friendly at times. He seemed so tenderhearted. How could it be?

Barry's flannel sleeve pressed her arm, and she looked up. "It was a nice evening," he said, stepping close to her. She could see the individual bristles on his stubbled chin.

"One of the best I can remember," she said. Without meeting his gaze, she moved away to gather the last two empty mugs.

"How about a walk in the moonlight?" he asked, following her.

She held Lane's mug and felt the rim, thinking she ought to go with Barry but feeling reluctant somehow. "I've had a busy day, Barry. Maybe tomorrow night."

He hesitated, pursing his lips and watching her carefully.

Angie lifted the tray. "Good night, Barry."

Still gazing at her, his expression blank, he lingered a moment longer before he headed outdoors to his quarters. Angie carried the tray to the kitchen. She felt bad about putting Barry off, but she wasn't in the mood for his light banter or his insistent advances. She was beginning to wonder if she'd ever been in the mood for them.

Coming in from the barn, Lane passed her in the hall without looking at her. He entered the living room. His sober face made Angie's heart ache.

Washing out the mugs, Angie wished she could ask Lane's advice about her mixed emotions for Barry, but it was hard to talk about something one couldn't define.

On her way upstairs she stopped in the living room doorway. Lane sat on the sofa, staring into the fire.

"Would you like something more to drink?" she asked.

He gazed at her until she wondered if he'd heard her question. "Do you remember Charlotte's eyes?" he asked softly. "I can't remember them. I know they were dark like yours, but I can't see them anymore." His brows drew together. "I lie awake some nights trying to see her in my mind the way I used to."

Padding into the room, she eased into a chair across from him. The fire popped, sending sparks in a shower against the metal screen.

"She had half-moon eyes," Angie told him, "with dark, thick lashes."

"That's right." His lips curved upward. "When she laughed, her eyes almost disappeared behind her cheeks." He drew in a slow breath and let it out. "I still miss her terribly. Maybe I always will."

"I miss her, too." She blinked back tears.

He rubbed his fingertips across his chin. "Until Saundra arrived, I didn't realize how gloomy I'd become. She's been through a lot of pain, too, but she's so pleasant, so easy to be around that a person would never guess she's had a rough past."

Angie pulled at her lower lip with her teeth. Hearing him talk about Saundra sent a strange uneasiness through her. She tried to shake it off.

Lifting his left ankle to his right knee, he leaned back, his arm across the back of the sofa. "I want things to be different around here. Next week I'm going to the smokehouse and pick out the biggest smoked ham for our Christmas dinner." He grinned. "I'm going to take the second biggest ham to town and trade it for some dress goods for Judy. She hasn't had a new dress since I can remember."

He looked at Angie, his dark eyebrows slanted to a peak above his nose. "How would we have survived without you, Angie?" He shook his head. "Poor Judy. I can't imagine what that child went through losing her mother like that, and me so tied up in my own grief I didn't even notice."

They talked late into the night, reliving sweet memories, discussing the future. Finally, reluctantly, Angie stood to say good night. Lane stood, too, and walked with her to the stairs. She took the first step up and turned back to speak with him.

Standing at almost his height, gazing into his eyes, her sentence died unsaid. With lips curved into an easy, natural smile, he had a soft expression she hadn't seen for so long. His strong jaw with a hint of evening stubble, the deep smile crinkles around his eyes.

How long they stood there, she had no idea. Finally she came to herself, and her cheeks burned. Muttering "Good night," she lifted her skirt and scuttled up the stairs to the shelter of her room.

When Angie closed the door, Judy turned over and sighed deep under the covers. Lighting a candle on the dresser, Angie pulled at the fastenings on her dress and slipped a flannel nightgown over her head, working quickly in the cold. She shoved her arms into a quilted wrapper and tugged at the hairpins holding her topknot in place, sitting in a chair to brush and plait her hair.

Her hands moved deftly while her mind dashed hither and yon like a frightened antelope. After awhile she settled down, and the image of Barry's uncertain face came to her. Guilt washed over her in waves. She had treated Barry badly tonight. He deserved more than she could give him.

Pulling off her engagement ring, holding it toward the candle flame, she thought deep and hard about her plotting and conniving. The time had come to be honest about one important fact. She could never wed Barry when she loved another man.

Chapter 13

Anxious to get the difficult task over with, Angie waited for an opportunity to speak to Barry alone the next day. At ten o'clock she spotted him going into the barn. Reaching for her coat, she told Saundra, "I'm going out for a minute. Would you mind taking the bread out of the oven for me? It should be ready in fifteen minutes."

"Of course, dear." Saundra jabbed a darning needle into her ball of wool and laid a mended stocking across the back of a chair. "Three finished and two left to do."

Tip met Angie just outside the door, his feathery tail high, his nose close to her heels. She scurried across the ranch yard, but when she reached the barn door, she slowed down and drew in a breath.

The structure's interior seemed dim after the brilliance of the winter sun. Angie paused inside, listening to the shuffling sound of rats skittering through the hayloft, smelling dust, manure, and hay. She paused by the horses' boxes to pat Sheba and speak to her. A rattle of metal led her to Barry in the feed room.

He looked up, surprise reflected on his face.

"Barry, we need to talk," she said, standing against the rough doorjamb, her mouth dry.

He held a handmade tin can scoop with a folded scrap of metal for a handle. Dropping it into a sack of grain, he said, "You're right. I've known for a couple of weeks that you've got some kind of problem with me. I'd like to know what it is."

Angie pulled in her lower lip. Where should she begin? Barry kept his distance, watching her face and waiting.

Finally she dove in. "Barry, sometimes people make decisions before they really think them through."

"I reckon they do at that," he drawled.

"Lately I've come to realize that—my feelings for you are what a sister feels for a brother, not—" Oh, why couldn't she just spit it out? Having him standing there staring at her didn't help any.

She twisted off his ring and stretched out her hand. "I'm sorry. I never wanted to hurt you."

Watching her, his expression calculating, he didn't reach for the ring. "You're jealous of Saundra, aren't you?" It was more of a statement than a question.

"That isn't it. Believe me." She stepped forward and touched his arm with her outstretched hand. "Here. I wish you all the best."

His lips tightened. "What will I tell Pa and Ma?" he demanded, a hint of desperation in his voice. "They're counting on us getting married and living in the new house." He closed his fingers around the signet ring and slipped it into his pocket.

"Tell them the truth." Turning away, she paused at the door, her heart heavy. "I wish we could still be friends. You've been my best friend since I can remember."

"Maybe someday, Angie," he said, his voice flat, his shoulders slumped. "But not right now."

Trudging to the house, she felt awful for hurting Barry by impulsively accepting his proposal. She'd been uncomfortable with the engagement from the start.

That afternoon the house felt warm and rich with the smell of freshly baked fruitcake. Saundra carefully wrapped each of her creations with a cloth soaked in fruit syrup, then packed them away in a tin to ripen until Christmas. While Saundra worked at the table, Angie stood by the stove, frying doughnuts. The doughnuts were to distract the men from the fruitcake, else little would be left for the holiday.

At supper Barry bent low over his plate, his face sullen. Angie couldn't bear to look at him, and Saundra kept trying to cheer him up. "How about a game of chess after supper?" Saundra asked. "We haven't played for more than a week."

"Maybe tomorrow," he said. "I've had a hard day. I want to go to bed early."

She looked at Lane with a teasing smile. "Would you like to play? Or are you too scared?"

His lips formed a half smile. "Who said I was scared?"

"Well, you didn't finish the last time we played."

He chuckled. "I guess that cuts it. You're on."

Angie took her sewing to her room that night. All that was left to complete the dress was sewing the bodice to the finished skirt.

At ten past eight Angie tied the last knot on her thread and snipped it off. Finally the dress was ready to try on. She should have been excited but felt only a quiet sadness as the fabric slipped over her head.

Folds fell around her feet in a deep green cascade that looked almost black by candlelight and felt cuddly soft, like a warm blanket. She ran her hands over the close-fitting bodice and fluffed out the skirt.

With a gentle knock Saundra appeared in Angie's bedroom doorway with Judy beside her. They looked at the dress, excited. "It's finished!" Saundra cried, happily moving around Angie and fastening the back for her.

"You're beautiful, Angie," Judy said, her eyes glowing.

"That style is almost like the dress I wore for my first Harvard party," Saundra said. "That one had white lace edging the collar and the cuffs."

"I'm going to make some wool braid to trim it," Angie said, adjusting the cuffs. "This skirt ought to have six petticoats at least."

Judy bounced on the edge of the bed. "I want one with eight petticoats."

"'Patience is a virtue,'" Saundra told her, smiling.

"I know that one by heart," the girl interrupted, wearily.

"I've been learning a few things on that subject myself," Angie admitted.

"You look sad tonight," Saundra said. "Did you and Barry quarrel?"

Angie sighed. "I broke our engagement this afternoon."

Saundra's face grew concerned. "So you did quarrel." She clasped Angie's hands. "Things will be all right tomorrow. He'll apologize."

Angie shook her head. Wispy tendrils swept her forehead. "I don't think so, Saundra. We agreed that we weren't meant for each other."

Judy leapt from the bed and almost bowled Angie over. "Does that mean you can stay with me, Angie? You can really stay?"

The child's intense relief brought tears to Angie's eyes. She put her arms around her and squeezed hard. For Judy's sake, she'd stay on as Lane's housekeeper for another ten years just so she could mother this dear child.

For the first time since her talk with Barry, her heart felt lighter. She rested a cheek against Judy's braided hair and breathed a thankful prayer.

"I believe I'll turn in," Saundra said when Judy turned Angie loose. She sounded a little sad.

Angie disentangled herself from Judy and turned her back so the girl could unfasten her buttons. "Good night, Saundra. Thank you for your help."

At the door the other woman hesitated and then turned back. "I'll get up to start breakfast in the morning, so don't hurry down." With a gentle smile she closed the door.

Judy laid her head against Angie's shoulder. "You know something?" the girl asked.

"What?"

"Papa's going to be glad you're staying, too."

Under a mound of wool blankets and quilts, Angie lay awake that evening with Judy snuggled close beside her. She felt the girl's soft rhythmic breathing and sensed something inside her had relaxed. Angie had done the right thing. It felt so good to know that she had. Her eyes drifted closed, and she slept.

Deep in the night Angie's eyes flew open, every nerve tense, on the edge of panic. What had happened? Something had awakened her, and she couldn't tell what it was. Darkness filled the room like thick syrup. Though her eyes strained to see, it was her ears that went on full alert. She felt that horrible numbness that comes with fear.

Something terrible and frightening had happened just now. Was it a nightmare that had brought her fully awake?

She didn't move. Waiting.

Then she heard it. The distinct creak of the loose board on the fourth step from the bottom. Lane must have gotten up to fetch a drink from the kitchen. That must be it.

But her nerves wouldn't settle down. Moving slow and easy so she wouldn't awaken Judy, Angie slipped from the covers, trying not to shiver as she pulled on her thick black robe and found her shoes on the freezing wood floor.

She had to know who was moving around in the house. Something was wrong. Or was it? Maybe Saundra had trouble sleeping and went downstairs for some milk.

Grabbing a candle and matches, she dropped them into her deep pocket. *You're losing your mind, Angie,* she told herself. *There's nothing wrong. You had a nightmare. Admit it.*

But the feeling of dread wouldn't leave.

She eased open the door of her room and tried to peer outside. The hall was as dark as her room. She closed the door behind her, holding the latch so it wouldn't click. Padding four steps straight ahead, her hand touched the wall, and she turned toward the stairs.

Maybe I'm having a nightmare now, she thought. *Maybe this is a crazy dream where I know I'm dreaming but I can't wake myself up.*

When her hand touched the banister, she stopped to listen. A soft rustle came from the kitchen. Taking four quick steps down, she leaned over the banister, peering at the kitchen door to see someone's light.

Only blackness lay ahead. If Lane or Saundra had gone downstairs, they would have lit a candle. Angie pressed a fist to her mouth so the scream wouldn't come out. She had to find out who was there.

Avoiding the fourth step, she slid her right shoe along the wooden baseboard and followed with the other shoe, moving her weight smoothly until she reached the hall table. Despite her care, the edge of her robe caught the corner of a pewter plate in a stand near the edge. It crashed to the floor.

The next instant the kitchen door flew open to let in a brief chilly gust then slammed shut. Hard shoes thumped across the porch and disappeared.

Angie dashed to the door and held the curtain away from the window. Her mind formed a dozen questions simultaneously. Who was it? An Indian? They hadn't had Indian trouble for more than five years. A tramp? Not likely this far from town. What had they wanted? There were no valuables in the house. No one would ever imagine there were. What could an intruder be looking for?

Trembling, she turned away from the door. Suddenly she wanted to be back safe in her room. Feeling her way along, she hurried back upstairs and slid in next to Judy. She lay on her back, shaking, her teeth chattering from a fit of nerves.

Everything in her wanted to believe that a stranger had violated their home, but she couldn't make herself accept it. Tip hadn't barked.

The next morning Angie lingered under the covers fifteen minutes later than usual, enjoying the soft warmth, dreading the intense cold waiting outside her quilt. Had the previous night's episode been a nightmare? It had seemed so real.

The smell of coffee and bacon drew her out, and she hustled, shivering, into a gray dress. When she reached the kitchen, Lane, Barry, and Hans sat together drinking coffee. None of them looked as if they'd slept well.

"How would you like your eggs this morning, sir?" Saundra asked Lane at the breakfast table. Wearing a pale blue dress, she brandished a spatula and smiled sweetly. "Scrambled or over easy?"

Lane set down his coffee cup. "Scrambled, but not too hard."

She arched an eyebrow, watching Barry.

"I'll take the same," Barry added. He glanced at Angie standing in the doorway then turned toward Saundra.

Angie knew he was trying to hide hurt feelings, and her heart ached. She wanted to blurt out her nighttime experience, but she didn't. She would wait and talk to Lane later.

"Scrambled for me too," Hans said. He had his face bent down and seemed to be studying the ridge on his enamel plate, one thumb feeling its edge.

Angie studied Hans's face. Had Lane been right? Had she asked him to bring someone dangerous into their home? Last night she'd been almost certain that Hans was the offender, but now that she saw his sadly troubled eyes, she couldn't believe he was a villain.

Chapter 14

I make the best eggs this side of the Rockies," Saundra said, flashing a smile as she whisked eggs to a froth and poured them into a sizzling skillet.

Barry grinned. "I had some of your eggs last Monday, and I have to agree."

Angie's attention focused on Saundra. She seemed livelier. She had a laughing slant to her eyes. What had happened to Saundra since last night? Had she been the person in the kitchen?

Angie rejected the idea the moment it came to her. Saundra wouldn't be sneaking around in the dead of night. She had full access to the house already.

Lane looked beyond Angie to his daughter in the hall. "Hurry up, slowpoke," he called, teasing. "I'm your driver this morning, and I want to leave early. I've got business in town after I drop you off."

Feeling invisible and totally miserable, Angie pulled out a chair and sat. "I'll take my eggs over light, please," she told Saundra.

"You're next in line," that day's cook said, scraping eggs onto three plates and delivering them with a flourish. She opened the oven door and reached inside for a pan of golden biscuits.

Sniffing appreciatively, Barry waited until the biscuit pan landed on the table, then forked one onto his plate. Hans followed suit.

Judy dropped her school bag by the door and took a seat. "Three more days 'til Christmas vacation," she said glumly.

Lane grinned and touched her shoulder. "You'll live through it. Before you know it, the break will be over, and you'll be going back to school again."

She shot him a horrified glance. "You think that makes me feel better?"

Chuckling, he sampled his eggs. "Saundra, can I fetch you anything from town?"

"No, but I'd like to do some Christmas shopping sometime."

His face showed interest. "Why don't you come along with me today?" He glanced at Barry. "You two can look after that piece of broken fence, can't you?"

"Sure, boss." Reaching for a second biscuit, Barry split it and dipped his knife into the butter bowl.

"I hate to leave you with the dishes," Saundra told Angie.

"You made breakfast," Angie replied, making an effort to keep her voice light. "You can choose some fine green wool for my braid trim while you're there."

"Of course." Untying her apron, Saundra hustled out of the room. "I won't keep you waiting, Lane."

"No hurry."

Angie stared at her plate. That wasn't what he told Judy a few minutes ago.

Ten minutes later she sat alone, listening to Tip's bark and the fading sound of clopping hooves with rattling iron wheels on frozen earth.

For the first time in her life, Angie-the-fixer felt completely helpless. After trudging through her morning chores, she set some white clothes to soak in a washtub of scalding water and climbed the stairs slowly. In her mind she saw Lane and Saundra laughing, close together on the buggy seat. She wanted to grind her teeth, to scream, to beat her fists against a wall.

Worst of all, Angie knew she had no one to blame but herself. In Bible days Rebekah had lost her beloved son, Jacob, because of her conniving. Had Angie lost Lane as well?

Lying on her bed, Angie wanted to pray. She felt ashamed to ask for God's help, but what else could she do? Desperately unhappy, she buried her face in her pillow—begging for mercy and soaking the goose down with hot tears.

Her tears spent, she fell into a twilight doze. And suddenly came full awake. It was the same feeling she had last night.

She scooted off the bed and lunged for the door. This time she didn't have to sashay around in the dark. She was going to find out who was doing this.

She flew into the kitchen and skidded to a halt, almost nose to nose with Barry. He held the broom.

"What's gotten into you?" he asked, his voice gruff. "You chasing a rabbit?"

Her cheeks flamed. "I thought I heard something."

Heavy sarcasm colored his reply. "You did. I shut the door." His expression creased. "Say, you're white as a ghost. What's wrong? You getting sick, too?"

"No." She said it a little too loud. "I thought I heard someone downstairs—that's all." She moved to the washtub and picked up a white shirt.

Still holding the broom, Barry reached for the door latch. "You're getting strange. You know that, Angie?" He lifted the broom. "I'm going to sweep out our bunk room, if that's all right with you."

Angie stared at him and didn't respond. She was too wrought up to deal with Barry's cynical comments. She may as well let them pass.

When he left, she dipped the shirt into the warm water and rubbed it slowly across the ridges of the scrubbing board. Maybe she *was* imagining things.

Trying to turn off her skittish thoughts, she worked steadily until time to get lunch for the men. They came in half an hour late.

"May I help you with something this afternoon, Miss Angie?" Hans asked when he'd finished two roast beef sandwiches. "I'd like to polish the fireplace for you if you don't have anything else you'd like me to do."

Angie hesitated. She felt uneasy at being alone with Hans in the house all afternoon.

"I'm going to work on that halter I'm plaiting for Lane," Barry said. "Would you mind if I sit by the fireplace in here?"

Angie let out her pent-up breath. "That would be fine, Barry," she said, giving him a radiant smile.

He looked at her, uncertain. Still watching her, he stood and pushed in his chair. "I'll—I'll fetch my horsehair in the barn." He turned away to open the door, looked back at Angie once more, and went out.

"I can help you with the dishes first," Hans said, gathering plates from the table.

"Uh—thank you, Hans," Angie said. She moved as though in a hurry, avoiding his gaze. "The polishing cloth and linseed oil are in the pantry," she told Hans when Barry returned. "You can find it."

Hans's head bobbed, and he disappeared behind the pantry door. Within three seconds he returned with the supplies in his hands and left the kitchen.

As soon as he left, Angie's heart rate slowed to normal. She rinsed her dishpan and flung the water over the porch railing into the yard. So far Hans's promise of a kitchen drain hadn't materialized.

The afternoon passed with Angie finishing up the men's overalls and socks, her least favorite part of washday. When the last of them were on the line, she trudged to the living room to sit by the fire. Her hands were red and chapped with cold from hanging clothes on the line. Her nose felt numb.

The men inside sat in cozy silence. Hans had his nose inches from the gleaming mantel, his hand working in rhythmic strokes. Barry sat in a chair nearby, his fingers working the tight braid and stopping now and then to slide on some beads. He looked up when Angie came to the door.

She spoke first. "I'm finished with the wash, and I thought I'd sit down for a few minutes."

"Help yourself," Barry said, nodding to the chair across from him. "I'm enjoying the Christmas tree. See the way the firelight shines on the ornaments?"

"You're not the only one enjoying it," Hans said. "This is the best Christmas I've had since my wife passed on." He turned to smile at Angie, his cheeks glowing red from the warmth of the fire. "Welcome, Miss Angie. Come in. Sit down and rest your weary bones."

Angie sank into the chair and sighed. "It's been a long day." She passed a hand across her brow. "I didn't sleep well last night."

"I didn't either," Hans said. "In the middle of the night, I came inside the house to get a glass of milk. My mother used to give us milk when we couldn't sleep." He glanced at Angie. "I hope you don't mind."

Angie turned to look him full in the face. "Was that you I heard?"

"I'm afraid so." He looked sheepish. "I'm terribly sorry to disturb you. Please forgive me."

"That's fine," Angie said, leaning back in the chair and closing her eyes. "I'm just glad to know it was you and not a spook."

Barry chuckled. "Since when do we have spooks?"

Angie didn't laugh. Since when indeed.

※

Greeted by Tip's happy barks, Lane's buggy rumbled into the ranch yard late that afternoon. Weary at heart, Angie continued setting the table.

Saundra swept into the room, her complexion blooming from cold and excitement. "You must come upstairs and see what we bought," she said, setting an armful of brown-wrapped packages on the end of the table so she could take off her wraps. "Quick, before Judy comes in. She stayed outside to toss a stick for Tip."

Angie came along quietly. Inside the room Saundra took a second look at her. "Are you feeling well? You look flushed."

"I'm fine. What did you want to show me?"

Laughing brightly, Saundra pulled at the brown cord tying the biggest package. "I should have taken your word for it, Angie, when you said Lane would forget to be shy after awhile. He's perfectly charming." She drew the paper away and handed Angie a bundle of pink wool challis, a fine light cloth.

"For Judy?" Angie asked, feeling the soft fabric.

"Lane asked me to make her a dress like they wear in the city these days." She pulled a sheaf of newsprint from another package. "I bought this from the shopkeeper's wife for a penny." She handed her a month-old copy of *Frank Leslie's Illustrated Newspaper.* "I thought it would give us some ideas."

Sinking into a chair, Angie opened the paper, supper forgotten. "Are they really wearing short dresses with bloomers in public?" she asked, shocked at the drawing before her.

"Not many people do, but I saw a few back East."

Turning a page, Angie held the paper toward Saundra so she could see too. "This one looks nice. A wide collar and the waist coming down to a point in front." She looked up. "Can you show me how to make that kind of waist?"

Judy's voice called up the stairs. "Angie! Where are you?"

"We'll start tonight after she's in bed," Saundra promised, taking the newspaper from her.

"Oh dear, I forgot to put supper on the table. I hope the roast isn't overdone." Angie laid down the fabric and headed out of the room. "Here I am, Judy," she called, closing the door behind her.

Barry waited in the kitchen when Angie arrived. "Where's Saundra?" he asked.

"She'll be down in a few minutes." Angie opened the oven and pulled out a roasting pan filled with beef and potatoes. Rising steam blasted her cheeks and made her draw back.

He hovered around the doorway, watching the stairs. "There you are, Saundra," he said at last. "I was wondering if you have time to walk to the barn with me. There's something I'd like to show you."

Saundra glanced at Angie. "Do you need my help?

"Go ahead," she said, spooning potatoes out of the pan and piling them into a bowl. "Dinner will be ready in twenty minutes."

Saundra reached for her cape, but Barry quickly lifted it for her and wrapped it around her shoulders. After she buttoned up, he offered his arm.

"Well, aren't you the gentleman today?" she asked with a teasing smile.

"Today and every day." He cast a sly glance at Angie then smiled widely at Saundra.

Angie saw his glance. What was he trying to do, make her jealous? When he opened the door, a cold blast of wind swept through the room. Angie hardly felt it. She was boiling inside. Barry had done that to make her mad. He acted so childish sometimes.

When Lane came inside, Angie's first impulse was to tell him about her experience the night before, but she held back. Hans had already admitted that he had been in the kitchen. Telling Lane about it might simply get Hans dismissed. Angie didn't want that to happen. She thought that Hans was telling her the truth about why he'd been in the house, and she was afraid that Lane might not see it that way.

One question kept bothering Angie, though. If Hans had been in the kitchen to get some milk, why had he drunk it in the dark? When she'd looked into the kitchen, she had seen no candle or lantern there. Did Hans have the eyes of an owl?

Chapter 15

The next morning Angie got a jolt when she came downstairs and found Lane and Saundra with their heads together in the hall. She caught a couple of whispered words as she passed.

An expression of suppressed excitement on his face, Lane asked, "What do you think?"

"Wonderful!" Saundra replied with a quick nod and brilliant smile.

Forcing herself to move away, Angie's mind replayed the snatch of conversation. She crossed the kitchen—pushing up her sleeves—poured scalding water into the metal dishpan, and added a little cold water to it, trying to keep her mind off the couple in the hallway.

A few minutes later, Lane helped Saundra into her cape. They crossed the yard talking excitedly with Tip sniffing at their heels. Heartsick, Angie watched through the window until they disappeared into the barn.

Lane and Saundra were still inside the barn when Barry returned from driving Judy to school. He unhitched the horses, led them to their stalls, and then strode to the house, white gusts puffing from his mouth with every step.

"Where's Saundra?" he asked Angie.

"In the barn. She and Lane went out half an hour ago."

His brow creased, and he glanced out the window as though expecting to spot them through the weathered walls across the yard. "I just came from there. I didn't see them."

She shrugged and turned away.

"Have you got any coffee?" he asked. "I'm frozen."

"There's still some in the pot. Help yourself." She kept her back to him, deftly drying dishes and stacking them in the cupboard.

He poured the last of the strong brew and set the pot on the back of the stove, moving again to the window. "What are they doing out there?"

"Why don't you go and see, if you're so worried?" His fretting was getting on Angie's nerves.

Still wearing his coat and hat, Barry finished his coffee close to the warm stove, circling to the window every few minutes. Suddenly he clanged his tin cup to the table. "There she is." He jerked the door open and banged it shut behind him.

A minute later he returned with Saundra at his side. Her hand on his arm, she laughed. "Don't you have chores today?"

"I'll be finished by noon. Lane doesn't want to do any more logging until after the holidays."

"Well, after lunch I guess I could play one game with you." She patted his arm, a teasing slant to her eyes. "Now run along. I've got lots to do."

Grinning, he pulled his hat lower in front and strode outside.

Saundra gave Angie a woman-to-woman look. "I hope you don't mind, Angie."

"Why should I mind? Barry and I were never right for each other. I'm just glad I found out before the wedding."

Saundra pulled at the fingertips of her gloves and put them into the pocket of her cape. "I'm going right upstairs to get that challis fabric." She hung the cape by the door. "If you're finished, we can cut Judy's dress out, no?"

"That's what I thought, too."

Swishing her dishcloth in hot, soapy water, Angie shooed those pesky men-worries to the back of her mind. Only two days of school left before Christmas break. After that there would be no chance to work on Judy's dress during the day without giving away the surprise. Working quickly, Angie scrubbed the already-clean tabletop and dried it with a vengeance.

That evening and every evening for more than a week, Angie lingered downstairs after the others retired, hoping to have another chat with Lane. Unfortunately, he worked outside too late for her to see him. Each morning after breakfast he and Saundra would stroll across the yard and disappear behind closed doors, sometimes for more than an hour.

"They're locked in the tack room," Barry said, pacing in the kitchen.

"Have you asked Lane what they're doing?" Angie asked, trying not to laugh at his agitation as she kneaded a pearly lump of bread dough. "They must be working on some kind of Christmas project. What else would they be doing?"

"He won't tell me. I mentioned it to him three days ago, and he ignored me. Saundra won't tell either."

"Don't you think you're making a problem out of nothing?"

"It's not that I don't trust Lane with Saundra." He flicked strong fingers through his shaggy hair and sighed. "You're the last person I should be talking this over with, Angie."

She gave the dough a hard push with the heels of her hands. "We used to be friends, Barry."

He flung himself into a chair. "Saundra's different from any girl I've ever met."

"Lane seems to think so, too." The words slipped out before she could stop them. Angie clamped her lips shut.

"Oh, you've noticed it, too, huh?" He sat up straighter, watching her face for clues.

"Simmer down, Barry. There's nothing you can do about it. If she likes Lane, that's that."

"I'd like to punch his nose in." He glared at the bread dough as if it had a strong jaw and mild blue eyes.

Judy sailed into the kitchen, a pair of mittens in her hand. "Punch whose nose, Barry?"

"Never mind." He lifted his hat from the chair beside him and slammed outside.

Pinching off a large handful of dough and forming it into a loaf shape, Angie wished she could take her own advice.

"What's wrong with Barry?" Judy asked, taking the seat he'd just left.

"It's not something you need to know right now," Angie said softly. Hoping to change the subject, she looked at the brown mittens in Judy's hand.

"What do you have there? Did you finish your father's Christmas present?"

Judy held them high. "You think he'll like them?"

"He'll love them." She slid four loaf pans into the oven. "I have some calico scraps in my trunk. Can we wrap them tonight?"

Judy bounded out of her chair, calling as she skipped down the hall, "I'll put them in my handkerchief box so no one will see them."

That evening Lane surprised Angie by coming back to the kitchen after he'd gone out to the barn for an hour after supper. With Hans cheering them on and laughing, Barry, Saundra, and Judy played Blind Man's Bluff in the living room while they waited for Angie to join them for charades.

"Are you busy?" Lane asked. He had a look of secret anticipation on his lean face as he stepped close to her. Feeling the cold flowing from his clothes, she wondered how he kept from freezing in the unheated barn night after night.

"No, I'm not busy. Why?"

"Could you come to the barn for a few minutes?"

"Surely. I'll tell the others not to wait for me." She tugged her apron strings as she hurried down the hall.

Standing on opposite ends of the room, Barry and Saundra nodded without speaking when Angie told them to go ahead without her. Judy wore a blindfold, her hands outstretched, in the center of the carpet. Hans sat at his usual spot by the fireplace.

"Dress warmly," Lane said when she returned. "I set up a small coal burner out there, but it's still bitter cold."

"It's a wonder you haven't been sick again." She pulled on her coat and reached for a thick shawl.

Eyebrows raised slightly, he looked down at her. "I'm not ready to retire to a rocking chair yet." His slow grin made Angie's stomach flutter.

"Neither is Hans," he continued. "That man can outwork Barry and me hands down." He opened the door, and they stepped outside. On the porch he paused. "He said something strange this morning."

"What was it?" Angie blurted out.

"Barry and I were talking about how we needed to get water to the lower pasture. With the field so big, the cattle have to walk too far to get a drink. It takes beef off of them before sale time."

"Hans wasn't in the conversation at all," he went on. "He was just listening. Then all of a sudden he said, 'Why don't you clean out that old spring in the hollow?' "

Angie gasped. "What? I never heard of a spring down there."

"Neither have I." He took her arm and stepped off the porch. "Let's get to the barn. It's too cold to stay out in the open like this."

"How did he know about the spring?" Angie asked.

"I asked him that. He said he used to work for some people who owned this place about twenty-five years ago. That's how he knew the ranch was here when he came to us. He needed shelter and headed for our house, hoping some friendly folks had moved in."

Angie shoved her hands deep into her pockets. "Well, that puts a new light on things, doesn't it? That's why he was interested in the house and what we'd done to it since we came here. What do you know!"

They crossed the yard in comfortable silence, two people who knew each other so well they didn't need to fill the quiet spaces between them.

At the barn door, Angie asked, "Why didn't he tell us this when he came? It would have been natural for him to tell us."

Lane shrugged and pulled the wooden handle on the plank door. It creaked open. "Who knows? Maybe he didn't think it was important."

The barn felt eerie inside. Lane's moving lantern opened a tiny path of yellow in a sea of thick, furry darkness. Animal smells and soft shuffling noises closed around Angie's senses.

"I thought the tack room would be the most private," he said, pulling at a creaking door. "Judy never comes near here this time of year." He set the lantern on a worktable made of rough lumber.

Angie caught her breath, her eyes wide. Before her stood a three-foot-high chalet as detailed and perfect as a real one. The first story was made of stone and the second two of wood with a wide, hip roof covering the top two levels. It had long, oak shingles and a tiny stone chimney, shutters with a design carved into them, and greased paper across mullioned windows.

"I asked Saundra to draw me a diagram of a German alpine chalet." He nodded, a satisfied look on his face. "She's got a great memory for detail. Every day she remembers something new to make it more authentic." He stepped around the table. "Look at this side."

Open, it showed the interior: the bottom floor for work and storage, the second for cooking and gathering, the third for sleeping. Tiny furniture sat huddled in almost every room.

"I got out Charlotte's doll furniture," he said. "She wanted to save it for Judy when she was old enough not to break it. It's been in a box in the attic all these years, and I just now remembered it." His eyes glowed when he looked at Angie. "You think she'll like it?"

Her face creased into a wide smile. "She'll adore it."

He grinned. "Sorry to keep you in the dark for so long. I didn't want Barry to spill the beans, so I didn't tell you either for fear you'd accidentally mention it to him."

"You didn't know?" Angie said, twisting her hands. "I broke our engagement. I thought Barry told you."

His eyebrows lifted. "The last two weeks he hasn't said anything to me besides talking about work." He tilted his head, still watching her. "You know, he sure has been acting strange lately. Maybe that's why. You must have broken his heart."

"Hardly," she said wryly, wondering how Lane could have missed Barry's calf-eyed looks at Saundra.

He sent her a puzzled look then turned to the project before them. "I'll bring the dollhouse inside on Christmas Eve. You or Saundra can arrange the furniture then. Saundra is knitting covers for the beds."

"I have some fabric scraps for curtains." Angie leaned over to peer inside. "How big are the windows?"

"Two inches by three. The downstairs windows are double wide."

They spoke about the project until Angie started shivering and they had to go inside. Her heart warmed toward Lane for taking so much time over Judy's gift. He truly had changed.

When they reached the house, Angie played one game of charades with the family before Judy had to go up to bed. Tonight Angie went upstairs with her, carrying an iron pot containing one of the bricks she'd heated at the fireplace. With the bedcovers icy in the unheated room, they had to have something to warm it up. Angie felt unusually tired. Getting so cold in the barn had sapped her energy.

She helped Judy fasten her gown then quickly changed her own clothes. The room was cold enough to form ice on the water in the pitcher beside the bed. Her feet on the flannel-wrapped hot brick, Judy snuggled into the covers and promptly closed her eyes.

Before Angie climbed under the biscuit quilt that night, she opened the trunk at the end of her bed and dug deep. Triumphant, she pulled out a piece of dotted Swiss and one of blue gingham. Thrusting her hand down on the other side, she touched a small wooden box and grasped it.

Lifting its hinged lid, she saw a tiny china tea set gleaming against dark velvet, another reminder of happier days. Angie set the small box on top of the trunk's inner contents and closed the lid with a gentle smile. This Christmas would be one that Judy would never forget.

She pulled the thick quilt over her and settled into the snowy sheets, already partially warm from Judy's presence and that deliciously warm brick.

Why hadn't Hans told them before about his living on the ranch years ago? Was he playing some kind of deep game? She pictured his twinkling blue eyes and his ready laugh. He really had cried the night Saundra prayed. That wasn't pretend.

But then he had come into the house and stayed in the dark—if that really had been Hans in the kitchen when she came downstairs that night. She sighed. It was so confusing.

Judy rustled beside her. "Angie?" she asked.

"Yes, honey?"

"What is Hans looking for?"

Suddenly wide awake, Angie asked, "Why do you say that?"

"This afternoon he was digging into the back of the closet under the stairs. I think he was tapping on the wall. I saw him when I ran in after school."

"Did he see you?"

"Yes. He told me he was looking for some polishing cloths to put blacking on the stove." She snuggled into Angie's side. "What is he looking for?"

"Now that you mention it, he does seem to be looking for something, doesn't he?" She brushed Judy's hair from her cheek. "I don't know what it could be."

"I'm going to find out," Judy said sleepily. She turned over so that her back faced Angie. "I'm going to look, too."

Judy made the promise while mostly asleep, but she kept her word. Her first day of Christmas break, she disappeared into the far corners of the house. Angie saw what the girl was up to but didn't mention it to anyone else. Let Judy entertain herself for a few hours. What could it hurt?

Chapter 16

After lunch Judy dried dishes for Saundra with a dab and a promise, impatient to be back to her tapping and probing upstairs.

"Do you need any help, Miss Angie?" Hans asked when the other men returned to the barn. "Lane doesn't need me this afternoon. I could clean out the cellar for you if you don't have anything else to keep me busy."

"It's freezing cold down there," Angie said. His suggestion brought up a hint of suspicion. In the few weeks he'd been with them, Hans had worked in every sector of the house except the bedrooms and the attic.

"I don't mind the cold," Hans said, smiling widely. "Once I get moving, the exercise will keep me warm."

"Let me go down and take a look at it with you," she said finally, giving the table a last swipe with a wet cloth.

"Judy and I will finish here," Saundra said. "Go ahead with Hans." The German lady sent a warm smile toward their newest hand. "I'll bring you down a hot cup of coffee in a while."

"Danke," he said, returning her friendly look.

Angie lit a lantern for herself and one for Hans. "It's pitch black down there. No windows," she told him. She paused and glanced at him. "I expect you know that."

He nodded. "I cleaned out this cellar once before, about"—he squinted—"thirty years ago." He grinned. "Do you think it needs it again by now?"

Angie smiled. "I haven't cleaned it myself. There never seems to be time for a project like this." Holding the lantern away from her body, the other hand outstretched to keep a stray spiderweb off her face, she descended the stairs slowly and carefully.

The cellar had stone walls. Whitewashed many years before, they were now gray and streaked with a thick coating of grime. Along two sides, plank shelving held jars of various fruits and vegetables. A red rubber ring edged each tightly sealed glass lid. The jars shone in the lantern light, some of them green-tinted and some of them clear.

To the back of the cellar stood an ancient washstand, the one Angie had Barry haul to the yard each spring. Rusty tools lined one wall. A broken picture frame and a half-finished cradle sat atop a pile of discarded junk, a pile that had been there as long as Angie had lived on the ranch. Most of it had been there when Lane bought the place fourteen years before.

"Help yourself," she told Hans. "You can make a burn pile beside the barn to get rid of most of that." She looked at the junk heap. "Just show me what you're carrying out as you pass through the kitchen." She set her lantern on a shelf nearby. "Judy may be down to help you later. She loves to dig into old stuff and get dirty."

Hans nodded. "She could bring down a broom and a duster, please." He looked at the foot of the stairs. "I see a bucket there. I think that's all I'll need for now."

Angie climbed the stairs, uneasy and scolding herself for being so. What kind of trouble could Hans get into down there? It wasn't as if they had jewels scattered among the junk.

Instead of helping Hans, Judy continued her inspection of crevices and crannies above. By the evening of the second day, Angie wondered how long the child would keep up her search.

Judy came to supper that night with her cheeks flushed and a shine to her eyes. "Are you feeling well?" Angie asked, concerned. "You look as if you may have a fever."

Judy shook her head until her braids flapped around her face. "Nope. I'm fine." She plopped into her seat at the table. "After supper I'll help with the dishes," she announced.

Angie glanced at her. Something was definitely up.

When the last dish was dried and in the cupboard, Judy sidled up to Angie. "Let's go up to our room," she whispered and set off down the hall.

Angie dried her hands and followed at a more mature pace. Saundra came behind her then veered into the living room to join Barry and Hans, who played checkers before the fire.

"What is it?" Angie asked Judy the moment she closed her bedroom door behind her. "Did you find anything?"

Judy held something behind her back. Her eyes were wide and gleaming. "Look!" She held out a suede-wrapped bundle, dusty and cracked with age.

"Where did you get that?" Angie took it from her and sat beside her on the edge of the bed.

"The back of Daddy's closet has a loose floorboard. I pried it up and found that."

Angie unfolded the packet carefully. Inside lay several brittle, yellowed pages folded together into a tight wad. "I'm afraid to open the papers up. They may break."

"They won't," Judy said, sitting next to Angie. "I already opened them."

Angie laid the pages on the quilt beside her and slowly pulled them open. Some of the words disappeared into the deep cracks where the folds had been. She held a letter and a crude drawing. The letter was dated September 16, 1850, twenty-two years ago.

> To the person who finds this,
> You have just found a treasure.
> Being the fool that I am, I caught gold fever almost one year ago and left my dear Eliza to care for this place with only one ranch hand, a difficult job for a hearty man. But how much more for a frail woman with a five-year-old child to care for?
> Eliza was never strong in body, but I was so bullheaded that I wouldn't listen to her when she cried and begged me to stay at home. I went to California with a mob of other empty-headed husbands and fathers.
> (Here the words disappeared into a fold.) . . . returned last week with my saddlebags full of gold, I found Eliza in bed with consumption. Jared had died two months before of fever, and my beautiful Eliza was soul sick with grief. First she had lost me and then our child.
> Oh, God, forgive me!
> I brought back twenty thousand dollars in gold, more than I ever dreamed of seeing, but it has become a curse to me. I will not benefit from it.
> Eliza died in my arms this morning. This afternoon I will bury her behind the house and ride away from this cursed place. I'm leaving the gold for you, whoever you are. You

may have it with my blessing. May it bring you more joy than it brought to me.

I had to dig for the gold, and so will you. I've made a rubbing of the spot where the gold is buried deep inside the bowels of this house. Dig for it, my friend. (Another line lost in the paper's fold.) *. . .drawn a map, but that would have been too easy.*

Study the rubbing and think hard. If God wills, you will find it. Take it. Just remember—no amount of money in the world can replace the ones you lo. . . (The words smeared here.)

The letter was signed with a shaky hand: *Amos Nissley.*

Angie let the yellowed page rest on her lap. She and Judy had their heads together, alive with shock and excitement.

"Where could it be?" Judy asked. "I've already been over most of the house." She bounced on the bed. "Oh, Angie! Papa would be able to pay off the ranch! We've got to find that gold for him."

Angie shuffled the papers and brought up the rubbing. It looked like an oddly connected spiderweb, disjointed and asymmetrical. "Judy, does this look like any spot you've seen around the house?"

Judy stopped bouncing and pressed her face toward the paper. "I looked at it for a long time before lunch, and I couldn't figure it out. What is it, a map?"

"It could be, but I doubt it. There's no direction or landmarks to go by." She turned the paper over. "It's a rubbing, Judy. He put the paper over a spot and ran his pencil back and forth across it to pick up the texture."

"The fireplace stones!" Judy cried. She would have dashed out the door, but Angie caught her arm.

"Wait a minute!" she said. "Slow down. I've got to think."

"What?" Judy demanded, sinking back to her seat on the bed.

"I'm thinking about Hans. Do you think he knew about this? The fireplace has fascinated him since he came here. I had convinced myself that I was imagining things, but now I'm not so sure."

"How could a lot of gold be hidden in the fireplace?" Judy asked. "The stones are solid. And if the gold was inside the fireplace, it would have melted by now. Gold is soft." She nodded wisely. "We learned that in school."

"Maybe a few of the fireplace stones are loose and could be pulled out," Angie said, turning the paper around in her hands. "The trouble is, there's no way of telling which is the top and which is the bottom of the paper."

"How much does Daddy owe on the ranch?" Judy asked, hunching close to the mysterious paper. "Is it a lot of money?"

Angie nodded. "Almost a thousand dollars." With her index finger she traced the pattern on the paper without actually touching the page. "This is our ticket to freedom from the banker, Judy," she said. "Maybe God sent it in answer to our prayers."

She laid the paper down and looked directly into Judy's face. "I'm going to trace this pattern so you can have one to take with you. I want you to keep looking, Judy. I'll help you when I have time."

She put her hand on Judy's chin and looked deeply into her eyes. "Don't let Hans or anyone else know what you're up to." Her mouth quirked in on one side. "Your father would think we're two silly children. Barry will hoot and holler about how we've got gold fever. I'll never live it down with him if we don't find it."

Her expression grew sober. "And I'm not sure what Hans will do. If he's really looking for the same thing we are, we'd best be careful. This kind of thing can get dangerous."

Judy looked up at her, scared and delighted at once. "You think he'd murder us in our beds for the gold?"

"Don't say that!" Angie said. Abruptly she stood up. "This isn't a scary story that kids tell around a campfire, Judy-girl. This is real life. Don't let your imagination run wild." She stepped to her bureau and pulled open the top drawer. "I'll trace this and get back downstairs. Saundra probably needs me in the kitchen. I can't let her do all the work. She's still a guest, you know."

"She doesn't seem like a guest," Judy said, watching Angie lay a clean sheet of paper over the rubbing. "Things have been so fun since Saundra came, haven't they?" she murmured.

Angie moved to the window to press the pages against the sunlit glass. "Things have been *fun* all right. I don't know what I'll do if they get any more lively." Her short pencil moved quickly across the page. In a moment she handed the finished tracing to Judy. "Happy hunting!" she said.

Judy skipped out the door.

Angie stared after her a moment before she moved from the window. She carefully folded the papers together as they had been and returned them to the suede holder. Lifting the straw tick, she slid the packet under it and smoothed the quilt.

Her steps lagged on her way downstairs. Was Hans after the gold? If he was, how had he found out about it? He said he'd been on the ranch thirty years ago. That would have been 1843, before the tragedy in the Nissley family. Before the letter.

He could have been there when Amos returned. He could have known about the gold. Why hadn't he stayed then and found the gold after Amos Nissley left? Why had he waited so long to come back for it? How many men would suffer through twenty-five years of hunger and cold when he knew a fortune lay within his reach?

Angie sighed and ran her hand slowly down the banister. Maybe someone else had already found it. Lane had bought the ranch from a pipe-smoking old woman, the last of her family. She'd made the living room and kitchen her home for more than ten years. When Lane bought the house, the upstairs had looked like the cellar looked now—the dust an inch thick and thousands of spiders setting up housekeeping in the bedrooms.

Angie passed the closed living-room doors and paused at the kitchen, her eyes on the cellar door standing open to her right. Hans was downstairs right now, probably prying into the floor. Her mouth went dry. She had a sinking feeling in her stomach. What would he do if she surprised him while he had the gold in his hands? Hans looked friendly enough, but some folks went crazy when that much money was at stake.

Why hadn't she listened to Lane and let him fire Hans before all of this came up?

"Angie, what's wrong?" Saundra asked. She knelt in front of the oven door, her hands holding a blackened cleaning cloth. "You look like you're about to faint." She moved as though to stand up.

"No, Saundra." Angie swallowed, trying to force her voice to sound normal. "I'm fine. It's nothing, really."

"I just took Hans some coffee," Saundra said, reaching into the far recesses of the oven with the cloth. "He's got that cellar looking swept and new. You should go down and see it."

Angie shuffled to the cellar door and knocked loudly on the wall. "Hans? It's me." She stepped down the stairs. "How are things coming?"

Bending over the last of the refuse pile, Hans straightened, his smile intact. "This is the last of it, Miss Angie," he said. "I made a little pile over there by the stairs so you can decide if you want to save any of those things."

"Uh—that's fine, Hans." She swallowed again and tried to sound natural. "It looks wonderful down here." Gingerly she moved down the stairs to check out the stack of bent iron and scored wood beside the bottom step. A few minutes later she straightened. "Move these things to the barn," she said, pointing to a bent plow handle and a bucket handle. "The rest you can bury or burn."

She started to climb the stairs then turned back. "Would you mind doing the same thing in the tack room? It's not as bad as this was, but it's really dusty, and there are some old harnesses and things that need to be thrown out."

Hans's gray head bobbed. "Of course, Miss Angie. I'll start on it when I finish here"—he glanced around—"tomorrow or the next day."

"Thank you, Hans," she said mechanically and moved up the stairs. She wanted to give him something that would keep him busy away from the house. The tack room would be worth at least one afternoon, maybe two.

Two hours before suppertime, Judy climbed to the attic. She came to supper with dust balls in her hair and cobwebs in her eyebrows. Laughing, Angie pointed to the washbasin beside the back door. "Help yourself, child," she said. "You need it more than your daddy and Barry tonight."

At that moment Hans appeared in the same dust-covered condition.

Saundra's gentle laughter came from where she set the table. A flood of German followed, and Hans chuckled.

Angie kept her back turned to the pair, her chin down, as she dabbed Judy's braids with a damp cloth. What were they saying? The foreign tongue had taken on a sinister sound. Now that she thought about it, had Hans's coming here been such a coincidence? He and Saundra sure did seem friendly.

Wait a minute, Angie, she told herself. *You were the one who brought Saundra here. That Saundra would know a former hand from this very ranch is stretching things until they snap.* She hung the cloth on the rack beside the basin.

"That's better," she said, patting Judy's damp head. "Please set out the forks and spoons while I fill the mugs with coffee, hon. Lane and Barry will be freezing. Hans looks cold, too. The cellar isn't heated."

"What about me?" Judy said, turning big eyes on Angie. "I've been in the—"

Angie's elbow in the girl's side stopped the sentence. Lowered eyebrows and a frown brought up an understanding pucker to Judy's face. The girl clamped her lips and reached for Barry's enamel mug on the table. She handed it to Angie.

"I'll give you half a cup with lots of milk," Angie told her. "It won't hurt this once." She glanced at Hans and Saundra who were checking out the creamed chipped beef simmering on the stove. They hadn't seemed to hear Judy's blurted-out statement.

Moving around the table with the coffeepot, Angie filled cups. Her side vision kept track of the German couple beside the stove. What were they whispering? Even if she could hear them, she wouldn't understand a word.

Barry burst in the door, letting in an icy draft. Lane filled the doorway behind him. The men rushed inside, and Lane closed the door.

Lane pulled off his gloves. "Smells like snow out there. We put up the rope to the barn just in case."

"There's plenty of split firewood," Barry added, shedding his sheepskin coat, "thanks to the hard work of Hans and me." He hung his coat on a peg. "What's cooking?" he asked, moving to the stove. Hans immediately stepped back and found his seat, leaving the spot beside Saundra open.

Angie watched the older man's quick movement. His face was set. Whatever he felt about Barry's attention to Saundra, Hans wasn't giving it away. His face was almost too still.

Angie moved to her seat. "I told Hans he ought to work at cleaning out the tack room when he has time in the afternoons. Is that all right, Lane?"

He looked at her for ten seconds before answering. "Fine," he said, as though half hearing. "It needs cleaning, no mistake." His eyes turned toward Angie for a long minute, and she suddenly felt heat rising from her neck to her cheeks. Then he picked up his coffee and took a small sip. Sighing, he set it down. "Just how I like it," he said, "hot and strong. Nice going, Angie."

Angie moved her fork half an inch to the right then pushed it back beside her plate. "Saundra made the coffee, Lane. Not me."

"Oh! Sorry for giving your compliment to someone else, Saundra," he said, smiling at the woman at the other end of the table. "Nice coffee."

Angie tried not to stare at him, but she couldn't help sneaking a few glances. She hadn't heard him talk so much at the table for years. She touched her brow, a definite headache coming on.

That evening an exhausted Judy climbed the stairs to go to bed twenty minutes earlier than usual. Lane went up with her. Barry and Hans bundled themselves in coats and hats, their scarves about their faces, and headed for the barn. The cold had sapped everyone's energy. With the gloom of night coming on so early now, bed seemed like the best place to be.

Angie and Saundra lingered by the fireplace. Reaching into her needlepoint sewing bag, Saundra held up Judy's gown to show its wide sleeves and gathered skirt to its full effect.

Angie clasped her hands. "Saundra! Judy's going to have heart failure when she sees it. It's the loveliest thing she's owned since she was four years old."

Saundra smiled, her face glowing in the firelight. "I can't wait to see her face." Folding the dress in her lap, Saundra said, "You know, Judy's the dearest child I've ever known. She's so full of life and so terrifyingly honest." She chuckled softly then murmured, "I'd love to have her for a daughter."

Angie's face stiffened. She looked down to watch her hands pleating her skirt. "Saundra—"

"Yes?" Those beautiful blond eyebrows lifted slightly.

Angie licked her lips and forced herself to go on. "Has Lane said anything to you about marriage?"

"Marriage? Not yet." Perfect lips curved into a dreamy smile. "He'll get around to it in time. No man could write those letters and not be thinking of marriage." With precise care she laid the dress over her arm and stood. "I'm going to iron this and hang it in my closet until Christmas. I can't bear to fold it into a package. Is that all right with you, Angie?"

"Oh—yes, fine," Angie murmured. "Thanks for being so good to Judy, Saundra. She loves you."

Saundra patted the cloth dripping from her arm. "And I love her," she said with a soft smile.

Angie felt a fleeting impulse to tell Saundra the truth, but the next moment the German woman was gone. Angie didn't have the heart to follow her to the kitchen to tell the awful tale. If Lane ever found out what Angie had done to get Saundra out here, he would tan her hide and hang it out to dry.

Chapter 17

The next afternoon Hans finished cleaning the cellar and climbed the steps for the last time. Angie was rinsing the scrubbing board and washbasin on the back porch when he passed her.

"The job is finished," he said, beaming at her. Angie turned toward him, her face still.

"Thank you, Hans," she said quietly. "I'm sure Lane will be glad to have you working in the barn now."

His expression slowly changed to concern. "Is something wrong, Miss Angie? Has Hans done something bad?"

He said it so anxiously that Angie almost laughed. This man must be an actor or something. "Not at all, Hans. You've been a real help. I don't know how we would have made it through this winter without you."

"God sent me," he said softly, nodding. "I know He did." With a short good-bye he struck out toward the barn, back straight, stout legs pumping, a man with a reason for going to his destination.

Quickly Angie propped the scrubbing board inside the washtub and pulled open the back door. The cellar door stood slightly ajar like the open mouth of a sleeping giant.

Lighting a lantern, she stepped inside and pulled the door shut behind her. Saundra had gone upstairs to rest awhile. Tired of searching, Judy lay on their bed with Angie's copy of *Ivanhoe*, the only novel in the house. Angie had a few minutes to herself. She intended to make the most of it.

The cellar was transformed. Even the walls were free of dust. The room smelled of fresh lime that Hans had sprinkled on the floor. Holding the lantern high, Angie pulled a folded page from her deep skirt pocket and flipped it open. Finding the right combination of shapes seemed impossible. In seconds her eyes blurred. She couldn't tell one stone from another.

Her arm grew tired of holding the lantern so she set it on a nearby shelf, squinted in the dimness, and kept searching. She held the paper up so that it caught a feeble ray of light from the lantern. Foot by foot she held the tracing up to the wall, seeking a match for the fist-sized shapes drawn there.

The cellar seemed like a logical place to look for the gold. The letter had said deep inside the bowels of the house. The cellar would definitely match that. And the cellar had no windows so it was always dark. That would make it easier to hide something. Who in the world would ever pass the time studying the stonework in the walls of a dusty, gloomy cellar? No one except crazy Angie.

Her feet grew cold. Her eyes grew weary.

Not watching behind her, she tripped over a small shovel propped against the wall and dropped the paper. It fluttered toward the center of the room and landed in a pool of lantern light. Angie bent over to retrieve it and suddenly dropped to her knees.

She reached out to swivel the paper a little and bent closer. There it was! The disjointed spider web had lain at her feet all the time.

She pried at the stones with her fingers but got nowhere. After thirty years of lying underfoot, they may as well have been one unit. Those stones wouldn't budge without a pick or shovel and a man's strength.

"Angie?" Saundra's muffled voice came from overhead. "Angie?"

Angie folded the paper and stowed it in her pocket. She picked up a jar of peaches from the shelf, lifted the lantern handle, and climbed the stairs. "Here I am," she called.

Angie let the peaches speak for her when she reached the kitchen.

"Would you like me to make some cobbler tonight?" Saundra asked, eyeing the jar. "A cobbler would taste good with the pork roast we're having."

Angie nodded and handed her the jar. "I'm a little tired, Saundra. This was a long washday. Would you mind if I rest half an hour or so?"

"Don't even ask that!" Saundra told her, setting the peaches on the table. "Supper is all but finished. I'll mix up the cobbler in no time at all."

"Thanks, Saundra," Angie said, already in motion toward the stairs. Her head was reeling, and her eyes ached. She wanted to cry and shout at the same time. Wouldn't Judy be excited when she heard about it?

When Angie reached her room, Judy lay on her pillow, the heavy book dropped to the bed beside her. Angie eased onto the quilt and lay back with a deep sigh. Maybe telling Judy wasn't the thing to do. The child was so excitable; she'd surely give away the secret.

Angie let her eyes drift closed. Maybe she should tell Lane the whole story. If only she could get him alone without the others knowing about it. Before she realized it, she fell asleep and didn't wake until she felt Judy's hand on her shoulder.

"Angie? Do you want to come down for supper?" the child asked. "You've been sleeping a long time."

Angie sat up, her chin sagging against her chest. She pushed hair off her face. "I'll be right there. Just give me a minute to wake up." Disgruntled, she stood and shoved her feet into her stiff shoes. So much for talking to Lane. With supper already on the table, the evening was all but over. He'd probably play a game of checkers and turn in after that. She couldn't follow him into his room to talk to him, could she?

Running fingers upward toward her bun to smooth a few stray ringlets, she headed to the stairs. Her chat with Lane would have to wait. But how could it? Christmas was less than seventy hours away.

✷

The next day was December 23, and Saundra and Angie met in the kitchen before dawn. They planned to make pies and sticky buns all that morning and apple strudel in the afternoon. They'd spend Christmas Eve making pies and cleaning the turkey Lane would butcher for them that morning.

"I hope the men don't mind coffee and biscuits for breakfast," Angie said, pulling the wooden flour bin from under the counter. She felt so strange, as though she were watching herself from a high window, as though she were only acting like Angie McDonald. The real

Angie was bouncing up and down on tiptoe and begging for a chance to catch Lane alone so they could talk.

Saundra waited for her to finish dipping out flour and then reached for the bin. "Christmas dinner will make up for the small meals today and tomorrow," she said.

Adding saleratus and salt to flour in a bowl, Angie looked up to see Judy stumble into the kitchen, half asleep and wearing a woolen robe, her braids like twisted strands of barbed wire. Judy was never at her best in the morning.

"What brings you out so early?" Angie asked her.

"I want to help with the sticky buns," Judy said, sitting at the table, chin on hand.

Angie barely suppressed a grin. "We could use two extra hands—once you dress and comb your hair."

Judy made a sleepy, pouty face and slid out of the chair. A moment later they heard her door thump overhead. Ten minutes later Judy raced back into the room wearing a brown dress that was badly in need of ironing. Her hair hung in twin zigzag braids. The three ladies worked feverishly for the next two hours then set breakfast on the table.

After the meal Lane stood and reached for his coat. Angie dipped her floury hands in the washbasin and grabbed a towel. She had her cape around her before the door closed behind him.

"Lane?" she called, closing the door firmly. "Can I talk to you for a minute?"

At the bottom of the steps he turned. "What's wrong?" he asked, concerned. "What's happened?"

She moved closer. "I need to tell you something. Let's move away from the house. I don't want anyone else to hear."

Still watching her, a crease between his brows, he waited for her to join him, and they moved toward the lane. The wind had a bite that wouldn't let them linger too long.

Angie pulled the cape around her and wished she'd taken time to put on her coat as well. "Judy and I discovered something I think you should know about." She told him about the suede packet, the letter, and the diagram. "Judy and I have been scouring the house to find a pattern that matched the rubbing on that paper."

He shifted his feet. "This sounds like one of Judy's fairy tales."

"Well, I think I found the place," Angie told him. "I was looking at the stonework in the cellar, and I think I found the pattern on the floor. Only I'll need help to dig up the stones. They're packed in tight."

Lane drew in a breath and let it out in a white cloud that drifted over Angie's head. "I'll come in later, and we'll have a go at it."

She handed him the folded paper. "Here is the pattern. It's about three feet from the wall next to the shelf full of peach jars. You'll see it. I'll leave a lantern for you on the shelf inside the kitchen door."

She shivered. "We'll have to make up some kind of excuse for your being down there. I really don't want Hans or Saundra to know about it."

"Why not?"

She shivered again. "I think Hans was the ranch hand mentioned in the letter. I think he came here to find the gold himself."

"You don't say!" He tugged down the left flap on his wool hat. "Angie, you're knocking me off balance with all this." He gazed at the sky for a moment and looked back at her. "I'll help the men with the chores and then set them to mucking out the stalls. That should take them most of the morning."

Angie turned toward the house. "I'm freezing! I'll see you later!" She set off at a trot, her teeth set against the chattering she felt coming on.

"Whew! It's cold out there!" she gasped, blinking at the rush of heat that hit her inside the kitchen. With the cookstove going full throttle, the change in temperatures was dramatic.

"What were you talking to Daddy about?" Judy asked. She had a rolling pin in her hands and a lump of flattened bread dough in front of her on the floured table. "Why did you go outside to talk to him?"

Angie slipped off her cape. "Children shouldn't ask questions this close to Christmas," she said, a mysterious lilt to her voice. Hanging the cape on its hook, she stepped up to the table. "Now let's see—where was I?" She briefly washed her hands, carefully dried them, then dipped them in the flour bowl and squeezed off a lump of dough.

When Saundra left the room a few minutes later, Angie whispered to Judy, "Don't ask any more questions. Your dad is coming in to dig in the cellar later on this morning. I think I found the pattern down there. We don't want anyone else to know."

Nodding wisely, a smile tugging at her mouth, Judy mouthed the words "all right" and sprinkled brown sugar over the wide band of dough before her on the table. Angie slid a bowl of raisins over to her then reached for a lantern and a match.

Around ten o'clock Lane came inside, his cheeks pink, his nose red. Without a word he picked up the lantern and matches Angie had left on the shelf near the back door. He opened the cellar door and disappeared. It happened so smoothly and fast that Saundra didn't see him. She was facing the stove stirring a small pot of dried apples and raisins simmering in brown sugar syrup—the filling for her strudel.

Angie checked the last pan of sticky buns in the oven and decided to leave them in five minutes longer. With a feed sack dishcloth, Judy rubbed at hardened lumps of dried dough that stuck to the tabletop like glue. The girl sent Angie an excited smile and received a warning scowl in return.

Lunch consisted of warmed-up stew and leftover biscuits from breakfast. Angie set them on the back of the stove as Saundra and Judy set off for the chicken coop with a basket.

The moment they stepped off the porch, Angie was at the cellar door. "Lane? Did you find anything?" She skittered down the stairs.

Lane stood beside a pile of stones, dirt scattered across the floor. At his feet lay a small hole.

"I spent an hour getting the stones loose," he said. "It's taking longer than I thought." He propped the shovel under his forearm.

She stepped closer. "Saundra and Judy went to fetch the eggs so I have a few minutes."

He picked up the shovel, thrust it into the dirt, and stepped on it with a heavy work boot. When he lifted it, a sagging bundle hung off the side of the mound of dirt.

"What's that?" Angie cried, lunging forward. She grasped the bundle and pulled it free. "It's heavy!" The sack fell to the earth with a distinct thud, too weighty for her to hold up.

Angie fell to her knees, forgetting all thoughts of keeping her skirts clean. Lane squatted beside her. They tugged at the leather bag and finally got it open.

Chapter 18

Moving to a clear spot of floor, Lane turned the sack over and shook it. Dirty black lumps fell out.

"It's not gold," Angie said, deflated. "What is it?"

Lane pulled a small sheath from his pocket and drew out a knife. He picked up a lump and cut into it. Standing, he held it up to the lantern.

Angie gasped. A yellow sheen glistened in the light. "It *is* gold!" She grabbed Lane's arm. "Lane! The ranch! You can pay for the ranch!"

Still holding the nugget up, he turned his face toward her, meeting her gaze. Suddenly suspended in time, Angie forgot to breathe. She still had hold of his arm, but she forgot to let go. She saw the small creases beside his eyes from long years in the sun, his long, thin nose, his sensitive mouth that had turned down into a deep frown for so long. Too long.

His face came closer until she could almost feel his breath.

"Angie?" Judy's voice came from the kitchen above.

Gasping, Angie grabbed a jar of pears and headed for the stairs. She almost forgot to raise her skirts and did a little two-step at the bottom riser. Somehow she made it to the top and grabbed the latch. She stopped an instant to wet her lips and swallow.

Stepping into the kitchen, she tried to force her voice to a normal level. "Here I am," she said.

Saundra stood by the coatrack, smoothing her hair over her ears where one strand had sprung free. "Oh, pears will taste good for lunch," she said. "I think it's almost time to call in the men."

"Let's set the table, Judy," Angie said. "Then we'll call them."

Angie kept her face turned away from Saundra, afraid that the other woman would notice her warm cheeks and shaking hands.

"I'm going upstairs for a minute," Saundra said, still fussing with her hair. "I've got to find a hairpin."

Angie waited to hear her shoes on the stairs before she moved three steps down the cellar stairs. "Saundra's going upstairs. Now's your chance to come up."

Below her, Lane shoved the dirty sack under a shelf and reached for the lantern. He dusted his pants as he moved.

"What did you find, Daddy?" Judy asked when he reached the kitchen.

He set down the lantern and moved to the hand-washing stand by the door. "We'll take about it later, chicky," he told her. His voice had a not-now tone that held back Judy's anxious questions.

Instead the girl skipped to the back porch, put her hands to her mouth, and called for Barry and Hans to come for lunch. A triangle and metal rod hung beside her, but she ignored them.

The rest of the day passed without a hitch. Saundra made strudel while Angie and Judy watched with interest, trying to memorize each step.

The men had more leftover stew for supper but this time with corn bread.

"What variety!" Barry commented, dipping his wedge of corn bread in buttermilk. "Stew for lunch and stew for supper." He grinned at Judy. "Is it stew for breakfast, too?"

Saundra smiled. "That depends on how much you leave in the pot tonight."

Hans picked up the stew pot and handed it to Barry. "Eat hearty, my friend. I've been hankering for shepherd's pie."

They all laughed.

Barry dipped a spoonful of stew into his bowl. Lane followed suit.

"What's on the top of your list for tomorrow, Boss?" Barry asked Lane. "It's Christmas Eve."

"I've been thinking about riding down to the lower forty and checking out the pines down there."

"In this weather?" Barry asked. "It's near zero."

Lane laughed and leaned back in his chair. "Just kidding, Barry. I wanted to get a rise out of you."

"You don't have to tease him to make him mad," Judy piped up, her eyes on Saundra. "Just pay attention to—"

"Judy!" Angie cried. "That's enough!"

The girl clamped her mouth shut and tried to act sorry, but a telltale gleam in her eyes told the real story.

Barry ignored her. "How about chess after supper?" he asked Saundra.

She gave him a weary smile. "I'm sorry, Barry, but I'm too tired tonight. I'm going up to bed. It was an early morning today, and there's another one yet to come."

"Christmas will be early, too," Judy said. "We open our presents at dawn." She smiled at her father. "Always."

He reached out to touch her cheek. "Right, chicky."

"I'll help with the dishes," Hans said, standing to gather bowls and cups. He spoke a few words of German to Saundra.

"Thank you, Hans," Saundra said in English.

His kindly smile shone down on her like a benediction. Her smile deepened.

"Uh-hmm." Barry cleared his throat, a flush growing on his stubbled jaw.

Saundra stood and smoothed her skirt. "Maybe we can play a game tomorrow," she quickly told Barry. "Good night."

"Good night," Hans said, still watching her.

"I'll play chess with you," Lane told Barry. "If you want me, that is."

"Fine," Barry said dourly, getting to his feet. "I'll set out the board." He stumped toward the living room, his boots heavy on the wood floor.

Lane paused in the kitchen door. "Would you mind making another pot of coffee for me, Angie? I'm kind of cold tonight."

She turned from the dishpan to look at him. Lane hardly ever drank coffee at night. "Sure, Lane. I'll put it on now."

"Nice job on the cellar, Hans," Lane said. "It hasn't looked that good since we bought the place." He paused. "Say, did you notice that funny low spot on the floor?"

"Low spot?" Hans asked, pausing from his work. His head tilted. Suddenly serious, he studied Lane's face.

"It's right beside the shelf of peaches. I'm going to take another look at it in the morning." He turned away. "Thanks for the coffee, Angie."

Hans set a cup on the cabinet shelf and reached for another. His hands were shaking.

Angie wearily moved through the dishwashing routine. What had Lane meant? Had he gone back downstairs while Angie took a nap that afternoon? Why had Lane said that to Hans? What was he up to?

She wanted to go after him and make him tell her all about it. On the other hand, after that tense moment in the cellar earlier, she had a sinking feeling in her middle at the thought of another private conversation with him. It was a combination of fear and intense longing—fear that she was imagining his interest in her and intense longing to be with him. The way things were going, how could she stand to live in this house much longer? How could she stand to leave? What a muddle.

She dipped hot water from the reservoir in the back of the stove and scooped coffee grounds into the coffeepot. Reaching into a small can under the sink, she dipped up a few broken eggshells and added them to the pot.

Lane and Barry were deep into their game when Angie brought a mug of coffee to the living room and set it down beside Lane at the game table.

"Would you like some coffee, Barry?" she asked.

"No, thanks. I'm going to turn in after this." He moved his queen.

"Hans went to the bunk room," she said. "He's been a godsend, always so willing to help."

"Right," Lane said, a touch of irony in his tone. He moved his rook. "Checkmate."

"What?" Barry cried. "How did you sneak up on me like that?"

"Sorry, old man," Lane said. "You've been half asleep all evening. Maybe we'll have a rematch tomorrow night."

Barry stood. "I'll have a better partner tomorrow night," he said significantly. "Good night." With that, he marched out of the room.

Lane picked up the box and started putting the pieces into their slots. "What did he mean: a better partner?" he asked Angie.

She slid into the seat across from him. "You know he has a mad crush on Saundra. That's what he meant."

He paused to look at her, black king in hand. "Doesn't that bother you?"

"No." She said it easily. "Barry and I were never meant for each other, Lane. I don't know why I ever thought we were."

"You were desperate," he replied, "to get away from me."

Her jaw dropped. "No, I wasn't!"

"Now who is telling fairy tales? You must be taking lessons from my daughter."

Angie swallowed and stammered. "Every girl dreams of having her own family, her own knight in shining armor." She looked at him. "But that's not the way I feel now. Believe me."

He finished packing the game box and shut the lid. "I know, Angie," he said softly. "I haven't been easy to live with all these years." He leaned closer, his eyes dark and probing. "I want things to be different from now on. I'm going to start looking ahead instead of back. For Judy's sake—and for yours."

"Angie!" Judy's sleepy voice came from overhead. "I'm thirsty!"

"I'd best go up to her," Angie said, standing. "The water pitcher must be empty again." She scurried to the kitchen, filled a jar with water, and hustled toward the stairs. When she passed the living room, Lane sat sipping coffee and staring into the fire.

Angie must have slept too long in the afternoon because that night she couldn't close her eyes for ten seconds at a time before they popped open again. She tossed and wiggled, trying to get comfortable. Finally Judy mumbled something and lifted her hand.

Not wanting to awaken the girl, Angie slid out from under the quilt and found her shoes by searching with her bare toes. She bundled into her woolen robe and moved to the window.

A full moon shone on the yard below to make deep, eerie shadows that moved with the wind. She pulled the belt on her robe tighter and started to turn away when a darting movement caught her eye. What was that? She strained to see.

A wide, thick form moved across the ranch yard with a steady tread. The person was too big to be slim Barry. It had to be Hans.

Angie's heart started to pound. She gripped the belt on her robe as though holding to a lifeline. The figure disappeared below her. He seemed to be moving to the back porch.

Angie slipped off her shoes, her feet tingling against the icy floor. She padded down the stairs, avoided the squeaky step, and waited at the bottom step, her eyes on the dark kitchen.

A feeble moon glow shone through the windows but didn't give enough light to see even a shadow of movement. A faint click told her that someone had just entered the kitchen.

Her senses tensed to an excruciating pitch. What if he became violent? Hans seemed so gentle, but who knew what happened to a man when gold was involved?

A hinge gave a soft groan. The cellar stairs.

Angie took one step away from the stairs, her hand still on the newel post. Suddenly a strong arm slipped around her waist from behind, a wide hand clamped around her mouth. She squeaked.

"Shh!" sounded softly in her ear. It was Lane. For two full minutes he held her and didn't move. After a while Angie relaxed against him and felt his heart thumping against her left shoulder.

"It's Hans," he whispered finally. "I wanted to give him time to start digging."

"What about the gold?" Angie murmured.

"I moved it." He loosened his grasp on her waist. "Let's go."

Moving swiftly and surely, he lifted a lantern from the hall table and struck a match. The hallway sprang to life under the soft glow. Lane reached the cellar door in two strides, flung back the door, and bolted down the stairs.

"What are you doing?" he cried.

Hans dropped the shovel and backed away, his hands upraised. "I–I—don't shoot!"

Lane stared at him. The only gun Lane Phillips owned was a hunting rifle that hung in the tack room. "I asked what you were doing," he repeated, the lantern held high to catch the man's face.

"I'm–I'm—" Hans's eyes bulged. He took a step backward.

Watching from the stairs, Angie wondered if the German man was about to have a heart attack or a fit of apoplexy.

"You'd better let him sit down," she said. "He can tell us about it upstairs, can't he?"

Lane shook his head. "He can explain right here. Hans, you'd best start talking if you want to spend the rest of the night in a warm bed. I'll put you out to walk to Chancyville if you don't speak up."

Hans ran a shaking hand across his face. "It's so terrible, Mr. Lane. It's too terrible." He sounded close to tears. "I'm not a thief. You've got to believe me."

Lane didn't waver. "If you're not a thief, what are you?"

Hans dropped his hand. "I'm a poor ranch hand with no family, no connections, no hope for the future. I've spent my whole life going from one job to the next, working for food and shelter, working for a few cents a day. Is it so wrong to want more than that?"

"Were you here when Amos Nissley lost his wife?" Angie asked.

Hans stared at her, shocked. "How did you know that?"

"We found a letter he left," she said, stepping lower on the stairs. "Amos went to the gold fields and left his wife with one ranch hand to take care of this place. You were that hand, weren't you?"

Hans nodded. "I was a young fellow then, just off the boat from Germany. I had enough money to ride the train this far, and then I had to get off. Mr. Amos gave me a job. He was a good man. He had a fine family. That little boy was a jewel." Tears glistened in Hans's eyes. "It almost killed me when the little fellow died. His poor mother ended up in her grave because of it."

"What happened after that?" Lane asked.

"Mr. Amos came home in time to bury his poor wife. I came into the house and found him sitting at the kitchen table with a loaded gun in his hand. I think he was about to shoot himself. I grabbed the gun and got it away from him." He drew in a breath.

"When he calmed down, Mr. Amos told me that the gold had destroyed his family. He wasn't going to take a single nugget with him when he left. He said that the gold was cursed, and he was going to bury it where it wouldn't be found for years.

"He planned to leave the ranch and find a buyer. He had me take the cattle to town and sell it to the drover. I was to keep a hundred dollars and mail the rest to him in care of General Delivery in Deadwood. That's what I did. I never came back here, and I never saw him again."

"Why did you come back now?" Lane asked.

"All these years I've thought about the gold. There was a lot of it, a big sack full. I saw it."

"Why didn't you come back right away?" Angie asked.

"I did. But Mr. Amos had sold the ranch to a tough bunch of brothers. They all carried Winchesters and warned off anybody they didn't know. When one of them pointed a gun at me and told me to move on, I moved on." His Adam's apple bobbed as he swallowed.

"Then this winter I ran up on some bad times. My job played out before cold weather had even set in. I had no money saved to see me through the winter. So I set off walking across the country and prayed that the ranch sat empty or else that a good family lived here now, one that would give me a job and a place to sleep."

Hans looked down, shame on his heavy features. "You were the answer to my prayers. And now look at what I've done to you."

Lane spoke. "You haven't done anything to us, Hans. The gold doesn't belong to us."

"But it does," he said. "You bought the ranch and everything here. If the gold is still here, it should be yours. I should have told you about it." He paused. "Once I got to know you,

I almost told you about it—except—"

"Except what?" Angie asked, watching him. "Why couldn't you tell us?"

Hans shrugged. "It was just a foolish man's dream, Miss Angie. I'm too ashamed to tell you about it." He looked up at Lane. "Are you going to send me away now?" he asked. "I'll fetch my bundle from the bunk room and go if you tell me to."

"He'll freeze," Angie said to Lane. "It's below zero out there."

"He's not going anywhere." Lane sounded bone weary. "Let's go up to the kitchen and talk about this some more." He motioned to Hans, and the German man edged by him to the stairs. Angie led the way with Hans behind and Lane coming last.

Chapter 19

Lane set the lantern on the table and pulled out a chair. He and Hans sat across from each other.

"There's still some coffee," Angie said, lifting the pot. "Or there was. It's empty."

"I drank the last of it," Lane told her. "I wanted to make sure I didn't fall asleep when Hans came in."

"You knew he'd come?" she asked.

"I intended to catch him digging in the basement and then send him away."

Hans stood up. "I'll go now."

"Sit down," Lane said abruptly. "You're not going anywhere."

Hans sank back into the seat.

Angie sat next to Lane. "What about the gold?" she asked.

"You found it?" Hans blurted out.

"Yesterday," Lane told him. "It was buried in the cellar where you were just digging."

"Amos left a drawing to help us find the spot," Angie added.

Hans sagged with disappointment. "I thought it might be behind a couple of loose bricks in the fireplace," he said, his face creased in misery, "or under a loose floorboard. Oh, what a fool I was. I've betrayed you good people after you were so kind to me. What a rotten man sits here before you. You should whip me and send me away into the night to freeze." He pulled a red bandanna from his pocket and blew his nose loudly.

"Judy found the letter and the drawing," Angie told him when he fell silent. "Then Lane and I found the gold."

Lane paused, watching the picture of dejection before him, considering his next move. "How about if we divide it?" Lane asked. "You get half, and we get half."

Hans stared. "You'd give half to me?"

"Of course. You took care of Nissley's wife and son while he was gone, didn't you? You earned it." Lane leaned his forearms on the table. "I don't understand why he didn't give you more to help you get a start when he sent you away."

"He thought the gold was cursed," Hans said. "I've never seen a man so beside himself with grief. He blamed himself for leaving them. He wanted to die, too."

"Poor man," Lane murmured, gazing into the darkness.

"You're wrong. I don't deserve anything," Hans said, more spirited. "I don't deserve anything at all."

Angie spoke up. "Hans, we don't always get what we deserve. If we did, none of us would be very happy, would we? God sent His only Son, Jesus, to die for us when we didn't deserve it. The Bible says, 'But God commendeth his love toward us, in that, while we were yet sinners, Christ died for us.' He loved us when we were wicked sinners, Hans."

The German man's eyes filled with tears. "That's so beautiful. My mother was a church-woman in Germany. She used to read the Bible to me every night. That same passage some-times." He shook his head. "I didn't pay attention to what she was trying to tell me. When she died, I sold the cottage and bought a ticket to America. All I could think about was getting rich. People said that the streets in America were paved with gold.

"Gold again," he went on. "After almost thirty years, I've found nothing but hard work and heartache. I wish now I'd stayed in Germany and worshipped my mother's God. She was poor but so happy." A single tear slid down his cheek.

"You can still believe, Hans," Angie said. "You can trust Christ now, tonight. We can pray together right now."

"I would like to," Hans whispered. He leaned his face into his hands. Quietly he said, "Dear God, I know I don't deserve anything from You but punishment. I'm ashamed to pray to You. There's no one left to help me. Please forgive me of my wickedness. I don't want the gold anymore. I only want to take Jesus for my Savior. I know You will take care of me." He stayed in silence for a moment then blew his nose again.

Angie swallowed back her own tears. The night had ended far differently from how she had expected.

Lane spoke, and Angie glanced at him. She was surprised to see his eyes glistening. His expression had turned from anger to compassion. "It's late, Hans," he said. "We're all tired and wrought up. How about if we settle this tomorrow? Go on out to the bunkhouse and get some rest."

Hans's gray head bobbed. He dabbed at his eyes. "Ya, Mr. Lane. Ya. And thanks again." He stood and grasped Lane's hand, pumping it rapidly. "Thanks a hundred times."

Lane freed himself from the man's strong grip and stood. "Get some sleep now. We'll settle everything tomorrow."

When Hans left, Angie stayed at the table. Lane stood in the center of the room as though uncertain of his next move. He gazed at Angie as if he wanted to say something but didn't know the words. Finally he moved toward the hall. "I'm dead on my feet, Angie. I can't think straight. I've got to get some sleep. Good night."

Picking up the lantern, she followed slowly. Her bare feet were numb blocks of ice. After all the excitement, she doubted she'd sleep before dawn. And there was still so much baking to be done. She'd be dozing over her pie dough in the morning.

In her room she blew out the lantern and crawled under the quilt with her robe still on. Her toes touched the still-warm brick at the foot of the bed, and she sighed deeply. The next instant she was asleep.

When she opened her eyes, the sun peered over the horizon, and Judy was nowhere to be seen. Angie dressed and hurried downstairs. "Sorry I slept so late," she told Saundra when she reached the kitchen.

"Don't worry," the German woman replied, smiling. "Judy and I have everything under control, don't we?"

Judy had flour on her nose and right cheek. "Right!" she said proudly. "I crimped the edge of the piecrust by myself. Saundra showed me how."

Angie was impressed. She picked up a lump of dough and dropped it to the table. "Looks as if I ought to have a lesson on that myself, Saundra. I usually just push a fork into the dough at the edge of my pies. How do you make such an even rope like that?"

They worked steadily until four pumpkin and three apple pies stood on the counter to cool, and it was lunchtime.

Lane was first inside to wash up. Drying his hands on a towel, he moved near Angie at the stove. No one else was close enough to hear. "I divvied up the you-know-what with Hans," he whispered to her. "He didn't want it, but I talked him into taking half. Everything's settled. He's staying on for a while."

"Good!" Her voice was low but intense, filled with relief.

"What are you talking about, Daddy?" Judy asked, coming closer.

He tugged at one of her braids. "No questions—"

"I know, no questions this close to Christmas," she finished. She moved to the table and plopped into her seat.

Lane shared a secret smile and a wink with Angie. He took his seat at the head of the table. Just then Hans came in with Barry. He had a quietness about him that hadn't been there before.

After washing his hands, the German man came to Angie and held out his hand. When she clasped it, he said, "You saved my life, Miss Angie. I'll never be able to thank you enough."

"Hans, I'm so happy for you." Angie squeezed his hand. "You were right. God did send you here. I'm so glad He did."

He turned loose of her hand and pulled out his chair. Already at the table, Saundra watched Hans sit down then looked a question at Angie. The look on Saundra's face told that she knew something significant had happened, but she couldn't tell what it was.

Lunch conversation was subdued, as though everyone sensed that something had changed. Near the end of the meal, Lane speared his fourth biscuit and reached for the apple butter. "Saundra, do you have time to come to the barn with me one last time after lunch?"

"Of course, Lane." She finished her coffee and pushed back her chair. "I need to fetch something from my room first."

Immediately Barry's expression soured while Hans's turned watchful.

Angie had an overwhelming urge to giggle. Those men were like a picture book with no words to tell the story. No words were necessary. She glanced at Saundra. The woman had captured the heart of every man in the house except the one Angie had intended for her. Angie turned her eyes toward Lane, who finished off his biscuit and reached for his coffee cup.

On the other hand, maybe Lane was smitten, too. Who could tell? Why wouldn't he love Saundra? She was beautiful, refined, sweetly feminine. All the things Angie wasn't.

Her mind went back to the warm moments she'd shared with Lane during the past week. What did they mean? *Probably nothing,* she told herself. *Angie girl, you have a good imagination.*

Warmly wrapped in coat, cape, and scarf, Saundra left the kitchen with Lane, her face turned upward to smile at him. Angie tried not to watch, but she couldn't help a peek out the window after they left. She watched Lane carefully skirt the large patch of ice in the center of the yard where a mound of snow had melted and puddled during a few warm hours yesterday afternoon and then frozen solid last night.

"I'll fetch wood for the pile beside the house," Hans said, setting his empty bowl on the counter by the washbasin. "The cookstove has a raging appetite this time of year." He shrugged on his coat and was gone.

Pausing beside the door, Angie took her first good look at Barry since the meal began. He sat, shoulders slumped, chin on his hand, toying with the last bit of shepherd's pie on his plate.

Hopeless irritation swept over Angie. "Stop sulking, will you, Barry? You're acting like a child."

His expression darkened. "What do you know about it?"

"I know you're making a fool of yourself. Try to take things in stride for once in your life. Everything is a crisis to you."

Judy looked from Barry to Angie, her mouth open.

Scraping back his chair, he grabbed his coat, shoved one arm into a sleeve, and lunged outside. Huffing out a white cloud, he paused on the porch to finish pulling on his coat and button the sheepskin garment about his throat.

Angie stood by the window and wished back her words as she watched his stiff back move toward the porch steps. If she hadn't been so tense herself, those heated words never would have been said. Why did she always take out her own frustration on others?

Judy joined her at the window. "Why are you and Barry so mad?"

"We're not mad, Judy." Angie sighed. "It's hard to explain. Sometimes things happen to make people's nerves get frazzled, and then they snap at each other."

"What are you frazzled about?"

Angie touched Judy's nose. "What are you, a question box?"

Angie's gaze wandered back to Barry. He circled around the wide patch of ice in the center of the yard. Glancing up at a row of long icicles hanging from the roof before him, he rounded the corner of the barn.

At that moment Lane and Saundra entered the ranch yard. Saundra no longer held Lane's arm. Smiling, delighted, the German woman pointed toward the house's roof, glanced at Lane, and looked back up. Still pointing, she veered away from his side toward the center of the yard.

Sighting along the angle of her upraised finger, Lane spoke to her and laughed.

Suddenly Saundra's arms went up as her feet slid out from under her. She landed on the ice in a most unladylike position.

Chapter 20

O h, no!" Judy cried. "Did she hurt herself?"

Angie raised fingertips to her mouth, her face close to the pane, concerned that Saundra was all right but at the same time wanting to laugh at the shock on Saundra's face. It was so out of character for the little lady.

Stepping carefully to keep himself from falling, Lane reached Saundra and tried to help her up, but she went down, screaming, a second time.

Barry jogged into view. Heading for Saundra, he knocked Lane over and sent him sprawling full length. Barry knelt beside Saundra, taking her hands.

Lane lunged up. He had his feet planted far apart, elbows back, chest out. Angie slid into her coat and yanked her cape from its peg. She flipped it over her shoulders as she stepped through the door. Judy found her coat and soon followed.

"What do you mean shoving me like that?" Lane demanded, stepping close to Barry. Angie had never seen Lane so angry.

"Why did you let her fall?" Barry said, thick accusation in his voice. He stood and helped Saundra slowly to her feet.

She brushed off her skirt. "My ankle hurts."

Barry put his arm about her waist. "Here, lean on me." He glared at Lane. "You don't seem to care much about what happens to her. All you're worried about is yourself."

"What do you mean by that?" Lane demanded. "You came charging in here like a *loco* bull and knocked me flat. What do you expect me to do, forget about it?"

"When a man's in love, he should look after his lady," Barry bawled, "and you haven't."

"Who said anything about me being in love?" Lane growled back.

Saundra froze. She watched Lane with a wary expression.

Angie's fears came into full bloom. There was Barry overreacting again. She wanted to run across the yard and clamp her hand over his mouth. Instead she gripped the porch railing and stared.

Lane spoke each word slowly and distinctly. "I haven't gone after a woman since Charlotte died."

Barry flushed and didn't answer.

Angie's heart pounded like a tom-tom. Judy gripped her hand until it hurt.

Saundra suddenly found her tongue. "What about all those love letters you wrote me?" she demanded, her voice growing more intense with every word. "What about asking me to come hundreds of miles to meet you and see your ranch?" The German accent grew thicker with every word.

Lane's eyes grew round. "You must have been dreaming, ma'am. I haven't written a letter in ten years."

Saundra's mouth formed a perfect O. She drew in two hard breaths, her breast heaving, took a shaky step, and slapped Lane full in the face.

Grasping her arm, Barry pulled her a short distance from Lane, looking from Lane's red cheek to Saundra's flashing eyes. "Say, what's going on between you two?"

Lane's lips formed an iron line. He said to Saundra, "You were writing to Angie. She's your pen pal. Right?"

Her voice shook when she answered him. "No! You are."

All eyes turned toward the porch. Angie stood in a pool of misery, its icy waters washing over her until she thought she'd drown. She couldn't say a single word. Beside her, Judy started to cry.

Skidding on the ice like a fledgling ice skater, Lane reached the edge of the frozen puddle and stretched his long legs toward the barn. Angie led Judy inside the warm kitchen, hugging her and trying to hold back her own tears.

"Go to your room," Angie whispered to her. "I'll take care of everything."

Sniffling, the girl set off toward the stairs. Angie sank into a chair, covered her eyes, and waited for the ax to fall.

Moments later Barry and Saundra stepped into the kitchen with Hans close behind them. They stared at Angie as if she'd just sprouted a second head. Saundra had tears on her cheeks.

Staring at the tabletop, Angie spoke softly. "I put that ad in the paper because Lane was so horribly lonely. Judy needed a mother. And"—tears sprang up—"I wanted to have a life of my own." She paused, groping for words. "I never meant to hurt you, Saundra."

"Lies always hurt." Her words were heavy and guttural. She looked from Barry to Hans. "One of you will take me to town, no? I can't stay here another day."

Chin high, Saundra mounted the stairs as scalding tears spilled onto Angie's cheeks. Her shoulders shook with silent sobs.

"I'll take her in the buggy," Barry said.

"No, I will take her," Hans countered. The men stood toe to toe. Each had a determined look in his eye.

"I'm taking her," Barry insisted.

Hans let out a stream of German. Without pausing, he switched to English. "I will take Saundra anywhere she wants to go. Anywhere. Even if it's California."

Barry raised a tight fist. "What did you say?"

Saundra's voice broke into their argument. "Hans will take me to the hotel in Chancyville," Saundra said. "Barry, would you kindly help him with my trunks?"

With a final glare at Hans, Barry sidled past Saundra and headed for the stairs. Hans was close behind him.

Drumming hooves pounded across the yard. Angie darted to the window. Through bleary eyes she saw Lane astride Dan, galloping across the field toward the timberline.

What must he think of her now? If only she'd prayed and waited instead of manipulating the situation herself. What a tangle! What a disaster!

Saundra moved closer to the window. She watched Lane ride away then moved to stand beside the cellar door, her face turned away from Angie, as still as a statue.

The men brought down the trunks and set them on the porch. Saundra walked with them to the barn.

Angie hurried upstairs to hold Judy, who was still crying, and rock her gently as though she were two years old again. When her sobs subsided, Angie lay next to her on the bed, eyes closed. What would become of Judy now? What would become of scheming Angie?

A few minutes later Judy whispered, "They're going." Her breath came in hiccups. Her head lay on the pillow. "Hear the horses?"

Angie moved to the window. "Barry's got Dan and Sheba hitched to the buggy. I hope Hans doesn't have any trouble with them. Sheba doesn't take to strangers, and Hans hasn't been here very long."

Soon after the buggy disappeared down the lane, Barry cantered away on Molasses, his own horse. Watching him go, Angie wondered if he would ever come back. Poor Barry had suffered a lot at her hands as well.

"Angie," Judy wailed, drawing Angie's attention back to her, "I'm so scared of what Papa will say when he comes inside."

"I know." She smoothed the girl's tawny hair, trying not to think about Lane out in the woods. She dreaded his return almost as much as his daughter did.

"Judy, what we did was wrong. I should have never pretended that your father put the ad in that paper. I should have never signed his name to those letters."

"What's going to happen to our happy Christmas?" Judy asked, tears flowing afresh.

"I don't know. We'll have to wait to hear what your daddy says when he comes home. All we can do now is pray."

Holding Judy close in her arms, Angie squeezed her eyes shut and cried out to her heavenly Father. "Dear God, I know I did wrong. I confess my lies and my scheming to You. Please forgive me and work this situation out for good. In wrath remember mercy."

"Bring Papa home safe," Judy added, tightening her arms around Angie. "Please help him to forgive Angie and me."

Judy lay back on the bed and closed her eyes, relaxed. Sliding to her knees beside the bed, Angie continued praying for more than an hour.

At one forty-five, Hans brought the buggy back and stayed in the barn.

Lane came into the house at ten past two.

Angie left Judy sleeping and paced downstairs to meet him, her heart thudding dully as if it didn't care if it kept beating or not. Standing in the kitchen, white about the lips, Lane's blue eyes held an icy chill that froze her to the marrow.

"How dare you?" His voice shook with repressed emotion.

Staring at him, she couldn't answer.

"Did you honestly think that you could force me to fall for someone *you* chose? Did you think I'd go along with such a plan just because you wanted me to?" He moved toward her. "Come on—tell me! Just what did you expect me to do?"

She moistened her lips. "I was hoping that once you met Saundra, you'd—"

"I'd be a good little boy and marry the woman." He paced toward the stove and back to the door. "Just what do you think marriage is, anyway? You say you'll marry Barry, and then suddenly you change your mind. You try to hook me up with a woman you've never even seen before."

"Saundra's very nice." A bit of Angie's spirit returned. "She did a lot for us. You can't deny it."

"That's not the point, Angie." He faced her, his expression like granite. "You schemed and lied and connived to fix something that didn't need fixing. And you got my daughter involved in your treachery as well."

"I'm sorry."

"Oh, that makes it all better!"

Her temper flared. "What more do you want me to do? I explained to Judy that I was wrong. I'm apologizing to you. What more can I do?"

He turned toward the door, yanked it open, and was gone.

Pressing a fist to her mouth, she watched him bolt to the barn. She stood, staring at the barn door as if it could give her the answers she so desperately needed.

Lane's angry words rang through her brain again and again. She was a liar and a cheat. She was a bad influence on Judy. He couldn't stand to be near her.

A lone tear trickled down her face. One thing was clear. She must leave. She couldn't stay here any longer.

Chapter 21

Brushing away tears, Angie threw a few things into a small carpetbag, moving carefully so she wouldn't awaken Judy. Her maiden aunt in Denver kept asking her to come for a visit. The elderly lady would gladly welcome her.

Emptying her bureau drawers to fill her trunk, Angie stuck a small leather wallet into her pocket. Twenty carefully hoarded dollars would get her out of an impossible situation and see her through a few weeks until she found work.

She glanced around the room and paused at the sweet face nestled on the pillow. What would Judy do when she woke up and found Angie gone?

Letting out a pain-filled gasp, Angie darted out the door, afraid she'd lose her nerve. She paused on the porch, considering her next move. She didn't want to take Lane's buggy, and Sheba's saddle was locked in the tack room. Gripping the handle of her small bag, she set off down the lane at a brisk pace. If she hurried, she'd make it to town before dark.

Under a brilliant afternoon sun, the ground showed damp patches, and the rough road lay dotted with dark puddles. Trying vainly to keep her skirts clean, Angie tramped on, blocking out thoughts about her future, ignoring her cold, aching feet. She shifted the bag to her other hand and plodded on.

When she reached a crossing, she saw a buggy rumbling toward her from the west. Rounding the corner, it paused beside her.

"Need a ride, Angie?" whiskery old Mr. Hawkins asked, wheezing. His plump, white-haired wife sat beside him. "We've been visiting with the grandchildren, and we're heading back to town."

"Thank you. That's where I'm going." She handed up her bag and climbed aboard. The seat felt so good against her aching back.

"Something wrong with your horse?" Mrs. Hawkins asked with a kindly smile.

"No, ma'am."

"Lane sick again?"

"No, ma'am."

A heavy silence followed. Angie hated to be rude, but she couldn't share her situation with the whole town. She kept her head turned as though watching the landscape, but all she could see were Lane's cold blue eyes and a child's sleeping face against a pillow.

A sudden icy wind shook the buggy. Angie pulled her shawl closer around her coat and shivered.

At Angie's request Mr. Hawkins stopped in front of the train station. Mumbling a feeble thanks, Angie stepped down and hurried inside. Five minutes later she'd made arrangements for a wagon to collect her trunk and tucked a ticket into her pocket.

She hurried toward the hotel restaurant, anxious to get out of the cold. Her feet were numb. Her ears and nose burned.

Sliding into a seat at a corner table, she laid her case on the floor near her feet, clasped her hands in her lap, and closed her eyes. Her train left at midnight. How could she bear to leave? Her whole life was wrapped up in Lane and Judy. What a foolish girl she'd been last summer when she imagined she wanted to get away.

A moment later a dark-haired girl with brown-flecked teeth stopped beside her. "We have beef and beans with a pone of corn bread or Irish stew and biscuits."

"Stew will be fine," Angie said. "And some hot tea, please."

The food tasted good, though not as good as Angie's own cooking. She took her time, savoring each bite, dreading the long wait ahead in a cold depot. Finally she had no choice but to leave. She glanced at a grandfather clock beside the door: six-thirty.

Laying a quarter and a nickel on the table, she paced to the lobby and stiffened when she reached the doorway. Saundra sat on a sofa near the desk, her toe tapping against the thin carpet, her face incredibly sad. She spotted Angie, stared, and turned away.

For a long moment Angie stood in the doorway. She felt so sorry for Saundra. Her hopes had been dashed. Her future was as uncertain as Angie's own.

Finally Angie stepped across the room and sat beside the German woman. "Saundra, I want to apologize again for what happened. I asked you to come here because I wanted someone to care for Judy. I did want you and Lane to be happy, too." She felt the texture of her carpetbag through her thin gloves. "I wish you could believe me."

"Why aren't you at the ranch?" Saundra asked, her voice tight.

"I'm leaving on the midnight train. Lane was so angry with me that I can't stay at the Flying P any longer." Saying it brought fresh pain to her heart. She blinked away tears. Her voice cracked. "You brought laughter into the house again, Saundra. You woke Lane out of his terrible depression. I'm everlastingly grateful for that."

Saundra turned to her and laid her gloved hand over Angie's. Her voice softened. "That's where you're wrong, Angie. You did all those things."

"Me?"

She nodded, her eyes wise and kind. "You were brave enough to want to make a change." She smiled sadly. "I am not saying you were right in how you did it, mind you."

Saundra drew her hand away, her expression lightening. "I'm taking a job as hostess and manager at this hotel starting the day after tomorrow."

"You'll be alone for Christmas?" Angie asked.

That familiar playful look sparkled for an instant in Saundra's eyes. "Hans is coming to the hotel to take Christmas dinner with me. He said he has something important to talk to me about." Gazing at Angie, she grew serious. "In a way this whole mix-up has done me good. I had built up an image in my mind that wasn't real. The man I came out here to meet was a phantom, a paper figure. He wasn't Lane Phillips. But if I hadn't come, I would have missed Hans."

"What about Barry?" Angie asked. "I thought you were interested in him."

Saundra shook her head slowly. "Barry is a nice boy. One of these days he'll meet the girl of his dreams." She leaned toward Angie to say confidentially, "You weren't that girl, Angie, and neither was I. Barry has some growing up to do before he's ready for real love."

"So did I," Angie murmured. "I'm so glad we didn't marry each other. It would have been a disaster." She touched Saundra's arm. "I wish you all the best, Saundra," she said warmly. "God bless you and keep you." A few minutes later she said good night and headed toward the depot.

For five hours Angie paced from the window to the door in the tiny, deserted waiting room. Several times she sat down for a moment and then stood up again. Lane's angry words wouldn't let her rest. They rang through her head until she wanted to scream. *How dare you! You schemed and lied and connived. . . .*

When the wagon with her trunk arrived, she hurried outside to see it ticketed. Drawing her arms close to her body, she rushed back to the feeble warmth of the depot. At a quarter to twelve, a whistle announced the arrival of her train. Soon she'd be far away from a million painful memories.

She pushed through the door and crossed the wooden platform, her carpetbag in hand.

"Angie!"

She wheeled and saw Lane running toward her. His hat blew off, but he didn't stop to retrieve it. "Angie, wait! I have to talk to you!"

Her heart pounding, her mouth dry, she stopped near the train steps, both hands gripping the handle of her bag. Had he come to berate her again? She couldn't bear any more abuse from him. Clenching her jaw, she waited for him to reach her.

He stopped before her, his face lined with fatigue and worry.

"I have to get on the train," she said tightly. "If I miss this one, I'll have to wait two days until the next."

"Just give me a minute, Angie, please." He gasped for breath, one hand on her arm above the elbow as though holding her from running away. "I came to apologize. Judy told me the whole story." He paused to take a long breath. "I'm sorry I spoke so harshly to you. My pride was hurting something awful, and I took it out on you."

She stole a glance at his anguished face and looked at the floor again, biting her lips. "I ruined everything: our family, our Christmas, everything."

His voice urgent, he said, "God had a reason for it, Angie, despite the misguided way it happened. We both learned some hard lessons He's been trying to teach us for a long time."

Hope poked a tiny hole of light into the darkness that blanketed her spirit. Looking up into his anxious eyes, she felt tears well up in her own. This was worse than another scolding.

"Please don't cry," he said. "I didn't come here to make you cry."

She tucked her chin down.

He lifted it gently. "Don't go away, Angie. Come home with me. Judy needs you. I would have come earlier, but she was hysterical, and I couldn't leave her. She cried herself to sleep."

She shook her head. "I can't go back with you. Not even for Judy." Her voice broke. "Too much has happened. I'm not the same girl I was before Saundra came."

"Will you stay for me?" he asked, moving closer. "I've been so caught up in self-pity that I didn't realize how important you are to me. I need to apologize for that, too. You've been so good to Judy and me, and I've made your life miserable."

"That's not true," she said, shaking her head. "These have been the happiest years of my life. Only I've been too stupid to realize it. I ruined everything." She tried to free her arm from his grasp, but he held on.

"Angie, please listen to me," he said, desperation in his voice. "It's time to let go of the past and look toward the future. Charlotte would want us to be happy. I know she would." He moved closer to her, his voice softening. "You're full of fun and laughter. You're impatient and quick-witted and alive."

With her head still bowed, tears coursed down Angie's cheeks, silent and thick.

He touched her chin. "I love you, beautiful Angie. Won't you please marry me and come home? I'll never know another day of happiness if you get on that train. I can't face tomorrow without you." The train whistle blasted a final warning.

Stifling a sob, she nodded. He pulled her into his arms, and she melted against him, tasting her own salty tears on his lips, feeling the warmth of his love down to the core of her soul.

"Let's wake the parson," he said close to her ear as Engine 534 rumbled out of the station. "We'll take him home with us, wake up Judy, and say our vows in front of the fireplace." He held her to him. "Please, Angie. Say you will marry me tonight before I lose my mind."

"Now who's impatient?" she asked with a breathless laugh. She blinked away the last of her tears, still reeling under the wonder of it all.

He pulled back to look into her eyes. "Will you do it? Will you marry me tonight?"

"Yes, Lane," she said. "With all my heart."

He let out a loud laugh, a triumphant sound, and kissed her again. Arm in arm they strode to the buggy, faces shining. Pausing at the door, Lane chuckled. "I can't wait to see Judy's face when she sees you. Talk about a special Christmas! This year we all get an unexpected surprise."

RIBBON OF GOLD

by Cathy Marie Hake

Dedication

To all of my dear Christian sisters who long for a godly
husband, yet still fill their lives with joy and service
as they wait for the Lord's timing and will.

Special thanks to Rick Randall of the Boott Cotton Mill
National Park. He graciously shared a wealth of information
and helps keep this part of our nation's history alive
as he works in the weaving room there.

*"I am the door: by me if any man enter in, he shall be saved, and shall go in and out,
and find pasture. The thief cometh not, but for to steal, and to kill, and to destroy:
I am come that they might have life, and that they might have it more abundantly."*
JOHN 10:9–10

Chapter 1

A scream pierced the loud roar of the steam engines and clack and whoosh of the looms. Isabel Shaw whirled around as she yanked the ten-inch shears from the cloth sheath at her waist. Four hasty, desperate hacks freed Mary's brown cotton skirt from the take-up gear on the machine.

Kathleen hurriedly snatched the ragged scrap before it stopped the loom or caused an unsightly flaw in the cotton cloth. "Whew!"

Isabel gave Mary a quick hug and half-shouted in her ear, "You did fine! You're one of us now." She glanced down at the ragged hole in Mary's dress, then meaningfully at her bun. "Aren't you glad you pinned up your hair?"

Mary nodded and accepted the bobbin Kathleen grabbed from a box by their feet and thrust into her hands.

"Keep up, honey. We'll help you." Every word they spoke had to be shouted to be heard. Isabel guided Mary's shaking hands, steadying them as they popped the old bobbin out of the nearly empty shuttle and deftly thrust the new one in place.

Mary lifted the alderwood shuttle that was shaped like a bottomless canoe to her lips, then sucked the loose thread through the small hole near one of the copper-tipped ends. After she placed the shuttle firmly into the far right-hand side of the race, she gave Isabel a wobbly smile.

"You're catching on quick!" Isabel carefully held in her own deep blue calico skirt as she turned back to her own machines. Closely packed as the looms were, she'd learned to mind her skirts when she moved in order to prevent being snared.

In unison, the trio resumed weaving the thirty-inch-wide shirting at Steadman Textiles. Machines continued to roar, and they put off a greasy odor that mixed oddly with the smell of the thread. Since untreated thread snagged and broke, they dressed the cotton thread with potato starch to make it stronger. The odor saturated the brick walls and wooden floor, and Isabel longed for a breath of snow-fresh air.

Beneath her skirt and single flannel petticoat, she felt her stocking slip down. *I can't take the time. I'm already in trouble for helping Mary.* Isabel considered herself lucky to have stockings at all. When she went to help the girls at Kindred Hearts Orphanage with their sewing after church the previous Sunday, its headmistress, Amy Ross, discreetly passed the paper-wrapped black stockings to her. Amy explained that a wealthy woman had generously left a few charity baskets. Isabel knew the extra-long stockings wouldn't fit petite Amy or any of the older girls. Since she was tall and her last pair of stockings looked far beyond redemption, the sagging new stockings reminded her of how God provided for her needs. She just wished she had tied her garter tighter.

Nimble fingered, Isabel replaced her own bobbins and saw to setting the hooks attached to a leather strap weighted with a bell-shaped metal piece. The temple hooks kept the web of her fabric snug. Down the line she went, only to start again as soon as she finished her last. A bobbin lasted just five minutes. It took rhythm for her to keep up with the speed of the machines, and the mishap made it hard to catch up.

Eleven-year-olds lugged in baskets with more thread, and empty bobbins went into one bin to be dragged away by slightly younger girls. Isabel took care not to step on them when they crawled past to pull those heavy bins.

The warm, filling porridge from breakfast sat heavily in her stomach. Though known for being a pinchpenny, Ebenezer Steadman had considered feeding his workers well to be a sound business investment. He'd arranged for the boardinghouse tables to groan beneath the weight of good food for his workers. When she'd first come to work at the mill two years ago, Isabel enjoyed the same hearty breakfasts she'd eaten back home—eggs, bacon or sausage, freshly baked bread, and plenty of creamy milk. Since Mr. Steadman passed on—ostensibly to be with the Lord—the mill's overseer had ordered severe changes in how things ran. Delicious meals and extras at the dining tables disappeared overnight. Pasty porridge, stews made with gristly meat, cheap corned beef, and day-old fish now dominated the menu. Though Isabel didn't approve of gossip, she couldn't help wondering if Mr. Jefford was tucking the saved money into the pocket of his expensive, new, double-breasted coat.

She shook her head to rid herself of the uncharitable thought. Instead, she continued to diligently tend her looms and pray for Mama and each of her siblings in turn. Originally, Isabel had left her family's farm in New Hampshire and come to work at Steadman Textiles so money could be put aside for her brother's education. David hoped to be a doctor someday. A bright boy, he showed every promise of bettering himself with advanced learning.

Then Papa died, and her plans had changed. Isabel sent almost all her pay home so Mama could keep food on the table, and David set aside his dreams and took an apprenticeship with a cooper. The beat of the machines rang out a cadence to her prayer. *Lord, be with them. Take my love to them. . . .*

✳

Carter Steadman sauntered down the long catwalk. He sensed his snail's pace tried Harlan Jefford's patience. Though aware his overseer was a busy man, Carter didn't consider it too much to expect a thorough inspection. He'd arranged in advance for this tour of the mill, and he didn't want to rush from room to room. After the improvements and innovations he saw in England, he wanted to institute several changes at his family's mill. He'd have to be selective about which alterations to make first. Changes, he'd discovered, were best accepted if introduced gradually. Judging from Jefford's scowl, Carter decided those changes would have to be presented with a shipload of tact.

Below him, the looms operated in mesmerizing synchronicity, creating fabric at a dizzying rate. His brows knit. Carter stopped and counted the stroke speed. Tapping the toe of his sleekly polished boot, he kept beat with the rhythmic machinery.

Whale oil lamps overhead cast a dim glow upon the workroom. For fear one might cause a fire, buckets of water sat at the ready by the windows. Warp threads strung from the backs of one hundred metal-and-wood looms, looking like a million harp strings. They protested loudly each time the rear beams clanked up and down. Shuttles carrying the weft threads zoomed across the warp threads, and beater bars slammed the weave tight. Finished cloth wound onto the front beams of the machines into fifty-yard bolts.

Here and there, weavers had tacked or pasted pages to their looms or the windows so they could read a quick snippet as they worked. With the looms operating at top speed, no one truly had an opportunity to read, so those pages stood as a reminder of dusty, forgotten dreams.

Jefford propped his forearms on the metal rail and nodded toward the floor. "I've kept everything running just as your father ordered."

"Even the speed?"

"Ayuh. Upping the speed yields three hundred more bolts of cloth from No. 14 yarn each day." He drummed his palms on the rail proudly. "I get 250 yards from each loom each week."

Carter strove to appear unruffled as he leaned against the rail and watched the women tend the looms. Speeding up the machinery was a simple matter of adjusting a few levers; speeding up the workers took more finesse. If the overseer occasionally issued the command to accelerate work to meet a special order, Carter might consider it, but he counted it unsafe to push the workers at this pace on a daily basis. "So you run the looms at maximum capacity at all times?"

"A mighty poor overseer I'd be to do otherwise."

Tamping down his temper, Carter reminded himself Jefford boasted working for the mill for a fair length of time. During those years, he'd obeyed the mandates given him—but those orders had come from an owner who rarely troubled himself over the needs of others. If Jefford displayed that same loyalty to Carter's plans, the mill would benefit. *I'll give him a chance.*

Watching the bustle below, Carter realized the workers seemed to cover a fair distance in their movements. His eyes narrowed. "How many looms apiece?"

"Three, most often. Some, I can stretch to four."

Carter's molars grated. "Three or four?"

Jefford shot him a bland look, then added, "Beginners are on two for the first week or so. If they can't handle three by the second week, they're turned out."

Some changes can't wait. Carter watched the women scrambling to keep pace with the machines and decided he'd finish the tour, then demand speed and loom assignment adjustments.

Just as they prepared to continue, a cry sounded. A quick scan of the floor revealed a flurry of activity among three women who then rapidly separated and got back to their weaving. Carter suspected the middle one had gotten snagged in the machinery and her friends hastily freed her.

Jefford squinted and read aloud, "Row Sixteen." The tone of his voice promised retribution. He turned to Carter. "Mr. Steadman—that is, your father—made the policy no one could leave her loom for any reason without permission."

"Frivolous causes, I agree with. In this case, however, they rescued a worker. I consider the purpose quite reasonable."

"Begging your pardon, Mr. Steadman, but you cannot expect these women to think the matter through. We'll have pandemonium if we let them start to decide for themselves when they can stop working!"

"Row Sixteen did a fair job helping the center worker and resuming duty. Since I approve, you needn't take any action against them."

The overseer nodded curtly. His face reflected disagreement.

Carter crossed his arms and studied him for a long moment. "You've served at Steadman Mills a long while, haven't you?"

"Seven years." Chest puffed out with pride, Jefford added, "And every year's turned a better profit than the last one!"

Carter headed down the catwalk again. "If you have weavers handling three looms apiece, we must have fewer workers and the boardinghouses must have vacancies."

"No, sir. While you was away, your dad replaced the old looms with modern ones. Faster, better technology—more profit in that, you know. He scooted the looms all up a bit tighter and added in six more rows. I've kept every machine busy, so the boardinghouses are full."

No wonder that woman got caught in the machine. Carter stopped. His hands tightened around the metal rail. "How often do the workers get snagged in the works or injured?"

"Haven't bothered to count." The overseer shrugged indifferently.

Carter hit his limit. Before the day was done, he would let Jefford know that as the new owner, he expected changes. He wasn't going to delay them, after all.

Chapter 2

Carter saw blatant disregard for the workers' safety from the room where the raw cotton was cleaned, to the thread room, through the weaving room, and on to the fabric finishing. He didn't expect the mill to be a Sunday picnic, but he refused to allow the current situation to continue.

He stood at the doorway to the kitchen of one of the boardinghouses and watched the women wolf down their midday meal. Accustomed to refined dining, he felt a bolt of disbelief. These women engaged in no gentle conversation and never paused between bites. The meal of corned beef, cabbage, and bread seemed simple but plentiful. They'd not return to work hungry. Still, he couldn't help thinking that eating so fast might well cause indigestion.

The contrast between this meal and the feast he and Jefford shared just an hour before jarred him. Admittedly, duckling might be far too difficult to roast for this many women, and Jefford might well have ordered an especially fine meal to impress the new boss. . . .

The bells chimed, interrupting his musings. All of the women rose and carried their plates to wooden boxes at the end of each table. Like a chain of postulants in a nunnery, they obeyed the bells that regimented their lives.

Carter drew a gold pocket watch from his paisley silk waistcoat pocket and noted the time. Twenty-five minutes. He cocked a brow and looked at Jefford, then shot a meaningful glance at his timepiece.

"No use wasting daylight by having them dawdle over their meal."

Just then, a tall brunette passed by and captured Carter's attention. Fine-boned and graceful, she looked and moved like a queen. She carried her own plate and another, as well.

He smiled. Seeing her was the first pleasant thing he'd experienced all day.

Her voice lilted softly as she promised the pale teen beside her, "Tomorrow, your fingers won't be so stiff and sore. You're doing fine."

Unaware of his presence, the younger girl plucked at a sizable, ragged hole in her brown skirt. "But my clothes! I can't do anything about them, because I promised Aunt Amy I'd give most of my pay to her!"

"Beneath our aprons, many of us have tattered skirts," the first reassured. "You're not alone in that. Kathleen and I will help you mend it before you walk home."

"That we will," the third woman said. "And Amy would never expect all of your money."

Lazing against the doorsill, Jefford declared, "They get along well enough. Not many troublemakers."

His attitude had grated on Carter's nerves all morning. Even if Jefford held no compassion whatsoever, couldn't he understand these women would work better if treated well? On a simple business level, it made sense to invest in a happy workforce. Even if greed were his sole motivation, Jefford should be able to see that much. Carter refused to accept such an attitude, and he was about to show this pompous man just how different things were going to be. He paced off and stopped the trio. "A moment, please."

The youngest looked stricken and blurted out, "It was my fault, sir. Please don't punish them for helping me!"

The other two drew closer to her in an instinctively protective move and stared up at him. Their somber expressions sliced through his heart. Something inside twisted. He'd frightened her. Carter asked the pretty brunette, "Are you from Row Sixteen?"

"Yes, sir, we are."

"Your names?"

She blinked, and he noted how her huge brown eyes glistened. The others huddled closer still. *All of them are frightened, as a matter of fact. These women are so accustomed to harsh management, they expect me to castigate them. They did nothing I wouldn't have done myself.*

"I'm Isabel Shaw, sir." The plates in the dark-haired beauty's hands rattled a bit as she tilted her head to the right. "Mary Tottard," then to the left, "Kathleen McKenna."

"Don't you think I didn't see what happened this morning." Jefford set his hands on his hips and scowled at them. Other women hurriedly slid by and left the boardinghouse's dining hall.

Isabel wet her lips. "Sir, it's Mary's first day to mind her own loom."

"She understood the rules. She also knows the penalty—as do both of you," Jefford asserted.

"But in this case," Carter inserted smoothly, "you were right to react so quickly." He cast a glance at Mary's ruined skirt. "You're not wearing an apron. On your way back to the floor, go help yourself to a remnant."

All three women rewarded him with relieved smiles, but Isabel cast a wary glance at Jefford.

Carter gave the overseer a cool look, then turned to address the women. "You other ladies are welcome to a piece, as well."

Isabel blinked in astonishment. "Sir, I can make do just fine with my apron; but if you don't mind, I'd take a scrap so we can make a few dolls for the girls at the orphanage."

Her charitable response took him by surprise. Carter tilted his head to the side and stared at her for a long moment. "Miss Shaw, I'd be pleased if you'd take a length for yourself and some for the orphans. How many dolls are you making?"

A beautiful flush painted her cheeks. "Mrs. Ross has sixteen girls, sir. A bit over a yard of cotton would be enough for us to make sure each of the young ones has a Christmas doll."

"Take an additional yard apiece for them—not just the plain solids, either. Make them fancy pieces from printworks. That way, the girls can learn to stitch some pretty little clothes and blankets. . .and," he stressed, "be sure to take a piece for yourself."

She almost dropped the plates. "Oh, sir, you're being so generous, but I wouldn't want you to get in trouble."

Carter wanted to chuckle. Clearly, Miss Shaw didn't know his identity—a surprising fact since the Steadman males bore a strong resemblance to one another. Tall, broad of shoulder, and square-jawed, he resembled his father with the exception that his dark brown hair hadn't a single hint of silver to it. Had she never seen his father? He set those thoughts aside and found her concern for him quite charming. So was her selflessness.

He didn't want to embarrass her, so he turned to the overseer. "Mr. Jefford is more than able to approve of this."

"Oh, God bless you, sir!"

"Yes, God bless you!" the other two said in unison.

Once they were out of earshot, Jefford heaved a deep sigh. "Mr. Steadman, that was a terrible mistake. You've been abroad and don't understand the way of things anymore. Every last woman on the floor is going to be looking for a handout now. This is a business, not a charity!"

Carter reined in his temper and strove to face his overseer with a modicum of civility. Getting him to institute changes would likely be difficult, and inspiring him to cooperate would require finesse. "You've shown me the mill all morning, Jefford. The productivity of Steadman Textiles would stagger smaller minds than ours. A few paltry yards won't be missed, and as it aids orphans, it's a worthwhile charity."

"Your father believed charity began at home." Jefford's thinned lips made it clear he agreed with that theory.

"Farmers in the Old Testament left grain in the fields so the widows and orphans could glean. God blessed them for it. So far as I can see, the Lord's blessing will carry me a far sight better than hoarding a few remnants."

Jefford hitched his left shoulder in a gesture that might have looked careless, had the motion not been so tense. "Whatever you want, sir. You're the owner now, since your father stuck his spoon in the wall."

※

"Nice, white muslin, Kathleen! Look at this." Isabel held up a two-yard length of fabric from the rainbow stack on their bed in the boardinghouse. The remainder of the pile gaily tumbled across the colorful nine-patch quilt that covered the double bed they shared. "Why, the girls will be delighted."

Kathleen laughed. "Amy is going to be more excited than all of her little ones."

"I know. Let's tell Amy we'll make the dolls, and we'll let her have three yards so she and the older girls can sew doll clothes for the young ones. That way, they'll all have a part in the gift."

Kathleen sat cross-legged on the other side of the bed and took the pins out of her twisted coronette, releasing an abundance of black curls that bounced down her back, then sprang back up to curl in abandon around her shoulders. At times like this, Isabel knew her Scottish friend must have left a trail of swains behind when her father decided to sell his New England farmhouse and move the family to Indiana, sending Kathleen to the mill to help them financially until they got settled in their new home. Oblivious to Isabel's admiring look, Kathleen stared at the fabric and wondered aloud, "What about the older girls? Some of them are beyond doll age."

"We'll use some of the fabric to make them aprons. Ginger can help us decide who'd like which piece best."

"Aye, and ye can use the scraps to teach the wee girls to quilt dolly blankets," Pegeen said as she plopped down on her bed. She yawned deeply. "I dinna ken how the both of you find the strength to sit there by the lamp in the evenin' to work. I'm worn down to a nubbin' by the day's end."

After slamming the lid down on her lap desk, Grace blew on her letter to dry the ink. The dark expression she wore promised a biting comment. "Didn't you listen to the sermon on Sunday? Christians are obliged to do good works."

"Ach! I sit there the whole while, daydreamin'. Spinnin' in her grave, she is, my mama—her daughter darkening the doors of any church not named after the Virgin or a saint. If the dragon who runs this boardinghouse didn't herd us all out to her verra own church, I'd not go, and well you know it." Pegeen wrinkled her nose. All of the mill workers had to attend church, or they lost their positions. "I need every last cent so I can bring me sister o'er."

Isabel and Kathleen exchanged a quick glance. They made no secret of their faith, and they had made a pact to pray for their two roommates since neither sought salvation. Instead of arguing, Isabel simply said, "The idea of having the girls quilt is lovely, Peg."

"She just goes to help at the orphanage so she won't miss her little sisters so much." Grace folded her letter with a savage sweep of her hand. "Face it—we're all here because our families need money. Nothing like being a beast of burden so someone else's life improves."

When the boardinghouses designated for the Irish lasses filled to capacity, Isabel and Kathleen offered to take Pegeen into their room. Grace arrived a year later, and she pitched a fit when she learned she'd have to share not only a room but a bed with an immigrant. Disgruntled because her stepfather sent her to the mills to earn funds for his son's education, she'd been alternately rude and sullen. Others felt fortunate to have their positions, but Grace grumbled constantly. Close quarters and the differences among the four roommates made for some challenging moments.

After Grace left the room, Kathleen leaned forward. "We're not going to let her sour tongue get to us, Isabel."

"We haven't, yet," Isabel whispered.

Kathleen picked up a length of mauve cotton that had a wispy green vine every few inches. "Who does this remind you of?"

"Mauve—Amy. Definitely Amy." Isabel sighed. "There's not enough for an apron unless we piece the straps."

Kathleen folded the length and carefully set it aside. "We'll do that. If I don't miss my guess, Amy's spent every last cent she has on those girls. It's well past time she got something new for herself."

"I made my sisters dolls last Christmas. I still have the papers I used as a pattern." Isabel knelt by the small oak chest of drawers all four of them shared and searched for the pattern she'd made. For a moment, her heart ached to cuddle her sisters again. It had been two long years since she'd seen them, but she couldn't spare the dollar it would take to travel home and back again. The thick packet of letters in the drawer testified to the passage of time and served as a reminder that Mama loved her and needed her help.

A glittering gold ribbon wrapped around the letters. Grandma carried that ribbon in her bridal bouquet, and Mama did, too. By rights, Isabel's older sister should have gotten the ribbon; but Hannah and Abe surprised everyone in church one day by standing up and asking the parson to wed them. Hannah carried no bouquet to tie with the cherished ribbon. She'd happily pledged her vows and gone home to live in the little cottage on the outskirts of the village where her husband sharecropped.

Last Christmas, Mama sent the precious ribbon with a sweet, sweet letter—she'd apologized she hadn't managed to scrape together a few cents for a gift, but postage would add on a cost she could ill afford. Instead, she'd tucked her beloved ribbon of gold into the letter with the pledge to pray for Isabel as the sun's first rays streaked the morning sky.

Each time Isabel touched that ribbon, she felt close to her family. Her three little sisters and Mama would need her to send money home for many years to come. Isabel's heart grew heavy when she realized she probably wouldn't ever carry the ribbon in a bridal bouquet.

Chapter 3

Carter pulled his thick, black wool greatcoat tighter and headed across the courtyard toward the office. The five o'clock bell chimed, calling the employees to work. He hoped Jefford would be self-indulgent enough to sleep a bit later. After all, the last thing Carter wanted was for the overseer to hover while he examined the books.

Last evening, Carter's mother expressed her irritation when he stated his plan to return to the mill again today. "Your father paid others to see to that. So do you. Indeed, you pay them exceedingly well. The profits are such that we've been able to live comfortably. Stay home. Belinda Atherton and her daughters are coming to tea tomorrow."

Another good reason to be at the mill. Carter had hastily turned down the invitation.

He left the house early, before his mother could involve him in her matrimonial machinations. Her idea of a suitable wife revolved around wealth and breeding. She'd be delighted to match him with a brainless, simpering girl whose only interests were shopping and attending soirees. Carter wanted nothing to do with a "biddable" socialite; he had more important issues to mind. Mother, bless her compassionate soul, would understand—especially if he went home for supper tonight and shared with her his plan to wait on God's timing instead of rushing to the altar. At the present, cotton—not courtship—demanded his attention.

Virtually nothing had changed since he left except that Jefford ran the mill even more harshly. Carter and his father parted on less-than-comfortable terms. Father felt betrayed when Carter stated he fully understood and supported the mill workers in Lowell, who went on strike and took other actions to protest low wages, long hours, and poor working conditions. His father's anger rose even higher when Carter stated that he held similar concerns about Steadman Textiles. Mother soothed Father's fury by suggesting Carter merely hadn't enough knowledge of the world to understand the situation. They'd sent him to Europe with the expectation he'd go on a Grand Tour, rub elbows with idle, rich young men, and come to see the benefits of his station in life. Instead, he'd spent his time visiting other textile factories and making notes of techniques and labor management.

When he received word that his father died at a card table from a violent heart spell, Carter knew the time had come for him to return to Eastead. For all of Father's wealth, he'd not been able to take a cent to his grave. Carter mourned the fact that his father stayed so busy seeking wealth, he'd never sought the Lord. The young man resolved to set a different course for his own life.

Then, too, Carter felt a heavy burden weighing down on his shoulders. It fell to him to recompense his father's wrongs. God was the God of justice. The Bible clearly warned the sins of the father were visited upon the son. Aware he bore the responsibility of making restitution and appeasing God's pending wrath, Carter vowed to do all that was in his power to cancel the curse and receive God's blessing.

The office building door was unlocked, so Carter pushed it open and hastily lit an oil lamp on the small table beside the door. Half a dozen strides carried him to the bookkeeper's office. He inserted a key into the lock and let himself in. He'd not let Jefford know he possessed a key. At first, he'd been willing to believe the overseer had tried to be a diligent steward of the responsibilities he carried. Now, he couldn't be sure the overseer warranted his trust, so until he inspected the books and records, Carter chose to keep some matters to himself. The moment Jefford arrived today, he'd realize the new Steadman owner held keys—but by then it would be too late to doctor the financial records.

Carter put the lamp on the corner of the cherrywood desk and took a seat. For the next two hours, he pored over the books. Indeed, the records showed impressive business accomplishments—Steadman Textiles averaged six million yards of cloth each year. Carter knew a pound of cotton yielded three and one-fifth yards and that a bale of raw cotton usually weighed 361 pounds. Quickly scribbling on a nearby slate and using those facts, he checked the figures in the ledgers. Indeed, everything checked out as it ought.

Heavy footsteps made him aware he'd soon have company. Carter turned around in time to catch sight of the mill's overseer as he crossed the plank floor with a lumbering gait.

"Mr. Steadman! Had I known you wished to review the books, I'd have brought you here yesterday." Harlan Jefford gave him a brisk nod as he peeled out of his stylish, heavy wool coat.

"I appreciated the tour you gave me. I didn't want to take more of your time while I went through the mundane matters."

"I do my best to see to each and every detail." Having hung his coat on a brass wall hook, Jefford stepped over to the desk and jabbed a beefy finger toward the ledger. "The books prove it. Even after your father died, I kept the mill going and made sure it brought in just as much as when he'd been here to inspect the finances."

"There's no doubt Steadman Textiles turns a remarkable profit. Your zeal is noteworthy." Carter watched his overseer's chest puff out with pride. Sweeping changes would no doubt irk this arrogant man. That didn't matter. Carter had taken the reins, and he wasn't about to let someone else decide on the path. "As you're so capable, I'm counting on you to help make the changes go smoothly."

"Changes?" Jefford's shoulders stiffened.

Carter gestured toward a hard-backed chair. "This is a good time to outline the reorganization. Have a seat."

Shaking his head sagely, the overseer dragged the chair across the plank floor. Its legs scraped in loud protest, then the seat creaked under his considerable weight. He leaned back and jutted his chin toward the desk. "Those books show Steadman Textiles is turning the best profit it ever has—far and away above what the other mills are doing. Tampering with a good system isn't wise."

Carter stared at him.

Jefford shifted uncomfortably. "Begging your pardon, sir, but you've been gone a good long while. I mean you no disrespect. Give yourself a month or so to get a feel for how things run around here. No need to rush into things."

"Your concern is duly noted," Carter said in a soft tone that would have warned anyone who knew him that he was doing his utmost to rein in his temper.

Jefford's head bobbed, and a patronizing smile accompanied his next words. "Your father and I built a good system here. He approved of how I run things."

"My father and I disagreed on some of those issues. I am now the owner. I expect your full loyalty and cooperation." Carter closed the ledger, having seen enough. He stared straight at the overseer and watched the man's jaw tighten and his face grow florid. He didn't know Jefford well enough to guess whether the reaction indicated wounded pride, frustration, or anger.

"You know Steadman Textiles inside and out. You will be pivotal in instituting the revisions."

"No one knows the mill better."

Carter couldn't be sure if Jefford had agreed with his praise or was making a point of stressing his own significance. "Several of the changes are beneath a man of your importance in the scheme of things around here."

Jefford tugged at his gold silk waistcoat. He looked more like a prosperous bank owner than a mill overseer. "Your regard does me proud, sir. I consider it my duty to keep on top of things—everything."

"Agreed. That's why we're meeting now."

"Things changed while you was away. Used to be farmers' daughters who worked here. Nowadays, I get them Irish gals. More than a third of the workers are potato eaters." A glint lit his eyes. "Willin' to work for less, too."

"So that is why the pay dropped from $3.50 a week to $3.25?"

"Ayuh." A smug smile crossed Jefford's face.

"And you're still charging $1.25 per week room and found."

"The boardinghouses are better than what those lasses ever had back home." The overseer leaned forward. "Saving a quarter per worker each week adds up to a tidy sum. It boosted the profits. Your father came up with that notion himself."

"I am not my father." The iron in Carter's voice made it clear things would change. "Pay is to be brought back up to $3.50 a week, effective today."

Jefford's eyes bulged. "For all but the Irish, right?"

"For all of the women. The book of Ephesians says, 'Now, therefore, you are no longer strangers and foreigners, but fellow citizens with the saints and members of the household of God.' I'll not hold with treating the Irish women any differently than the others."

"If that's what you order."

Though Jefford's tone made it clear he disagreed with the decision, Carter didn't care. He suspected the overseer wouldn't be any happier with his next words. "There are other issues we need to address at once."

Chapter 4

"M r. Jefford looks like he sat on a pincushion," Kathleen whispered to Isabel as they gathered in the aisles of the weaving room.

Isabel shot her a quicksilver smile, then turned her attention back to the overseer. Standing on an overturned salt box, he stuck out above all of the women's scarved heads. His brows beetled into a dark vee, and he kept huffing like a steam engine coming up to speed. Never before had the women been ordered to gather for a meeting before the day began. If the overseer needed to make an announcement, he waited until mealtime so as not to lose a moment of labor.

Hands on his hips, he clipped out loudly, "Henceforth, you will all tend only two machines. . .one machine for the new laborers for the first fortnight."

Isabel drew in a surprised breath. Only two looms?

"That better not mean he's cutting pay again," the woman behind her grumbled.

Oh, if it does, I won't be able to send Mama enough to take care of everyone back home!

"Rows One through Eighteen will work their usual stations, but Nineteen through Twenty-five are to fill in the gaps formed by the reduced responsibilities."

Mary let out a relieved sigh. Isabel grabbed her hand and squeezed it. They wouldn't be separated.

"Now get to work." Jefford scowled and flapped his hands like he was shooing away a flock of pesky hens.

Weaving felt different that morning. Isabel couldn't decide what gave her the odd sensation her world had changed. Perhaps it was because she didn't have to scurry madly about to tend three looms. She still needed to work at a steady pace, but even then, it almost felt like her job had slowed from a horse race to a hayride. Mayhap 'twas that her threads didn't seem to break as often at this speed, so she didn't have to tie as many weaver's knots. Then, too, Pegeen now wove on her other side, and her cheeky smile had a way of lifting Isabel's spirits.

Midmorning, a pair of men came into the weaving room. Instead of leaving the windows closed as was customary, they opened each of them a few inches for almost an hour. The fresh air smelled and felt wonderful.

As the women filed down the stairs on the outside of the building to go to dinner, Kathleen tilted her head toward the blackened brick walls. "Now can you beat that? All along, Mr. Jefford said the breeze would dry out the room and make the threads break. Hasn't done anything at all."

"It blew out some of the hot oil and the thread's stale potato starch smell." Mary's deep brown pelisse parted as she reached around to retie the length of pink-and-white-striped fabric that served as her new apron. "I'm ever so grateful."

"The air's so wet from the snow, it couldn't dry anything out," Kathleen decided.

"Hot and humid—that's what they want," one of the women behind them said. A smash piecer, she knew more about the weaving room than anyone else. "Get a room dry or cold, and the threads snap all over the place. What with the steam heater going, they could leave the windows open on days like this and we'd all be better off."

Isabel compressed her lips, then cast a look around. "I'm worried. If we're not weaving as much fabric, then profits will fall. They'll either pay us less or dismiss some of us."

"Saints preserve us! I hope not!" The woman in front of Isabel turned and gave her a stricken look. "I'm needin' that money to fetch my sister here. I figured 'twould take me another four months to earn her passage. If they cut our wages. . ."

"And the orphanage needs money," Mary added. "Last night, Aunt Amy told me she expects me to keep a fair portion of my earnings, but if they drop our wages, I'm going to try to keep her from finding out. It costs a fair amount to feed all of us girls."

"Speaking of food," Kathleen moaned, "I hope we get something better for lunch today. You know I'm not one to complain, but we used to eat well. They're holding out the same dollar and a quarter each week for room and found, but the meals aren't half as good as they used to be."

Isabel shuddered. "I agree. I know I ought to be thankful for a full plate, but they're buying the cheapest food they can now. I couldn't gnaw through the gristly meat in the stew last night."

"Aunt Amy makes such good food." Mary sighed. "She didn't get cross with me about my ruined dress. She just gave me a hug. I'm glad I still get to live at Kindred Hearts."

"Did you tell her about us making dolls for the girls for Christmas?" Isabel slipped into the dining hall and shed her cape.

"Oh, yes! And Ginger is so sweet. She offered some of the yarn in her knitting bag so we could make hair. If you make the dolls and faces, we'll match the hair for each of the girls."

"Oh, can't you just see red looping curls on Patty's or brown ones on Ruthie's?" Isabel laughed as they all sat at the table. "We ought to match the color we embroider the eyes, then, too."

Moments later, the kind, dark-haired man from the previous day strolled over and stopped by the head of their table. He flashed an urbane smile. "I see you got an apron, Miss Mary."

"Oh, yes. Thank you, sir!"

Isabel paused a moment from passing a bowl of potatoes to Kathleen. She smiled at him. "And we thank you, too, for the fabric. We'll be making lovely dolls."

"At the risk of being thought an eavesdropper, I'll confess I overheard you discussing them. It occurred to me, you might need cotton to stuff the dolls. I delivered a roll of batting to your boardinghouse."

"How thoughtful of you!"

"It was nothing. I'll be here, moving the looms for the next week. Perhaps you could bring the first one in so I can see how she turns out."

"It's the least I could do," Isabel murmured.

Kathleen twisted around. "Moving looms? Why?"

The man gave her a puzzled look for a moment. "I thought you'd been told we're removing some of the looms."

"No." Isabel gulped. "Is there a problem? Are the mills cutting back?"

His hazel eyes darkened, and he clamped his lips together.

"I don't mean to put you in an awkward position, asking you to reveal your supervisor's plans," she stammered. "It's just that we all count on every bit we earn. Most of the women here are trying to put by money to send a brother or son to school. Some are saving to bring a relative over from Ireland."

"I understand." He nodded and cast a glance about the room.

"That's me," one woman volunteered. "I'm bringing me sister over. We were hoping she'd find a job here at the mill when she came. Isabel—her mama's a widow and has a flock of bairns back home, and Mary shares her pay wi' the orphanage."

"God blesses those who see to the widows and orphans." The man's smile warmed enough to melt an icicle in an instant. "Put your trust in the Lord, ladies. He'll provide."

Once he walked off, Isabel quickly finished dishing up her meal and ate. When she went down the center walkway in the mill, she spied the kind stranger in a knot of other workmen. Tall and broad shouldered as he was, he stood out even in their midst. Throughout the rest of the day, she caught occasional glimpses of the men through the swirling lint as they unbolted looms from the floor and dismantled them.

If the mills were turning out less fabric, using fewer machines, and serving cheaper food, then Steadman Textiles must be in trouble. Before fear overtook her, Isabel thought, *Trust in the Lord. . . .* From the looks of things, she was going to have an opportunity to exercise her faith.

✄

Two days later, Carter looked to the side as he finished rolling up a blueprint. "Miss Isabel," he said in greeting to the young woman who stood before him.

A shy smile touched her lips as she held out a doll. He didn't bother to look at the toy— he could barely take his eyes off the woman. A becoming flush tinted her cheeks, and several tiny wisps of her rich brown hair spiraled at her temples and nape. Queen Esther couldn't have been half as lovely. Realizing he bordered on being rude for staring, he focused his attention on the doll. After he set aside the blueprint and wiped his hands off on the thighs of an old pair of heavy broadcloth pants, he accepted the toy.

"Betty's barely two. Amy took in her baby sister, too." Isabel smiled lovingly at the doll. "Little Betty's hair is that same shade of chestnut, and I embroidered brown eyes to make them match hers—only hers are so big and pretty."

"The doll is splendid." Carter didn't try to hide his grin. "Can't say I ever held one before, but if little Betty is half as sweet as this, I'm surprised someone hasn't adopted her."

"She's far cuter, but she has a limp. Amy Ross gets an occasional inquiry, but folks are generally looking for a healthy older girl to watch their younger children or use as a maid. Amy won't let the girls work until they're sixteen. Most of her girls are fine, but Betty has a limp, and Ginger is nearly blind."

He thoughtfully fingered the little loops of reddish-brown yarn that made a mop of curls. "How many children did you say she has?"

"Sixteen. Mary Tottard is the oldest. You met her the other day and let her have material for an apron. She and Veronica are the only ones who work."

The pink-and-white-striped dress on the doll jarred his memory. "I see you're clever about using scraps."

"Every scrap counts." Her smile sparkled with joy. "I can't thank you enough for talking Mr. Jefford into allowing us to have the material. He always admonishes us about the little things adding up around here. This time, those little bits of fabric will add up for the orphans."

"I thought the remnants and seconds were always donated to worthy causes."

Her brows arched. "Why, no, sir. They're sold in the company store."

Disgust twisted through him. *Why did I expect this would be any different? Every rock I pick up has slime under it.*

At every turn, Carter discovered ways his father and the overseer squeezed every last penny of profit imaginable from the mill. How much money could one man want? His family lived in luxury, yet his father cut the wages of these women, then sold them flawed goods in order not to take a complete loss. *Yet another sin of his I need to atone for. . . .*

"Look at that," one of the women exclaimed as she walked in. "Isabel, you made another doll. Will you get to take this one home to your sisters?"

Isabel's smile faded a bit. "No, I'm afraid not."

The woman patted her arm. "It's sweet of you to send Christmas gifts to them."

"We're making dolls for the girls at Kindred Hearts. If you'd like to join us, you can come to my room any evening."

After the other woman walked off, Carter gently set the doll into Isabel's arms. He watched how she nestled it close. For some reason, she looked so right with that baby doll cradled to her bosom. Tenderhearted as she was, she'd be a very loving mother. "I could get you more fabric so you could make them for your little sisters, too."

"It's kind of you to offer, but I used my fabric allotment to do that last Christmas." The steam engines started to chuff. "I need to get back to my looms. I didn't mean to take up so much of your time."

"Hey you! Get busy. I don't pay you to angle for a husband. And you—the women are off-limits. Get those last machines out of here and—" Jefford's voice came to a strangled halt when he drew close enough to see around the loom's frame.

Carter stared at him coldly. The bell to begin work hadn't yet rung. He'd seen Isabel oil her looms already, so she'd prepared for the day.

"Mr. Steadman—" Jefford stammered and cleared his throat.

"*Steadman!*" Isabel's eyes widened and the color drained from her face. A second later, two bright pink spots appeared in her cheeks. "I'm sorry I bothered you, sir." She turned and dashed off.

Chapter 5

Carter rolled down his shirtsleeves as Jefford stammered. "Begging your pardon, sir. I didn't realize it was you. I never would have—I mean, I was just trying to make sure. I don't let the workers flirt or trifle with one another here—"

Carter lifted a single finger, and the other man fell silent. "What time is it?"

The overseer fumbled to retrieve his pocket watch, then faltered, "Five until the hour, sir."

Just then, the bell to begin work rang. The supervisor stepped onto his stool and pulled a cord. Above him, a leather belt shifted onto a tight pulley, and every loom in the room groaned and rattled into action. The floor rumbled beneath their feet.

Carter tilted his head and squinted at the ceiling. "Am I to assume you've weaseled five extra minutes in the morning, just as you have at the dinner hour?"

Jefford had to lean close to hear the question over the din. He shouted back, "By your father's orders!"

"Ten minutes a day, six days a week." Carter glared at him. "That's an extra hour of work each week."

"We pay them by the week, not the hour," Jefford pointed out as he shifted from one foot to the other.

"I'll have to think about how to make restitution. You're to personally adjust the chimes so they ring true to time." Carter walked off, climbed the stairs, and strode across the catwalk. He looked down at the floor of the weaving room and gritted his teeth. *How do I make up for the way these women have been cheated? Dad had so much—couldn't he at least pay them and deal with them fairly?*

The looms were operating at normal speed instead of at the frantic pace of a few days ago. As he and the workmen had spaced out the remaining looms, safe room existed for the weavers to tend to their labors. Those facts should have brought him satisfaction, but they didn't.

He looked down at Row Sixteen. At their first meeting, he hadn't revealed his identity to Isabel Shaw. He'd originally assumed she knew who he was, then refrained from introducing himself once he realized differently. At some point, he should have said something, but he hadn't. Regrets assailed him.

All she wanted to do was thank me for letting her help the orphans. . .and she got embarrassed for her sweet intentions and nice manners. She didn't get to take the dolls to her own sisters last year and doesn't plan to go see them again this Christmas. How long since she went home for a visit?

The women who worked in Lowell wore clothing comparable to fashion plates. As he came home from Europe, he'd ridden through Lowell and noted how those women, dressed in their stylish designs, could easily blend into the merchant class of the Continent. He squinted as he studied the women below him. What had Isabel said? *Beneath our aprons, many of us have tattered skirts.*

Were those words mere consolation, an exaggeration, or a revelation that the workers preferred to keep their better garments to wear away from the mill?

Then again, there seemed to be two distinctly different groups of women here. Some came to benefit from the after-work classes and library and were able to save their wages for a brother or son's education. Others—like Isabel—sent almost every last cent home to distressed families.

When the bell sounded for the midday meal, Carter discreetly stood off to the side and watched the women head for the tables. He specifically came to Isabel's boardinghouse, partly because the women had already seen him there, so his presence wouldn't be cause for comment. Most of all, Carter chose that house because he found Isabel so appealing, he'd take any chance or excuse to be closer to her.

From a spot beside the door, Carter studied the sleeves and hems of the women's lint-covered gowns. He meant no disrespect, but he needed to collect facts. Jefford didn't have a sympathetic bone in his body, and the women likely wouldn't be bold enough to complain to Carter, so he silently observed the condition of their clothing. Just before he turned to leave, he watched Isabel for one last moment. Weak noontime sunlight slanted from the window and brought out the sparkle in her beautiful eyes. Even dressed in worn calico and dusted with lint, she reminded him of a queen.

Isabel lay in bed and stared at the ceiling. She couldn't get to sleep. "Kathleen?" she whispered in the dark.

"Oh, so you're awake, too?"

"Likely I'm purple from pinching myself to see if I'm awake."

Kathleen muffled her laughter. "Then you'll match the material for your new dress."

"As long as I don't match the pumpkin pie we had at supper, I'll be happy."

"Could you believe that? It's been months since we had such a meal." Kathleen folded her hands behind her head and stared at the ceiling. "Fine food and new clothes. I hardly know what to think."

Isabel rolled over and knew exactly what to think. Carter Steadman's hand and heart were behind all these changes. She stared at the fabric draped over the foot of their bed. A length of plaid in plum and two shades of blue lay there, waiting to be made into a new dress. Beside it, a dove gray-and-black stripe shimmered dully in the moonlight. Isabel selected it for Mama—since she'd been in mourning for two years, gray would be proper. Right beside those pieces, the verdant green dress length Kathleen chose for herself made a cheerful swag atop the amber calico.

"Kathleen, I ought to be ashamed for asking, but could we maybe work on our dresses tomorrow instead of the dolls? We have almost a month to go before Christmas."

Kathleen chuckled. "I was trying to find a way to ask you the same thing!"

Grace sat up and grumbled, "I'm tired. Will you just hush up? Just because you were both here long enough to get two lengths, you don't have to gloat."

Two dress lengths. . .and they weren't even to be counted against the two yards the Steadmans gave to each worker at Christmas! If that weren't enough, a grim-faced young Mr. Steadman had stood before everyone that afternoon.

"You have my personal apology. I've discovered the bells were set wrong. I've calculated you all worked about an hour extra each week."

Everyone stood in the yard, uneasy with his revelation, but careful not to voice discontent for fear Jefford or someone else would note dissenters and blacklist them.

Carter Steadman went on. "I owe the workers here restitution. Pay will be brought back up to the wages noted in my ledger from two years ago. You will each be paid double this week, and tomorrow will be a holiday for you. Just as I expect your best efforts and loyalty, I'll do my utmost to deal with you fairly."

His admission astonished Isabel. If his honesty and humility weren't enough, his restitution stunned her. The whole yard rang with cheers. Once the clamor died down, Mr. Steadman added, "For those who have worked here less than a year, you may have a dress or shirt-length of fabric. Those who've worked here longer may have two."

Lying in the dark, Isabel remembered every word he'd said. Tomorrow would be like a holiday—they'd have a day off work to use at their leisure. "Imagine, we're off on a Saturday!"

Grace threw a pillow at her. "Isabel, I declare, the minute we blow out the lamp at night, you start chattering."

"Sorry, Grace. I did that back home, too." She started to laugh. "Oops. Sorry. I was talking again."

※

"Mother, were you aware Father was selling the seconds and remnants to the workers instead of donating them to charity?" Carter sat across the supper table and waited for an answer.

"Why, no, dear. We rarely discussed business." She took a sip of tea, then smiled. "You could ask Mr. Jefford. Your father trusted him implicitly."

"I don't mean to hurt your feelings, Mother. You'll hear things are changing at Steadman Textiles and for good cause. Father and Mr. Jefford agreed on despicable practices."

"Despicable? Now, Carter, I know you didn't agree with your father at times—"

"Mother, word is going to get out. I'd rather tell you these things myself than have you hear gossip from others. The workers have been cheated—blatantly cheated. The chimes didn't ring true time, so they've set to work early, gotten off late, and had shortened mealtimes. Because the Irish girls are so desperate to earn money to bring family over, the wages were dropped."

"Oh, Carter!" She placed her hand to the bodice of her black bombazine mourning gown. "This is shameful."

"I agree." He gave her a grim smile. "I'm setting things right, but I felt it only fair to warn you, there may be comments about the changes being made. I also needed to ask where the seconds used to go so we can resume donating them to worthy causes."

A frown marred her brow. "I couldn't rightly say. Since Amy Ross started running Kindred Hearts, I was certain we'd been donating material to the little orphans."

He shook his head as he sliced the savory roast beef. "I made inquiries. As a matter of fact, one of the weavers offered to sacrifice taking a length for herself so she could have material to make dolls for the children for Christmas. I rode by the orphanage today, and though the girls all looked happy as could be, they wore frocks that were patched and threadbare."

"This cannot continue—we must do something at once!"

"My thoughts precisely. I'd like to gather up some material for the children to have new frocks and small clothes. Would you like to deliver it?"

"Of course I will. I'll get buttons, ribbons, and thread, too." The creases on her forehead smoothed as the serving maid carried in dessert plates. The aroma of apples and cinnamon wafted through the room, and Carter thought that was the cause of his mother's pleasure until she coyly added, "I could ask Belinda Atherton to accompany me. You missed seeing her daughters, Carter. They're both comely girls and quite accomplished."

"Mother, please don't try to play matchmaker."

"Someone has to. I want grandchildren, Carter. It's high time for you to marry a nice girl and start a family."

"I suppose you have a bevy of suitable prospects." He sighed.

"Now that you mention it. . ."

"Hold on." Carter held up both hands in a horrified gesture. "The mill is going to keep me busy for some time. I'd like to ask if you'd help me with the charity issues instead of parading eligible girls by the door at every opportunity."

"I could do both, you know."

Chapter 6

Two girls bracketed Isabel on the shabby red velvet settee in the orphanage's parlor. She worked with each of them as they cross-stitched alphabet samplers while she cuddled little Betty on her lap. "Alys, you did a wonderful job on that line. You're running out of floss. Knot that and rethread your needle. What color would you like to use?"

"Rose, please. It's so pretty!"

"Aye, now." Ginger's knitting needles clacked in a steady rhythm. "That's our Alys for you—always loving rose the best. I always know 'tis her comin' me way when I see her pink dress."

Kathleen winked at Isabel. They'd arranged with Amy and Ginger to give them hints about the girls and what colors to use for their dolls.

One of the older girls sat on the floor, whipstitching an orange patch she'd cleverly cut to look like a fish to cover a small hole in the bodice of a little dress. Kathleen sat on another settee, cradling the baby and helping the twins with their samplers.

A few minutes later, Amy lifted Ruthie onto a small cherrywood end table so she could measure her dress to see how many inches of a strip from a flour sack she needed to insert to stretch it to a decent length.

When someone knocked on the door, Mary hopped up. "I'll get it, Auntie Amy." A second later, Isabel heard her squeak, "Mr. Steadman!"

A minute later, Carter Steadman and his mother came into the parlor. He smoothly reached down, helped Amy to her feet, and greeted her warmly. "I'm so sorry to hear you lost Jason. He was such a good friend and a fine man. He'd be proud of you for opening your heart and home to all of these little girls."

Amy gave him a warm smile, and her voice barely quavered at all. "Mrs. Steadman and Carter, what a lovely surprise. I miss Jason terribly, and I'm so sorry for your loss as well."

"I should stop clackin' these needles and get tea, Aunt Amy." Ginger set aside her knitting and chuckled softly as she rose. "I recall me dear granny saying tea is better than sympathy."

Mrs. Steadman managed a watery little laugh. "Tea would be lovely."

"While you visit, I'll take care of things," Carter Steadman murmured to his mother. He then nodded politely to Isabel. "Miss Isabel, it looks like your little friends are talented with their needles."

"Yes, they are." She hoped she didn't sound too silly. Seeing him at the orphanage shocked her.

He turned and greeted Kathleen by name, then met Veronica. To his credit, he didn't treat them as lowly weavers in his factory. His manners were impeccable, and he managed to momentarily excuse himself while they all tried to cover their surprise with small talk.

Moments later, he came back inside the parlor with two large, paper-wrapped packages under his arms. He set them down, left, and returned with two more.

Quite commendably, Amy had taught her charges fine manners. Two of the older ones took the initiative to bring in chairs from the dining room, and the twins had already hopped up so Mrs. Steadman could sit on the settee with Kathleen. Though the girls desperately wanted to know what the packages contained, none of them asked. As Carter straightened up from setting down the additional packages, Alys popped off the settee she shared with Isabel. "You can have my place, Sir. I'll go help with the teacups!"

Isabel couldn't quite imagine sitting next to her employer. Their social circles didn't overlap. She started to rise. "I'll help—"

"I'm sure Amy has plenty of help in the kitchen already, Miss Isabel." Carter smiled at her, then brushed his knuckles over Alys's cheek. "Thank you for the seat, Little One." As Alys giggled and skipped off, Carter started to lower his tall frame onto the dainty settee.

"Wait!"

He jolted up straight and gave Isabel a baffled look.

"The needle," she warned. "Alys stuck her needle in the cushion."

He chuckled. "Better this needle than one of the wicked-looking knitting needles that lively redhead was wielding!"

Isabel hugged Betty a bit closer and reached to pluck the needle from the cushion. His fingers and hers met. "Better no needle at all," she said as she pulled her hand back.

He sat beside her, and Isabel tried to tuck in her full skirts, but holding Betty made it impossible. So did the horsehair crinoline and flannel petticoats. Seemingly oblivious to the way the full skirts of her Sunday-best, cabbage rose dress brushed his pant leg, he turned his wide shoulders a bit and gently threaded his fingers through Betty's curls. "This must be Betty."

"Why, Carter, however did you guess?" Amy asked.

"Miss Isabel described her perfectly." He looked about the room. "She told me each of the girls at Kindred Hearts is very special."

Isabel let out a relieved breath. She'd feared for a moment that he'd accidentally say something about the dolls and ruin the girls' Christmas surprise.

"That's Isabel, to be sure. Always has a kind word on her lips," Amy said.

"'Specially at nighttime," Kathleen tacked on. "Blow out the lamps, and she chatters like a magpie!"

All the girls giggled, and Carter gave Isabel an amused look, then winked. *Some of us know when to keep quiet.*

Isabel couldn't help laughing. She relaxed a bit and watched as the girls hastened to show Mrs. Steadman their sewing projects. Amy and Kathleen kept a steady patter of conversation, so Isabel decided she'd better put this lone man in a room full of women and girls at ease.

"We're so grateful for the changes you've made at the mill, Sir."

"I've done nothing other than give the workers their due." He let out a long, heavy breath. "I have a lot to atone for."

Isabel gathered Betty a bit closer and murmured softly, "Sir, you're making changes—good, fair changes. None of us holds you to account for what your father did."

"God does."

She gave him a startled look. "I don't understand—"

"The sins of the father are visited upon the son. The Bible states it clearly. I'm doing my best to make amends." His jaw hardened, and he shook his head. "I didn't mean to mention any of this. Forgive me."

Isabel blinked at him in utter astonishment. His admission caught her completely off guard. Unsure what to think of such a declaration, she shifted her hand a bit to subtly pat his upper arm. "Please don't apologize for saying what weighs heavy on your heart. The Bible tells us to bear one another's burdens."

He wound one of Betty's curls around his forefinger. "I still have plenty to do." He untwisted the ringlet and started to play with another as he changed the subject. "Do you come here often?"

"Every Sunday afternoon. Kathleen comes, too. I love children."

He looked about the parlor and studied the girls. One by one, they showed his mother their sewing projects and beamed at the praise she lavished upon them. "Sixteen girls," he mused. "I don't know how she manages it."

"Amy has them organized and does a wonderful job. We come to help with sewing, but I always go back to the boardinghouse feeling like she and her girls gave more to me."

Betty stirred, so Isabel readjusted her a bit and smoothed down her butter yellow frock. She still couldn't quite fathom that an important man like him had remembered something as inconsequential as a little orphan's name.

"She must be heavy. Would you like me to carry her to bed?"

"Oh, thank you, but no. Betty takes her nap in my lap each Sunday. The baby Kathleen is holding is Betty's little sister. Someone offered to adopt the baby, but Amy wants to keep them together. Betty has already lost her parents. . . ."

"Excuse me, Mr. Steadman." Ginger's voice sounded over a chorus of giggles. "Susannah was asking you if you'd be takin' a wee bit o' cream or sugar in your tea."

"Now let's see. . . ." He drew out the words as he stared at the ceiling and tapped a finger on the cleft in his chin. That finger came away and delved into the pocket of his coat. He pulled out a small paper packet. A distinct, sweet fragrance wafted from it. "This time of year, I always like to have peppermint in my tea. Would anyone else like to try one?"

Like a flock of sparrows after a fistful of crumbs, the girls flitted to him. He winked and told the first, "Give one to each of the ladies for me. If you put it in the cup before Mrs. Ross pours the tea—"

"Who's Mrs. Ross?" a little voice piped up.

"Auntie Amy," whispered another.

Carter pretended not to notice and continued, "The hot tea will melt the peppermint and sweeten your cup."

"Auntie Amy," Ruthie asked, "may we do the thing for them?"

Amy gave her girls an indulgent smile. "Perhaps another time."

"What thing?" Mrs. Steadman asked.

"They've been acting out parts of the Christmas story each evening."

"Could we do it, please?" Patty begged. "The man could be Joseph. We never got a real man to be Joseph before."

Carter leaned forward and looked past Isabel, straight into Patty's big blue eyes. "I've never been Joseph. What do I have to do?"

"You have to forget what everyone else thinks and care about what God wants you to do. You take Mary on a trip, but you walk and let her ride the donkey 'cuz she's tired. Next, you get to kneel by Baby Jesus. Then you're 'posed to feel lucky 'cuz He's good, so He forgives you even when you done bad things in the past. See? That's God's Christmas present to us."

In a matter of moments, Carter Steadman, owner of the influential Steadman Textile Mill, had a clump of little girls surrounding him. He played his part with notable enthusiasm and skill. He didn't even bat an eye when the wagon became a donkey. With true gallantry, he lifted "Mary" on and off the "donkey," then tenderly helped her wrap a doll in a blanket. Isabel smiled as he calmly hiked one of the twins onto his shoulder so she'd stop whacking him whilst she flapped her arms as angel wings.

When he knelt at the crate that served as the manger, he didn't fold his hands in prayer. Instead, he spread his arms wide. The "animals," "Mary," and another angel all crowded in to be included in his hug. In a rich baritone, he began to sing, "While Shepherds Watched Their Flocks by Night." Everyone joined in.

Isabel mouthed the song, but the words didn't register. Instead, she ached for her employer. He knew the Christmas story, but he hadn't fully accepted its meaning. He'd been so busy trying to atone for his father's wrongs and earn his place in God's kingdom, he hadn't allowed himself to accept the gift of grace God provided by giving His Son. If only he could understand God appreciated deeds done in love, but they weren't necessary for atonement. The price was paid—and represented right there in front of him in the form of a blanket-wrapped doll.

Carter Steadman's rich baritone contrasted with the girls' sweet sopranos, and the words finally registered in Isabel's heart. "Good will henceforth from heav'n to men, Begin and never cease, Begin and never cease."

Lord, please loosen the chains in his heart and make him feel free to accept Your good will.

❋

After Kathleen blew out the lamp that night, Isabel heard her humming that same tune. She closed her eyes and promised herself she wouldn't talk tonight—but it was so hard to stay silent. Memories of how her employer had humbly knelt on a tattered carpet and pretended with those girls tugged at her heart.

He'd been trying so hard to prove to himself and everyone else that he wasn't going to be like his father, and his methods of restitution could only be considered more than generous. In the past two weeks, he'd increased their pay, given them an extra day off, provided cloth, and made sure the meals improved considerably.

Couldn't he see he'd never be like his father? Carter Steadman displayed too much integrity, too much humility to ever put himself or greed above others. Odd, how he'd already proven the vast difference between his ways and his father's, yet he hadn't proven it to himself.

Isabel snuggled deeper under her covers. If only he'd stayed long enough to watch the girls open his packages! Instead, he'd escorted his mother from the orphanage without saying a word about the paper-wrapped bundles he'd delivered. Amy waited until the girls cleared away the teacups and plates, then she clipped the strings on the first package.

A veritable rainbow of fabrics and ribbons and a wealth of buttons spilled out. The girls squealed with glee, and Amy's pretty gray eyes went silver with tears of gratitude. If only Carter Steadman could have seen the joy his gift gave to others. . .and if only he could accept that God gave His gifts as freely. Just as the girls hadn't earned a thing from their bene-factor, so he would never earn a thing from God. No matter how hard he tried, how many good deeds he performed, God's infinite grace was all that mattered.

Father, reveal Yourself to him. Free him from the bonds of his past and let him come to understand the sweetness of Your Christmas Gift. Reach his heart and teach him we are reconciled through Christ, not through our works.

"Isabel?" Kathleen propped up on her elbow and whispered, "Are you talking to yourself again?"

"Praying."

Kathleen muffled a giggle. "I'm praying, too—that no one asks you to sing a duet in church with Mr. Steadman."

Chapter 7

Production is dropping," Jefford grumbled as he walked through the weaving room. "The carding, spinning, and weaving have all slowed down."

"Quality is much higher," Carter countered. "With the No. 30 yarn, we get thirty yards of cloth per loom per day. It sells for more. Printworks are putting out extraordinary designs, too."

"Hmmpf." Jefford cast a surly look out the window. "Winter means fewer hours at the looms. During summer, we get fourteen, but now—"

"Ten now." Carter's voice went steely. "Eleven in the summer. No more."

"Profits are going to drop. Can't run a successful business like this. You cut their hours, increased their pay, and slowed production. Your father—"

Carter's hands clenched into fists at his side. "My father's choices are not mine."

Jefford shrugged. "You own the place." He cast a look about the weaving room, then said, "We're in for more change, too. Daisy is leaving to be married. I'll need to appoint a new head weaver."

"Kathleen McKenna."

Brows furrowed, Jefford shook his head. "I had my eye on a few others."

I have no doubt you did, Carter thought sourly. He'd already considered several possibilities. Isabel was exceedingly patient—which made her an excellent trainer. Still, the women looked to Kathleen to speak for them. She'd represented them well regarding a concern over a problem with badly wound bobbins last week, and she had a level head on her shoulders. Carter wanted a Christian woman who would be diligent and loyal to him. He wasn't about to let Jefford plant someone in that position.

Jefford shifted and pushed the issue. "I know these women. Decisions like this take extensive knowledge—"

"Kathleen McKenna," Carter ordered implacably.

"Your own father passed her by last year when the position opened."

"Mr. Jefford, if one of the employees goes counter to your order, what becomes of her?"

"I dismiss her at once."

"In that aspect, we are alike." Carter stared pointedly at the overseer. "I've given you an order."

Carter walked away. Machines around them muffled Jefford's comment, but Carter made out, "just like your father." Though tempted to wheel around and fire him, Carter resisted the urge. He refused to rage as his father so often had.

His boots pounded out every step toward the office with determination. *I will not be like my father. I refuse to. Bad enough, the sins of the father are passed on to the sons. I have enough to atone for. When I have a son, I want his legacy to be blameless.* He looked around. What more could he do to expunge his father's greedy acts?

"How are you doing on the dolls?"

Isabel looked up and gave her employer a smile as she swallowed a bite of fresh, fried codfish. He often passed by and spoke to the women. He frequently came to her table, but since he'd assigned Kathleen as head weaver, it made sense that he'd sometimes show up at their boardinghouse to contact her. Still, he must have a warm heart, because he not only checked with Kathleen about some detail about the day's order or a problem, he'd also chat for a few moments about something quite ordinary and pleasant.

He chuckled. "I caught you with your mouth full."

Isabel smiled after she swallowed. "We need to put the finishing touches on just a few more dolls, then we'll be done. The girls will be so happy, sir."

"I've no doubt of that."

"Amy is allowing the older girls to stay up a bit later so they can make a dress for the dolls. That way, they get to be part of the secret."

He nodded, then asked, "What of those girls?"

"Aprons. We've made one for each of them." Isabel averted her gaze. Staring at this handsome man defied propriety.

He lifted her hand and ran the pad of his thumb over her fingers. "You must be nimble-fingered to get so much done."

Isabel looked up at him, startled at his touch. Her hand tingled and her heart sped up at that light contact.

"Aye, and look at how pretty her new dress is," Kathleen chimed in.

"Very becoming, indeed."

"Thank you, sir," Isabel mumbled as she pulled her hand free from his disturbing hold. "All of us are grateful for your generosity."

"You have laudable skills with the loom and needle." He never took his eyes off her. Though his words could have included every woman in the boardinghouse's dining hall, Isabel fought the notion that he meant to aim them specifically at her. Yet he maintained eye contact. "You earned that fabric."

"Your surprise delighted Amy and the girls," Isabel murmured.

His mouth crooked into a rakish grin. "So I gathered. She wrote me a note, and the girls got together and drew a picture of our nativity play." He turned to Kathleen. "As for you, Miss Kathleen—you displayed admirable expertise that afternoon when you organized them for the play."

Kathleen shrugged. "Amy needed to tend the baby. I'm accustomed to herding my brothers and sisters about." She accepted the bowl of succotash. "Ma always said I had a bossy streak."

His lighthearted chuckle and the fact that he'd addressed another worker eased Isabel's uneasiness. She spread butter on a slice of hot-from-the-oven bread. "You made a wonderful Joseph, Sir. It's hard to say who enjoyed the Christmas pageant you put on more—the girls or the adults who served as the audience. Your voice is exceptional. If you attend church regularly, Parson Hull will be after you to sing a special."

He gave her a baffled look. "Of course I'll attend each Sunday."

Isabel cringed. She'd meant no offense, but since his father rarely attended, she hadn't been sure if the new owner was much of a churchgoer.

Before she could say anything, he added, "Perhaps you'd like to make that a duet with me, Miss Isabel."

She felt her cheeks go hot as she laughed self-consciously. "Sir, my singing is likely to cause parishioners to seek repentance so they can put an end to such punishment."

He chuckled as he walked away.

Kathleen nudged Isabel and murmured, "I think he's sweet on you."

Isabel dropped her fork. "Kathleen!"

"I'm serious. He's quite a catch."

"Not for me. I'm just a worker; he owns the whole place." Isabel hissed, "So help me, Kathleen, don't you dare breathe another word of that nonsense. He's far above my station, and that kind of scandal could get me dismissed. My family needs me to work—"

"If you married him, you'd have plenty of money," Kathleen singsonged under her breath.

"The day I marry, it will be for love, not money." She sighed. "But I doubt that day will ever come."

❈

Isabel fingered the golden ribbon after she slipped Mama's most recent letter into the packet. Just because Isabel wrote and told her of the changes at the mill, Mama's letter now asked questions a simple mill girl couldn't answer about her employer. . .she hinted such a man would make a fine husband. Between Mama's note and Kathleen's teasing, Isabel worried maybe she'd somehow revealed the secret feelings she'd begun to have for him. The very thought anyone might detect she felt a special fondness for him terrified her. What if she were so transparent, she was making a fool of herself and he detected it?

In the privacy of her room, for just a moment, she allowed her imagination to fly free about Mama and Kathleen's opinions regarding Mr. Steadman's interest in her. Surely, they were wrong. Still, thoughts tumbled through her mind. *Oh, to have such a fine man interested in me, to call me his own! I long to be married and have children. . . .*

Isabel shook her head. Carter Steadman was so unreachable, he might as well be in China. He'd wed some wealthy young darling of high society. Imagining for even a moment that someone of his class would stoop beneath his station to court a mill girl would lead only to heartbreak.

Isabel shoved the drawer shut, walked over to the small bedside table, and moved the candlestick aside. She took a sheet of foolscap from the drawer and dipped her pen. "Dearest Mama," she began. A wave of loneliness washed over her.

❈

"Carter, I'm counting on you to come speak to my Missionary Benevolence Meeting this week."

Carter hung up his coat and gave his mother a wry look. "I scarcely think the women would consider England a heathen country. Why would my trip there be germane to mission work?"

Her smile drooped, and it caused him a pang. She'd endured months of grief alone, waiting for word to reach him and for him to return home. Even now, she permitted herself only very limited social connections. Carter crossed the floor with a few long strides and gave her a kiss on the cheek. "But for you, I'll do it."

Wednesday, Carter plastered on a smile and accepted a third cup of tea as he juggled his fork and a plate loaded with a mountain of tea cakes and silly looking confections. If the Atherton girls didn't drown him in tea, Blanche Smythe might well bury him under desserts. Every last mama and eligible daughter in town filled the main floor of the Steadman home. "Excuse me, ladies," he murmured as he swam through a sea of skirts that swirled like the colored glass shards of a kaleidoscope.

"Carter," Mrs. Henly gushed just before he reached the door, "your talk positively inspired us—didn't it, Elizabeth?"

Elizabeth's fat sausage curls bounced as she emphatically nodded her head and hastily swallowed something. The years of Carter's absence hadn't treated Elizabeth kindly. Gawky and gap-toothed, she didn't shine among the butterfly set of Massachusetts society.

Carter wanted nothing to do with this after-speech parade of prospective wives, but he'd always held a rather tender spot in his heart for Elizabeth. He forced himself to remain long enough to exchange a few inane pleasantries, and the look of sheer gratitude on her face tugged at his heart.

"Oh, Mr. Steadman!" Blanche Smythe headed toward him with another plate of food.

Elizabeth deftly swiped the first plate from Carter and handed it to her mother, then snatched his teacup and emptied it in the potted palm. Though she hid her smile behind her fan, the twinkle in her eyes let him know their childhood friendship had endured.

Carter tilted his head back, let out a full-throated laugh, and barely waited for Blanche to reach them. "Ladies, you must excuse me for leaving you, but I have matters I must attend at the mill." He nodded at Elizabeth. "It was especially nice to see you again, Miss Henly."

He made his escape and headed for the mill. That whole morning might have been a fiasco, but Elizabeth's assistance made it worth the lost time. It did him good to see her sense of humor was just as sharp as it had been when they were children. He chuckled to himself, then sobered again at the blatant truth: Mother wanted him wed, and she'd no doubt make it a crusade. He'd gotten an updated look at the girls she fancied as candidates, and not a one appealed to him. When the time came for him to marry, he didn't care for silks, pearls, and curls. He wanted a woman with heart.

A woman like Isabel Shaw.

Snow started to fall, and he lengthened his stride. Isabel. He'd been enchanted with her from their first meeting. She'd been so embarrassed when she discovered his identity, he knew full well she had no designs on him. Indeed, she'd about died ten deaths when he sat on the settee next to her at the orphanage. He walked past the buildings and headed into the office. After closing the door, he prayed, "Father, make Your will known to me regarding a wife. Give me a wife who delights in the Word and adorns herself with love and humility instead of braids and pearls."

Just then, a knock interrupted him. "Sir? Mr. Steadman—are you there?"

"Yes." He turned as the door opened. Isabel Shaw stood in the opening.

Chapter 8

"Your cousin's ship docked early," Isabel announced as she looked down at her employer, sitting behind his desk.

"Which one?"

"Maxwell." As soon as she identified which cousin, Isabel realized he wanted to know which ship. She hastily added, "This time, it's the *Resolute*. The *Reliant* isn't due for almost two weeks."

Carter nodded. "That makes sense. Last I heard, the *Steadfast* was bound for Europe. Did you come just to tell me Maxwell is here?"

Embarrassed she'd been so caught up in his presence that she failed to give the full message, Isabel blurted out, "Kathleen's busy with a jammed shuttle, so Mr. Jefford sent me. He wants permission to speed up the looms and keep us late so we can meet the order."

Isabel watched as her employer rose from behind his desk. She'd always been self-conscious about her height, but around him, she felt almost dainty.

He reached for his greatcoat and hat, then frowned. "Where is your wrap?"

"Oh." She let out a small laugh as she brushed a few errant snowflakes from her sleeve. "I just dashed over. Since Mr. Jefford, himself, tripped the levers to stop my looms, I presumed I'd best make haste."

"Going from the heat of the weaving room to the cold of a snowstorm is liable to cause you a nasty chill." He draped his heavy coat about her. "Let's go see what Maxwell and Jefford want."

Though she could have demurred and refused the coat, Isabel relished its warmth. She grabbed the lapels and held it shut as Mr. Steadman walked by her side, across the courtyard, and into the weaving room. Once there, she started to shed the coat; but Mr. Steadman rested his huge hands on her shoulders and kept it in place as he looked for Jefford. He dipped his head so his lips almost brushed her ear as he half-shouted, "Did he mention where we should meet?"

"No, sir. Your cousin—the Shipping Steadman—"

Even over the clatter and roar of machinery, she could hear him laugh. "The Shipping Steadman?"

Isabel nodded and amusement threaded through her. "They've named each of you Steadmans, you know. You're the Cotton Steadman, Mr. Maxwell is the Shipping Steadman, and his brother is Little Steadman."

"Lucas wouldn't appreciate that. He'll be out of medical school soon. I rather doubt he'll want to be considered as anything other than Dr. Steadman."

Just then, Mr. Jefford and Maxwell Steadman came over. Isabel tried to ignore the odd, assessing looks in their eyes as they spied Carter's hands upon her shoulders and her still burrowed in the folds of his wondrously warm coat. She shed the greatcoat at once.

Before she could slip back to her machines, the Shipping Steadman bellowed above the din, "So you're Isabel. Aunt Vivian told me to send you home to her. The carriage is out by the west entrance for you."

"What's this?" Carter asked.

Maxwell shrugged. A rapscallion's smile tilted his mouth. "At sea, everyone follows my orders; on land, everyone follows your mother's."

Isabel cast a baffled glance at both cousins, then looked at Mr. Jefford. "My looms—"

"Go," he barked.

"Get your coat and bonnet first," Carter ordered.

"Yes, Sir." She scurried away, confused by this odd turn of events.

�֍

Isabel nestled the doll in her arms as she stood on a splendid Turkish carpet in the ornate Steadman parlor. Large gilt-framed portraits, elegant chandeliers, and russet velvet draperies made this place look more like a palace than a home. A handful of servants quietly set the mansion to rights in the aftermath of some sort of party, but one of the maids had shown her here. Isabel couldn't decide whether she should sit or stand as she waited for Mrs. Steadman to arrive. She'd never spoken to Mrs. Steadman other than that Sunday when they'd chanced to meet at the orphanage. *Why did she send for me, and why did the driver stop off at the board-inghouse and make me go get this doll?*

"Isabel, how lovely to see you."

Isabel spun at the sound of the dulcet voice and saw Mrs. Steadman entering the room. Isabel smiled. "Mrs. Steadman, I–I . . ."

"Do have a seat." Mrs. Steadman gestured toward an elegant floral tapestry chair by the marble fireplace and took the matching chair, which sat at a close angle. "I've asked for tea to warm us."

"How gracious of you."

Mrs. Steadman leaned a bit closer. The whisper of her black silk mourning gown and scent of her expensive French perfume underscored her social standing, yet she almost greedily reached for the doll. "May I, please?"

"Of course." Isabel handed over the little doll she'd finished making only the night before. Designed to resemble Patty, it bore blue eyes and carroty hair. "We're making them for the little girls at Kindred Hearts."

"Ohhh," Mrs. Steadman breathed, "she's adorable. Simply adorable." She played with the yarn braids, examined the embroidered features, and admired the ruffled little dress. "You sew magnificently."

"Thank you, ma'am."

"When Carter told me what you were doing, I hoped I might have finally found someone to help me." Mrs. Steadman carefully propped the doll beside her as if she were a treasured friend instead of a bit of yarn and remnant cloth. Then she lifted a basket from beside her chair. "I have the dolls that belonged to my grandmother and mother, as well as my own. I fear they were more loved than cared for."

Puzzled, Isabel sat and waited for her to continue.

"Here." Mrs. Steadman withdrew a porcelain-faced doll. Though the head was still in good condition, the dress needed mending, and a detached porcelain leg had been tied about the waist with some twine. "This was Grandmama's. I was hoping maybe you could repair her."

Isabel examined all three dolls. She nodded confidently. "Yes, all three can be mended. They're delightful."

"Oh, wonderful! You must begin as soon as we finish our tea."

Isabel reverently ran her finger over the belt on one of the older dolls. "My grandmother carried a ribbon similar to this in her bridal bouquet. It carried the same embossed roses, but it was gold, not silver."

"Oh, so she kept it?"

"Yes. My mother used it in her bouquet, too." Isabel forced a bright smile, though deep inside she felt a twang of sadness for the fact that for her, the ribbon would hold letters instead of a bridal bouquet. "I should be able to fix these pretty little dolls quite quickly."

"Oh, no. Don't rush. I want you to take your time. Clearly, you're deft with a needle, but I confess I'm a bit lonely these days." She waved her hand dismissively. "Missionary Benevolence met here today, yet now that everyone has gone home, the house feels all that much more empty."

Isabel gave her a sad smile. "My condolences for your loss."

Mrs. Steadman blinked a few times and took a bracing breath. Her smile trembled a bit. "Stitch slowly, my dear. I'd count it a favor."

"And precisely what schemes are you up to now, Mother?"

She laughed merrily and patted his shoulder. "Now, Carter, never let it be said I've ignored your preferences. I saw the way you looked at Isabel at the orphanage. I'd have to be blind to miss the way you lit up in her presence. When all of the young ladies were here for the missionary meeting, you didn't show a speck of interest in anyone other than Elizabeth Henly, and you've always been like a doting brother to her."

He quirked a brow and stayed silent. She hadn't wasted a moment. He'd barely escaped from that gaggle of socialites before Mother sent for Isabel.

"I'm determined to see you happily wed and make sure that I have several grandbabies to cuddle. Clearly, you cannot court Isabel at the mill, so I've concocted a perfectly legitimate reason for her to be here. You'll simply show up for supper, and after dining, we'll visit before you escort her to the boardinghouse."

"Mind you, I'm not complaining in the least, but I confess, I am surprised. I have distinct recollections of Father talking about how Grandfather disowned Uncle Esau for marrying beneath him."

Mother sighed. "That was a shameful chapter in the family history—not on Esau's part, but on your grandfather's. Esau's bride was a charming girl who came from a sound family, but your grandfather wanted him to marry to bind the Steadmans to another society family. He put money and power above his son's happiness. More the fool, he."

"I don't know Isabel well enough—"

"Which is why I'll arrange for you to spend plenty of time with her here. It will all be quite proper."

Carter bent down and brushed a kiss on his mother's cheek. "You've made my life far easier. Now instead of having to divide my time between convincing you she'd make a worthy wife and courting her, I'll have you as an ally and be free to direct my attentions on her alone."

His mother laughed. "You're already so smitten, the girl hasn't a chance."

"Yes, the last one is finished." Isabel set down her fork and blotted her lips with the napkin. After two days, she'd lovingly repaired all three dolls.

"Not quite." Mrs. Steadman shook her head. "I sent Bernice to the attic. She found Grandmama's doll trunk. There's another doll, and several of her little frocks are in dire need of restoration."

Carter chuckled. "Isabel, once Mother gets a notion in her head, it's impossible to divert her."

Beneath the table, Isabel pleated her skirts with her fingers. Though the days here were far easier and Mrs. Steadman's company quite pleasant, the best part of the arrangement was the wonderful evening meals spent with Carter. He was so interesting and easy to converse with.

Nonetheless, this couldn't continue. Isabel had obligations to meet. She ventured, "Perhaps I could take one piece back to the room with me and work on it each night after I'm done at the mill."

"Oh, I simply couldn't bear to have those taken from under my roof."

Carter frowned at Isabel. "Are you unhappy here?"

Heat flooded her cheeks. "Oh, no, sir!" Her fingers clenched tightly together, trapping the material into a scrunched ball. *I'm never happier than in your presence. . . .* She tamped down that thought before it imprudently left her lips. She had no call to be mooning over any man—let alone her employer! Embarrassing as this was, she had to stick to business and speak up—for Mama's sake.

"Then what is it?"

Isabel trained her gaze on the handsome cleft in his chin and cleared her throat. "I need to work. For my family. Mama—"

"Just a minute." He leaned forward and locked eyes with her. The candleglow made his hazel eyes look like molten gold. "Of course you're to draw wages for sewing."

"I should have realized. . . ." Playing with a jet button at her throat in agitation, Mrs. Steadman gave her an apologetic look. "I'll send a note to Mr. Jefford at once. He'll see to it, Dear." She then turned to her son. "Our Isabel sends her wages home to her mother and three little sisters."

"I'll speak with Jefford directly." Carter must have sensed her discomfort in discussing the crass matter of finances at the table, so he mercifully changed the topic of conversation. "It occurred to me this afternoon as we reset the looms in Building Three to do toweling that if Amy's girls needed clothing, she probably could use towels."

"Sheets, too, son," Mrs. Steadman urged.

They moved on to the parlor for a leisurely after-supper discussion, and the Steadmans asked Isabel several questions about the orphanage. Though both huge and lavishly appointed, the mansion seemed warm and comfortable. Isabel truly enjoyed retiring to the parlor with them and sitting by the fireplace, conversing for an hour or so each evening.

Carter eventually cast a look at the window. "It's not snowing now. Would you rather I take you back in the carriage, or would you like to walk tonight, Isabel?"

"Oh, I can walk alone, sir."

"Piffle! Carter, walk her home. A bit of fresh air would do you both good. Isabel, Bernice found my mother's pelisse when she went to the attic. It's warmer than yours. I insist you use it. We can't have you catch a chill. She was a stately woman, just like you—willowy and tall. It should suit you perfectly."

When Carter helped her into the midnight blue pelisse, Isabel felt like a princess. "Oh, this is too grand," she whispered. "Mrs. Steadman, I don't think you should loan it to me."

"I don't think so, either." Mrs. Steadman smiled. "It's not a loan. I want you to keep it." She laughed at Isabel's gasp. "Dear, that fits as though it were made for you. I'm so pleased it suits you so well."

"Please explain to her," Isabel begged Carter.

"There's no one here who can wear it, Isabel." Carter gently lifted the hood over her hair and let his fingers linger on the fabric at her temples for a moment. "Besides, a beautiful woman like you deserves pretty things."

Chapter 9

As if the gift of the garment hadn't been enough of a shock, Carter Steadman's compliment completely overwhelmed Isabel. Before she could stammer out her thanks, Mrs. Steadman bustled between them and gave her a quick embrace. "I'll see you in the morning. Now off with you."

Moments later, Isabel walked alongside her employer. The scent of chimney smoke filled the crisp air. Moonlight sparkled on the new fallen snow that crunched beneath their boots. Her new pelisse warmed her heart every bit as much as her body. "Your mother is such a kind woman."

"Yes, she is. How she and my father ever wed is beyond me. For every thread of kindness she wove, he unrolled a bolt of oppression." He held aside a branch so she wouldn't snag on it.

"Mr. Steadman—"

"Call me Carter, Isabel—at least away from the mill."

She looked at him, then nodded. Was this an invitation for her to say what was on her heart? She'd felt God pushing her to tell Carter something, but if he took it the wrong way, it could ruin the unique friendship they'd begun to forge. Not only that, he was still her employer, and if she offended him, it could threaten her job. *But Carter's not that kind of man. . . .*

Isabel cast a glance at him. "Carter, might I say something personal?"

He stopped and gave her a heart-melting smile. "You can say anything you'd like."

God, please give me the words. . . . "You mentioned something back at the orphanage, and it's bothered me."

"What was that?"

"You feel the sins of the father are visited upon the son. I think you're working far too hard to try to buy your way into God's good graces."

He frowned. "The Bible is clear about the legacy a father leaves."

"True, it was. . .in the Old Testament. In the New Testament, Christ made a new covenant. God claims us as His children by grace. Any of our works and deeds are simply to be an offering of thanks and a help to one another. Your father's sins were his, Carter; God looks on your soul and knows your heart. He'd never punish you for your father's deeds."

"I'm not blameless."

"None of us are. None of us gets what we deserve. If we did, we'd all be doomed. Instead, we are saved by grace."

"Of course we are."

"I don't mean to judge you, but I wonder if you've given Him your soul, but not your heart."

He gave her a baffled look. "What do you mean?"

Isabel drew in a bracing breath as she prayed for the Lord to use her. Carter hadn't cut her off so far—in fact, he was pursuing the conversation. Had the Holy Spirit been preparing his heart for this very conversation?

Carter reached up and gently tugged her hood a bit closer about her. "Isabel, I told you, you could say anything you wanted to."

"Christ paid the price already, Carter. Nothing you do will add to His sacrifice."

"I know that. I've accepted Christ, Isabel."

"When you accepted Him, God forgave all. From the things you say, I get the feeling you claim the pardon from sin; but walking with Him can be so much more than that—it is receiving the Father's love and consolation."

Carter grimaced and let his hands drop to his sides. "My own father was harsh. Thinking of God as my Father brings to mind reproof, not compassion."

"Maybe it's time for you to leave the past behind." Isabel grabbed his hands and squeezed them. "Stop letting yesterday be an anchor that causes you pain and regret. You accepted His pardon; I'd love to see you experience His peace."

❋

Sunday passed. Though the others all reported to the mill on Monday, Isabel went to the Steadmans' home. For the next three evenings, Carter walked her back to the boardinghouse. Each time, he offered his arm so she wouldn't slip on the icy ground; but as they neared the boardinghouse, he took care to keep his hands clasped behind his back so he'd not give anyone cause to tease Isabel or cast aspersions on her character.

That restraint cost him dearly. He'd far rather hold her hand or wrap his arm about her shoulders. The most he allowed himself was to help her with her hood—it allowed him a fleeting opportunity to feel the softness of her luxurious hair. Yielding to his attraction would put them both in an impossible position, so he governed his actions.

Each evening, they spoke more openly about a number of things. He asked about her family and she heard about his years in England. They spoke about the mill and the orphanage, but she never again brought up spiritual matters. Carter felt grateful she left him to ponder those matters on his own. Intensely personal as they were, he needed time to contemplate what she'd said and meditate over what the Bible revealed.

Now as he walked her back to the boardinghouse, he quietly said, "I need to go out of town for a few days. I worry about Mother being alone, and she enjoys your companionship. Are you going to the orphanage after church on Sunday?"

"Yes."

Carter waited for a moment, but because she made no offer, he forged ahead. "Why don't you invite her to go with you?"

Isabel gave him a startled look. "Sir, that isn't done."

"Isabel, you and she get along so well. Because she's in mourning, she isn't socializing except for church-related events. She'd be glad to have an opportunity to get out."

"But I'm just a mill girl."

Carter shook his head and tilted her face up to his. "How can you be so wise about forgiveness, yet you ignore all the verses about us all being equal in God's sight?"

"Even if I got beyond that, others wouldn't. Your mother is a fine lady. The women in her social circle are far above—"

"You underestimate your worth," he growled. Tempted to dip his head and brand her

136

with a kiss, Carter denied himself. Instead, he gruffly took her arm and quickened his pace to the boardinghouse. When he returned home from this trip, he was going to set Miss Isabel Shaw straight.

Fired? Isabel couldn't believe her ears. She tilted her head to the side and faintly said, "I beg your pardon?"

Mr. Jefford leaned forward in the chair and set his beefy hands on top of Mr. Steadman's desk. He'd called her in to the office, and she'd wondered what he was up to. He snarled, "You heard me, all right. I told you to pack your belongings and be out of the boardinghouse by supper."

"But why?" His leer gave her the shivers.

"You knew the rules when you signed on. We demand our women be of the highest moral quality. It's come to my attention you're keeping company with a gentleman late in the evenings. Brazen hussies taint the good name of—"

"Mr. Jefford!"

He waved his hand. "I won't hear another word. All you'd do is lie. Pack and leave by supper. Now go. I have work to do."

Isabel wiped away hot tears, but more trailed down her cheeks. Her vision blurred as she folded her new plaid dress and put it into the portmanteau on top of her Sunday-best, cabbage rose dress. Last, she put in the bundle of letters from home. The gold ribbon mocked her. She couldn't even keep her job—how would she ever keep a man?

"Isabel, I can't believe this." Kathleen stormed back and forth.

"Oh, believe it," Grace sneered. "She reached too high. Thought she was better than the rest of us, going over to the owner's house. He skulked away and had the overseer do the dirty work of discharging her."

"Hush," Pegeen hissed at her. "Isabel's a good woman. You have no call to be mean to her."

"This is wrong." Kathleen spun around and shook her head. "Wait until Mr. Steadman gets back."

"I c–can't. Mr. Jefford told me I had to be gone by supper."

"Then go to Mrs. Steadman!"

Isabel shook her head. The very notion that Mrs. Steadman might hear such scurrilous accusations mortified her. The woman had such a tender heart, she'd probably blame herself. "Even if things were settled, Mr. Jefford would make my life a nightmare."

"You're one of the best weavers. What about somewhere else?"

Isabel hitched her shoulder. "Mr. Jefford dismissed me without a certificate of honorable discharge. No other mill will take me on." She didn't add on the rest. No one would hire a woman reputed to be a mill owner's cast-off mistress.

"It's been two and a half years since I saw Mama and my sisters. David, too. I'll go home and see what work I can find there."

Her last possession was her Bible. Isabel held it to her bosom, then went across the room and somberly held the leather-bound book out to Pegeen. "You've learned to read this year. I want you to have this."

"Oh, no, Isabel. I—"

"It would bring me comfort, knowing I've left it with you. Mama has a Bible I can share."

Once Pegeen accepted the Bible, Isabel pulled on her bonnet and the pelisse Mrs. Steadman had insisted she keep. Pride made her want to return it; common sense dictated she keep it and take her own cape home for Mama or her sisters to use.

A week's wages were knotted in her handkerchief. She couldn't afford to spend the money for a coach ride back home. Luckily, one of the other girls was going home to take on a teaching position, so Isabel would ride in her wagon all but the last two miles.

Isabel tried to muffle her sob. She lifted her portmanteau and whispered to Kathleen, "Write me. Tell me how the girls liked the dolls, and say good-bye to Amy for me."

Kathleen hugged her close. "God go with you."

Carter briskly strode into the weaving room just minutes before the day was to begin. While he'd been gone, he'd spent considerable time pondering Isabel's comments about God's grace. After he'd prayed and felt released from the burden he carried, Carter rushed through the rest of his business so he could come share his joy. He made up his mind, and he didn't believe in wasting his time. As soon as he spied Isabel, he...

She wasn't at her looms. Where was she? He scanned the area again. A new lass with hair the shade of untanned leather struggled to tie her apron about her ample waist. The wide-eyed way she gawked about made it clear she felt overwhelmed.

Mary had begun to oil the loom before them, the whole time explaining in a patient tone what she was doing.

To the other side, Kathleen looked up from preparing her own looms to glower at him.

His heart gave a sudden jolt. He'd assumed Isabel hadn't extended an invitation to his mother and had skipped church on Sunday because of her sensitivity to the difference in their social standing. Was she sick? He demanded hoarsely, "Where is Isabel?"

"Gone home." Mary's eyes welled up with tears.

"What?"

Chapter 10

"You can't be serious!" His mother quickly folded a few garments and shoved them into a black leather valise. "I hope you discharged Jefford at once."

Carter shoved his feet into riding boots. "I barely let him grab his coat and hat before I got rid of him. Maxwell delivered the cotton, and I laid out the orders for the next week late last evening. James Roland can oversee the mill, and Kathleen can keep charge of the weaving rooms for the next few days 'til I get back."

"With Isabel," his mother tacked on.

"With Isabel," he confirmed in a definitive voice. He'd gotten her address from Kathleen, and he was about to go claim his woman.

"Isabel?"

"Yes?" Isabel sat on the mattress and plaited her sisters' hair for bedtime. The threadbare flannel of their nightgowns made her heart twist. Over the past two and a half years, how many thousands of yards of cloth had she woven, yet her own little sisters went to sleep in thin-as-air gowns on a frigid night.

"Do you s'pose Baby Jesus got poked by the hay in His manger?"

She forced a laugh. "I don't know." After she tied a bit of string about the last braid, Isabel took her cape and spread it over the mattress. "This'll keep the hay from jabbing you. Now hop in and we'll say prayers."

The small cabin shook as the front door slammed. Abe probably just got back after checking the animals. He made a meager living by sharecropping, but he and Hannah had been good enough to take in Mama and the girls. Still, with him, Hannah, and their baby, that had been burden enough. Isabel knew there wasn't room for her here—but she had nowhere else to turn.

"Isabel, come down here."

She startled at the sound of Carter Steadman's voice. Peering over the loft at him, she called, "What are you doing here?"

He folded his arms akimbo. "Strange, but I was wondering the same thing about you. Come down, and bring your coat. We're going outside to talk."

"It's cold out there!"

"Which is why I told you to bring your coat," he said with excessive patience.

"We can sit by the fire inside."

Isabel wasn't sure if she heard his mutterings correctly. "Obtuse and stubborn" seemed to be mentioned, but whatever the rest of the words were, Hannah and Mama drowned them out with their muffled giggles. Abe looked entirely too entertained. Unwilling to provide more amusement for them, Isabel took the pelisse Carter's mother had given to her and tucked it under her arm.

Just as she started down the ladder, Carter growled, "Are you trying to break your neck? Drop that thing and use both hands."

All three of her sisters lined up by the loft rail and twittered.

Isabel flung the piece so it hit him square in the chest, then scurried down before he could say another word. "Mr. Steadman—"

"Carter," he corrected as he spun her about and wrapped her tight. He then nodded his head toward Mama. "Mrs. Shaw, I presume."

"Indeed." Mama smiled at him.

"Ma'am, I intend to drag your daughter outside and talk some sense into her. Before I do, I'd best mind my manners and propriety enough to declare my intentions. I'm Carter Steadman, and I can provide well for her. I love her and aim to ask for her hand, so if you have any objections, now's the time to speak up."

"Carter!" Isabel spluttered.

He kept his hands clamped on her shoulders.

Mama looked to Abe. Abe took a moment to take Carter's measure, then asked, "Are you a God-fearing man?"

"Aye, and a God-loving man, as well."

Abe nodded. Mama smiled, and all of the girls cheered.

Carter swept Isabel straight off her feet and headed for the door. Hannah opened it and before she could catch her breath, Isabel found herself sitting on a crate in the barn.

Carter knelt beside her. "Isabel, I already proclaimed my love for you back in the house. I can't apologize, because though such tender words would best be said in private the first time, I'm willing to shout them to the world. A man can't hope for a treasure better than a godly wife. I'm asking you to be my bride."

Isabel ducked her head in disgrace. "Mr. Steadman, you and I both know the gossip was untrue. You needn't be gallant and do this to salvage my reputation."

"Jefford's opinion holds no sway. Everyone who knows you knows better than to put any store by his accusations."

"Then you can see your noble proposal is unnecessary."

He gave her a tender look. "I think it's essential."

Isabel wrapped her arms around herself. "Carter, we both know your propensity for trying to cover someone else's wrongdoings with a good deed. I thought you'd grown beyond that. Proposing to me is—"

"The most selfish thing I've ever done. I want you for my own. I want to come home to your gentle words and sweet laughter each night. We'll give my mother a dozen beautiful grandbabies. Don't you understand, Isabel? I couldn't risk ruining your reputation, so my mother and I plotted a way to allow me to court you under proper, albeit contrived, circumstances."

"I can't imagine this."

"You'd better. Before I left, I'd already asked Parson Hull about the best date for a wedding. You're all I could ever hope for in a wife. Don't you hold any feeling for me?"

"Yes! But I'm just—"

"Mine." He kept her from saying another word by kissing her.

✶

They spent the next three days with her family. Carter rolled up his sleeves and worked alongside Abe on farm chores. He gave her little sisters piggyback rides and took Isabel out on a walk to choose a Christmas tree.

David came home from his apprenticeship for Christmas. He and Carter bunked down in the barn loft. That first night, Isabel feared they'd be too cold. Hannah merely laughed. "How could you forget all of the quilts Mama made you sew?"

"Mama—I wrote and told you to—"

Mama wrapped her arm about Isabel's waist. "I couldn't sell them, Honey. See? I knew you'd need them."

Carter bedded down under three of those quilts that night and marveled that Isabel had worked so hard on such beautiful quilts, only to tell her mother to sell them off. The sacrifice staggered him. She reminded him of the widow in the Bible who tithed her last mite. *Father, thank You for giving me such a wonderful, loving woman to be my wife.*

The next morning, he took Isabel for an early morning stroll. She kept her eyes on him, a fact that pleased him no end. . .until they came upon a specific tree. They paused, and Carter finally urged, "Sweetheart, turn your head to the right."

There, the special gold ribbon dangled from a branch. Tied to it was a ring. "Merry Christmas."

"Oh, Carter, I love you!" Isabel threw her arms around his neck and kissed him.

A month and a half later, they kissed at the altar. The golden ribbon dangled from Isabel's bridal bouquet. Her heart overflowed with joy. Carter had continued to do good deeds, but they came from the fullness of his heart instead of as an attempt to appease God's wrath. His mother's support eased Isabel's entry into what might have seemed snobbish society—and a sweet young woman named Elizabeth Henly quite helpfully taught her how to dispose of the ofttimes undrinkable punches and teas in strategically placed potted plants.

Kathleen caught the bridal bouquet, and as she and Mama helped Isabel change into her going-away gown, Kathleen returned the ribbon. "Someday, your own daughter will cherish it, too. Keep it for her as a symbol of how God fills our lives with love."

LIGHT BECKONS
THE DAWN

by Susannah Hayden

Dedication

For the people who have been beacons of God's light in my life.

Chapter 1

Verdant, plush green gave way to the worn, well-trod trail. The meadow behind the lighthouse, speckled with rainbow-hued wildflowers, faded behind Joshua Wells as he nudged his sluggish gray mare toward the lumber camp. Although the miles between the lighthouse and the camp could be traversed in an hour by horseback, Josh felt as if he were moving across time, not mere landscape. As he left the lighthouse, he left more than sixty years of nineteenth-century heritage; as he neared the camp, he approached an unknown future that in less than two decades would take the northern Wisconsin peninsula into the twentieth century

For eight long years Josh had missed the journey. At seventeen, he had announced to his older sister, Lacey, who was running the Wells household during their mother's illness and father's consequent depression, that he was leaving to go away to school. All along he had insisted that he would come back to the isolated locale where they had been raised in the shadow of a lonely lighthouse, but no one had believed him because few people who left ever did. Josh's twenty-one-year-old twin brothers, Joel and Jeremiah, were nearly finished with college in Madison, and they were not coming back and no one had ever expected they would. But Joshua had always known that he would come back, no matter what anyone said. The lumber camp needed a doctor.

As the oldest son, Joshua bore the weight of expectation that he would become the next lighthouse keeper in the Wells family, a tradition maintained through three generations. But as a young teenager, Joshua embraced a different dream, and he went away in order to become a doctor. Joshua was convinced of the area's need for a doctor. He had seen many tragic lumber accidents; and the small towns springing up along the shores of the northern peninsula were hours away from medical care. Now they had a doctor. His practice was small and erratic. Weeks might pass with everyone in good health and not more than a scratch to clean up, leaving Josh time to dream about the town that the camp might become or to pitch in with the physical labor of the lumberjacks. But, in the blink of an eye, all that could change and Josh would be entwined in emergency care where his years of training were exactly what was needed.

Today had been a slow one. With no pressing medical emergency demanding his time or expertise, Dr. Joshua Wells had been sent by his sister to check on their father, Daniel, and their youngest brother, Micah. Daniel Wells tended the lighthouse in which Lacey, Joshua, the twins, and Micah had been raised under the stern hand of their mother, Mary Wells. She had died shortly after Joshua left home. In Josh's mind, the stroke and debilitation that had taken her life were one more reason why the peninsula needed a doctor. After his wife's death, Daniel Wells had sunk into a spinning depression, but with time and Micah's burgeoning passion for the lighthouse, he had begun to function again. Daniel no longer sat in a chair, staring for hours at a time. He once again applied his spit-and-polish standards to the brass fixtures of the lighthouse and kept impeccable watch over the rocky waters in his charge. Meticulously, he taught Micah everything the sixteen-year-old boy would need to know to someday tend the lighthouse himself. But even after eight years, the light was still gone from Daniel's eyes and the spark missing from his step. Lacey insisted that she and Joshua must check on Daniel and Micah at least once a week, and she persistently counseled Micah to come to the lumber camp for help any time he thought their father was regressing.

After Mary's death, Lacey had stayed in the lighthouse with her brothers and father for as long as she could. But Travis Gates had at last finished building a home for her, and then he married her and carried her off to the lumber camp. Many times since then she had crossed the miles back and forth, checking on Daniel and making sure her brothers completed their schooling under her tutelage. She was still supplying lesson plans and books for Micah. Joel and Jeremiah had done well enough to earn scholarships for college; Micah could go, too, but he did not want to.

Sixteen-year-old Micah Wells was a younger version of his father. The deer-specked meadow around the lighthouse thrilled him as much now as when he was seven years old, the solitude did not bother him, and Micah could not imagine his life anywhere else. Of the five Wells children, Micah alone still burned with a passion for the lighthouse, and he would be the fourth generation of Wellses to carry on the tradition of being an official lighthouse keeper. In his midfifties, Daniel still had many years before retirement, but Micah would be ready when the time came for him to assume the job.

Long before anything else, the lighthouse had been on the peninsula, standing regally at the peak of the cliff. For months at a time, it was inaccessible by water, especially in severe weather. The generations of Wellses who had lived there had long ago learned to conserve the goods brought to them by the supply boat, for they could never be sure when it would come again. In recent years better roads to the northern peninsula had been built; and with each passing year, even the path between the lighthouse and the expanding lumber camp was better defined.

Daniel Wells had been raised in the lighthouse; his siblings had left, but he had stayed and raised his family there. Now most of his children were gone; only Micah would stay and possibly produce another generation of Wells children in the old lighthouse.

As the lumber camp came into view, Joshua raised his eyes. He hated to call it a camp, for it was not really a camp anymore. It had one dirt street and a series of recently constructed permanent buildings. But it was not really a town, either. None of the permanent buildings would exist if it were not for the lumber industry thriving at the north end of the peninsula. As the cities in the southern part of the state grew and prospered, the demand for lumber increased. The thick, rich forest to the north seemed inexhaustible. Trees were milled into planks for homes and tables and chests and chairs and office buildings. But Joshua believed that the lumber camp would someday be much more than it was now. He could already see the progress that eight years had brought.

When in his teens, Joshua had worked as a lumberjack in the camp. He remembered the days when men slept in lean-to shelters and worked for weeks on end without decent food. Gradually buildings began to spring up, and the bunkhouses kept the men out of the elements. A cook arrived and demanded that the dining hall be enclosed and have a roaring fireplace at one end. The lumber camp manager, Tom Saget, dared to build a house and bring his wife and daughter to live in the camp. His daughter, Abby, had married Peter Regals, a lumberjack, and together they built another house. And Joshua had begun to see that the camp could become a town—that in fact the transformation was inevitable. The change was far from finished. But in his mind's eye, Joshua could see the finished picture: rows of homes, a church, a real school for his sister, Lacey, to teach in, a bank, mercantile shops—and a doctor's clinic.

While Joshua could not return to the lighthouse and be content there like his brother, Micah, he never regretted for a moment that he had come back to the peninsula. He had a natural talent for medicine, especially for the fast-thinking, quick-acting care needed in an emergency. When he finished his medical training, he had three job offers that would have given him a comfortable living in a civilized city, but he had turned them all down.

And then there was Priscilla, who had very nearly lured him away. His heart still twinged when he thought of her dark curls and shining eyes and the lilting laugh that enchanted everyone she met. She was a woman of far more depth than she let the world see: intelligent, articulate, opinionated, daring. But she would not come to the lumber camp to live, and Joshua could not do anything else but return. So last year they had parted sorrowfully, and Joshua had come home to his future.

Joshua was at the edge of the camp now, at one end of the single road that served as a center of social gatherings and business activities. The foreman's office stood prominently at the center of the cluster of buildings, while his home was at one end of the road. Across the way stood the dining hall, followed by a short row of houses and shedlike structures. Six bunkhouses were set back away from the road but with easy access to the dining hall. Completing the layout, at the far end of the road was a stable that housed the workhorses needed to haul the heavy lumber from the forest to the water, where it was floated south to a full-scale mill. Tom Saget who ran the lumber operation, also ran a small mill as a supplementary business to lumbering.

Josh was certain that mill operations would expand drastically before much longer. Soon the camp would have its own mill. Tom Saget, and his son-in-law, Peter Regals, had lobbied for years with the company that owned the lumber business. Machinery had been arriving for months, and soon the skilled workers to run the machines and mill the wood would come. And they would bring families, and they would need shops. Next would come the craftsmen, who could make furniture to ship all over the state. Excitement rose in Joshua's chest as he thought of what the future would bring.

"Hey, Josh!" a voice boomed and broke Joshua's reverie.

"Peter!" Josh called back. "What are you doing here? Don't you have work to do in the office?"

Peter grinned. "Lacey and Abby sent me out to wait for you."

"What Abby wants, Abby gets," Joshua said playfully.

Peter looked sheepish. "They wanted to be sure you came straight home."

Josh nodded. He slid off his horse and held the reins lightly as he fell into step with Peter. "I know. Lacey wants to know how Papa is. She always sends me to check on him, but she wants to be the judge of whether he is really all right."

Peter shrugged. "Can you blame her? After what she went through taking care of your mother while she was ill and then looking after Daniel when he could hardly put his shoes on for himself?"

Josh nodded again. "I know. And Micah is like her own son instead of her brother. But Papa and Micah are both doing fine. Don't you have to go back to the lumber office?"

Peter shook his head. "I'll finish my paperwork tonight."

"Does Tom know you're gone?"

Peter chuckled. "He indulges his daughter even more than I do."

"So there are some advantages to being married to the boss's daughter?"

"Only because I work hard and get the job done in my own way. I can't just count logs all day. I have to have time to dream."

"I know what you mean." Peter and Joshua had spent hours dreaming together before Josh left for school.

"I have some new drawings for you to see," Peter said. "I'll meet you at Lacey's house in a few minutes."

With a wave, Peter darted back to the office. Josh nodded with satisfaction, for seeing Peter's latest drawings of what the town might look like was always a treat.

Chapter 2

When Joshua slung his lanky legs around the corner and into his sister's kitchen, Lacey Wells Gates raised an eyebrow at him. "You look more like Mama every day," Joshua said, laughing softly.

Lacey threw an enormous mound of biscuit dough down on the polished pine table. "That's not a bad thing. Now that I am a mother myself, I have a much greater appreciation for Mama's ways than I did when we were young," she said. She dug the heels of both hands into the dough and pushed with the automatic motion of years of kneading bread dough.

Joshua looked around. "Where are my adorable nephews, anyway?"

"Napping," Lacey answered, "and I want to make sure it stays that way."

Joshua lowered himself into a chair. He eyed the biscuit dough, unsure how long he would be able to restrain himself from pinching a bite. Mama had always disapproved of that habit. On the right day, Lacey would allow his indulgence, but his dilemma was that he was unsure of his sister's present mood.

"Adam is too old for naps, isn't he?" Josh asked. "Six-year-old boys don't take naps."

"They do when they don't feel well. He has nearly whined me out of my mind today."

"Maybe I should take a look at him." Joshua assumed his best doctoring expression.

"When he wakes up. If you go in there now, you'll wake up Caleb, too. And three-year-old boys do take naps."

"Yes, Mama, I mean, yes, ma'am."

Lacey swatted at her brother with a hand covered in flour. Josh ducked and grinned.

"So?" Lacey said, kneading her dough.

"So, what?"

"So, how are Papa and Micah?"

Joshua shrugged. "Papa is Papa and Micah is Micah."

"What is that supposed to mean?"

"It means they are not any different than they were last week or than they will be next week. They're fine."

"Mama was fine one day and an invalid the next," Lacey reminded her brother.

"Come on, Lacey. You know that if anything like that happened to Papa, Micah would be over here lickety-split."

"It takes half an hour, even at a gallop. And what if you weren't here? What if you were off on one of your circuits to the towns?"

Joshua sighed. "They're fine, Lacey. Micah is as excited as ever about that old lighthouse, and it's good for Papa to be teaching Micah all he knows."

Lacey nodded and sighed. "You're right. Papa was so depressed for so long, I sometimes have a hard time believing that he's all right now."

"He still misses Mama, even after all these years, but he's so much better. I really don't think you need to worry as much as you do."

"Are they coming for supper?"

"I was supposed to invite them for supper?" Joshua asked innocently.

Lacey's eyes widened. Josh grinned.

"Yes, they're coming for supper. They won't be far behind me. Your biscuits won't be wasted on Micah. Papa says he eats like a horse now."

"He's a teenager. I can remember when Mama said the same thing about you. And she was right." Lacey folded over the dough and began to knead again.

"Peter said he would meet me over here with some new drawings," Josh said, changing the subject.

Lacey turned to stir the stew on the stove. "That's right. Abby and the kids are coming, too."

"For supper?"

Lacey nodded.

"No wonder you're making so many biscuits."

"A triple batch. I want some left over to pack in Travis's lunches. He spends nearly every day in the forest these days and doesn't make it home for lunch."

Joshua pinched a bit of dough and dropped it in his mouth. Lacey laughed. "I was wondering how long you could wait."

Chagrined, Josh avoided his sister's gaze and changed the subject. "Can't Travis eat the camp food when he's in the forest all day? I thought the men took lunch with them."

Lacey scowled. "He used to, until Lars Peterson got fed up and quit cooking. All the men are complaining about the food since he left. Now Travis would rather eat cold biscuits."

Suddenly, the back door swung open and a blond-headed ball of energy, about four feet high, whizzed past Lacey before she could stop him.

"Nathan, wait!" she called futilely. "The boys are sleeping!" With a groan, she reconciled herself to the fact that they would not be sleeping much longer.

Nathan's mother, Abby Regals, appeared in the doorway, breathless. Her five-year-old daughter, Francie, was attached to her skirt and moving in tiny steps; her eighteen-month-old boy, Nicholas, was squirming in her arms.

"I'm sorry, Lacey," Abby said plaintively. "He's over here so much he doesn't think he has to knock or be invited in. I just couldn't stop him from charging ahead of me."

"You know your children are like more of my own," Lacey said. She wiped her hands on a towel and reached to take Nicholas out of Abby's arms. He seemed fascinated by something on the ceiling and pointed and grunted persistently. Lacey tilted her head back, because she had no idea what was so interesting about the beams over their heads.

Abby gently tried to get Francie to let go of her skirt. The little girl loosened her grip enough to allow her mother to sit down and then put the child on her lap.

"How's Adam?" Abby asked.

"Still not himself," Lacey answered.

A crash and a wail from the room above them brought Joshua to his feet. "That's my cue," he said. "Dr. Josh will find out how Adam is." And he left.

Nicholas was through being held. "Down," he demanded, and Lacey complied. She set a fry pan on a throw rug and tried to interest him in that.

Abby smiled at the scene. "When we were little girls living miles apart, we were dying to see each other more often. It's hard to believe that we ended up living next door to each other in. . .in. . .in a lumber camp, of all places."

Lacey laughed. "We both swore we would never marry lumberjacks. We were going to get out of this place once and for all."

"Well, with two husbands and five children between us, it looks like we're pretty settled here."

"I don't know what I would do if you weren't here," Lacey said. "You and Peter forged the way when you built your home and stayed here."

"We have five homes now," Abby remarked. "And my parents are planning to add on again, you know."

"No, I didn't know. Why?"

Abby laughed. "I think they want some escape from the noise when the grandchildren come to visit."

"Peter and Travis have done a beautiful job with our homes," Lacey said, "but those two other homes are hardly more than shacks. I feel sorry for the wives who live in them."

"Bridget and Moriah don't have children yet," Abby said. "Their husbands are working hard, and those homes will be ready for families when the babies start to come along."

"At least we knew what we were getting into when we married lumberjacks and moved here," Lacey said. "Those poor women from the city. . .I can't imagine how they're coping. In the city they could have electric lights, even a telephone. They could go to church on Sundays and have ice delivered to their homes."

"You've never said you wanted all those things," Abby said.

"I don't. I'm used to life without them. But it's different for Bridget and Moriah."

"I talked to Bridget just the other day. She's doing very well but she's caught the virus."

"The virus? Is she sick?"

Abby laughed. "No, she's fine. I mean she's caught the one-day-we're-going-to-be-a-real-town virus."

"Oh, that," Lacey said, relieved. "Then I guess she'll be okay, after all. Speaking of the dreaded virus, I wonder where our husbands are. I understand Peter has new drawings."

"Yes, you'll love the sketch of the school this time. He wants it to have two rooms, not just one."

"Two rooms! He must be planning on a lot of students."

"He is. He's building for the future, not just what we need right now."

"Mama, I'm sick," a little voice said.

Lacey spun around to see six-year-old Adam standing in the doorway and looking droopy. "I know you are, sweetheart," she said. "Did Uncle Josh come see you?"

The boy nodded. "He wanted me to open my mouth so he could look down my throat."

"So did you open your mouth?"

He shook his head emphatically. "My throat is private."

"It is?"

"Uh-huh. Uncle Josh shouldn't look at people's private places."

"Sweetheart, Uncle Josh is a doctor. We've talked about this before. You must let him look at your throat."

Again Adam shook his head. "Not going to."

Lacey sighed. "Then how about if you drink some tea with honey? Maybe that will make your throat feel better."

Now he nodded. Lacey turned and put the kettle on the stove. On the floor at her feet, Nicholas pounded the bottom of the frying pan with his open hand.

"He's going to break it, Mama," Adam said anxiously.

"No, I don't think he can break the pan," Lacey answered. She put some loose tea in a strainer and leaned against the counter to wait for the water to boil.

Francie finally slid off her mother's lap. "Where's Caleb?" she asked.

Lacey turned to Adam. "Is Caleb awake?"

Adam nodded.

"He's upstairs, Francie. You can go find him."

With her tiny steps, Francie moved slowly across the kitchen. When she had finally passed into the next room, Lacey turned to Abby. "How long has she been walking like that?"

"A few days. It takes me forever to go anywhere with her."

Lacey furrowed her brow. "Maybe Josh should have a look."

"I suppose it wouldn't hurt. But I think it's just a phase. Two weeks ago she skipped everywhere she went, and before that she rolled somersaults all over the house."

"It's probably nothing then." Lacey sank wearily into a chair. Nicholas scooted under the table, dragging the frying pan with him.

"Mama, I'm sick," Adam repeated.

"Yes, sweetheart, you are."

"I don't feel good."

"I know. Come here and sit on my lap."

He shook his head. "I'm not a baby."

Baby or not, he looked like he was ready to cry. Lacey patted her lap, but he refused to come.

The water boiled and Lacey got up to make tea. She put a generous helping of honey in it. Adam shuffled over and took a seat at the table. As Lacey set the tea in front of him, Joshua returned.

"How's the patient?" he asked.

"What's the diagnosis?" Lacey countered.

Joshua shrugged one shoulder. "That's a little difficult to say without a look at his throat. But he seems to have a slight fever."

Lacey nodded. "I thought so."

"Up! Up!" Nicholas demanded, and Joshua scooped him up off the floor.

"Uh-huh, Lacey, I think you'd better check the stew," Josh said.

Lacey flew across the kitchen, wooden spoon in hand. She peered over the bubbling pot and breathed with relief. "It's okay, but I'd better get back to the biscuits."

"Here, let me help," Abby said, snatching an apron off a hook next to the back door. Lacey produced a rolling pin and began to flatten the dough she had kneaded.

Joshua shook his head as he held the squirming Nicholas, who was now hanging upside down from his arms but did not want to be put down. "It's a wonder you ever get anything done," Joshua said, with sincere admiration. "This place is chaos."

"What's chaos?" Adam croaked.

"That means a place where everything seems out of control," Lacey explained quickly.

"I'm not out of control," Adam asserted.

"No, of course you're not," his mother agreed, as she rolled her eyes above his head at Abby and Josh.

Nicholas slid a little too far out of Joshua's arms and landed with a thud on his bottom. He squalled, stunned.

"Nicholas is out of control," Adam said.

Chapter 3

The back door swung open once more, and the already busy kitchen got busier. Lacey's husband, Travis Gates, filled the doorway as he entered. Close behind him was Peter Regals, with a roll of wide papers neatly tucked under one arm.

Peter kissed Abby on the top of the head and stooped down to scoop up the wailing Nicholas all in one motion. Travis bent his dark head down to greet his weary wife with a kiss. Joshua watched as his sister's eyes met those of her husband. He could see the light that flashed between them. Both of them, weary from a long day, still spoke a wordless language that said they were glad to see each other. Peter and Abby looked at each other with similar expressions.

Josh looked from one couple to the other and felt afresh the pang in his heart—Priscilla. He tried to imagine her in this setting, a kitchen bursting with friends and family. She would have smiled at everyone, engaging the adults with her wit and charming the children with her playfulness. Everyone would like her; everyone always did. But Priscilla would not be doing what Lacey was doing—simmering stew, baking biscuits, and soothing a sick child all at one time, after having spent several hours teaching squirming children. The maid that Priscilla had had all her life would have dealt with the cooking and soothing, while a tutor handled the teaching. After a calm and civilized meal in the dining room, Priscilla would suggest a stroll through the streets. He had strolled the streets with her on many occasions. But here there were no streets to stroll, and the neighbors were all gathered in this house at the moment. No, Priscilla would not fit in here.

But who would fit in? The lumber camp was hardly the place to meet a prospective bride. Would he have to do what his father had done so long ago and venture to one of the cities to find a bride who would fit in at the camp better than Priscilla? Joshua had left the peninsula the first time in order to become a doctor. He had not thought much about marriage in those days. Meeting Priscilla had been quite accidental, and nearly two years had passed before he realized she regarded him as a prospective husband. He had allowed his own affection to grow guardedly, suspecting that he would be disappointed in the end—and he was.

Peter balanced Nicholas, who was now sucking his thumb and sobbing only intermittently, on his one hip and laid his roll of drawings on the table across from the mound of biscuit dough.

"No, no, no," Lacey protested as she scooped up the papers and thrust them back at Peter. "It's far too crowded in here. Take those drawings in the other room, please."

"We'll go to the dining room," Travis suggested.

Lacey shook her head. "Not there, either. I'll need to set the dining room table for supper soon. We won't all fit in here."

Travis sighed and smiled. "Is the living room floor all right?"

"Perfect." Lacey turned back to her biscuits. "As soon as Papa gets here, I'll bake these and we'll be ready to eat."

"Can I come?" Adam asked in his most pitiful voice.

Travis furrowed his brow and considered his son. "What's wrong with Adam?"

Lacey raised her eyebrows at Josh, who shook his head. "I can't be sure if he won't let me look in his throat."

"Adam?" Travis prodded gently.

Adam adamantly shook his head. "I don't want anyone to look at my throat. Can I see Uncle Peter's new pictures?"

Travis reached out his hand for his son, and together they trailed after Peter into the living room. Josh followed, also.

Peter squatted on the floor and unrolled his papers. The drawings of a small town had become familiar to everyone in the house, but each time Peter presented them for inspection, they had become a little more complex. Peter pictured a dozen small streets dotted with homes and a main road where the shops and offices would be. Adam snuggled under Peter's arm and put his face over the center of the map.

"I've thought about putting the school here," Peter said, pressing his finger into an intersection. "Lacey is already working hard with Nathan and Adam, and it won't be long before Francie and Caleb are ready for school, and then Nicholas."

Josh raised an eyebrow. "I'd like to see a school as much as anyone else, but we have only five children."

"We're planning for the future," Peter reminded him. "Someday there will be many more families with children living here. If we build the school first, they will be more likely to want to come here."

"You have a good point there, I suppose. If we want people to see we're a town, we have to look like one."

"Right," Travis agreed. "That's why we need a church, too."

"One thing at a time," Peter said. "For a while, the school might also be the church."

At the rap on the front door, Adam sprang up. "It's Grandpa!" He ran to the front door and heaved it open as quickly as an ill, scrawny six-year-old boy could. His grandfather's arms were waiting when he threw himself into them.

Daniel Wells lifted his oldest grandchild and pressed him against his chest. With his hand on Adam's cheek, he said, "You feel warm."

"I'm sick, but Uncle Joshua doesn't know what's wrong with me."

"What kind of doctor is he, then?" Daniel's eyes twinkled as he looked at his own son.

"I won't let him look at my throat," Adam declared proudly.

"That's not being fair, is it?" Daniel said.

Adam looked thoughtful, but he did not open his mouth for inspection.

Micah Wells followed his father into the room. Joshua looked on with pleasure at the young man his brother had become. As a child Adam's age, Micah had often tugged on Joshua's hand to pull him into the meadow behind their lighthouse home so they could look for deer and butterflies. Now, Micah had his father's broad shoulders and height, but he still had those sensitive blue eyes that were now being trained to scan the water swirling below the lighthouse for crafts in distress. Micah had the intensity to do the job well.

Micah pointed at the drawings. "Do you have something new?"

Peter pulled a sheet out from under the large map. "I've done a sketch of the building that would be a school and church. Here's the outside and here's what it might look like on the inside."

"Lacey should see this," Travis said. He turned his head toward the kitchen. "Lace!"

She appeared a moment later.

"Come see the school," Travis said.

Lacey kissed her father and waved at her brother, then squatted to inspect the drawings.

"I know I'm just an old man who lives in the lighthouse," Daniel Wells said, "but from what I hear whenever I come this way, not everyone is so keen on the idea of turning the camp into a town. They say that if they had wanted to live in a city and take a bath every week, they would have stayed in Milwaukee."

"I know who you're talking about, Daniel," Peter responded. "Troy Wilger makes a lot of noise, but there aren't so many men following him as he would like us to believe."

Travis agreed. "I think most of the men are in favor of developing the camp further. A lot of them came up here looking for work so they could save some money. But this is beautiful country up here. Why shouldn't they be able to settle here and raise families?"

"Well, you're a city boy and we managed to snag you," Daniel said. "So I guess there is hope that others will want to stay."

"It's inevitable," Peter insisted. "This area is too rich in natural resources not to attract people. Why shouldn't we plan for growth right from the start? We've already begun doing simple millwork here, and already we're more profitable. Travis's father is very close to closing a deal for a partnership with a major mill to move in here. And once the finished wood is more easily available up here, furniture makers and other craftsmen will be attracted to this area."

Lacey squinted at the drawing. "How many people will this building hold?"

"How many do you want it to hold?" Peter countered. "We could make it bigger."

"I couldn't begin to guess how many children we might have in a few years," Lacey said. "You're the one who has such a clear picture of the future."

"Don't forget your husband," Peter said. "Without the investment his father has already made here, we couldn't even think about next year, much less ten years."

Lacey smiled and nodded. Peter was right. Travis had come nine years ago on a secret scouting mission for his father. He had left temporarily to persuade his wealthy father to invest money for roads and basic mill equipment. And then he had come back to stay and build a future. Travis worked with Tom Saget, Abby's father, to carefully administer the generous investment his father had left in his hands. If the mill became successful, the senior Mr. Gates would more than make his money back.

"And then there's Josh," Travis said. "How many new towns can boast that they already have a doctor?"

Peter poked at the map. "And right here is where the new doctor's clinic is going to be."

Lacey gave a mock gasp. "You mean my brother is going to move out of my extra bedroom?"

Joshua eyed his sister. "When do we start building, Peter?"

"By midsummer," came the answer.

Joshua snapped his head around, surprised. "Really?"

"Really. I've organized a small crew, and we'll get that building up in no time. You'll have a waiting room and an exam room and a couple of rooms in the back to live in, just what you asked for."

"You're serious, aren't you?"

"Absolutely. After that, the school."

Lacey chuckled. "You might want to do something about the mess hall first. Old Lars left it in quite a jumble when he stomped off."

Peter and Travis shook their heads. "What got into him?" Peter asked. "How could a camp cook just up and leave one day between lunch and supper?"

"I don't know," Travis said. "But you're right. He left things in a mess. The new cook is not going to be happy."

"When does he come?" Joshua asked.

"Any day now," Travis responded. "His name is Percy Morgan."

"Is he any good?" Lacey asked.

"He doesn't have a lot of experience, but he comes with good references."

"Have you met him?"

Travis shook his head. "No. I didn't have time to go around looking for a cook. I hired him through the mail. I offered a three-month trial period. If he doesn't work out, we'll look again."

"Uncle Josh?" Adam said softly. He moved in a wilted way out of his grandfather's arms and toward his uncle. His face was flushed and his eyes bright.

"Yes, Adam?"

"You can look at my throat now."

Chapter 4

Impatiently, Lacey Wells Gates waited for the water to boil. Another glance at the clock told her that her household would awaken soon—too soon. Lacey had hardly slept all night. Adam's flushed cheeks had turned into a full-fledged fever that left him thrashing in his bed and calling often for his mother. The cough had begun around midnight.

Not wanting him to disturb three-year-old Caleb, Lacey had taken her older son and settled him on a pallet on the dining room floor. The voice of motherly experience told her that it was pointless to go back upstairs to her own bed, so she had settled in beside her son and snatched a few minutes of sleep whenever he dozed off. Now she wanted the water to boil so she could have a cup of tea in peace before the family awoke and so the water would be ready when Adam needed another dose of tea and honey.

Joshua found his sister slumped at the kitchen table, waiting for the water to boil. "How is he?" Josh asked, his voice low to avoid waking the sleeping Adam in the next room.

Lacey raised her weary head. "He's been calmer the last couple of hours. Thank you for checking on him during the night."

"I didn't really do anything," Josh answered. "He needed his mother more than he needed a doctor."

"Still, it was reassuring to me to hear that you don't think this is a serious infection."

"I don't think it is," Josh answered guardedly, "but it's still important to keep him quiet. The best cure is rest. And keep Caleb away from him as much as possible."

Lacey sighed. "I'll try. But you know Caleb. He gets into everything he has a mind to get into."

Josh chuckled. "Your job is far harder than a lumberjack's!"

The kettle whistled at last, and Lacey got up to fix her tea. She turned her head at the sound of footsteps on the stairs.

Travis entered the kitchen and kissed his wife gently on the forehead. "I'll sit up with him tonight," he said softly.

"Do you want some breakfast?" she asked.

Travis shook his head. "I'll get something later."

"What will you get?" she challenged. "There's no camp cook."

"Matt Harden is doing his best with the breakfast duty these days," Travis said. "It will encourage him if I eat his food."

"Yes, it will encourage Matt," Joshua said, laughing, "but it may make you sick. The rumor is that you should stay away from his scrambled eggs."

"I'll keep that in mind," Travis answered. "Probably he hoards his eggs too long, trying to get enough to feed fifty men."

"He needs more chickens, but he keeps cooking the ones that lay the best."

"That reminds me," Lacey said, "Adam is too sick to feed our chickens."

"I'll do it," Travis assured her.

Outside, a horse whinnied and the wheels of a carriage clattered to a stop. The sound so common in a city area was almost unheard of on the northern peninsula.

Joshua raised an eyebrow. "Who is that, so early in the morning?"

Travis shrugged. "We'd better go see."

"If it's Micah, you let me know immediately," Lacey said sternly.

"Micah doesn't have a carriage," Joshua reminded his sister.

The horse whinnied again, this time more loudly.

Josh and Travis left the house and stepped into the broad, dusty street outside the house. A few men straggled out of the mess hall and wandered down the street, curious about the early morning intrusion on their routine.

A man in a frayed brown suit stepped down from a rickety carriage and absently looked around for a post to tie the horse to, but there was none. He then stooped to inspect the axle of his carriage.

Travis furrowed his brow. "I don't recognize the fellow," he said. "Do you?"

Josh shook his head. "Could it be the new cook?"

Travis's eyes brightened for a second, then narrowed. "There's a woman with him. Percy Morgan never said a word about bringing a wife."

"Does it really matter?" Joshua asked. "After all, we're trying to attract families."

"We don't have living quarters for a married couple," Travis reminded him.

"She could be his daughter," Josh speculated. "He seems quite a bit older than she is."

"We haven't got housing ready for a father and daughter, either," Travis said.

"I'm amazed that they got here in that carriage without breaking a wheel. The roads are rough."

From the height of the carriage, a young woman surveyed the growing crowd. She was dressed in a plain dark green dress and wore sturdy boots and a brown leather jacket. A broad-brimmed hat hid most of her features, but Josh could not help but notice the piercing black eyes.

"We'd better find out who they are," Josh said, and stepped toward the unlikely pair. He approached the carriage and extended his hand to the crouching man. "I'm Dr. Joshua Wells."

The man looked up sideways at Josh and did not stand to receive the welcome. "Nobody warned me about the roads up this way," he muttered.

"Most people come in on horseback or with a sturdy wagon," Josh said lightly. "We don't see too many carriages up here."

"I thought I heard the axle crack, but I guess it's all right." Finally the man stood. He looked around. "This place is at the end of the world."

Josh was puzzled and glanced at Travis, who had joined him next to the carriage. "Surely you were warned what conditions were like," Josh said.

"Why would I be warned of anything?" the man asked.

"You are Percy Morgan, aren't you?" Travis asked.

"No. I'm not Percy Morgan, and apparently you don't know much about Percy Morgan." Travis was taken aback. "We've not met. I hired Mr. Morgan through the mail to be our camp cook. We don't get many visitors here, so when you arrived, we assumed you were Mr. Morgan."

The man threw back his head and roared. He glanced up at the woman in the wagon. "You got them good, lady, I'll say that for you."

Josh and Travis glanced at each other, both agitated.

"Sir," Travis said, "if you are not Percy Morgan, perhaps you would give us the pleasure of introducing yourself."

The man shook his head. "It's not me you want to meet. I'm just the sucker who agreed to drive the lady all the way up here."

"The lady?" Josh said, turning to the woman in the carriage.

"That, my dear fellows, is Percy Morgan!" The man roared hilariously once again. He moved around to the back of the carriage and pulled on a trunk. With a smooth, experienced motion of visible exasperation, he heaved it off the carriage and dropped it. Dust swirled into a small cloud and quickly settled again. "And this, my friends, is all the worldly belongings of Miss Percy Morgan."

"Miss Percy Morgan?" Travis echoed faintly.

"You heard me," the man said. "Now if you don't mind, I'll be on my way. We drove most of the night through these back roads to get here. But from the looks of the place, I'm better off to turn around and go home now than look for any refreshment here."

Hearing her cue, Miss Percy Morgan stood up, stepped off the carriage, and landed lightly in the street. "Thank you, Mr. Booker. You've been most indulgent."

With laughter in his eyes, Mr. Booker looked at his customer. "I sure hope you know what you're doing, young lady." He swung himself up into the seat and snapped the reins of the horse. In another minute, he was gone.

Several dozen lumberjacks now stood in the street, staring at Miss Percy Morgan. Matt Harden emerged from the mess hall, spatula in hand.

"Travis, who is this and why is she here?" Matt demanded.

"Ah, Matt," Travis began awkwardly, "apparently your relief has arrived."

"What do you mean?" Matt barked.

"This is Percy Morgan," Travis answered. "The new cook."

"You never said the new cook was a girl," Matt said, scowling.

"I, ah, was unaware of that myself," Travis confessed, eyeing Percy Morgan. "You never mentioned that in our correspondence," he said to her softly.

"You never asked." She met Travis's gaze, daring him to question her further.

Her voice was firm and fierce, but Josh thought he heard a hint of fear embedded in arrogance. Percy Morgan took off her hat and shook free her long, wavy black hair. It fell across her shoulders, framing the creamy complexion of her face. Josh watched her shoulders rise and fall with her even, controlled breaths, as she held her head up straight and surveyed the gawking crowd.

"Travis Gates, you did this on purpose!" Troy Wilger pushed himself forward through the crowd. His ragged brown hair grew well past his shoulders and his beard had not been trimmed in months. His astonishment that the new cook was a woman evolved quickly into overt hostility. "This is all part of your plan to civilize us. You think you can bring a woman in here and make us all behave ourselves and mind our manners."

"Troy," Travis interjected, "I assure you I had no knowledge that—"

"Don't give me that!" Troy interrupted. "You don't make mistakes. Not like this."

"I wouldn't say it's a mistake," Travis defended himself, "perhaps just a misunderstanding. I'm sure we can work things out. Miss Morgan is very well qualified to cook for all of you."

"Do you mean you're going to let her stay?" Matt Harden challenged.

Travis forced himself to laugh. "I thought you were eager to be relieved of your culinary duties, Matt."

"I don't see how this can possibly work," Matt retorted. He waved his spatula in the air and turned his back.

"We won't know that unless we try," Travis insisted.

Josh's eyes were fixed on Percy Morgan. Her head never moved; her shoulders never twitched; her eyes never flinched. Her fingers held firmly the rim of her hat, and her feet stayed locked in place. *She has guts,* he told himself. *She really wants to do this.*

"She has to go," Troy Wilger shouted.

"We signed a contract," Travis said simply. "Three months' trial."

"Don't talk to me about contracts," Troy retorted. "This is a matter of integrity. She didn't tell you the truth about who she was."

"She answered all the questions I asked," Travis said. "And I promise you, her answers were quite satisfactory. Now perhaps one of you would help me with her trunk."

Troy thrust himself farther forward and lunged toward the trunk. "I'll help you, all right." With his powerful arms, he picked up the trunk and threw it toward Travis and Percy.

Instinctively, Joshua grabbed Percy's arm to pull her out of the trunk's trajectory, but she lost her balance and tumbled to the dirt. Indignant, she leaped to her feet and, as she did so, Josh heard the ripping sound. Although the trunk had not hit her, as Troy intended, it had landed on the edge of her skirt when she fell, and now her skirt had a huge rip along the bottom.

Josh jumped into action and pushed the trunk off of her garment, but the damage was done. The men in the street roared in amusement as Percy Morgan tried to fix her skirt, showing then the first hint of her being flustered since her arrival.

Troy Wilger, though, was not satisfied with her embarrassment and he lunged at Percy. This time Josh was not quick enough. Percy's slight frame was no match for Troy, and she tumbled backward, her head struck the side of the trunk, and everything went black.

Chapter 5

Travis and Joshua hurled themselves at Troy Wilger and intercepted further assault on Percy. With his hands firmly planted on Troy's chest, Travis pushed, forcing the angry lumberjack to step backward or lose his balance.

"Miss Morgan!" Joshua dropped to his knees over the limp form of the newcomer. "Miss Morgan! Can you hear me?" Gently he slapped her cheek, but she gave no response. He put one hand under the back of her head, his fingers finding the slender nape of her neck.

"Is she all right?" Travis called over his shoulder.

"She's unconscious," Josh replied. Then he looked at his fingertips, damp and red. "And she's bleeding."

Matt Harden pushed his way past Travis and dropped his spatula in the dirt. "I'll help you move her," he said. "I may not think it's fitting for a woman to be camp cook, but she didn't deserve that."

"Take her to my house," Travis instructed.

Troy seemed to settle down. With a last disgusted look at Percy Morgan, he stomped off toward the mess hall.

"I'll deal with him later," Travis said, irritated. "What about Miss Morgan?"

"We'll take her home where she'll be out of further danger."

Matt moved toward Percy, but Joshua put his hand up to stop him. "Thank you, Matt, but I can manage."

"I want to help."

"Then get her trunk and take it to her room."

Joshua slipped one arm under Percy's shoulders and the other under her knees and easily stood up. *She hardly weighs anything.*

Travis fell into step beside him. "There's a cot on the back porch," he told Joshua. "Lacey put it out there so Adam could rest in the afternoons."

"That will have to do," Joshua said. "I wish that clinic Peter has sketched were already built."

Moving quickly but smoothly, they retraced their steps to the Gates house and circled around to the sheltered back porch. Joshua laid Percy on the cot and reached for her limp wrist. "Her pulse is a little fast, but regular," he announced, "and she seems to be breathing well."

Lacey appeared from the kitchen. "What happened out there?" she demanded.

"Troy Wilger and his gang," her husband answered, "and their usual barbarian behavior."

"And who is this?" Lacey asked, pointing at Percy.

"This is Percy Morgan," Travis answered.

"The cook you hired?"

"One and the same."

Lacey shook her head, a sly smile breaking on her lips. "You never mentioned that—"

"I didn't know," Travis said, cutting her off.

"I think we've established that Travis didn't know he was hiring a woman," Joshua said, "but she's here and she's hurt."

"I'm sorry, Josh. What do you need?" Lacey asked.

"A cool cloth and my medical bag."

"I'll get them," Travis said, and he disappeared into the house.

Lacey unfolded a quilt on the end of the cot and spread it over the still-unconscious Percy Morgan. The rosy color had drained from Percy's face, making her coal black hair appear even richer in tone. Her small features were smooth and well placed on her oval face.

"She's quite striking," Lacey observed. "I can imagine how Troy and his friends would feel about having a woman this attractive around."

Joshua did not answer. He took Percy's pulse again.

"On the other hand, you would think some of the men would be glad to have an attractive, unattached woman around. Things might be more interesting here for her than she imagined when she accepted the job."

Joshua glanced up. "What's taking Travis so long?"

"I'm here, I'm here." Travis came through the door and handed Josh a cool, damp cotton cloth.

Joshua gently pressed the cloth against the side of Percy's head, in the back under her black hair. Immediately he felt the warmth of the blood oozing into the cloth. He pressed on the wound with three fingers as he brushed away strands of hair to see what he was doing.

"What else do you need?" Lacey asked.

Joshua shook his head. "I'll be fine. The bleeding doesn't look too bad. If she doesn't come to soon, I'll use the smelling salts."

"I'd better go and see how the other men are taking the news," Travis said, "if there's nothing else I can do here."

Joshua nodded. "Go. We'll be fine."

"Mama!" came a plaintive cry from the kitchen.

"Is that Adam?" Joshua asked.

Lacey nodded. "His throat is worse."

"Just try to keep him quiet and comfortable. I'll look in on him later."

"Are you sure you don't need anything else?" Lacey asked, glancing over her shoulder at the kitchen door.

"No, she should wake up soon."

"Mama!"

"I'm coming, Adam," Lacey said, stepping toward the door.

Joshua repositioned the cloth. The bleeding seemed to be slowing.

Percy groaned and turned her head. "Where am I?" she asked as her eyes opened reluctantly and stared into the brown of Joshua's eyes.

Holding her gaze, he studied the size of her pupils. "You're going to be okay," Joshua said. "It's just a bump on the head and a small cut. The fact that you've regained consciousness so soon is a good sign."

"I have a headache bigger than the Civil War," Percy said, "but you didn't answer my question. Where am I?"

"You're on my sister's back porch, if you must know."

"Are you really a doctor?"

"Board certified."

"You have a sister?"

"Yes."

"And she has a back porch?"

"Yes, a small one." Josh was pleased that his patient appeared capable of sustaining coherent conversation.

"This doesn't sound like such an uncivilized place." Percy slowly moved her legs toward the side of the cot.

"I don't think you ought to move just yet," Joshua cautioned.

"But I want to," Percy answered.

"You just said your head hurt."

"It does. But it can't possibly hurt any more if I sit up." She had her legs over the side of the cot now and began to push her torso up. With a sigh, she leaned back against the side of the house and, after a moment, the view was in better focus. She looked out at the vegetable garden and henhouse. The scene was sharply different from the view of her old backyard. Although unfamiliar, it seemed oddly inviting. "It's a nice back porch."

"Here, let me change the cloth," Joshua said, taking away the blood-soaked cotton and replacing it with a clean rag.

"I guess that's why my head hurts so much," Percy said. She slipped her fingers in under his, took hold of the cloth, and nudged him away. "I can do this."

"Perhaps I failed to impress you with my assurance of board certification." His fingers still covered hers.

"I'm sure you're fully qualified. It's just that I'm not hurt all that badly."

Reluctantly, Joshua let go. "When it stops bleeding, I want to have a closer look at that gash."

Percy moved her head slowly from side to side. "I'm fine. Did I hear a child crying?"

"That's my nephew."

"So you have a sister and she has a back porch and a son."

"Two sons, actually."

"As I said, this doesn't sound like such an uncivilized place."

"I'm sorry that you got such an uncivilized welcome."

Percy scrunched up her forehead. "Why were they so angry? I'm a good cook. They'll see."

"It's a long story," Joshua said. "Don't take it personally."

Percy made a feeble attempt to laugh. "I am attacked within five minutes of arriving and you tell me not to take it personally?"

"I see your point. After you're here awhile, you'll understand better. Troy Wilger. . .well, he has his own ideas about how things should be done around here. It has nothing to do with you."

"Except that I'm a woman."

Joshua unrolled a bandage. "You represent change. Troy doesn't want change."

"But the camp needs a cook."

"Yes, it does. But you're not the kind of cook Troy had in mind."

"What did he have in mind?"

Joshua gently moved the hair off the base of her skull, exposing the wound. He inspected it thoughtfully. "I'll have to wrap that somehow," he said. "The wound is small. It should close within a couple of days."

"You're avoiding my question," Percy said. "What kind of cook did Troy have in mind?"

"Oh, somebody more rugged, a little rough around the edges, somebody who doesn't care for city ways."

"City ways? Up here?"

Joshua chuckled. "We're not all barbarians."

"No, of course not," Percy said, flushing. "After all, you are a real doctor."

"That's right. I even went to the city for training."

She looked around the porch. "You don't seem to have an office."

"I'm working on that," he said.

"I suppose that would be the city way to do things."

Joshua laughed aloud now. "Yes, it would. But I happen to be in favor of doctors having proper offices, with the right medicine and equipment."

"I thought this was just a lumber camp. Why does your sister with a back porch and two sons—and presumably a husband—live in a lumber camp?"

"That's a complicated question, but I suppose the simple answer is that she wants to."

"And you?"

"Me?"

"Surely you have other opportunities, better places to go."

Joshua shrugged. "If this is such a bad place to come to, why are you here?"

Percy hesitated ever so slightly. "Don't change the subject. Why do you live in a lumber camp? Why is there a house here?"

"We have several houses, actually, and several families."

"So this is not really a lumber camp?"

"Yes, it is. And no, it isn't."

Percy raised a questioning eyebrow.

"It has been a lumber camp. But it doesn't always have to be just that."

Percy nodded slowly. "I'm beginning to understand. Troy Wilger likes things the way they are, but not everyone does."

Joshua smiled. "Your deductive reasoning skills seem to be intact. I guess we can be sure that there's no permanent damage to your brain." He bent to examine the wound once more, pushing her thick, wavy hair away. Black, silky strands slipped through his fingers, and he had to hold her head more firmly. "Hold still now," he instructed, "and let me bandage this."

"I could do that," she insisted.

"Humor me," he responded. "Let me prove to you that I'm a real doctor."

The door from the kitchen creaked open, and Lacey stepped out onto the porch. "Oh, good, you're awake," Lacey said. "I'm Lacey Gates."

Percy could not turn her head to greet her hostess, but she said, "The sister with the back porch. Nice to meet you."

"Excuse me?" Lacey said, confused.

Josh chuckled but made no explanation to his sister. "That's right. And the older son is inside with a sore throat, and the presumed husband is trying to smooth things over with the men."

"Presumed husband? I assure you, my husband is quite real. I haven't the foggiest idea what you're talking about," Lacey said.

Josh caught the twinkle in Percy's eye and did not respond to his sister.

"The son with a sore throat is asking for Uncle Josh," Lacey said.

"I'll be in soon. I just want to get Miss Morgan settled."

Chapter 6

Your nephew needs you," Percy said as she stood up awkwardly. She had more of a headache than she wanted to admit. "Just point me in the direction of my trunk, please."

"Nonsense," Joshua protested. "When I said I wanted to get you settled, I meant I wanted you to be comfortable on this cot so you could rest. Perhaps later in the day we'll move you."

"I've intruded on your sister quite enough," Percy insisted. No matter what her welcome had been like, she was determined to make an impression of competence.

"You were unconscious for several minutes," Joshua reminded her. "I think it is premature for you to be up walking around."

"I'm perfectly fine. I have only the slightest headache remaining, and I'm sure a cup of tea will take care of that."

"Then let me fix you one. Lacey keeps a fine assortment."

Percy waived away his efforts. "I came here to run a kitchen. I'm sure I can manage a cup of tea."

Joshua sighed and snapped his medical bag shut. "Miss Morgan, are you always this stubborn?"

"Generally," she admitted. She had good reason for her stubborn streak, but she was not about to explain it to this stranger, no matter how sincere he was in taking care of her.

"What is the harm in letting someone look after you for a short while?"

"It's simply not necessary."

"If you're afraid of what the men may think if they hear you're hurt—"

"I'm not concerned in the least with what the men may think," Percy cut in. "It's simply not necessary for anyone to look after me at all. Now, please, be so kind as to direct me to my quarters."

"All right," Josh said in resignation. "But it's against my better judgment."

"Dr. Wells, please."

"Yes, yes, come this way. I'll walk you over."

"I told you that it is not necessary for you to coddle me. Just point."

"At least let me walk you to the front of the house. From there you can see where I'm pointing."

Percy marched down the steps of the porch and led the way around the side of the house, resisting the urge to clasp her aching head between her hands. From her new vantage point, she scanned the street. "I see where we came in," she said. "That must be the mess hall over there."

"Yes, it is," Josh confirmed. "There's a small room in the back. Your trunk should be waiting for you."

"Thank you, Dr. Wells."

"My name is Joshua." He hesitated. "I'm afraid the room is not much. It's quite small, and I don't know whether Travis had it cleaned out after the last cook left. The window doesn't open properly, and there's no lock on the door."

"Will I need a lock?" Percy asked sharply.

"I hope not," Josh answered softly. "But if you would like one installed, let me know."

Percy chuckled. "And you'll go right down to the hardware store and get one, won't you? I must have missed that shop on my tour of the city."

Josh laughed, too. "It might take a few weeks, but we could get one. And anything else you need—staples, kitchen supplies, pots. With enough time and patience, we can get whatever we need."

"I'll keep that in mind." She offered her hand to him firmly. "Thank you, Joshua Wells. I hope that someday I will have the opportunity to repay your kindness."

Josh shook her hand gently. "Thank you, Percy Morgan. And if you need any more medical attention, you know where to find me."

She raised her eyebrows and looked around. "You can't go far."

"I do ride an occasional circuit to other places just as obscure as this one. But I'm not usually gone too long."

"Good day, then." She turned on one heel, lifted her skirt out of the dirt, and, with her head held high and her eyes straight ahead, she strutted across the street. The handful of men still standing in the street watched curiously, but no one spoke to her.

As Percy reached the mess hall, her heart was in her throat, but she was determined that the men staring at her would not unnerve her. She would ignore them until she felt ready to be in control of an encounter. With her lips pressed hard together, she pulled open the door to the mess hall and began to take stock of her new surroundings.

Travis Gates had told her by correspondence that the mess hall was a fairly new building. For years the men had eaten under a makeshift shelter, their fare prepared over an open fire, and this happened only seasonally. Gradually more and more men began to stay on the peninsula year round, and the lumbering continued as steadily as the harsh winter would allow. Travis had been instrumental in constructing an enclosed building that could house the men for meals and provide shelter and camaraderie when the weather kept them from working. This was the building that would be Percy Morgan's world, her workplace, her home.

Percy walked slowly through the dining area, admiring the craftsmanship of the tables. They were plain and functional, but beautiful in their simplicity and solidly built. The chairs, though of a half-dozen different designs, were just as well made. Percy had grown up in a home filled with fine furniture and she recognized craftsmanship when she saw it. Her mother would have been pleased to have a table and chairs of this quality in her home.

She came to the kitchen. No doubt Matt Harden had done his best to manage the unfamiliar territory, but he had left chaos in his wake. A greasy film covered everything in sight. Pots and dishes were stacked haphazardly around the room. The floor looked as if it had not been swept in three months. She would speak to Travis about the condition of the kitchen, Percy decided. She at least deserved to begin her work with reasonable conditions. Travis could assign a couple of the men to scrub down the kitchen and put things in order at her direction.

On the other hand, she told herself, some of the men were already inclined to throw her out. If she caused a stir about working conditions, they would find more reason to complain about her. She was here on a three-month trial basis and was determined to give Travis Gates no cause to exercise his option to let her go. No, she would have to tackle this job on her own. It would not be the first time she had taken on such a task, although she had learned these skills fairly recently.

Cautiously, she began to open cupboards and inspect the contents of the shelves. Flour, beans, lard, more flour, more beans. If she wanted to serve vegetables, she supposed she would have to grow them herself. She wondered if it was too late in the spring to put in a garden. And perhaps there was some dried meat hanging in a place she had not yet discovered. She would have to have something more than flour and beans to work with.

She hated to admit it, but her head was throbbing. In her trunk she had some chamomile tea, which would soothe her aching head and frazzled nerves. She also longed for a long, hot bath, but knew that that was out of the question and would be for as long as she stayed at the camp. Lugging the buckets of water, heating them, and filling a tub would be her own labor, not that of a servant. Percy did not suppose she would have time for such indulgence very often.

Percy pumped the handle above the sink, wondering if there really was water flowing straight into the kitchen. Delightfully, there was! It was cold, clear, and sweet, apparently coming directly from a well. She splashed her face with her eyes wide open. Feeling momentarily refreshed, she looked around for a kettle or a pot clean enough in which to boil water. She found one that looked a little less dubious than most of the others, pumped some fresh water into it, and set it on the stove. The coals were still hot from breakfast, and the woodpile, though depleted, was nearby. Swiftly she stoked the wood and stirred up the fire. It would not take long for the water to heat.

Now she wondered where her small sleeping room might be. A narrow door off the kitchen looked likely. She pushed it open and peered in. The room was dim, even in the daylight, which puzzled Percy. Travis had obviously gone to great lengths to build a very workable kitchen—although dirty at the moment—and a pleasant dining hall. Why was the cook's room so disheartening? Percy stifled her self-pity with determination and took inventory of the room.

An oil lamp sat on the bedside table and she lit it. Even though it was midmorning and the sun was shining, she thought the light would help. Now she could see that a great shade tree stood right outside the window. Although it made the room dark, the shade surely kept it cool in the hot summer.

Joshua was right. It was small. The room held only a narrow bed that was hardly more than a cot, the small bedside table, a chair that had probably come from the dining room, and a row of hooks for clothing. It was at once clear that Percy would need to keep her trunk in the room for additional storage. Though her wardrobe was far from lavish, she had more than a pair of overalls to hang on a hook.

Her trunk had been placed with care along the only unoccupied wall in the room. Percy went to it now and opened it. She rummaged past the few books she owned—a Bible that had belonged to her grandmother, a book of poetry, and two novels—and felt between the layers of her clothing for the tin of chamomile tea. She sighed as she wondered if there was a cup clean enough to drink out of anywhere in the kitchen. Her head ached and she longed to lay it down on a soft, clean pillow. But of course she did not have a soft, clean pillow. In her determination to get the job, she had neglected to discuss with Travis what personal items she should bring with her. The bedding looked serviceable for the time being, but it would have to be washed before she would actually sleep in it. Perhaps she should have accepted Joshua Wells's invitation to spend the day on his sister's back porch. That might have given someone a chance to come over here and see the sad state of affairs.

No self-pity, Percy told herself sternly. She glanced down at her torn skirt. A skillful seamstress could probably mend the tear at least well enough to wear the garment for working in the kitchen. But Percy was not a skillful seamstress. She was fortunate to have learned to cook, and her own fetish for orderly surroundings dictated that she learn to clean. But she had never learned to sew.

Briefly she wondered whether Lacey Gates was handy with a needle and could perhaps mend the skirt. In the meantime, Percy decided she could at least change her clothes. She extracted a gray poplin skirt from her trunk and quickly traded it for the torn garment.

The water was boiling. Percy peered into the depths of a dark cup and decided it was safe to drink from it. She took the tea back to her room and sat on the edge of the bed. It was actually quite comfortable. Percy took her torn skirt and spread it out over the pillow. That would have to do until she felt up to scrubbing the bedding. She set the tea on the bedside table to steep and scooted back on the bed. Maybe Joshua was right; maybe she did need to rest a bit more. Her head beat like an African drum. She let her eyes close as she leaned her head back against the wall.

"Miss Morgan?" a voice called from the kitchen.

Percy scrambled to her feet, her head screaming with every movement. She had not heard footsteps. "I'm here," she answered.

"I wonder if we might have a word."

It was Travis Gates. She recognized his voice from the encounter in the street that morning. If he had any notion of sending her away, he had another thing coming. They had signed a contract.

"I'm just settling in," Percy said as she stepped back into the kitchen. She regretted that she had not yet sipped her tea.

Travis smiled in a friendly way. She decided he was not there to send her away. At least not yet.

"I am sorry to disturb you," he said. "You've already had quite a morning."

"It's no trouble. What can I do for you?"

"I'm afraid I have some rather disturbing news."

So he was going to send her away!

"It's about supper," Travis continued. "Matt Harden refuses to prepare another meal. I explained to him your condition and that you were not likely ready to step in just yet, but he won't hear a word of it."

"Nonsense," Percy said emphatically. "I'm perfectly fine. The men need dinner and I'll cook it."

Travis nodded gratefully. "That would be very kind of you. And then perhaps we should have a more specific discussion about your duties."

"Yes, of course."

"Are the accommodations acceptable?"

"Yes, certainly."

"I looked in that room a few days ago." Travis smiled slyly. "I'll ask Lacey for some clean bedding and bring it over after lunch."

"That's not necessary."

"It's the least I can do after the welcome you received this morning."

"I'm quite fine."

"I'll see you after lunch, then."

Travis turned around and gingerly stepped across the sticky floor. Percy put a hand to her throbbing temple and decided that she needed that tea more than ever.

Chapter 7

Aweek passed. Percy had never been so tired in her whole life. She had personally scrubbed down the kitchen and dining hall from corner to corner on her hands and knees, breaking from the task only long enough to prepare three meals a day for the fifty or so lumberjacks. Her days began before dawn. She could make enormous batches of pancakes or biscuits in her sleep, and it often felt as if that was what she was doing. The men left for the work sites very early, and breakfast had to be ready precisely on time. She could spend two hours cooking, and fifty men would whiz through and inhale the meal in nine minutes or less. Someone would grab the crate of packed lunches, and Percy would be left with dishes and cleanup and a deadline for getting supper ready. At the end of the day, just when she was ready for stillness and quiet, the men would come in, ravenous and rowdy, and their boisterousness would send her spinning.

On the first day that she was alone with the monstrous kitchen, Joshua came by and he scowled when he found her on her knees, scraping crusted pancake batter from the floor. It was hard to tell how long it had been there, but its texture and color suggested a very long time. Percy had assured Josh that there were no lasting consequences to the incident in the street on her first morning and refused to allow him to check her bandage. It was not bleeding, her head had stopped hurting, and she had far too much to do to lie in bed as he might have liked her to do. After a few minutes of awkward conversation that never seemed to veer from the cut on her head, Joshua left, but his parting words were a stern warning not to overdo.

When Percy was alone again, she scraped at the pancake batter a little more slowly. She would have liked it if Joshua Wells had stayed longer, but at the same time she knew she had driven him off with her impertinence.

At least three times every hour Percy admitted to herself that she ached and was tired and felt overwhelmed by what she had undertaken. But she was determined not to admit it to anyone else. She simply pressed on with the task of transforming the mess hall into an orderly, functioning state so that the next time Dr. Wells came by, he would see that everything was under control.

✼

One day Travis Gates came by to ask what supplies she needed. She gave him a list, grateful for his promise to get them as quickly as possible but knowing that it might still be several weeks. Her mind whirled with the challenge of providing some menu variety with the limited supplies on hand. She hoped for several hundred pounds of potatoes to arrive sooner rather than later.

Once she proved her industriousness by cleaning the mess hall without a whimper of complaint, she intended to approach Travis about having someone dig a garden where she could put in some vegetables. And the dozen scrawny hens in the coop behind the mess hall might provide enough eggs for pancakes or dessert cakes, but she dreamed of having enough to scramble eggs for breakfast twice a week.

Percy had noticed Lacey Gates and another young woman weeding a vegetable patch between two houses. It must have been the garden that Percy had seen from Lacey's back porch. Lacey and her companion seemed to converse pleasantly and easily as they worked, while their children of various ages roamed around, exploring the meadow and creek behind the short row of buildings. From a distance, Lacey Gates struck Percy as being competent and unflappable. Her children were as mischievous as any children, Percy supposed, but Lacey seemed to handle them with an admirable, gentle firmness. She worked in the garden swiftly and expertly, hung her tidy wash on Wednesday afternoon, and steered her children toward the kitchen with minimal resistance when it was time to prepare the evening meal. Her companion, whom Lacey judged to be about the same age as Lacey and a few years older than her own twenty-one years, seemed to hear a different drummer as Percy observed them in the street. She arrived at the vegetable patch after Lacey was already hard at work, and her wash was more likely to be laid out over the railing of her front porch. Even her children giggled and romped more energetically than the Gates boys. Despite their differences, the two women appeared clearly companionable.

Travis Gates had told her that there were two other young women, new brides who were lonely themselves, and hinted that it would not be as difficult as she imagined to find friendship in the camp. But Percy had not taken time to socialize with her new neighbors beyond returning Lacey's morning wave several times. As it was, she fell into bed each night exhausted by the day's labor. The thought of having to be polite and engaging with other civilized people overwhelmed her. Her mind was focused on the job she had come to do, and she had not expected to have friendships with other women at a lumber camp. Despite the clear availability of four other young women, Percy could not muster the energy to be sociable and so she made no attempt.

Dealing with the lumberjacks was another matter. She had to face the whole lot of them morning and evening, but nothing dictated that she had to be sociable. Every time Matt Harden came into the mess hall, he looked as if he wanted to say something, but he never did. She looked him in the eye and waited, but nothing came. After the first two days, Percy paid no attention. If he had something to say, he should just say it, she told herself. She was far too busy to try to urge it out of him. Troy Wilger glared at her each time he passed through the line and consistently found something critical to say about the food, generally in a very loud voice. But Percy could not help noticing that he came back for seconds more frequently than anyone else. She was sure she would please his appetite once she had a full range of staples available.

Most of the other men scrutinized her more silently. As they filled their plates at the serving table, their eyes were more often on her than the food. She refilled the platters as quickly as they emptied them. If anyone stared at her, she stared back fiercely and intently. Once Troy Wilger had caught her staring down a younger lumberjack and roared hilariously and within seconds the whole mess hall shook with laughter at the standoff. Percy blushed with fury but did not break her glare. Finally, the man moved on through the line. The laughter heightened, but this time the young man blushed. After that he did not look Percy in the eye again, and not many others did, either.

At the end of the first week, Percy sat cross-legged in the middle of her bed and brushed her hair. Most of the time, her long, coal black hair was pulled tightly behind her head for it simply was not efficient to have it flowing around her shoulders while she cooked and cleaned. But she did not forget she had beautiful hair. She stroked it each night with slow, thorough, long movements that kept the hair thick and lustrous. Her father had had the same beautiful thick, wavy, black hair and the same fair complexion Percy had. She remembered standing beside him as a little girl, looking into a mirror and giggling at the resemblance. She had taken such pleasure in it in those days.

But that's as far as it goes, she told herself now. *I got your hair, Papa, but I don't have to have any of the rest of you. And I don't want any of the rest of you.*

Without getting up, she tossed her brush into the open trunk. The giggling little girl in the mirror was someone else—at least it felt that way sometimes—and those memories belonged to another lifetime. Percy Morgan no longer had the luxury of indulging in sentimental moments. Giggles were not only childish but irrelevant to real life, at least to the adult life into which she had grown.

It was late. Dawn would come soon and it was imperative that she sleep. But still she feared that she would not.

Chapter 8

One morning a week later, the men burst through the mess hall door in a pack, as they had done every morning. Percy was ready for them; her days had fallen into a routine that improved steadily. The breakfast rush, which came so early in the morning, took her less by surprise every time. Exhaustion still enveloped her each night, but its onset came later and later. She might soon wish that she had something pleasurable to read in the evenings. She could reread her favorite novels, of course, or her book of poetry, the three volumes that sat on her nightstand. Her grandmother's Bible was still safely tucked away in the trunk. Grandmother would never let a day pass without reading it, but Percy had long ago given up the habit of looking for encouragement in its pages. Percy had always thought her grandmother's habit a sweet one, but after what had happened in her family, she was not sure God was someone from whom she cared to hear. Perhaps Lacey would have a book to loan her.

Percy had worked sixteen days in a row and for the first time would have an afternoon and evening off. She and Travis had agreed that twice a month she could prepare a cold supper during the day and the men would look after themselves for the evening meal. Travis even promised to assign a cleanup crew so she would find no surprises when she returned late in the evening.

The question was, though, what would she do with an entire afternoon and evening off? There were no restaurants to eat in, no concerts to attend, no parks to stroll through; and it would hardly be restful to hole up in her dingy room and pretend not to hear the commotion in the dining hall. Percy supposed she could lace up her sturdiest boots and go for a hike to explore the countryside around the camp. She had seen very little of it so far because getting the mess hall and kitchen into some semblance of order had demanded her full concentration. During the last few evenings, she had begun to imagine ways to make her small bedroom more comfortable and appealing. But she had not yet wandered off the dirt road that ran through the camp.

While she served one plate after another with sausage, biscuits, and gravy, Percy's mind planned out the details of the rest of her day. The noise and commotion that she had found deafening on her first morning barely got her attention today. She nodded somberly at the men who greeted her, averted her eyes from the ones most likely to make lewd remarks, and worked rapidly. The sooner they had their breakfast, she told herself, the sooner they would be ready to go. In the corner by the door stood the crates packed with their lunch—bread, cheese, ham, cookies, jugs of tea. She wanted to add apples to the daily lunch menu as soon as Travis could arrange to get some. Percy supposed a farmer farther south on the peninsula might be able to supply them. Apples were not something that would require sending an order to a big city.

Having inhaled their morning nourishment, the men swarmed out just the way they had swarmed in twenty minutes earlier. The mess hall was empty and quiet except for the sound of Percy clearing tables, loading dishes onto a cart, and pushing it to the kitchen. With an exasperated sigh, she realized she had forgotten to put on the big pots of water to heat so she would have hot water for cleaning up. Now her day's schedule would be delayed by at least half an hour. Percy pumped water into smaller pots, dumped them into the larger pots until they were full, stirred up the embers in the stove, and shoved in three more pieces of wood.

On an impulse, and perhaps because she was feeling agitated about the irregularity of the day, she decided to take a walk while the water heated. The mess hall was situated toward one end of the short street that ran through the camp. She would walk briskly up one side of the street and back down the other, and as she went she would look for trails or paths that she might want to follow later. Resolutely, she wiped her hands on a dish towel, removed her apron, straightened her blue cotton skirt, and headed for the door.

The day outside was golden, the energy of spring still in the air but the strength of the morning sun bringing a promise of summer. The trees had filled out nicely with their leaves and blossoms, sending sprays of color across the road. The last wagon of lumberjacks had just rumbled out, and the dust had not quite settled in the street. Percy observed that a light sprinkling would help to tamp down the dirt without turning it to mud, the way many spring thunderstorms did.

She headed up the street. By now she knew what all the buildings were: three nice houses where real families lived; two lean-to structures where young brides waited patiently for their husbands to have time and money to build homes; the offices of Travis Gates, Peter Regals, Tom Saget, and a few others who helped to manage the business activities of the camp. Behind the mess hall were the bunkhouses where most of the men slept and at the far end, the stables and barn. Various other outbuildings dotted the landscape, and Percy knew there were more temporary shelters spread around the lumbering area.

She marched up one side of the street, making a mental note that one day she would visit Travis Gates in his office. In that professional setting, she would tell him what she needed and her plans for improving the diet of the men over the next year or so. No doubt he would be surprised to hear her talking in terms of next year; she was almost surprised herself. But she was determined to make this job work, despite the odds against it. And to do that, she had to think about the future in a way that sounded real.

Percy reached the stables, crossed the street, and started back down the other direction. Halfway back to the mess hall, she heard her name and looked up. Lacey Gates stood a few feet beyond her with a small boy in her arms.

"Good morning!" Lacey called.

"Good morning," Percy answered.

"I'm glad to see you out. I'm sure you've been busy getting settled in, but I was hoping we would have a chance to get better acquainted."

"Thank you for your unexpected hospitality on my arrival," Percy said sincerely.

"My porch is your porch," Lacey answered lightly, "any time you get hit on the head. How is your head?"

Percy touched her fingers to the spot that had been bleeding. "I'm quite recovered. It wasn't really so bad after the bleeding stopped."

"I'll be sure to tell Josh. He's been wondering."

"Oh, has he?"

"Yes. But he seemed hesitant to make a pest of himself."

"I was grateful for his help," Percy said, knowing that she had not acted very grateful on the day of her arrival or the time that Josh had come to check on her.

"This is my son, Caleb," Lacey said, turning the toddler on her hip to face Percy. "He's three."

"And you have an older one?"

"Adam. He's six. He's at my friend Abby's house."

"Abby. So that's her name. I've seen you weeding your garden together."

Lacey nodded. "I'm afraid we may have planted a bigger plot this year than we can handle. But the children are getting old enough to learn a bit about gardening. We'll soon put Nathan and Adam to work."

"It's nice that the kids have each other to play with," Percy remarked.

"Yes," Lacey agreed quickly, "and it's nice that they live so near each other. Abby and I had to go through a lot more trouble to see each other when we were small."

Percy perked up. "How long have you known Abby?"

"Nearly twenty years," Lacey answered, "since we were about nine."

"I had no idea anyone had been living in this camp so long."

Lacey laughed. "It wasn't this way twenty years ago. When Abby's father and mother moved here and brought her along, everyone thought it was scandalous. But I was delighted. I lived over at the lighthouse, several miles away. I had four brothers and no sisters. Abby and I were bosom friends as soon as we laid eyes on each other."

"And now you both live here, as neighbors."

Lacey laughed again. "When we were thirteen, we promised each other we would never marry lumberjacks. We were going to follow our dreams to the big city. But here we are—and very happy."

"It's ironic," Percy said. "I grew up in a city with thousands of people around me, and I can't think of anyone that I've known for twenty years."

"No one?"

"No, not anyone."

"Surely you must have some family, perhaps cousins or other relatives?"

Percy shook her head.

"I have cousins scattered around the state," Lacey went on. "Some of them came to visit us in the lighthouse, but that hardly ever happened. It was too hard to get to us in those days. If anyone came, they had to stay for weeks or months. We visited my grandmother in Milwaukee a few times when I was a child. I suppose I have other relatives that I don't even know about. You probably do, too." Lacey looked at Percy expectantly.

Percy shrugged. Why was Lacey so interested in her family tree? She did not offer any further information.

"I'm glad I caught you out and about," Lacey said brightly. "Travis tells me you have the evening off."

"Yes, that's right."

"Do you have plans?" Lacey said, grinning.

Percy could not help but laugh. "Well, it will be difficult to choose among the many entertaining options available to me. I thought I might take a hike and carry a picnic supper."

"Let me make you an offer you can't refuse."

"What would that be?"

"Come to our house for supper. You've already seen the back porch. Now you can see the rest of the house."

Percy's mind formed the words to decline the invitation, but before she could get them out, her heart overwhelmed her. She was lonelier than she wanted to admit. "I would love to do that," she said. "What can I bring?"

"You cook for fifty men twice a day and pack a lunch for them to take to the work site. I don't think you need to worry about bringing anything to our table."

"Perhaps one day I'll be able to return the favor," Percy said. "In the meantime, it would be delightful just to sit down to a nice meal without having to multiply a recipe times ten."

"We'll see you about six o'clock. That will give you time for a late afternoon hike, if you still want one."

"Thank you. I think I will try to do a bit of exploring."

"Stay to the trails, and you won't get lost. Most of them lead to places where the lumber has been cleared."

"I'll be sure to be careful."

Caleb's patience wore out and he squirmed to be put down. "Let's go, Mama," he said.

"Okay, Caleb. We'll go. Say good-bye to Miss Morgan."

"Good-bye, Miss Morgan," Caleb said obediently, already pumping his little legs to move down the street.

Percy waved good-bye and stood still for a moment. She was caught off guard by what had just transpired. She had not realized how anxious she was to know some of the other people in the camp, but like a neglected orphan, she found herself warming to Lacey's overtures of friendship. If there were others like Lacey, the camp would not be such a difficult place to live, after all.

Chapter 9

Percy wished for a mirror. Surely no one would think her vain for wanting to be sure her buttons were straight and her hair in place. But she had no mirror in her small room and she would have to do the best she could to dress for dinner at the Gates house. Percy had not seen an image of herself for several weeks, but from the way her sky blue dress fit her around the waist, she could tell she had lost weight. Hoping that her face did not look too thin, she pinched her cheeks for color.

The invitation to dinner had brought more nervousness than Percy thought reasonable. Why was her stomach so unsettled? Perhaps it was because she wondered if Joshua Wells would also be at dinner. Lacey had not said anything about Josh when she issued the invitation, but Percy knew he lived there and supposed he took his meals there much of the time.

She wore her hair flowing freely around her shoulders. She hardly ever let it hang loose; it was too much in the way of her work. And in the city, where she had grown up, a young woman of twenty-one would be thought childish if she let her hair hang free. But Percy was not in a city and she was in a lumber camp. Her intuition told her that city expectations would not necessarily carry over to this setting. She knew that her jet black hair was her most striking feature, and she wanted to feel pretty tonight. She stroked through her hair one last time, smoothed her skirt, and was ready to leave.

Down the street a few minutes later, she slowly ascended the steps of Lacey's front porch. It was swept clean, with two bowls of pink petunias brightening the corners. Percy felt welcome, but the swarm of butterflies in her stomach doubled. She raised her hand to knock, but the front door swung open before she could.

"You're the lady from the street," announced a child whom Percy presumed to be Adam. She had already met Caleb, and this boy was clearly older.

"And you're the boy with the sore throat," Percy retorted playfully.

Adam scowled. "It's not sore anymore."

"And I'm not in the street anymore," Percy said. "Your mother invited me to dinner."

"We're having mashed potatoes."

"Delicious. Mashed potatoes and. . . ?"

"What do you mean?"

"Mashed potatoes and what else? No one eats just mashed potatoes."

"I do."

Lacey appeared behind her son. "Adam, let's invite Miss Morgan inside."

Adam hesitated a moment, glanced at his mother, and complied. "Please come in, Miss Morgan." He shuffled to one side and turned to walk away.

"We're working on manners," Lacey said softly as she gestured that Percy should enter.

Percy chuckled. "How about coming around the mess hall one evening with your lessons in manners?"

Lacey smiled. "I want to make sure Adam learns his before he gets any ideas about becoming a lumberjack."

"You don't like lumberjacks?"

"I married one," Lacey answered. "It's not the occupation so much as the setting. Standards do seem to get lax way up here. I was rather hoping that the presence of a pretty, unattached young woman would influence some of the men to be more mindful."

They walked through the house toward the kitchen.

"I suppose some of them have," Percy said. "One or two of them are trying to muster the courage to speak a flattering word to me. I see it in their eyes."

Lacey laughed aloud.

"Can I help you in the kitchen?" Percy asked. "I'm very good at mashing potatoes."

"Yes, but you do it for fifty people. There will only be six of us tonight."

Six, thought Percy. Lacey, Travis, their two sons, and herself would make five. So Josh would be there, after all.

"Besides," Lacey continued, "I invited you here to give you a break from the kitchen. The food is almost ready. I'm just waiting for Travis and Josh to come through the door."

As if on cue, the front door opened again, and the two men entered. Joshua set his black medical bag on the floor next to the door in a way that seemed habitual. "Miss Morgan, what a delightful surprise," he said. His eyes caught hers with sincerity.

"Your sister invited me to dinner when we met in the street this morning," Percy answered. She liked his eyes. An ordinary shade of brown, they nevertheless had a shining quality that caught her by surprise each time she saw them.

"I'm so glad she did."

"Travis," Lacey said, "if you can help the boys wash up, we'll be ready to eat."

"On my way," Travis said, and headed for the stairs.

"Why don't you two go on into the dining room," Lacey said. "I'll just see to the food."

Josh put his hand lightly on Percy's elbow and steered her toward the dining room.

"I see you had your medical bag with you," Percy said. "Was there an emergency today?"

Josh shook his head as he pulled out Percy's chair. He had learned his city habits well. She seated herself as gracefully as she could.

"No emergency. I make rounds a couple of times a month in some of the other places on the peninsula where people are beginning to settle. I was gone overnight, actually. It's a rather long circuit to cover in one day."

"Then you must be exhausted."

"I'm ready for a good hot meal, that's certain." Josh took his place beside Percy as Travis and the boys made their noisy entrance. Travis settled them smoothly, and the boys sat with their hands in their laps waiting for food. Lacey came in with a platter of sliced ham and the potatoes, and a promise to return with the peas and biscuits.

The boys sat across from Percy and Josh, and Lacey and Travis sat at the ends of the table. Suddenly, Percy was caught with her eyes open as everyone else closed theirs and lowered their heads. Awkwardly, she did the same.

"Father God," Travis said smoothly, "we're grateful for the gifts that You bring us every day, and tonight we're especially grateful for the gift of having Miss Morgan with us. Thank You for bringing her to our community, and bless the time that we have visiting with her tonight. Amen."

Percy felt the blush rising in her cheeks. No one had ever thanked God for her presence before.

"You like that word 'community,' don't you?" Josh said to Travis as he passed the mashed potatoes to Percy.

"Don't you?" Travis retorted.

"It's a fine word," Josh agreed, "especially for a place like this."

"What do you mean?" Percy asked. "A place like this?"

"Every year we look less and less like a lumber camp, but we're not really a town. 'Community' is a good in-between word."

Percy served herself some peas and shrugged. "I hear the men in the mess hall talking about this sometimes. But I don't see what all the fuss is about."

Josh raised an eyebrow.

"What I mean is," Percy continued, "if the camp...the community...is meant to become a town, it will. There won't be any way to stop it."

"So you believe in God's will, one way or the other?" asked Travis.

"I don't know very much about God's will," Percy was quick to say. "I don't know very much about God at all. I just believe that some things are out of our control. No matter how much we try to control a situation, things happen. There's no stopping it."

Lacey put a spoonful of peas on Caleb's plate, despite his protest. Then she turned to Percy. "Let me ask you another question. Do you think that you can make something happen if you want to badly enough?"

Percy was quiet. "No, I don't think so," she finally said softly. "What happens, happens."

"Can God make something happen?" Josh asked.

Percy shrugged. "I don't know. I suppose He could if He cares. But God is...I don't know if God cares." She regretted the words as soon as she spoke them.

"I want more mashed potatoes, please," Adam said as politely as he could manage. "Please pass them to me. I can serve myself."

Travis set the bowl in front of Adam, who plopped an enormous mound of potatoes on his plate. Then he added a tiny bit more...and just a little more.

"There. That's enough," he announced.

Everyone laughed.

Percy was glad for the change in subject. She had not meant to express her doubts about God aloud in a roomful of strangers.

"How are you liking your work, Miss Morgan?" Josh asked.

"I'm slowly getting squared away," she answered, relieved that he did not pursue her earlier remarks.

"The men are raving about your cooking," Travis reported, "behind your back, of course."

"Of course," Percy echoed, smiling. "To tell me to my face would be almost like being glad I came."

"You have a good attitude. I appreciate that."

"I have a lot of ideas for how we could give the men a better diet," Percy said. "I would like to plant a vegetable garden, but it would have to be rather large to feed fifty men. We could plant herbs, too, so everything would not taste so bland. And if I had a second pair of hands in the kitchen at mealtime, I could offer more variety."

"Didn't the cook used to have an assistant?" Lacey asked.

Travis nodded. "No one seems to want the job right now."

"Those silly men don't want to be told what to do by a woman," Lacey said irritably.

Travis's eyes twinkled. "They'll never manage marriage if they don't get over that."

"What about one of the new brides?" Josh suggested. "Maybe both of them."

Lacey shook her head. "What they need is friendship, not more work. Keeping house in those lean-tos is no picnic, and they both hope to begin building soon."

"Well, perhaps I'll ask around among the men again," Travis said. "Percy should have help."

"That was easier than I thought," Percy said pleasantly.

"Getting Travis to agree with you is not the hard part," Josh reminded her. "We still have to find someone who would like the job."

"Until we do, I'll press on by myself. I'm going to mark off a garden plot tomorrow."

Percy looked across at Adam and burst out laughing. He had energetically attacked his mound of potatoes and had eaten a good portion of it. But a V-shaped clump hung from his chin like a white beard. "Perhaps when this community becomes a town, you'll find a good barber for your son."

Chapter 10

Not a scoop of mashed potatoes remained in the bowl, and the bread basket was empty, but there were some peas left. Everyone had eaten their fill and the boys had wandered into the living room to play.

"This is a beautiful home," Percy remarked to her hostess. "And you've decorated it wonderfully. You have a flair for the artistic."

"Thank you," Lacey said, "but most of the credit belongs to my husband and my friend Abby's husband. They built it and they wouldn't settle for anything less than the best in craftsmanship."

"I can see that they are skilled. We had a carved crown molding like this in the house I grew up in, and my father always told people it had come from Europe."

"Ah, your secret is out," Travis said, smiling. "You're a civilized city girl, after all. Do you miss all the finery?"

"I'm quite content to be here," Percy said sincerely, without further explanation about what had brought her to the camp.

"Do your parents still live in that home?" Lacey asked.

Percy hesitated a split second. "No," she finally said, "they've moved on." She lifted her eyes to the large dining room windows dressed with a rich burgundy tapestry. "Did you make these draperies yourself?"

"Yes, she did," Travis answered proudly for his wife. "My mother-in-law, before she passed away, made sure Lacey could do just about anything."

"She just thought of it as doing what was necessary," Lacey said.

Percy was relieved that her question about the draperies had successfully shifted the focus of conversation. What had possessed her to bring up her childhood home in the first place? Danger lurked in places where she began to feel comfortable. She would have to be more careful.

"What else did she teach you?" Percy asked, trying to make sure the conversation did not circle back to her family.

"Cooking, gardening, wood chopping. She did it all."

"Did she grow up on a farm?"

"No, actually she was a city girl, too, like you. My father wooed her up here to the end of the world. Thirty years ago, there was very little this far north except the lighthouse. We had to be even more self-sufficient than we are now."

"Who taught her how to get along so well?"

"Experience," Lacey answered quickly. "Especially after she started having children, she had to learn very quickly."

"Don't forget that your mother is also the one who made a teacher out of you," Travis said.

He turned to Percy. "Mary Wells taught all five of her children, and they are five of the most well-rounded people I know."

"I think Lacey deserves the credit for Micah's education," Joshua said. "She helped a lot when Micah was small and then picked up where Mama had left off when she died. But Mama probably would have insisted on teaching me a medical course if she had not become ill and died before I was ready for medical school."

Percy turned to Josh and smiled. "She sounds like a wonderful mother." Images of her own mother floated through her mind, a mother who knew very little about what the private tutors might be teaching her daughters and who was as isolated from realities of the world as if she had lived in a lighthouse.

"Mama was very strict," Josh was saying. "We did not always appreciate that as we were growing up, but I can see now that it gave us the determination that we needed to do what we're doing now."

"And what exactly are you doing now?" Percy teased.

"Building a town," Josh declared emphatically.

"Or at the very least a community," Travis added. "Right now, I would like a community with a softer chair." He pushed back from the table.

"Go on into the living room," Lacey said, as she stood and began stacking plates. "Get comfortable, and I'll bring coffee."

"I'll help you," Percy offered. She picked up the empty mashed potatoes bowl. "I guess we don't have to worry much about the leftovers."

Lacey laughed. "Adam's favorite food. He won't be pleased when he finds out that there are enough peas left to have them again tomorrow."

"Are these from your garden?" Percy asked as they walked with their loads toward the kitchen.

"I canned them last year," Lacey explained. "I can't wait for this year's crop to be ready. There's nothing like sugar snap peas, fresh from the pod."

"Perhaps you'll help me plant my garden," Percy said hopefully. "I've never actually had a vegetable garden before."

Lacey burst out laughing. She set her armful of plates beside the sink. "You sounded like such an expert when you asked Travis about putting in a garden."

Percy shook her head. "No expert, just being sensible. I have to have more than an occasional ear of corn if I'm going to cook properly, and a vegetable and herb garden seems like the most economical way to improve the diet for the men in the long run."

"You're right about that. We can get a lot of food in cans now, but fresh is always so nice. Travis should be impressed that you are thinking ahead and trying to keep costs down at the same time."

"So you'll help me?"

"Yes, I'll be delighted to help, and I'll tell Abby that she's got to help, too."

"Can you mark it off with me in the morning?"

"Certainly."

"Good. Then I just need to find someone willing to work with me to look after it."

Lacey took the serving dishes from Percy's hand. "Go on into the living room."

"But I'll be happy to help you clean up," Percy said.

"No thanks. Not now, at least. I'll make coffee and join you in a few minutes."

Percy could see that Lacey was not one to be argued with. She turned to go into the living room. She stood under the hand-carved crown molding and soaked up the scene before her eyes.

Travis sat in a chair that was obviously his favorite, his feet up on an ottoman, with a book in his lap. But he was not reading it. He was watching Joshua and the boys. Josh sat cross-legged on one side of a checkerboard, while Adam squirmed around on the other side.

"You've got me now," Josh said dramatically. "I don't know how I'll ever get myself out of this predicament."

Adam howled with pleasure.

"My turn, my turn," Caleb insisted.

"You're not playing," Adam said emphatically.

"Of course he is," Josh said, grabbing Caleb and pulling him into his lap. "If I ever needed someone on my team, it's now."

Caleb gave his brother a smug, satisfied look.

"What shall we do, Caleb?" Josh asked. "Should we move this one or that one?"

The three-year-old boy put a pudgy finger on a red checker. "This one."

"This one? Are you sure?"

Caleb nodded.

"All right, we'll move this one." Josh slid the checker diagonally one space.

Adam whooped and he swept down his hands to double jump his uncle and come in for a king.

Caleb turned around and patted his uncle's head. "It's okay, Uncle Josh. Next time."

"That's right. We'll get him next time."

The lump in Percy's throat was so big she could barely swallow. What a wonderful picture of a man with his children—only these were not Joshua's sons, but his nephews. She could not imagine he could be any better with them if they were his own. Travis looked on with a smile, much more interested in his sons than his book.

The house she had grown up in may have had hand-carved European crown moldings and expensive arrangements of fine furniture, but it did not have what she saw before her eyes right now. She herself had learned to play checkers by reading a book and deciphering the rules and illustrations on her own. She had practiced against herself until she could predict all possibilities. But her father would never have come home from the bank and then spend his evening playing checkers with young children, much less seek obviously futile advice from a three-year-old boy. He rarely even stayed in the same room with his daughters after the somber, formal evening meal, preferring instead to withdraw to his study until long after Percy and her sister had been sent upstairs to bed. Percy had learned at a very young age not to disturb her father when he went into his study. But that was then, and this was now. What did it matter, anyway? she asked herself.

"Can we play again?" Adam asked. He looked at his uncle with the same hopeful brown eyes that Josh had.

"Sure, we can play again," Josh answered. "This time, Caleb gets to make the first move. Maybe we'll be luckier."

They started setting up the game and Percy took a step forward. "Who taught you how to play checkers?" she asked Josh teasingly.

"My father," he answered. "But it looks like I could use a few more lessons."

Adam did not want to stop playing, so he set up one game after another. Percy could not help but be drawn into the competition and, by the time they were finished with dessert and coffee, Percy was sitting in for Josh, having proved herself to be a worthy opponent for Adam.

As Percy played, though, she kept one ear cocked to the adult conversation. Travis was mulling over whom he might ask to work in the kitchen with Percy. Josh was pressing to move forward with some new construction, following Peter's latest drawings. So far the people responsible for the lumbering business were responsible for the growing community, Josh remarked. But soon the community would need its own mayor. The people who lived in the town should have some say in how it developed.

Percy had no plans to leave any time soon, but, at the same time, she had not thought about the future of the camp. She wondered if she would ever be personally interested in how it developed.

The time came when Percy faced Josh over the checkerboard, with everyone else cheering over their competition. With most of the pieces removed from the board, she knew she had him cornered before any one figured out the strategy. She could make a subtle move and lose the game graciously in another three or four moves or she could easily win it within three moves. As she contemplated her choice, Percy glanced at Josh's gentle face and comfortable smile. He was a good, kind man who deserved to win. But she had earned this win; she had not practiced by herself all those years for nothing! So she made the move that would bring her victory, but Josh did not immediately realize the impending defeat. When it came, though, he groaned but accepted it graciously, catching her eye with the twinkle in his.

Percy lingered in the warmth of the Gates home as long as she dared without being impolite. The butterflies in her stomach had long ago disappeared. Even as she moved her feet down the porch steps and across the street, she felt the reluctance of her body to leave the congenial, welcome atmosphere of that simple living room. At the back of the mess hall, she sighed and then opened the narrow door to her little room. She thought of Lacey's rich burgundy draperies. Perhaps after the garden was in, she would ask Lacey to teach her to sew. If she could learn to cook as well as she did out of necessity, she might also conquer sewing.

She removed her dress, hung it on a peg, and pulled her simple cotton nightdress over her head. For so many years, she had not allowed herself the luxury of an evening like this one. It was not a fancy evening—they had eaten simple food and played simple games—but it was the best evening Percy Morgan had had for years. She had felt welcome—and she had almost forgotten how good that could feel.

Chapter 11

The promise of a real summer infused the air. As Percy bent over the washtub behind the mess hall, scrubbing her kitchen towels and rags and the aprons that protected her few dresses, sweat trickled down her temples. In an attempt to keep the sweat from dripping down her neck, she scrunched up one side of her face, but without her hands free, there was little she could do to control the rivulets of perspiration. Even before plunging her hands into the scalding wash water, the close, humid air had Percy feeling like a shriveled human blister, and it had curled her hair in sticky knots around her face. She imagined that with a proper brushing, the hair framing her face could be arranged in a very flattering way on a day like this. But she had no time for brushing and she still had no mirror in her room. She certainly did not feel very attractive, hunched over a wash basin with her hair roughly knotted at the back of her neck to keep it out of her way, her sleeves shoved up past her elbows, and her blouse unbuttoned at the neck to catch the rare hint of a breeze.

Percy had not expected such miserable weather for late spring; actually, she was not prepared for it at all. Lacey told her that this was just the beginning of a brutal summer. Lacey's description of the extreme summer weather had seemed exaggerated to Percy and she had been determined not to be frightened off by it. Surely the proximity to water would have some cooling effect. Where Percy came from, being near the ocean made all the difference. But Lacey was proving to be right; Percy should never have doubted the word of someone who had spent twenty-eight years living here. She longed for a walk along the water, closer to the areas where the men were out logging. Perhaps then she could hope for a flutter of a breeze. Between the hot kitchen and the labor of laundry, Percy found little relief from the heat and humidity. She could only imagine what it must be like for the men, laboring unsheltered in the hot sun for long hours each day. Each night they returned to the mess hall, wilted and somber, until refreshed by nourishment and cold drinks.

If this was only the beginning, Percy hated to think what the rest of the summer might be like. It certainly would not remind her of the summers of her childhood. There would be no leisurely games of croquet on the front lawn. Actually, no one in the lumber camp had a front lawn, least of all the mess hall where Percy's cramped quarters were squeezed. There would be no tall glasses of lemonade carried out to her by the family cook, no fanciful games with her little sister under the shade of a spreading oak tree, no books to tickle her imagination. This summer would be work, all work, and Percy could not allow herself to imagine anything different.

True to her word, Lacey helped Percy mark off a vegetable garden the day after their dinner together. While Lacey and Abby had put in their garden weeks ago, Lacey was quite optimistic that it was not too late for Percy to grow a few things, if she was careful what she planted. The garden plot was not large. Percy had wanted a plot four times as large and Lacey had laughed aloud and told Percy that she was not talking about a garden but a farm. Percy had argued that she needed a large plot in order to raise enough vegetables for all the men, but Lacey insisted that what Percy had in mind would be far more work than one person could handle, even if that person was the stubborn Percy Morgan. Reluctantly, Percy yielded to Lacey's advice. She had cornered off one section for growing herbs; even if she could not produce enough vegetables to feed fifty men all winter, she could at least flavor the food she prepared with more variety.

As much as Percy hated to admit it, Lacey's caution made sense. This was her first garden, after all, and perhaps there was more to the task than simply planting, watering, and enjoying the sun. At the moment, she did not find the sun very enjoyable and would have preferred to water herself rather than vegetables. Once the garden was planted, she would be obligated to weed it, also. Already Percy was planning how she might alter her routine in order to work the garden in the cooler evening.

In the past, she had not thought too much about gardens. Her own mother had spent many summer days on a lounge chair in the middle of a flower garden, but as Percy reflected on the memory, she realized she had never seen her mother actually work in the garden. A quiet, unobtrusive older man came in periodically to tend to the garden. He produced beautiful, exotic flowers that Percy's mother proudly displayed as if they were the work of her own hands. As she was growing up, it had never occurred to Percy to wonder where her vegetables came from, and she was never curious where the cook had gotten them from in the first place. In fact, she spent much of her childhood wishing her vegetables would go away.

Percy's mother had not done a lot of the things that Percy now did every day. It was a good thing that she had occasionally watched when the wash was done, Percy reflected, for she had turned out not to be completely helpless. Her observation skills and quick intelligence put her in good stead when she had to learn something new rapidly and furtively.

Percy squinted at the sun and realized immediately that she had to return to the stifling kitchen because the men would be appearing for their evening meal any moment. She abandoned the wash, thinking that she might return to it later in the evening when it might be cooler anyway.

Inside the mess hall, Percy barely got the food off the stove and onto the large serving platters before the men came tumbling in. After a quiet day with her own thoughts, their noise jolted her. Today they entered with even more rambunctiousness than usual, and Percy immediately realized that it was not friendly camaraderie. The voices were pitched loud and boisterous. Her eyes wide and alert, she pushed through the swinging doors that led from the kitchen to the main dining room. The food line had begun to form, and Percy could see immediately that the men in line were those who preferred quiet and solitude at the end of the day. They were not likely to be involved in the argument growing rapidly behind them.

Quickly, Percy began to serve food. Knowing that she had plenty, she heaped large servings on the plates. Normally she simply set out a stack of plates and let the men serve themselves. Today she tried to create a diversion of her own, keeping one eye on the men huddled by the door who seemed not to be interested in eating. Troy Wilger's face was as red as she had ever seen it, and Carson Gregory had his nose right up against Troy's.

"I'm afraid I'm not used to the heat and humidity you have here," Percy said loudly and with contrived cheerfulness. "I can't imagine how you men have the stamina to work in the heat all day long."

Two men quietly took their plates and headed for a table in the corner. No one responded to Percy's attempt at conversation.

"It will be quite a challenge for me," she continued, even more loudly, "to come up with some meals that will refresh you when you come in for supper."

The shuffling by the door swelled alarmingly. Men lined up behind Troy and Carson.

"What's going on?" Percy finally asked quietly as Matt Harden came through the line. "What are they so upset about?"

Matt scowled. "It's this town business. Peter Regals was out at the site today talking the way he always does."

"What do you mean?" Percy had barely met Abby's husband, but he had not struck her as someone who would incite a crowd. Josh and Lacey seemed to like Peter's ideas.

"He had some crazy ideas about a town government," Matt explained reluctantly. "Something about how everyone should have a say in how things are done around here."

"Isn't that good?" Percy asked. She gave Matt an extra scoop of mashed potatoes.

Matt shrugged. "Peter says the family that owns the lumber company is not trying to own us body and soul. A real town up here would be good for all of us, but some of the others, well, they're not convinced."

"No?"

He shook his head. "They figure Peter and his father-in-law and Travis Gates will run things the way they want them, no matter what the rest of us think."

The smack of a fist against a jaw interrupted their conversation. Carson Gregory stumbled and fell back against a row of chairs, scattering them with a clatter. Immediately, he scrambled to his feet and charged at Troy Wilger. With his head bent low, Carson slammed into Troy's midsection, but the hefty tall man barely moved under the impact of the smaller, lighter man. Instead, the two of them entwined their arms and pushed and twisted their way across the room. In only a few seconds they had broken through the food line and began circling the food table. Their tussle showed no sign of letting up; determination burned in both their faces.

"Stop that right now!" Percy demanded, but they ignored her.

The men in line, not wanting to heighten the hostility, stepped back. The entourage surrounding Troy and Carson followed the struggling pair across the room and crowded around the table. Percy was forced to leap out of the way herself.

Troy got the upper hand and planted his massive hands firmly on Carson's shoulders. With one great shove, Troy threw Carson through the air. Carson came down with a crash on the serving table, which gave way and split down the middle. Percy's serving dishes clattered to the floor, spilling chicken and potatoes. The pies she had labored over all afternoon splattered the floor and were flattened as Carson landed on top of them.

Ignoring his bleeding lip and the apples and potatoes stuck to his backside, Carson scrambled to his feet once again and lurched at Troy. Troy deftly stepped out of the way, and the angry Carson plunged into another row of chairs. The men watching began to cheer. Carson came up swinging. Clearly, there was no way he could win a fight against Troy Wilger, but Percy could see the fire in his eyes and he was not about to give up. Around her, men laughed and cheered, oblivious to the fact that their own meals had been lost to a fight that most of them cared little about.

Percy whirled around, dashed into the kitchen, and returned with her heaviest iron pot and spoon. Fiercely she banged the pot like a drum. Some of the men began to chuckle at her, but she ignored them. Using the pot as a shield, she ventured toward Troy and Carson. One way or another, she was going to stop this fight.

Her opening came and she took it. She aimed low. With all her might, she slammed her heavy metal spoon into Troy Wilger's kneecap. He stopped and stared at her. Knowing that he was more likely startled than actually hurt, she wasted no time making her point.

"I don't care whether this is a town or not," she shouted. "I do know that it is not a zoo, and I will not have you acting like wild animals in the middle of my dining room."

Percy glared first at Troy, then at Carson. "I made one supper tonight and I don't intend to make another one. The two of you can explain to your buddies why they have to go to bed hungry tonight. As for me, I'm finished for the day!" She threw down her pot and let it clatter and roll across the floor; it echoed rancorously around the room. "I'm going out. When I come back, I expect that this mess the two of you have created will be cleaned up. I'd better not find a sliver of apple on this floor or a splinter of wood from the table you ruined. Clean it up! I mean it!"

She spun around and marched out the front door, feeling the stares that followed her on the back of her hot neck but refusing to acknowledge them.

Outside the door, she was just ready to let her shoulders sag with the weight and frustration she really felt when she spotted Josh Wells coming around the corner.

"What's going on?" he asked. "What's all the commotion?"

Percy kept her shoulders rigid and her head high. Without breaking stride, she replied, "Nothing I can't handle."

Chapter 12

Percy stayed away for long, exhausting hours; she certainly was in no hurry to return to the mess hall and face the remains of the chaos to which she may have contributed. The evening was warm and sticky, so she had no need for shelter. From her perch on a boulder tucked at the edge of the woods, she could see the dim lights of Lacey and Travis's home. Percy knew she would be welcome there, but somehow the thought of being with other people exhausted her. Besides, she did not want Travis to charge over and let the men believe she had tattled on them. No doubt Josh had gone into the dining hall to see why she had flown out the way she did. Travis and Lacey would hear about the fiasco soon enough. Instead, she sat alone, her arms around her knees, and stared up at the night sky.

What was out there? she wondered. Were the planets real? Could they really be hanging in the black space that overwhelmed her? Was God real? Was He out there somewhere? Mrs. Higgins, her Sunday school teacher for most of her childhood, had assured Percy and the rest of the class that God was indeed out there. But Percy was not so sure. If He was, then why had her life taken the turns it had? Why had she ended up breaking up fistfights in an obscure place instead of entertaining suitors in a more genteel setting?

Eventually Percy trudged back up to the mess hall. In her haste to leave, she had not thought to take a lantern with her, and she was guided only by the stars she found so mysterious. With a grimace on her face and reluctance in her hands, she pulled the door open and entered. Blackness greeted her, just as deep as the blackness outside. She crept along the side wall to a window ledge where she knew she would find a candle to light. By its dim flame, she peered around the large room. The tables were upright with chairs pushed in neatly. The serving table, splintered by Carson Gregory's smashing fall, had been removed. Pots, platters, and leftover food were gone from sight. The room looked as if nothing unusual had happened that night—except that one table was missing. With a sigh of disbelief and relief, Percy crept through the immaculate kitchen and went to bed.

In the morning, Percy served breakfast as usual and did not speak of the previous evening. Troy Wilger and Carson Gregory clearly avoided her, coming to the newly designated serving table to pick up a plate of pancakes and staying only as briefly as necessary. Percy set a platter of fresh pancakes in front of Troy but said nothing. The other men were reserved. Few lifted their eyes to Percy's. Her glare dared anyone to approach her.

Later, as Percy worked in the garden, meticulously preparing the ground for the vegetable seeds Travis would bring, Lacey approached with a grin on her face. While no one was speaking to Percy, apparently the men were speaking to each other. Troy and Carson's behavior was extreme, but expected, according to Lacey, and they had come to blows before. But no one had expected the spitfire that Percy had shown. Lacey found it hilarious that the men had complied with her demands that they clean up after themselves. According to what Lacey had heard from Josh, who had gone into the mess hall to investigate after passing Percy, Troy and Carson had done most of the cleanup work themselves. Percy was the talk of the town, so to speak.

But Percy did not want to be the talk of the town. She simply wanted peace and order in the dining hall. So, over the next few days, she proceeded with her usual routine, including the added task of tending to the garden. The dirt oozing between her fingers was strangely comforting, and keeping her fingers busy and her eyes focused helped to stem the swirling in her mind. Her nerves needed calming, especially today. She had accepted an invitation from Lacey to spend the early afternoon at the Gates home with Lacey, Abby, and Bridget and Moriah, the two young brides living in lean-tos while their husbands prepared to build homes. Abby's mother, the first woman to come to the lumber camp more than twenty years ago, would also join them. Percy had baked a pie, which was cooling in the kitchen. Knowing that she had only a few minutes left in solitude, she breathed deeply of the earthy air and exhaled slowly.

As she let out her sigh, Percy was jolted by the raucous sound of a horse and wagon careening down the street. What she heard was no gentle trot and the rhythm of turning wheels. It was a full gallop and the clatter of a wagon being stretched beyond its capacity. The shouting voices demanded immediate attention. Her heart thumping, Percy sprang to her feet and hustled around to the front of the mess hall.

"Where's Josh?" Matt Harden demanded. "Find Josh!" He dropped the reins and hurtled himself off the wagon bench. The horse seemed agitated, but he paid no attention.

"What's happened?" Percy asked urgently. She followed Matt as he hurried around to the back and then hopped up into the wagon bed.

"An accident with the saw," Matt answered. "It went out of control. He's hurt bad."

Matt huddled over the victim and Percy strained to see who the injured man was. She saw the ashen face of Troy Wilger.

Peter Regals was in the street now, and Travis Gates was right behind him, having left the office where they both spent their days.

"We have to find Josh," Matt repeated. "He's bleedin' bad."

"I'll go look for Josh," Percy offered. "He must be at Lacey's house."

Peter shook his head. "He's gone on one of his circuits. He left this morning."

Matt flashed a look of anxiety. "There can't be anybody who needs him as much as Troy does right now."

"He's been gone a couple of hours," Peter said. "I don't know if we can catch him."

"We have to try," Matt insisted. "That old mare of his is half blind. He can't have gone all that far in two hours if he was stopping to check on folks. He said he came back to doctor us, and right now Troy needs a doctor. Which way did he go?"

"He usually heads straight south first," Peter answered. "There's a woman in a little place along the harbor who's due to have a baby any day now. My guess is that he went to check on her."

"I know the place," Matt said. He grabbed at the wagon hitch and set the horse free. "Take him somewhere," he instructed. "Make him comfortable. I'll be back with Josh."

Matt jumped on the horse and galloped off. Peter scrambled up into the wagon and put his hand under Troy's head.

"Where is the wound?" Travis asked, unwrapping the blanket from around Troy.

"It's his leg," Peter exclaimed. "It's cut deeply. Someone had the good sense to tie a tourniquet above the wound."

"His clothes are drenched," Travis said. "He's already lost a lot of blood."

"What can we do?" Percy asked.

"Matt is right. We should take him somewhere and get him comfortable?"

"Where?"

"Wherever we take him, he'll have to stay awhile," Peter said. "He's going to need a lot of care."

"I'm afraid our back porch just won't do," Travis said. "Besides, it's too far up the street. Matt took the horse. We don't have time to fetch another one to hitch the wagon to."

Travis and Peter looked at each other, then at Percy. "We'll have to take him to the mess hall," Peter said. "We're right here in front of it."

"Yes, and there's plenty of water and clean rags," Travis said. "We can start trying to get him cleaned up so Josh can see what he's doing."

"The mess hall?" Percy echoed faintly.

"Percy," Travis said gently, "I'm afraid we're going to need your bed for a while."

"My bed?" Indignation rose within her. How dare they invade the only private space she had—and for Troy Wilger!

"I know it's an inconvenience," Travis said. "But right now, taking him there makes the most sense."

"You're right," Peter agreed. He placed his hands under Troy's shoulder. "Help me carry him. Percy, you get the door."

Numbly, she followed their instructions. She held open the door as Peter and Travis carried Troy as quickly and gently as possible, then she led the way back to her little room. They laid him on the bed.

"We need rags," Travis said, "and hot water. Do you have any on the stove?"

Percy rallied. Travis was right. The mess hall was well supplied to care for the injured man. "Yes, of course," she said. "I'll be right back." She scurried into the kitchen and scooped up a handful of dish towels, knowing that she might never again be able to use them in the kitchen. She filled a small pot with water and returned to the bedroom as quickly as she could. "Here, start with these. The water is not hot, but I'll put some on to heat."

"Troy!" Travis called loudly. "Troy, can you hear me?"

There was no response.

"He's out cold," Peter said. "He's lost too much blood. We've got to get these clothes off of him and make sure the bleeding has stopped. Percy, bring me your kitchen shears."

Once again Percy followed instructions. Then she returned to the kitchen long enough to stoke up the stove fire and pump water into a pot. Back in the bedroom, she found Peter and Travis slicing through the sticky mess of Troy's denim pants. She grimaced and her stomach lurched as they exposed the wound. The saw had cut deeply into Troy's thigh.

"How could this happen?" she asked.

"That doesn't matter right now," Peter answered. "We just have to take care of him and pray that Joshua gets here soon."

Percy's head spun as she looked at the clock on her bedroom wall. How much time had passed since Matt took off in search of Josh? It couldn't have been more than a few minutes, but it already felt like hours. A few minutes earlier, she had been anticipating a leisurely afternoon with the few other women around her. Now a man she strongly disliked was lying on her bed, helpless and at her mercy. In a moment, her life had changed.

She closed her eyes against the thought of what this change might mean. She had not yet recovered from the last time that her life had changed in an instant.

Where was Josh?

Chapter 13

For more than three hours, Peter, Travis, and Percy tended Troy Wilger, whose consciousness rose and fell at random intervals and endured only briefly. When he was awake, the unbearable pain and blood loss soon drove him to the respite of unconsciousness again. While he lay limp on the bed, Peter and Travis huddled over his wounds. They had cut away his soiled dungarees and stemmed the bleeding enough to loosen the tourniquet and restore circulation to the leg. The wound gaped open, ugly and vicious. The blood flow was no longer rapid, but the fact that it still seeped concerned everyone. They changed the cloths every few minutes. Percy was running out of clean rags to offer.

Peter and Travis speculated on the facts of the accident. Had Troy been working the saw and lost control? His years of experience made that seem unlikely. Was Carson Gregory on the other end of the saw and had he deliberately become aggressive? They hated to think Carson was capable of such maliciousness. Peter and Travis shook their heads in befuddlement, realizing the pointlessness of their speculation. They would have to wait until they could gather the facts. Besides, what they needed most right now was not an explanation but a doctor.

Every few minutes Percy restlessly raised her eyes to the door frame, hoping to see Josh. Several times one of the vigil keepers went outside to look down the street, hoping to catch sight of him and signal where he should come. Finally, Josh exploded through the front door. Percy heard his thundering steps as he crashed across the wooden planks of the mess hall floor. Her heart in her throat, she met him in the kitchen.

"What happened?" he asked urgently as he pushed his way past her.

"We're not sure. We thought Matt might have told you."

He shook his head. "There was no time. He only said that it was very bad."

"It is."

By this time Josh had squeezed into her little bedroom to see for himself. Travis and Peter lurched to their feet. With Troy on the bed and four people standing, the room was crowded. Josh pushed his way past the others and knelt at the side of the bed to examine the wound.

"Matt was right," he soon announced. "It's a serious wound."

"Will he lose the leg?" Peter asked anxiously.

Josh sighed. "I hope not. I'm going to try to sew it back together. Let's pray there's been no chance for gangrene to set in." He set his medical bag solidly on the floor beside him and swiftly opened it.

"How much help will you need?" Travis asked.

"I need one of you to stay," Josh answered without looking up. "It's too warm and dark and crowded in here with all of you here. Travis, you and Peter go find out what happened. Percy can stay with me."

Percy was about to protest, but Travis cut her off. "Good. I would like to ride out and see if anyone saw what happened. If I hear anything that leads me to think this was intentional—"

"Don't jump to conclusions," Peter warned. "Accidents happen, even to someone as experienced as Troy Wilger."

Travis blew out his breath. "You're right. But I do want to get the facts straight. If it was an accident, we want to be sure it won't happen to anyone else."

"Percy, I'm going to need better light," Josh said, ignoring the interchange between Travis and Peter. "See how many lamps you can round up."

"Of course," she choked out in response. "And I'll pull back the curtains as far as they'll go to let in the daylight."

"Yes, yes." Josh was fishing in his bag for supplies. "Has he been conscious at all?"

"A few times, but only briefly."

Travis and Peter had left and it was up to Percy to report on Troy's condition and care. She lit the light at the side of her bed and scraped the table across the floor closer to Josh.

"I have two more lamps in the kitchen," Percy said. "I'll get them."

Josh nodded but did not speak. His fingers gently probed the wound. When Percy returned with the extra lamps, he said, "You did a good job cleaning up the wound."

"Peter and Travis did that," Percy quickly clarified. "I just brought them water and clean rags."

Josh's eyes went briefly to the pile of blood-soaked rags in the corner of Percy's bedroom. The bedding was streaked with blood and the mud caked on Troy's clothing. Her counted cross stitch throw pillow was tossed haphazardly on the floor in the far corner. Travis and Peter had repositioned her trunk in order to sit on it, and when Josh arrived, he had shoved it out of the way. Now it sat cockeyed across the center of the room.

"I'm sure this is not quite the décor you had in mind for this room," he said.

Percy shrugged. "It'll clean up." Hours ago, she had resigned herself to the reality of what was happening, bizarre as it was.

"You're being a good sport about this invasion of your home."

Percy laughed. "I didn't really have a choice." She was caught off guard by Josh's reference to her room as her home for she had not yet come to think of it in that way. Although she had nowhere else to go, no other place to call home, and had no plans for leaving, she had not thought of this room as "home" in her own mind. Would she ever? Would she ever know the feeling of being at home again?

"It's a good thing he's unconscious," Josh said. "This is going to hurt."

"What if he wakes up?" Percy asked, suddenly panicked.

"Let's pray he doesn't. And if he does, we'll use ether. Look in my bag for a small pair of scissors," Josh instructed. "I'm going to start stitching. I'll need you to help cut every now and then. Get in here as close as you can so you can see what I'm doing, but don't block the light."

"But I'm not. . .I've never—"

"Percy, I need your help."

Josh's tone was clear. He was not leaving her any choice, any more than she had had a choice about any of the day's events so far. Swallowing hard, she knelt on the floor next to him, feeling his shoulder against hers.

Josh worked on the wound and Percy hardly breathed as she watched him sew the gaping hole together, layer by layer. At his instruction she snipped, cleaned, adjusted the light, wiped his brow.

Finally, they finished. Josh rocked back off his knees and sat on the floor cross-legged. He held his bloodied hands carefully out away from his body.

"Here," Percy said, thrusting a pot of water toward him. It was no longer hot, but at least Josh could rinse off. "I'll heat some more."

"Thank you," he said.

Percy put another pot of water on the stove. She returned to find Josh shaking the water off his hands and she handed him a clean towel.

"You could use some of this water yourself," he said.

For the first time, Percy looked at her own hands and clothing. The dress was a dark one and perhaps the blood stains would not show too badly after it was washed.

"I'm sorry about all this mess," Josh said.

"It's not your fault. I'm just glad you got here."

"I wish I had been here sooner. I could have made my rounds tomorrow."

"You can't possibly know when something is going to happen here. I heard you went to check on a pregnant woman."

He nodded. "She's fine, but her time is getting close."

"You did the right thing to go."

"I'm going to insist that Peter begin building the medical clinic he's been promising. He must start right away."

"Even if you had a clinic," Percy pointed out, "you would have been away."

"Perhaps. But you and Peter and Travis would have had a proper place to take Troy and the right supplies to help him until I got there. People have to know where to find help. Matt could have taken Troy straight to the clinic. And I need proper working conditions for situations like this." He gestured around. "Bright lights, a place to operate, a bed where a patient can recover and I can stay close."

A groan coming from the bed snatched their attention. Percy watched, her own eyes wide, as Troy opened his eyes and stared at her. "What's she doing here?" Troy asked gruffly.

Josh looked at Percy. "Has he spoken before?"

She shook her head. "This is the first time."

Josh turned back to Troy. "You should be thankful she's here. She's been very conscientious about taking care of you."

"I didn't ask her to."

"You were not in a position to ask anybody anything," Josh said harshly. "Just be grateful someone was around to look after you."

"That's your job," Troy muttered.

"You've been unconscious a long time," Josh said. "This is one time when you don't need an argument."

"What happened to my leg? It's throbbing with pain."

"The wound was very deep and I had to sew it back together. I'm hopeful for a full recovery."

"Where am I?" Troy grunted.

"In Miss Morgan's room, behind the mess hall," Josh informed him. "Another reason why you should be grateful to her."

"I want to get out of here."

Josh shook his head. "Oh, no. You're not going anywhere for quite a while."

Percy's heart lurched. What did Josh mean? Surely he was not going to leave Troy Wilger in her bedroom!

Josh looked at Percy. "I'm sorry, Percy. But he's very, very weak. I can't move him for several days, maybe even a week."

She gulped. "So you want him to stay here? In my room?"

Josh nodded. "I realize it's an extreme inconvenience, and I'll do my best to make it up to you. I'm not sure where we'll take him for the recovery period he's going to need, but at least for the time being, he must stay here. I'll stay with him much of the time, of course."

"But. . .but. . ." Percy could not put words around the cloud of feelings that swirled inside her mind. Joshua's reasons for usurping her room were quite legitimate, but to have the only private space she had taken from her seemed equally unreasonable.

"You can stay in my room at Lacey's house," Josh explained, as if reading her thoughts. "You can move in over there right now, if you want to. Plan to stay a few days. Travis can explain to Lacey, if he hasn't already. I'm sure she'll understand."

Percy hardly knew what to say.

"Why don't you get a few things together," Josh said softly, "at least enough for tonight. You can always come back for whatever you need."

Of course Josh was right, Percy told herself. What he suggested made perfect sense. She looked from Joshua to Troy, who was drifting back to sleep.

"Just take what you need," Josh repeated. "Don't worry about the mess. I promise it won't be here in the morning. Just go on over to Lacey's."

Percy gasped. "Oh, no! I was supposed to go to Lacey's hours ago. She invited me for the afternoon with the other women. I made a pie to take."

"You could still take it."

Percy glanced at the clock, suddenly mindful of time. "I barely have time to make supper for the men. They'll be here before I know it."

"I wish there were someone else who could do that for you," Josh said gently. "You must be exhausted." Josh's weary face, lined with worry about Troy Wilger, nevertheless looked at Percy with sincere concern.

Percy's knees were weak, her stomach lurching, her head pounding. Yes, she was exhausted. "I'll be fine," she said a little stiffly. "I'll check on that hot water so you can clean up properly. Then I've got to get back to work."

Chapter 14

Percy thought the men would never finish the biscuits and sausage gravy she had hastily thrown together for supper. Since she usually served that meal for breakfast, she got a few strange looks as men came through the line. But she had needed something that she could make without thinking, without calculating or multiplying ingredients. Finally, the last dishes were cleaned up and put away. Percy was exhausted.

Little noise emanated from the back room while she worked in the kitchen. Every so often she would hear the shuffle of Joshua's feet as he moved across the room and checked on Troy more closely. She had taken them food while the men ate. Troy was too weak to sit up for very long, but he ate hungrily and gratefully before dropping off to sleep again. Now Percy remembered that she had not gone back in to collect their dishes. Wiping her hands on her apron, she entered her bedroom-turned-clinic.

"I came for the dishes," she said softly, picking them up.

"I'm sorry," Josh responded. His haggard face showed the strain of the day. "I should have brought them out to you. I guess I dozed off myself."

"It's no problem. But I finished all the others, so I think I'll leave these till the morning."

"The biscuits were superb. I can see why the men like your cooking."

"Thank you."

"Troy is sleeping soundly. When you get your things together, I'll walk you over to Lacey's house."

"That's not necessary. I can manage."

"I'd like to do it."

Percy started to protest further, but stopped. He was looking at her with his clear, honest brown eyes and she believed him. "All right. I'll just be a few minutes."

Percy left the dishes in the sink, soaking, and tried to focus on what she would need overnight at Lacey's house. Opening up her trunk and extracting a nightgown and other personal items was awkward, although Josh discreetly kept his eyes turned in another direction. Percy quickly picked up a clean dress—she still wore the blood-soaked one—and her hairbrush, stuffed everything in a pillowcase, and announced she was ready to go.

Josh stood up wearily.

"You really should stay here," Percy said. "You're dead on your feet. Anyone can see that."

"The fresh air and a few moments of exercise will do me good," Josh said.

"Where are you going to sleep? I haven't got any other bedding to offer you."

"Remember the army cot on Lacey's back porch? I think there's room to squeeze it in here for the night."

Ah, so that was it, Percy thought. He hadn't really wanted to walk me down the street. He just wanted a cot. She swallowed the tart reply that leaped to her mind.

After a last glance at Troy, they left through the front door. The night was warm and sticky, as were all the nights now. But the sky was cloudless and glistened with the light of the galaxy.

"Look at that sky," Percy said amiably. If he insisted on walking her down the street, she might as well make the best of it.

"It's pretty amazing," Josh agreed. "Even more amazing is the thought that the Maker of that sky was in your bedroom today."

Percy looked at him sharply. "Are you talking about God?"

Josh was amused. "Do you know someone else who could make a night like this?"

Percy did not respond. She had been taught to believe that God made heaven and earth, and she supposed she did believe that. But that God would be involved in what had happened that day was beyond acceptance.

"I can imagine that looking after Troy was not an easy thing for you to do," Joshua said gently. "He's been openly hostile toward you more than once, and he can be quite a trouble-maker. Yet you took him in and cared for him."

"I didn't have much choice," Percy said abruptly. "Peter and Travis insisted on carrying him in there. And you insisted that I stay and pretend to be a nurse."

"You did very well," Josh said, smiling in the dark. "You could have just walked away and refused to help."

"The thought did occur to me," Percy admitted.

"You might have even thought that Troy Wilger got just what he deserved," Josh said.

Percy did not want to admit aloud that she had thought that exactly when she first saw who the wounded man was. "He does seem to be more trouble than he's worth sometimes," she said cautiously. "Travis and Peter seem to be quite indulgent of behavior that many would find unacceptable. For some reason, they must think he's worth all the trouble he causes."

Josh paused a moment before responding. "Aren't we all more trouble than we're worth? By God's grace, people put up with us, even love us sometimes."

Not me, Percy thought. *I have to earn my way every step that I take. I don't ask for an ounce of anyone's grace, much less God's.* Aloud, she said, "I prefer to believe that I don't go around causing chaos and havoc everywhere I go."

Josh laughed. "I would say that your mere arrival here a few weeks ago caused consider-able chaos and havoc."

Percy was glad the night hid her blush. "Don't misconstrue my words. That's not the same thing at all. I'm not anything like Troy Wilger. And neither are you."

"At some level, we all are," Josh said softly. "But thankfully, that's not the end of the story."

Percy wanted to continue her adamant protest against a comparison between her and Troy Wilger, but they had arrived at the Gates house. She pressed her lips together to compose herself and told herself she should have brought the pie still sitting in her kitchen. It might have made coming over here under these circumstances less awkward.

"Lacey and Travis will still be up," Joshua said confidently as they started up the front porch steps. "I'm sure by now Travis has explained to Lacey why you didn't show up with the pie this afternoon."

Lacey was in fact still up, reading by lamplight in the living room. She welcomed them warmly and listened with rapt attention to the report that Joshua gave on Troy's condition.

"Thank God he's going to be all right," Lacey said when Josh finished. "And thank God that you were there, Josh. Even just last year, he would have had to be taken south and the trip might have killed him. And Percy, thank you for staying to help Josh. Don't worry about what you missed this afternoon. We'll do it again soon."

"It may be a few days before I can move Troy," Josh explained to his sister. "I'm going to take the cot and stay over there with him. Percy can stay in my room, if that's all right with you."

"Of course it's all right. I'll go up now and change the bedding."

"Don't go to all that trouble," Percy protested. "If you give me the sheets, I'll change them."

"Don't be silly. You're my guest. Sit down and relax. There's tea on the stove if you want it."

Lacey flew into action and armed Josh with a pillow and blanket to go with his cot, and she had changed the sheets on Josh's bed before Percy knew what had happened. It seemed like only a few minutes later that Percy found herself standing in the middle of Joshua Wells's room, with the bed invitingly turned down and a lamp glowing softly on the nightstand. On top of the dresser Lacey had left a wash basin of steaming water. Percy glanced down at herself and began to peel the soiled dress off. Grateful for Lacey's thoughtfulness, she scrubbed her face and arms. By the time she pulled her nightgown over her head, she felt almost refreshed. She turned around to survey the room more carefully.

Percy had not seen this room on her previous visit to the house. By most standards, it was not a large room, but compared to her own quarters, it was enormous. The double-sized bed had a thick, lofty mattress and was covered by an intricate, colorful quilt. Percy wondered if the quilt was the handiwork of Lacey or her mother. A small bookcase in one corner held a range of medical books and another stack sat on the desk across from the bed. A plain pine wardrobe no doubt held the simple collection of clothing that belonged to Dr. Wells.

Josh kept his room neat, Percy concluded. Lacey had hardly been up here long enough to change the bedding, much less straighten up the room. No, Josh was orderly and thoughtful in private, just as he appeared around other people.

Percy sat on the edge of the bed and let out an involuntary squeal. It was softer than anything she had slept on for years, ever since. . . She refused to let her mind conjure up the picture of her childhood bed and the reason she had left it behind. But a moment of envy told her it would be difficult to go back to her own bed after a few nights here. She pulled her legs up from the floor and curled them under her in the softness. From her comfortable spot, Percy examined the nightstand. Another stack of medical books made her smile. Joshua surely was absorbed by his profession, even as limited as his practice was. Then she saw the Bible. It looked well thumbed and familiar, like her grandmother's Bible looked. So he was serious about that, too, Percy said to herself. Well, if he had lived the life she had lived, maybe he would have a different perspective.

She picked up the leather volume, not unlike her grandmother's Bible. It seemed to fall open naturally to the middle, to Psalm 27:1: "The Lord is my light and my salvation; whom shall I fear? the Lord is the strength of my life; of whom shall I be afraid?"

Percy read no further. She was afraid, even if she admitted it to no one but herself. But for this one night, perhaps she could feel safe. She turned away from the Bible and let herself sink into the glorious oblivion of the featherbed.

Chapter 15

Percy soon grew afraid that she would become too accustomed to the comforts of Joshua's room and Lacey's home. The bed was soft, the sheets clean and cool, the quilt an obvious heirloom.

She awoke the first morning well rested from sleeping in the spacious featherbed. In the haze of the early morning consciousness, for a moment she thought she was in her old bed, the one in the room with the wallpaper of neat rows of tiny blue flowers. She expected to open her eyes and see the eyelet curtains and the breakfast tray with tea and toast. But the confused memory lasted only a second. Percy jolted to full consciousness and bolted out of bed, sure that she had overslept. She darted across the room and threw back the plaid cotton—not white eyelet—curtains and judged the sun. Her heart slowed its pounding. She was not late. If anything, she had awakened early. Swiftly and quietly, she dressed and left the house.

At the end of the day, Joshua insisted that Troy, although much improved, was not ready to be moved. And there was no place to move him to anyway. As diplomatically as he could, Josh impressed upon Percy that her quarters would have to serve as the infirmary until Troy was strong enough to rest on his own in the bunkhouse. Josh would not predict how soon that might be, so Percy returned to the Gates house for another night. It was nearly bedtime for the Gates boys by the time Percy arrived, but Adam successfully pleaded permission for one game of checkers.

"Grandpa is coming tomorrow," Adam announced.

"Oh?" Percy responded as she slid her checker closer to Adam's side of the board.

"He's coming for lunch," Adam explained. "Why don't you have lunch with us, too?"

Lacey interjected immediately. "That's a wonderful idea. Take a break from that garden of yours and enjoy a meal that you didn't have to cook."

"Oh, I don't know. I wouldn't want to get in the way of a family visit."

"Nonsense," Lacey insisted. "Papa wants to meet you, anyway. We've been telling him stories."

Percy smiled awkwardly, embarrassed. "I hate to think I've done anything worth telling stories on."

"My father is easily entertained," Lacey said.

And so Percy found herself at the Gates house for lunch the next day. Lacey prepared a menu that would appeal on a hot day: a fruit tray, bread with cheese and jam, and cool tea poured over ice chipped off the block in the icehouse.

"Oranges!" Percy exclaimed. "Where did you get oranges from?"

"Travis brought back a dozen from his last trip. I'm sure he would have brought six dozen for you if he had been able to get them."

"I'll just enjoy a few orange slices here and not mention to any of the men that I had them."

"Thank you for your discretion," Lacey said amiably.

"Can I help you set the table?"

"Thank you. There's a clean tablecloth hung over the back of that chair."

Percy hardly finished laying out the dishes before the front door swung open. Adam and Caleb heard the familiar creak and tumbled down the stairs and into their grandfather's arms. Daniel Wells feigned weakness, collapsed to his knees, and allowed them to knock him over. Giggling, Caleb positioned himself squarely on his grandpa's chest. From his prostrate position, Daniel grinned up at the triumphant little boy.

"My turn, my turn," Adam demanded as he straddled his grandfather and nudged Caleb out of the way.

Watching the scene from across the room, Percy asked Lacey, "How often does your father come to visit?"

"About once a month," Lacey answered. "In between, we go over there. The trail has become so well worn over the years that it is a much easier walk than it used to be."

"It's several miles to the lighthouse, isn't it?"

Lacey nodded. "Several miles to a whole different world."

"What do you mean?"

"When Josh and I were little, the lighthouse was all we knew. We could roam for miles and not see anyone but our family for months at a time. Then the lumber camp came in. Abby's family moved in and things began to change. Twenty years ago no one would have guessed that there would be an argument about forming a town government here."

Daniel Wells drew himself to his feet, with one squealing boy wrapped around each leg. "Is that argument still going on?" he asked.

"It gets more animated all the time," Lacey said. "Josh is taking care of someone who was hurt in an accident with the saw, but Travis thinks there may be more to it than that."

"I'm sorry to hear that," Daniel said genuinely. "I know as well as anyone how difficult change can be, but fighting about it doesn't help anything." He lifted his eyes to Percy. "You must be the Miss Morgan I have heard so much about. One of the nicest changes I've seen in the camp in a long time."

"Thank you, Mr. Wells."

Gently shedding the boys, Daniel crossed the room and kissed Lacey's cheek. "We haven't had one of our talks on the lighthouse balcony for a long time. I miss that."

"Mmmm," Lacey agreed, smiling pleasantly, "I do, too. Next time I come over, let's ask Micah to take the boys out in the meadow to look for deer, and we'll go up the lighthouse."

"Don't wait too long," Daniel said. "I know how you sometimes let things build up inside you."

Percy felt a lump in her throat swell. Was this caring, gentle man really Lacey and Joshua's father? He seemed to know his daughter well. Percy could not imagine ever having a conversation like this one with her father, Archibald Morgan. He would never have known if her feelings were pent up inside her. He barely noticed whether she was in the house or not. He preferred not to engage in conversation outside of his study, and children were strongly discouraged from entering the room where he withdrew to brood. Daniel Wells did not hesitate to speak to the point. Percy could remember being thoroughly confused about what her own father was thinking. She was never even sure that he actually liked Percy or her younger sister. What they did or did not do with their pent-up emotions was certainly no concern of his.

"I'm not holding anything in, Papa," Lacey assured her father. "I'm quite happy. I promise you."

"Good. I'm glad to hear it. Now let's have that lunch before your sons tackle me and tie me to a post."

That was all the cue they needed. Adam gasped. "Caleb, let's find some rope!" And they were off.

Percy watched, wide-eyed. Was he serious? Was Daniel Wells really going to allow his grandsons to tie him up? She had never thought much about what kind of grandfather her own father might be, but she was certain he would not surrender to the ropes of two little boys. As it was, though, she doubted she would ever find out what sort of grandfather her father might be. She seriously questioned whether she would ever have the opportunity to have children of her own. And, of course, she had no idea where to find her father, even if she wanted to. His unknown whereabouts were not a problem, though, since Percy could not imagine the circumstances under which she would want to see her father again. After what he had done, what would be the point? No matter what her mind told her, though, Percy could not quite dissolve the lump in her throat as she watched Daniel Wells with his grandsons.

"I hear you are quite the checkers player," Daniel said to Percy. "Perhaps after lunch we can have a game. But you'll have to let Adam be my special consultant."

Percy fought for words. "I'd be honored. Certainly, we'll have a game. Caleb can be on my side." Archibald Morgan would never have suggested a game of checkers, much less agreed to take on a small child as a teammate.

"I'll get the food," Lacey said.

"I'll help," Percy added hastily, for she did not want anyone to see the mist that filled her eyes.

Chapter 16

Troy Wilger's health improved, but his attitude did not. For four days he occupied Percy's room, grumbling nearly every moment that he was conscious. When Lacey sent over clean sheets, Troy wanted nothing to do with them, even though he had been sweating and twisting in the bed for two days and the bedclothes were so damp and tangled he could hardly find a loose end on which to pull. When Percy heated water for Josh to give Troy a sponge bath, Troy nearly knocked the basin from her hands. It was all Josh could do to keep Troy in bed and resting. Troy repeatedly muttered about his wounded dignity and refused to accept the seriousness of his injury. Josh hardly dared leave the bedside for fear that Troy would try to get out of bed and demand his independence—and rip open his wound. And, of course, Troy had nothing pleasant to say about Percy, even as he commandeered her room and devoured the plates of food that she dutifully carried in at regular intervals. Each time Percy recalled that Josh had compared her to Troy, saying that at some level everyone was as much trouble as that hateful lumberjack, she was infuriated anew. Some day, she determined, she was going to challenge Dr. Joshua Wells on that remark and set him straight.

Percy occupied Josh's room for each of the four nights that Troy was in her room. Lacey kept a pot of coffee hot so that when Percy arrived in the evening they could sit together and relax for a few minutes. On the third evening, as they tidied Lacey's kitchen after drinking their coffee, Percy's heart caught in her throat. Lacey was no longer treating her as a guest but as a friend. Despite her city background, precious little friendship had ever graced Percy's life, unless she counted the brief attachment she had had to the gardener's daughter. She hardly knew how to respond to Lacey's gracious informality.

On the last evening, Adam and Caleb got into a frightful scrap that made Percy's childhood arguments with Ashley, her younger sister, seem like polite conversation. But Lacey responded with firmness and authority, and the boys soon restrained themselves. Even a flareup of sibling rivalry reminded Percy how different this home was from the one in which she grew up. Her own mother would have looked helplessly at the governess to resolve the conflict. Fortunately, her disagreements with Ashley had been rare. Their shared intuition about the tenuousness of their family's relationships bound them together in a silent pact. Also, Ashley was so much younger than Percy and they had very little over which to compete.

After watching Lacey discipline her sons, Percy went to bed with a heavy heart. *Will I ever have another chance to soothe Ashley?* She wanted to so badly, but it seemed a hopeless dream.

�֍

Percy was relieved when Josh informed her that he was moving Troy to the bunkhouse and arranging for a rotation of people to take care of him. Troy was out of immediate danger, but he had to be watched or he would do something foolish and find himself under Josh's unrelenting eye once again.

Josh had done his best to keep Percy's small room tidy. After living in his immaculate room for four nights, Percy expected nothing else of him. He removed his army cot and replaced her trunk along the wall, and repositioned the side chair and nightstand, which he had been using as a table for his own meals. The room looked as it usually did. Still, Percy felt compelled to scrub everything in sight. She remembered in too much detail the scene of Troy's arrival: the streaming blood, the anguish on the faces of Travis and Peter, the enormous knot in her own stomach that nearly immobilized her. Scrubbing would make the room clean again and, more importantly, it would make the room hers again.

As modest and lonely as the room was compared to the warmth of the Gates home, Percy was relieved to be on her own again. She could easily imagine living among the physical comforts of Lacey's home. After all, while the Gates house seemed quite sophisticated for the lumber community, it was modest compared to the Morgan family home. Percy had no altruistic determination to live under harsh conditions for the rest of her life. Yes, she could imagine and even welcome the physical comforts of a real home. It was the less tangible dimension of the Gates home that would overwhelm her if she were not careful. Could such an atmosphere be true and lasting? She doubted it. So it was better, much better, that she was in her own room once again. Here there was nothing to trigger the memories of her own childhood, nothing to remind her how she had come to live under such curious circumstances in the first place.

She also welcomed the return of her demanding routine. Travis still had not found anyone willing to work with her in the kitchen and garden, but Percy was determined not to relax her ambitions. No matter how physically taxing, she would have a vegetable garden and a clean, well-operated kitchen.

On the fifth day after the accident, Percy set about taking inventory of her supplies and planning menus for the next week or so. She had a craving for potato soup, and she had been hoarding tinned milk for weeks in order to have enough to make a hearty, thick soup. With enthusiasm and a quick step, she crossed the kitchen and opened the cupboard door. Her taste buds were already savoring the soup. She would serve the men and clean up and then sit in the peace and quiet of the mess hall with her own evening meal. Percy reached into the cupboard. Her hands found the tins, but the pile did not feel right. Surely the stack should be taller! Puzzled, she peered into the cupboard—probably one-third of the cans of milk were missing. She had counted them just two days ago and was certain there was enough for the potato soup.

Percy frowned as she turned away from the cupboard. She had taken meals to Josh and Troy regularly and offered extra food in between meals, for which Josh had seemed grateful. Josh should have had no reason to raid her cupboard. Besides, he could not possibly have had use for so much tinned milk.

Curious now, Percy opened another cupboard door. The supply of beef jerky that she sometimes used in the packed lunches was there but, like the milk, it was considerably diminished. Again she told herself that Joshua could not possibly have consumed the quantity of food that was missing. But who would have? If some of the men were sneaking into the kitchen and removing food, she would have to ask Travis to put a stop to it. She planned her meals carefully, making the most of the supplies available, and she simply could not have people coming and fixing themselves snacks whenever they wanted to. Why would such a problem begin now, she wondered. Perhaps it was because people knew that she was not staying in the building at night. But they knew Josh was there, and certainly the men would not think he would approve of their stealing food.

Percy pressed her lips together in a hunch. Outside, in the back of the building, was an outside entrance to the cellar. She kept the potatoes down there in the cool darkness. Surely someone looking for a snack would not raid the potato stash. There was no way to cook them in the bunkhouse, although Percy supposed that anyone could go off into the woods, build a small fire, and roast potatoes.

Taking a burlap sack with her, she went outside to the cellar doors and pulled them open. The cellar was dark and, as always, it took a few minutes for Percy to be able to see when she descended. She was careful that the doors remained wide open behind her. Enough light filtered down the rough stairway that she knew she would be able to gather potatoes as soon as her eyes adjusted to the dimness, so she did not bother with lighting a lamp. The potato supply was substantial. Travis had found a good source and bought a wagonload of potatoes. Percy had portioned them out so that most of the potatoes were at the rear of the large cellar, while a smaller pile was handy at the bottom of the stairs.

While she waited for her eyes to adjust, Percy studied the shadows at the back of the cellar. Something looked different, darker than usual, but she could not quite decide just what was different. Out of habit, she reached down for the potatoes, expecting to easily fill her bag. She stopped almost immediately. The pile was far too small. Percy was positive that quite a few potatoes were missing.

Pensively, she began dropping potatoes into the sack. *Something is wrong. What is it?*

She turned and peered into the grayness of the cellar and a shadow at the back of the cellar moved. It was almost imperceptible, but Percy was sure she had seen something.

"Who's there?" Percy demanded. She dropped her sack and reached for the broom that she kept parked against the wall.

The shadow rushed past her, nearly knocking her down in the rush up the stairs.

Percy scrambled to regain her balance and began the chase. No one was going to raid her cellar and get away with it that easily. She charged up the stairs, only steps behind the intruder.

In the open sunlight, the trespasser broke into a sprint across the uncluttered land behind the mess hall. Waving her broomstick, Percy chased him as hard as she could. He clutched a bundle to his chest as he ran. Whoever he was, he really was stealing her food.

Out of breath and outdistanced, Percy finally had to give up. He had gotten away and she had not recognized him. He was not one of the lumberjacks. He was young, probably not more than fifteen, she judged, and skinny as a rail. She turned back to the cellar. This time she paused to light a lamp on the ledge just inside the door and carried it down the stairs.

Percy looked around carefully for she knew exactly what ought to be in the cellar. Two jars of green beans were missing and some cherries she was saving for pies were gone. An apple core gave evidence that the thief had been too hungry to wait until he carried off his loot.

Percy could not imagine who the boy was, but she could remember, painfully, doing something not so different herself when her survival was in question. Whoever he was, he was desperate.

Chapter 17

After that, Percy watched her provisions carefully and wondered how long it would take to get a lock on the cellar door if she decided that she needed one. She had seen with her own eyes that there was an intruder, but she hoped that being discovered would frighten him off. On the other hand, discovery had not always deterred her when she had done the same thing. It only made her quicker and more sly. She was not proud of those days, but at least they had not lasted long—only for a few weeks after Ashley was gone and Percy had struck out on her own. She always hated the thought of stealing anything and, after what her father had done and the way the family had been treated, Percy had wanted nothing more than to prove everyone wrong. Desperately, she had hoped for an alternative to the cunning schemes that had flooded her mind, but none had come. For those few weeks, she had succumbed to something she hated. Perhaps the boy she had seen was not so different.

Lacey came to help in Percy's garden, after having spent much of the morning working in her own patch. Seeds had sprouted, their delicate leafy greens a testimony to the life and nourishment that they would bear. Some days when there was not much work that really needed to be done in the garden, Percy would simply sit among the plants and dream of the day when her labors would yield a lush harvest. On the day of Lacey's visit, they pulled out the random small weeds that had survived the tilling process and sprung up once again.

"Judging from the number of green beans you planted," Lacey said with a twinkle in her eye, "you must have quite a few recipes that require them."

Percy chuckled. "I may have gotten carried away."

"We'll find out when canning time comes."

"I know even less about canning than I do about gardening," Percy admitted.

"I suspected as much," Lacey said. "But you're a quick learner. You seem to pick up whatever you put your mind to."

Percy did not answer. She was thinking, *If only you knew how much I've had to learn.* But she could not tell Lacey.

"Josh was asking about you the other day," Lacey said.

"Oh?"

"He wondered if you were comfortable while you were staying with us."

"I hope you assured him that I was quite spoiled."

"He would only say that you deserved to be spoiled."

"He would?" Percy was stunned.

"I believe I know my brother quite well," Lacey said, her lips twisting mysteriously to one side, "and I would have to say that he seems to have a particular regard for Miss Percy Morgan."

Percy blushed. "Don't be silly. I've never given him any encouragement."

"Is that what city girls are taught to say when a man shows an interest?"

"No. . .I mean, I don't know. Josh doesn't. . . What makes you say. . .?" As hard as she struggled, Percy did not seem able to complete a single sentence because what Lacey was inferring took her completely by surprise. Finally, she managed to say, "Can we talk about something else?"

"Sure. You choose the subject." Lacey said, hiding her smile and lowering her head to concentrate on a weed.

"Someone has been stealing from my provisions," Percy said abruptly.

Lacey's head snapped up. "Have you told Travis?"

Percy shook her head. "I will if I have to, but the boy might not come back."

"Boy? Not one of the lumberjacks?"

Again, Percy shook her head. "I'd never seen this boy before. He's young, probably younger than your brother Micah, and skinny as a rail. I thought maybe you would know him."

"What did he look like?"

Percy shrugged. "Brown hair, I think. I didn't really get a look at his face. I caught him in the cellar and it was too dark to see him well. He ran out ahead of me, so I saw only his back."

"Which way did he go?"

Percy pointed into the woods. "That way."

"Mmmm," Lacey said thoughtfully. "I suppose he just took off in whatever direction would get him away from you without drawing attention to himself. I can't imagine who it is. Josh hasn't mentioned any families up this way, but we could ask him. He might know."

"Whoever he is, he took several jars of beans, so I may need the ones I've planted."

"What was that?" Lacey asked, looking up and scanning the back of the mess hall.

"What was what?" Percy followed Lacey's gaze.

"I saw something."

"A person?"

"No, not a person. But a shadow."

"Are you sure?"

"Positive." Lacey rose to her feet and brushed the dirt off her hands. "I want to investigate."

"Do you think it might be the thief?"

Lacey scrunched up her face. "If it is, he's not a very smart thief. Coming back here in broad daylight is asking to be discovered."

They peered at the back of the building but nothing stirred.

Percy was on her feet now, standing beside Lacey. "Are you sure you saw something?"

"Absolutely," Lacey insisted. Suddenly she lunged forward. "There it is again." She broke into a trot and Percy stumbled through the dirt after her. Lacey kept her eyes fixed on what she had seen. "You go around that way," she said to Percy, pointing to the far side of the mess hall. "Don't let him run out into the street." Lacey was in a full run now.

This time Percy had no broom handle in her hands and she wondered what she would do if she did come face to face with the thief. Nevertheless, she followed Lacey's instruction and she cut around to the other side of the building, glancing around for a weapon as she ran. Just as she rounded the corner at the front of the building, she snatched up the biggest rock she could spot in the dirt. She was fairly confident she could raise it and strike with one hand if necessary.

The boy was pressed up against the front of the building, his face blanched and his lower lip quivering almost imperceptibly. Percy lowered her stone for he was no threat to her.

"I've caught him," Percy called out as Lacey rounded the other side of the building.

"Is it the same boy?" Lacey called back.

At the sound of her voice, the boy wheeled around and faced Lacey. He said nothing. From behind him, Percy saw his shoulders rise and fall with rapid breath.

Lacey stopped in her tracks. "TJ?"

The boy nodded.

Percy came up close behind him to face Lacey. "Do you know him?" she asked, incredulous.

Lacey nodded. "This is TJ Richards. He was once a student of mine."

"I hope that not all of your students have turned out to be thieves." Percy regretted her words as soon as she spoke them, but they were already out. *How many times have I endured such comments about myself?*

Lacey stepped forward to embrace TJ. "I'm sure there's an explanation."

TJ returned the embrace wholeheartedly. He spoke for the first time. "I've been watching you. I wanted to be sure it was really you."

With one arm around TJ's shoulders, Lacey turned toward the door. "Percy, let's go inside and give this boy a decent meal while he tells us why he is stealing your green beans and potatoes."

TJ ate with gusto everything that Percy put in front of him. He was pitifully thin and bony. She opened one of her precious tins of milk and let him have the whole thing, along with some ham and biscuits left over from breakfast.

"It's been eight years," Lacey said. "That would make you sixteen now. I remember that you were the same age as my youngest brother, Micah."

Percy could hardly believe the boys were the same age. Though slight of build himself, Micah was far more robust.

As he consumed the last of the ham, Lacey spoke gently. "TJ, tell us why you're here. Somehow I don't think this was an accident."

He shook his head. "No, it's not an accident. I came looking for you."

"How did you find me?"

"I've been studying maps of Wisconsin for a year or more. I remember all the stories you used to tell us about growing up in the lighthouse and the dangers of the lake."

"Why have you come?" Lacey asked softly. "Your father?"

TJ grimaced. "He doesn't know where we are."

"We? You mean—"

"Sally and Mama are with me," he said simply.

"You've been stealing food to feed your family?"

He nodded. "I remember the day you found me hiding while my daddy was drunk. You wanted to take me home with you."

"I remember. You wouldn't come because you thought he would start in on your sister if you left, and you didn't want to take Sally away and break your mother's heart."

"You told me that day that you figured I was God's business. I never forgot that. And you said that God had made me your business, too."

Lacey nodded. "I remember." She turned to Percy. "TJ's father drinks nearly all the time, and when he's drunk he beats up on TJ. But TJ didn't want to leave and put his mother and sister in danger."

"I can take care of them now," TJ said. "I'm older and bigger. I can get a job and support them, and I can stand up to my daddy if I have to."

"How did you convince your mother to leave? I didn't think she ever would."

"She didn't want to at first," he admitted. "But I told her I was taking Sally, and she would have to choose between Sally and Daddy."

"She chose Sally."

He nodded. "I saved and planned for months. She knew I would really do it."

"Where are your mother and sister?" Lacey asked urgently.

"In the woods. We have a place there."

"A place?" Lacey asked skeptically.

"We brought a piece of canvas with us, and we have some rope. I made us a tent."

Lacey stood up. "We must go get them and bring you all here immediately. I won't have you living in the woods for a moment longer."

Chapter 18

Lacey meant business. "The boys are at Abby's. Give me a minute to run down and tell her I'll be gone."

Before Percy could protest, she was left alone with TJ. He scraped his plate nervously.

"Do you want more to eat?" she asked.

"No, ma'am," he replied softly, not lifting his eyes.

"Are you sure? I have plenty more."

"Thank you, ma'am. I'm grateful for the meal."

"How long has it been since you've had a real meal?"

TJ blushed. "Well, my mama can do some amazing things with potatoes and a campfire. But I guess that's not the same as a real meal."

"Your mother and sister will be eating better before long, too."

TJ swallowed hard but said nothing.

"How long has it been since you left home?"

"We've been on the road about six weeks," TJ answered. His voice was barely audible. "But that place was never home to me. I aim to make a real home now. Even if it's just a piece of canvas in the woods, a home should be safe, a place where you know you belong."

Percy choked on the lump in her throat. This boy was barely sixteen years old, the age she had been when home as she knew it fell apart. But, to her envy, he had an understanding of what a home ought to be.

TJ cleared his throat. "I'm sorry about the food, ma'am." Now TJ lifted his sincere blue eyes and looked straight at Percy.

They are beautiful eyes, glowing islands of hope on a face of despair. Percy sighed. "It's all right."

"I knew it was wrong, and if I'd been on my own, just me, I mean, I wouldn't have done it. But my mama and Sally. . ."

Even when she was on her own, alone, Percy had snitched food. How could she judge TJ for wanting to feed his family? "Don't worry about it, TJ. You'll find a way to make it right." That's what she had done. Percy had never been caught like TJ, but she had wanted to make things right. She rose to clear his dishes from the table and her memories from her mind.

Lacey was back soon. "Let's go. TJ, lead the way."

Percy was speechless at Lacey's determination to help. No doubt her day was already full of other obligations, and what Lacey planned to do with three extra people Percy could not imagine. But she was throwing that all aside to offer solace to a family she had known for only a few months more than eight years ago.

"Are you coming?" Lacey asked Percy.

"Yes, of course," Percy quickly answered. Somehow that seemed to be the right answer. She could hardly believe that the thief who had raided her precious tinned milk had moved her so, but she was and she could not refuse him help. *How old is his sister*, she wondered as she thought of her own sister, Ashley, who would be thirteen now.

They went out the back door, crossed the garden, and were soon into the woods. TJ seemed confident about where he was going. He moved skillfully and silently along a path that was invisible to Percy. He meandered such that Percy would have been hard pressed to duplicate the route. Clearly he had been determined to stay hidden until this moment. Having found Lacey Wells Gates, he was ready for revelation.

"North and a little bit west," Lacey mused. "Are we headed to that spot with the big rocks? The three boulders that come together in a sort of triangle?"

TJ flashed a look of surprise, then relief. "I guess when you live your whole life in a place, you know all the ins and outs."

"I'm sure you knew every hiding place in Tyler Creek," Lacey said. "I found you in more than one, remember."

"I remember. And yes, we're going to the place where the boulders are. They give pretty good shelter, and we hung the canvas."

"You've spent your last night there, I promise you."

TJ looked at Lacey with more gratitude than Percy could imagine mustering. The truth was no one had ever given her reason to be that grateful. When she was sixteen and suddenly estranged from her upbringing, no one had offered her solace and shelter. How different might things have been if someone had. She would never know.

At least TJ knew where his sister was. He was doing his best to care for her and keep her safe. Percy had not been able to do that for Ashley. *Ashley!* her mind cried out. *I'm sorry!*

"Surely your father knows you're all gone by now," Lacey was saying. "Do you think he'll look for you?"

TJ shrugged. "I don't know. He'll be right angry, I'm sure, but I don't know if he cares enough to come looking."

"He might not care for you," Lacey said gently, "but he may be infuriated at having been tricked."

"I don't know if he can stay sober long enough to figure out where we went."

"But he might," said Lacey.

"Yes, ma'am, I suppose he might."

"And there are plenty of people in Tyler Creek who know where I came from."

"Yes, ma'am."

"We'll just have to be very careful, that's all. We won't let him find you."

"Yes, ma'am. Thank you, ma'am."

"We're almost there, aren't we?"

"Yes, ma'am." TJ paused. Percy and Lacey stood behind him.

Before them were the three boulders Lacey had described. They were perhaps eight feet tall and lopsided enough that they did indeed lean into each other. With the help of long sticks stuck in the ground, a worn piece of canvas was stretched over the opening in the midst of the boulders. Percy could see a small bundle tied to one of the makeshift poles and the evidence of a small campfire within a ring of small rocks. Three tin plates sat on the ground just outside the ring.

"I don't see them," Lacey said urgently.

"They probably heard us coming."

"So they're hiding?"

"Yes, ma'am."

"But we want to help, not hurt them!"

"Yes, ma'am. But I told them not to trust anyone, not until we found you."

"Will they come out if you call?"

TJ formed his lips to give a low, melodic whistle. It did not last long, but it was a distinct sound. The three of them stood motionless and watched. Slowly, two thin, weary forms appeared from behind the large boulder on the left.

"Sally!" Lacey called out as she began to move forward.

The smaller form lurched into a trot and headed directly for Lacey. "Miss Wells, is that really you?" Sally said as she threw herself into Lacey's arms.

"It's me, it's me." Lacey stroked the girl's head pressed against her shoulder.

Tears sprang to Percy's eyes. She judged the girl to be only a couple of years younger than TJ. She was small, but had the roundedness of young womanhood. Her long brown hair was matted and needed a serious cleaning and brushing. Her dress was patched in at least a half-dozen places and was clearly too short and too tight across the shoulders. The toes on her left foot showed through the flap that resulted from torn stitching. But seeing Sally Richards in Lacey's arms was a beautiful sight.

Percy's own arms ached to hold Ashley just that way. Would she ever be able to?

Lacey now opened her arms to Alvira Richards.

"I'm so sorry I wouldn't let you help us all those years ago," Alvira said, sobbing softly. "I know you meant only the best for us."

"Yes, I did," murmured Lacey, "and I still do. You're coming home with me, all of you. This time I'm going to do exactly what I wanted to do eight years ago. I don't always understand God's timing, but I'm glad he's given me another chance to care for you."

TJ smiled. "So you still think God made us your business?"

"More than ever. He brought you right to me! How could I think any differently?"

"I'm right grateful for your help," Alvira said, "but I'm mindful that the three of us can be a handful of trouble."

Lacey shook her head. "Don't worry. We'll figure it out. My boys can bunk in with their uncle, and you and Sally can have their room for the time being. We'll get TJ a job. I happen to have some influence with the man who does the hiring! You'll be on your feet before you know it."

Lacey turned her attention to the makeshift shelter and Percy took up the cue. "Let's get your things together," Percy said. "What can I carry?"

TJ looked at her sheepishly. "Well, ma'am, there are a few jars of green beans and a sack of potatoes. Perhaps you'd be interested in them."

Percy smiled broadly. "Yes, I would. And I would be especially interested in any tinned milk you might have lying around."

"Yes, ma'am, we have that, too."

Chapter 19

After breakfast the following day, Percy rushed through her cleanup routine, anxious to go back to Lacey's house and see what the next step would be for Alvira and her children. She wrapped a batch of fresh cinnamon rolls in a napkin, tucked them in a basket, and set off down the street.

"The lady from the street is here," Adam announced. "I think she wants to see the lady from the woods." Lacey, Alvira, TJ, and Sally were gathered around the kitchen table enjoying midmorning coffee.

Percy narrowed her eyes and glared playfully at Adam. To Adam she would always be the lady from the street.

"I'm glad you came over," Lacey said warmly as she pulled another chair up to the table for Percy. Caleb crawled up onto his mother's lap as she sat down again. "You can help us make a plan for how we're going to take care of our new friends."

Lacey spoke so easily of friendship. After trekking back to Lacey's house with the meager belongings of the Richards family, Percy had heard more of the story of Lacey's connection with TJ and his sister. Her stomach wrenched as she listened to the stories of drunkenness and beatings and how Bert Richards behaved in public as if he were the model father. The account reminded Percy of another father who was far different than he led people to think.

Percy turned to Alvira. "I hope you enjoyed sleeping in a real bed," she said, remembering the four luxurious nights she had under the Gateses' roof. She herself had spent the night wrestling with her memories and now hoped that her sleeplessness did not show in her face.

"I was afraid I wouldn't sleep a wink," Alvira said hesitantly, "what with all the excitement yesterday. I haven't been sleepin' all that well lately, ever since. . . . But I slept like a well-fed baby."

"That's good to hear," Lacey said. "I intend for you to be fed well and to sleep well every night from now on."

"Perhaps these will help," Percy said, placing her basket of cinnamon rolls in the center of the table.

"You made these?" Sally said, her eyes wide. "Mama, these look just as good as yours."

Alvira laughed. "I don't suppose a body gets a job as a cook unless she can cook. If we eat those, we'll be headed for sweet dreams again tonight." She reached out to pinch off a piece of cinnamon roll.

"I don't remember the last time I slept as well as I did last night," Sally said, helping herself to an entire roll. "Maybe not in my whole life."

You slept because you felt safe, Percy thought. *I remember the weeks of not sleeping, of wondering how long I could stay where I was, the hungry, exhausting days.*

"It was right kind of your boys to give Sally and me their room," Alvira said to Lacey.

"Oh, it was nothing. I'm sure they thought it was great fun to bunk in with Uncle Josh. They've been talking about it all morning. The sofa may have been a bit uncomfortable for TJ, though."

"It's a whole might better than a mattress of pine needles," TJ responded brightly. Then he sobered. "But I know I can't sleep on your sofa permanently. I aim to get us a place to live as soon as possible."

"Around here that means building a place," Lacey informed him seriously. "There aren't any empty houses or abandoned farms like there might be down south."

"What did Travis say?" Percy asked, knowing that Lacey must have used her influence on her husband to try to better the lot of the Richards family.

"He promised to give TJ a job," Lacey said brightly. Then she laughed. "He wanted to assign TJ to work with you in the kitchen, but TJ wasn't sure he wanted to do that."

Percy glanced at the sheepish TJ. "No offense, ma'am. I ain't proud of what I did and I reckon I have some debt to work off in your kitchen. But I'm the man in the family now, and I aim to do a man's work."

"Am I really so frightening?" Percy teased. "I promise not to chase you with a broomstick again."

TJ blushed. "No, ma'am. It's just that I hiked all the way up here from Tyler Creek because I had my mind set on being a lumberjack."

"Then you should be a lumberjack," Percy agreed. *If only I had believed in myself that much when I was sixteen.*

Alvira said, "I'm proud to see my boy doing a man's work."

"From what I see, you have every reason to be proud of your boy," Percy said softly. Had anyone ever been proud of her? It seemed that every word spoken stirred up memories she thought she had long buried.

"Josh was about TJ's age when he started working in the camp," Lacey commented. "You might be sore for a while, TJ, while you build up your muscles, but I know you can do the job."

"TJ's right, though," Alvira said somberly. "We can't impose on your hospitality. Your boys may think it's fun to sleep with their uncle, but he might think different. A man deserves to have his home just the way he likes it."

Percy sighed. Her father certainly always had his home just the way he liked it. She hoped that Josh was somehow more congenial in the face of last night's invasion.

"Once TJ starts working," Lacey explained, "he can stay in the bunkhouse with the other men. You and Sally are welcome to stay here as long as you need to."

Alvira shook her head adamantly. "No, ma'am. You have a very big heart. I understand why my boy wanted to come all this way to find you. But we have to stand on our own feet."

"But there are no houses," Lacey protested.

"We have our canvas," Alvira said. "We'll find a place closer into town that we can pitch a tent."

Lacey chuckled "My husband would be pleased to hear you call this place a town."

"I remember when Tyler Creek wasn't much more than this."

"Mama," TJ said, "Tyler Creek is still just a speck of dirt on the map."

"Town or no town, I don't want you living under a piece of canvas," Lacey said insistently.

"Beggin' your pardon, ma'am, but we can't stay here," Alvira said, just as insistently. "It wouldn't be right."

"What about the shed?" Percy suggested.

"The shed?" Lacey echoed.

"Yes, the one behind the mess hall. It's got a few old tools in it and scraps of lumber. I never see anyone go in there."

"I'd almost forgotten it was there!" Lacey exclaimed. "But you're right. We could clean that place up and there would be plenty of room for a couple of cots."

"I'm going to build a real house," TJ said, "but it might be that this is the best we can do for now."

"A real house could take years to afford," Lacey said. "The shed will keep your mother and your sister out of the elements in the meantime. That was a good idea, Percy. And I have another one. Why not have Alvira work for you in the kitchen?"

Percy perked up. "Really?"

Lacey turned to Alvira. "What do you think? Sally says you can make cinnamon rolls as good as these. I'll bet you have a whole book of recipes in your head."

"Well," Alvira said reluctantly, "I reckon I do know how to cook. But I can't imagine getting paid to do it. I've never had no job."

"I've never had a job," Sally said, correcting her mother's grammar. "Miss Wells, I mean Mrs. Gates was our teacher. We should speak right."

"I'm glad you said that, Sally," Lacey said, "because that's the rest of my idea. Sally, I want you to finish your schooling. You're fourteen now, right?"

"Yes, ma'am."

"What grade were you in when you were last in school?"

"The sixth grade, ma'am."

Lacey pressed her lips together thoughtfully. "We'll have some catching up to do then. But we'll work on it. I want to see you get your eighth-grade certificate."

Sally's eyes lit up. "Really? You'd be my teacher again?"

"Absolutely. We'll start tomorrow, if you like. I'll listen to you read and see how your arithmetic is, and we'll make our plans from there."

Sally jumped out of her chair and threw her arms around Lacey, who was still holding Caleb.

"Hey!" Caleb protested the confinement of so many arms entangled around him.

Sally stepped back, laughing. "When we left home, I thought that was the end of school for me. I'll study hard, I promise. I'll be the best student you ever had."

Percy stood up awkwardly and moved toward the stove, acting as if she wanted a cup of coffee. She didn't, really, but she did not want anyone to see her face just then. How different the story would be for TJ and his family, compared to her own. She had longed for someone to merely speak a kind word to her, much less offer her housing and a job. But no one had. Week after week she heard only harsh words, blaming words, a tone that urged her to stop being such a bother as quickly as she could. She admired TJ's independence and fierceness because she understood it, and she knew exactly what would compel him to clear a path for his mother and sister.

Coffee cup in hand, she turned around and observed TJ from behind. If only she had been as successful in her own quest. If only someone had reached out to her with just one kind gesture when she was sixteen. Maybe things could have been different.

Ashley, her heart cried out, *I'm so sorry.*

Chapter 20

Having Alvira's help changed Percy's life. The after-meal cleanup was done in a snap with Alvira, and sometimes Sally, too, helping. The garden, which had sprouted very nicely but now needed frequent weeding, was not so intimidating. Alvira seemed to know just what to do to keep the birds and insects away. Clearly she was experienced at raising her own vegetables and squeezing every ounce possible from the harvest. She hauled water for the wash, scrubbed the kitchen floor, gathered eggs. Every afternoon after her lessons were finished, Sally appeared to work beside her mother. Percy had to say very little in the way of instructions. Alvira proved to be a proficient cook, even with making fifty servings at a time. More than once in the two weeks since Alvira began working, Percy had awakened to find that Alvira had breakfast nearly ready and that Percy was free to doze for another thirty minutes. She hardly knew what to do with such a luxury. In more than eight years she had not truly been free to sleep as late as she wanted.

Two weeks and three days after finding Alvira in the woods, Percy woke to the smell of brewing coffee and sizzling bacon. She turned over and buried her face in the pillow once again, tempted to let Alvira handle the entire breakfast. She pictured the flapjacks Alvira would make, fluffier than her own. After weeks of being perpetually tired, Percy could almost rationalize sleeping later and letting Alvira take the brunt of the early morning work, but the thought was fleeting. Meals for the men were her responsibility and Alvira was there to assist her, not to coddle her. Without any further self-pity, Percy rose, freshened up with the water that had stood in the basin on her dresser overnight, and dressed in the soft gray dress that had become her favorite work dress. By the time she entered the kitchen, Alvira was mixing flapjack batter.

"I was just about to bring you some hot water when you came out," Alvira said.

Percy smiled. "Thank you, but it's been years since I had anyone to bring me hot water in the morning. I suppose I've given up the habit."

Alvira looked puzzled. "Don't you heat it for yourself? I've never had anyone bring it to me at all, least not regular."

Percy blushed and looked away. Why did she let such things slip out? "It was a long time ago. At this time of year, the water doesn't turn icy overnight, so I don't really mind. But it was sweet of you to think of me."

"Why don't you sit down here and let me put some breakfast in front of you? You can have the first of the flapjacks and eat while they're fresh. I don't think you eat nearly enough, for someone who cooks for a living."

Percy briefly considered her waistline. Her skirt still hung awkwardly, but not so badly as last year. The hard-earned weight she had lost when she first arrived had come back. If Alvira only knew how bad things had been at one point in time. She glanced at the bacon, tempted.

"Alvira, you're a wonderful help," she said, "but you must not overwork yourself. You're here to help me, not replace me. There is plenty of work for two." She reached for an apron and tied it over her gray dress.

Alvira turned several strips of bacon and added some new ones to the pan. "I'm so grateful for this job. I just want to be sure I do right by it."

"You're doing just fine. I don't know how I ever got along without you."

"It's my first job, you know. I never really had a job before."

"You don't have a thing to worry about. You're wonderfully competent at everything you put your hand to. I only wish I could have said that about my first job."

"A fine lady like you ought to be livin' in a nice house with folks to look after her," Alvira said. "I know what brought me here, but I can't quite fathom how you ended up here. I can tell you have more breedin' than most."

Percy took a stack of tin plates from the cupboard and set them on the rolling cart that she would later push into the main dining room. If she were to tell Alvira about her father and what had become of her family, her new friend might not think so much of her fine breeding.

"I suppose we all just do the best we can," Percy said casually. "Perhaps breeding has little to do with how we fare."

"I knew it!" Alvira's eyes lit up. "You are a lady of fine breedin' but something awful happened. That's what brought you here."

"I needed a job, and the camp needed a cook," Percy said flatly. "That's what brought me here."

Alvira turned back to the flapjack batter. She splattered a drop on the griddle to test the temperature; it sizzled appropriately.

"My TJ believes that God brought us here to find Miss Lacey. He's believed that ever since that day that she told him God had made it her business to look after him, even when no one else would stand up to Bert and his ways. Can't say that I argue with Him." She dropped a generous spoonful of batter on the blistering griddle. "It does seem that God made the way plain for us to find her again, and now look at us. Sally's back in school and TJ and me are workin'."

Alvira prattled on as she made one batch of flapjacks after another and Percy assembled plates, cups, and silverware on the rolling cart. There was no question that Alvira had blossomed during the last two weeks. She was beginning to gain needed weight, despite all her vigorous work, and her cheeks were almost rosy. Alvira talked more every day, making Percy think that she had bottled up her thoughts and feelings for years. Now nothing could keep everything that was in her from streaming out uncensored.

Percy remained guarded. It would be easy enough to be caught up in Alvira's gushing. The story she told reminded Percy far too easily of her own. Alvira seemed not to mind if everyone knew the smallest details of her life. Years of being afraid of what others thought of her because of her husband faded quickly into a natural infectious gregariousness. Still, Percy chose her own words carefully.

After breakfast Josh appeared. Alvira was quick to offer him the last of the flapjacks and bacon. "I promised Lacey I would check up on you," Josh said to Alvira as she scurried around the kitchen. "If you would slow down a minute, I might like to check your pulse and have a look at your eyes."

Alvira waved him away. "I've never felt better in my life. I don't need doctorin'."

"You've been under a great deal of stress the last few weeks, what with leaving your home and the long journey up here. We have to be careful about your health."

Alvira set a plate down in front of Josh. She sobered suddenly. "No, you got that wrong. I was under a heavy burden before we ever left Tyler Creek. But it's been lifted away by folks like you."

Josh squeezed Alvira's hands. "We are but vessels of the One who bears your burden. God brought you to us, and we're grateful."

Alvira turned away to hide the tear in her eye. Percy swallowed the lump in her throat.

"How's that man you been tendin'?" Alvira asked.

"Troy Wilger? He's coming along nicely, actually. He should be able to go back to work in a few more weeks."

"Is he as cantankerous as ever?" Percy asked.

Josh smiled and nodded. "I'm afraid so."

"Someone always seems to come for his meals, so I haven't seen him in quite awhile."

"I'm sure he prefers it that way," Josh said. "He still bellows on and on about how much he hates progress. Some of the men have been referring to our little strip of buildings as 'town' and he hates that. We'll always be a camp in his mind."

"I don't see how it much matters what you call yourselves," Alvira said. "Camp or town, you're the folks that took me and my children in when we had no place to go. That's what matters, that you folks have tender hearts."

"That was beautifully put," Josh said. "Thank you, Alvira."

Alvira turned away, embarrassed. "I got chores to do."

"Alvira, take a short rest," Percy said. "You've been working for hours already."

"Not till the washing is hung," Alvira said. "I'm going to find the scrub board." And she left.

"Do you want any more to eat?" Percy asked. "We have a bit of cold bacon left."

Josh shook his head as his eyes followed her around the room. "How are you, Percy?" he asked. "Alvira is not the only person I wanted to check on."

"What do you mean?" Percy asked.

"We haven't seen much of you lately, and when I have seen you, you seem withdrawn."

"Do I?"

He nodded. "I was hoping Alvira's help would make things easier for you."

"It has, tremendously."

"Then why does it seem that you've gone deeper into your shell since she arrived? Alvira and Sally have been visiting in the evening, but Adam is wondering why the lady from the street doesn't have time for a game of checkers. I am, too."

Percy looked into Josh's dark, pondering eyes and nearly let go. Fleetingly, she wondered what it might feel like to tell her story, to unleash the stirrings within her.

"Tell Adam I'll come over soon." She avoided looking at Josh, moving instead toward the sink with his empty dishes.

"What shall I say when he asks why you have not come before now?"

She sighed. "It's a long story, Josh."

"My morning is unscheduled."

She looked at him again. If she could tell anyone, it would be Josh. But no, she could not. She was on her own now and she had to stay that way. Telling him the truth would ruin everything.

Percy shook her head. "I'm sorry, Josh. Let's talk about something else. How is work on your clinic coming?"

Josh paused a long moment before answering. Percy pumped some water into the sink to cover the silence. "The lumber is piling up," he finally said, "and I believe we have agreed on a final version of the drawings."

"Will you have good living space?"

"I'll have two rooms in the back, a bedroom and a small sitting room, with space for a small kitchen. The front of the building will be a waiting room and an exam room, plus another bedroom for caring for patients who require an overnight stay. Peter's plans are drawn in a way that would make it easy to add on a second story later."

"It sounds like a very good arrangement," she said stiffly. She was sincere, but could not control her voice.

"I'm trying to convince Peter to use any scraps or cast off boards to help improve Alvira's situation."

"That's thoughtful of you. Perhaps he could build her something more adequate than the shed."

"That's what I'm hoping. It shouldn't have to cost a lot."

They conversed for another fifteen minutes. Percy could feel Josh's eyes on her the entire time, no matter where she moved about the room. Working hard to keep her tone light, she dared not look him in the eye for fear that her story would tumble out against her will.

Chapter 21

Alnd after that," Percy said a week later as she and Alvira finished their midmorning coffee, "we should take an inventory of what is left in the cellar. Travis will be sending for supplies soon. We need to have a list ready."

They sat together in the vacated mess hall, their empty coffee cups on the table between them, along with evidence of blueberry muffins and a coveted orange.

"I've been thinkin' that—" Alvira did not get to finish her thought. Outside, a stack of lumber thundered to the ground, making them both start. Alvira gripped the edge of the table.

"That's the wood for Josh's clinic!" Percy said. She jumped up and scurried toward the window. "It was stacked next to the dining hall temporarily. I wonder what would make it fall."

"An animal, maybe," Alvira offered.

"I hope no one was hurt."

"Woman! Get out here!" bellowed a voice.

Percy stopped in her tracks, midway across the empty dining room.

Alvira gasped and jumped out of her chair. "It's Bert!"

"Your husband?" Percy was incredulous. "How did he find you?"

"I didn't think he could," Alvira said weakly. The color drained from her face. "We were careful and moved around every couple days till we got here."

"Are you sure that's him?"

Alvira nodded, her jaw clenched tight. "When you live with a man like that for twenty years, you know his voice even before he opens his mouth."

"Woman! Don't try to hide from me. I know you're here!"

"Nothing will stop him now," Alvira moaned. "I might as well go out there and spare everyone a lot of trouble."

"Don't you dare! You haven't come this far to give up that easily. He can't even be sure you're here."

"He might have spoken to one of the men out at the work site," Alvira said. "I just pray he didn't see TJ."

A multitude of scenarios flashed through Percy's mind. "TJ is safe as long as he stays with the other men. It's you I'm worried about. And Sally."

"Sally!" Alvira gasped anew. She began to run toward the front door.

Percy grasped Alvira's elbow as she flew past and stopped her. "You can't go out there," Percy said firmly.

"But Sally!" Alvira protested.

"We'll find her. She's at Lacey's for her lessons, isn't she?"

Alvira nodded mutely.

"Lacey won't let anything happen to her."

Outside, drunk and full of rage, Bert Richards kicked violently at the tumbled lumber, sending several planks clattering down the street. "I know she's here somewhere!" he shouted. "Bring me my woman!"

Motioning to Alvira to stay in the center of the large room, Percy moved stealthily toward a window on the front wall. If she ever wished there were curtains, it was now. She pressed herself against the wall and peered out into the street for her first glimpse of Bert Richards. He was about fifty, with gray-streaked brown hair that grew well beyond his collar and matched a beard that had never been trimmed. In one hand was a bottle, and he gulped greedily from it. When he had drained it, he smashed it to the ground.

"Woman!" he yelled.

Just then Travis and Josh emerged from the lumber office and, with confident strides, approached Bert. He took an angry swing, which Josh ducked.

Secretly relieved to see Josh but also anxious for him, Percy turned back to Alvira. She was determined that the frightened woman would not see her own fear. "Travis and Josh are out there. Let them try to talk to him. This is our chance to go out the back and go get Sally."

Alvira needed no further prompting; together they hurried across the dining room, through the kitchen, and out the back. Then they ran and in less than a minute, they arrived at Lacey's home and pushed open the back door.

Startled, Lacey looked up from the kitchen table where she was bent over a book with Sally.

"Your daddy's here," Alvira blurted out to her daughter.

Sally burst into tears.

Lacey pushed her chair back and jumped up. "Don't worry! We'll hide you!"

"Where?" Alvira asked weakly, bending to put her arms around the sobbing Sally. "He'll find us here sooner or later."

"But you won't be here. I sent the boys over to Abby's this morning so I could work with Sally. There's nothing to keep us from leaving right now." She slammed her textbook shut and took off her apron.

"Where are we going?" Sally asked, wiping her face with the back of one hand.

"To my father's. Bert won't find you there."

"What about our things?" Alvira asked.

"We can't worry about that now. We just have to get you out."

"I want to take my books," Sally said, having regained her composure. "I want to keep studying."

Percy looked at the thin girl with the big eyes. Three weeks of tutoring had changed her countenance. Fear had momentarily overtaken her, but Percy could still see the striking difference that lessons with Lacey had made. Sally's face exuded determination and perseverance.

Lacey nodded. "Yes, take your books. If you need anything else, I'll bring it to you later."

"Shouldn't we get horses?" Percy asked, imagining the long miles to the lighthouse.

"There's no time," Lacey responded. "We can't risk being seen."

She was right, of course.

"How long we gonna be there?" Alvira asked.

"As long as you need to be."

"With your pa? Alone?"

Percy saw the panic of scandal in Alvira's eyes. "Alvira, you have to keep yourself safe. You'll be safe with Mr. Wells."

"You won't be alone, Mama," Sally said. "I'll be there, and Miss Lacey's brother is there."

Alvira still looked uncertain.

"We have to get out of here," Lacey insisted. "I don't know how long Josh and Travis can hold him off. You must stay with my father and brother until we can manage something more suitable."

Mutely, Alvira nodded.

And they were out. They flew across the yard and found a trail. Years of trekking back and forth had taught Lacey every inch of the landscape. Now she guided the small entourage through the untrampled forest bed paralleling the main road but hidden from it.

Percy stumbled along behind the others, not sure why she was going—Sally and Alvira were safely in Lacey's care and there was little more Percy could do—but compelled nevertheless to go. Her feet tumbled along in an irregular rhythm. The group spoke little; all energy was focused on moving quickly and quietly through the forest, out of range of Bert Richards's raucous shouting. At the same time as she hoped in her heart for Alvira's safety, Percy hoped that it would not come at the expense of Josh or Travis. Had they been able to turn Bert away? Or had he harmed them and set off on a rampage through the woods?

When she caught sight of the lighthouse, Percy slowed her step for just a moment. Its majestic white, red-trimmed tower rising above the lake was just as Josh had described it once, and it beckoned to her now, calling her to safety, just as it beckoned to the ships that faced treacherous winter waters. Perhaps it meant that the story of Alvira and TJ and Sally would end in a better way than the story of Percy and Ashley and Myra had. Perhaps they would find the solace and refuge that Percy and her sister and mother had not found.

Long before they reached the house, the back door opened and Micah and Daniel Wells emerged and hurtled toward them. "What is it?" Daniel called when he was within shouting distance. "I can see that something is wrong."

"Papa, I need your help," Lacey said breathlessly as she allowed her father to embrace her. "This is my friend, Alvira, and her daughter, Sally. They need a safe place to stay."

Daniel nodded. "Joshua mentioned them when he was here last week. What's happened?"

"Bert's found the camp," Lacey said. "How he managed to track them here, I can't imagine, but he has. But he doesn't know where the lighthouse is. Maybe he doesn't remember that I came from here."

Micah relieved Sally of her burden of books. "If he shows up here, he'll have to get past Papa and me. And that won't be easy."

"I'm counting on that."

With tears in her eyes, Alvira looked at Daniel. "I'm a stranger and you're taking me in. How can I ever make it right with you?"

Daniel touched Alvira's shoulder gently. "There's no need to worry about that. Let's just pray that you're safe here."

Micah's mind was already figuring. "I'll move downstairs to Lacey's old room, and Alvira and Sally can have the big room upstairs."

"Oh, I hate to put anyone out," Alvira protested.

"I don't mind," Micah assured her. "It will be fun to have company in the house." He glanced sideways at Sally. "Especially someone near my own age."

Sally blushed but smiled. "Maybe we can study together. Lacey says you're a good student. I'm having trouble with math."

"I'll help you." Micah fell into step with Sally and the two of them took the lead walking back toward the house.

They entered through the back door, and Percy found herself standing in the kitchen that Lacey and Josh had grown up in, looking at the table where Lacey had taken her lessons as a child. Through the doorway in the other room, she could see a piano and remembered that Joshua had reluctantly admitted that his mother had insisted that he learn to play. Above them rose the lighthouse. Josh had spoken to her of filling the lamps with whale oil, trimming the wicks, polishing the brass, shoveling coal into the kitchen stove, and hauling supplies up the side of the cliff every few months when the supply boat's owner remembered to come.

Lacey and Josh had not had a coddled childhood, not at all like Percy's. They had been isolated from a real community and expected to work hard from the time they were small children. Yet they had grown into adults who could open their hearts and take in a stranger and her daughter seeking safety. And Alvira and Sally were not the only strangers they had taken in, Percy reminded herself. They had taken her in, too.

Chapter 22

A few hours later, TJ clattered into the dining hall. Percy had not been back very long herself. The waning afternoon had finally demanded that she return for the evening meal, and she and Lacey had traversed the trail once again. Percy now held a half-peeled potato in her hand, with one eye on the clock, wondering if she would make the mealtime deadline. She raised her eyes to meet TJ's when he entered the kitchen.

"I can't find Sally," he said. "I came to see if Mama knows where she is. I'm worried that she wandered off."

Percy set her knife on the edge of the sink and turned to face TJ.

"Your mother is not here, but Sally is safe," she said, wiping her hands on her apron. She spoke cautiously. "Have you been out at the work site all day?"

TJ nodded. "I just got back. I like to see Sally before supper, but she's not in the shed. It doesn't look like she's here, either."

"So you've been gone all day?" Percy verified.

"Miss Morgan, what's the matter?" Anxiety rose in TJ's voice. "Did something happen to Sally? Where's Mama?"

"Everything is fine. It's just that. . .your father was here this morning."

"Daddy? Here? How?" Percy saw the color drain from the boy's face as he asked the incredulous questions.

Percy gestured that TJ should sit at the small kitchen table and she quickly recounted what had happened in the street that morning.

"Where are Mama and Sally now?" TJ asked.

Percy hesitated. She and Lacey had agreed that it was best if no one knew where Alvira and Sally had gone. "I have to ask you a question first," Percy finally said.

"Yes, ma'am."

"Do you want to go and stay with them?"

"Stay? You mean, give up my job?"

Percy nodded. "Temporarily. I'm sure Travis would take you back when it's safe."

TJ raised his roughened and calloused hands for inspection. "Finally my hands don't hurt every time I bend my fingers. Finally I'm earning some money to take care of my family. I can't quit now."

"I understand, and I think that's the right decision. But unless you want to go into hiding, I can't tell you where your mother and sister are. Lacey and I believe that it is safer for all of you if no one else knows."

"You have to tell me!"

She shook her head firmly. "No. You might try to go there. And what if your father is still lurking around in the woods watching you?"

227

"I'll be careful."

"I know you would be careful. But he managed to find you here when no one thought he would. We can't risk having him follow you."

"I won't go, I promise. I just want to know where they are."

Percy stood up and picked up her knife to resume peeling potatoes. "I'm sorry, TJ. I promised Lacey."

She looked at his crestfallen face and knew exactly how he felt. Nevertheless, she maintained her resolve. "You trust Lacey, don't you?"

He nodded. "More than anybody except God. She showed me how to trust God."

Percy was not sure what to make of that remark. She had learned from other people not to trust anyone. But she believed TJ.

"TJ, if you truly trust Lacey—and God—then you have to accept what I'm saying. Hopefully the separation won't last long. We just have to be sure your father has given up."

Heartbroken, TJ left a few minutes later when it was clear that pressing Percy further would yield no more information. Percy allowed herself to sink into a chair and slump her head down on the table. She hated denying TJ's request. In her mind's eye, she saw herself at an age not much older than he was, standing in her cousin's parlor, demanding to know where they had sent Ashley and no one would tell her. It was for Ashley's own good, they said. She had not believed them then, so how could she expect TJ to believe her when she said the same thing? If the look on his face was any indication, she was not sure that all his talk about trusting God would make any difference in the end. She hoped it would.

Somehow Percy muddled through the evening meal, avoiding TJ's eyes as he came through the serving line. He sat apart from the other men, ate quickly, and left. Acutely missing Alvira's company, she cleaned up after the meal and began laying out what she would need in the morning. When she heard footsteps crossing the main room, she intuitively grasped the handle of an iron skillet. The footsteps slowed on the other side of the door, in the darkened dining room. Percy tightened her grip.

"Who's there?" she called out.

The footsteps resumed, moving steadily closer.

"Who's there?" Percy demanded.

"It's me," came the soft voice of Joshua Wells, just as he pushed the swinging door open and stepped into the kitchen. He raised an eyebrow at the poised skillet.

"You should have come to the back door," Percy said brusquely, "so I could see it was you."

"You're quite right. I'm sorry if I frightened you. May I come in?"

Percy let out her breath and set the skillet down. Inwardly she was relieved to see him, to see for herself that Bert Richards had not harmed him. "Yes, of course. I have some coffee on the stove, if you'd like."

"That would be nice, if it's no trouble."

Percy moved to a cupboard and took down a cup and filled it. She set it in front of Josh, who had taken a seat at the table. "Is there something I can do for you?" she asked.

Josh caught her eyes and held her gaze. "I was wondering if I could do anything for you," he said gently. "You've had quite a day."

Percy ached to slump into a chair and weep, but instead she methodically pulled out a chair and lowered herself gracefully into it. "It has been an eventful day," she agreed. "Did Bert

Richards hurt you this morning?"

Josh shook his head. "Not really. He was too drunk to throw a decent punch. It's amazing he ever found his way up here, as soused as he was."

"Apparently he has moments of sobriety during which he thinks quite clearly."

"It would seem that way. He stumbled around the street, banging on doors and screaming for Alvira. I was grateful than when we got here, you were gone. Thank you for taking Alvira out of here."

"It was the only thing to do. She's in a safe place now." Had Lacey told Josh where the refugees were? Percy wondered. She supposed that Josh might guess before long, but she resolved to say no more to Josh than she had to TJ.

"No one saw you leave," Josh said. "Travis was surprised to find Lacey gone when Bert headed toward the house. How four women managed to disappear together into the woods without being seen, I can't explain, but I'm glad you did. When we found Lacey and Sally gone, we knew you and Alvira were in safe hands, too."

"Lacey is the one who managed the whole escapade," Percy said. "I'm not even sure why I went along. I wasn't needed, not even to carry anything."

Josh shrugged. "There are different ways of being needed. I'm sure Alvira was glad you were there. She's become quite fond of you." He picked up his coffee cup and took a deep sip of the steaming liquid.

"Oh?" Percy was not sure how to respond. She stood up to pour herself some coffee, suddenly wishing to keep her hands busy.

"Anyway," Josh continued, "I just wanted to be sure you were all right."

"I'm fine, thank you." She seated herself at the table once again.

"You greeted me with a frying pan," Josh reminded her. "Are you sure you're all right? Do you feel safe here?"

"Considering Bert Richards's state of mind, I think a few prudent precautions are in order. How did you finally get him to leave?"

"He got even angrier when Travis would not let him near the house. He was just sure Lacey was hiding Alvira, and for all we knew, she could have been. But Travis stood his ground, and Peter had gone to his house to look after Abby and the children. So Richards was not getting anywhere. He cursed up a storm and finally left."

"Did he threaten to come back?"

Josh nodded. "I believe he will be back."

"Then it was wise of Lacey to take Alvira and Sally away."

"She wouldn't tell me where they are." Josh looked at her hopefully.

Percy smiled slyly. "Lacey and I made a pact, so you won't get anything out of me, either."

"Well, I have my suspicions."

Percy did not respond. She could not help if Josh's intuitions proved correct, but she would keep her word to Lacey and not be the one to tell him.

Josh pushed his chair back. "I suppose I should be going. I hate to leave you here, though."

"I'll be fine."

"It's not too late for a game of checkers over at the house."

"Adam will be in bed soon," Percy said.

"I wasn't thinking of inviting him to play," Josh said, catching her eyes. "I'll be happy to walk you back over here later."

Percy shifted her gaze. The pull to go with Josh to the Gates house was a strong one—too strong. She was not sure she could trust herself over there anymore, especially after a day as trying as this one. Surely she would say too much and regret it later. She shook her head.

"I really ought to stay here and get a few more things done. After all, I won't have Alvira in the morning and there was so much that didn't get done today."

"If I can't do anything for you tonight, I'm sure I can be of service in the morning." He stood up and moved toward the back door.

"That's not necessary. I managed on my own before Alvira came."

"I'm not offering because it's necessary, but because I want to. I'll see you bright and early."

He left before Percy could protest further. And she was not sure she wanted to protest further. She picked up the iron skillet and took it into the bedroom with her.

Chapter 23

Each report that Lacey brought back from the lighthouse was more encouraging than the one before. Alvira was thriving, her cheeks rosier by the day and her countenance more serene. Daniel's garden kept her occupied and outdoors much of the time, but she did not neglect the indoors. Anxious to earn her room and board, she fastidiously cleaned every nook and cranny of the house, mended worn clothing, and polished the heirloom furniture until she could see Daniel's smiling reflection in every room. Sally, likewise, blossomed. With Micah to set a vigorous academic pace, she threw herself into her books more deeply than anyone could have imagined possible. Lacey temporarily excused Joshua from any visits to the lighthouse and went herself, every few days. Bringing new lessons for Sally, she could barely keep up with the rapid progress the girl made. Even Micah and Daniel seemed invigorated by the presence of their guests. Lacey reported to Percy that she had not seen her father so happy in years, and Micah seemed delighted to have someone in his own age bracket around the house.

"It won't be for much longer," Lacey told Percy one morning three weeks after Alvira and Sally had been secreted away. "Alvira is asking to come back to work."

"But you said she seemed happy," Percy answered.

"She is. She and Papa have struck up quite a friendship, but she wants to earn her own way. She enjoys my father's company and she doesn't want his pity. There's been no sign of Bert. Alvira is starting to think he gave up and went back south. She wants to come back to work."

"When?" Percy asked. She was anxious to have help again. The summer was pushing on and there was so much she wanted to do before the fall.

"I'll go get her on Thursday," Lacey promised.

"Three more days," Percy mused.

Lacey chuckled and left.

✤

Percy spent the rest of Monday and much of Tuesday planning out the work for the next several weeks. She could certainly make sure Alvira felt that she was earning her way. Tuesday's evening meal came. The men tousled their way through the line, eager for Percy's baked ham and scalloped potatoes. Taking delight in their pleasure, Percy stood behind the serving table and presided over the distribution of food. She made sure to fill a plate generously and set it aside for TJ, who was fetching firewood at his own insistence. He had undertaken the task every evening since his mother had left.

When the front door burst open unexpectedly, Percy jumped. A thick slice of ham slid off the serving fork and plopped to the floor. At the sight of the figure in the doorway, Percy felt herself become pale.

"Where is she?" demanded the roaring Bert Richards. "Where's my wife?" His soiled clothing bore witness to weeks of living in the woods. Dark angry eyes darted around the room.

"Ain't no wife here," Matt Harden returned fiercely. He glared at Bert defensively. "I don't know who you are and I don't much care, but Miss Morgan ain't anyone's wife."

"She's not the one I want." Bert lumbered toward the serving table. Percy inched backward involuntarily. "My wife was here. I know she was. Somebody here knows where she is. And I ain't leavin' until I find out where she and my girl went."

"I think you lost your trail, mister," Matt said, setting his half-filled plate down and turning toward Bert. "This is a lumber camp, not a refugee camp."

"I've been all over the backwoods of this state looking for my family. I believe I'll find them here. And you folks are going to help me or I'll give you a reason to help." Bert touched his hand to his hip and Percy saw the shape of what might be a pistol under his grimy clothing.

At the same moment, she heard shuffling in the kitchen. TJ! She heard the wood drop from his arms into the bin. Purposefully this time, she inched backward toward the door between the dining room and the kitchen. Under no circumstances must TJ come into the main room.

Matt stepped forward, accompanied by Carson Gregory. "Look, mister, whoever you are, this is by and large a peaceful place. We have our fights from time to time, but they're our own. We ain't looking to take on anyone else's."

Keep talking! Percy cried out in her mind as she moved slowly and quietly toward the kitchen. She heard TJ open the stove door and throw in a piece of wood. Next he would pump water to heat for washing dishes.

"I ain't askin' you to take on my fight," Bert Richards roared. "I'm just asking you to tell me where my wife and kids are."

At the door now, Percy leaned against it and pushed it open, slipping into the kitchen. She had no idea if Richards had noticed her. Swift action was the only alternative.

"TJ!" she whispered, taking his elbow and briskly guiding him toward the back door. He started to talk, but she silenced him with her finger to his lips. "Your father is in the dining hall. You have to get out of here. Go to Lacey's right now! Leave!" She literally pushed him out the back door and took a deep breath of relief as she saw him sprint around the side of the building toward the Gates house. She was tempted to sprint out after him, but if Bert noticed she was missing, there was no telling what he might do. TJ would go to Travis and Lacey, and help would be on the way. Bert was far outnumbered in the dining hall, but if he really had a gun, he would quickly have the advantage.

Quietly, her heart pounding, she slipped back into the dining room. As she surveyed the increasingly restless group, she was thankful for Lacey's wisdom in not telling anyone where Alvira and Sally had gone. Some of the men knew bits and pieces of her story and they knew she had fled an abusive husband. It was better for Alvira and the men that none of them could say where she was. Only Percy, out of fifty people in the room, knew the whereabouts of Bert's family and he was not going to find out from her.

"Where did you disappear to?" Bert demanded.

So he had noticed her absence.

"I was just checking on things in the kitchen," she answered evenly. Her voice sounded far more steady than she felt.

"Who's in the kitchen?" He lurched toward her, but Matt Harden stepped in his way. Bert pushed the smaller man aside, not easily, but successfully. Percy was backed up against the wall, Bert's face in hers. "If your mind is on the kitchen, then you don't realize the importance of my visit."

Percy did not answer.

"My guess is that you're in cahoots with that schoolteacher lady. You look like you'd be friendly with her."

Percy sucked in her breath and said nothing. Bert stank as if he had doused himself in whiskey.

"You gonna tell me where my woman is, or am I gonna give you some help?" He touched his hip again.

"I'll thank you to leave my dining hall," Percy said between gritted teeth. "You can see for yourself that your family is not here."

"You're gonna tell me where they are."

"No, I'm not."

"Yes, you are!" With a stealthy movement Percy would not have thought possible of someone so drunk, Bert reached into his pocket and pulled out a pistol.

"I will not be intimidated," Percy said insistently. "You will leave now or I'm sure some of these gentlemen will be happy to help you leave." She looked anxiously over her shoulder at Matt Harden and Carson Gregory. They were gesturing to each other, but they both caught her glance.

Bert Richards wheeled around, gun in hand. "I believe I have all the help I need," he said, waving the gun. "I promise you, it's loaded. Who's going to tell me where my family is?"

Percy looked around the room at the stone-faced men. They were not going to say a word, she could tell. Alvira's brief time among them had been enough to develop a protective layer of loyalty. But there was no reason any of them should be threatened for information they did not have.

"Don't bother with the men," Percy said. "They don't know where Alvira is."

"Ah, you know her name! So she was here!"

"It seems you've already ascertained that," Percy said briskly. "But she's not here now. So you might as well be on your way."

"I will be just as soon as you point me in the right direction."

"She's not going to point you anywhere," came a voice from the back of the room.

Josh! Percy turned to see Josh moving cautiously but steadily across the room. She had not even heard him come in, but his presence surely meant that TJ reached safety. Travis must not have been home or Josh would not have come alone, but surely he and Peter would appear soon.

Bert turned and leered at Josh. "You again. I thought you would have learned your lesson last time. You wanna get hurt again?"

Again? Percy thought, gasping inwardly. Had Josh hidden from her that Bert had hurt him the last time he stormed into town?

Josh put out his hand and continued walking toward Bert. "Give me the gun, Bert.

Hurting somebody is not going to help anything."

"You all seem quite happy to steal my wife away. Don't you think that hurts me?"

"I'm sure it hurts," Josh said gently. Percy believed he really meant what he said. "It's not easy to have your life turned inside out. Let's put the gun away and talk this through."

Percy held her breath. No one else in the room made a sound as Josh reached out for the gun.

With a jerk, Bert moved the gun from Percy to Josh's face. Josh's chin pointed up as he moved it away from the pistol. He was frozen in place.

"I'm done sweet-talkin'," Bert growled. "If you think I won't shoot this thing, you got a lot to learn." He cocked the trigger.

Percy's heart leaped into her throat. Josh! She had treated him so brusquely in all his attempts to reach out to her. As much as she regretted her curt demeanor, she never seemed able to help herself. Suddenly she wanted to start fresh, to make things right with Joshua Wells, to receive the good intentions that he offered her. *It can't end like this!* she cried out silently.

"Dr. Wells does not know where your family is," Percy said abruptly. "I told you, I am the only one who knows."

The gun turned back toward her. Percy breathed deeply. No matter what happened to her, she would not let Josh be hurt if there was anything she could do about it.

"Then you talk to me!" Bert shouted. "If you care about your friend, you'll start talking!"

Percy glanced at Josh, who shook his head almost imperceptibly. That was all the encouragement she needed. Instantly, inexplicably, she trusted his gesture. "You'll get no help from me of any kind," she said firmly.

The gun swung back toward Josh. At the same moment, Carson Gregory and Matt Harden lunged at Bert from behind.

Chapter 24

Instinctively, Percy's eyes squeezed shut. If Josh was to be shot, she could not bear to watch. She believed with every ounce of her being that Bert Richards was capable of pulling the trigger on that gun without remorse or pity. She had no idea what he was like when he was sober, and that did not matter much at the moment, for he was roaring drunk and angrier than she thought humanly possible. For a fleeting second she wanted to cry out that she would reveal Alvira's whereabouts to save Josh from further danger. But even if she had chosen to, the opportunity vanished instantly.

The combined weight of Matt and Carson and their precision in moving together gave Bert Richards no time to anticipate their action. Instead of a gunshot, Percy heard the thud as Carson and Matt knocked Bert Richards to the floor. Men all over the dining hall, freed from the paralysis that a cocked and pointed gun brings, pushed back their chairs and sprang to their feet.

Richards cursed loudly and thrashed against his attackers. Despite their momentary advantage, he would not be subdued easily. Percy forced her eyes open to see that he still waved the pistol in one hand. He gripped it, ready to shoot. Bert Richards was a strong man, more determined than ever in his drunken rage. One enormous boot kicked at Carson's head as Carson tried to restrain Bert's feet. Carson ducked the blows and persisted, clamping his hands down first on one ankle and then the other. Bert swung the pistol around Matt's head, somehow managing to keep a fraction of an inch ahead of Matt's grasping hands. To avoid a vicious blow to the jaw, Matt leaned backward, off balance. With a mighty one-armed jolt to Matt's chest, Bert sent the smaller man sprawling. Cursing continuously, Bert leered at Carson Gregory, still struggling to hold down his feet. Richards had gained the advantage he sought and Percy saw the monstrous contortion that his face took on and she was frightened all the more. Strength surged through his arms as he pointed the gun at Carson's face. Once again her eyes narrowed in anticipation of the gunshot.

From behind Bert, Josh threw himself at the big man and thrust his hands down on Bert's shoulders. His smaller size was no match for Bert's powerful torso and the two were soon entangled in a twisting wrestling match. Carson hung onto Bert's feet, but that did not stop Bert from rolling forcefully to one side. Ignoring his own pain, Matt scrambled to his feet and lurched toward Bert again. He joined the rolling fray, heedless of where the gun was now. Out of the side of her eyes, Percy could see a couple of other men moving in to help, but they could not cross the room quickly enough. Percy's common sense somehow overcame the urge to leap onto the tangled heap of men herself. If anything happened to Josh because she had kept silent about Alvira—she did not know if she could bear the thought.

Bert continued to threaten randomly with the gun. He needed no further provocation to pull the trigger, only the opportunity for a clear shot. The gun moved toward Josh's face.

Carson Gregory shifted his position for a better grip. For a moment, Percy could not see Bert or Josh and in that moment, the gun went off.

For an eternity of a second, the room was motionless.

Unimaginable scenarios flooded Percy's mind. Common sense failing her now, she pitched forward toward the tangle of arms and legs that was Josh, Bert, Matt, and Carson. She could not see Josh, but the sudden stillness was ghastly. Slowly, far too slowly for Percy's liking, the men peeled themselves apart.

First, Carson released his fought-for hold on Bert's ankles, stood up, and backed away. As he did, he shook his head at the sight before him.

"What happened?" Percy cried out.

As Carson stepped away, Matt pulled himself to his knees, breathing heavily. His eyes did not move from the scene before him.

Percy had reached them now and she forced herself between Carson and Matt. Josh was up on his knees, finally, bent over Bert with blood soaking the front of his shirt.

"Josh!" Percy gasped. "You're hurt!"

He shook his head and rocked back on his heels. "Not me. Him."

Percy blanched as she saw the blood spurting out of Bert's chest.

"Somebody clear off a table," Josh barked. "We have to get him up where I can see what I'm doing."

"You're not going to try to save this piece of trash!" Carson shouted, incredulous.

"I'm a doctor. This is what I do." Josh's answer was firm. "What you do is up to you."

Carson stood frozen in his place as Josh pulled open the front of Bert Richards's shirt. "Clear a table!" Josh repeated urgently.

Behind her, Percy heard men rapidly swiping dishes off the nearest long table and scraping chairs out of the way. They heaved the table toward the spot where Bert Richards had been transformed from intruder to patient. Josh had one hand tucked under Bert's back and was leaning over with his ear to the big man's mouth, listening for breath.

"He's still breathing," Josh finally announced, "but I can't find an exit wound. I don't think the bullet came out."

"What does that mean?" Percy asked.

"It means we have to go in looking for it." He caught her eyes. "Sorry, but it looks like we'll have to commandeer your dining hall again for a temporary medical facility."

Several men, including Matt Harden, stepped forward and together they hoisted Bert Richards's limp form to the table. Josh immediately turned him on his side for a better look at his back, peeling off patches of bloodied clothing along the way.

"Did you find an exit wound?" Percy asked, wanting to know but hardly able to look for herself.

Josh continued to probe Bert's back. Finally he shook his head and rolled Bert to his back. "Definitely not. It went in here," he said, pointing to the hole in Bert's chest. "Based on the angle of the entry wound and the way the blood is spurting, I believe the bullet may be near the heart."

"So what do you have to do?"

"I'm going in."

"Going in?"

"It's his only chance."

"Are you talking about operating? Here? Now?"

Josh looked at Percy steadily and spoke quietly. "Yes. That is exactly what I'm talking about. And I need you to help. Will you?"

Stunned, she nodded mutely.

"My medical bag is over by the door. Can you get it? Then see about getting rid of the onlookers. I'm sorry about their supper, but I can't have everyone loitering around while I work."

"Yes, of course," Percy said, moving toward the door to scoop up the black medical bag. She whispered some instructions to Matt and Carson, gesturing toward the food and the kitchen. As she turned back to Josh, she could see the men organizing themselves to bring some order back to the dining hall.

"There are some scissors in there," Josh said.

"I remember," Percy responded, reaching into the bag and pulling out the scissors Josh had used to cut away Troy Wilger's dungarees all those weeks ago. Now, without being asked, she used them to remove what remained of Bert Richards's shirt. Blood pumped out as fast as she could sop it up with the few rags that were in the bag. Percy slipped off her apron and laid it across Bert's chest. It turned a deep purple almost immediately. She looked at his ashen face. Under other circumstances it would be possible to believe that he was an ordinary patient, an ordinary man with a family who had succumbed to an accident and needed a doctor. At a moment of need, Bert Richards looked like anyone else.

"The blood just keeps coming," Percy murmured as she rearranged her apron to absorb more.

Josh removed a scalpel from the bag and positioned it between his thumb and forefinger.

"Are you sure about this?" Percy asked, half under her breath.

Josh was breathing rapidly. "I took some surgical training. I admit I don't have a lot of experience, but I had a case like this once." He glanced at her. "Are you all right? You look pale."

"You don't look so well yourself," she said gently, "but if you're ready, I'm ready."

"Here we go." And with that, Josh made the incision and soon had his hand deep in Bert Richards's chest.

"What are you looking for?" Percy asked.

"We have to stop the bleeding. The bullet must have hit an artery."

"Can you sew up an artery?"

"I can try."

Josh worked by touch, not able to see but moving his hand around gently inside Bert's chest.

"I need more rags," Percy said. "I'll get them."

Her hands and dress bloodied, she ran to the kitchen. Some of the men were still pressed against the walls of the big room and a few had gathered in the kitchen. Percy ignored their inquiring looks and focused on her task. She retrieved a stack of dish towels and dashed back to Josh. Bert looked noticeably worse. Blood dribbled down the side of the table and pooled on the floor. Josh was visibly agitated.

"Is he. . .?" Percy started to ask.

Josh shook his head. "I think we're losing him."

Chapter 25

They did lose him. Bert Richards expired on a wooden table in the dining hall on a muggy midsummer Tuesday night. The blood loss was rapid and voluminous, and it was only minutes after the gunshot when his heart stopped beating. Joshua Wells pulled his hand out of the man's chest and stepped back from the table. He opened his fist to show that he had indeed found the bullet, seconds too late. Percy lifted her eyes to meet his as they filled with the grief of a lost battle and a lost life.

"He's gone," Josh murmured. "I wanted to help him."

"You did everything you could." Percy reached out and grasped Josh's arm at the elbow. They were both sodden with the blood of Bert Richards. "You tried to save him. I'm not sure anyone else here would have done that. Besides, if he hadn't come in here with that gun..."

Josh shook his head slowly. "I know what you're thinking... that he deserved this. He was a wicked man and deserved what happened to him. But don't we all? Even when we bring things on ourselves we can hope that by the grace of God mercy will prevail."

Percy raised an eyebrow at such a philosophical response at this burning moment. She was fleetingly reminded of the time Josh had compared her to the wickedness of Troy Wilger. But this was not the time to pursue a theological discussion. Instead, she put her arms around Joshua Wells, whom moments earlier she had feared losing, and she breathed relief that he was not the man on the table.

Josh returned the embrace. "Thank you for helping," he murmured into her ear. "It was the only chance he had."

"And you were willing to give it to him."

Suddenly self-conscious, Percy glanced over her shoulder at the row of men pressed against the far wall. Most of the men had scattered as soon as Bert was hoisted onto a table and Josh extracted a shiny scalpel from his bag. But a few had stayed to witness Josh cut open Bert's chest and plunge his hand inside. The men were pale now, one or two slumped into chairs. They were too busy holding onto their stomachs to notice her embrace with Josh.

The front door opened. Travis and Peter burst in, then stopped in their tracks. "What happened in here?" Travis demanded.

Josh pulled away from Percy and gestured weakly toward the table. Percy realized how rapidly the entire incident had happened. When she sent TJ off to safety, she expected Travis and Peter would come right away. And they had. But those few minutes had been enough to bring tragedy. Haltingly and briefly, she explained what had happened.

Josh sighed. "I'm glad you're here. We'd better move him and clean up."

"I'll heat some water," Percy mumbled and turned numbly toward the kitchen. Percy, Josh, Travis, Peter, and a small crew of men worked long into the night, erasing any clue of what had transpired.

The community was stunned. Fistfights broke out occasionally, and the danger of an accident with the machinery or lumber loomed over them always. But never in the camp's short history had a stranger thundered into town wielding a gun and then ending up with a sheet over his face.

In the morning, Travis went to fetch Alvira and Sally, bearing the mixed news that they were safe but at the expense of Bert's life. Their return to the camp, although a day earlier than planned, was somber. TJ held his mother and sister tightly as they sobbed, their shoulders racking with relief that their flight to freedom had come to its destination and sorrow that any glimmer of hope for restoration was now gone. That afternoon, Bert was buried quietly and unceremoniously in the first grave adjacent to the camp land. TJ refused to be present; and as soon as the last shovel of dirt was thrown over the hastily made pine coffin, Sally ran sobbing back to the shed she shared with her mother.

Percy walked with Alvira from the unmarked grave back toward the camp. "I never wished him dead," Alvira said.

"No one would blame you if you had," Percy said softly, remembering that more than once she had pondered that it would have been better if her own father had died than to do what he had done. She might still be with Ashley and their mother might have survived widowhood with more grace than she had brought to the shameful events they had endured.

"He was my husband and I once loved him. I wasn't always afraid of him. But he changed. It was like the demons got hold of him and he turned into someone I didn't know. But I never wished him dead, not ever, not a single time."

Percy put her arm around Alvira's shoulders. "I'm sure you didn't. That would not be your nature."

"I know folks thought I should stop putting up with him years ago. Miss Lacey thought that when TJ was just eight and she saw what was happening to him. I'm sure she thought I was weak, and I was."

Percy squeezed Alvira's shoulder. "No one is judging you now. You don't need to judge yourself so harshly."

If only she had learned that lesson herself. Not a day went by that Percy did not wonder what she could have done differently, any small thing that might have spared Ashley's being sent away.

Alvira sighed deeply. "Well, he is dead now and I'm not sure I'm sorry about that. I'm supposin' that makes me a horrible person, just as bad as he was."

"Alvira, don't. What you're feeling is normal; it's understandable. He treated you dreadfully."

"But I shouldn't be glad he's gone."

"You should be glad that you're safe now and your children are safe."

"Runnin' and hidin' all the time is no way to live," Alvira murmured.

"No, you're right about that." Percy had had her share of running and hiding. She wanted to be finished, but she knew she was not.

The camp is the best hiding place I've found, she thought, but lately she had more and more trouble hiding from herself, much less anyone else.

Daniel Wells was waiting at his daughter's house when Percy and Alvira returned to the row of buildings. He looked gently upon Alvira and opened his arms to her. Unmindful of the roomful of people, Alvira walked directly to Daniel and received his embrace. He held her tightly as she buried her head in his shoulder.

Percy glanced at Josh, who in turn glanced at Lacey.

Alvira returned to working with Percy in the dining hall and took charge of the garden once again. But now, instead of working every waking moment of the day, she accepted an occasional afternoon off. She wanted to be free to see Daniel when he came to see Lacey, which now seemed to be at least once a week, sometimes more. Little time passed before Lacey, Josh, and Percy realized that it was not his children that Daniel came to see. After a perfunctory game of checkers with Adam or a lunch with Lacey, Daniel seemed to prefer a long afternoon stroll with Alvira.

One day Lacey insisted that Alvira and Percy join them all for lunch. Percy could see for herself the looks exchanged between Daniel and Alvira. When Lacey rose to clear dishes and carry them into the kitchen, Percy sprang up to help her; Josh was right on their heels.

"Did you see that, Lace?" Josh asked.

"You mean the way his eyes look?" Lacey responded.

Josh nodded. "He hasn't had that light in his eyes—"

"In eight years." Lacey finished her brother's thought. "Not since Mama got sick."

"What do you think this means?" Percy asked.

Lacey laughed. "You might not have your kitchen help for much longer."

Josh nodded. "Papa probably never thought about marrying again. He would never have gone looking."

"But when God puts someone in your path the way He put Alvira at the lighthouse," Lacey said, "it's hard to ignore."

The door between the dining room and kitchen opened. Daniel stuck his head in. "You're talking about me, aren't you?"

The trio looked shocked, then burst out laughing. "Yes, we were, Papa," Lacey finally said.

"I thought so. You should have been back long ago for more dishes. Come back in here and I'll give you something to talk about."

They regrouped around the table, joining Travis, the boys, Sally, and Alvira, who looked strangely nervous.

Daniel took Alvira's hand. "When the minister comes again," he said simply, "we want to have a ceremony. Nothing fancy, so don't outdo yourself, Lacey. After that, Alvira and Sally will move to the lighthouse."

"Papa!" Lacey exclaimed. "How wonderful!" She kissed her father's cheek and embraced Alvira. "Does TJ know?"

Daniel nodded. "He gave his blessing last week."

"Miss Lacey," Sally said, "does this make you my sister?"

Lacey grinned. "I suppose it does, in a way. I always wanted a sister."

The smile on Percy's face was sincere, if strained. What she had hoped for had come true. Alvira's story would have a happy ending. She would be cared for and treasured as she deserved. It was Percy's own story that strained the smile. Could anything turn her story around?

"Percy?" Suddenly she heard Josh's voice piercing through the resounding congratulations. "Are you all right?" His brown eyes, guileless and clear, held her, even from across the table; he was asking because he truly wanted to know.

She choked and said, "Yes, of course."

Chapter 26

Josh moved toward Percy. "I'm afraid I don't believe you," he said softly. No one else heard what he said. "You don't look yourself."

She shrugged. "It's the announcement. Alvira is going to marry your father and move to the lighthouse. It will be hard to find someone to replace her."

Josh raised an eyebrow, skeptical. Percy ignored him. Plastering a smile on her face, she hugged Alvira and Daniel enthusiastically.

"I'm very happy for both of you," she said lightly. And she did mean it, despite what Joshua might think. "But I'm afraid I'm going to have to cut short my celebrating. I have some things I must do before supper."

"I should be helping you," Alvira said.

"No, no," Percy countered. "You stay and enjoy your afternoon. Come back to work when you're ready."

After a quick round of farewells, Percy successfully excused herself, but she did not head back to the dining hall. Instead, she stumbled into the woods behind Lacey's house. Sobs welled up inside her, unsubsiding, relentless. Racing against the rising force, she hurried her footsteps. Percy Morgan wanted to be far away from anyone else when the dam burst. Weeks, months, even years of grief pressed against the controlled facade she had erected and lived within. She tramped into the forest, mindless of where she went, not seeing the chipmunks that used to startle her with their scampering or the spreading tree roots that threatened to trip her. Putting one foot in front of the other more and more rapidly, she pressed on blindly.

At last she fell to the ground, exhausted, and gave way to the tidal wave within her. Her shoulders heaved with her sobbing and the torrent that came from her eyes spilled down her face and splashed the ground beneath her. The sounds that came from her mouth were foreign to her. Not in five tumultuous years had she allowed herself such release, such protest, such catharsis. Percy lay flat on the ground, her head buried in her hands. It mattered not that the light beige of her dress became layered with black earth. Percy was not thinking of the moment when she would have to pick herself up and return to camp to prepare an evening meal. At the moment, she hardly thought it possible that she could do so. It seemed more likely that she would rise and circle around the camp and keep on walking till her feet carried her far away from this place where the truth was so unendurably present.

She did not hear the footsteps behind her. When he spoke her name, she raised her head awkwardly and looked around. "Joshua!"

"Yes, it's me. I told you I didn't believe you."

Percy sat up and began wiping tears from her cheeks with the back of one hand. She was unable to speak.

Josh sat in the dirt beside her and opened his arms. Without even the slightest hesitation,

Percy allowed herself to fall against his chest. With his arms around her, he stroked her black hair with one hand. Josh said nothing for the longest time. He simply held Percy as she shivered with grief. Gradually, the tears subsided, the shaking dissipated, and Percy began to feel composed. She pulled herself upright, out of his embrace.

"I'm sorry," she said. "I don't usually. . .it's just that. . . well. . ." An explanation for her uncharacteristic lack of control seemed impossible. She returned to wiping tears off her face.

Josh smiled gently. "As fond as I am of Alvira, somehow I think this has a greater cause than just the loss of your kitchen assistant."

Percy sighed heavily. "It's a long story."

Josh shrugged. "I have time. I have a feeling it would do you good to tell your story."

Percy pulled her knees up under her chin and wrapped her arms around them. "I've never told it before. I'm not sure where to begin." She could hardly believe she heard herself speak those words, so contrary to her resolve that her past would not get in the way of her future.

Josh stretched his legs out in front of him and leaned back on one elbow. "How about if you start with why you know a lot about hand-carved European crown moldings but not so much about ordinary vegetable gardens."

Now Percy laughed through her tears. "It's just that while I was growing up, we had a lot of crown moldings, but I never saw where the vegetables came from. The cook brought them in, I suppose."

"The cook?"

"Yes, we had a cook and two maids and a gardener who looked after my mother's exotic idea of a garden."

"Two maids and a gardener?" Josh echoed.

Percy nodded. "And of course there was always a governess about the place, lest my sister and I run off to some corner of the house where we were not permitted to play."

"I didn't know you had a sister."

A cloud washed across Percy's face. "I did have one. I'm not sure if I still do or if she would want to acknowledge being related to me after all these years."

"How many years?"

"Five. Almost six."

Josh waited patiently for Percy to continue. For a fleeting moment, she considered cutting the conversation short and jumping up to lead the way back to the mess hall. After all, she still had an evening meal to prepare. But Josh's shining brown eyes cut through her resolve. With a sigh, she plunged in.

"I grew up in Connecticut. At the time I didn't know it, but we were quite wealthy. My friends all had the same standard of living. As a child, I didn't know anything different."

"What did your father do to earn such an income?"

"He was a banker. The president of a bank, actually. He worked all the time. We hardly saw him. I think that was part of why my mother was so withdrawn. She placed far more value on those flowers of hers than they were worth. I can see that now. She just needed something to devote herself to, since my father did not seem to care if she was around. Mother always talked about how she had failed to give him a son, as if that might have made things different. Some of the money was Mother's, actually. She had inherited a tidy sum when they married. Her family has had money for generations. The Percy name had to be steadfastly upheld by money."

243

"Percy is a family name?"

Percy nodded. "My mother's maiden name. I think I was supposed to be a boy to carry on both the Percy and the Morgan names. I disappointed them both from the start. Anyway, the money was Mother's, but she trusted Father implicitly. As soon as they were married, she signed everything over to him and never gave it another thought.

"Then one day Father announced he had to go to Chicago on bank business. He did that from time to time, so it was not unusual. But this time he did not come back. Mother waited weeks for word from him, and none ever came. We found out what he had done from another bank officer."

"What had he done?" Josh queried.

"He had been embezzling bank funds for years, more than a decade. He did have a meeting set up in Chicago, but he never got there. He just disappeared with all of Mother's money and hundreds of thousands that he had taken from the bank. It wasn't until after he disappeared that anyone really studied the books he kept. He had also mortgaged the house, which was my mother's. It was the Percy family home, and he mortgaged it heavily, then left town with the money. The bank foreclosed almost immediately. Mother had no way to repay the loan, of course. There was nothing left in their account. Father had taken it all, every penny. We had to move out, but we did not really have any place to go."

"Where did you end up?"

"My mother had a second cousin, Louise. They had known each other when they were little but had not been close as adults. Mother never really liked Louise, but what were we to do? We moved to New Jersey to live with Louise."

"Something must have happened there, or you would not have ended up here," Josh said, prodding her to keep going with her story.

"Mother was simply too frail. She hated that we had to go to Louise, and while Louise did take us in, she was none too happy about it. She never let a day go by without reminding Mother what a scoundrel she had married. Mother just started to disappear. At first she claimed exhaustion from the ordeal and wanted to rest for hours at a time between meals. Then she started coming out of her room only in the late afternoon. Eventually she did not come out at all, not even for meals. My little sister, Ashley, and I took food in to her and pleaded with her to eat. We wanted so much for her to get better and to stand up to Louise. But she never did. She just grew weaker and weaker every day until one morning she did not wake up. I'll never forget Ashley's scream."

"Ashley found her?"

Percy nodded.

"How old was she?"

"Seven. A seven-year-old girl should not wake up to find her mother dead."

"No, surely not," Josh agreed.

"After Mother died, Louise was even more irritated with me. I look a great deal like my father, and she blamed me for his actions."

"That hardly seems fair."

"Nevertheless, that is what happened. Louise found a boarding school somewhere in the Midwest and shipped Ashley off one day while I was out of the house. She wouldn't tell me where."

"That must have been awful!"

"It was. I begged and begged to know. She insisted it was for Ashley's own good, that the only way to save Ashley was to separate her from the Morgan family completely. But I was sixteen, nearly grown. I suppose Louise thought it was too late to redeem me. She simply said that I would have to leave."

"She threw you out?"

Percy nodded. "She gave me one week to make some plans, then told me I was on my own. She gave me enough money for room and board for about a month."

"And you've been on your own ever since."

"I gave her money back. Just left it on the doorstep one day. She hated me. I didn't want to touch her money."

"I can understand."

"I got a job washing dishes in a restaurant. It seemed to be the only skill I had. I hadn't been raised to actually work for a living, after all. I was supposed to marry into another rich family, multiply the family fortune, and live happily ever after. But after what happened, the young men who used to come calling didn't even want to mention my name."

"So how did you learn to cook?"

"By watching in the restaurant while I washed dishes. I didn't care what work I did. I only wanted to find Ashley. I knew she was somewhere in the Midwest. I thought perhaps she was in Chicago. All I know is that the school was called Miss Bowman's School for Girls."

"That isn't a lot to go on."

"No, it isn't. I never found Ashley. I worked in one restaurant after another in Pennsylvania and Ohio, just trying to keep moving west. Finally in Indiana I applied for a job as a cook, rather than washing dishes. They didn't ask for references. They only watched me cook. I got the job. And you know the rest after that."

"What about Ashley?"

Percy shrugged. "I never found her. I wish I could, but I don't think I can. Louise sends all my letters back unanswered."

Josh looked puzzled. "You're not likely to find Ashley way up here. So why did you come?"

The tears began again, slowly. "I've given up," she whispered hoarsely. "I can only hope she's happy. She's almost thirteen now. Perhaps she found someone at the school who would really care for her. And I hope deep in my heart that she knows I had nothing to do with banishing her."

"I'm sure she does. You must not give up hope, Percy."

A tear slipped off Percy's face and dribbled down her collar. "I hoped for as long as I could. I can't anymore."

Josh reached for her and took her in his arms again. "When you are weak and powerless, that is when God is strong and mighty. You must not give up hope, but you must hope in the right thing."

"I don't know what the right thing is anymore."

"When TJ was eight years old, Lacey told him that he was God's business. Look how that sustained him. You're God's business, Percy Morgan. He sent me here today just as surely as He sent Lacey into TJ's life all those years ago. You must always hope. And we will find Ashley."

Chapter 27

When Percy awoke the next morning, she could hardly believe what had happened in the forest with Joshua. As her mind moved into its morning mode, rising to awareness of the day's tasks, her pulse quickened at the implications of what she had done. No longer could she hide behind a facade of competence. No longer could she insist that she was fine to his probing eyes and expect that he should believe her.

Unexpectedly, relief washed over her. She got out of bed, reached automatically for her gray work dress, and began to dress. On the floor in a heap was the beige dress she had worn the day before, soiled with the forest earth. Percy stooped and picked it up. She fingered the hem, which had trailed in the dirt for miles until it was black, and reflected on her flight. Running from Daniel and Alvira's happiness had been an irresistible impulse, an overwhelming wave that she could not contain. But after five long years of running, she was finished. Josh had gently turned her back toward camp, taking her hand in his as they retraced the rugged miles together. Now, on this morning, instead of waking with fear and regret, she relished the relief that someone, especially Josh, at last knew the truth.

After breakfast, Alvira insisted on cleaning up by herself and she shooed Percy out the door with instructions to relax and enjoy the morning. The impulse to protest was fleeting. Instead, Percy stepped outside into the sunshine and wandered aimlessly toward the garden. The green beans were doing well and there would be plenty of radishes and onions. She was anxious to know how well the carrots were growing and she fingered the lacy green topper of a plant at the edge of the patch. Would it hurt to pull up just one carrot to see how the whole row was faring?

"If you pull it up to see how big it is, you can't put it back."

Percy spun around to see Joshua standing, smiling, at the far end of the garden. "The carrot," he said, gesturing toward her fingers on the carrot top. "I used to pull them up to see how big they were getting. It made Mama mad, but I was so curious I couldn't help myself."

Percy smiled. "I assure you, I have no intention of doing any such thing."

"But you are curious, aren't you?" Josh walked slowly toward her between the tomatoes and the bean stalks.

"Yes, I confess I am. I want to know if there really are carrots under there."

"Mama always told me that I had to have more patience and give God time to do His work."

"I guess that's one way to look at it." *If you believe in God,* she added silently.

Josh sat in the dirt beside her. "Some things you just have to take on faith and wait."

"For how long?"

"Until it's time."

"And how will I know when it's time? I suppose Lacey will tell me when it's time to dig up the carrots."

"The carrots, yes. The other things you'll have to figure out by yourself."

Percy fell silent. Josh knew her whole story now. So Percy knew that he meant what he said.

Josh ran his fingers in the soil and let the dirt drizzle through his fingers. "I remember the day you rode into town, so to speak," he said, "with that crotchety carriage driver."

"Mr. Booker."

"Yes, Mr. Booker. I remember thinking that there was something remarkable about you right from the start. After all, you talked him into bringing you up here against his better judgment. After everything you told me last night, I think you are all the more remarkable."

"You do?" Percy looked up to catch his eye.

"Absolutely. You're determined, hardworking, resourceful, organized, and brave."

Percy had no response. Her heart beat faster at the thought that Joshua Wells thought she was all those things.

"Do you remember the night I walked you to Lacey's, after you were brave enough to help me with Troy?"

Percy nodded.

"We talked about the stars," Josh continued. "I remarked that the Maker of the Stars had been in your little bedroom that night, helping us care for Troy. I may think the world of you, Miss Percy Morgan, but what the Maker of the Stars feels about you is what really matters."

Percy pursed her lips. "As I recall, on that same night you also told me that I was just as much trouble as that wretched Troy Wilger."

"That's right. I did say that. None of us is really any different than Troy."

"How can you compare yourself to Troy Wilger?" Percy protested. "You risked your life when Bert Richards burst into the dining hall. You tried to save Bert's life when the others were ready to leave him to die. Troy wouldn't have done that."

"No, probably not," Josh agreed. "But Troy doesn't look at the stars much. He doesn't know the Maker. That's the real difference."

Percy was silent for a long time. She remembered the well-thumbed Bible she had seen on Joshua's nightstand that night. At last she said, "And you do know the Maker?"

He nodded. "When I look at those stars, I don't just see their light. I see the One who gave them light. And that's who was in that room with us that night with Troy, and at that table in the dining room with Bert. And in the forest with you last night."

Percy sniffled and held back her tears.

"The Maker sent me to you last night," Josh said, "just as He sent Lacey to TJ and Alvira eight years ago. You've been afraid I would turn my back on you if I knew the truth, haven't you?"

Percy nodded. "Everyone else has," she croaked. "I'm sorry for all the times I rebuffed you. I knew you were trying to be my friend. It's just been so long since anyone did that for me. I didn't know what to do."

Josh shook his head. "Your father failed you, Percy. Your cousin, Louise, failed you. Your friends failed you when you needed them most. But not the Maker. It's understandable that you would hesitate to trust other people to care for you. You've had to look out for yourself all these years. But the Maker of the Stars is on your side, Percy Morgan. You haven't tried depending on Him." Josh put his hand on a carrot top. "I believe there is a carrot growing in the ground under this. And so do you, or you wouldn't be tempted to dig it out early. Some things you take on faith."

"You say that so easily."

He shrugged. "I'm preaching far more than I meant to. But when I saw you hovering over the carrots with that hopeful look on your face, I couldn't help myself." Josh stood up and brushed the dirt off his trousers.

Percy squinted up at him. "Did you and Alvira plan this?"

"What do you mean?"

"She practically chased me out of the kitchen, as if I was going to be late for an appointment, and almost as soon as I sat down here, you came along with your little sermon."

Josh's brown eyes twinkled. "No, Alvira and I did not plan this. Someone else did." He turned and strolled away, hands leisurely in his pockets.

Percy watched him walk away. Once again, relief washed over her.

Chapter 28

The garden gave a good harvest. Percy learned to can. The cellar was stocked for the winter. And Alvira prepared for her wedding.

As the summer sun burned through July and August, Percy labored in the heat of the day and sought refreshment in the cooler air that came with nightfall. Her garden became a favorite spot, because it was out in the open, away from trees or structures. From the carrot patch, she could easily see the night sky. Resolutely, she resisted the temptation to check on the carrots' growth. Lying on her back in the garden, against the cool earth, sometimes with Josh next to her, she dared not even try to count the stars she had not noticed during the spring and early summer. Caught up in work and anguish, she had not raised her eyes often to the gemmed, sparkling field of black in those weeks. Now she often would stare at the stars, wondering, was the Maker of the Stars looking back at her?

When she pondered Joshua's growing companionship, which she no longer rebuffed, Percy celebrated a gift. A gift of friendship; a gift of confidence; a gift of faith and hope. Laughter, not the cautious sort but free laughter, returned to her face. Her grandmother's Bible had been promoted from the bottom of the trunk to the bedside table. A great deal of what she read still puzzled her, but she continued to read.

Still, she ached for Ashley and kept herself from surrendering to happiness without word from her cousin, Louise. Joshua had carried through on his promise to help find Percy's sister. In the most official language he could muster, he had written to Louise, imploring her to reveal information about Ashley's whereabouts. When his letter was not immediately returned, as all of Percy's had been, Percy allowed herself a glimmer of hope. But the letter eventually was returned, unopened, by the postal service, with the notation that Louise was now deceased.

That night, Percy huddled in her room in blackness, the curtains drawn against the moonlight, the lamp extinguished, until Josh came to her to insist that they had not reached the end of the trail. There were other relatives, he said, and there must have been an attorney to settle Louise's estate. They would persist until they found Ashley. With his arms around her, he lifted her to her feet and led her outside to see the night sky. The Maker of the Stars, he repeated, had not abandoned her. She longed to believe.

❋

Daniel and Alvira chose to marry facing the western sky at sunset, in the meadow behind the lighthouse, on an early autumn evening. The visiting minister joined Peter and Joshua's dream of a church for the emerging town, but for now, the people would have to settle for his occasional visits for official acts.

Daniel and Alvira faced the minister, with Lacey and Travis, Peter and Abby, Josh and Percy, TJ, Sally, and Micah gathered around them. Abby's children squirmed some, but Adam and Caleb Gates were ecstatic about acquiring a grandmother, and they paid rapt attention to the brief service. The same minister had presided over the unions of Peter and Abby, and then Lacey and Travis two years after that.

Looking past the minister while he gave a brief homily, Percy's eyes wandered to the lighthouse. Against the glowing orange sky, it glimmered in the evening air with freshness and life. Daniel maintained an immaculate tower. Josh and Lacey had both told her stories of ships that had crashed around in dark, treacherous, winter waters below, depending on the light that came from the top of the tower to beckon them toward safety. Somehow she knew what those shipmasters must feel like—the anxious searching in the midst of a swirling storm, the unpredictable heavings of a craft powerless against the wind and waves. Would a small light at the top of a distant tower really be enough to guide the way to safety and calm sailing?

The minister said, "You may kiss the bride," and Daniel gladly complied.

Adam tugged on Alvira's skirt. "Are you my grandma now?"

She scooped him up. "I would be delighted to be your grandma." Caleb clamored into her embrace as well.

Percy felt Josh at her elbow. "It was a lovely ceremony," she murmured, "and a lovely time of day for it."

"Papa has always liked the sunset," Josh explained. "He knows that the darkness comes next, and says that should make us appreciate the gift of light all the more. I think finding Alvira after all these years alone, well, it's a new dawn for Papa, a new gift of light."

"Yes, a gift of light," she echoed softly. "The ships must feel that way about the lighthouse when they pass at night and the weather is bad."

"The trick is not to look at the weather, not to mind the darkness," Josh replied. "They have to watch the light at all times, keep it in their sight, aim toward it."

"I imagine the night can be very long out there."

"Yes, but the lighthouse is a beacon of safety and the dawn always comes."

"Yes, I suppose it does," Percy murmured. "If they make it through the night."

Josh paused. "You'll make it through your night, Percy. The dawn will come."

She looked at him, wordless, suddenly filled with belief. Perhaps he was, after all, right about the Maker of the Stars.

The small wedding entourage began making its way toward the house for cake and refreshments. Josh put his hand on Percy's elbow to guide her. "I talked to Peter about modifying the plans for the personal quarters behind the clinic," he said casually.

"Oh? But he hasn't even finished building the clinic yet."

"That's why I thought I should talk to him now," Josh explained. "I want to add several more rooms—a proper kitchen, another bedroom, maybe even a dining room."

"That sounds more like a house than a clinic."

"Perhaps you're right. But I'm going to need more space, at least enough for two people to live in without falling all over each other. And I hope there will be children later."

She stopped in her steps and turned to stare at him.

"We can always add another story. I wonder if you would like to see the new floor plan."

"Me?"

"Yes, you. I was rather hoping that you would consent to being the other person living behind the clinic. Perhaps the next time the minister comes around, it will be our turn."

"Our turn?"

"To marry."

"Marry?"

"Yes." He took her hand in his. "Percy Morgan, will you marry me?"

She fell into his arms and only when she heard clapping did she realize that the others were listening.

"Does this mean the lady from the street is going to be my aunt?" Adam asked his mother.

Lacey grinned at Percy expectantly.

Percy smiled at Adam. "I would be delighted to be your aunt."

THE RELUCTANT SCHOOLMARM

by Yvonne Lehman

Study to shew thyself approved unto God,
a workman that needeth not to be ashamed,
rightly dividing the word of truth.
2 TIMOTHY 2:15

Chapter 1

A s Christa Walsh started down the steps of the train, the man in front of her turned to race back up. She reached for her hat lest it be jarred off.

Male voices began singing, "For He's a Jolly Good Fellow" accompanied by a harmonica. Looking ahead, she saw two men, one tall and one short, beneath the sign above the depot, confirming this was Grey Eagle, the closest she could get by train to her destination high in the Blue Ridge Mountains of western North Carolina.

The man in front of her cast furtive glances over his shoulder while stammering, "Pardon me. . . I. . ." The greenish cast on his face wasn't caused by the reflection of the vest he wore over his white shirt. Maybe he was motion sick. The train had chugged higher and higher around curves. The smoke and people odors in the coach hadn't been all that pleasant either.

A man's voice behind her sounded annoyed. "Ma'am, sir, could you step aside, please?"

The tall singer rushed to her. With a slight bow, he held out his arm. She had the strange feeling she should respond by placing her hand on it. The green-vested man now held her suitcase. The short singer grabbed his arm.

At least the strap of her smaller bag still lay across her shoulder. Her arm pressed the bag closer to her body in case the singers weren't as innocent as they seemed. She'd heard tales about highlanders not liking their territory being invaded by flatlanders and referring to city folks as highfalutin' with their 1910 conveniences that hadn't reached the mountains.

The logical explanation for the singers, however, was that they were welcoming some important personage. No thanks to her fellow passenger, they stood in the way of others trying to exit the train.

Christa placed her gloved hand on the tall man's arm and moved forward, not wanting to mess up their parade or this welcome.

She and the panicky-looking man were being escorted across the yard toward the depot, where the bearded man in overalls was still playing the "Jolly Good Fellow" tune.

The welcoming committee was quite small—only three people. The depot was small, too, compared with her hometown of Hendersonville. A welcoming committee there would have been a band of a dozen or more men in uniform and perhaps a chorus of women and children. Horse-drawn taxis would meet an important personage. Men and women would dress in their finery. These men wore simpler attire—everyday work clothes.

When they reached the depot porch, Christa took her bag from the strange man. Now that they were out of the way, she thought it exciting that she might see a celebrity while waiting for Uncle John to show up.

The short singer began talking to the weird man, but before Christa could catch what he was saying, the tall singer said, "Jeb Norval here. Ah!"

His "Ah!" kept her from introducing herself. Her gaze followed his. Coming up the road, raising a cloud of dust, was a horse-drawn wagon with a big red ribbon tied around the horse's neck.

"Whoa!" The driver drew up and looked down at her. "Black Bear Mountain, next stop!"

Christa looked up. He nodded like he knew her. Was this her transportation? "You. . . know John McIntyre?"

He looked as if the question were an affront to his intelligence. "Why, ma'am, I don't just know him. I beat him in a game of checkers ever now and then. Can outhunt 'im, outshoot 'im, and if need be outrun 'im." He laughed heartily, jumping down from the wagon.

Christa thought he might have out-aged 'im, too, considering his head of snow-white hair and the cottonlike puffs on his jaw.

He bowed, then stuck his thumbs behind his red suspenders. "Clem Carmichael at your service, ma'am."

Christa responded favorably to the smiling man with his twinkling eyes. He obviously enjoyed life. She hadn't. . .in a long time. But this was not the time for thinking about that.

She offered her gloved hand. "I'm Christa Walsh. So pleased to meet you. This is some taxi service."

"The least we can do, ma'am. Here, let me help you up."

"I need to get my suitcase."

"Which one?" the weird man asked. "I'll get it for you."

Surely this man wouldn't want to steal a woman's luggage. "The tweed one."

Clem Carmichael took her small bag and set it in the wagon, then held out his hand to help her up. She lifted her skirt slightly, stepped up, and took the seat behind the driver's. The man who'd gone for her suitcase hoisted it and a black bag into the back of the wagon, then jumped up and sat beside her.

She stumbled on her words. "You. . .you're going to Black Bear Mountain?"

"Don't have much of a choice." He made it sound like a fate worse than death.

Clem Carmichael spoke briefly with the singers. Christa wished she could stay longer to see the important person emerge from that train. Why would they come here? From the few things she'd heard about Black Bear Mountain, she'd concluded it was a backwoods place.

Well, for whatever reason, her uncle John couldn't meet her, but he sure made nice arrangements by sending his friend to fetch her. How sweet of him to think of the red ribbon.

To her surprise, when the driver climbed up into his seat, the two singers and harmonica player went to the side of the depot, unhitched horses, and rode out in front of them.

She looked back. The conductor shouted, "All aboard!" and a couple got on. The train began grinding away, puffing smoke from the stack. Leaving the station.

Had she missed something?

"Giddy-up," Clem Carmichael said, flicking the reins. "The real celebration is at Bear Cove," he explained, looking back over his shoulder. "You know my Dora, Doc."

Now what did that mean? His doradoc? Was that a name? A person? Place? Or was. . .

She slowly turned her head toward the green-faced man, who quickly turned away. "Are you ill?"

He took a deep breath and faced her. His dark eyes seemed to say that was an understatement. He exhaled heavily. "Quite!"

"Perhaps," she said with a lift of her chin, "you should see a doctor."

His growl was not happy. Looking worse by the moment, he leaned back against the seat and mumbled, "I can't believe it. This can't be happening."

She had to ask. "He called you Doc?"

He nodded.

"You. . .are the celebrity?"

His gaze met hers. "No," he said. "You are."

Chapter 2

D r. Grant Gordon had seen varied responses to all sorts of injuries—broken bones and even the insides of a man blown away by rifle shot. But he wasn't sure he'd ever seen a more baffled expression than was on the face of this woman.

This should not be whatever her name was. This should be Adelaide Montgomery, his beautiful blond, blue-eyed fiancée from Asheville. Or—he corrected his thought—his fiancée-to-be. The only thing lacking was a ring on her finger. That would happen after he made the final payments to the jeweler.

His fellow passenger wasn't really the celebrity, of course, since she was not Adelaide Montgomery. A little scrutiny revealed she was likely a couple years older than Adelaide. Definitely darker. Medium-brown hair, wide surprised-looking eyes. Would her dark eyes dance with golden fire if he obeyed his sudden urge and asked her to be his fiancée?

He understood that crazy impulse—it was the product of desperation. This situation could ruin his career in the cove. Over the past few years while waiting for Adelaide to be ready for marriage, he'd won the people's trust. He'd started out as one of them, but after going away to university and medical school, he had to prove he didn't have highfalutin' ideas.

In Asheville, he had to do the opposite and prove himself intelligent, competent, and without backwoods ideas.

He'd given the impression that he and his intended would come to the cove because that's what he wanted and what Adelaide had implied. Promised, in fact!

What he hadn't counted on was the predicament that had delayed Adelaide's arrival. He'd determined to return to the cove and explain things. That was before these greeters had assumed this woman seated next to him was Adelaide.

He drew in a deep breath and prepared to explain. However, the only words he uttered were, "I'm truly sorry."

✕

Sorry? Christa thought a more apt word would be *crazy.*

Or else she was!

Her brother, William, had said she was doing a dangerous thing, traveling alone on the train to a backwoods place she'd never seen.

Her sister-in-law thought her motives noble, but Christa had a feeling Bettina would be glad to have her out of the house and shop. The woman had wished Christa well and warned her not to talk to strangers.

Now, Christa sat behind a stranger in a wagon that was taking her to Uncle John's and taking this strange man. . .where?

She was about to ask when he took a letter from his pocket. She tried to see what was on that pink sheet of paper upon which was scrawled a feminine script. As if aware of her intent, he tilted the paper, studied it, then returned it to his pocket. He sighed heavily.

Whatever his problem, it wasn't hers!

She would not respond to his "celebrity" remark, in case he wanted a discussion of whether being the preacher's great-niece gave her celebrity status and rated a couple of singers, a harmonica player, and a horse with a red ribbon.

Dear Uncle John was treating her as special, so she would simply enjoy it. With that resolve, she looked at the scenery.

Everything was lushly green in mid-June. The air cooled the higher they went. At times, the thick forest prevented the midafternoon sun from filtering down on the road. She wouldn't want to be out here alone at night. Her previous thought resurfaced. She was in this secluded place with two men she didn't know—strangers!

She had seen nothing but trees and mountains for quite a while, one piled behind another until they faded into the horizon. Where were the houses? She'd noticed a few near the train station at Grey Eagle, and farther out she'd noticed a few buildings making up a small town with a main street, a hotel, and several houses.

Occasionally she glimpsed a log cabin or a plank-board house, or smoke curling from a chimney back in the forest.

She began to wonder how far back into these mountains they were going. She leaned forward. "Mr. Carmichael!"

Wearing that friendly smile, he looked over his shoulder. "You'll have to speak up. I'm a little hard of hearing."

She leaned closer. "I was wondering how much farther to Uncle's John's?"

"Oh, a few miles as the crow flies. 'Course we don't take the same route as the crows." He laughed. "But we'll be there directly."

Clem Carmichael then described what a fine preacher her uncle John was. "Too bad he can't be here for the festivities."

Christa looked at the doctor, whose gaze lifted to the sky as if pleading for help. She leaned forward again. "Festivities?"

"I don't want to give anything away. I guess John was in too big a hurry to get down to Flat Creek Community for their revival meetings to tell me you're his niece. But we sure are glad to have you here in the cove."

Christa wondered why. A light began to dawn. Of course! Uncle John must have told him she wanted to find unique mountain-made handcrafts to sell at the shop in Hendersonville.

"When is Uncle John coming back?"

"Later tonight. Has to preach here tomorrow, it being Sunday and all."

She was disappointed it wouldn't be sooner but understood her uncle had obligations. At least she had a place to stay.

"Did Uncle John leave a key?"

"Don't need no keys around here, Miss Walsh. Nobody's got anything anybody else wants, 'cept maybe some food. John would give anybody his last bite. No need to steal it."

Christa leaned back and tried to relax.

That wasn't easy. The weird man beside her had just learned she'd be at Uncle John's alone—and without a key to lock the door.

Grant realized he had another problem after hearing that John McIntyre wasn't in the cove. The depot hadn't been the place to explain the mix-up because, yes, Grant did know Clem's Dora. Sending Clem and the singers to the station indicated this was only a preliminary welcome.

Nevertheless, a hope grew within. Maybe this would be a quiet dinner for Clem and Dora, Grant and his fiancée. He would explain the mistake, and they would laugh. Dora would be pleased she could do this nicety for the preacher's niece.

Soon they rode out into a clearing. The horse trotted along on level ground. A line of children held a long WELCOME TEACHER banner. In front of the church stood women and a few men who began to sing "She'll Be Comin' 'Round the Mountain" to the sound of the harmonica and the rhythm of their hands.

No, this would not be a quiet dinner for four.

Chapter 3

W hoa, Nelly!"

Christa knew this was no welcoming party for her, although "Doc" had implied so.

She could not explain this situation, so she might as well stop trying. Clem was thoughtful to bring her to this celebration instead of to her uncle's empty house. Besides, this was a good way to meet people and ask about their crafts.

The doctor stepped down and turned to assist Christa. His strong hands easily encircled her waist. By the time her feet touched the ground and he had moved aside, a regal-looking woman with silvery gray hair stood in front of her, smiling. She hugged Christa. "I'm Dora Carmichael, dear."

Christa thought the woman must have been a friend of Aunt Sadie's. They were about the same age. Maybe as a tribute to Sadie, who had died six months ago, and to their beloved preacher, the celebration really was for her. Back here in the cove, any change might be an excuse for a celebration.

"I'm pleased to meet you, Mrs. Carmichael. I'm Christa Walsh. I'm here—"

"Finally!" Dora Carmichael gushed. "Just follow me!"

With a flourish, the woman turned and strode up a path bordered by at least fifty people. They applauded, and the children chanted, "Teacher, teacher, teacher" in unison.

Dora must be a teacher.

Dora looked over her shoulder. "Come on, Grant, and get your dues. You're responsible for this."

Grant stepped up beside Christa. She realized he must be the teacher. He had admitted he was a doctor, and she had thought his degree was in medicine. But it must be academic.

"This is the worst day of my life," he said. "I'm sorry to drag you into it."

She tried not to feel scared. "Are they going to tar and feather us?"

He drew in a deep breath. "Worse."

When she stopped, he shook his head. "Not you. I'm the one who's going to be run out on a rail."

"You just came in," she said.

"That's where I made my mistake."

Christa followed his gaze. They stood in front of the church, and the others were following.

Dora loudly declared, "We have waited a long time for this. Our dear children have suffered from the lack of a teacher for more than a year. Now our prayers are answered."

Grant's eyes met Christa's for an instant before he shut them and shook his head. If he didn't want to be a teacher, why was he here? Come to think of it, why was she standing beside him?

"Grant told us he would persuade his intended to come and teach our children."

His intended? Where was she? Christa could only stare at Dora, who said, "Let's thank Grant and welcome the new teacher, Miss Christa Walsh."

"Hip! Hip! Hooray!" the crowd cheered. "Hip! Hip! Hooray! Grant! Grant! Christa! Christa!"

"Miz Dora," the doctor choked out, just as Christa said, "I feel rather faint."

Dora ignored Grant and addressed Christa. "Oh, my dear, you've had a long trip, and this hot sun doesn't help. You don't need to make a speech now. You can talk to the people during our potluck."

Dora led her around the side of the church.

Christa wondered if the train ride up the mountain had done something to her mental processes. Perhaps she had caught whatever disease Doc had. Amidst the women welcoming her, children trying to talk to her, and Dora gushing about her, she tried to figure this out.

Doc. . .or Grant. . .was the teacher.

Christa was John McIntyre's great-niece.

But Dora Carmichael hadn't said that. She had said that Christa was Grant's. . .intended? She had to do something. "D'y'all know John McIntyre?"

Dora stopped in her tracks. "Oh, honey, he's our preacher. You know him?"

"I'm his niece. Great-niece, I should say."

Dora placed her hand over her heart. "Oh, my dear. If you're kin to John, you have to be great. He's the dearest man. We all just love him."

The other women nodded, expressing similar sentiments.

Dora huffed. "I could just box that Grant Gordon's ears. He wouldn't say much about you. But word got around that he was bringing his fiancée here to teach. Now we have a double reason to celebrate. A teacher! And kin to John McIntyre. Just wait 'til the others hear this. You're balm to a sin-sick soul, child."

Christa wondered whose sinful soul Dora referred to. Before she could say she was not a teacher and could not be, they had reached white cloth-covered tables supported by sawhorses.

"Say grace for us, Clem," Dora said.

"Let's bow our heads," Clem said in a loud voice, "and thank the good Lord for the blessings of this day and what it means for our children's future."

They bowed their heads. His prayer echoed across the mountains as if the entire cove was being blessed. When he said, "And thank You, Lord, for this young lady who has come to fulfill Your purpose," Christa sneaked a peek at the doc.

His glance met hers. He grimaced and shut his eyes tightly.

"Here, dear. Take a plate. You go first behind the children."

Christa raised her head and looked into Dora's eyes, which held a hint of mischief. She must have seen Christa and Grant peeking at each other. She would think. . .what everyone already seemed to think. . .that they were. . .promised to each other. Feeling flushed—and not from the sun—Christa took the empty plate and followed the children and their mothers.

A woman on the other side of the table spoke. "We think the world of Pastor John." The man behind the woman nodded. Christa smiled. She could not explain the teacher part, but she was glad they were accepting her as Uncle John's kin. Without further hesitation, she filled her plate with fried chicken, green beans, sliced tomatoes, corn on the cob, and corn pone.

"Let's go over to that table," Dora said. "You're the guest of honor, and we don't want your pretty outfit to get messed up."

Christa followed her to a table shaded by a tall oak. She sat on a bench facing tombstones in the cemetery beyond the backyard. Grant strode up. It took all her strength not to ask what in the world he thought he was doing.

Dora patted the place across from Christa. "You sit here, Grant. Across from your sweet lady."

Since none of the other women were wearing hats, Christa removed hers. She looked steadfastly at the man, then glanced at the graveyard, hoping he got the idea that if he continued this farce, he might end up there.

Something flickered in his eyes as if he found the idea amusing. At least he got her point! He looked slightly repentant. "Could I get you ladies something to drink?"

"I'm going to need something to be able to swallow this," Christa said.

He held his breath.

Dora laughed. "They do know how to put on a spread. Some of the girls managed to get some tea and make it for this special occasion. We know city girls like tea."

"Thank you." Should she partake of this hospitality? Wouldn't refusing be cruel after all the trouble they'd gone to? They obviously accepted her as Uncle John's niece. Doc could explain the rest.

She stared at him. "I would like tea, please."

He glanced at Dora, who nodded and took the seat next to Christa. Dora gasped. "Oh, look. Just in time."

Christa looked up to see Uncle John on a fast-galloping mount. He hopped down, tied the reins to a stake, and rushed forward.

Clem and some other men stopped him and talked. He reared back at one point as if hearing something unbelievable. His smile broadened, and he strode toward Christa, chuckling, his thumbs at the lapels of his suit coat.

Christa scooted off the bench, ran, and fell into his arms. Now they could put an end to this charade.

Her uncle's embrace felt warm and comforting, reminding her of her daddy's hugs. She wanted to nestle there and bask in the feeling. However, she stepped back, and he placed his hands on her shoulders.

"My, it's good to see you," he exclaimed. "How long has it been? Two years? Sorry I didn't meet you, but I didn't know you were coming. I just got your letter on the way back from Flat Creek," he explained. "The mail had been held up because of storms last week." His eyes twinkled. "They don't deliver to your door up here."

Christa felt her smile was stuck. He didn't know she was coming? Then the welcome at the depot had nothing to do with her.

"And to think, my little niece is a teacher. And engaged. Well, glory be!"

Before she could protest, he looked beyond her. "And here's the lucky fellow."

Chapter 4

Grant felt helpless. He should have known better than to confide in Clem that his fiancée would graduate from college this year and might become the cove's teacher after their marriage.

He should have had better sense than to go to Clem's son, who was a jeweler in Asheville. He should have known the son would tell Clem about the ring, Clem would tell Dora, and Dora would turn possibility to fact. That woman had a way of turning a kitten into a bobcat.

The pastor would know how to ease things without upsetting this crowd. Grant set the glasses of tea on the table and hurried toward Christa and Pastor John.

John spread his arms wide. "Well, you ol' rascal. Who would of thought we'd end up kinfolk?" He laughed jovially, then added, "Son!" Obviously, someone had already given the pastor the news.

Grant suffered through the embrace while staring into Christa's eyes. Her chagrin had changed to amusement. She had an ally in her uncle. He could see his well-planned future dissolving before his eyes.

John released him long enough to put an arm around his shoulders. "I need to get me some of those victuals, son. Have you eaten?"

"No. But I'd like a word with. . .um. . ." Miss Walsh hadn't given him permission to address her by her first name. Instead of saying "Christa," Grant finished, "your niece."

John chuckled. "I understand. She's a beauty like my Sadie was. Has that same reddish-gold hair when the sun shines on it."

The brown did have a reddish-golden sheen. Quite. . . impressive. But Grant had no business looking at her as his fiancée. She was not Adelaide.

Pastor John went off toward the food, chuckling. Grant turned to Christa. "How are we going to handle this?"

✻

"We?" Christa crossed her arms. "I have no idea how you're going to handle this."

She kept her voice lowered and spread a smile on her face for the benefit of onlookers. The doctor looked like he might have a heart attack. "All I want is for you to tell them that I am neither your fiancée nor the schoolteacher."

He nodded. "Before this is over, I'll tell them."

"Think they'll be sorry they fed me?" She gazed longingly at her plate. "That is, if I ever get to eat."

"Go ahead," he said. "I'll fill my plate. I'm sure Pastor John will sit at our. . .your. . .table. I'll relate the situation to him and the Carmichaels. The custom is to have a few welcoming speeches. They will expect me to introduce you since I know you best—"

"You don't know me!"

"What I mean is, they expect me to introduce Adelaide. Instead, I will explain the mistake."

"How will they take it?"

"They'll be disappointed. Especially the children."

Christa frowned at the food. They had prepared it for the person they thought she was. She had to eat. She had to show appreciation. Besides, she was starved. She returned to her seat at the same time Dora Carmichael stood.

"I'm going to get some of FannieMae's blackberry cobbler." Dora picked up her plate. "You'd better eat, young lady. You can't live on love. And you're going to need your strength."

Christa needed some now. She tackled the food before anything else could interrupt. Her solitude didn't last long. While children ran off to play, women and a few couples came by to greet her.

Dora returned with cobbler for them both. Uncle John and Grant were talking with several men.

"From what I could overhear," Dora said, "there's trouble up the mountain. Rifle shots rang out. Jim thinks the revenuers might have found the still."

Christa perked up. This was more like the stories she had heard about these people. But she mustn't judge. Likely, they'd heard unsavory stories about city folk, too.

She finished her dinner and tasted the dessert. "*Mmmm*, this is good."

Dora nodded. "FannieMae is the expert with blackberries. She picks 'em all over the cove. Makes pies and cobblers and sells some down at Grey Eagle."

"Is she here?"

"No. Her daughter, LulaMae, is expecting a baby any time now."

Christa noticed fewer children running around. The crowd had thinned. "Grant said there would be speeches."

"That's the practice if a visiting preacher comes. And when Grant came back to us, we wanted to hear what he had to say. Oh, don't look so worried." Dora patted Christa's arm. "We won't do that since everybody has already met you, and your being John's niece is recommendation enough. We're just hoping you're going to like us."

"Oh, I do like you," Christa said. "Everybody is so nice."

Uncle John joined them, holding a plate piled high with food. "I'm sorry, Christa. Grant's gone up the mountain with Jim."

Christa gasped. "He's. . .gone?"

"Now don't you fret none, child," Dora soothed. "He'll be just fine. Neither the revenuers nor the moonshiners want to hurt Grant. He'll be there to help in case anyone gets shot."

That wasn't what worried Christa. She feared that if this tangled situation dragged on, Christa Walsh or Grant Gordon—or both—would get shot.

✦

Two hours later, horse's hooves sounded outside Uncle John's door. Christa opened it before the doctor had a chance to knock. At least this glum man took things seriously, unlike Uncle John, who had gone from a hearty laugh to intermittent chuckles over the misunderstanding about her being Grant's fiancée and the schoolteacher.

When Grant stepped inside the cabin, Uncle John's laughter started again.

Christa closed the door. "Uncle John, it's really not that funny."

"Now, Christa, don't deprive me of this. I haven't had such a good laugh since before Sadie got sick. She got her dander up at the slightest thing, just like you."

Was that a compliment? She folded her arms across her waist. "I don't consider this slight, Uncle John. Unless the doctor here. . .sets this straight, I can't face these people again. They're going to think I'm as devious—"

Grant straightened. "Now wait just a minute."

Uncle John chuckled again. "Let's discuss this over supper. You eaten, Doc?"

"Nothing all day."

Uncle John turned toward the kitchen. "Dora made us bring home enough to last a week."

Grant motioned for Christa to precede him.

Uncle John set a plate and milk on the table.

Grant closed his eyes to pray.

Christa waited for him to look up, then spoke. "It's time for an explanation."

Uncle John held up his hand. "Now hold on a minute. Did anybody get shot up the mountain?"

Grant chewed, then swallowed. "Nope. A black bear came down where children were playing. Men were shooting to scare it away. Apparently no revenuers are nearby, and the still's intact."

"They weren't trying to kill the bear?" Christa asked.

"Just scare him away."

"Then maybe we won't get shot."

Grant's eyebrows lifted. "They'll probably chase me up Rattlesnake Ridge or shoot me—whichever they have a hankering for."

Did the doc have a sense of humor? On second thought, maybe that was no joke.

Christa watched Grant eat. He had manners, unlike a few people she'd seen at the potluck. After several bites, he took a gulp of milk.

He licked his lips, then spoke. "The only explanation I have," he said, "is that I went to Asheville to get Adelaide and instead was given a letter saying she couldn't come today." He stabbed a bite of tomato.

Christa's words halted his fork in midair. "When is your fiancée coming?"

"In about a week when she and her parents return from Charleston." He poked the tomato into his mouth.

Uncle John leaned over the table. "Christa graduated from college."

Christa's suspicions were alerted. "What are you saying, Uncle John?"

Spreading his hands, he looked deceptively innocent. "You could teach for a week, Christa. That would keep both of you in these people's good graces, and later they can laugh about the whole situation."

Christa could hardly believe the expectant look on her uncle's face and the gleam of hope in the doctor's eyes.

"Well, I'm here for crafts, not teaching. Explaining the truth is"—she pointed at Grant—"his responsibility."

Uncle John spoke softly. "The Lord brought you here for a reason, Christa."

She slapped her hands against the table. "If the Lord brought me here, Uncle John, then He smokes a lot, chugs loudly around the mountains, and doesn't smell too good."

Any other time, she might have thought the doctor had a nice laugh. But she didn't want to give any indication she would consider Uncle John's ridiculous suggestion. After the men's laughter subsided, Uncle John said what one might expect from a preacher. "God doesn't always do what we presume, Christa. He often works in mysterious ways His wonders to perform. That's what the Good Book indicates anyway."

Rather than respond, she stood and walked to the window above the sink, taking in the view of red tomatoes on stakes, green cornstalks, and yellow squash peeking through huge green leaves.

She'd tried to believe verses that said if you ask you'll receive. She'd asked that Roland would come to his senses. She'd asked that she find crafts that would make her brother and sister-in-law think she could be an asset to the business.

But that had all gone by the wayside.

Chapter 5

That blackberry cobbler seemed to call Grant's name, however, his desire for a solution to his problem was greater. Christa's reaction to Pastor John's suggestion that she teach indicated she wouldn't provide the answer.

John's next question presented further complications. "Just what is the situation between you and your intended, Grant?"

Grant looked at a spot on the table. "Pride is part of it. I bragged too much to Clem's son, Frank, when I bought that ring." He looked up. "You see, Frank and I were rivals in our younger days, whether it was over school, coon hunting, or girls. Then Frank went to the city, got married, and got a good job."

He might as well admit the whole truth. "I told Frank I was marrying the prettiest girl in Asheville, the daughter of a well-known doctor. To prove it, I took Adelaide to pick out her ring."

John spoke kindly. "You mean you stretched the truth, Grant?"

"I didn't lie about Adelaide being lovely and charming, or about her dad's status. But when I'd go to make payments, I gave the impression she'd definitely be coming to the cove to teach." He unclasped his hands and felt the coolness of the wood beneath his palms.

"The reality is that Adelaide was to come to Bear Cove to see the school and meet the people before making a decision. But when it became known that Adelaide was coming to the cove today—probably through Frank to Clem and Miz Dora—the news got around, and everyone assumed she was coming to start teaching."

John stroked his chin. "Generally, I'd say this was not a church matter. But it's come about because people jumped to conclusions. I can allow for your explanation after Sunday's service. They're expecting school to start Monday morning."

"Thanks." Grant breathed easier. "I'll be at school Monday morning in case anyone doesn't get word."

John huffed. "The way news travels around here, I suspect they'll hear."

Christa walked over to the table. "Not everyone will take this well—and those little children who were introduced to me. . ." She touched her forehead. "Oh, I can't do this. I'm going home tomorrow."

Grant leaned back. "Afraid you can't do that."

She had a pert way of lifting her chin. "And who is going to stop me?"

He tried to conceal his amusement. "No train comes into or leaves Grey Eagle on Sunday. Unless you hitch a ride or walk, you'll have to wait until Monday."

Her eyes sparked flaming arrows. She apparently did not find him amusing.

Pastor John looked up at Christa. "Don't make any decision until after church tomorrow. Why, I'll even let you announce your purpose in being here. They'll be disappointed about the school, but they've waited over a year already. Another week won't hurt."

She shook her head. "I can't do that. This was not my doing."

John sighed. "I think the good Lord just gave me a new sermon for tomorrow—on bragging, gossip, rumor, and jumping to conclusions." He nodded, then gazed at Christa. "They'll look upon you just as warmly as they did at the potluck. Many of them would love to sell their crafts in the cities. If this is the Lord's will for you, Christa, it will work."

Grant watched her mouth open, but no words came. Was she about to cry? Suddenly, she walked past the table. "Excuse me. I'd like to take a walk before dark."

"Don't go far, Christa," John said. "As soon as the sun goes behind the mountains, darkness falls quickly and so does the cool night air."

Christa looked out the window and up at the sky, where the light was already fading.

John's gaze followed hers. "You have about thirty minutes or so of daylight. A nice walk would be up to the church and along the creek that runs behind it. A few cabins are out that way, belonging to some of the people you met today."

Grant heard the front door close, then brought the bowl of cobbler closer. "I'm sorry I've brought this on your niece, John."

"Give it all to the Lord, Grant. He works in mysterious ways. But do me a favor. Soon as you finish that cobbler, go find Christa and make sure she's all right."

❋

Christa walked from marker to marker, reading inscriptions. Many bore only a name and the dates of birth and death. She stopped at a larger tombstone that marked Sadie McIntyre's grave.

A twig snapped. She turned. Grant stood there.

"If you want me to leave, I will."

"No." She faced the tombstone again. "It's all right."

"You must have loved her very much," Grant said. "The cove people did."

"I didn't know her well," Christa confessed. "Before she became ill, they visited a couple times. She wasn't able to come to my parents' funeral, but Uncle John came. I was surprised and honored when he came to my graduation."

She touched the tombstone. "We couldn't come to Sadie's funeral because of the snowstorm."

"Yes," Grant said. "We were isolated here for several weeks."

The tombstone felt cold to her touch. "All this reminds me of how different things would be had my parents lived."

"How different?"

She saw no reason not to confide in him. They'd have no more than this brief encounter. "Had they not died, my brother would have remained in Charlotte as an accountant. But he felt obligated to take over the family business. According to him, a mere coed couldn't handle it."

"It's a crafts business?"

"Yes. More tourists come in each year now that the trains run from major cities. They like to take back souvenirs."

"So your brother doesn't let you work in the shop?"

"Oh, I can work. But he manages it, and he has a new wife." She looked toward the treetops.

Grant's "Hmm" seemed to confirm what she thought. A new wife would easily replace a sister in her brother's heart.

"Don't get me wrong. William and Bettina are good to me. I get to live with them, help with the cooking, cleaning, and running the shop." She regretted the resentment in her voice.

"I see," he said. "Your trip here is to make them sit up and take notice."

"Well, to show that I'm not just another hired hand. I have a better idea of how to handle that shop than Bettina."

"Bettina is your brother's wife?"

"Yes. She's lovely and charming." As soon as she said it, she recalled it was how he had described Adelaide. She turned quickly and tripped over a stone.

He reached out and grasped her arm. "Charm has its place," he said. "But you could match anyone in the lovely department."

Christa stepped away, and his arm fell to his side. This man who had ruined her chances to prove herself in this cove implied she was. . .lovely? He likely was trying to redeem himself for all the trouble he'd caused.

For an instant, she was speechless; then she focused on the grave markers. "Most of these are for babies and young children."

"Too many children die because of ignorance, superstition, or lack of a doctor's care. I want to help these people."

She looked at a marker. "This bears the name of Gordon."

"My little brother died of scarlet fever. There was no doctor to attend him."

"I'm sorry," she said.

"Thank you. That was many years ago. Pastor John says the Lord works in mysterious ways. I don't understand all that God allows. But I know my brother is in heaven. His death helped strengthen my resolve to become a doctor. Good comes from the worst of things, if we trust in the Lord."

She gave a short laugh. "That's great advice from a man who can't find a way to tell people his fiancée has been delayed. Where was your trust today, Doctor?"

Chapter 6

Grant stared at the ground. The changing light began to bathe the markers with color. "Come with me," he said.

A slight hesitation preceded the lift of her chin, but she walked beside him out of the graveyard and along the creek. Water rushed over the rocks, making small waterfalls and white foam, emitting a clean, fresh scent.

Surefooted, he stepped on a rock and held out his hand, unconcerned with city protocol that a gentleman wouldn't touch a lady's hand without her wearing gloves.

For an instant, her gaze rested on his hand; then she reached out. With one hand in his, and the other lifting her skirt to her ankles, she stepped out in her dainty shoes. They eased their way across the creek.

On the other side, he let go and led the way through the thick forest, heady with the smell of pungent pine.

"Oh my," she said, when they walked out into a clearing. "This is so unexpected."

She steered clear of thorny stems to touch wildflowers in the glade. She stopped at a great outcropping of rocks that revealed treetops and other mountains far below and beyond.

Her face lifted toward the brilliant sky where yellow became gold, orange turned red, and blue deepened. The orange sun peered over a mountain. The glow touched her face, shone in her eyes, and caressed her brown hair with a halo of reddish gold.

All the emotions he had seen in her face—chagrin, resentment, hurt, irritation—flew away like the few birds in the sky. Her expression held perfect peace and awe.

She whispered, "I've never seen anything so beautiful." She found a level spot on a boulder and sat down.

He sat near her, drew his knees up, and rested his forearms on them. "This is my favorite place. I can relax and be in tune with God. Remember how insignificant I am and how great He is. Coming here renews my trust in Him."

Her face turned toward his. With a slight movement, their shoulders would touch. He remained quite still, seeing the deepening color in her eyes, on her face, and the way the cool breeze blew a few strands of hair against her cheek. She had a perfect nose, lovely lips. They were slightly parted. He thought he knew why her eyes held a question and a challenge.

"You asked me about trust," he said. "When I was in Asheville and things didn't work out the way I wanted, I failed to trust, to stand up like a man and speak out. I let pride get in the way."

Feeling her fingers lightly on his arm, he glanced down, and she moved her hand away.

She spoke softly. "You were brave to go up the mountain, knowing your life could be in danger."

"That's easy. It's those women with their potlucks who scare me."

Christa laughed. Grant joined her and marveled at the sound echoing against the mountainsides.

"Well, Doctor," she said. "I'm afraid, too. They were pleasant, but when they find out I'm not the teacher, I'm afraid there's going to be some righteous anger."

"They've already accepted you, Miss Walsh."

"Christa," she said softly.

"Christa." The name tasted clean and cool in his mouth, like sparkling spring water. "What are you thinking?"

He told her what he was thinking about her name.

She opened her mouth in surprise, then looked out at the darkening landscape as the sun hid its face behind the mountain. "Thank you."

He stood. "It's getting cool and will be dark soon. We should go back." He held out his hand and helped her stand.

Strange, he had planned to bring Adelaide here. Instead, she was more than three hundred miles away. Perhaps she had watched the sky change colors over the ocean.

He didn't mean to compare Christa with Adelaide, but the comparison lay in his thoughts. Adelaide wouldn't walk with a man she didn't know or hold his hand to cross a stream. He couldn't image her stepping out onto those rocks or sitting down on the boulder in her fine dress. Adelaide would not travel alone on a train.

Christa had an entirely different lifestyle. She had no parents to whisk her off to Charleston. Even if she had, he doubted she would go anywhere with her parents instead of visiting the man she planned to marry.

Adelaide should be here with me.

Adelaide should be here with him, Christa thought.

But she wasn't. And Christa was enjoying this male companionship. Her impression of Grant Gordon had changed. He was a capable man with an honorable profession. Yet he was vulnerable to hurt and uncertain about some things. She could identify with that.

She wondered if something like this had happened with Roland. Had he taken an innocent walk and noticed the attributes of another woman, just as she was doing with this man beside her?

She could imagine how easily one might find another appealing. Were Grant Gordon not engaged, she might entertain serious thoughts.

He led the way back through the forest and took her hand again as they stepped on the rocks to cross the creek. His hand felt warm and strong.

Twilight had come. Stars twinkled in the darkening sky, and a silvery moon appeared. The evening was pleasantly cool. The leaves in the maples and oaks whispered.

Upon passing the graveyard, Christa realized something. "Most of the graves are marked several years ago. Are there fewer deaths now?"

He looked down at her. "Yes. For several years the cove had no doctor."

She liked the way the moonlight lay on his hair and on his rugged face. "So your being here has made a difference."

He smiled. "Having a doctor nearby does that. Also, education helps. Parents are eager for their children to be educated. That's why they jumped to the conclusion that you're the teacher and why I was reluctant to disappoint them. Would you like to see the school?"

"Uncle John—"

"He knows I came looking for you. He said he'd had a long week and was going to turn in."

"Oh. Then yes, I would like to see the school."

The shadows lengthened as the moon brightened. They walked past the church and onto a dirt road. Faint light glowed from the windows of several cabins. "That one is mine," Grant said. "The bigger one across from mine is the Carmichaels'. Teachers have always had a room in their cabin."

"There were more than one?"

"Not at one time," Grant said. "Sometimes the teacher borrowed a horse and rode to homes way back in the cove. Sometimes he stayed with a family for weeks and taught the children. But..." He drew in a deep breath. "Most teachers couldn't handle that for any length of time. Teaching here takes a lot of time, and there's very little pay." His gaze met hers. "In terms of money, I mean." He looked ahead toward the trees. "The pay comes in different ways."

Christa could understand that. A doctor, a teacher, or a preacher could feel proud of making a difference in people's lives. "Do any of them send their children away to school?"

"The closest is at Grey Eagle. That's too far to take children in all kinds of weather, and it costs too much to board them there. And too, the children in Grey Eagle stay out of school when their parents need them to help with crops, cattle, pigs, chickens. They're needed for that here in the cove, too, but these people will take what teaching they can get when they can get it."

"That's admirable," she said.

"Wasn't always like that, Christa. The railroad coming as close as Grey Eagle has brought an awareness of a world outside the cove." He gestured ahead of them. "There's the school."

The land had been cleared. She could imagine children playing there. Moonlight bathed the small building on the rise of the hill. A couple of wooden swings hung on long ropes tied around the limbs of two tall oaks.

She followed Grant up the steps and onto the narrow porch across the front of the building.

"Just a minute," he said when they reached the doorway.

He went inside, struck a match, and lit a wick. Light from a lamp on a table in front of the chalkboard brought the room into view. A narrow aisle separated the two sides. Several desks were reminiscent of ones Christa had used in the early grades. She suspected they were donated. Men of the cove likely had built the benches and narrow tables.

Two windows were on each side. She couldn't find anything to comment about and felt no need to walk around. The impression lodged in her mind was "bleak."

"There on your right," he said, "is the bell that summons the children to school."

A bell no larger than a good-sized pear sat on a narrow ledge. "I wouldn't think the sound of that little bell would travel far."

He smiled. "You could stand in this doorway, yell, and your voice would travel over these mountains and return to you. God knew what He was doing when He created echoes.

He knew people back in these coves wouldn't have the advantage of things city-folks have like timepieces and telephones."

She should say something. "I–I see this is only one room."

"The cove men built it several years ago. Before that, school was held in the church." He turned down the wick, leaving the room in shadows created by moonlight filtering through the windows. Christa walked onto the porch. Grant joined her and braced his hands on the banister.

"After the last teacher left, Sadie taught until she became ill. Years ago, the Carmichaels sold their house in the city to come here as missionaries. They're responsible for bringing your aunt and uncle here, as well as teachers. But age and illness have limited their activities. They are encouragers and have servant hearts. Their main income now is from raising chickens and selling them here and in Grey Eagle."

What about this place made people like Uncle John, Aunt Sadie, the Carmichaels, and Grant want to spend their lives here? She looked out at the schoolyard with its two big oaks. "It's certainly beautiful."

His voice was soft as moonlight. "You're a city girl, Christa, like Adelaide. I know this schoolhouse is backwoods compared with those in the city. Do you think she will like it here?"

Christa looked at the mountain vistas beyond. Would Adelaide like it? To be around people who put service to others ahead of themselves? To be in a place where so many anticipated her coming? To be loved by children eager to learn? To have an attractive man with an honorable profession love her? Would she like it?

Christa looked at the moonlight on his handsome face. "Yes," she said softly. "I think she will love it."

She walked down the steps and into the yard. She heard his voice behind her. "Christa." She turned to face him.

"We got off to a bad start. But I hope you have forgiven me. Do you suppose we could be friends?"

Chapter 7

The scene looked liked Saturday reversed. The forest that had swallowed up people and kept them overnight, now released them back onto the lush green lawn and into Sunday morning sunshine. The children looked freshly scrubbed—boys with their hair parted and plastered down, and girls in pigtails or curls. Most of the men wore coats despite the warm temperature.

They came quickly, eagerly, holding children's hands. They nodded to each other or spoke with dignity and reverence. The women wore plain hats or scarves on their heads. Miz Dora, strolling beside Clem in a suit coat and top hat, wore a fancy hat that complimented her frilly blouse, cameo broach, and black skirt. Christa breathed easier at the sight of her, having feared she looked too fancy in her store-bought dress and hat with its colorful silk band and small flowers.

From her place inside the church at a window, she saw a couple wagons pulling up. Grant came riding across the clearing. Christa hastened to the bench where Uncle John said she should sit—up front.

The church reminded her of the schoolhouse—small with one aisle down the middle. The differences were a pulpit instead of a teacher's table and benches with high backs.

Uncle John stood at the doorway, greeting people. She had come early with him to ring the first bell, as he called it. When he rang the second bell, people had about five minutes until the service started.

Christa wanted to see the church in case she didn't have another opportunity. Her gaze moved to the wooden cross on the wall behind the pulpit. She looked down to her gloved hands rather than think about what took place on that old rugged cross. She believed Jesus had died for her as He had for the entire world. But did He really work in one's daily life? If so, what had she done to cause Him to withhold His blessings from her?

A tap on her shoulder brought her attention to her surroundings. "Oh, good morning, Miz Dora."

"Good morning, Christa, dear. Your outfit is adorable."

"Thank you. So is yours."

Dora leaned forward and whispered, "I bought this in Asheville. I believe in wearing my finest to the Lord's house."

Christa smiled and glanced around, wondering if she'd be able to meet these people's eyes after Grant made his announcement. She heard his voice along with Uncle John's.

Soon, he sat beside her. She glanced over, and their eyes met. Her breath caught. Why did he sit beside her? She supposed it would look strange for him not to sit beside his supposed fiancée. And he had an announcement to make.

Besides that, they were friends.

Last night, when he'd asked, she had held out her hand in agreement. But friends. . .for how long?

After Roland told her about his change of plans, he had said, "We can still be friends, can't we, Christa?"

"Of course," she'd said and forced a smile. That had been followed by half a day in her room, drenching her pillow with tears. Bitterness had taken root in her heart. The feeling she had for Roland was not friendship.

And now, although she and Grant shared a songbook and she thrilled to the sound of his baritone voice, she wondered what kind of friends they could be after his fiancée arrived.

Adelaide would fill his time, heart, and mind.

Christa would go back to being a woman past marriageable age who had no purpose in life beyond taking a few highland crafts back to the city.

But for the moment, she sat beside a most appealing man. Everyone else other than Uncle John thought the two of them were in love, would be married. For the few minutes of this service, she would bask in that thought while being conscious of the warmth of his arm brushing against hers as they shared the songbook. She was this man's fiancée.

She would be. . .until he made his announcement. She slowly turned her face toward Grant. His head turned toward her. Their eyes met. For an instant, he seemed startled, then an expression like that of a dear friend crossed his face, and she thought a trace of color tinged his bronzed cheeks.

She saw him swallow as he again faced the front. His shoulders rose slightly.

So what if he thought her brazen. He had allowed these people to think she was his fiancée. For however long Uncle John preached, that's what she would be. When all one had was memories, she would savor this one. And for the first time, she hoped the sermon would be quite long.

Grant wondered what Adelaide would think of his taking Christa to his private place. To have held her bare hand, looked into her eyes, and asked for her friendship.

Adelaide had had a conniption fit when he'd commented that her cousin was quite attractive. She would never accept Christa being his friend. How could they be friends, anyway? She would be here a week. A few days. Until the train left tomorrow.

Could people be long-distance friends?

Sure.

Just as there could be long-distance fiancées. If someone was in the heart, it didn't matter if one was in Charleston and the other in Bear Cove. Was Adelaide in church thinking of him?

He could tell John was winding down. Grant had planned a speech. There'd been a mistake, he would say. This woman whom you have taken to your hearts is not my fiancée and she's not the teacher. No! That would never do—saying what Christa Walsh was not.

He would have to keep the attention focused on himself, not Christa.

Was that possible when during the entire service his eyes had been on Pastor John but his sensibilities had focused on the smartly dressed, lovely young woman beside him—his. . .friend?

Pastor John finished. He asked anyone who had anything to get right with the Lord to come and kneel at the front of the church.

Everybody stood. They were singing about when we all get to heaven what a day of rejoicing that will be.

Grant kinda wished he was there already.

John stared at him. Grant willed himself to stand.

"Pastor! Doctor!"

The singing stopped. A man with blood covering the front of his shirt ran down the aisle. Fear filled his eyes, and his breath was shallow. "Doc, it's my son." Both men ran up the aisle. The bloody man looked wild. "He nigh got his hand cut off down at the sawmill. He's out in the wagon."

Uncle John spoke loudly. "Let us bow before the Lord."

He prayed for Birr Morgan and his son as Grant ran out to the injured boy.

At the *amen*, everyone rushed out. Grant jumped down from the wagon. "Take him to my cabin." The boy looked deathly pale and rocked back and forth in the corner of the wagon, holding on to a bloody rag wrapped around his hand.

Birr Morgan jumped up onto the wagon, picked up the reins, and commanded the horse to go forward. Grant mounted his horse, calling out, "I could use some help."

Dora turned to Christa. "I'm sure Grant would appreciate your help. You'll be called on many times."

Here they were, the two best-dressed women in the crowd, picking up their skirts and racing across the yard. Soon they reached the dirt road. Christa looked at the older woman, who might have been a track runner. "Nobody else seemed eager to help."

Dora raised her eyebrows. "That's Birr Morgan. He had a bad experience with a church-goer who got lumber from him, then left town without paying. He's had nothing to do with churchgoers since then. Makes them pay before he'll load their wagons. They take that as an affront."

"But surely they won't hold that against the boy."

"They'll say if Birr had been in church, this wouldn't have happened."

The doctor's cabin was spotless. He began telling the women what to do at the same time he calmed the boy and his dad.

After giving the boy something to dull the pain, Grant cleaned the wound.

"How bad is it, Doc?" Birr Morgan kept asking.

"I'm trying to determine that," Grant said more than once.

The boy looked scared. "It's gotta be all right, Doc."

"Yeah," Birr said, "I'll need him at the sawmill."

"Then I don't want it well," the boy said. "I told you, I'm no good at the sawmill."

"You'll learn, boy."

Christa wondered about Birr Morgan's stern look. Was he only concerned about work?

When Grant asked, Dora handed him the sterilized instruments. He talked while examining the wound. "Looks like it cut the flesh across the palm. The cut on the thumb is deeper but not into the bone. That will heal just fine." He sutured the wound, then wrapped the hand in gauze. "Todd, we'll have to keep close watch on this. You need to follow my instructions about keeping it clean."

He addressed Birr. "You have him working at the sawmill before this is healed, and he could get an infection. Then there's a real problem." He paused. "Understand?"

Birr nodded.

Uncle John stood by the doorway.

"If you don't need us anymore, we'll leave, Grant," Dora said.

"That's fine. Thank you two, very much."

Birr Morgan interrupted. "I want to say something, and it's fine if you womenfolk hear it." He glanced around. "You, too, preacher."

He shifted uncomfortably, then stuck his thumbs behind his suspenders fastened to the waist of his worn pants. "I'd like to trade for your services, Doc."

"Sure," Grant replied without hesitation.

"Don't have any extra money right now," Birr said. "Need some supplies and repairs. I know you and Miz Dora here always wanted this boy in school. He learned a lot of foolishness that time I sent him. But he ain't no good to me in the sawmill like this."

Todd's eyes lit up, and all traces of pain left his face.

His dad continued. "He's got these highfalutin' notions Miz Sadie put in his head a long time ago. I don't need no education to run my mill. But things are changing, and my boy will have to deal with them townspeople. So, as a favor to you and your woman here, I'm gonna let my boy come to school."

The quick nod of Birr Morgan's head indicated he'd sacrificed his son as payment for his medical treatment. "His cutting his hand and all, pertnigh scart the daylights outta me. And I'm responsible. Just because I don't attend church don't mean I can't say when I'm sorry." He nodded at his son.

"Thank ya, Pa."

Grant and Birr Morgan shook hands on the deal.

"I. . .need air." Christa hurried from the cabin.

Dora followed. "Are you all right, dear?"

"I'll be all right." She would. As soon as she could get out of this place where she'd become a living lie.

Chapter 8

Christa stopped when Uncle John called her name. He caught up with her. When they were out of earshot of others, she could hold back no longer. "Uncle John, how could you and Grant let Mr. Morgan make that kind of deal? Have you forgotten? I am not the teacher, and I'm not. . . anybody's woman."

"It's a breakthrough for Birr Morgan to allow his son to get some schooling. To turn down Birr's offer would destroy that man's pride. It was a favor to Grant, and to—"

"His woman!"

Uncle John sighed. "Well, Christa. Sometimes it's best to remain silent. Grant will answer for his actions or lack of them."

"He certainly will."

Uncle John chuckled. Christa looked at him sharply.

He took on an innocent look. "That accident is working to change Birr's hardheadedness. Yes, indeed. The Lord works in mysterious ways."

So did a few people around here. Namely, her uncle and Dr. Grant Gordon.

When they reached the door of the cabin, Christa faced her uncle. "Maybe I should write to Adelaide and tell her not to bother coming to the cove. Tell her we already have a teacher—and Grant has his woman!"

She expected her uncle to tell her to ask the Lord's forgiveness for such an outburst. Instead, he laughed heartily. "You do remind me of my Sadie. Put spark in our lives, she did." He sighed and grew serious. "You bring joy to me, Christa. I stay busy, but I get lonely. It's good having a woman in the house."

Uncle John liked having her here? She liked being here. . . except for the deception.

They ate lunch, then Uncle John said he was going to his bedroom. "Sunday's the only day I can take a nap and still sleep all night."

She was washing dishes when Grant arrived. She offered him the leftover vegetable soup and corn pone.

He ladled soup into a bowl and sat down. Christa wiped her hands and sat across from him. If she had married Roland, they would be sitting across from each other like this.

She corrected that thought. Roland would never live in a rustic cabin in a backwoods cove. He wanted and needed attention. He was a banker now, married to the bank president's daughter. He wore suits with a watch's gold chain hanging from his vest pocket. He was fast becoming a man of means.

She did not want to sit across a table from such a man.

That idea startled her. Was she getting over Roland?

Grant looked over at her. He must have heard her intake of breath.

He wiped his mouth with a cloth napkin. "I'm sorry. I must have been eating like a pig.

I eat fast. Most of my meals are interrupted by someone needing help."

"I like seeing someone enjoy a meal I fixed, even if Uncle John insisted I open a jar of vegetable soup Sadie put up instead of taking time to cook from scratch."

He ate more slowly and kept peeking over at her. This mature man had a way of looking like a lost little boy. "Did John explain the importance of my accepting Birr Morgan's trade?"

"Enough to make me know you find it of the utmost importance. But something else is troubling me. I'm wondering—Grant, do you really have a fiancée?"

That's not what he expected her to say.

Did he have a fiancée?

He thought so.

He was making payments on a ring. Adelaide had said she'd come to the cove to check it out. "Of course I have a fiancée. Surely you don't think that's not true."

The look on her face reminded him that he hadn't told the truth in two days. But emergency situations had prevented his confession. He continued to stare at Christa when she took his empty bowl and carried it to the dishpan.

He picked up his glass, downed the rest of the milk, then went over to her. He picked up a towel and took the dishes from the rinse pan, dried them, and set them aside. "While I was eating, Christa, I was thinking of a solution."

She scrubbed a dish. "You mean there is one?"

"Sure. I'll be at the schoolhouse in the morning before eight o'clock. I'll tell everyone as they come."

"They're going to be terribly disappointed, aren't they?"

"Yes," he admitted. "But they'll handle it, Christa. And when Adelaide arrives, they'll be captivated by her charm."

She stiffened. "You think these people need charm?"

He realized his mistake. Christa must think he meant that she had no charm. She didn't have the kind of charm that Adelaide had. She had different qualities. "They're already captivated by your enthusiasm for life, Christa. Your outgoing nature. Your—"

He'd almost said, "your appeal." But it wouldn't be fitting for an almost-engaged man to speak that way to another woman.

She scoffed. "Oh, Grant. You don't have to flatter me. I know I'm not the kind of charming young lady who bats her eyelashes, has honey in her mouth, and makes a man fall at her feet. I'm a spinster in her early twenties."

He shrugged and grinned. "The attributes you mentioned are not the only ones that attract an old man like me—in his midthirties."

He picked up the bowls and put them on a shelf. He had been in his early thirties when he'd fallen for Adelaide. He had to admit that eyelashes and honey weren't a bad combination.

He glanced back at Christa. He must not contemplate her attributes, however.

He closed the cabinet door. "Christa, meet me at the schoolhouse in the morning. After I tell the parents you're here for crafts, you can talk with them."

She lifted her chin. "Dr. Grant Gordon, even if I have to walk, I'll be out of this cove tomorrow before the school bell rings."

✻

Clang. . .ang! Clang. . .ang! Clang. . .ang!

Christa couldn't believe she was standing in the doorway of this one-room school-house, ringing the bell. It not only rang; it echoed around the mountainsides and returned as if the sound were trapped, reminding her of exactly how she felt.

How was she going to tell these people to take their children home?

Grant had come by early, saying LulaMae was having her baby. The midwife sent word that it hadn't turned right. She needed the doc and the preacher.

Christa stepped into the front room just in time to see Grant and a boy disappear from sight. Her uncle turned to her. "I have to go."

"What about school?"

"Maybe Grant or I will return before school starts. If not, you can. . . ." He lifted his hands helplessly. "I honestly don't know, Christa."

She stared at his disappearing back, then at the wooden door. The quiet was deafening, until the hoot owl scared the wits out of her. No, she'd already had the wits taken out of her by Dr. Grant Gordon and his inability to speak up. Now her uncle was in cahoots with him.

So, here she stood in the schoolhouse doorway, swinging this bell as if she were the schoolmarm. Once they knew, these people would never forgive her.

The sun rose over the mountain in all its glory, and the forest thrust forth children, all sizes and ages. They came across the clearing and from down the road. They hastened up the road from the direction of the doctor's cabin, and some came from behind the church, through the graveyard.

Why had she rung that bell?

Facing a black bear would be easier than facing the parents of these children.

Parents?

"Wh–where are your parents?" she asked as several children came up to her with expectant faces.

"School ain't fer them, ma'am," said a red-headed, freckle-faced boy who looked to be eight or nine years old. "And we ain't babies. We can come by ourselves."

"Of course," she said.

His smile spread from ear to ear. "Name's BillyJoe Davison, ma'am."

Christa hoped the children mistook her grimace as a smile. She felt no joy.

A girl as big as Christa came holding the hands of a younger boy and a girl who didn't look a day over four years old.

They kept coming.

She kept willing Grant or Uncle John to show up.

They didn't.

A fair-haired boy of about seven came right up to her. "The preacher said to tell you Ma had a baby girl. The baby's doing fine, but Ma ain't feeling so good."

"Well, I'm sure the doctor and the preacher will take good care of her."

"Yes, ma'am," he said. "Ma shore is proud to have a girl. She named her FloraMae. Right purty, ain't it?"

"Very pretty." Christa was glad he focused on the baby instead of his ma, who wasn't doing too well. Maybe she should tell the children she wasn't doing too well and send them home.

She saw a wagon in the distance. A child wouldn't be driving a wagon to school. But explaining to one parent wouldn't solve anything. She could at least give the impression she was a teacher. "Children, go in and take your seats. Um. . .little ones in front and bigger ones in back."

They obeyed as if she knew what she was doing.

She recognized Birr Morgan in the wagon. "Here he is, ma'am. Just like I said."

She tried to smile. "I see." Todd climbed out of the wagon, careful not to use his injured hand. "Thank you, Mr. Morgan."

He touched the edge of his floppy brimmed hat and nodded, then went back the way he'd come.

"Teacher."

Christa looked at Todd. In the doctor's cabin, she hadn't paid attention to his looks. Before her stood a young man taller than she. He had the most vibrant blue eyes, and his blond hair gleamed in the sun like corn silk.

"Teacher, this is one of the happiest days of my life. If I'd known cutting my hand would get me in school again, I would have done it on purpose." Color blushed his cheeks. "That is, if we'd had a teacher here."

Christa had to tear her gaze away from him. His resonant voice was as impressive as his looks. She remembered that Uncle John, Miz Dora, Sadie, and Grant had wanted this boy to get an education. She didn't know what his abilities were, but she couldn't imagine that he should be hidden away in a sawmill.

Hours later, she had to admit she'd enjoyed getting to know the children and their interests and making lists of their names, ages, something about their families, how much education they'd had, and what they knew. They sang a couple songs together, and Christa was struck by the pure beauty of Todd's voice.

At noon, she dismissed them for recess and to eat the lunches they'd brought. She had no lunch. She couldn't imagine what had detained the men unless LulaMae had grown worse.

Excited voices sounded from the schoolyard. She reached the doorway as BillyJoe rushed up. "Teacher. Come look."

She hurried onto the porch. Children were gathered around. BillyJoe pointed to the ground. Her breath caught at the sight of a man slumped over at an odd angle.

"Grant!"

Chapter 9

"Huh! Wh–what?"

Grant sat up, groaned, and began massaging his numb leg. He waved away the giggling children.

Christa stood in front of him. "What are you doing on the ground, Grant?" She looked at his leg. "Are you hurt? Shot?"

My, she was pretty in that white shirtwaist and red skirt. "I was sleeping." He stood in spite of his tingling leg. "When I heard Todd singing, I couldn't interrupt. I closed my eyes to thank God that Todd has this chance, and I fell asleep. Christa, we can't let him go back to hiding away in a sawmill."

"We?" Christa crossed her arms.

Grant blinked. "I mean the people in the cove. The boy has great talent."

"I agree."

He yawned. "Um, you want me to teach the rest of the day?"

"You're dead on your feet, Grant. Go home and rest. Apparently, you don't get much of that."

"You're right. I am sorry about all this, Christa. I'll set it straight. Just wait and see."

"I'm waiting." She tapped her foot.

He grinned, climbed on his horse, and looked down at her. "You look like a schoolmarm."

"I am not a schoolmarm."

"You still look like one. All stern, as if you'd like to give me a whack with the ruler."

He rode on home. Yes, she did look like a schoolmarm. But next week, Adelaide would be standing there.

He supposed he was just too tired to feel elated about that.

Christa dismissed school at 3:00 p.m. She found Uncle John in the backyard, where he'd wrung a chicken's neck and was pulling out white feathers. His smile was warm. "I had to take a nap after being awake most of the night, Christa. The least I can do is fix you a hot supper. You must be tired."

"Honestly, Uncle John. I haven't felt so exhilarated in years. Oh, Uncle—"

He held up the chicken by its legs. "If you're going to talk about school, go fetch the doctor. Invite him to supper. He and I can finish out the week. Dora claims she can only teach Bible and music, but she always pitches in wherever needed. We should know what you did today."

"Yes, you're right."

She walked quickly up the dirt road to Grant's cabin and knocked.

"Just a minute," he called. He opened the door, buttoning his shirt. His hair was damp from being washed. A mass of dark curls fell over his forehead. She liked the looks of this. . . friend.

He readily agreed to come to supper.

They walked down the road in the late afternoon sunlight.

"How are LulaMae and FloraMae?"

"The baby's perfect." The softness in his eyes turned serious. "But LulaMae has been fighting a bronchial cough. I couldn't give her strong medication until after the baby was born. I needed to stay and make sure she would be okay. You understand, don't you, Christa?"

She nodded. "I hope the parents understand when they learn their children were taught by an imposter."

"Do you know what your uncle John said?"

She grinned. "That God works in mysterious ways?"

Grant chuckled. "Well that, too." He stuck his hands in his pockets. "He said that you're a lifesaver."

"Maybe a lifesaver for myself, Grant. Today, I stopped thinking about what's gone wrong in my life. I thought about the children. They're bright and talented. But their abilities will go to waste if they're not trained. When you didn't speak up, it wasn't because you're a coward, but because you care."

His glance met hers. "I do care, Christa."

They reached Uncle John's cabin and were greeted by the wonderful smell of chicken frying. Grant and Christa set the table, then pulled out chairs and sat down.

"Todd wants to write songs," Christa said. "He brought some with him written on old scraps of paper. He hides them from his dad, who thinks songwriting is a waste of time."

Uncle John turned from the sizzling chicken. "You seem to have found out a lot about him, Christa."

She smiled. "He volunteered that information after class today while waiting for his dad. He left the papers with me. He has the tunes in his head but can't put notes on paper." She sighed. "I don't know how to help him with that."

"I don't know music," Grant said. "But I'd like to see what he's written."

Christa nodded. "We got to know each other. The children are eager to hear about city life—what the houses are like and the kind of work people do. I wrote down their names and what I thought important." She laughed. "Except the boy who said he's not supposed to tell what kind of work his pa does."

Grant laughed and nodded when Uncle John said, "Must be the Spiller boy."

Christa assumed the boy's reluctance had something to do with moonshine—and not the kind that comes from the sky.

After supper, Uncle John insisted on washing the dishes. "You two talk over that school-work, and I'll listen."

Grant refilled their coffee cups. "I'd like to see your notes, Christa, since I'll be teaching tomorrow." He motioned toward her notepad. "Let's take a look."

She took a sip of coffee, then opened the notepad.

The sun's rays were slanting through the kitchen windows by the time they finished. Grant had moved closer to her to better see her notes. She had written students' names, a rough description of where they lived, how much schooling they'd had, who could read, who knew their ABCs and numbers, their hobbies, and what their parents did.

Grant studied her pages for a long time, making Christa feel defensive. "I tried to make it a fun day so the children would like learning. A child should show respect but not be afraid of a teacher." She hoped she'd done something right. "Do you think this will help Adelaide?"

Both men stared at her as if she'd spoken in French or Latin. Uncle John rubbed his chin and glanced at Grant.

Grant looked thoughtful, then said, "Unequivocally." He leaned back in his chair. "Do you have any suggestions about what should take place tomorrow?"

"Well, yes. I thought I'd test them. Not grade them, but tell them the spelling bee and the numbers quiz is practice for the real tests after they study. That way I—I mean you—can divide them into grades. Also, you should find out what they know about life beyond the cove and about history."

He pushed away from the table. "I'd like to check on Todd's hand. Would you go with me?" She hesitated, and he added quickly, "We can discuss how we might help him."

※

Grant returned to John's front yard with his horse and medical bag. Christa had changed into a riding skirt and had taken the pins from her hair. It fell in waves below her shoulders. Her face glowed with happiness as he reached down to scoop her up behind him.

He glanced at John, who stood looking at them with raised eyebrows and a finger against his lips as if holding back words, such as the Lord and His mysterious ways.

Grant acknowledged John with a nod and turned the horse in the opposite direction. Whether it was the Lord or the day at school, he knew John was pleased with Christa. She was learning, as Grant had after losing his parents, that getting involved with the problems of others lessened your own. She had taken over the school quite successfully.

He liked the change in her. And he liked the feel of her behind him, holding onto his shirt, and the sound of her voice telling him about the need for books, writing materials, and lesson plans.

Earlier, he said she looked like a schoolmarm. Now, she talked like one.

The Morgans lived a couple of winding miles away. Several hunting dogs greeted them. Todd came onto the porch, and Elvira Morgan stood in the doorway. She invited them inside.

Elvira kept a clean cabin. Maybe because she had only one child. After having Todd, she had had several miscarriages.

Elvira poured tea for them at the kitchen table. Grant unwrapped the bandages from Todd's hand. "It's red and raw, but that's to be expected. Keep it clean, and no lifting."

Elvira sat at the table. "Oh, Miz Christa. Thank you for coming to teach. I know what this means to Todd. I once had the kinds of dreams he does about singing." She blushed. "My voice wasn't near as good, though."

"Now, Mrs. Morgan," Grant said, "your voice stood out above the others in church."

"I always did love singing." She looked at Christa. "It's no secret, Miss Christa, that my pa left Ma with a passel of younguns and went off and joined a band down in Tennessee. We heard he done real good. I vowed I'd never do a thing like that." She glanced at Todd. "And I told my boy he has to mind his pa 'cause family's more important than singing."

"Some people manage to have a family and enjoy their music, too, Mrs. Morgan," Christa said.

Elvira looked surprised. "They can really do that?"

Christa nodded.

Grant wrapped gauze around Todd's hand. "It sure would be nice if you and Todd sang in church again."

Elvira agreed. "I learnt Todd all the songs I know. He makes some up, and we sing them to the tunes of church songs. But we don't let Birr hear us. He says them churchgoers ain't no count since that one done 'im wrong."

Christa spoke up. "Does he feel that way about Uncle John and Grant and the Carmichaels?"

"Oh, no. But he says they have to be decent, being the preacher and missionaries and a doctor." She touched Christa's arm. "And I know you're good, Miss Christa, just by what you done for my boy today. You give him hope."

Grant tied a knot around the gauze. "Does he feel the same about the women at church?"

Elvira leaned back. "Well, no, Doctor. He don't do business with no women. But they's married to the men."

"If you were there, I reckon there'd be one good woman who was married to a good, honest man."

Grant watched her eyes light up. "I could say that to Birr. I can up and tell 'im what the church needs is some good woman like me." She laughed. "You know I'm funning with ya."

"You have a nice way about you, Mrs. Morgan," Grant said. "I wouldn't be a bit surprised if you have that husband of yours back at church in no time."

Todd grinned.

Grant's good feeling left after they left the cabin. Christa walked so fast, he feared she might ride off and leave him stranded. "Did I do something wrong?"

"You encouraged them to come to church where there are good, decent people like you and me." She got up behind him on the horse. "So how will they feel when they find out we're liars and deceivers? The good teacher won't even be at school tomorrow."

The mountain air cooled as the sun set, but the coldness he felt was from the stiff figure seated behind him.

They returned to John's cabin beneath a darkened sky. She didn't protest when he raised his arms to lift her down. Maybe she, too, missed their earlier togetherness.

She stood in front of him. He gently turned her face up toward his. "There's no way I can tell people the truth until they're gathered in church on Sunday."

He braced himself for her reaction before adding, "Is there a chance, Christa, that you would consider teaching for the rest of the week?"

Chapter 10

Christa hardly heard the *clang...ang* of the bell. A different tune sounded in her heart and mind. Last night, she'd looked into Grant's face bathed in soft moonlight. How could she say anything else? "Grant, I will be honored to continue with the children because...we're friends."

After an interminable moment, he had pressed her hands gently. "I'm grateful to you."

Christa felt pleased that she could let go of resentful memories of Roland and replace them with thoughts of a man who had shown her that he was competent, confident in his work, yet vulnerable when it came to disappointing adults and children.

The first child came bounding out of the sunlit horizon, bringing Christa back to her own sense of mission. She would give her best efforts to being a schoolmarm.

The week went all too quickly. Grant came a couple times and talked to the children about science and chemistry. Uncle John commented on a Bible story before lessons began. Dora helped Todd lead the hymn singing. Christa wrote the words on the blackboard with chalk so they could see how the words looked. The children were like sponges soaking up everything being taught.

Dora helped her plan the Friday exhibition for parents.

Friday dawned clear and warm. They practiced most of the day.

Grant and Uncle John set up tables outside for refreshments provided by Dora and Clem. Adults arrived before 3:00 p.m.

Christa told the children they had nothing to be nervous about, despite her shaking hands and tremulous voice. At three o'clock, she had the children stand on the porch, the steps, and the ground. Parents stood opposite them.

Todd led the other children in a welcoming song. The parents applauded, then Christa greeted them. She had the younger children sing the ABCs. Older children recited the multiplication tables. They all quoted the Twenty-third Psalm. Christa didn't want any child to perform alone in case they become embarrassed by making a mistake. That is, no one but Todd.

He sang "Amazing Grace." His high tenor reverberated around the mountains as if an entire chorus of angels had joined him, and nature itself had decided to praise the Lord. The adults didn't move a muscle or blink an eye. Tears streaked many faces.

When Todd finished, complete silence followed. Finally, a man shouted, "Amen." Others began saying "Amen" and "Praise the Lord" and applauding.

Todd smiled. He had told Christa he was going to sing to the Lord, no matter what his pa might do.

Christa gave out report cards for the week's work. She wrote only praise for what each child had accomplished, whether learning no more than "ABCDEFG" or as much as the older girl who did long division.

The program was a huge success. Children and parents glowed with pride and happiness.

Then came the moment Christa had been dreading. First, she told the parents how much she appreciated them letting her teach. "I've never had a more fulfilling week in my life." She paused, feeling tears threaten her eyes.

The faces in front of her expressed respect and admiration. That would soon change. She looked at Grant. "The doctor has something to say."

❋

Grant had prayed and thought but still wasn't sure what to say. He faced the adults. Christa stood by Pastor John, who put his arm around her shoulders.

Grant began. "I have an announcement."

All sound faded except the gossiping birds in the big oaks.

The words came easy when he praised Christa for what she had meant to the children during the past week, how the program reflected her love for the children and her efforts to discover their capacity for learning. "There could be no finer teacher," he said. Applause erupted.

Silence returned when he said, "However, there has been a misunderstanding."

He reiterated what happened from the moment he got off the train, and how he'd wanted to find the right time to tell the truth. He'd been called away for emergencies both times.

Their gazes remained fixed on him. He prayed their anger and disappointment would be toward him and not Christa.

"Christa Walsh is not my fiancée, which means she's not the teacher you expected."

He heard a few gasps but continued. "She came to visit her uncle John and to find crafts for her brother's shop in Hendersonville. She thought her uncle had sent Clem to fetch her. She had nothing to do with this deception, and I hope you won't blame her."

He lifted his hand to silence the escalating mumbling. "Adelaide Montgomery is my fiancée and a teacher. She and her parents will arrive tomorrow."

Pastor John came and stood beside him. "My niece told me about the situation that first night at the cabin. Doc planned to set things straight on Sunday morning." He reiterated some of what Grant had said. "But if the misunderstanding hadn't happened, then the children would have been without a teacher this week. And nobody can deny Christa has been about the best teacher we could have."

Grant doubted anyone would take issue with that. A little of his confidence returned. "What Miss Walsh has done will be turned over to Miss Montgomery. Miss Walsh came here for crafts. So to show appreciation for her week of teaching, maybe you will want to share with her."

Uncle John laid his hand on Grant's shoulder. "And we can thank the Lord for Grant's not speaking out sooner. Otherwise these children would still have been underfoot this past week."

The people laughed.

Uncle John continued. "The Lord works in mysterious ways. Let's bow for prayer."

At the *amen* Miz Dora stepped up. "Now it's punch and cookie time."

Grant expected to receive a few verbal punches. He hoped Christa would be spared. Just then, he saw Birr Morgan making a beeline toward her.

Christa could hardly believe it. Children stopped to say they wanted her to be their teacher, then ran off to play. Women told her about their crafts and about people who made the finest quilts, whittled beautiful wooden animals, tatted the fanciest doilies, dried the prettiest flowers, and made souvenirs from rocks.

Birr Morgan walked up, staring at her. Elvira and Todd hurried to stand next to him. Others stepped back.

Christa thought Birr's removing his hat and holding it in front of him was a sign of respect. But she dreaded what might follow when he said, "Miss Walsh. I'm plumb dumbfounded." At least, he wasn't toting his rifle.

He looked her in the eye. "I knowed Todd could sing but not like that. I ain't never heard anything so beautiful. My woman could sing pretty, too, and I don't normal say things like this, but she needs to hear this. Todd, too."

Christa identified with the uncertainty in Elvira's and Todd's eyes.

"That singing today wasn't like guitar and banjo singing. Or even church singing. It was citified. I've heard citified singing so I know what I'm talking about. I was mighty proud of the way my boy stood up there, waving that stick I made 'im, and them children singing in time with it. I think maybe I've been selfish, taking Elvira away from the music she was fond of."

Elvira caught hold of his arm. "Oh, no, Birr. I made my choice. You was it. I loved you more than I loved singing. And there ain't a thing wrong with your banjo picking. I sing to that."

Birr stood a little taller. Then he looked away from the softness in Elvira's eyes. Christa thrilled at the love they had for each other. "So," he said. "I think my woman is right. She made her choice, and it was me. I reckon Todd needs to make his choices hisself. But he's only sixteen, and first I want him to know a trade in case he don't make it in the city with singing."

"Oh, Birr." Elvira's arms went around him.

"Now hold on, woman. People's looking."

She stood close. "You're just the best man I ever knowed, Birr Morgan."

He cleared his throat. "Well, anyway, Miss Christa. Feel free to help my boy. And if you ain't going to be here, you can tell that new teacher." He spoke softly. "You might want to know. I make a few craft-like pieces out of my wood."

Christa felt she must surely look as happy as that family. How mistaken she'd been thinking that Birr Morgan was the meanest man she'd ever seen. He had a tender heart, and dearly loved his wife and son. The way some things turned out sure was beginning to look. . . mysterious.

When the crowd dwindled, Dora came up and handed Christa a glass of punch and a cookie. "You're such a hit, Christa, with everyone. I don't know how they'll get along without you. And I tell you this. . . ." She leaned closer. "We're not having another welcoming like we did for you."

Christa didn't know if she should thank her for that. "I appreciate all you've done for me. And I didn't mean to deceive anyone."

"Oh, we know that. We're just glad to have you here. Maybe you can help the new teacher."

Being a substitute would make her feel like she had after Roland jilted her and all her friends were getting married.

After she and Uncle John went to his cabin, she told him that the women, and even Birr Morgan, were eager to share their crafts. "But Uncle John, I've imposed on you long enough."

"Imposed? Girl, it's a joy having you here. And I'm selfish enough to want you to stay."

"Oh, Uncle John, I'll spend a day or so gathering a few things to take back for William. Then I should leave."

He nodded. "You'll have to stay long enough to see what Miss Adelaide looks like, now won't you?"

Chapter 11

C hrista chose the royal blue suit she'd worn when she came to the cove, the dressiest outfit she'd brought. Even so, she'd be no match for the lovely, charming Adelaide.

She sat in the front row at church. Would Grant escort Adelaide down the aisle and seat her beside Christa? Everyone must be as curious as she to see the woman who had won their doctor's heart and would be the real teacher for their children.

Where were they? Church was no place to make a grand appearance after everything started. Uncle John asked Todd to stand up front and lead the singing.

When they stood, Grant slipped in beside Christa. A quick glance didn't reveal any charming woman standing with him.

During the service, his hands moved to his knees and he'd lean back and take a deep breath. At times he crossed his arms.

When Uncle John asked for those who had a decision or special request to come forward, Grant walked to the front. "I have an announcement," he said.

❋

Grant didn't like speaking about his personal life in public, but he owed these people an explanation. He'd simply state the facts.

"The Montgomerys didn't arrive yesterday," he said. "Instead, a telegram came. Adelaide's grandfather suffered chest pains. Dr. Montgomery can't make the trip until he's sure his dad is all right. Adelaide can't travel alone all the way from Charleston."

Only Christa could help in this predicament. "Miss Walsh," he said, "Could you stay on until Miss Montgomery arrives?"

With her head held high beneath that pert little hat, she walked up and stood beside him.

When Christa said, "I am reluctant," Grant felt the disappointment in the room. "Because," she continued, "I love it so. I will be honored to substitute until the real teacher comes."

The congregation broke into applause.

Uncle John stepped up. "The Lord. . ."

When they returned to their seats, Grant whispered, "How can I ever thank you?"

Christa tried to reject the words from Browning's famous poem. "How do I love thee? Let me count the ways."

Grant's words and her thoughts had nothing to do with love.

He was thanking her for saving him from humiliation. For a while longer, however reluctantly, she would be a schoolmarm.

❋

Christa made up her lesson plans and continued to use Uncle John, Dora, and Grant to help. She didn't think she rated any praise. The important thing was teaching the children as best she could.

She'd never before felt so useful. Others could probably do the job much better than she. But they weren't here.

And she was.

The following Sunday when Grant sat beside her in church, unaccompanied, Christa supposed Adelaide might never come. She reprimanded herself for that selfish thought. Adelaide's grandfather could still be ailing. . .or worse.

Uncle John must have had a similar thought. "Instead of waiting until the end of the service for the doctor's latest announcement," he said from the pulpit, "we'll have that first. Otherwise if he were called away early, we wouldn't know what's going on in his life."

Grant stood and announced that Adelaide's grandfather was improving. Adelaide and her parents would arrive on Monday.

Christa peeked at him. He didn't look at her. There was no applause. He said, "Well, um, that's it."

He returned to his seat. Uncle John motioned for Todd to lead the singing.

When Christa and Grant stood, sharing the songbook, he didn't sing. She supposed his mind was with his Adelaide.

✂

Grant stared at the dark clouds hanging low in the sky. A storm was rapidly rolling over the mountains. It would be gone by morning. Weather would not prevent the Montgomerys from arriving. He would meet them tomorrow and rent a carriage to bring them to the cove.

Would Adelaide fit in the way Christa had?

Would Todd and his parents feel as comfortable with Adelaide?

A week ago, Grant had written to Adelaide that a teacher was filling in for her. He'd mailed some of Todd's songs and told her of the boy's exceptional talent.

The dark clouds moved closer. Grant turned to leave. Walking into the woods, he heard a rumble of thunder, saw a movement.

"Christa?"

"Oh!" She tugged. "I'm caught."

Grant loosened her skirt from the thorny twig. "A wild-berry bush."

"Thank you." She smoothed her skirt and stepped away from the bush. "Sorry. I didn't mean to intrude. I thought you would be home, making arrangements. I just wanted a last look."

He should have said there was a storm coming. But that was no way to treat a friend who had done so much for him. He took hold of her arm and smiled. "You could never be an intrusion. Come look."

They walked out into the glade.

"It's even beautiful with a storm approaching," she said.

"Yes. You should see it when the clouds are below this glade." He knew that might never happen. "I was just thinking about the house I want to build here."

"Oh, this belongs to you?"

He nodded. "This is directly behind my cabin, separated by the woods. I've thought my cabin could be a clinic someday."

"I suppose you were thinking about your cabin and your life with Adelaide."

He stared at the mountains below. "Yes," he said finally. "I was." He took a deep breath.

"Dr. Montgomery was my mentor and entrusted his daughter to me. I owe him everything."

All was quiet except the wind rustling in the trees.

He knew this was difficult for Christa. She loved the school and the children. "Will you stay in the cove? You've come to mean so much to. . .everyone."

"I'm glad I got to teach. I'm going to miss it."

Shadows on her face reflected the darkness he felt at the thought of not seeing her, teaching with her, sitting with her in church, watching her relate to the children. "I don't want to lose y—"

A crack of thunder stopped his words. He'd almost said he didn't want to lose her. He now said, "I don't want to lose your friendship."

He barely heard her voice above the rising wind. "You'll be busy with Adelaide, and I'll return to Hendersonville."

He felt like a tree, rooted to the ground. He wished she would turn, run away from him, before. . .

Following another loud roll of thunder, she stated the obvious. "It's raining!"

"You're kidding," he said as the cloudburst showed no mercy.

They ran through the forest and across the creek, not bothering with stepping stones. They laughed and sloshed past the graveyard, splashed beyond the church, and hurried to John's cabin.

As if having a mind of their own, his hands came up to her shoulders. Her rain-spattered face lifted toward his. He didn't intend it, but their cool, wet lips touched.

Then as if lightning had struck, they pulled away.

She said, "Bye," and fled inside. He remained staring at a closed wooden door, getting soaked.

How could he ever forget this storm?

This storm that raged within his heart.

Chapter 12

Christa and Todd stood outside the school as the newcomers strolled across the schoolyard. Christa glanced at the middle-aged woman and Dora but could not take her eyes from the lovely young woman walking with them. Blond curls peeked out beneath a pink-flowered bonnet that matched her pink and white dress.

The pretty girl came right up to Christa and reached for her hands. "You have to be Miss Walsh. Grant and the Carmichaels think the world of you. They told me about your being mistaken for me. It's so funny. But I must scold Grant for not telling me how pretty you are."

Christa couldn't help but respond favorably to the compliment accompanied by the sweet smile and shining blue eyes. "And you'd be Adelaide Montgomery. Grant did say how lovely you are. I'm pleased to meet you."

Adelaide turned to the other women. "This is my mama, Jane Montgomery."

The woman hugged Christa. "We're all so grateful to you, my dear. Grant told us how disappointed the people in the cove would be without all you've done."

Christa could see where Adelaide got her charm. This smartly dressed, congenial woman reminded her of her own mother. "I'm sure I've benefited more than the children. Let me introduce Todd Morgan."

Adelaide shook Todd's hand. "Oh, you're the talented young man Grant told us about. I have shown your songs to a music teacher in Charleston. He is so impressed that he has made this trip with us."

Todd's eyes sparked with excitement. "A music teacher came all the way from Charleston?"

Adelaide nodded. "He's with my papa and Grant right now, and he wants to talk with your parents."

By Todd's adoring look, Christa felt he had lost his heart to Adelaide. With their blond hair and blue eyes, they could pass for brother and sister. His smile broadened. "There's my pa now."

Adelaide did not seem put off by Birr Morgan's rugged looks. He climbed down from the wagon and took his hat off before shaking her pink-gloved hand.

Birr, Todd, and Adelaide engaged in conversation. Christa would have liked to listen, but Miz Dora spoke. "I've managed to convince Adelaide and her parents to stay with me and Clem tonight. That way, Miss Adelaide can get an early start with you in the morning."

Adelaide bade the Morgans good-bye and turned to Christa. Apparently she had overheard Dora. "Oh, Christa, I do want you to tell me all about the children and what you've done. Grant says it's remarkable." She smiled delightedly.

Dora invited them all for supper. "Christa, you and Pastor John are welcome to join us. Dr. Montgomery, Mr. Warren, and Grant will be there."

"Thank you," Christa said, "but I'm sure Uncle John is already fixing our supper. And

I need to make sure I have everything ready for Miss—"

"Miss nothing," Adelaide said. "I'm Adelaide to you. I think we could be great friends."

Christa couldn't imagine that anyone would turn down an offer of friendship with Adelaide.

But she also couldn't imagine sitting at supper watching Adelaide and Grant glow with love for each other. How could she consider staying here and have her mending heart break again?

�✻

At the depot in Grey Eagle, Grant and Adelaide had kissed each other's cheeks. She was so beautiful. He felt guilty. Not only had he betrayed his fiancée, he'd betrayed Christa's trust in him. Mrs. Montgomery hugged him, and Dr. Montgomery shook his hand. Then Adelaide introduced a young man in a dark suit as Charlie Warren, the music teacher from Charleston.

Grant was pleased that the man was impressed enough with Todd's song to visit him in the cove but thought him young to have much experience. However, as Charlie and Dr. Montgomery rode along with him on their rented horses ahead of the carriage in which Adelaide and Mrs. Montgomery rode, Grant soon discovered the young man's accomplishments.

Charlie had been a child protégé and traveled as a concert pianist, but his love was teaching music. "I feel that the Lord wants me to give back to others the kinds of opportunities I have had. I want to see if Todd is one I should mentor." He addressed Grant. "I understand that is what Dr. Montgomery did for you, and now you're of tremendous value in this cove."

Grant admired Charlie Warren's dedication to the Lord and to others.

After the three men toured the cove, they visited the Morgans, where Charlie talked to Todd about his music. Upon returning to the Carmichaels, Clem and Dora insisted the Montgomerys and Charlie stay with them instead of riding back down to Grey Eagle after supper.

"Charlie's welcome to stay with me," Grant said.

Charlie accepted the offer.

Adelaide linked her arm through Grant's and teased, "You didn't tell me your Miss Christa was so young and pretty."

Grant felt warmth rise to his face. "Well, yes, I suppose she is."

Adelaide surprised him by saying, "I like her. Very much. I'm eager to observe her tomorrow in school."

During supper, Grant halfway listened to the conversations. He kept reminding himself of Adelaide's attributes. Yet he couldn't keep his mind on Adelaide. When he needed words most, they didn't come.

What could he say?

That while promised to one woman he found another. . . appealing.

Appealing?

To say the least.

But he must face facts. His feelings for Adelaide had grown over time. His feelings for Christa had come suddenly, unexpectedly.

Things weren't working out the way he'd planned—in his life or in his heart.

Christa lay awake. The past weeks had been wonderful. She'd gained a purpose, a love for children, a new confidence in her abilities. She'd replaced her bitterness and resentment of Roland, William, and Bettina with an admiration, respect, and even love for so many.

Grant and Adelaide were now together, and Christa thought Adelaide would be a wonderful teacher. The Morgans and the Carmichaels liked her. So would the children.

She prayed that God would forgive her for ever harboring a hope that she might be the one in Grant's heart. She never wanted to feel sorry for herself again, be selfish, or wallow in negative thinking.

She finally slept but awakened several times and prayed about her apprehension concerning the day to come.

At breakfast, Uncle John prayed that she might have courage.

After he said, "Amen," she poured maple syrup on a flapjack. "Thank you, Uncle John. I'm afraid I don't have much courage."

"You have more than you think, Christa. You see, courage isn't bravery. Courage is taking action even though you're afraid or apprehensive. You've faced fears head on, and God has used you in a wonderful way."

"I've resisted all the way."

"No, Christa. You acted in spite of your reluctance. You've put others ahead of your fears. You put Grant's reputation ahead of your own. The Lord answered your prayer for help."

"Oh, Uncle John. For so long I didn't trust Him to answer. I wanted Him to bring Roland back, to make William and Bettina see that I was responsible and make me the proprietor of that shop."

Uncle John smiled and put his hand on hers. "He had something better in mind for you."

She nodded. "Yes, but why would He do this for me when I was not trusting Him?"

Uncle John leaned back. "To prove that He loves you. You're His child."

That was a good feeling. To know that God loved her. Uncle John loved her. "I've learned a lot, Uncle John. But it's over now."

"Don't worry about that." He pointed his fork at her. "God has a way of teaching us new lessons all through life."

Christa smiled. Lessons could be hard. Sometimes you didn't pass the test.

On the other hand. . .sometimes you did.

"Don't worry," Uncle John said. "I'm coming to school with you this morning. As pastor, I need to meet these people."

Shortly after ringing the school bell, Christa's commitment to courage almost failed. Walking across the schoolyard were the Carmichaels, June Montgomery, and two men who would be Dr. Montgomery and the music teacher.

Behind them was Grant, giving his full attention to Adelaide, who had one hand tucked around his arm and the other holding a sunshiny yellow parasol above her pretty face. She looked like everything in her world was just perfect.

Chapter 13

Christa abandoned her careful lesson plans. The visitors should see for themselves what the children had learned.

The children performed much as they had for their parents. Having an audience brought out their best. She asked the music teacher, looking handsome in his citified suit and tie, to speak to the class. He accepted graciously and talked about various kinds of music, from banjo picking to opera to his own instrument—the piano.

Charlie Warren asked Todd and Adelaide to sing with him a song he and Adelaide had sung at church in Charleston.

Todd's voice was by far the best of the three, but the trio sang beautifully. Christa was again struck by the fair hair and blue eyes of Adelaide and Todd. Their appeal was enhanced by the tall, dark-haired man. Todd was dressed in everyday clothes, but Christa could visualize him dressed up, singing on a stage before a huge audience, delighting them with his voice.

Christa stood near the doorway and stole a glance at Grant along the wall near Dr. Montgomery. Both men seemed entranced as the trio gave a theater-worthy performance in a one-room schoolhouse.

She was thankful she had been a part of Grant's life during the past weeks, helped make things easier for Adelaide, and played a part in the life of a boy with exceptional talent.

She had done her best, in spite of her reluctance.

Now, she must step aside for those who could do better than she.

�֍

Christa dismissed school at noon so she could talk with Adelaide. Charlie Warren took Todd home. The other adults praised her for how well she had taught the children.

Grant came over and thanked her. Christa nodded, afraid to do more than glance at him.

Uncle John moved to her side. "I think it's lunch time," he said.

Dora heard him. "All of you are invited to my house for lunch."

Adelaide spoke up. "Grant, why don't you make yourself useful and bring a plate for me and Christa. We need to talk about things."

He looked as if a weight had been released from his shoulders. "I'd be glad to."

"And I'd be glad to accept your lunch invitation, Miz Dora," Uncle John said. He turned to Christa and winked.

Christa stared at the adults walking between the two oaks. Why did Grant seem as strange and unresponsive as the day she first met him? Did he think she would fall apart because she'd no longer be teaching? Did he suspect how she felt about him? Likely, he was regretting that brief kiss. She thought he'd regretted it the night it happened.

Adelaide spoke. Christa turned. "I'm sorry. My mind was elsewhere."

"Oh, I understand," said Adelaide. "I was saying that you obviously love these children and have done a wonderful job with limited resources. How do you like cove life? I know this one-room schoolhouse is quite different from what you've experienced in the city."

They walked toward the classroom. "It's hard," Christa admitted. "The living situation is rustic. No electricity except closer to Grey Eagle. No stores to buy food or clothes. Pump water for a bath."

A part of her wished it would seem too hard for Adelaide. But she wanted to be honest. She stopped on the porch. "I love it here. You will, too, I'm sure. The benefits are seeing these children so eager to learn."

Adelaide's face lit up. She did a fancy little dance step. Her blond curls swung around her pretty face. Then she rested her hand on the banister. "I know Grant loves this place. It's closer to his heart than anywhere. Can you see that his work is making a difference?"

Christa looked away from the light in Adelaide's eyes. She answered as truthfully as she could, trying not to feel the emotion that welled up in her.

Grant needed a helpmeet to welcome him home. He needed someone to talk to, to understand, to care, to have supper ready, to warm his bed. She turned back to Adelaide. "The graveyard out back of the church is just one testimony to the effectiveness of his work here. The mortality rate for babies has decreased by half in the past few years. Oh, Adelaide, you can teach women about hygiene. That will make such a difference."

She saw the pleasure on Adelaide's face. She almost expected the lovely girl to shout. She had done some good after all. She had helped settle in Adelaide's mind that she was needed here, would love it. Yes, she had done something good for the man she. . .called friend.

Adelaide grabbed Christa's hands. "Oh, thank you, Christa."

They continued talking about everything. Christa would love to have a friend like Adelaide. But she knew that would be possible only if her feelings for Grant vanished. That seemed about as unlikely as the mountains ahead of them disappearing.

They were laughing and talking about city life when Grant brought their food.

"You're not eating with us?" Adelaide asked.

His brow furrowed. "I'm talking with your dad about the medical needs here."

"Hmmm, I see. That's more important than us."

"No, but it is important."

"I'm teasing you, Grant."

He nodded and glanced at Christa. She smiled down at her plate. Instead of thinking about what she might want for herself, she thought of how she'd felt when Roland had jilted her. She would not wish that kind of experience on anyone, particularly the lovely Adelaide.

While they ate lunch, Adelaide surprised her. "Christa. Could I ask a favor? Could you finish out this week for me? I'm just not ready to jump in and teach. But I would love for you to show me the church and a little of the cove."

"I'll be glad to. But don't you want Grant to do that?"

"I learned a long time ago that Grant and my dad forget everything else when they discuss medicine."

Christa and Adelaide spent the afternoon walking through the cove. They talked to adults and children. After they returned late that afternoon, Christa was afraid Adelaide might not completely understand how busy Grant was as the cove's only doctor. She relayed some of that information.

"Oh, I'm aware of how much the people here need him, Christa. Last night he had to go help a cow deliver her calf." She laughed. "I guess Grant has to be a veterinarian, too."

"The animals are important to these people. Milk isn't delivered to one's porch."

"Christa, don't you think Grant is about the most wonderful man a girl could want?"

Christa feared the warmth flooding her face must be visible. But Adelaide kept talking. "I'm so glad we spent this time together. I've had questions about teaching here. Now, I'm sure of where I belong and what I should do." Her blue eyes shone. "Friend to friend, will you tell me something?"

"If. . .if I can."

"Do you believe in love at first sight?"

This girl was obviously very much in love. Adelaide had known Grant for years. Christa had known him for a short time.

"I don't know about just a look," Christa said. "But I do think love can happen very quickly."

Adelaide laughed delightedly. "Sometimes in spite of ourselves, right?"

Christa nodded

Adelaide took Christa's hands in hers. "You can't imagine, Christa, what our conversations today have meant to me. Now, I need to go see Grant." Her pretty yellow skirt swirled gracefully as Adelaide turned and hastened down the road.

Christa would have preferred Adelaide to not have asked about falling in love. And she wished she could have said, "No, you need to know a person for a long time."

But Adelaide, offering her friendship, had deserved the best answer Christa could give.

Chapter 14

When Christa came home from school on Wednesday, Uncle John set a cup of coffee for her at the kitchen table, sat adjacent to her, then said the Montgomerys, the music teacher, and Grant had left the cove.

"What? Why?"

Christa had thought it strange that Adelaide hadn't made an appearance at school but supposed she and Grant had a lot of plans to make. That would be why Adelaide asked Christa to finish out the week of teaching.

Maybe something wonderful had happened for them—like their deciding to elope.

Or maybe something terrible happened. "Is it Adelaide's grandfather?"

He shook his head. "I don't know. Grant said they had to catch the train and he'd explain when he returns. Dora and Clem visited later. They only know the Montgomerys graciously thanked them for their hospitality."

On Friday, Miz Dora stopped by to say Grant had returned, but before she could get anything out of him, he was called away to a logging accident.

Determined to be useful, Christa spent Saturday visiting those who made crafts.

When she sat in the front row of church Sunday morning, she thought she heard Grant's voice, but he did not sit beside her. Perhaps he sat farther back with his fiancée—the real schoolmarm.

Uncle John stood up and announced, "After the service, some matters need to be addressed. I hope you'll all be able to stay. Now, let's get on with our worship."

Todd led the singing. Uncle's John's sermon seemed shorter than usual. No one came forward for special prayer. Uncle John said, "Our doctor has an announcement."

Grant walked to the pulpit. Christa prayed she'd conceal her emotions, particularly if he announced that his fiancée had become his wife.

She looked up when he described an important doctors' meeting in Asheville. Dr. Montgomery hadn't planned to attend, but a situation arose that changed his mind. At the meeting, the doctor made an impassioned plea for funds and equipment to turn Grant's cabin into a clinic. They would appeal for a doctor just out of medical school to come and train under Grant.

Christa joined in the applause. She was happy for Grant. His dreams were coming true. Oh, how she wished she could see these things materialize.

"I'll need men to help renovate the cabin," he said, "and women to help with furnishings."

Birr Morgan spoke up. "We'll do what we can at the sawmill. Free of charge."

"It'll be hard with crops coming in," Jeb Norval said, "but me and my boys will help."

Other offers sounded throughout the church.

"One more thing," Grant said. "The Montgomerys have a commitment from the

Asheville church to send school supplies. Mr. Warren, who is eager to mentor Todd when the time is right, has also promised help from Charleston schools."

After taking a deep breath, Grant cleared his throat. "Miss Montgomery plans to take a teaching position in Charleston."

Christa stared. What did that mean? Would Grant leave the cove after he trained another doctor?

"I think, if Miss Walsh will continue at our school, we need to make a bigger commitment to her than one day or one week at a time. She deserves better."

Others agreed, but Christa focused on her gloves when Grant walked past her up the aisle.

Dora stood. "Christa, do you have something to say? You know we want you here as teacher."

Christa had thought this was what she wanted. Now, she wasn't sure. "I need to think this over."

Dora smiled. Uncle John looked tenderly at her.

Clem nodded. "Jeb had a good point. We were so eager to have a teacher, we wanted the children in school even though it's summer. But you men want to help with the clinic. Children are needed to help bring in the crops. A few weeks off school might be good."

Grant spoke up. "That would give Miss Walsh time to get her crafts and think about teaching permanently. Since she has been so gracious to teach for us, we should let her make the decision about the school schedule."

Sounds of affirmation sounded.

Christa stood. "At school tomorrow, I'll send notes home with the children about the schedule."

The meeting ended. Adults expressed their wish for her to be the teacher.

When Christa went out into the yard, a few men were walking away from Grant. He acknowledged her with a nod, then headed toward his cabin. She supposed he had plans to make that didn't include her.

Men came at daybreak to start renovating the cabin. Clem and Dora, who insisted Grant live with them while the work took place, left on Monday morning for Asheville. Christa left on the same train with craft samples for the shop. She had sent notes home with the children that school was dismissed until further notice.

"Will she come back?" Grant asked John when they stopped for the lunch that women brought to the work site.

Christa's uncle gave Grant a long look. "I didn't ask." He proceeded to fill his plate.

Grant sensed that a lot of meaning lay behind that simple statement. He followed John and absentmindedly spooned food onto his plate. "I haven't asked, Pastor John, because I didn't want to influence her decision."

"What decision, Grant?"

Grant stared after him, feeling the impact of that question. By his silence, he'd gotten Christa into teaching. Now, by silence, he'd likely driven her away.

For the rest of the week, he worked with the other men from daybreak 'til dark, then spent the nights in the Carmichaels' cabin, wondering where they were. What was Christa doing?

Should he go to Hendersonville and find out? Or wait here forever, wondering what might have been?

He felt lonely in church Sunday. The Carmichaels hadn't returned. Christa wasn't sitting in the front row.

On Monday morning, he told the men to quit working on the clinic at noon and tend to their crops and businesses.

In the afternoon, he stood outside the depot when the train pulled in. Holding his bag and a ticket to Hendersonville, Grant headed for the train. He stopped when Dora and Clem exited, followed by Christa, wearing the same questioning expression he'd seen when he first ran into her.

"You going somewhere, Grant?" Dora asked

Where he was going depended on Christa.

He took Christa's suitcase from her hand. "For now, let's just say I've come to welcome each of you home."

His heart skipped a beat when Christa smiled at him and said, "It's good. . .to be home."

Chapter 15

Grant remembered his first ride with Christa in Clem's wagon. Out of desperation, he'd wanted to ask, "Will you be my fiancée?"

Now he wanted to ask the same question from a desire to spend the rest of his life with her.

If he did, she would likely get that suspicious, confused look again. However, when he stopped by Pastor John's and asked if she'd like to see the progress on the clinic, she agreed to go.

He asked about her trip to Hendersonville. She answered politely. They even talked about the weather. Had she lost trust in him because he'd kissed her while engaged to another woman? Was she leaving the cove, meaning the end of their relationship before it really had begun?

The tension vanished when they reached the clinic. Her enthusiasm rekindled his as he explained each room. She walked across the hardwood floors, commented on the waiting room, looked into the treatment room, and touched cabinets. He led her to the addition at the back that would be sleeping quarters for his assistant.

"This is fine, Grant. Even if you don't get an assistant right away, this is so much better since patients will be able to come here."

He agreed. "And the cove people will appreciate it because they helped build it. That's the difference between here and the city. We don't take things for granted."

"I learned that from teaching," she said. "No one takes teachers for granted. That makes it so worthwhile."

Hope sprang in him. He opened the screen door, and they went out into the backyard, smaller now because of the extension to the cabin. They walked toward the gurgling creek. Maybe she wouldn't hear the pleading in his question. "Does that mean you will stay on as teacher?"

He stepped on a stone in the creek and held out his hand. She hesitated, then tilted her head and smiled. "I can do it." She lifted her skirts slightly and stepped from one stone to another. His foot slipped. Hers did, too, and they grabbed each other's hands. Laughing, they reached the other side without filling their shoes with water.

"I could have done it," she said, "if you hadn't done that silly dance on the rocks."

Ah, it felt good to have her behave in that spunky manner again. "Sure you could." He couldn't resist adding, "But holding onto someone else helps one's balance."

Maybe he shouldn't have looked into her eyes then. She ducked her head slightly and walked ahead of him into the woods. In the coolness and the shadows, he tried to regain that sense of togetherness.

"For your information," he said, "I plan to build a bridge over that creek. Since I'll be living in the glade, I'll be called upon come hail or high water and don't want to wade neck deep in the creek."

She laughed. "Good idea." How grand that he and Adelaide would have a beach home in Charleston and a mountain home in Bear Cove.

They walked into the glade. He watched her look out over the lush green mountains beneath a deep blue sky where the late evening sun hid behind a distant cloud. He wondered if she'd come here to say good-bye—to the cove and to him.

He stood beside her, and she looked at him, a gleam of gold touching her eyes. "Being here has been good for me, Grant. I love the people, the children, and the sense of purpose I've gained. When I arrived, I wanted to do well and make a difference, but it was mainly about me."

She turned toward the tranquil view. "I needed to know what was best. I asked God for a sign."

"And He gave you one?" That sounded like he doubted, so Grant added, "Of course."

She nodded. "I realized William and Bettina's acceptance was genuine. They loved the crafts and want to purchase them. And I no longer resent Roland. Maybe he did fall in love with the banker's daughter instead of her money." She shook her head. "I thought the Lord giving me insight into my own self-centeredness and taking away my resentment was the sign."

Just as he figured she would say her place was in Hendersonville, she added, "But it wasn't."

The sun hadn't brought that glow to her face; it came from inside. He needed to pray for what was best for her, in spite of what he wanted. But what she was saying made him want her even more.

She faced him. Amazement tinged her voice. "Dora contacted me. Their former church invited me to talk about the school. I was scared but knew they might sponsor a teacher, so I told them about the children and about Todd. They were so impressed. Oh, Grant!"

She pressed her hands to her chest. "I am now the official cove missionary-teacher, sponsored by a church in Asheville."

Emotion flooded Grant's eyes. "Christa, this is wonderful. You're perfect for this. I knew it that first week."

She looked down. "Even with that, it wasn't easy. I had to ask myself if this was God's will. I had to be able to say I would teach even if those I. . .those close to me were not here. Suppose Uncle John and the Carmichaels left. And you. . . ."

Was she about to say, "Those I love?"

His heart thudded. "Christa, I'm not going anywhere."

Her gaze met his. "But Adelaide's in Charleston."

He nodded. "She's in love with Charlie Warren."

"Oh," she said. "Are you. . .heartbroken?"

"I was concerned, Christa. I didn't want to hurt her. I do love her. But when you came into my life, I began to realize that I'm not in love with Adelaide. When I couldn't seem to get the words out right, she informed me about the difference between loving someone and being *in* love with them."

Christa nodded. "She asked me if I believed in love at first sight."

He dared believe what he saw in her eyes. "What did you say?"

"I said I believed in love coming quickly."

His hands moved to her shoulders. "I think that's something she and Charlie Warren learned. I know it's something I learned, even though I fought it. I'm in love with you, Christa."

She came into his arms. "I'm in love with you, Grant."

After a kiss that, this time, neither ran away from, he drew a deep breath and held her close. "May I tell the world I have a fiancée, she's the schoolmarm, and her name is Christa Walsh?"

"Please do."

He moved away, faced the view, and shouted. "I'm in love."

Christa shouted, "Me, too."

The mountains echoed back, "love, too" so many times that it began to sound for all the world like, "true love true."

❋

A week later, Christa and Grant traveled to Asheville and chose her engagement ring. They rode to Hendersonville and visited William and Bettina, who were delighted with Grant and the engagement. They returned on Monday.

A few weeks later, they joined the Carmichaels at Adelaide and Charlie's wedding in a big church in Asheville. The summer sped by quickly. The clinic was finished. A new doctor lived in the addition and studied under Grant.

Whenever they could, the men of the cove worked on the log house in the clearing where Grant and Christa would live after they married.

William and Bettina had placed orders for crafts that gave many a renewed sense of purpose. Christa couldn't imagine getting married anywhere other than in the little church in the cove where Uncle John preached.

She spent what time she could planning for school, which would begin in the fall. The wedding was set for a week before classes started.

The wedding day arrived—a beautiful, clear, warm day. Clem and Dora organized the reception to be held in the churchyard.

The little church was packed with some standing around the walls and others outside looking in the windows. Christa had invited a couple of her married friends from Hendersonville. Some of Grant's acquaintances from Asheville came, including Dr. and Mrs. Montgomery, who said Adelaide and Charlie were living in Charleston and getting ready for the new school year. They sent their love and a generous monetary gift.

After Bettina walked down the aisle and took her place as matron of honor across from Clem as Grant's best man, Todd sang, "O Perfect Love."

Christa couldn't imagine anything more perfect than William walking her down the aisle and saying, "I, her brother, do," when Uncle John asked, "Who gives this woman to wed this man?"

Uncle John then said, "We are gathered here to join this man and this woman in holy matrimony." He cleared his throat and paused, looking from Christa to Grant and back again. "I must add something to this ceremony. The Lord works in mysterious ways. . . ."

Christa and Grant smiled, then gazed into each other's eyes. She was asked a vague question and said, "I do." Grant did the same.

Uncle John pronounced them man and wife. "You may kiss the bride."

Grant and Christa turned toward each other. She felt his arms come around her, and she lifted her face to his, not the least bit reluctant.

SCHOOL BELLS
AND
WEDDING BELLS

by Colleen L. Reece

Dedication

In memory of my mother,
who ruled her students with a rod of love,
and all the one-room schoolteachers
who taught lessons in life,
as well as from textbooks.

For my thoughts are not your thoughts,
neither are your ways my ways, saith the LORD.
For as the heavens are higher than the earth,
so are my ways higher than your ways,
and my thoughts than your thoughts.
ISAIAH 55:8–9

Chapter 1

Boston, Massachusetts—late 1890s

Sunlight burst through spring-gray clouds and streamed through the magnificent stained-glass windows of the anteroom in Boston's most prestigious church. It turned Meredith Rose Macrae into a living mosaic. Blue, green, and rose shimmered on her white satin gown and the coronet of orange blossoms anchoring her bridal veil, then caressed her white prayer book dripping with ribbons and lilies.

A warning growl of distant thunder mingled with the well-modulated tones of the costly organ in the sanctuary, an unwelcome reminder that March—which had come in with lamb-like meekness—might well depart with the temperament of a roaring lion.

Twenty-seven-year-old Marcus Macrae, Boston born and bred and a tall, dark-haired replica of his twin sister, clenched his hands and fought the storm of anger hidden beneath his fine wedding clothes. *Lord, how can I tell Merry? Will it break her heart? Her spirit?* He glanced at the young woman who had been a law unto herself from early childhood, then he surreptitiously stole a look at his pocket watch. What little hope he had clung to had departed. Herbert wasn't coming.

Herbert. Marcus straightened the strong fingers that had automatically clenched into fists. He'd despised Herbert Calloway from the moment he met him. Marcus shook his head. Not a fitting sentiment for a minister of the gospel, but it was a simple fact of life. How many times had he ruefully muttered to himself, "If I had a dollar for every hour I've spent on my knees asking forgiveness for feeling this way, I'd be richer than Croesus." His outbursts were always followed by, "Too bad I'm not. I'd abduct that sister of mine and hide her somewhere until she could see Calloway for what he really is!" Time and Marcus's many prayers did little to warm him toward his future brother-in-law. Herbert's supercilious manner, slicked-back hair, and dapper black mustache that resembled a misplaced third eyebrow fired Marcus with the primitive desire to mop up the floor with the man. How could Merry love him?

Marcus shook his head and stared at his twin, seeing her not as she was on what should be the happiest day of her life, but the way she had been as far back as he could remember. . . .

Meredith Rose Macrae had charted her life's course before she was ten. School and finishing school. Travel. Love, marriage, children, and a storybook happily-ever-after. Even as a child, the ebony-haired girl with the direct blue gaze had a way of getting what she wanted. Marcus watched with a great deal of amusement as his twin achieved her first three goals right on schedule. Before God called him to higher purposes, he had accompanied Merry on her jaunts all over the world. The hordes of hopefuls who pursued the well-to-do young woman failed to touch her heart. Neither had Marcus met a woman with whom he wanted to spend the rest of his life.

Before it seemed possible, their twenty-third birthday arrived. Marcus would never forget that day in May when his sister came to him in a panic. He had just made a life-changing decision in the seclusion of the richly carpeted, wood-paneled library and was considering how best to break the news to Merry. Would she understand, or would it create the first real rift of their lives, and color the future?

"What am I going to do?" she demanded, wringing her hands and dropping into a tapestry-covered chair beside the massive fireplace with its cozy fire. "It has been wonderful flitting about the world. I never dreamed my traveling would so thin the ranks of eligible suitors! Marcus, if something doesn't happen soon, I'm in serious danger of becoming an old maid."

The idea was ludicrous; laughter spilled from Marcus like water over Niagara Falls. "You, an old maid? Hardly!"

She raised her chin, and her expression chilled. "I fail to find anything humorous about the situation." A quiver in her voice alerted her brother to trouble.

"My word, you're really serious, aren't you?" Marcus could scarcely believe it.

"Yes. Percival Vandevere just got engaged. So did Howell DeWitt and—"

Marcus gasped. "Don't tell me you considered marrying one of those fops!"

"Both are high on the social register," she retorted.

"Neither has ever done an honest day's work in his life and their family fortunes were acquired by less than honorable means," Marcus snapped. "If Father were still alive, he'd squelch that idea in a hurry."

"I have to marry," Meredith Rose reminded him. "It's what women do."

"Why? You can stay single and keep house for me, old dear," he teased. "Besides," Marcus added fiercely, "I'd rather see you marry a working man than anyone like Vandevere or DeWitt."

Disbelief shone in his twin's blue eyes, followed by scorn. "I? Marry a working man?" She delicately shuddered and turned up her nose. "I hope you aren't going to disgrace the Macrae name by taking up with some common girl who doesn't know which fork to use at dinner."

Marcus leaned back in his luxurious chair. "You really are a snob, aren't you?"

Angry color flared in her smooth cheeks, and she leaped to her feet. "I am *not* a snob. I just know what is expected of me. I pray you do, as well."

Marcus knew the moment had come. Not the ideal time for his confession, but it could wait no longer. "Sit down, please, Merry. I have something to tell you."

Apparently mollified by his refusal to be baited, she flounced back into her chair. "I hope it's good news."

Heart pounding, Marcus leaned forward and rested his hands on his knees. "The most wonderful news in the world, as far as I am concerned." He wistfully added, "I hope you think so, too. You said you pray that I will do what is expected of me. For months I have been asking for enlightenment to find out just what that is."

His sister's mouth opened in a little round *O*, but she remained silent.

"Do you remember when we invited Jesus into our hearts when we were very young?" Marcus began, praying that she would understand what had happened to him.

Her eyes opened wide. "Of course, but what does that have to do with—"

"It has everything to do with it, Merry. I believe with all my heart that God is calling me to serve Him by becoming a minister." His ringing voice filled the library. "I also want to learn at least the rudiments of medicine."

"A minister! *You?*"

His blue gaze never left hers. "Yes. I know I'm not worthy, but I intend to be." Unable to stay seated, he stood and paced the carpeted floor. "Until now, I've played the part of an idler." He felt shame suffuse his face. "Don't misunderstand. I've enjoyed our life of ease—of being with you in all kinds of delightful adventures. But through it all, I've felt hollow. Even going to church hasn't filled the emptiness inside me."

She stirred in her chair and looked perplexed. "I've never heard you speak like this before. Are you sure you aren't just bored?"

"I thought so at first. Not now. I've been studying the Bible, especially the lives of the disciples and others whom Jesus called to serve Him. I want to be one of them."

The tick of the ancestral clock on the mantel sounded loud in Marcus's ears. *Tick tock. Tick tock.* Ticking off the seconds while he waited in suspense. *Please, God, help her accept my decision, even if she cannot comprehend.*

Seconds became minutes before Meredith Rose answered. When she did, it was with outstretched hands and tear-wet lashes. "Dear Marcus, if God is calling you to serve Him, serve you must." She smiled.

He grasped her hands and knelt by her chair. "Thank you." It was all he could get out.

After a long moment, a small voice asked, "What about me? Your decision doesn't find me a husband."

For the second time that day, Marcus's laughter swept through the room. "No, it doesn't, but don't you see, Merry? If God wants us to have mates, He can send them at just the right time. All we have to do is pray and wait."

❦

"Herbert isn't coming, is he?" His sister's voice yanked Marcus from the past back to the present.

"He may just be late," Marcus reminded her.

She shook her head. "That's unlikely. He prides himself on being prompt at all times. Or at least sending a message when he is delayed."

The door burst open. A man Marcus remembered seeing with Calloway stepped inside. "Mr. Macrae? A message for you." He proffered a sealed white envelope and started out.

"Wait. There may be an answer."

The man's lips set in a grim line. "Begging your pardon, sir, but I was told there would be no reply." He went out, closing the door behind him.

"What on earth was that all about?" Meredith Rose demanded.

Marcus tore open the envelope and removed the crested notepaper inside. Fury rose until he thought he would choke. "What a rotter!"

"What does it say?" She snatched the page. Face whiter than her gown, Meredith Rose maintained a remarkably steady voice as she read the message aloud: " 'By the time you get this, Gwendolyn Arlington and I will be married. Although she is much younger, under the circumstances, I am sure you will understand. Herbert Calloway.' " The signature had the peculiar little flourish he always used.

The humiliation in his sister's face struck deep into Marcus's soul. Yet a spark of hope ignited when he saw the flush of anger that crept from the high neck of her bridal gown and drove away her pallor. Perhaps pride was more involved than love.

"What a coward! He didn't even have the courtesy to address this to me." Meredith Rose jerked the lace mitts from her hands and shredded the page. For a moment she stared at her engagement ring with its enormous, sparkling diamond surrounded by a galaxy of lesser stones, then tore it from her finger and flung it to the floor.

"It was always too ostentatious, anyway," she said through gritted teeth. "I wonder how that cat Gwendolyn Arlington will enjoy wearing it." Her eyes flashed. "I'm surprised he sent word before I got to the altar." She paused. "What did he mean by that cryptic 'under the circumstances'?"

Marcus recoiled. His pain intensified. Surviving Herbert Calloway's desertion was one thing. Facing the shattering news Marcus had planned to withhold until she was safely married was another. To gain time, he stooped, picked up the ring, and shoved it in the breast pocket of his tailored coat. "Time enough to talk about that when we get home. Will you be all right until I tell the minister there won't be a wedding?"

"Yes." She stumbled to a nearby chair.

Marcus chucked her under the chin the way he had done when they were small. "Brace up, old girl. Things could be worse. What if you had married the cur, then found out what he really is?" The horror that sprang to Merry's eyes added fuel to Marcus's kindled hope that the blow was more to her pride than the loss of love. He quickly added, "God has delivered you from a lifetime of misery," and strode out—trying to decide whether to throttle Calloway or fervently thank him.

Chapter 2

Marcus Macrae's words rang in his sister's ears. *"What if you had married the cur?"* Then, *"God has delivered you from a lifetime of misery."*

Meredith Rose shuddered at her narrow escape and stared at the floor. She wanted to shriek to the high heavens. If God had really wanted to spare her, why had He sent Herbert Calloway into her life? *Did God send him, or was it all your own doing?* her sense of fair play protested. She squirmed, remembering the aftermath of that fateful May day when she was twenty-three....

When Marcus announced he'd been called to become a minister, she'd known nothing would ever be the same. She and Marcus had clung to one another from the time they could toddle, especially after their parents died in a railway accident when the twins were in their late teens. He was the dearest person on earth to her—and the only one she allowed to call her Merry. "It's too frivolous for my position," she protested.

Marcus only laughed, his eyes crinkling at the corners in the way that always lifted her spirits. He made a low bow. "Your will is my command, Miss Macrae."

"If you are going to play court jester, I suppose you may call me Merry," she told him in a long-suffering tone of voice. "You will, anyway."

"Yes, Your Majesty." He bowed again.

A rush of love for the brother who always seemed much older than she filled her. "You may call me anything you wish, Marcus." She anxiously peered into his face. "Just so nothing ever comes between us. It won't, will it?"

His mirth fled. "No, Merry. We are two against the world now that Mother and Father are gone. At least until we marry, you are first in my world."

"I feel the same," she murmured, comforted by his promise.

Their deep and abiding love for one another continued untroubled—until Marcus's call to serve. Meredith Rose instantly recognized their relationship must irrevocably change. She would always hold a special place in her twin's heart, yet she would no longer be first with Marcus. God had replaced her. Even though she knew it was as it should be, a sense of loss pervaded the innermost parts of her being. Marcus could no longer be the willing companion in whatever pleasures she conjured up, free as a butterfly in summer to take off at a moment's notice. He must study and prepare.

"What about me?" she asked. "Your decision doesn't find me a husband."

His reply sank deep into her heart. "If God wants us to have mates, He can send them at just the right time. All we have to do is pray and wait."

Meredith Rose secretly pondered Marcus's words, wondering if he could be right. He certainly sounded confident, but she wasn't sure. Why should God do anything for her, when she had done so little for Him? After asking Jesus into her heart, her religious life consisted of attending formal service on Sundays and contributing to the needy. She also lent her name to various charities. In the light of Marcus's decision to follow the Master, her own contributions seemed insignificant.

Weary weeks became restless months. Meredith Rose chafed at being denied her brother's company because of his need to study but she wisely never let it show. She also began to dream and scheme toward the day when Marcus would occupy the pulpit of a noted Boston church. The Macrae name could open gates padlocked against others less fortunate. In the meantime, her own life had grown dull and flat.

In desperation she turned to God, beseeching Him for favors, deserved or not.

Nothing happened.

She continued to beat on the doors of heaven. "Can't you hear me, God? I really need Your help, now that You've taken Marcus away from me." The prayer sounded childish even to her own ears, so she hastily added, "It's not that I begrudge losing him to You. Well, at least not much. It's just that his involvement leaves me with too much time on my hands. Please, won't You change my life, too?"

A few weeks later, it appeared her prayers were being answered, at least in part. Miss Grenadier, founder and director of the exclusive Miss Grenadier's School for Young Ladies, which Meredith Rose had attended, came to call. "Miss Macrae, I hope you don't find it presumptuous of me to ask, but would you consider teaching for us?"

The woman twisted her gloved hands. "We are in desperate need. Having your name on our faculty will ensure we can attract students from the best families. I remember how popular you were with both fellow students and your instructors. We would love to have you join us."

Meredith Rose's first inclination was to respond with a haughty and resounding no. Before she could speak, a thought stole into her mind. *Don't be too hasty about turning her down. Teaching would at least relieve your boredom while you're waiting for God to send you your Sir Galahad.*

The idea was too strong to be ignored. "What would my duties be?" She laughed carelessly. "It's been a long time since I diagramed sentences or worked fractions."

Miss Grenadier's eyes gleamed with obvious satisfaction. "Oh, we have others to handle those subjects. We need you to teach our girls more important things: elocution, deportment, music, painting—I remember how skilled you were with the pianoforte and brush—that kind of thing. In short, you'd help us turn out real ladies, like yourself."

The flattery piqued Meredith Rose's interest. "How soon will you need to know?"

The woman looked troubled. "We are really shorthanded." She sniffed. "The former teacher was terribly inconsiderate! She resigned without giving proper notice in order to marry. Can you imagine?" She rushed on. "Would you be able to give us an answer in a week?"

When Meredith Rose nodded, Miss Grenadier clasped her hands and said, "I am so thrilled! Just the thought of having you become one of us is. . ." She left rejoicing, as though Meredith Rose Macrae were already "one of them."

"What have I done?" the young woman wondered. "Do I really want to teach, even those enjoyable activities?" She looked around the library, feeling the walls were closing in on her. "At least I'm not firmly committed."

That evening before Marcus began his nightly studies, Meredith Rose told him of the position she had been offered.

"Take it," he advised. "You'll do a great job." He sighed. "I know these last months haven't been easy. You need something on which you can focus, Merry. Something into which you can pour your time and energy. You aren't cut out for sitting idle. You don't care for heading up charitable drives or doing volunteer nursing."

She shook her head in disgust.

He grinned at her. "Why not give it a try? If you don't like it, the school won't be any worse off than it is now."

The next day Meredith Rose became "Miss Macrae" and entered a life as far from her former indolent existence as Boston from Australia.

"I like it," she reported to Marcus at the end of the first week. "I actually like it." She laughed deprecatingly. "Of course, if I had to teach such mundane lessons as grammar and the multiplication tables, it would be a different story!"

"Always taking the easy way out," he teased, but she could see he was pleased that she no longer moped around home. Now when Marcus studied at one side of the beautiful library, she busied herself at the other. She hunted out music for the girls' chorus, who would do her proud in an upcoming presentation. She pictured herself in a rich sapphire velvet gown, bowing before beaming parents and accepting their gratitude. Recitations from the classics as well as original essays from the brightest students would be included. All were designed to bring even more glory to Meredith Rose and show the world how fortunate Miss Grenadier's School for Young Ladies was to have her on its staff.

Despite her new interest, despite the smashing success of the presentation and others like it, prayers for God to send a husband who would change her life even further remained in the teacher's heart and often on her lips.

A year slipped by. Another. No Sir Galahad appeared, although Meredith Rose continued to remind God she was still waiting. Marcus completed his ministerial studies and began his preaching career, studying medicine on the side. To his sister's dismay, he refused a desirable offer from a prominent denomination in favor of working with a small church on the outskirts of Boston.

"I know you had your heart set on my occupying a high position, Merry," he said sadly, "but the people at Community Christian need me. Those attending First Central don't." All her pleading that the powerful and the mighty deserved to hear the gospel as well as the poor and humble didn't change his mind.

Now she saw him less than ever. Whenever Pastor Marcus—who steadfastly refused to be called Reverend—wasn't conducting services, he was counseling families, visiting the sick, or searching out food and shelter for the needy. At his urging, Meredith Rose accompanied him now and then but decided she was too delicate for the sights, sounds, and smells of social work. "Besides," she reasoned, "I'm providing service to the girls I teach."

Once, in a moment of depression, a sigh so deep she felt it began at her toes and crept upward escaped. Perhaps teaching was all she would ever do. All the other girls in her social set had married. Most had babies. Why had God denied her the joy of being a wife and mother? The thought planted itself in Meredith Rose's mind and haunted her. In less than two weeks, she would be twenty-seven years old. Crop after crop of debutantes had entered society and taken her place, leaving her to wither on the vine, an object of pity among those she once called friends.

"I suppose it's Your plan that I become like Miss Grenadier," she accused God in the privacy of her lavishly furnished bedroom one night. Half-expecting a rebuke, she bitterly added, "Deliver me from such a fate! Nothing could be worse." At least she still had her beauty. The mirror above her brocade-skirted dressing table attested to that.

"If only my life would change!" she complained.

The very next day a new dancing master reported to Miss Grenadier's Finishing School for Young Ladies. Single, sought-after by eligible young maidens and their overly eager mamas, Herbert Calloway was reputed to be disgustingly rich. When the black-haired, black-eyed young man met Meredith Rose, he bent low over her hand and clicked his heels together. "Mademoiselle Macrae? It is indeed my pleasure."

His admiration warmed her lonely heart and melted the reserve with which she usually greeted strangers. "Coincidences like this just don't happen," she told herself. "Herbert's coming is surely an answer to my prayers."

A time of enchantment followed. Herbert overwhelmed her with admiration. A few months later the Boston newspapers formally announced nuptials for Miss Meredith Rose Macrae and Mr. Herbert Calloway would be held the end of March.

When the long-awaited day came, Meredith Rose awakened to brilliant sunshine. Distant clouds warned that the capricious month was not yet over, but she only laughed at their gloomy rumblings.

Somehow the hours passed until she reached the church and donned her wedding dress, chosen over the objections of the dressmaker who had trotted out samples of far more elaborate frocks. Gowned in white satin and dreams, she waited in the anteroom, visualizing the moment when Marcus placed her hand in Herbert's and she took the vows that would bind them together forever. Then the note arrived. . . .

"Ready, Merry?"

Her brother's voice calling her back from her thoughts made her feel she had returned from a long journey, one so wearisome she dared not speculate about what "under the circumstances" meant. "Yes. Take me home."

Chapter 3

Every *clop clop* of the matched pair of white horses that proudly pulled the closed carriage from First Central Church to the Macrae home accused Marcus. *You should have told her. Why didn't you tell her?* He impatiently thrust the accusations aside. What was done was done. Self-recrimination couldn't undo the past. He must focus on how to tell Merry what the ominous words *under the circumstances* meant—but not here. Not while she sat stiffly beside him in a wedding gown as crumpled as her former dreams.

When they reached their spacious home, he silently helped Meredith Rose from the carriage and waved the driver away. She started up the walk, paused, and glanced at the scowling, gunmetal clouds that had changed from warning to reality. A bolt of lightning split the sky, followed by window-rattling thunder. Glad for the diversion, Marcus threw his arm around his sister and called above the tumult, "Quick! We need to reach the porch before the rain starts!"

They made it with only seconds to spare. A silver torrent of rain that changed to hail descended. From the shelter of the wide porch, the twins watched the storm. After it passed on and a patch of apologetic blue sky appeared, Meredith Rose said in a shaken voice, "Look." She pointed to a shimmering rainbow above them that arched across the city of Boston. They watched until it disappeared, then her blue gaze turned to Marcus. "As soon as we get out of these abominable clothes, you can tell me what else is going on. It would be nice to think the rainbow is a good omen, but I know you too well not to recognize Herbert's desertion is only part of something bigger." Before he could reply, she slipped inside and hurried up the stairs.

With a prayer for wisdom, Marcus slowly went to his room and changed into comfortable clothes. "Abominable is right," he muttered, flinging his wedding apparel onto his bed, then hastily retrieving it and hanging it up properly. Under the circumstances, he couldn't indulge in recklessness of any sort, even discarding despised clothing. *Under the circumstances.* Strange. He had never hated the words until today. Now they stood for heartbreak and the rocky road ahead.

The ring of the telephone shattered his reflections. A few moments later, there was a discreet knock at his bedroom door. "A call for you, sir," a servant announced.

"Thanks. I'll take it here." He picked up the phone on his bedside table. "Macrae. Arlington? You have some nerve, calling me at a time like this!" Marcus paused, trying to make sense of what the distraught man on the other end of the line was saying. "I see. . . Yes. . . A sorry mess indeed, and one you brought on yourself." He paused again. "I understand. God help you, Arlington!"

The line went dead. Marcus didn't know whether to rage or rejoice. Romans 8:28, a favorite Scripture verse, came to mind: "And we know that all things work together for good to them that love God, to them who are the called according to his purpose."

Heart lighter than it had been for days, Marcus went back downstairs to the library.

Meredith Rose was already there, clad in a simple white muslin gown scattered with tiny blue flowers and some frilly stuff around the neck and on the pockets. It made her look more like a little girl than a rejected bride-to-be. A blazing fire cast dancing shadows on the walls, and the soft lighting lay like an aura of peace over the room. Marcus dropped into his favorite chair, passionately wishing it could be like any other day when they gathered by the fire to share secrets, joys, and woes.

"Marcus, do you know why Herbert did what he did?"

He drew in a deep breath, held it, then slowly released it. This was no time for evasion. "Gwendolyn Arlington's banker father betrayed client confidence. She evidently passed the news on to Calloway."

Meredith Rose's white brow wrinkled. "What does that have to do with us? What on earth could Mr. Arlington say that would cause Herbert to elope with Gwendolyn?"

Marcus gritted his teeth. The dismay and anger that had attacked him when Arlington first summoned him and broke the news that figuratively blew things to bits returned. "Money. There's no easy way to tell you this, Merry. A few days ago, I learned our trusted family solicitor had been ill. Wanting to make sure our holdings would be well cared for, Mr. Simpson turned them over to his brother. He didn't dream what kind of man he was putting in charge." Marcus paused in an effort to control his feelings and continue with the story.

Meredith Rose's face turned to parchment. Shock filled her face. "You don't have to say what happened. The brother absconded with our funds."

"Yes." Marcus pounded his knee with one hand. "If I'd only known sooner I might have been able to salvage at least something—"

She acted as though she didn't hear him, but her eyes darkened to the color of the night sky. "So when Mr. Arlington found out, he told his daughter," she said in a mocking voice. "And of course, Gwendolyn *couldn't resist* telling Herbert." She shook her head. "I still don't understand why it should matter. Everyone knows Herbert Calloway is wealthy, far more than we are—were."

Marcus sprang to his feet, clenched his hands into fists, and delivered the final blow. "Everyone knows wrong. While I was upstairs changing, Arlington called. It seems Herbert Calloway is a charlatan. He duped Miss Grenadier and others into believing him to be a man of unlimited means and worked his way into Boston society in order to find a well-to-do wife!"

Meredith Rose stared at him. For a moment, she didn't move. When she did, she shocked her brother beyond belief. Instead of showing anger or pain, her lips twitched. Her eyes sparkled. Laughter exploded as if from a cannon and filled the quiet library.

Marcus felt his jaw drop. Had she taken leave of her senses? "Are—are you all right?" he stammered when he could find voice enough to speak.

"All right?" Another peal of laughter came, along with a rush of tears that obviously didn't spring from sadness. "It's the joke of the year. Don't you see?" She took a dainty hand-kerchief from her pocket and dabbed at her eyes. "Gwendolyn Arlington, who shouted to the housetops that I was odd because I didn't want bridesmaids at my wedding, is married to an unscrupulous man who hoodwinked her into an elopement." She went off into more gales of laughter. "Talk about poetic justice; Gwendolyn has it."

Marcus joined her. "Arlington is beside himself," he managed to get out between chuckles. "What's hurting him the worst is that it's his own fault. If he'd kept his mouth shut about business affairs, he wouldn't have Herbert Calloway for a son-in-law."

"So that's what Herbert meant by 'under the circumstances.'" She sobered. "Just how bad is our financial situation, Marcus?"

"It couldn't be worse," he succinctly told her, hating what he had to do, yet relieved by her reaction to Herbert's conniving. "We've lost everything."

She looked around the library. "Even the house?" Her voice quavered.

"Even the house." Marcus squirmed and dropped his head into his hands. "Several months ago, a friend of father's came to me. He had fallen on hard times and desperately needed a large sum of money in order to save his business. I placed a mortgage on the house so I could help him out. I hoped you'd never need to know."

Meredith Rose looked as if she'd been turned to stone. "Can't he pay you back?"

"No. Fire destroyed his business, and he had no insurance. We could have squeaked by if Simpson hadn't stolen our funds. Now there is no way to pay the mortgage. I'm sorry, Merry. So sorry."

She slipped from her chair and knelt by him. One hand stroked his dark hair. "I would rather give up everything than not have you willing to help those in need," she fiercely told him. "I can stand anything as long as we have each other and are together."

Hope flared within Marcus. "Do you really, truly mean that? Even though we've lost our home, our place in society?"

He saw her swallow convulsively before she said in a flippant tone that didn't conceal her sincerity, "Just call me Ruth. 'Whither thou goest' and all that." She pressed her cheek against his hair. "I'll follow you to the ends of the earth, if necessary," she whispered. "I mean," she hastily amended, "to the outskirts of Boston." She wrinkled her nose. "I can't say I'll like it, but at least it's better than being married to a scoundrel!"

Marcus seized both of her hands in his. "Meredith Rose Macrae, you're a brick, and I'm proud of you." He fell silent, dreading the next few minutes. His twin had just survived two devastating blows. God help her be able to come to terms with the final jolt.

"Do you remember the old saying about things, both good and bad, coming in threes?"

Her hands tightened on his until he wondered why she didn't cry out in pain. She raised her chin in the way she had done since childhood when faced with something new and strange.

"Fire away," she ordered. "So far today I've been jilted and informed we're penniless and will be living in a—well—let's call it a less-than-desirable neighborhood. Nothing could be worse." Her eyes widened with fear, and she released his hands. "Unless you're planning to elope, join the Foreign Legion, or you have some life-threatening illness, I should be able to handle it."

"None of those, thank God," Marcus fervently said. "The thing is, we won't be living out near Community Christian Church."

Meredith Rose jumped to her feet. Radiance erased every trace of worry from her lovely face. "You rascal! You saved the best for last. The rainbow *was* a good omen. I don't have to guess what the third happening is. You've been called to a new church. How exciting! When do you start? How long have you known?" She blinked wet lashes. "Why didn't you tell me?"

Marcus's heart thudded. When they were toddlers, he had popped a huge soap bubble his twin had blown with soapsuds and her little clay pipe. A bubble that shone iridescent and beautiful. Now he must do the same thing, only this time Merry was no crying child to be comforted by blowing a new and larger bubble.

Marcus quietly said, "Sit down, please." If his life had depended on it, he couldn't have kept from sounding somber.

Apprehension replaced the joy in her face, and she obediently resumed her seat in the chair opposite his.

"For several months I've felt dissatisfied with where I am serving," Marcus began. "It started when I read stories of how desperately both ministers and doctors are needed in faraway places." He ignored his sister's gasp. "The more I prayed about it, the more I realized God wanted me to go where I am truly needed, where there is no one to replace me should I not be there. I didn't tell you because I felt once you were married, you could accept my leaving and the loss of our money far better."

"But I'm *not* getting married," she protested. "Now you're going to Africa or India or someplace like that. We promised to stay together, Marcus. How can you do this? What will I do? What kind of God would call you somewhere I can't go?"

"He hasn't, old dear," Marcus burst out. He leaped from his chair, pulled her to her feet, and executed a wild dance around the library. "God has called me somewhere you *can* go." Exuberance for what lay ahead spilled like salt from a saltcellar. "It will be an adventure; one unlike any we've ever experienced. My call is to Idaho. A little mountain town called Last Chance."

"*Last Chance?*" She sounded appalled. With a cry of distress, she tore herself free from her brother's arms and raced upstairs, where she flung herself down on her bed and raged, "God, are You some kind of monstrous joker?" The words *you asked me to change your life* flew into her mind, but she fiercely rejected them. No loving God would send anyone—especially her—to a place called Last Chance.

Even though the name perfectly described Meredith Rose Macrae's present situation.

Chapter 4

Briton Farley slid from the saddle of his favorite stallion. He dropped the reins to the ground so the buckskin would stand, and then strode to the edge of the promontory that overlooked the mining town below. He had discovered the lonely spot years earlier and returned again and again, especially when he had a knotty problem to work out.

Brit had seen the spectacular Bitterroot Range that separated Idaho from Montana on the east blanketed with winter snows, etched against fiery sunrises, tranquil beneath cloudless, sapphire skies. Tawny head bared in respect, Brit had quoted Psalm 19:1 countless times: "The heavens declare the glory of God; and the firmament sheweth his handywork."

Today, troubles as abundant as the red, yellow, and golden leaves he trod distracted him from nature's wordless appeal. Brit stared across at the mountain peaks and dolefully whistled "Lone Prairie," then laughed when his horse nudged his shoulder.

"Too bad you can't talk, Nez Percé," he told his horse. "You'd be reminding me there's no problem worth stewing over on a day like this." He yanked off his Stetson, unknotted his colorful kerchief, and mopped his face. Never in the eight years since he had first come to Idaho had he seen a more exquisite Indian summer. It stretched over the land like a blanket of peace.

Brit hunkered down on his boot heels and breathed in the evergreen-scented air. Eight years. He sighed. It didn't seem possible. Thoughts of the decisions shouting to be made faded. So did his present surroundings. He closed his eyes and allowed himself to drift back. Back to life on the Rocking F in Texas. To untroubled days with his father, whose tawny hair, amber eyes, and catlike grace had replicated themselves in Brit. . . .

Michael Farley had become everything in the world to his small son when Brit's mother was stricken with fever and died. "It's just you and me and God now, Brit," he'd said.

"I don't like God. He took my mama," Brit had burst out. If he lived to be older than the Bitterroots, he would remember his father's reply and the pain in his voice.

Strong arms wrapped around him. "We don't always like what God does, but we need to remember this: God loved us so much He sent His Son to die on a cross so all who believe in Him and invite Jesus to live in their hearts can live with Him. Your mama can't come back to us, but someday we'll go to her. She will be waiting for us in a place so beautiful the Bible says we can't even imagine it!"

The child turned it over in his mind. "What if she isn't happy?" His lip quivered. "What if she forgets us?" He buried his face in his father's shirt.

"She won't forget us," Michael assured. His voice softened. "And Son, she could never be unhappy in the presence of God. The wonderful thing is, we can have that presence with us, too. All we have to do is ask for it."

Brit looked into his father's face, not understanding. Yet the lines of sadness that had etched themselves so deeply when Christine Farley fell ill were miraculously smoothed out. His expression reminded Brit of how the world looked after the sun came up over the low hill to the east and filled the sky with glory. It brought comfort. As long as Daddy looked like that, everything would surely be all right.

Years passed: busy, happy years. Father and son worked as harmoniously as blades on a fine pair of shears. They survived drought and losses and made the most of the good years. They doubled their landholdings and increased their herds. Just after Brit's twenty-first birthday, his father signed the ranch over to him.

"I may live to be a hundred." Michael Farley's weather-beaten face opened into a broad smile. The crinkles at the corners of his expressive eyes deepened. "It doesn't matter. You're ready to take full responsibility." He leaned back in the comfortable, hand-hewn chair that had occupied the same spot in the rustic living room as far back as Brit could remember, then propped his feet on an ancient stool. "Speaking of taking responsibility, when are you going to get married and give me grandchildren? Christine and I were married with you on the way by the time I was your age."

Brit felt himself redden. "I'm too busy for girls," he said gruffly.

His father gave a knowing smile. Golden motes danced in his eyes. "Oh? According to bunkhouse gossip, you could tame and marry just about any pretty little filly for miles around. Is that the problem? Too many to choose from?"

"No." Brit nodded toward the wedding picture of his parents that graced the mantel over the huge stone fireplace. "I won't marry until I find one like her."

Michael's feet came down with a *thump*. "God willing, somewhere in this world there may be another lass as good and sweet as your mother. Don't pay any attention to my wanting to hear the patter of little feet here in the ranch house. Never marry until you find the woman God intended you to have; then don't let anything stop you."

"Just as you did."

"Yes." Michael stood, crossed to Brit, and dropped a powerful hand to his shoulder. "If she is like Christine, she's well worth waiting for."

They were the last words he ever spoke to his son. That afternoon his galloping horse stumbled and fell, crushing her rider. Michael never regained consciousness. . . .

Nez Percé whinnied.

Brit reached up and stroked the buckskin's black mane, feeling he had just returned from a long journey. Trained to never make decisions in a hurry, he had stuck it out in Texas for a year after his father died. Then Brit knew it was time to move on. Determined to make a fresh start wherever God led him, Brit sold out lock, stock, and barrel. He left most of his money in a trustworthy bank, reasoning it could be obtained when needed by means of a telegram. Scorning railroads, he saddled the sorrel he had withheld from the sale of his stock, mounted, and rode away. He didn't look back. The ranch was no longer his. His parents' wedding picture rested in the bottom of his saddlebags. God went before and beside him. Nothing else mattered.

Curious about the reports of gold, copper, and silver strikes in Idaho, Brit decided to head north and west. The many faces of America captivated him, especially the towering mountains so unlike those in his home state. He missed the companionship of others, so he hired on now and then at ranches along the way. Yet none appealed to him enough to stay in one place a sufficient amount of time to make lasting friends or to satisfy the belief he would know where he belonged when he got there. And—God willing—find a wife.

"What kind of girl would look at a ragamuffin like me?" he ruefully wondered when he reached Boise. To avoid trouble on the trail, he had deliberately made himself as nondescript-looking as possible. "Not that I want one who judges a man by his trail appearance. Or takes up with him for his money." He grinned. No one seeing Briton Farley in his present state would dream he could buy a nice little chunk of Idaho!

He ended up doing just that. After scouting much of the state, he fell in love with the panhandle area southeast of Coeur d'Alene. Forests abundant with game offered food and shelter. Brit stumbled across a down-on-his-luck, half-starved prospector who needed a place to winter. Grizzled and talkative, Charley January agreed to help Brit build a house in return for a grubstake come the next spring.

"Mind if I put up a sign?" the whiskery fellow asked when they finished the snug log house. "I've prospected all over. Made and squandered enough gold an' silver to have kept me 'til I died." He scratched his head. "Don't 'zackly know why, but I feel this may be my last chance to strike it rich."

Touched by the old man's sincerity, Brit agreed. A few days later, a whimsical, tipsy-looking sign appeared in front of the cabin: LAST CHANCE. POPULATION 2. It was all Brit could do to keep from laughing and hurting his new companion's feelings.

When spring came, Charley January asked permission to prospect on Brit's land before moving on. "If I find anythin', you can give me what you think's fair," he said.

"I'm going to run cattle and horses, Charley, but half of the profits from any ore you discover are yours," Brit told him.

"Ya-hoo!" January waved a rusty pick in the air. "Son, we're gonna be rich."

To Brit's amazement, the unlikely prophet's prediction came true. After months of fruit-less searching, Charley took shelter one night in a cave on Brit's land. The next day he came tearing into the cabin. He had found silver.

It was the beginning of change. The strike proved rich beyond belief. Tents followed by log cabins sprang up like mushrooms. When the miners saw there was no sign of the ore petering out, they brought their families to Last Chance.

To Brit's dismay, the growing town looked to him for leadership. He was elected pres-ident of the school board before Last Chance had either school or teacher. He was also appointed to track down a teacher, a doctor, and a minister. The closest church was Cataldo Mission—Idaho's oldest building—near Kellogg. Built by Indians during the 1850s and 1860s, it was too far away for residents of Last Chance to attend.

Men pitched in, and in short order built a log schoolhouse. The womenfolk prettied up the attached living quarters with cheerful curtains and mail-order rugs for the floor. "In case our teacher has a wife," they said. Brit planned for a church to be constructed if they could find someone willing to do more than take one look at Last Chance and flee as if the devil were after him.

After searching for more than a year, a teacher was found. Unaccustomed to miners and their ways, he left the following spring. Two more followed his example, and complaints poured in about the current teacher. Brit had also been unable to interest a doctor or a minister. He told Charley January in exasperation, "If I'd known I would become the town father, I'd never have let you prospect on my land."

"It ain't so bad." Charley hooked his thumbs beneath his bright red suspenders and smirked. "Fer the first time in my life, folks r'spect me. Besides, since this is *our* town, we kin keep a lid on things, leastwise inside the city limits. Like not lettin' saloons get started." He scowled. "O' course, we ain't got no say who does what out of town. That's why we need a parson right bad." His scowl deepened. "A new teacher, too. T'other day when I was passin' the school, what did I see but that whey-faced feller chasin' two boys around the building, coattails a-flyin'. The rest of the students were chasin' after the teacher. He ain't fit to teach, if you ask me." Charley looked apologetic. "I know you did the best you could, but our younguns need dis-*sip*-line, an' that poor excuse fer a man can't handle it."

Brit sighed, feeling the weight of the world descend on his shoulders. Again. "I know. I thought maybe he'd be better than nothing, but I was wrong. I also kept hoping he might improve. Wrong on that count, too. I'll send out some more notices and see if we can get a nibble. Practically anyone would be better than what we have now." He grabbed a pencil and scrawled, WANTED. *A minister. A doctor. A teacher. If you're any of the above and looking for employment, contact Briton Farley, Last Chance, Idaho.*

What felt like an eternity passed before anyone contacted Brit regarding his advertisement in newspapers across the country. At last a lone letter came. The school board president peered at the return address: Marcus Macrae, Boston, Massachusetts.

"Boston?" Brit snorted. A previous applicant from the East Coast was a misguided store clerk who wanted to come west and hunt buffalo and fight Nez Percé Indians in his spare time! The man was evidently so dumb he didn't know the Nez Percé War had ended in 1877, after Chief Joseph led about eight hundred of his people in a desperate, one-thousand-mile trek toward Canada. Thinking they were safe, they stopped to rest just forty miles from the border and freedom. Chief Joseph's words when he surrendered after a five-day battle became legend: "I will fight no more forever."

Brit hadn't even bothered to answer that application.

He started to toss the Boston letter aside, but curiosity about its writer won. He tore open the envelope. A picture of a smiling young man with a steady gaze fell out. Brit grunted. Marcus Macrae, whoever he was, didn't look like a misguided soul. Or a store clerk bent on killing Indians and buffalo "in his spare time." Brit withdrew the letter and began reading:

Dear Mr. Farley,

I wish to apply for the position of minister in your town. I believe God is calling me to Last Chance. I have studied medicine to some extent, so I can be of assistance if your town is still without a doctor.

A list of qualifications and several references followed, then he added, "I will be available in April."

Nez Percé whinnied, bringing Brit out of his reverie. A chill in the air warned day was dying. He'd best do what he came up here to do and get back to Last Chance. Brit bowed his head.

"Lord, this Marcus Macrae looks intelligent and sounds honest. He also appears too good to be true. Besides, what other choice do I have?"

A hush fell over the forest—and the feeling Brit had learned to trust and follow all his years of seeking the Master's will. He stood, gathered up the reins, and swung into the saddle.

Tomorrow he would start a one-word message on its way to Boston: *Hired.*

Chapter 5

Every *clackety-clack* of railroad wheels between Massachusetts and Idaho added to Meredith Rose Macrae's misery. Marcus's growing pleasure about the new life on which they were embarking only deepened her depression. She hadn't seen him so excited since he first felt called to the ministry. She stared out the window as the chugging engines pulled her away from everything familiar. To her distressed mind, the train became a monster bent on devouring the shining tracks over which it sped and making it impossible for her to return to her former life.

"Not that I want to," she whispered during a solitary moment when Marcus left to get her a drink of water. Rage sent blood coursing through her body. From the moment staid and proper Boston learned of the Macraes' misfortune, society slammed its doors against them. Not only society. When Meredith Rose told Miss Grenadier she'd be able to finish out the term since she wasn't getting married, the woman looked down her nose and said icily, "Impossible! We have replaced you and Mr. Calloway with more suitable instructors."

"How dare you class me with that charlatan?" Meredith Rose blazed.

"I really don't care to discuss it. Good day, Miss Macrae." Miss Grenadier swept from the room, pulling her voluminous skirts around her as if afraid of contamination. Others did the same. Overnight, the formerly sought-after Macraes became outcasts. Only a few brave souls dared buck the tide of public opinion to come calling. Meredith Rose found it difficult to greet them cordially, and soon even their visits ceased.

"Cheer up, old dear," Marcus told her, with a pat on her shoulder. "No one in Last Chance will give a snap of their fingers for Herbert Calloway or Miss Grenadier and her School for Young Ladies." His eyes twinkled. "We'll follow Jesus' advice to His disciples in Luke 9:5: 'And whosoever will not receive you, when ye go out of that city, shake off the very dust from your feet for a testimony against them.'"

The idea conjured up such a vivid picture in Meredith Rose's mind that she burst into laughter. Yet as the end of life as the Macraes knew it drew to a close, there was neither time nor inclination for laughter. Even Marcus hadn't realized how badly their finances had been damaged. Tight-lipped, he and Merry watched piece after piece of fine china and furniture be sold for what seemed a mere pittance and carted away. The dressmaker greedily allowed Meredith Rose to return her wedding gown since it had never been seen in public but at a greatly reduced price.

The day of departure dawned showery and glum. The twins boarded their train. Neither looked back. Marcus took his sister's gloved hand. "We still have each other," he comforted. "And God."

Meredith Rose wordlessly squeezed his fingers. Yes, they did have each other. God? She shrugged her shoulders beneath the dark blue broadcloth traveling gown she'd chosen for her plunge into the unknown. Maybe someday she'd recognize the good Marcus said came from hard situations. Not now. Not when the mournful train whistle sounded like a voice crying *a-way, a-way*, as they began their exile.

✶

The trip west was filled with surprises. Rolling hills gave way to farmlands, then terrain so flat it seemed to go on forever. Weary of straining her eyes looking for something to break the monotony, Meredith Rose's first glimpse of the foothills that led up to the majestic Rocky Mountains left her speechless. Interest stirred. Marcus had said Last Chance was in the mountains. Would they be like this?

At last they reached Idaho, but the worst was yet to come. The decrepit excuse for a stagecoach that would carry them on the last lap of their journey little resembled any conveyance fit for human occupation. Meredith Rose felt like howling but gritted her teeth and climbed inside, nearly tripping over two large extended feet.

"Sorry, ma'am." The feet folded back like an accordion. "Ignatius Crane. At your service."

More like Ichabod Crane, Meredith Rose thought. She seated herself in the far corner of the stage opposite the tall, thin, middle-aged man whose graying hair and colorless eyes did nothing to enhance his horse-like face. She didn't dare look at Marcus, who was muffling laughter with a loud cough.

"Who you be?" their traveling companion asked.

"Marcus Macrae. This is my sister."

"Oh. The new parson." Ignatius's down-turned mouth quirked up. "Good. I'm headed for Last Chance myself. This'll give us time to get acquainted." He turned to Meredith Rose. "What's yore front handle?"

She gave him a stare cold enough to freeze Niagara Falls. "I beg your pardon?"

He sighed. "Ain't that just like an East'rn'r. Yore moniker, lady. Yore name."

"*Miss* Macrae." She longed to add, "If it's any business of 'yores,' " but bit her tongue. Uncouth as he was, Ignatius Crane was the first person she and Marcus had met from Last Chance—perhaps one of Marcus's parishioners. A prayer that he didn't represent the general population of their new home winged upward.

Ignatius doubled over in mirth out of all proportion to her reply. "I done heerd tell that folks from Baw-stun had fancy ways. Don't you worry, little lady. I'll see to it folks treat you right." He tucked his chin into his high collar. "What Ignatius Crane says in Last Chance goes." Pride oozed from him like pitch from a pine.

"Are you one of the town fathers?" Marcus asked.

Meredith Rose wanted to pinch him. The last thing she needed in the rocking, jolting coach was a monologue from the only other passenger aboard.

The thin lips changed to a smirk. "You might say that. Me 'n' Brit Farley just about run the town." He stroked his jaw. "School board and all."

For the first time since she left Boston, Meredith Rose experienced a moment of pure enjoyment. If only Miss Grenadier could see Ichabod–Ignatius. She would shrink in horror from this caricature of a man announcing he was the member of a school board!

The amusement didn't last. Long before Last Chance "hove into sight," as Ignatius inelegantly put it, Meredith Rose's body ached from the jouncing of the stage. She leaned back and closed her eyes, aware of Crane's carping voice going on and on. She did come to attention when Marcus asked, "Have you found a new teacher yet?"

"Nary a one. Yore sister don't happen to be one, does she?"

"She—"

A sharp elbow in her brother's ribs cut off a confession that could do irreparable damage. Meredith Rose leaned forward, forced herself to don her most charming smile, and said, "Mr. Crane, since you are evidently such an important part of Last Chance, do you happen to know where my brother and I will be housed?"

He parted his hair with a bony finger and beamed at her. "Folks take turns offering board and keep, but when I found out the parson was bringing a lady, I just up and says to Brit Farley that it weren't fittin'." He drew himself up pompously. " 'You can't have a real Baw-stun lady shifted from pillar to post,' sez I."

Marcus's eyes brimmed with laughter. "What did Mr. Farley say?"

"Brit? He done agreed with me. Seein' as how we ain't got no teacher right now, you'll stay in the rooms built onto the back of the schoolhouse."

Meredith Rose thought she had heard wrong. "You mean, live in a schoolhouse?"

Ignatius blinked. " 'Course. It's right nice, ma'am. The womenfolk. . ." He rattled on, extolling the virtues of the schoolhouse living quarters. He ended with a triumphant, "If you decide to stay, and I shore hope you will—it ain't every day Last Chance gets quality folks like you—we kin build you a cabin in no time once we get a teacher."

Meredith Rose weakly sank back against the seat, wondering, *What next?*

The opening words of a favorite hymn came to mind. *"My soul in sad exile was out on life's sea. . . ."* She closed her eyes. The last time she'd heard the song was when a highly paid quartet sang it in the church she'd attended since childhood. Her heart had thrilled to the powerful words of the chorus:

> *I've anchored my soul in the Haven of Rest,*
> *I'll sail the wide seas no more;*
> *The tempest may sweep o'er the wild, stormy deep;*
> *In Jesus I'm safe evermore.*

Would there ever be a haven of rest for her again? A place free of tempests where she would feel safe? Certainly not in Last Chance, Idaho. A plan began to take root. She would survive this miserable situation, no matter what it took. Despite his zeal, Marcus would surely grow disheartened if the man opposite them typified those with whom he must work, and he would be willing to go elsewhere. Even now the unpleasant fellow was spouting what was obviously the gospel according to Ignatius Crane. Meredith Rose had never heard such sanctimonious drivel. Her lip curled. She'd met conceited men before, but this scarecrow clearly wanted to be king of the cornfield.

She opened her eyes just enough to observe him through her lashes. Uneasiness filled her. Between his proclamations to Marcus on everything from the way a man should preach to thinly veiled contempt for Brit Farley, Ignatius was sending bold glances her way. The proprietary look in his face sickened her, and she drew her skirts as far away from him as possible.

Just like Miss Grenadier.

Meredith Rose flinched. Her body felt like it was on fire. Where had that odious thought come from? The two situations were farther apart than Idaho and "Baw-stun."

Were they really? She had withdrawn from a fellow human being as surely and as haughtily as Miss Grenadier had done from her. Memory of the humiliation brought shame. Meredith Rose peeked at Ignatius to see if he had noticed her movement, then breathed a quick prayer of thankfulness when he continued to ramble on to her brother. Lout that he was, this man should never have to suffer the way Meredith Rose Macrae had suffered when Miss Grenadier marched out of the room as if fleeing from a contagious disease. Too tired to think, she fell asleep against her twin's shoulder, only to be roused by Marcus's voice. "Wake up, Merry. We're here."

"So that's what yore name is. Mighty purty." Ignatius Crane's nasal drawl drove sleep away. "We don't hold with Miss-in' and Mister-in' folks out here."

Meredith Rose's temper flared. Parishioner or not, town boss or not, school board member or not, she wasn't going to take this churlish man's guff. "You will either address me as Miss Macrae or refrain from addressing me at all," she spit out.

The admiration she had seen in his eyes changed to an expression that sent a trickle of fear down her spine. Being provoked was no reason to lower herself to this man's level. The way his eyes narrowed brought back a long-ago memory of Marcus saying, "There are some people who are better to have as friends than enemies." Was this the case with Ignatius Crane? If so, what had she done?

Hating the need to retreat, for the second time she forced a smile. "Please don't take it personally," she told the now-belligerent man. "It's just that no one has ever called me Merry but my brother."

He gave her a suspicious look, but she was saved from having to say more by the stage-coach driver's loud, "Whoa, you miserable critters," and a deep masculine voice calling, "Did you get them, Len?"

"Shore did, and she's a looker." A hearty laugh followed.

Meredith Rose cringed. The stagecoach door jerked open. A strong hand reached in.

"Marcus Macrae? Miss Macrae? Welcome to Last Chance. I'm Briton Farley."

Chapter 6

The respectful way Briton Farley spoke her name did much toward settling Meredith Rose Macrae's qualms about Last Chance. So did the deeply tanned hand that gripped Marcus's. It hinted at strength and security. Whatever else this western man turned out to be, he would be a rock in time of trouble.

Don't be a ninny, she silently chastised herself. *You know nothing about the man except his name.* Yet eagerness to see if Mr. Farley's face lived up to his hands and voice, plus the desire to look well for Last Chance, caused her to straighten her gown and adjust her hat to the proper angle. Fortunately, Marcus had stepped out of the stagecoach, followed by Ignatius. It gave her a moment to collect herself.

Taking a deep breath, Meredith Rose attempted to stand. Unfortunately, she hadn't counted on the toll the long trip had taken on her normally athletic body. Her right foot buckled, and she gave a little moan.

Marcus's head reappeared in the doorway. "What is it, Merry? Are you all right?"

"I'm fine," she retorted, "except my silly foot's asleep." So much for appearing dignified. " 'Pride goeth before a fall,'" she muttered, stamping to restore circulation.

Marcus roared, then Briton Farley's richly amused voice said, "It's actually 'Pride goeth before destruction, and an haughty spirit before a fall.'"

Astonished by the remark, Meredith Rose took her brother's arm and stepped down from the stagecoach. What kind of man not only knew Scripture but wasn't afraid to quote it in front of the driver, Ignatius Crane, and the large crowd behind him? She looked up. And up. Briton Farley topped her brother's six-foot height by more than two inches. Her own five feet seven seemed puny beside him. April sunlight glistened on his bared head and turned his hair to pure gold. The sun was reflected in his laughing amber eyes and enhanced his wide, white smile. Even his worn but spotless work clothes didn't detract from the fact that outside of Marcus, Briton Farley was the finest-looking man she had ever seen.

A vision of Herbert Calloway shimmered in the air between them. The inadequacy of her former fiancé to measure up to this western rancher/miner/president of the school board/town father brought an insane desire to laugh. How outraged Herbert would be to know the woman he'd jilted in the dusty street of an Idaho mining town comparing him unfavorably with Briton Farley!

Meredith Rose could feel a smile lifting the corners of her mouth. She impulsively held out her gloved hand. "Thank you for the correction, Mr. Farley," she said demurely.

"Again, welcome to Last Chance." An unreadable expression crept into his eyes. Before she could identify it, Ichabod–Ignatius's nasal tones clanged in her ears like an unwelcome gong. "No need fer that, Brit. I done welcomed her."

Meredith Rose's attention shifted to the scowling man, who glanced in her direction and added significantly, "Keep this in mind. I seen her first."

"Don't you be pestering Miss Macrae," a buxom woman called from the crowd. She elbowed her way to where the Macraes stood. "I'm Katie Reilly. I own Katie's Kitchen." She nodded across the street at the buildings. Crisp, red-checkered curtains at the shining, many-paned windows made the café attractive. "If Ignatius comes around wanting to court you like he's done every other unmarried girl and woman in town, you let me know. I'll take my rolling pin to him."

A wave of approval and laughter swept through the on-lookers. Marcus solemnly shook hands with the restaurant proprietor. "With a protector like you, Mrs. Reilly, my sister should be well cared for." He spun toward Crane amidst a second round of crowd approval. "I believe in turning the other cheek, but there's also a time to smite the enemy. Do we understand each other?"

Ignatius jerked his head in the semblance of a nod but didn't back down. Meredith Rose found herself torn between humiliation, the desire to shriek, and the need to blink back tears at the championship from Marcus and Katie Reilly. "Th–thank you." She turned to Briton Farley and asked, "If Icha–Mr. Crane bothers me, will you smite him or take a rolling pin to him, too?" Her hand flew to her mouth. Had she lost her senses, along with her good intentions to treat Ichabod–Ignatius courteously?

The rancher's smile faded into a grim line. His eyes looked molten gold. "I'll do more than that," he vowed, glaring at the man who had attempted to stake a claim to the new minister's sister, with or without her permission. His rigid stance warned Meredith Rose that although Brit resembled a sleeping mountain lion, when roused, he could be equally dangerous. His voice cracked through the silence like a bullwhip in the hands of a master. "No one, I repeat, *no one* is to force unwelcome attentions on Miss Macrae. Understood?"

Meredith Rose expected Crane to slink away like a whipped puppy. Instead he smirked and demanded, "Does *no one* include *you*, Brit?" He smirked again.

The mood of the crowd changed to an angry rumbling. It expressed more loudly than words the esteem in which the town of Last Chance held Brit Farley. The big man clenched his hands into fists and crouched as if preparing to spring. Primitive feelings Meredith Rose hadn't known she possessed rose within her. Her fingernails bit into the palms of her hands. For one mad moment she hoped Brit would pound the repulsive Crane until he cried for mercy.

Her defender slowly relaxed. One tawny eyebrow raised. "As a member of the school board, I'm sure you understand the meaning of *no one*," he quietly said. He offered his arm to Meredith Rose. "Now if you folks will come with me, I'll show you where you'll be living." He smiled at the crowd. "Pastor Macrae and his sister have had a long, tiring trip. There will be plenty of time for everyone to greet them later."

Katie Reilly sniffed. "*If* they stay, after what Ignatius just did."

Crane cast a malevolent glance in her direction, then stared at Meredith Rose. It took all her self-control to remain calm beneath his scorching gaze. Denied of the chance to "court" her, would he become her enemy—and Marcus's? Could he stir up trouble against them?

Marcus patted Katie Reilly's shoulder. "Let's just forget what happened. It takes all kinds of people to make a town." He offered the grin his twin believed could get him almost anything he wanted, and addressed the crowd. "There will be church this coming Sunday. I hope you'll all be there." He even gave Ignatius a friendly smile.

"We'll be there, Parson," a loud voice called. "Any man who stands up for his women-folk should be able to tell us something worth hearing!" A hum of appreciation followed. It warmed Meredith Rose's cold heart, but not as much as the strong hand that gently rested on hers for a moment before Briton Farley said, "Don't let Crane disturb you, Miss Macrae. He's actually harmless. Most of the folks here are good people, rougher than you're used to, but kindhearted and real."

"I'm surprised at the amount of brick and frame businesses," Marcus confessed. He gestured down the street that stretched before them. Meredith Rose's gaze followed his pointing fingers, then traveled to the wooded slopes surrounding the town. All the way from Boston, she had tried to form a picture of where she and Marcus would be living. So far, there seemed to be nothing to dread. The town nestled between the mountains like a baby in the folds of a blanket. She could hear the distant rumble of machinery that must belong to the mines, but it wasn't close enough to town to be more than a reminder of why Last Chance existed.

"We are making a real town here." Brit grinned. "It's a far cry from the day my old prospector friend Charley January put up a sign in front of the log house he helped me build. It read: LAST CHANCE. POPULATION 2." He hesitated. "After you settle in, I want you to come out to my ranch." Again the unreadable expression Meredith Rose had seen when they first met came into his eyes. After a moment, he said, "Please forgive me if I stare, Miss Macrae. You remind me of someone who once meant everything to me." Sadness darkened his gaze.

Meredith Rose's spirits had been rising at finding out Last Chance wasn't as bad as she'd expected. Now they plummeted. Had the woman been his wife? He had obviously never gotten over his loss. *Why should you care?* she fiercely demanded. *He is nothing to you except the tool that brought you to Last Chance. The sooner you convince Marcus that God really isn't calling him to work here, the better. What are you, a silly schoolgirl to be attracted by a sunny smile and a man who springs to the aid of maidens in distress? A modern Sir Galahad, riding on a white horse?*

For the second time that day, she blurted out words best left unspoken. "What kind of horse do you ride?"

Brit blinked. "My favorite is my buckskin stallion Nez Percé."

"What color is he?"

"Golden tan with a black mane and tail. Why?"

"I just wondered."

So much for fairy tales. Sir Galahad wouldn't have been caught dead on a buckskin horse, even if there had been such mounts in the days of King Arthur. She fell silent, lengthening her stride to keep up with Brit's long steps. Was she the same Meredith Rose Macrae she had been for the first twenty-seven years of her life? So far today she had endured a boor, found at least two new advocates, longed to see Ichabod–Ignatius pounded, and felt disappointed to discover a stranger's heart was held captive by a lost love. Yet she felt more alive than she had in years.

Perhaps it was the friendliness of the crowd who supported her against one of their own. Or the blue, blue sky and smiling sun. Whatever the reason, she felt ready to face whatever came next, even living in a schoolhouse!

When they reached the log schoolhouse sitting on a knoll and encircled by trees and wildflowers, Meredith Rose could scarcely conceal her curiosity. What would it be like inside? She didn't have long to wait. Brit flung open the door. The familiar smell of chalk mingling with the unfamiliar tang of forest sweeping through the open windows made her homesick. In spite of what had happened, she had enjoyed teaching at Miss Grenadier's School for Young Ladies.

She noted the carefully crafted wooden desks, so in contrast with pictures of early schoolrooms she had seen in magazines depicting backwoods schools. Open cupboards held a goodly amount of supplies. An American flag proudly stood at one side of the room; a large black wood-burning stove at the other. Meredith Rose's gaze turned to the teacher's desk. An open Bible rested on its polished surface.

"What a well-equipped school," Marcus burst out. "Merry, you could do wonders here!" Remorse killed his enthusiasm but too late. The cat was not only out of the bag, it perched on the teacher's desk and smirked at Meredith Rose.

Brit looked delighted. "Miss Macrae, don't tell me you're a teacher!" Words tumbled out like a mountain stream rushing to the sea. "Thank God!" He grabbed her hand and squeezed it. "You are truly an answer to prayer."

It took great effort, but she ignored his heartfelt exclamation and said, "I? Teach here? Preposterous! I'm sorry, Mr. Farley, but I'm afraid you will need to keep praying."

"How do you know God didn't send you unless you try?"

The question caught her unawares. She freed her hand and fumbled with her gloves. Putting all the chill she could summon into her voice she told him, "For one thing, I only taught such subjects as deportment, drama, music, and art."

"Fine." He beamed. "Our youngsters will be all the better for knowing those things as well as their ABCs. It won't be hard. There are only a few weeks left this term, and you'll have this summer to get ready for fall."

If anything in the world could have changed Meredith Rose's mind, it would have been Brit's golden smile, his absolute confidence in her ability, and his belief that God had sent her to Last Chance. She felt herself wavering. Should she consent to teach the short session with the understanding they must replace her in the fall?

His next words came like a deluge of ice water. They steadied her determination not to be swayed by this appealing westerner. "It isn't like you have to teach all forty-eight classes," he assured her. "The older students help by listening to the younger children's lessons."

Meredith Rose gasped. "Forty-eight classes?"

Brit looked surprised. "Of course. Six subjects times eight grades equals forty-eight." He ticked them off on his strong fingers. "Reading, writing, and arithmetic; spelling, history, and geography. Of course, if you add art and music and drama it *will* make a mite more work."

Meredith Rose weakly sank into a chair, wondering if the sound in her head could be God laughing. Eight grades in a one-room schoolhouse? Six subjects for each grade? A 'mite more work' if she added art and music and drama? From wedding bells to school bells in a few short weeks. It was enough to make her want to tear her hair and catch the first stage out of town.

Chapter 7

How do you know God didn't send you?" Brit Farley's challenging words beat in Meredith Rose Macrae's mind. Marcus didn't help. "Give it a try, old dear," he said. "Children here have the right to learn. You can teach. It's as simple as that." His eyes darkened to the color of the Idaho night sky. "Besides, we can use the money."

Meredith Rose gasped. "Are we that hard up?"

"We're all right so far, but my salary is partially dependent on the offerings. Teaching would also keep you from being bored." He waved one hand around their living quarters. Although rough compared with Boston, the small living-room and kitchen combination and the two minuscule bedrooms were comfortable. The cheap but cheerful curtains, rag rugs, hand-hewn furniture, and blazing fire in the small fireplace gave a warm and cozy feel. "You certainly won't be spending much time doing housework!"

Meredith Rose opened her mouth to indignantly deny any intention of teaching in Last Chance, then quickly snapped it shut. If she were to persuade Marcus to leave, they would need money until he could find a church elsewhere. Even the small amount she would earn in the few weeks remaining in the spring term would help. "I–I'll think about it," she promised, even though her soul revolted at the idea.

A thunderous knock sounded at the door leading outside of their quarters. Meredith Rose burned with resentment. Were she and Marcus to have no privacy?

"It's Katie Reilly," a voice called. "Preacher, we need your help."

Marcus flung the door open. Katie stumbled inside and held out the small boy she carried. Blood oozed between her fingers from the child's flannel-clad shoulder. "It's Sammy, my youngest. I told him and told him to stay out of the street." She gulped. "He didn't—and a horse kicked him."

"It weren't my fault, Katie. Honest." The grizzled old man who had followed Katie inside looked ready to burst into tears. "He tore out of the café and fell right in front of us. My horse tried to jump over him, but his hoof hit Sammy."

"Aw, Ma, I ain't gonna die," the red-haired urchin protested. He squirmed and stared at Marcus. "Brit Farley says you know how to fix folks." Meredith Rose marveled at the total trust and hero worship in Sammy's eyes.

"Let's see what we can do." Marcus pried Katie's fingers free from her son's shoulder and set the boy on the kitchen table. "Bring my medical bag," he told his sister, sliding the blood-soaked shirt off Sammy's skinny body. "Not too bad, Mrs. Reilly. See?" He showed her the shallow groove. "This is going to sting, Sammy." Marcus swabbed the cut with antiseptic.

Sammy screwed his face into an awful scowl, but not one tear escaped. He gave Marcus an anxious, gap-toothed grin. "You'll tell folks I didn't cry, right? Men don't cry when they get to be six."

Meredith Rose was torn between wanting to laugh and wanting to scoop the child in her arms and hug him. She bit her lip and was glad that Marcus solemnly promised to make sure everyone knew how brave Sammy had been. He finished his task, put a soft bandage over the wound, and tied it off in a jaunty knot. "All done."

"Thanks." Sammy slid off the table and looked at Meredith Rose. "Hey, you're purty. Are you my new teacher? I heard Brit Farley tell Ma he was gonna—"

A strong hand covered the child's mouth. "Men don't snoop on other folks's conversations, and if they do, they don't repeat what they hear," his mother warned.

Of all the times for Katie Reilly to give Sammy a lesson in manners, why did it have to be now? Meredith Rose wondered. She would love to hear just what Brit Farley was "gonna" do about convincing her to teach school in the town he controlled!

"How much do I owe you?" Katie asked Marcus.

"Nothing. I'm not a real doctor."

Katie sniffed. "Maybe so, but we're right glad to have you." She led Sammy out.

"That goes for all of us." The old man held out a toil-worn hand. "I'm Charley January. Welcome to Last Chance."

Now that the crisis was over, Meredith Rose had time to observe him. Rough but clean clothes. Kindly eyes in a whiskered face. "Are you a prospector?" she asked.

"I was 'til I up and found silver on Brit Farley's land." Charley swelled with pride. "Me 'n' him went fifty–fifty. That's the kinda feller he is. Grateful fer me helpin' him build his log house. You gotta come visit us." He pumped Marcus's hand up and down.

Meredith Rose saw her brother surreptitiously flex his fingers when Charley finally released his grip. Evidently age and hard work hadn't diminished the strength in Charley January's gnarled hands. Or the steady look in his eyes. On impulse she said, "Would you like a cup of coffee, Mr. January?"

He brightened up. "I'm just plain Charley, an' I'd love one."

Two hours and countless tall tales later—most featuring Briton Farley as the all-conquering, bigger-than-life-and-twice-as-natural hero—Charley left, although obviously reluctant to do so. Meredith Rose stared at Marcus. "So this is Last Chance, where anything can, and apparently does, happen!"

"We knew it would be different."

"Different?" Laughter swelled and burst into the quiet room. "I never knew the meaning of the word until now!" Yet long after she lay in bed watching the brilliant stars in the cold night sky, Meredith Rose couldn't help wondering what it was about Briton Farley that inspired such trust in an old prospector and a child as young as the adoring Sammy; Sammy, whose innocent, "Are you my new teacher?" had touched a chord in her heart silenced by her former fiancé's defection. Maybe teaching for a few weeks wouldn't be so bad after all.

The next day Meredith Rose sent word to Brit that she would take over the school. The look of profound gratitude in his amber eyes when he appeared at her door to thank her sent a thrill through her unlike any she'd ever felt for Herbert Calloway.

"You'll never know what this means," he told her. "I thank God. By the way, I'll be there come Monday morning to introduce you." A lazy grin and raised eyebrow did little to detract from the candle lit in Meredith Rose's heart.

She spent all day Saturday frantically reviewing the material in the schoolbooks Brit brought to her. He had consulted with Sadie Reilly, the only eighth-grade girl that term, and painstakingly provided a list of the fifteen students and where each was in his or her studies. It helped immensely.

"Now if I can only keep one step ahead of them," Meredith Rose told Marcus.

"You can, Merry." Her brother rumpled her hair and frowned. "Now if *I* can only keep one step ahead of my congregation! From what I hear, they know their Bibles upside down and backwards, especially Brit Farley." He went back to studying.

Meredith Rose muttered, "So that's his secret!" but not loudly enough for her twin to hear. She did *not* need Marcus teasing her about undue interest in the town boss. Her own unruly heart was already accusing her of it.

※

Marcus Macrae need not have worried about his first sermon in Last Chance. After much prayer, he chose Matthew 13:44 for his text: " 'Again, the kingdom of heaven is like unto treasure hid in a field; the which when a man hath found, he hideth, and for joy thereof goeth and selleth all that he hath, and buyeth that field.'"

A ripple of surprise ran through the packed schoolhouse-turned-church. Heads nodded. This they could understand! They were dependent on finding treasure. Working mines fed families, supported local businesses, and provided shelter and clothing.

For almost an hour, Marcus held the attention of men, women, and children who had been taught church was a place to listen and not just be entertained. He closed with Luke 12:34: " 'For where your treasure is, there will your heart be also.'"

After a moment of silence he quietly asked, "Where is your treasure? Your heart? If it is not with our heavenly Father, all the silver and gold in the world are worthless." He bowed his head. "Lord, we thank Thee for Thy love and for the gift of Thy Son. In Jesus' name, amen."

The congregation's *amen*s resounded through the room and bounced off the rafters. Then Brit Farley stood. "Preacher Marcus insists that no offerings be taken during services." He shook his head. "Sounds mighty peculiar to me, but he says the Bible tells us to do our giving in secret." He held up a flour sack. "For those who can and choose to give tithes and offerings, this will be at the back of the room on Sundays. No one, not even our preacher or the deacons, will know who gives what." He strode down the aisle and hung the sack on a nail.

Meredith Rose heard a grunt of disapproval from Ignatius Crane. He had placed himself directly behind her and she had felt his gaze boring between her shoulder blades throughout the service. Evidently the new regime didn't meet with his approval. If she were a betting person, she'd wager the highlight of Ichabod–Ignatius's week was ostentatiously placing his offering in the plate for all to see!

People began collecting their belongings, then Brit said, "School will begin at eight o'clock tomorrow morning. Miss Macrae will be our new teacher."

Hearty applause followed. "Miss Macrae" wished the floor would open and swallow her. She'd hoped to begin teaching without fanfare. So much for her hopes. "I'll be there to observe you for a few days," an unwelcome voice said in her ear.

Meredith Rose whirled. "That will not be necessary, Mr. Crane," she said in her iciest voice. "I am sure I can teach without your interfer—without your help."

He smirked. "Nevertheless, I'll be there. We've had bad luck with our teachers. As a member of the board of directors, I'll make sure our younguns are taught proper."

She cast an imploring look at Brit, handsomer than ever in his Sunday suit.

"Once Miss Macrae has time to settle in, I'm sure she will be happy to invite the school board members to visit," he said easily. He smiled, but again Meredith Rose sensed a readiness to pounce if necessary. "Tomorrow morning I will introduce her, then make myself scarce. She needs to *and will be* left on her own. By the way, I've been meaning to talk with you about. . ." His voice trailed off as he firmly edged Ignatius away, leaving the new teacher filled with gratitude.

❋

From the time Meredith Rose rang the school bell the next morning, then took her place behind the hand-hewn teacher's desk, she became the object of adoration from even the most unruly students. She attributed it to Brit Farley's warning that if they made trouble for the new teacher, they would answer to him. And to Sammy Reilly's loud praises about how Preacher Doc "fixed" his shoulder. In any event, long before the spring term ended, the young woman found herself actually anticipating each new day and searching for ways to keep her students interested.

She also discovered the heart she had vowed to never again give away pounded like a war drum each time Brit Farley stepped inside her classroom. She found it amusing to note the number of flimsy excuses he used to ride up on Nez Percé just as school was letting out. Sometimes it was to make sure she had enough school supplies. At other times, he wanted to know what progress this or that student was making. Meredith Rose came to look forward to his brief visits.

When the term ended and summer came, Brit was busier than ever with his ranch and mines. She seldom saw him except on Sunday at church and sometimes not even then. Rumors of trouble in other areas reached Last Chance: stories of miners' strikes that turned ugly. Wallace, Idaho, had faced such troubles a few years earlier. Tension mounted during a mining labor strike. Soldiers pitched their tents in a vacant lot close to brick and frame businesses in order to keep the peace.

"God forbid such a thing will come to Last Chance," Marcus told his twin.

Fear clawed at her. If it did, would Brit be in danger? In the space of a single heartbeat, realization came. She cared far more for Briton Farley than she had been willing to admit, even to herself. In the privacy of her room, she chastised herself severely. "What have you, a Boston lady, to do with a man of the West? A gulf lies between you; a chasm wider than the miles stretching between Massachusetts and Idaho. He could never be part of your world."

You could be part of his, a little voice whispered.

Meredith Rose laughed scornfully. She, settle down in Last Chance, the wife of a rancher and mine owner? Never! Brit Farley had installed every convenience possible in his log home, including running water from a nearby stream. Yet it was still a primitive house in a wilderness that both drew her by its beauty and repelled her by the lack of amenities she had been accustomed to all her life.

That home could be glorified by love, the voice persisted. *Think of Brit Farley coming home to you at day's end. Think of meeting him at the door and lifting your face for his kiss. Think of him catching you up in his strong arms and keeping you safe from the storms of life. Think of bearing Brit's children: a tawny-haired boy with his father's amber eyes; a dark-haired daughter who looks like you and Marcus. Of raising them in God's Word to be His children. Marcus loves it here, and the people are generously supporting him. Why fight it, Meredith Rose?*

"Even if I could overcome my feelings about Last Chance, I'd never be anything more than second choice, chosen because I remind Brit of the woman who 'once meant everything to him,'" she protested, remembering the sadness in his eyes when he told her why he stared at her. Torn by the conflicting images that knocked at the door of her heart and threatened to undo her, Meredith Rose cried herself to sleep for what might have been, if Brit hadn't made clear his heart still belonged to his first love.

Chapter 8

The little voice that had whispered to Meredith Rose was right. Marcus had fallen in love with Idaho. He exulted in the long hours he put in visiting townspeople and witnessing of his Lord, helping those who were sick or afflicted with ailments and injuries within the scope of his medical knowledge. Last Chance had become his home.

When Zeb Perry and his wife moved to Last Chance with their daughter, Alice, Marcus's joy increased. Alice, a modest young woman whose fair face shone with the goodness that comes from within, attracted Marcus as no woman had ever done. He wisely bided his time but felt that God had directed his and the Perrys' footsteps to the isolated mining town for a reason. If the look in the blue eyes gazing up at him from beneath Alice's simple bonnet were to be believed, she cared for him, as well.

Yet Marcus's growing love was bittersweet. How would Merry react when he told her he wanted nothing more than to marry sweet Alice and spend the rest of his days serving in a place his twin hated? Would it mean separation? The thought left him miserable. Why must he be a wishbone, pulled between the girl he hoped to make his wife and Merry, his other half—the half who had promised they would never part. In spite of her being a good sport about the teaching, Marcus sensed Merry was also biding her time—waiting until she could convince him to leave Last Chance.

One evening when they strolled to a wooded knoll at the edge of town and watched the setting sun slide behind a high green hill, Meredith Rose spoke. "You're in love with Alice. Are you going to marry her?"

Marcus didn't quibble. "Yes, God willing."

The rosy afterglow filling the sky and reflecting on her face didn't hide the desolation in her eyes, but she quietly said, "I am happy for you."

"What about you, Merry? Will you stay? Our school still needs a teacher." He didn't dare add that a certain rancher-miner also needed her. Neither Brit nor Merry had been able to hide from him their growing feelings. They had started with a spark of attraction when she first stepped down from the stage. Brit would be good for his twin. Strong enough to curb her haughty spirit—as evidenced by the way he had coaxed her into teaching—he was also gentle enough to appreciate and cherish her.

Her shoulders drooped. "I know. The board of directors asked me to stay."

"I hope you will." Marcus took a deep breath, then delivered a blow he knew would shatter her dreams. "Merry, even if you leave, I can't. This is where I belong."

"You'll marry Alice, and there will be no place for me." She held up her hand to still his protest. "The town will build you a home. Unless I continue teaching, I can't live at the schoolhouse." Her blue eyes flashed. "Marcus, even if it means never seeing you again, I won't live with you and Alice. I won't be the spinster sister people laugh at behind her back!" She turned in a whirl of pink muslin skirts and ran, leaving her twin sick at heart and knowing only God could help him and Merry.

�֍

For two wretched days, Marcus and Meredith Rose avoided the subject ever on their minds. "Lord, is it wrong to pray she will change her mind?" he asked again and again. "I can't bear to think we will be separated." Mark 10:7 came to mind: "For this cause shall a man leave his father and mother, and cleave to his wife."

"I know, Lord," Marcus brokenly said. "But the thought of watching Merry board the stage and ride out of my life is more than I can bear."

Before anything was settled, the arrival of two slick strangers overshadowed the twins' personal problems. The strangers came with the sole intention of inciting the miners to strike against the Last Chance mine owners, Brit Farley and Charley January. Brit learned of their secret meeting from Katie Reilly. Sammy had been scrunched down under a table at Katie's Kitchen hoping someone might have dropped some change.

"They didn't see me," he told his mother. "They said they were gonna get the miners to strike an' show Brit Farley who's boss of this town." He clenched his grubby hands into small fists. "Just let 'em try!"

Brit and Charley echoed Sammy's inelegant response when Katie sent word. They burst into the meeting held in a stand of trees at the edge of town and confronted the troublemakers. "We deal with *our men*—not with the likes of you," Brit barked.

"We done told 'em that," a loyal miner called. A growl of agreement ran through the crowd. "We only came tonight because we wanted to hear what they had to say. You've always treated us fair an' square. That's good enough for us."

Charley wasn't to be outdone. He cackled and pointed to the road out of town. "Git." A grin spread across his grizzled face. "Y'might say this is yore Last Chance."

The troublemakers hightailed it away as if it really were their last chance, followed by a chorus of loud *haw-haws* from those they had considered easy marks.

✗

When Meredith Rose heard about the incident, she marveled at the miners' allegiance. For a fleeting moment she pictured Herbert Calloway inspiring such loyalty. The idea was so far-fetched she laughed until she cried. Thankfulness that she hadn't married the dancing master filled her. At times it was hard to remember what he looked like. Boston and her former existence seemed long ago and far away. Life in Last Chance might be crude but never by any stretch of imagination could it be called dull.

The little town went all out for Independence Day. On July 1, Sammy Reilly stopped his teacher in the middle of the street and asked, "Didja hear about the Fourth of July? Every year, there's a pick-a-nick out by the mine." His red hair waved in the warm afternoon breeze. "You never seen such food!" He rolled his eyes and licked his lips. "Chicken 'n' cake 'n' pie 'n' lemonade 'n' all kindsa stuff. We play games, too, an' at night the sky gets all lit up from fireworks." He danced around her in anticipation. "I can't wait!"

"I guess we'll have to," Meredith Rose told him.

He sidled up to her and looked into her face. "Are you gonna be my teacher again? Ma says she shore hopes so an' that if Brit Farley lets you get away, he's plumb loco. He ain't, is he?"

The pleading in the child's face prodded Meredith Rose into announcing a decision she had slowly been moving toward for several days. She couldn't leave Last Chance. It wasn't right to ask her twin for money the congregation had contributed for his upkeep. What little she had earned wouldn't get her far. If she stayed for the full autumn term and hoarded everything she made, she'd have a nest egg. "No, Sammy. Mr. Farley isn't loco. I'm going to be your teacher."

His skinny hand grabbed hers and squeezed. Then he let out a war whoop and sped away. "Hey, Ma, Teacher says Brit ain't loco an' she'll stay!" His voice echoed up and down the dusty street.

Katie Reilly appeared at the door of her café. "Well, that's mighty good news. Right, Brit?"

To Meredith Rose's chagrin, the tall, familiar frame of the town boss followed Katie out of the café. "Which? That I'm not loco, or that Miss Macrae is staying?"

"Both, you big galoot," Katie retorted. She sniffed. "Land sakes, my biscuits are burning." She shoved past Brit and ran back inside.

Unable to escape the man who purposefully headed toward her, Meredith Rose knew she had to brazen it out, but why did Brit have to learn she was staying like this? Before she could think of a casual remark, he halted in front of her, just long enough for a wide smile to creep across his tanned face. The next instant his powerful arms caught her by the elbows. He lifted her off her feet, then swung her in a circle. Her thin white gown ballooned about her. "That's the best news this town has heard in a month of Sundays," Brit rejoiced. "Miss Meredith Rose Macrae, I just plain love you!"

Her heart soared. Did he mean it? Really mean it? *Don't be stupid,* she told herself. *He's just glad to have a teacher for his precious town.* Yet all the rationalizing in the world couldn't crush the warm feeling his strong arms produced.

"So that's what's been going on," an accusing voice said. "No wonder you claim-jumped me when I said I seen her first."

Brit set Meredith Rose down but kept one hand protectively on her arm. She turned and gasped in horror, knowing who she would see. Ignatius Crane had a talent for popping up at all the wrong times, like some evil jack-in-the-box. She felt Brit tense and was astonished at his self-control when he said, "Just celebrating the fact we now have a teacher for next fall, Ignatius."

The man's colorless eyes gleamed with unholy glee and satisfaction. He self-righteously drew himself up into a symbol of smugness. "I doubt that. I intend to see that the board of directors and the parents of our younguns are aware of this shocking public display." He tucked his chin under until he looked like a plucked chicken. "Like teacher, like pupils, I al-wuz say."

Brit released Meredith Rose so suddenly she stumbled and nearly fell. In all the weeks she'd known him, never had she seen him like this. Woe to Ichabod–Ignatius! He had awakened a sleeping mountain lion.

Brit grabbed the vindictive man by his collar and lifted him off the ground. He shook him as a dog shakes a rat, then flung him down. "If you ever again say one word against Miss Macrae, I will personally see to it you leave town in a manner you will never forget. Now pick yourself up and get out of my sight before I lose my temper."

The words *before I lose my temper* were Meredith Rose's undoing. She laughed until she cried. Knowing it would make Ichabod–Ignatius hate her more than ever couldn't stop her. It was just too funny. So was the way her former would-be suitor scuttled away after a baleful glance at the cheering crowd on both sides of the street.

"May I see you home, Miss Macrae?" Brit dusted off his hands and grinned. Every trace of anger had fled, and his amber eyes sparkled.

"Thank you." She took the arm he offered, realizing the encounter had shattered her perspective. Was Brit seeing her for herself and not as a mere reflection of the woman he had loved and lost? *Please God, let it be so,* her hopeful heart pleaded.

Chapter 9

Briton Farley slid from the saddle and patted Nez Percé. He strode to the edge of his favorite promontory and hunkered down on a huge rock. "Now you've gone and done it," he rebuked himself. "What got into you? Grabbing Merry Macrae in the middle of town and blurting out that you loved her?"

Nez Percé nudged him. Brit stroked the buckskin's soft nose. "Learning she's going to stay isn't an excuse," mumbled. "It's a wonder she didn't run screaming her head off and thinking I'm worse than Ignatius Crane!" His face scorched with shame. "I've never even dared call her anything to her face except Miss Macrae." He pictured the rich black hair, the lake-blue eyes. "Merry. A lovely name for a lovely person. Will she ever give me the right to use it?" He sighed. "Her uncanny resemblance to my mother had me roped, tied, and branded the minute she stepped out of that creaking old stage."

Memory of a long-ago conversation with his father came to mind. *"God willing, there may be another lass as good and sweet as your mother. . . . Never marry until you find the woman God intended you to have; then don't let anything stop you."*

Brit groaned. He had found her, but even if Meredith Rose Macrae someday learned to care for him, would her love be strong enough to overcome her distaste for Last Chance? Brit bowed his head. "Thy will be done, Lord." It was one of the hardest prayers he'd ever offered.

A slight breeze crept across the promontory. It cooled the silent man's heated face and stilled the tumult in his heart. If nothing but friendship ever grew between him and Meredith Rose, he would still defend her against the Ignatius Cranes of the world. He rose, vaulted into the saddle, and turned Nez Percé homeward.

❃

Independence Day dawned bright and beautiful. Last Chance was in an uproar. It seemed everyone in town either rode horseback or were transported by wagon to what Sammy called "the pick-a-nick place." A gap-toothed smile showed his joy was complete as he plopped down between his teacher and "Preacher Doc" in the Reilly family wagon. Marcus looked equally happy when Alice Perry climbed in and sat down beside him.

Glad she'd been wise enough to wear a riding habit and could clamber in and out of the horse-drawn, straw-filled conveyance without a loss of dignity, Meredith Rose smiled down at Sammy.

"This is a new experience for us," she told a beaming Katie Reilly. "Marcus and I have never been on a hayride."

"It should be a straw ride," Sammy piped up. "Hay gets saved for the horses. This is straw." He hollered at the tall man riding beside them. "Ain't that right, Brit?"

"Right, Sammy." Brit Farley chuckled. "You're pretty smart."

"I oughta be." Sammy looked indignant. "I'm almost seven an' Teacher says—" He broke off and disgustedly added, "Aw, why'd *he* have to come?"

Meredith Rose glanced in the direction of the stubby, pointing finger. Her anticipation seeped away. Ignatius Crane had urged a horse as sorry-looking as its owner into an awkward gait and was in danger of overtaking the wagon.

Katie made a dismayed sound but quickly said, "Now, Sammy, it's right and proper for everyone to celebrate the Fourth of July."

Sammy scowled. "He never did before. He prob'ly thinks he can court Teacher. He can't." The child squared his skinny shoulders. "Me 'n' Brit'll see to that. Right, Brit?"

The steady look in Briton Farley's eyes made Meredith Rose's heart flutter. So did his quiet, "We sure will, if she says it's all right."

"All right?" Sammy scrambled to his feet and glared. " 'Course it's all right! Teacher don't want that long, tall drink o' water hangin' around her."

Marcus Macrae burst into laughter and pulled Sammy back down. "Whoa, there. You don't want to fall on your head." His eyes twinkled. "Know what? I'm pretty sure my sister is glad to have such good protectors. Right, Merry?" he parroted.

Meredith Rose felt herself grow scarlet. She kept her attention on Sammy and agreed, "Right," but Brit let out a "yippee-ki-ay" that set Nez Percé prancing. The look in Brit's eyes brought a flood of happiness. She turned toward her twin, knowing he understood. For the first time since the harsh words she had spoken had created a wall between them, she and Marcus were again part of a whole. Meredith Rose silently resolved they must never again be separated by anger or disappointment.

The ride to the chosen site sped by much faster than the pace of the plodding horses warranted. The world around her became more beautiful to Meredith Rose than anything she had ever seen. The air sparkled with sunlight. Birds sang praises to their Creator. Squirrels scampered, and rabbits nibbled on wild clover.

Lord, she prayed, *I never noticed before how wonderful it is. Do I feel this way because of Briton Farley? Suddenly all the obstacles between us no longer seem to matter. Was this Your plan, long before I asked You to change my life? I could be content here forever—if Brit loves me. Did he mean what he said that day in the street? Maybe he doesn't just want me to stay because the children need a teacher.*

She stared at the wild roses beside the road. All the costly bouquets she had received were no lovelier than the simple posies blooming where God had placed them.

The deepest peace she had ever known stole into her heart. If it were according to God's will, a rose would one day bloom on Briton Farley's ranch. A Meredith Rose.

A small hand tugged at her arm. "We're here, Teacher." Sammy grinned. "C'mon. I'm holler as a log, an' Ma brung fried chicken."

Meredith Rose didn't have the heart to correct his grammar. There would be time enough for that come September and the beginning of fall term.

Hungry people made a shambles of the carefully prepared picnic. Meredith Rose groaned. "I haven't eaten this much in years."

"You'll work it off," Brit promised. "It's almost time for games." He raised his voice. "If any of you want to see the mine, I'll take you now."

"We do." Marcus leaped to his feet and helped Alice Perry up. "Who else?"

"We're coming." Jovial Mr. Perry and his wife chorused.

"You all go ahead." Katie Reilly waved them off. "I'll pass. I've been in the mine." Several others murmured agreement, reducing the exploring party to less than a dozen. Ignatius Crane wore a long-suffering look but mumbled it was his duty to go. When they reached the mine shaft, Brit lighted a lantern and warned them to stay together; then he led the way inside.

To Meredith Rose's annoyance, Crane trod so closely behind her she thought he'd step on her boots. She determined to rid herself of the leech-like man, so she allowed the others to pass her and Sammy and round a bend. The light from Brit's lantern grew dimmer, casting feeble, flickering shadows on the craggy, timber-shored walls.

Anxious to rejoin the party, she turned to Ichabod–Ignatius and said in a tone so haughty both of her companions gaped, "Mr. Crane, if you don't stop following me, I am going to bring charges against you." What those charges were, she had no idea, but it sounded good. "You have pursued me from the moment we met. You will cease doing this immediately or take the consequences!"

Crane's mouth opened and closed like a fish out of water before he threatened, "I can make you sorry fer this. I'm a just man, but I've stood about as much from you as I'll take." He laid a clammy hand on her arm, and his eyes gleamed in the semidarkness. "You think you're gonna be our schoolmarm come September. Well, you ain't. Not when I tell the parents and board of directors how you've been breakin' the commandments God give us to live by."

Sammy snatched the man's hand off his teacher's arm and blazed, "You're loco. Teacher made us learn the Ten Commandments, and she ain't never broke 'em."

Crane smirked. "The second commandment tells folks plain as day we ain't to make no graven images or likenesses of anything in heaven or earth or water under the earth." He cackled, then sanctimoniously folded his arms. "I peeked in the winder of the schoolhouse and seen her a-drawin' pitchers of what she said the disciples mighta looked like. We don't want no one corruptin' the minds of our younguns. O' course, if you were a mite friendlier, I wouldn't tattle on you."

Meredith Rose did the worst possible thing. She giggled. If only Miss Grenadier could know her former art instructor was being charged with corrupting the children of Last Chance. Her high spirits crashed at Crane's expression. Blind, unreasoning terror attacked. She grabbed Sammy's hand and fled in the direction the others had gone. They rounded the bend. Instead of welcome lantern-light, only a faint glow brightened the way. Fear lent wings to Meredith Rose's feet but the *thud-thud* of heavy boots warned they could never outrun their pursuer.

Sammy tugged her to a stop. "This way." He pulled her into a dark passageway at the left. "We can hide 'til he goes past."

Meredith Rose stumbled after him, hoping Crane hadn't heard them turn.

He evidently had, for he called, "Don't go in there. You'll get lost."

"Aw, he's just talking so's we'll stop," Sammy whispered. "C'mon, Teacher."

With a prayer that Sammy knew what he was doing, Meredith Rose followed. Nothing that lay ahead could be worse than having Ichabod–Ignatius touch her again.

Chapter 10

Sure-footed as a mountain goat, Sammy Reilly led Meredith Rose Macrae away from Ignatius Crane and into the silver mine. "Don't be scairt 'cause it's dark," he told her. "I'll take care o' you."

"I'm sure you will." She strained her ears. The sound of Crane's footsteps had ceased. Never had she heard such silence than what prevailed in this velvet-black place. "Uh, Sammy." She cleared her throat. "How will we get back?"

His skinny hand patted hers reassuringly. "Easy. Brit says al-wus remember the way out. We'll make two left turns and two right." He sounded so confident that some of Meredith Rose's rising fear dwindled.

"How will we know when Icha—Mr. Crane is gone?"

Sammy snorted. "Huh! You won't catch him in here. I bet he's already sneaked out so's folks won't know he scared us. It won't do any good. I'm gonna tell Brit." He paused. "I told you him 'n' me'd take care of you."

She wanted to hug him but refrained, sensing his young manliness might be offended. "I do appreciate it," she solemnly told him.

After what felt like a century but couldn't have been more than fifteen minutes, Sammy announced, "We c'n go now." He took her hand and confidently led her back the way they had come. Before they arrived at the main passage, the welcome sound of Brit and Marcus's voices calling their names reached them.

"We're here, Brit," Sammy shrilled, stepping into the open with his teacher.

The lantern in Brit's hand shook as he held it high. "Sammy Reilly, what in thunder possessed you to take Miss Merry off like this?"

All the small boy's bravado crumpled. "I–I. . ."

Meredith Rose knew men often yelled when worried, but Sammy's woebegone face roused her ire. "Briton Farley, you should be thanking Sammy, not bellowing at him!" She ignored a sob rising in her throat, marched over, planted herself in front of Brit, and glared into his face. "Ignatius Crane frightened me, and Sammy helped me get away." The last word came out as a squeak, for Brit put both arms around her and kissed her like she'd never been kissed before. Thoroughly. Tenderly. Reverently.

"It's the last time he or anyone else will frighten you if I have anything to say about it! Meredith Rose Macrae, I love you as I have never loved any other woman. Will you marry me?" Without waiting for an answer, he kissed her again.

She felt she had at last come home. A loud *haw-haw* from Marcus, and Sammy's ecstatic, "Oh, boy, wait'll I tell Ma!" brought her to her senses and out of Brit's arms.

"Hold it, Pard. She hasn't said yes yet," Brit reminded Sammy. "Women have been known to say no. Or even change their minds."

Sickening reality shattered Meredith Rose's bliss. She stepped back, knowing her face was whiter than falling snow. "Is that what happened with the woman I remind you of? The one who m—meant e—everything to you?" How maddening that her voice broke on the last words!

A poignant light gleamed in the amber eyes. "Merry, that woman was my mother. She died when I was just a few years old."

Silence fell over the group but not for long. Marcus, the irrepressible, drawled, "'Wal, I reckon that'll be aboot all,' as the cowboys say." He glanced down at Alice Perry, whose blue eyes looked enormous in the dim light. "At least for now." Even the dim light couldn't hide the pretty blush that rose from the collar of her hand-sewn dress.

Sammy anxiously reminded his teacher, "You ain't said yes."

"So I haven't." She smiled down at him, then looked straight into Brit's clear eyes. What she saw there more than repaid all the heartache she had experienced over the last long months. "Yes, Brit, I will marry you. On one condition."

He straightened as if burned with a branding iron. "Which is?"

With a flash of clarity, she knew Brit thought she'd ask him to leave the town he loved and had founded to take her back to Boston. Boston? Twenty-seven hundred miles and a lifetime away. Heedless of their audience, she placed her hands on his shoulders. "It's just that I'd like for the school bell to ring on our wedding day."

"Is that all? I thought—"

"I know." She stood on tiptoe and kissed him. "I'd also like a Christmas wedding."

Brit tilted his head to one side. A delighted smile appeared. "Sounds good to me. Fall roundup will be over, which means time for a honeymoon."

It was enough for Sammy. "Ya-hoo," he screeched, racing out of the mine like a speeding bullet. The announcement of the brand-new engagement floated back. "Ma, ever'body, Brit 'n' Teacher's gettin' hitched come Christmas!"

Mischief shone in Brit's eyes and he glanced at Marcus. "Now all we have to do is run Ignatius Crane out of town and wait until December!"

"Amen to that!" Marcus heartily agreed, but they were deprived of the satisfaction of ridding the range of the unpleasant man. Ichabod—Ignatius, as Meredith Rose would always call him, had shaken the dust of Last Chance off his boots and departed for parts unknown long before the picnickers returned to town.

On Christmas Eve Day, sunlight burst through the December clouds and streamed through the windows of the living quarters behind the one-room schoolhouse in Last Chance. It rested on Meredith Rose Macrae in her simple white gown and veil.

The sound of those entering the classroom and taking their places for "Teacher and Brit's" wedding was music to the bride's ears. So was the joyous tolling of the school bell that summoned students to their studies and worshipers to church.

Marcus Macrae stood at the window, looking across the street to the close-to-completion home where he and his Alice would live after their wedding in the new year. A dedicated teacher and his family would occupy the schoolhouse quarters, and a church would be built in the spring. Marcus smiled. "Well, old dear," he said, "this is it."

Merry turned her radiant face to him. "If you had told me last March all this would happen, I wouldn't have believed it. I railed against God, Marcus, thinking He had ruined my life. All the time He knew where I—where we—belonged." She gave him a tender smile.

"I know, and I thank Him." A rush of love for his twin threatened to overwhelm Marcus. To cover the emotion-filled moment, he resorted to humor. "I could give you all kinds of brotherly advice," he began, "but I won't. Instead, I'll just say this. If you ever write the story of your life, you can call it *School Bells and Wedding Bells*. After all, you *are* a schoolhouse bride!"

The door flung open. Charley January, who would walk Merry down the aisle, and Sammy Reilly, Brit's best man, came in. "Time to get this shindig started," Charley gruffly said. He turned bright pink when Meredith Rose kissed his freshly shaven cheek. Sammy chortled, then went with Marcus to find Brit.

Meredith Rose picked up her bouquet of Christmas roses. Brit had smiled when she asked how he had managed to get them; then he quietly said, "I have ways."

She took Charley's arm and stepped into the schoolroom that held so many good memories. She stopped short. Fragrant cedar boughs tied with red ribbon framed every window. Fat white candles glowed with a lovely light—but it could not compare with the light in the eyes of the man who held her future in his strong but gentle hands. What cared she for satin gowns, priceless lilies, jewels, and fine houses? Her home would be a spacious log house that kept out the storms of life. She and Brit needed no "charm from the sky," to hallow that home. God had directed them to Last Chance to give them a new beginning.

And from his place at the front of the schoolroom, Brit waited for his bride. His heart swelled with love for the white-clad figure coming toward him. Surely no man had ever been more blessed. The God who had given His Son to the world had granted the desire of Briton Farley's heart by bestowing on him a "Merry" Christmas.

ROSE KELLY

by Janet Spaeth

Dedication

For my sister Pat, who understands me and still loves me!

Chapter 1

Jubilee, Dakota Territory—1879

*J*ubilee!

Only an inbred sense of decorum kept Rose Kelly from pressing her nose against the window of the train like an excited child.

She had been on this train much too long. Every shudder and shimmy made her tense, knowing that the dreadful grating of metal on metal was about to begin. She'd have no teeth left if the train didn't come to a complete stop soon. Her jaw ground right along with the shriek of the brakes and the wheels on the tracks.

The train grated to a squealing halt, and Rose tried to restrain herself from elbowing her way to the front of the passengers disembarking.

Jubilee!

Despite her exhaustion—who could sleep on a train that joggled and jiggled and screeched the way this one did?—she was anxious to see this place that would be her home for the next six months.

She'd been watching through the train window as Jubilee came into view. It was a tiny whistle-stop town in the Dakota Territory, a cluster of buildings huddled protectively together on the open prairie. In winter, such proximity might be a blessing. But now with the glorious summer sun pouring over the grassy expanse, such closeness seemed an excess.

The crowd surged forward, and she felt herself being propelled toward the exit. She grasped her signature bag, a tiny thing embroidered and beaded with pink and red roses, and let the movement carry her.

Suddenly she was squeezed out into the front, to the open door. . .and she stepped into air. The footing she thought would be there wasn't, and she dropped suddenly toward the platform.

The crowd pushed again, and in a most ungainly and unfeminine move, she was launched into a very solid shape. Two arms came out of nowhere, it seemed, and caught her just before she hit the platform's surface. Strong arms. Tanned arms. Muscular arms.

"Careful, miss."

She looked up into blue eyes that exactly matched the Dakota sky behind him. The wind ruffled his hair, as blond as summer wheat.

He quickly dropped his arms. . .and his gaze.

"Wanted to make sure you weren't injured," he muttered. "Are you going to be all right?" he asked, and she realized that she was still clutching his arms.

Rose considered her rescuer as she released her grip and adjusted the front of her traveling suit—quite the thing back in Chicago. This man might be a good resource for her needs.

"Is someone coming for you?" he asked, but his words were more a statement than a question, as if he already knew the answer. His forehead knotted into a frown. From the lines etched there, Rose thought that expression must be a perpetual state with him.

"No." She looked at her surroundings. Even with all the research she'd done before coming out, nothing had prepared her for this.

What she'd seen from the train had been deceptive. Jubilee was more than a nervous clump of buildings. It was a genuine town with genuine buildings and genuine people walking on genuine streets.

Oh, there was a rough, raw edge to it, but Jubilee was definitely a town that would still be on the map in a century or two.

"Miss?"

With a start, she realized that she remained standing in front of the train exit and was being buffeted by the other passengers trying to leave the train.

"Are they all coming here?" she asked as a passenger's oversized carrier bashed her leg. She'd have a large bruise there by nightfall.

Taking her arm, he adeptly moved her out of the human traffic. "Just for a moment." A trace of a smile lit those sky-blue eyes. "I suspect they're anxious to feel solid land under their feet."

"I know how they feel." Even though she was standing on a very flat, very stationary platform, her body still vibrated from the long ride. "This is the first real stop we've made today. The fresh air is wonderful. It gets a bit close inside the car after a while. I do believe I'd have gotten off even if this weren't my destination."

"You're visiting here?" Again, an inquiry that wasn't one.

"No." She pulled herself up to her full height. It wasn't much, just a bit over five feet. "I'm here on business."

A shadow of a frown wrinkled his brow. "Business? Here in Jubilee?"

His thoughts couldn't have been more obvious if his forehead were transparent. She could see him trying to figure out what kind of business would bring her to a town like Jubilee. Etiquette struggled with curiosity, and etiquette won. He did not ask. She did not tell.

"Do you have lodging?" he inquired. "The best hotel in this area is the Territorial."

It's also the only hotel, she thought but didn't say. She had reservations at the Territorial, choosing what she hoped was some degree of privacy that she might not get in a boardinghouse.

"Would you like some help with your bags?" he asked.

Her reporter's eye had already taken in not just the obvious physical attributes of the man but the subtleties, as well. He didn't seem to be dangerous or aggressive. Her instincts weren't perfect, but they were generally good. Yet a certain wariness was, of course, in order.

"I can hire a wagon. I'll need to do that anyway." She glanced around. "If you can tell me where I might find one?"

"Clanahan's down the street is really the only place where you might find something like that. He has a few that he picked up from folks abandoning their claims and going back east again."

She visually measured the distance against the weight of her bags, then surveyed her surroundings as she realized she couldn't possibly carry her belongings that far. The area looked safe enough, although one could never be sure.

He must have seen her indecision, because he said with a touch of amusement in his voice, "You do know that the Territorial is across the road, don't you?" He pointed to a brick building behind the station.

How could she have missed it? It was the tallest structure in town.

She easily found her two bags. They were the only pieces of real luggage left in the pile of cartons and wrapped bundles on the platform. He reached for both of them, but she was faster and grasped the smaller of the bags herself. "I can carry this myself."

He didn't answer, but she was sure she saw a flicker of admiration on his face.

The hotel was far beyond what she had imagined she'd find in Jubilee. Three stories tall, constructed of brick so new that it was still hard-edged and clean, it was a sentinel on the prairie.

"This is it," he said unnecessarily as they paused beneath the large sign: TERRITORIAL HOTEL. ROOMS.

She dropped her bag and secretly flexed her fingers. The handle had pressed into her palm so completely that her fingers were numb. Had the hotel been much farther, she might have had to swallow her pride and let him help her carry the bag.

"Thanks for your help." She stretched her hand—the one that still had feeling in it—toward him.

"You're welcome."

He turned and began to walk away. But he returned. "You might need some more help with these bags." He easily hefted them up and carried them into the lobby toward the desk, where he deposited them. "Matthew can take care of them from here," he said, motioning to the young man behind the desk. "By the way," he added, "I'm Eric Johansen."

"Rose Kelly. It's been nice to meet you, and thanks again for your help with my bags." She smiled at him as a terribly rogue thought drifted into her head: *Too bad you're only staying here six months, Rose Kelly. He's got awfully nice eyes.*

Eric watched her through the window as she dealt with the Territorial's desk clerk. Matthew would take good care of her. He was a fair and decent man—Eric had seen that side of him often in church.

He had known from the moment she stepped off the train—and into his arms—that she was traveling alone. Her gaze hadn't swept the crowd at the station; instead, she'd raised her eyes to the buildings and beyond. That single movement had been quite telling.

From the corner of his eye, he saw Mrs. Jenkins and Mrs. Simmons, their heads together and their eyes staring directly at him. They hid their mouths behind their hands, but he knew what they were doing—undoubtedly talking about him and pairing him up with the guest.

He realized he probably shouldn't have carried her bags into the hotel, but what choice did he have? He couldn't leave her standing on the street.

With a quick sweep of his hat, he acknowledged the two women. Perhaps a direct response was best to forestall the rumors that were certainly already making their way through town.

They could talk all they wanted to. He had no time for a woman in his life, not now and, really, not ever.

He turned back to the station across the street, aware of the fact that he'd totally forgotten to pick up the plow part that had come on the train.

No, he had no time for women. Not even for someone with eyes that sparkled with green and golden flecks and with hair that caught the summer sunlight like new copper.

He shook his head. Next thing he knew, he'd be abandoning farming for poetry.

It was time to bring his head back to earth. Fast.

Rose surveyed her room. It was more than she'd expected. Actually, it was quite lovely in a basic sort of way. Although it admittedly couldn't hold a candle to the suites of her favorite Chicago hotel, the extremely elegant Palmer House, it certainly outshone the grimy rooms she'd seen in New York and Boston. The absolute newness of it was quite charming.

She sank to the bed and took stock of her situation. It was amazing that she was even here.

She'd never had even the vaguest intention of coming out to the Dakota Territory to begin with. If only she hadn't overheard her editor, George Marshall, at the *Chicago Tattler* telling one of his male reporters that no woman could do what he had in mind.

Those had been fighting words, and she'd barreled right in, arguing with Mr. Marshall, the whole time having no idea what she was shouting about.

Her daddy had always said that Rose was born with the Kelly temperament—yell first, ask questions later—and while her mother sighed helplessly into her apron and turned back to an endless array of diapers and socks when Rose announced her plans, she'd caught a glimpse of a smile on her father's face. He was proud of her.

It was her natural inquisitiveness, he'd told his friends, that made her a crackerjack reporter, and he had puffed out his barrel chest proudly when he told them of her accomplishment. His daughter, he proclaimed, was heading off to the land of wonder and adventure—the Dakota Territory.

Her mother hadn't been so convinced. Although Katie Kelly was not one to speak up, especially against her husband, her face spoke volumes. One eyebrow could shoot, quite independently of the other, to her hairline to indicate displeasure. Her eyes, once a warm kitten gray, were now faded and dim beneath lines etched deeply over the bridge of her nose.

But Rose saw something in her mother's eyes that escaped the gaze of her rambunctious brothers—the way the eyebrows settled and the gray softened when a baby was placed in her arms. Rose had seen the work-worn hands smooth a delicate blanket, noted the pain as a callused finger caught a fragile thread. And the sadness with which the baby was returned to the mother.

Katie Kelly had wanted babies, grandbabies, but Rose had wanted more.

She wanted to live in a whirlwind of excitement, always moving, always on the go, always finding out about things.

When Mr. Marshall had almost laughingly offered Rose the job of covering the fashion gossip scene, she'd seized it eagerly. Almost every week she attended a party, and eventually the elite of the city took her presence at their functions as a societal coup.

Everybody wanted Rose Kelly at their gatherings.

She had done well, had earned the right to be a reporter, and she knew she was a pioneer in her field. She got letters every week from girls who wanted to be her when they grew up.

Now she wanted to do more.

The heated discussion she'd had with a bemused Mr. Marshall resulted in just that. She'd had to plead her case, even when she found out that at stake was a series of articles about homesteading in the Dakotas.

Truth be told, she hadn't wanted it, but when it sounded like Mr. Marshall was going to give the assignment to Jerrold Pugh, a whiner if she'd ever heard one—and a self-important whiner, to boot—she'd had to leap right in and wrench the assignment away from him.

And now she was here, ready to get to work. A shiver of excitement shot down her spine as she considered how to proceed.

Could it be that God had given her the subject of her articles? Might it be Eric Johansen? It was a splendid idea.

She stood up and went to the lace-trimmed window. Her room faced away from the center of Jubilee, and from her window, she saw an amazing green vista.

The summertime prairie looked like it had awakened from a long nap, stretched out its deep brown lengths, and sprouted.

She chewed her lip as she thought about Eric.

Rose wasn't ignorant of men. Not at all. Working at the *Chicago Tattler*, she was surrounded by men. Admittedly, most of them were cigar-smoking, middle-aged men whose primary concerns were how Chicago's baseball team, the White Stockings, were doing and whether the beer would be cold at Albert's, the neighborhood tavern.

None of them seemed to consider her as anything other than one of the fellows. The thought gave her pause, but she shook it off. It was better that than they notice her female attributes. At least this way she was considered an equal.

In most things. Now, this assignment. . .

Eric didn't seem to view her the way the fellows she worked with did. There was something different, something she couldn't quite put her finger on.

Unexpectedly she yawned. She was really quite tired.

During the entire trip, she hadn't been able to sleep deeply. All she could do was close her eyes and drift off a bit. Everything she saw from the train window was new and fascinating, and missing even a bit of it was out of the question. The journey was entirely too exciting.

Not that she intended to stay here. Once she was done being a paid tourist, she could go back to her rather comfortable home in Chicago and the excitement of a city that lived twenty-four hours a day. Meanwhile, she'd enjoy the peaceful calm of the prairie, where nothing moved except the grass in the wind.

She dropped onto the pristine pale blue coverlet and closed her eyes, just to think about her travels and her future and a man who seemed to be Dakota himself. . . .

Chapter 2

My first impression of the Dakota Territory was that it is entirely blue and green.
As I got off the train, I saw nothing but endless land that touched an equally endless sky.
The world here is hemmed in only by our limited imaginations.

Which came first—the growling in her stomach or the aroma of something wonderful wending its tempting way under her door—didn't matter. Rose woke up with a roaring hunger gnawing at her stomach.

What a dream she'd had! A train ride that seemed never to end, a land that sprawled under a sunlit sky, eyes that caught that blue sky...

She rubbed her eyes and took in her surroundings. The plain but clean hotel room. Her bags, still unpacked at the door. The absence of street sounds from her slightly opened window. Sudden realization washed over her.

It wasn't a dream. No, not at all.

Jubilee!

Rose sprang out of bed and pressed her nose to the win-dow. Yes, the glorious sunshine still poured across the prairie, and she fairly itched to get out there and take a look.

But first she had to attend to the scraping emptiness of her stomach. Some things didn't change, she thought as she checked her dress and made sure it wasn't too wrinkled to wear downstairs for dinner. One common trait of all the Kellys was what her father called "a healthy respect for the dinner plate."

Food first, exploration later.

She splashed water on her face and repinned her hair into its usual strict bun, which had gotten a bit scraggly during her nap. The only advantage of having the straightest hair in Chicago had been that keeping it styled was fairly easy. Her hair was never tempted to curl, so she'd made the knot of copper at the nape of her neck into her trademark hairstyle. Even for parties, she wore the same style and added a velvet bow as decoration.

She hadn't packed many velvet ribbons for her visit to Jubilee.

With a resolute poke of the final pin into her hair, she stood up straight, put her hands on her hips, and stared at her reflection in the gilt-edged mirror.

Her father's words came back to her. They'd been standing at the station, waiting for the train that would take her away for six months, when he pulled her close and boomed, "Well, Rose Kelly, you've done it now. You've put yourself in the midst of it, right into the wildest of the wild. The Dakota Territory. You won't be finding the parties and elegant dresses you're used to, not there." Then he grinned. "And I think, my darlin', that you're going to be the better for it. I'm proud of you."

Her mother had simply hugged her, tears pooling in her pale gray eyes. "God be with you." Six months. She could do it. She would do it.

The enticing fragrance of baked ham drew her to the dining room of the Territorial. It was small, with the tables placed close together. The tables were topped with clean, starched white cloths that looked like thick cotton, and the sole decoration on each was a simple glass set of salt and pepper shakers.

Just last week she'd had lunch with a social belle at one of Chicago's newest restaurants, a tiny place along the lakeshore with an unpronounceable French name, where she'd dined on pheasant sautéed in some lovely sauce.

The baked ham here, though, smelled just as delicious.

A table by the window was empty, and as she made her way toward it, conversation in the room ceased, and in unison all heads swiveled toward her. A more reticent person might have ignored the obvious reaction she was causing, but Rose Kelly had never been reticent.

She smiled at all of them. "Hello, everyone," she caroled. "Is the food good? It smells wonderful!"

The other diners relaxed and smiled in response and once again began to talk at their tables. She proceeded to her seat, satisfied. This, she'd always believed, was the way to live. Being straightforward almost always worked best.

Bits and pieces of their discussions floated toward her.

"Arrived today. . ."

"Chicago. . ."

"Eric Johansen. . ."

She tried not to be too obvious as she shamelessly eavesdropped. Her eyes lit with a puckish glow as she realized that her fellow diners were, indeed, already linking her with Eric. It was too charming.

Matchmaking, were they?

Interesting. . .

One last swing of the hammer, and the floorboard would be fixed. If only those Nielsen children would quit their constant wiggling during the service, the wooden slats might hold up better. They were the squirmiest young ones he'd ever seen.

But children would be children, he reminded himself, and no matter how rambunctious they might be, they were a blessing from the Lord. The Nielsens came to church every single week to hear the Word and offer praise, Michael and Grethe leading their seven children in a stair-stepped line. He could only imagine what it must be like to get seven children dressed for church.

He dropped his head and offered a quick prayer for the family: *Dearest Father, please bless the Nielsen family for their constant faithfulness to You.* He peeped at the mended board and added, *And help me not to be so judgmental about fidgety children. Amen.*

Voices from the kitchen at the back of the church broke his reverie. He knew that a group of women were there, scurrying around in preparation for Sunday's after-church dinner.

He sniffed the air appreciatively as a tantalizing aroma drifted his way. If his senses weren't deceiving him, the women were making *lefse*, the delicious Norwegian treat. Maybe they'd have some to spare—for a man who was giving up his Saturday evening to mend a floorboard. He stood, unfolding slowly as his muscles, cramped from bending over so long, relaxed.

"Hello!" he called as he limped back to the kitchen, the feeling in his legs slowly returning. He was getting too old to be sitting on the wooden floor of the church, bent like a broken spring. "Do I smell lefse?"

Mrs. Jenkins poked her head out of the doorway, her snowy hair a bit disarranged and a smudge of flour across her cheek. "Eric Johansen, you're just in time. We're trying out a new *takke* that Grethe just got from her family back in Bergen, and we've finished the first batch. We need your opinion."

He had to smile. Just two years ago, nothing she said would have made any sense, but now that he was totally immersed in this heavily Norwegian community, it was absolutely clear.

"What's a takke?" a woman asked behind him. "And where's Bergen?"

"Miss Kelly," he said, recognizing her voice immediately. The impish smile on Mrs. Jenkins's face told him that the gossip mill had already started turning, and he groaned silently. This was the last thing he needed now, just when the land was taking up almost every moment of his waking hours—except those used mending cracked floorboards in the church: a woman in his life.

He turned and pasted on what he hoped was a pleasant yet noncommittal smile, but the woman before him nearly took his breath away.

Early evening sunlight, thick and rich as it came through the single stained-glass window in the church, poured across Rose's shoulders and head, casting ruby and emerald and sapphire shadows on her russet hair. She looked as if she had stepped right out of heaven.

Whoa, Johansen. Bring it under control. He dug one fingertip into his thumb to remind him that this was no dream, and she was no vision, and as a matter of fact, they were standing outside the kitchen of Redeemer Church in Jubilee with an overly interested audience. "It's very nice to see you again. I trust you're finding your lodging to your liking."

"The Territorial is an ideal hotel for my purposes," Rose answered, and she tilted her head slightly, questioningly, for a moment. Finally he realized that she was waiting for him to step aside so she could go into the kitchen. When he did, she touched his arm lightly with a tiny hand.

He didn't dare move. That hand on his arm was unexpected, and he had no idea what to do. Leave it there? Brush it off? Step back?

It's not a spider, Johansen, he scolded himself. *What's the matter with you? She's just a woman.* Just a woman. Well, that was the problem right there.

"Thank you for your help. I truly do appreciate it," she said, apparently unaware of the effect she was having on him, and she dropped her hand.

Before he could answer, she swept past him toward Mrs. Jenkins. "Hello," she greeted the older woman, who grinned back at her with delight. "My name is Rose Kelly, and I'm visiting from Chicago. . . ."

Almost as if an invisible force pulled him, he trailed after her.

"Series of articles. . .homesteading. . .newspaper."

He didn't catch all of the sentences, but he heard enough to piece together what her purpose was in Jubilee. So she was a newspaper reporter. That made sense—he guessed.

She certainly didn't seem the kind to be happy on the frontier, though, carving out a life in a prairie-dust town like Jubilee. There was something about her that bespoke money and class and comfort.

Maybe it was that ridiculous little bag she carried. He had no idea what it contained, but it was too tiny to hold anything of value, like the tine from a harrow or a bag of oats or even a cheese sandwich.

Maybe it held her money, but he hoped not. Certainly she would have taken care of that aspect with Matthew at the hotel and put her funds securely in the Territorial's safe.

"I'll be here for six months," Rose was saying.

Six months? He found himself counting—and then shaking his head. She was planning to leave when winter had settled in? Whose idea was that?

"So tell me what a takke is." Rose looked around the kitchen, and he was sure that even the tiniest detail didn't escape her examination. "I've never heard of one before. Where's Bergen, by the way?"

Mrs. Jenkins looped her arm through Rose's and walked her across the tiny kitchen. "Bergen is a town in Norway. That's where Grethe Nielsen is from. A takke is a pan we use to make lefse, and she's letting us use hers. She'd be here now except she has seven children, so she has her hands full as it is. But she's the champion lefse maker of Jubilee."

"Lefse. That's a new one for me. How do you spell it?" To Eric's amazement, she opened the rose-embellished miniature bag and pulled out not only a pen but a notebook as well. "And what is it?"

Mrs. Jenkins's words were a background of sound as he leaned against the doorway to the warm kitchen and watched Rose learn her first lesson in Dakota living. "Lefse is a Norwegian pastry," the older woman began. "It's made of potatoes and flour and butter and cream and—"

"Potatoes?" Rose interrupted. "Potatoes? You make a pastry out of potatoes?"

She leaned over and studied the pile of potatoes at the end of the metal table as if they held the secret to eternal youth. With the blunt end of her pen, she gave one an experimental poke and made a note on her pad.

Eric suppressed a grin. *City girl,* he thought.

"Oh yes, and potatoes make a lovely thick mix." Mrs. Jenkins loosened her grip on Rose long enough to point to a pile of dough. "There's some already made up. We take a bit of the dough like this and shape it into a ball. Then we roll it out evenly, as thin as possible, and carefully pick it up and put it on the takke. That's the hot grill there. Yes, we use that stick to pick up the dough and to turn it on the grill so it doesn't tear. See how it slides under the dough and lifts it just so. . .And when it's done, we call in Eric to test it."

Rose turned toward Eric and smiled widely.

He stepped into the room and reached for the lefse that was still suspended on the stick. "Yum," he said as he tore off a piece of it. "Lefse is good anytime, but when it's still warm, then it's the best. Try it."

He offered her the rest of the flat bread and watched as she popped it into her mouth. Would she like it?

"We sometimes put butter and sugar on it," Mrs. Jenkins said.

"I don't know why," Rose said, finishing it. "It's so good. Interesting, though. It doesn't taste at all like potatoes."

Mrs. Jenkins smiled. "No, it doesn't."

"May I ask another question? Why are you making so much of it?" Rose pointed to the piles of already-prepared lefse on the counter.

Mrs. Jenkins expertly lifted and turned another piece on the grill. "We're having a dinner here tomorrow. You're welcome to come."

"May I? It sounds like fun!" One of the last rays of sunlight slanted through the door, illuminating Rose's smile even more.

Mrs. Jenkins beamed. "You'll enjoy it. You'll find plenty of good food. Most of the folks in Jubilee have Norwegian roots, and that's why we make so much lefse. We don't do much *lutefisk,* though."

The other women in the small kitchen laughed.

"Lutefisk?"

Eric shook his head in amusement. "They're teasing you. Lutefisk is a Norwegian dish, and while some people say it's wonderful, others refuse to eat it. Or to even be in the same room with it."

"Why?"

The women laughed louder.

"Well," he said, "it's rather. . .fragrant."

"But what is it?" Rose asked, her pen poised over her notepad.

"Mrs. Jenkins? Do you want to explain?"

The older woman said, "It's fish, usually cod, that's been dried and then soaked in lye."

The expression on Rose's face was wonderful. She looked from person to person, studying their faces. "You're joking with me, aren't you? There isn't any such thing as this lutefisk."

"I'm sorry, Miss Kelly," he said. "It's true. But most of us prefer lefse. There aren't any surprise ingredients in it, and it smells much better."

"Lutefisk? Sounds like it'd kill you," she muttered as she put her pen back in her bag.

"You might wish that, if you had to be around it," he said, and Mrs. Jenkins swatted him with a towel.

"Get out of my kitchen," she said, her words laced with laughter. "But first make sure that Miss Kelly knows that she's to come to the dinner tomorrow. I'm afraid she's fearful that there might be lutefisk."

"That'd be something to fear, all right." He turned to Rose. "There won't be any lutefisk tomorrow. You can expect chicken and ham and beef, but no lutefisk. Trust me. That stuff has a powerful stink."

"Eric, be nice." Mrs. Jenkins shook her finger at him. "Make Miss Kelly feel at home here. You're the first person she met in Jubilee, you know, and it should count for something."

Laughter bubbled through the woman's words, gentling the scolding with fond teasing. Rose tilted her head and smiled at him.

He could feel his resistance crumbling, and he knew he should simply say something vague that no one could read anything into, bid them all good-bye, and turn around and walk away. That would be the best idea.

Instead, his mouth opened, all by itself, and began to speak. "The dinner is being held here on the lawn after church tomorrow." He could feel the women's gazes locked on him, and without looking at them, he knew that they were all smiling as they watched the tableau unfold before them. The words continued to pour out of his lips. "If you'd like to join us, we'd sure be glad to have you."

No! No! He didn't want to do this. What was he think-ing? He knew the answer immediately: He hadn't been thinking.

Quickly he tried to recover his dignity—a task that was probably pointless, he thought, seeing the look on Mrs. Jenkins's face. "You may not go to church. I don't know. Especially out here in the Dakota Territory. We don't have the same grand churches you're probably used to in Chicago."

His words sounded ungracious, but Rose tucked her notebook back into that absurd little pouch and said, "Miss church? You must be joking. Patrick and Kathleen Kelly would have my own little head on a plate if I skipped a service. My parents raised me as a Christian, and I'm glad of it."

She looked directly at him, her eyes as green as a mossy rock, and added, "Everything I have, I owe to the Lord. Of course I'll go to church here. He doesn't forget me. Why should I forget Him?"

Chapter 3

Every community has its own spirit, its own identity.
The kind of place we call home tells us more about who we are than about where we are.
Likewise, this visitor finds definition of who she is by determining who she is not.

Rose leaned across the stove and studied Eric. Even this early in the season, his skin was tanned to a dark honey by the sun, and his fingers were work-hardened with cuts and scrapes. His trousers and faded brown work shirt confirmed the image of him as a farmer.

But underneath the earth-stained man of the prairie, she sensed something else. A very solid thread she couldn't identify bespoke of a life beyond the prairie.

He'd be perfect for the assignment.

"Excuse me, Mr. Johansen. Might we talk privately? I'd like to propose something to you."

As soon as the words popped out of her mouth, Rose regretted them. They'd come out all wrong—and with an audience, too. When would she ever learn to think first and speak second? She should have formulated her approach—that would have minimized the chances of his refusal.

This wasn't Chicago, she reminded herself, where she was known—and where her outspoken style was almost legendary. There, it didn't matter how blunt her words were. She was expected to speak her mind.

Here, though, she needed to be more prudent in what she said.

Mrs. Jenkins and the other women in the room exchanged a silent but expressive round of glances. Silent laughter shook their plump chests, and from the discreet elbow nudges and the peeks at Eric and then her, she knew what they meant. They were pairing her off romantically with Eric.

She lowered her eyelids and studied him surreptitiously. *You could do worse,* came the unbidden thought. *As a matter of fact, you'd be hard pressed to do better.*

Wrong! Wrong! She was here to work, not to find a man. Chicago was full of men. If she wanted to go shopping for love, she should do it there. But there was something about this man, something interesting. *Something,* she chided herself, *that makes him a good subject for my articles.*

She realized she was staring at him. His cheeks were flushed, and he seemed to be uncomfortable with the attention.

The women quickly averted their gazes and turned their attention to the smoking griddle.

His clear blue eyes were clouded with a hint of wariness. "I'm probably going to regret this," he said in a low voice, nodding slightly to the women huddled over the takke, "but let's step outside."

He led her out of the small church into the summer evening. "I'd lay my life down for those women," he explained as they walked toward the hotel, "but they've been scrutinizing every woman who's set foot in Jubilee. Apparently they think I can't get my own woman."

"Can you?" Aghast at what she'd just said, Rose clapped her hand over her mouth. "Oh, I am so sorry! I didn't mean . . . Of course you can . . ."

To her amazement, he grinned. "That's all quite encouraging, but the issue is really that I'm not in the market. I have no intentions of bringing any woman into my life."

"Why? What would be so wrong with that? Do you have something against women?"

He didn't answer but continued to walk.

Rose scurried to catch up with his long-legged stride. "Or is it marriage?" she persisted. "Do you have a grudge against marriage?"

He shook his head no. "Farming is my spouse."

"That's good!" Rose reached into her small pouch and took out the tiny pen and notebook. "Can I quote you?"

"Quote me?" His face sagged into a scowl. "Is that what this is all about? Can't someone just have a conversation with you without you taking notes? Is everything anybody says going to appear in that Chicago rag you call a newspaper?"

Rose had had this conversation many times before in the course of her journalistic career. Lately, of course, in the society pages, people had been anxious to see their names in print, so possibly she was a bit rusty on her technique. She was almost a household name in Chicago. Here, she was as anonymous as the next stranger to step off the train. She needed to be vigilant.

If she was going to get people to open up to her, to learn what really drove these homesteaders—this homesteader, in particular—she'd better not be as aggressive as she was in Chicago.

One thing she had learned during her time at the *Tattler* was knowing what approach to take. Eric Johansen would need some coddling, but he seemed too smart to be flattered.

"Let's sit down here," she said, touching his elbow as she moved toward a small bench in front of the post office. "Let me start where I should—at the beginning."

He settled uneasily on the wood-slatted bench. "Start."

"I believe you know I'm a reporter with the *Chicago Tattler*. I'm here for six months doing a series of reports about homesteading." She paused and flashed him her brightest smile.

He didn't seem to be swayed, but on the other hand, he didn't get up and leave. "So what does this have to do with me?"

"I'd like to focus on one homesteader so my readers will understand this whole Dakota Territory mystique better." Rose touched the little notepad and stared directly into his eyes. "I'd like the story I write on these pages to be yours, and—"

"No!" He sprang up, his face tight. "No! Absolutely not!"

"Why not?" She stood up, a mollifying hand on his wrist.

"Simply put, I don't want to."

She hadn't faced this kind of opposition since a short stint covering the women's crime scene. Quickly her mind sought another approach. Maybe he had an ego she could appeal to. "Mr. Johansen," she purred, "you'll be the featured subject. People from across the country will read about you. You'll be famous."

"Famous." He fairly spat out the word. "I'm a farmer. I dig in the dirt for a living. Who'd want to read about me?"

She moved in for the proverbial kill. "Our subscribers. The businessmen who buy a paper from a newsboy or a newsstand. Those who pick up a discarded *Tattler* from a sidewalk or a gutter and read it. Most of them will never make it past the Mississippi, but they wonder and dream about coming out here. They want to know what your life is like. They want to live vicariously through you."

He didn't respond, and she held her breath.

So much was riding on his response. He *had* to say yes. He just had to.

Birds chirped in the early summer evening, filling the huge silence with their twitters.

The fact that he hadn't told her to leave was a promising sign, and Rose clutched at the thought.

Just as he was about to speak, a voice interrupted him. "Eric Johansen! There you are! I've been looking for you to thank you for fixing that floorboard."

A tall thin man with a shock of amazingly blond hair had come up behind them. "No thanks are necessary. By the way, Rose, this is our minister, Reverend Wilton. And, Reverend, this is Rose Kelly. She's visiting Jubilee."

The minister smiled at her. "Ah, you must be the reporter I've been hearing so much about. All of Jubilee is quite abuzz with your presence. I understand you're from Chicago?"

"Yes, I am," she said, offering her hand to the stranger. "I'm planning to be here for six months, sending a series of articles about homesteading back to my newspaper, the *Tattler*."

"What a splendid idea! Did you hear that, Eric?"

"Oh, I heard," Eric answered dryly.

Rarely does opportunity present itself on a silver platter, Rose thought, *but when it does, who am I to pass up such a gift?* She saw her chance and took it. "I'm hoping Mr. Johansen will agree to be the homesteader I feature in the series. I think he'd be perfect."

The minister rubbed his hands together. "Absolutely! Eric, don't pass it up. All of us at Redeemer will be glad to help both of you on this project. I can assure you of our support."

Eric shook his head, and Rose's heart sank.

"It would be a splendid opportunity to help Jubilee grow into a real humdinger of a town," Reverend Wilton continued. "I suspect quite a few people in Chicago read Miss Kelly's newspaper, and just imagine how many of them her articles might inspire to head out here and join us."

Eric's mouth stayed drawn in a tight, flat line.

"They could shake away the close confines of the city and come out here to experience God's love under this great blue sky." The minister's hand arced in a grand gesture over his head. "Give it some thought, Eric. I'd do it, except I'm not homesteading."

Eric sighed, and his next words gave her hope. "Reverend, I'm—"

Before he could finish his sentence, Mrs. Jenkins and the others from the church kitchen had joined them and were all chiming in with their enthusiasm for the project.

Eric didn't have a chance.

"All right, I'll do it. But with limits."

The crowd cheered, and Rose barely restrained herself from joining them.

This was going to be a glorious six months.

Thank You, she breathed. *Thank You.*

Eric glared at the trees on the horizon as his horse plodded down the road. He scowled at the rabbit that ran across the road in front of him. He glowered at the hawk that swooped overhead.

What was wrong with him? Why couldn't he have just said no and been done with it? It wasn't like he had even considered being the subject of her articles. It wasn't possible. There were a million and one reasons why it wouldn't work, and every bit of him screamed out a warning: *Don't do it.*

There was only one reason why he should do it. But it was a terrible reason.

It had been a long time since his arms had held a woman. He didn't allow himself so much as to dream of love. But Rose—she'd been warm and solid and real. Suddenly his dreams seemed silly.

Too much was at risk to get involved with her scheme. He couldn't take the chance—and he certainly couldn't put his heart on the line.

But he'd made a promise, and there was no way he was going to back out on it. He'd committed himself to doing this, and he had to stay the course. He'd have to be settled with that decision.

He lifted his eyes to the cloudless sky and prayed. His petition had no words, just a sincere heartfelt appeal, and he knew God heard it.

The dirt road curved, telling him he was almost home. There was something wonderfully peaceful about that word. *Home.*

He knew every inch of it by heart, every board and nail. It was *his* house. The closest any woman had gotten to entering it was when one or two of the women from Redeemer had brought towel-wrapped dinners when he'd first begun building it, and even then, they'd only set a foot in the door.

He'd built the house himself, placing every board in the structure, every nail, every brick. It was made the way that suited him. Bookshelves lined two walls of the living room, and they were organized not by author or subject or even color, but by the date he'd read them.

There was one picture on the wall, a painting of the battle of Jericho. It had hung in his bedroom when he was a teenager, a gift from his parents right before they lost their lives from influenza, and it had hung everywhere he had lived since then.

Now, as he pulled into the yard, attended to his horse, and went inside, he saw his home in a different light.

For the first time, he noticed the dust on the table by the window. The sweat-stained kerchief tossed carelessly by the front door. His morning coffee cup still by his chair. His house was not woman-ready. She'd probably bustle in and start sweeping and dusting and cooking, and the next thing he knew, he'd have pink ruffled curtains in his kitchen.

He shuddered at the thought.

On the other hand, maybe it would be all right.

He and Rose had set boundaries for the next six months. They were simple. First, she could not shadow his every move. There was no way he could possibly get his work done if she were hanging around his neck like a clinging vine. Second, she had to respect his privacy. She was not to pry into his personal things, and snooping was definitely not allowed. Third, there would be no assumption of friendship. He was helping her out with her article, and that was the extent of it.

Eric groaned. It seemed so easy in theory, and so impossible in fact.

What *had* he done?

Rose woke early the next morning and quickly dressed for church.

"There's a dinner after the service," Matthew said at the desk of the hotel. "I'm planning to get over there for at least a while."

She grinned at him. "I understand they're serving *lefse*."

He nodded. "Miss Kelly, they always serve *lefse*."

She laughed. "I imagine they do."

It seemed as if everyone in Jubilee went to Redeemer, Rose thought as she walked toward the church, joining the steady stream of people who were headed in the same direction.

Mrs. Jenkins waved at her when she entered the church and motioned her over to sit beside her. Across the room, she caught sight of the back of Eric's head, his blond hair neatly combed. Reverend Wilton was a splendid minister, and his sermon about the joys of friendship was pleasant and inspiring and buoyed her already-elated spirits even higher.

After the service, she joined the throngs of worshipers who headed for the grassy area behind the church. "We're going to eat outside," Mrs. Jenkins explained, "since it gets a bit close inside during the summer with all the folks there and the cooking going on."

She led Rose to a table where others were already seated. "Everyone, this is Rose Kelly. I'm putting her in your hands because I'm on duty at the bread table."

Her tablemates began to introduce themselves. Freya and Lars Trease, both in their midthirties, ran the store in town. Lars was as thin as Freya was thick. Linnea Gardiner was the young teacher at Jubilee's school, and Rose recalled seeing her in the *lefse*-making group at the church. Linnea's lovely blond hair curled around her face in charming tendrils. Rose sighed silently. *Linnea had the hair she'd always coveted.*

She pulled herself up short on that thought. *No, not coveted—admired. Linnea had the hair Rose had always admired.*

Thomas Pinkley was Jubilee's doctor. Arvid Frederickson farmed north of Jubilee and usually had his wife and three children with him, but they were home with summer colds.

"I hear you're doing a story about us," Lars said. At first Rose thought he was frowning at her, but she realized that the lines over his nose were permanently etched there.

"A series of stories," Rose corrected him. "They'll certainly touch on all of you, but the main focus will be on a single homesteader."

Dr. Pinkley nodded. His silver hair and well-cut black suit made him look quite elegant. "I hear tell you'll be writing about Eric Johansen."

"That's our current plan." Rose's experience had taught her to limit what she told others when she was working on an interview but to always be ready with one question. "What can you tell me about him?"

"He's a good fellow," Lars said. "We're glad to have him in Jubilee."

"Jubilee got its start with the railroad," Linnea noted, "although it's probably a toss-up as to whether the credit for its growth should go to the railroad or the land office. People have been coming out here regularly to homestead, but there's no property left around Jubilee. It went quickly. You can't find better land than right here in the Red River Valley."

"The ground is rich and dark." Arvid dug in the grass with his toe and uncovered a patch of soil. "Look at that, Miss Kelly. You can't tell me you have earth that rich in Chicago."

The conversation was not going at all in the direction she intended, and Rose tried to steer it back.

"That's true," Rose agreed, "but I'm wondering why people would come to a place like Jubilee."

"I'm nearing retirement," the doctor said. "I wanted to finish up my medical career where I could retire and dig in the ground, plant some radishes and corn."

Freya Trease spoke next. "Lars and I came here from New York City. We had a store there, but the neighborhood started to go bad, and there was a fire, and. . ." Her eyes filled with tears, and her husband patted her hand awkwardly. She sniffed and finished, "Anyway, here we are and glad to be here."

"Me, I'm just a farmer with dirt in my bones," Arvid said. "The missus and I figured it'd be easier to coax a crop out of this river land than anywhere else, so we let Uncle Sam give us a parcel out here. All we've got to do is prove up, and with soil this rich, that shouldn't be a problem."

"What about you, Linnea?" Rose asked.

"I was in teachers' college in Rhode Island, and I'd just graduated when my parents decided to come out here, so I tagged along with them."

"These stories are so interesting," Rose said. "I think that's one of the things that drew me to newspaper writing—learning about people's lives. So you came for a variety of reasons, I see. How about Eric? Do any of you know why he came out here?"

"You could ask him," Arvid said practically, "but he might not tell you."

Rose sat up straight, all her reporter's instincts alert. "Why not?"

"Not polite."

She was baffled. Why wouldn't it be polite?

Dr. Pinkley leaned over and said in a low voice, "This is a land of new beginnings for all of us. As you've heard, each of us has our reason for coming out here."

"Aren't you curious, though?" she pressed.

He shrugged. "Not really. We all wanted a better life. Some folks were stuck in jobs that had no future. Others felt hemmed in, stuck in the middle of a city. I know at least one family came because of the grasshopper plagues in Minnesota. You've heard of those, haven't you?"

She made a face. "Yes, I have." Even in Chicago, the invasion of the hungry creatures that ate everything in their path was legendary.

"And," the doctor continued, "I suspect some left situations that couldn't be tolerated any longer. If someone wants to tell us, we'll listen, but Jubilee is all about the future. We don't revisit the past out here."

Rose couldn't have heard anything that made her more anxious to learn more. Telling her she couldn't know something just increased her curiosity.

As if on cue, Freya spotted Eric and motioned him over. "Come join us," she said when he neared the table, a heavily laden plate in his hand.

His blue eyes twinkled when he surveyed their table. "No plates? What is this, a table of sluggards? You'd better move. I've left some lefse for you, but it's going fast."

As they all stood up to go to the serving tables, Rose noticed that they had neatly maneuvered their chairs so that the only open spot was beside her.

His words came back to her, something about how the women of the church were trying to get him paired off. She couldn't resist a secret smile.

This was going to be a very interesting six months.

✳

"Wait, Mr. Johansen!" Eric turned in surprise. Nobody called him Mr. Johansen except for some of the children in town. He'd have to get her squared away on that, really fast.

He was leaving the church, his arms full of bundles of leftover food. He dropped them in his wagon and waited for Rose to catch up with him.

"I'm so glad I caught you," she panted. "I wanted to get a quick history from you before you left."

He tried not to react. "Why do you need to do that?" he asked, leaning over to pick an imaginary bit of dirt off the wheel of his wagon.

"It's common newspaper procedure," she said, a small frown marring her flawless forehead. "I was thinking I'd start with what drew you out here in the first place."

"I came here to homestead," he said. "Now I really have to be going."

He started to get in the wagon, but she stepped in front of him.

"Mr. Johansen—"

"Call me Eric. Whenever people call me Mr. Johansen, I look around for my father, and he's been with the Lord for twelve years now."

She smiled. "I see. That would startle me, too. But if you could tell me a few things about yourself, I'd certainly appreciate it."

"Miss Kelly—"

"Rose. Call me Rose. Can't you please answer a few questions? Why did you decide to leave wherever it was you lived before? What influenced you? Was it the advertisements for free land? Had you heard stories from people who'd already homesteaded?"

He knew how a trapped mouse felt—cornered, caged, and with no hope of escape. "Those are a lot of questions. You don't expect me to answer all of them, do you?" He summoned a smile—a fake one, but a smile nevertheless.

"Oh, you don't have to answer all of them. Just a few. Just one?"

"My past is not part of this," he said a bit sharply.

She tapped her foot. He couldn't help but notice it was a very small foot shod in an outrageously inappropriate style for prairie living. That pale purple leather wouldn't last a day in his farmyard.

"Just tell me a little bit. I don't like begging, but I'm going to have to do that. Please? Something?"

"No," he said. "Just no. Plain and simple no."

"Why not?"

His exasperation was edging to the point where he was going to say something awful. *God, help me out here, please. Give me the words I need.*

"I'll tell you how I chose Jubilee, but that's all."

Rose nodded. "I'll take it. Tell me the story."

"Well, there isn't really much to say. I chose it because of its name."

"You decided to come here just because this town is called Jubilee?" She looked at him disbelievingly and then took her little notepad and pen out of her purse and scribbled furiously.

He couldn't resist asking, "You know what that means, don't you?"

Rose snapped the pad shut. "Why, yes, I do, as a matter of fact. And that, my friend, makes you that much more interesting."

He watched as she marched back into the church. He'd probably done entirely the wrong thing by telling her, but maybe it was vague enough that she could use it in her story and leave his past alone.

It was true, though. A place named after the joyful forgiveness of sins and debt had to be the place for him.

How long this information would hold her was another issue. Once she started putting two and two together, this woman would come up with seven.

Chapter 4

A good day's work is a noble thing. Not every day, however, is a good day to work.
The soul needs nurturing the same as the body. We must feed our souls as well as our bodies.

Rose quickly found one distinction between Chicago and Jubilee. In the big city, Sunday was simply another day of the week. Life roared on as it did on the other six days. For the most part, shops were open for business, and while Rose might have had to go a bit farther to find a store that was open on Sunday, it was possible.

In Jubilee, however, things were quite different. Apparently the residents took the matter of keeping the Sabbath quite seriously. Rose stared at the Closed sign on Clanahan's Wagon and Livery.

"The only thing you'll find open on Sunday is the church," Matthew explained when she'd walked back to the Territorial Hotel.

"Everything else is closed?"

"Everything." The young man nodded so vigorously that his glasses slid down his nose and he had to push them back into place.

"What do I do if I have to have a wagon today?" she persisted.

"You wait unless you can borrow one from someone."

Rose leaned across the counter. "Do *you* have a wagon?"

Matthew laughed. "You go right to the point, don't you, Miss Kelly? I'm sorry, but I don't have a wagon or even a horse. I live here in town, and I walk wherever I need to go."

"Do you know anyone who can lend me one?"

"At the risk of being impertinent," Matthew said, "is this an emergency? Can't this wait until tomorrow?"

Waiting until tomorrow was a concept to which Rose had never subscribed. Too many ideas slid into nothingness when they were forced to linger.

"I'd like to take a ride through the countryside and watch some farming in action. Remember, I'm a city girl. I know nothing about this." She smiled in what she hoped was a winning fashion.

Matthew shook his head. "You'd have to travel quite a ways. You won't find anyone in the fields today, not here in Jubilee, that is. This is a day of rest."

She nodded. "I see." She turned away from the desk and walked over the rose-patterned carpet to her room, where she sank onto her bed.

So Jubilee was closed on Sundays, was it? She liked that, even if it was inconvenient at the moment.

"'Remember the Sabbath day, to keep it holy,'" she said aloud.

It was one of the Ten Commandments. She stood and crossed to the window. The midafternoon sun lit empty streets and shuttered stores. As far as she could see across the gloriously flat land, nothing moved—except a distant cluster of shapes. She squinted at the rebels. They were oddly shaped and seemed to be dressed in black and white.

What was this odd development in Jubilee? She stretched as far as she could and narrowed her eyes even more, until at last it all made sense.

Cows. They were cows.

She shook her head at her own silliness. She had a long, long way to go before she'd be at home here—if, in fact, that ever happened. Rose Kelly was part of the city, just as much as Eric Johansen was part of the prairie.

What was she to do with the remaining hours of her day? She reached for the leather-bound volume on top of the bureau. Maybe it was time to take another look at those commandments.

❋

Monday morning broke bright and clear. Eric groaned as the first slivers of light stabbed his eyes. He hadn't slept well at all, and when he had finally fallen asleep, his dreams had been restless.

After his morning devotions—he liked to start his day with something from Proverbs—he wandered into his kitchen and remembered the lefse he'd gotten the day before.

He rolled up a piece of lefse and stuffed it into his mouth. The women had made him a basket of food after the meal yesterday. It was almost as if they didn't believe he could cook for himself. He glanced around his tiny kitchen and grimaced. They were right.

The Sunday dinners were a real boon to him. By the end of the week, though, he often found himself having to eat his own dry bread or his pitiful attempts at stew.

He splashed some water on his face and stomped out to the barn. There was never enough time to get even with farming, he thought as he mucked out the stable. His horse whinnied softly, and he rubbed its soft nose. "Yes, fellow, you're going to have some lovely hay now."

This was his favorite time of day, this time in the barn with his horse watching him with those liquid brown eyes. They'd stand beside each other, him working and the horse observing, until at last he'd turn the gray into the corral and let it graze.

"Your lazy days are about to end, my friend," he said to the horse as he evened out the straw. "Soon enough we'll be in the fields all day long, you and me. The wheat's doing well."

He led the gray out into the sunlight and paused. "Well," he asked the horse, "what do you think of Miss Rose Kelly?"

The horse shook out its mane.

"That's right. I agree. This whole thing can't come to a good end. Why did I let myself get talked into this?" He sighed and headed toward the fence on the other side, which was leaning a bit.

The gray followed him, tossing its head a bit in the sunshine.

"This is the day which the Lord hath made. I suppose it's up to me to rejoice and be glad in it, isn't it?"

The horse didn't answer but bent its elegant neck to nibble some early clover.

"Tch, tch," Rose said encouragingly as she flapped the reins. The only horse Clanahan had available was Big Ole, a gigantic thing with hooves as large as dinner plates.

The wagon was as tiny as the horse was large, and as they rumbled down the road to Eric's house, she had the unwelcome thought that she was at the mercy of the beast. If he wanted to go right, then they were going right. She didn't seem to have much choice in the matter.

Eric's house was going to be easy to find, Mr. Clanahan had assured her. She was supposed to watch for a small brown house in a grove of cottonwoods. He'd also laughingly told her not to worry, that Big Ole would turn in there on his own to get a drink at the stream that ran next to Eric's house.

She looked at her surroundings as Big Ole led her along the road. Was the sky this blue over Chicago? Was it simply obscured by the black clouds that spewed forth from the smokestacks? And did the birds sing this powerfully in the city? All she could remember were the tiny sparrows and the pushy pigeons, not the songbird whose glorious melody washed over the prairie.

Her musings came to a sudden stop as Big Ole slowed his steadily clomping pace and turned in at what had to be Eric's house.

She sat in the wagon, but nobody came out. *He must be in the fields,* she thought, *but where?*

Rose gathered her skirt and carefully climbed out of the wagon. She contemplated Big Ole—should she tie him up? She laughed at the thought. If Big Ole decided to leave, there wasn't a tether in sight that could hold him.

She patted him tentatively on his haunch. "Good boy. Stay there."

"He's not a dog," Eric called from the barn door. He was wiping his hands on a cloth as he came toward her. "I see Clanahan gave you Big Ole." He ran his hand along the horse's neck. "He's a gentle giant, this one is. And reliable."

He unhooked the wagon and began to lead the horse to the pasture. "The stream winds through the pasture. He likes that stream water better than the stuff Clanahan gives him from the tank in town."

Rose had to run to keep up with his long strides. "Do you mind if we visit awhile?"

"I have work to do." His answer was short.

"I understand that. I could help you," she offered, trying to avoid the random tufts of grass that threatened her elegant little French heels.

The look he threw over his shoulder was icy. "Can you milk a cow?"

"No," Rose said brightly. "But I can learn."

He shook his head. "Perhaps another day. I have quite a bit to do, Miss Kelly, and although I've already agreed to be the subject of your articles, I still need to do my work."

"I understand. I'll be just as quiet as a mouse. You won't even know I'm here."

He let go of Big Ole's bridle, and the horse thundered happily into the pasture toward the gray that was already there, kicking up a clod of moist dirt that landed directly on her white blouse. Rose tried not to think of the stain that the soil would leave on the silk.

She knew her smile wouldn't fool him, but she tried anyway. "I've had worse things thrown on me."

His reserve melted for just a moment. "What kinds of things would a society reporter have thrown at her? Chocolates? Cakes? Champagne?"

"Ah, the three C's of fancy dinners. No, surprisingly, there have been times when people weren't glad to see me."

"That is a surprise," he said dryly.

She ignored his comment. "And I don't drink champagne. A reporter needs a clear head. Actually, I think I always need a clear head, so I stick with juice or water." Rose grinned. "But I never had any problems with chocolates or cakes."

The gray horse left Big Ole's side and came to join them, nuzzling Eric's pocket. "He wants a treat," Eric said, taking an apple out of his pocket. "Usually I wouldn't give him one so early in the day, but he'll trail after us if I don't. Right, fellow?"

"Is that his name? Fellow?"

Eric ducked his head. "He doesn't have a name."

She faced him, her hands on her hips. "Do you mean to tell me that you haven't named this beautiful animal?"

"Well, uh, you see, I—" His words stumbled out.

"I think he deserves a name." She stepped back and studied the horse. From the corner of her eye, though, she watched Eric. He hadn't smiled at all since she arrived. She couldn't stand that; she just couldn't. "You should name him something suitable, something that will make him proud."

She paused. "Something like Sir Gray Steed of the West."

That did it. He smiled, and Rose's heart soared.

"What kind of homesteader are you?" she asked.

He stopped and looked at her. "I do all right."

She shook her head. "Very funny. No, I mean do you have animals? Do you grow things?"

"I had some sheep once," he said, walking toward the barn, "but I didn't care for that."

"Why not?"

He led her into the darkness of the barn. It smelled of hay and horses—not an unpleasant smell at all. Eric pulled a pile of leather bindings from a shelf and handed them to her. "Here. Check these over for damage."

"Damage?"

"Make sure they're not coming apart."

"What am I looking for?"

"Tiny teeth marks," he answered. He picked up a burlap bag of something metal that clanked as he carried it to the barn door.

"Tiny teeth—oh. Mice. Nasty. Say, what's in that bag?" She tried not to think about what the dirty leather straps were doing to her white blouse. The spot from the dirt clod might have come out, but this pile was spelling certain doom for the fine silken fabric.

"Pieces of this and parts of that. Say, pretty soon the barn will become an oven. Come on, let's go outside to do this," he said.

"Sounds good to me." She staggered a bit under the load. It was heavier than it looked.

He moved two short stools from the side of the barn. "Have a seat."

The wind felt good on her face. She began separating the bindings and checking them over for weaknesses in the leather. "So why didn't you keep them?"

"Keep what?"

"The sheep."

"Oh, them." Eric rummaged through the burlap bag. "There should be a—oh, here it is. Well, sheep are good for two things: food and wool. Shearing sheep is quite a skill. If you don't do it well, neither you nor the sheep will come through the experience unhurt."

"Why not raise them as a food crop?"

He shook his head. "Nah. Not for me."

"I couldn't do that," she said. "Once I named them, I couldn't—"

"Named them?" For the second time that day, he laughed. "Named them? Rose, that's priceless."

She glared at him. "I don't see what's so funny about that."

"Never mind. To move on with your question, I'll tell you—this year I'm raising wheat. I tried barley once before, but it didn't do very well, so I'm sticking with wheat. By the way, it's spring wheat."

"Spring wheat is. . . ?" she asked, digging out her tiny notebook and pen from her bag, which she had attached to her waist.

"Planted in the spring. Winter wheat is planted in the winter."

"How can you plant wheat in the winter?" Her pen tore across the paper as she wrote furiously.

"It's actually planted in September, generally late in the month for better yield. I've heard winter wheat does better than spring wheat but that it's riskier since it's so cold up here during the winter, so I stick to planting spring wheat. Just about everybody up here does."

"That makes sense," Rose said, busily writing everything down in her tiny notepad. "When did you plant, by the way?"

"Well, this year I got in the fields a bit early. It was the end of April. Sometimes we don't get out there until May. It all depends on the weather." He gave a short laugh. "Everything up here depends on the weather."

"And when will it be harvested?"

"August usually. Want to see the field?" He dropped the metal components back into the bag. "I'm about ready to go for a walk."

"Sure!"

He led her to the field, and they walked along the peri-meter. "See?" he said, crouching down along the edge row. "It's looking good. Strong, healthy plants, and barring any hailstorms or tornados or extended thunderstorms or plant disease, we should have a good crop this year."

She knelt beside him, ignoring the mud that was sponging up on her skirt. The entire outfit was a disaster anyway.

"The rows are about half a foot apart at minimum, although we like to give them nine inches if we can," he explained.

He stuck a finger in the dirt at the base of one of the plants and dug a small hole. "The root systems are sturdy, which helps." He covered it back up and patted the soil into place.

"Do you plant with someone else?"

"No. Why do you ask?"

"You keep saying 'we.'"

"I guess I mean God." He stood up and brushed the dirt off his hands. "Farming isn't something a man can do by himself. Each little seed is a miracle. Inside it is another plant. I can't make a seed, and I certainly can't duplicate the wondrous marvel of germination when the seed sprouts, and then when it pushes through the soil, climbing up to live under the sun."

"Well," Rose said, "you've chosen your partner wisely, then."

A storm was moving in with the evening shadows, and Eric built a fire to protect against the chill that came with it. Once it was crackling heartily, he pulled his chair closer to the hearth and settled in with his Bible in hand.

He needed to get squared away with this business with Rose, and he knew no better way than to take his concerns to the Lord. First he turned to his favorite passage, Psalm 23. It reminded him of the land around Jubilee.

Since he'd come out here, he'd truly been restored, just as the psalm said. The comfort of this psalm had soothed his soul many times.

He leaned back in his chair and mulled over this sudden turn his life had taken. There was no denying that Rose was a beautiful woman. Did that have anything to do with his decision to go along with her harebrained plan? Surely he had better control of himself than that. He hated to think he was so shallow that he'd follow a woman's path just because she was lovely.

Maybe it was the energy she generated. When she was near him, he felt as if he'd been placed in the middle of a tornado and swept up in its wildly churning winds.

"Speaking of winds," he said to himself as a shutter rattled wildly. The storm was arriving.

He didn't bother with a coat. The only shutter that couldn't be closed from the inside was the one in front of the house, which would take mere moments to fasten securely.

Huge raindrops plopped heavily on his shoulders as he secured the shutter. The wind whipped at his face and tore at his shirt. He made his way to the barn, fighting the wind every step of the way, and made sure everything was protected.

One thing he really needed to do was finish that storm cellar, he thought as lightning tore across the sky and thunder rumbled loudly across the fields. It was still as rudimentary as when he'd first built it.

The night sky opened, and rain poured down, drenching him to the skin. Drops were falling faster than the ground could absorb them, and the water was pooling. He ran as fast as he could back to the house.

Inside, he was glad for the fire. He got out of his wet clothes and into some dry ones, and he returned to his seat in front of the hearth—and to the subject of his earlier musings.

Rose Kelly. She was going to be snooping around his house, asking questions. That would make any man nervous.

A knock on the door broke into his musings. Who could be coming by during such a storm?

He answered the door and was surprised to see Reverend Wilton. "Come in, come in! What are you doing out in that storm?" he asked.

The minister handed Eric his wet coat. "I had dinner tonight at the Frederickson house, and I misjudged the arrival of the storm. Arvid wanted to show me his new venture."

They both smiled. Arvid Frederickson was always on the search for something new that would make his life easier. Eric thought that if Arvid would put as much effort into farming as he did in trying to get out of it, he'd be a great success. Of course, he never spoke his thoughts out loud, but from the looks he'd seen on other people's faces, he knew he wasn't alone in his theory.

"What's his new venture?"

"Ducks."

"Ducks. Ah. I see. Have a seat, Reverend, and dry off in front of the fire. I was about to have some tea. As you see, I've been out in the rain myself. Can I make you a cup, too?" Eric asked as he headed for the kitchen.

"Tea would certainly take the edge off," Reverend Wilton said. "Thank you very much."

"So Arvid's decided that ducks are the way to go, has he?" Eric called from the kitchen. "Is he planning to sell them for food, or is he interested in starting a duck egg business, or what?"

The minister waited until Eric had come back with the tea. "I'm not sure. I'm not sure that Arvid's sure. But he's got his mind set on those ducks, and he's already ordered them. They'll be arriving any day now, I guess. And who knows? Maybe they'll be just the thing, and he'll make a fortune."

"Maybe." Eric knew his single word didn't sound at all encouraging, but he knew Arvid's history.

"Say, speaking of new arrivals in town, I hear that so far it's working out well with Miss Kelly," Reverend Wilton said.

"It depends on what you mean by 'working out well,'" Eric responded. "To be honest, Reverend, I'm uneasy about this whole business. She says she's just going to watch me work and ask questions, and she promises that I won't know she's there, but she was here today and—"

"And you knew it, didn't you?" The minister nodded understandingly. "Eric, are you concerned because she's a woman and you'd be working out here together—and often alone?"

"No!" Eric put down his mug of tea and paced across the room. "No, it's not that at all."

"Then what is it?"

Eric didn't answer at first. He looked out the window and said, "It looks like the rain is stopping. We got a good soaking, though. The wheat'll like that. And so will Arvid's ducks," he added with a wry laugh.

"You're not going to answer the question, are you?" Reverend Wilton drained the rest of his tea. "But I think you should really try to identify why you're so uneasy with Rose. She's not a bad person, you know."

"I know she isn't, but, Reverend, I could be asking the same of you."

The minister sat up, his mouth twitching as if a smile and a frown were struggling. "What do you mean by that?"

"It seems to me," Eric answered with a wink, "that there's someone in Jubilee who's got your eye."

Reverend Wilton put down his cup. "We're not here to talk about my personal life, Johansen," he said primly. "This conversation is about you—and Rose Kelly. Can you tell me why you're uncomfortable with her presence?"

Eric shook his head. "I don't know. Part of it is that—well, let's face it. Would *you* like to have somebody watching your every move?"

The minister stood up and patted Eric on the back before raising his eyes heavenward meaningfully. "I already do, Eric. I already do."

Chapter 5

A friend is a valuable commodity. Companionship is important to us;
without it, we shrivel as unwatered grasses in the hot sun.

Rose patted the tiny bag to make sure her paper and pen were there, gave her hair a final glance in the gilt-edged mirror, and left the hotel.

It was a glorious late June day. The sky stretched out "as infinite as God's goodness," her mother would say. Not a single cloud marred the clear blue that swept from horizon to horizon.

Pretty. Very pretty. And quiet. Very quiet.

Or was it? She stood stock-still, listening—and hearing. Beyond the immediate town, a horse clopped its way along a dirt road, its regular and slow hoofbeats muffled by the distance. A group of four crows argued about an abandoned bit of bread in the street before her. Somewhere in the houses behind the hotel, a man spoke and a woman laughed.

So much for silence!

Rose's steps led her to her first stop, the school. Linnea Gardiner knelt in front of the white-washed building, her face shaded by a large straw hat. With a soil-crusted trowel, she carefully dug a hole and then placed a tiny plant in it. Rose watched a moment before approaching her.

The young schoolteacher pushed a stray lock of blond hair back with dirt-coated fingers. "I'm glad you stopped by."

"Don't let me interrupt your work," Rose said.

Linnea laughed. "That's one of the reasons I'm happy to see you. I need to take a break." She stood up, groaning as she rubbed the small of her back. "I think I've been in this position too long. Would you like to come in for some iced tea?"

As they entered the schoolhouse, Linnea explained that she was doing her summer sprucing up of the building and its grounds. "I do the best I can during the year, but June is my favorite time. As much as I complain, I love planting flowers. It must be because of my name—Gardiner."

"You seem to have quite the green thumb. Do you plant around your house, too?" Rose asked.

Linnea shook her head. "I don't have my own house here. Someday I hope I will." She blushed a bit. "Right now I've only got a room in the Jenkins's house, but they humor me and let me stick my blossoms in the ground there."

"Is that the Mrs. Jenkins I met at the church making *lefse*?"

"The one and the same. She's wonderful. I know I should start looking for my own place to live—maybe start a claim or maybe push a certain somebody a little harder, if you know what I mean—but the Jenkins family has become my own. I love Mr. and Mrs. Jenkins as if they were blood relatives."

Rose nodded understandingly and smiled at the school-teacher. "So you have a fellow who's not being forthcoming?"

Linnea bent over the pitcher, but not before Rose saw a flush climb the teacher's fair cheeks. She poured them each a glass of iced tea. "Let me know what you think of it," she said. "I put some mint in it from the garden at the Jenkins's house. I think it perks it up a bit."

"It's terrific!" Rose said truthfully, taking a drink. "The mint makes it really refreshing. This is just the kind of thing a young wife should know about," she added teasingly, but Linnea looked away and said only, "Maybe."

It was time to change the subject, and Rose steered the conversation back to the matter of the flowers. "I'm impressed that you can do that and the flowers live. It must add a pleasant border to the schoolhouse."

"I hope they do. I enjoy them. But the drawback," Linnea said, sitting on the desk and staring ruefully at her hands, "is that my fingers won't be truly clean again until winter."

Rose put the glass on the desk and self-consciously tucked her hands under her tiny bag. Just a week ago she'd sat at the manicurist's at La Belle's Beauty Emporium and had her nails filed and conditioned.

The thought struck her that she wouldn't be back at La Belle's for another manicure for half a year. Her life was certainly changing.

"You're the talk of the town." Linnea's frank blue eyes met hers.

"I probably am," Rose admitted. "But within a week or two, I'll be last week's news."

Linnea grinned. "Make that a month or two. News lasts longer out here. There's not as much for it to compete with."

Rose sipped her iced tea. "How long have you lived in Jubilee?"

"Not quite two years. I came out with my family. They went back to Rhode Island last year. I stayed."

"Rhode Island is so far away. How did your family choose Jubilee?"

"Reverend Wilton's uncle was our next-door neighbor, and that's how it got started. I think I'm the only person west of the Mississippi who's from Rhode Island. Have you ever been there?"

"No, I have to admit that I haven't. What's it like?"

"It's not that much different, I guess. More water and trees. The buildings are older." Linnea chuckled. "Of course, considering that the oldest structure in Jubilee was built six years ago, there wasn't much competition."

"What do you think of Jubilee?" Rose didn't like asking so many questions. Even as a reporter, she preferred guiding people into talking to her, but this conversation with Linnea invited her questions. "Compared to Rhode Island, that is."

"I like it. The only thing that bothers me," the blond schoolteacher confessed with a surprising intensity, "is that sometimes it gets a bit lonely, especially in the summer when I'm not surrounded by the children."

"I hadn't thought of that," Rose mused aloud. "It seems like it might be even lonelier out on a farm, especially if someone was by himself, without a family to occupy him in the quiet hours. Or," she finished briskly, "maybe there aren't any quiet hours on a farm."

"There are. My parents tried homesteading, and my father said it about drove him mad to spend hours on end battling with the elements, trying to coax a living from the land. He couldn't stand that, and he couldn't stand the solitary days. One day he realized that he was so desperate for companionship that he was having a full-bore argument with himself—and losing, he claimed—and he left the plow right where it was, came back to the house, and announced, 'We're going back home.'"

"How did your mother react?"

Linnea's eyes sparkled with amusement. "She pulled out the trunks and said, 'I'm ready.' She'd never unpacked them except for the necessities."

"Interesting. I can't imagine what it must be like for those who are homesteading and living by themselves." She swirled the iced tea innocently.

"You mean like Eric?" Linnea smiled impishly. "I wondered when you'd ask about him again."

An uneasy blush began its telltale climb up Rose's throat, and she shook her head adamantly. "He's just the subject of my articles for the *Tattler*. I thought he'd be a good choice since he is alone. I find that intriguing."

"I'm sure you do," Linnea teased. "Actually, we all do. He's quite handsome, in a farming sort of way."

" 'A farming sort of way'? What do you mean?"

Linnea shook her head. "I've discovered that God put the land in some people's hearts. It's not in mine, but it is in Eric's. Part of Eric *is* Dakota. He belongs here on the land, digging in it. My digging is limited to gardens in town. Eric, though, he's planting his own roots, and they're going deep down into the ground."

Rose said good-bye to Linnea, promising to see her again soon, and left the schoolhouse, her head spinning with what she'd learned. None of this was what she'd supposed it would be, not a bit of it. She'd always hoped one of her stories would change someone's life. She'd never expected that life to be hers.

Linnea was one of the surprises. In Chicago, Rose had many acquaintances who wanted to see her, wanted to be around her, wanted to share their lives with her. But none of them, she now realized, were friends, and the hole in her life was now gaping.

When she'd talked to the schoolteacher, she felt an immediate bond that settled into her soul. She'd never really had a best friend to share confidences and laughter with, and her short time with Linnea made her hunger for that.

She straightened her stance, lifted her chin, and began to walk briskly. This was a silly, melodramatic train of thought, and it was over. If she didn't guard her thoughts better, she'd be dreaming of falling in love while she was in Jubilee, and that, she told herself, was absurd.

She'd never fall in love with Eric.

Who said anything about Eric? the silent voice asked. She couldn't stop the smile that curved her lips dreamily.

She might not make it through these six months if she didn't rein in her imagination. Becoming friends with Linnea was one thing. Falling in love with Eric was something else entirely.

With determination, she hitched her little bag closer and headed for her next stop, the mercantile. It was right in the center of the town, across from the bank. Even this early, Jubilee was settling into a traditional city structure.

After the brightness of daylight, the interior of the store was dark. The matter wasn't helped at all with the mounds of goods in the single window, blocking out most of the light. Rose blinked several times to get her bearings.

When her eyes became accustomed to the dim interior, she realized that this was nothing like the large stores she shopped at in Chicago. The small room was crammed with objects of all sizes, shapes, and hues. A table in the center of the store was piled with bolts of fabric. Vivid red calico, deep blue poplin, coffee-brown chambray, and delicate pink lawn created a kaleidoscope of color.

Barrels, boxes, cartons, and jars vied for room and were stacked on top of each other in precarious pyramids.

Over it all, the smells—pickles, flour, soap, oil, fish—blended into one.

"Miss Kelly!" Freya Trease rose, laboriously from her seat behind the counter, her ample figure swathed in a green sprigged apron. "It's good to see you again."

"Please call me Rose. This is a wonderful store."

"Thank you." Freya brushed an invisible speck from her voluminous bodice. "It's probably quite different from what you're used to in the big city."

"We have small stores, too." Rose picked up a roll of white lace and studied it. "This would be lovely as an edging, wouldn't it?"

"It would," Freya agreed. "Is there something in particular you're looking for?"

Rose put back the spool of lace. "Not today, but I know I will eventually. After all, I'm here for six months."

"Six months can be a lifetime, or it can pass in the blink of an eye." The plump shopkeeper wiped the counter with a cloth she pulled from her apron pocket. "This land will be the death of me yet."

This was exactly the kind of thing she was looking for. Although the focus of her articles would be the homesteader, insights into the lives of those who shared his community would make the stories come alive.

"Why do you say that?" she asked, trying to appear casual as she ran her hand over the edge of the pickle barrel.

"The dust from the fields," Freya said, showing Rose the smudged cloth. "But it's not as bad as during harvest."

"So living here is a real trial, is it?" Rose suggested, hoping that Freya would disagree—and provide her with a quotable line.

"It can be. The mosquitoes in summer, the blizzards and biting cold in winter—yes, there are times when I think that I was out of my mind to leave New York."

"Why do you stay? Because of the store? Your husband?"

Freya smiled. "I stay because this is the most beautiful place on earth."

Rose glanced out the window at the building across the street. The rough-hewn exterior was a marked contrast to the elegant sign grandly proclaiming it to be HOMESTEAD HONESTY BANK in black and gold script.

Beautiful? She'd heard that beauty was in the eye of the beholder, but there had to be something terribly wrong with Freya's eyes.

The shopkeeper laughed. "You don't believe me, do you?" She shrugged her well-padded shoulders and looked Rose directly in the eyes. "This is the perfect place for some people but not for everyone. We all have our own reward waiting for us, our final home, but I've found that God has settled us differently on earth. My ideal home may not be yours."

Rose knew where her ideal home was—her roomy apartment overlooking the crowded skyline of Chicago. The city teemed with life. Even though she'd just arrived in Jubilee, she knew she could never stay here.

The image of Eric Johansen floated into her mind, and she immediately corrected herself: She *could* stay here. Maybe.

"What do you know about Mr. Johansen?" she asked Freya, trying to make her words sound like an idle question. "He seems to be happy here."

Freya's face clouded. "He is. There's something holding on to him, though."

"Really? Why, I wonder what it could be."

"I don't know." The dust cloth snapped once more across the spotless counter and disappeared back into the roomy apron. "It's not my business."

Unspoken, the sentence continued, *And it's not yours, either.*

Experience had taught her to listen to what was not said, and Freya's comment increased Rose's curiosity. The shopkeeper didn't seem to know what dark event marked Eric's history, but the fact that she had sensed it was important.

Discovering a delicious tidbit like something mysterious in Eric's past was enough to add a spring to her step. She was like a bloodhound on the track of an enticing scent, and it led her right to the person of Eric Johansen himself.

Eric shut his Bible. There was something about reading the Word that reached into his soul and calmed him. Lately he'd found himself turning to it more for the comfort it offered him.

This was his fourth summer in Jubilee. His body was already tuned to the flow of nature in the territory, to the growing seasons that echoed his own. June was the month of new life. He'd come to anticipate this time when the earth burst into glorious green.

But now, instead of feeling great anticipation, he was unsettled.

What had he agreed to? Had he really said he'd allow Rose Kelly to follow him around?

He snorted. Fool woman. She'd probably break her ankle in a gopher hole or pass out from sunstroke or get bitten by a rabid skunk.

Or, he realized as he rose to his feet, those things would happen to him as he chased around after her, trying to save her. He'd be lucky to make it through these six months in one piece.

Enough complaining. He had some ducklings to pick up. Arvid had gotten to him, and in sympathy, he'd agreed to take a few ducklings. If he didn't get moving, they'd be full-grown ducks by the time he got there.

There was never enough time in the day, not in June. But he wasn't going to whimper and cry about that. He'd rather be busy. There was only so much time a man could spend with his thoughts.

The sun warmed the air, and he dropped his jacket back on the hook inside the door. He wouldn't need it.

"This is the day that the Lord hath made; let us rejoice and be glad in it."

The Good Book certainly had that right!

"Go down that road until you see the cottonwood with the bent trunk. Take a right. After a while, you'll see a granite rock on the left. Go a mile or so past that. The road curves a bit, and then it'll fork. Head left, and the first farm on the right is Arvid's. You can't miss it."

Matthew pushed across the counter the scrap of paper on which he had sketched the way to Arvid Frederickson's farm.

Rose took it and stared at it. It seemed simple enough. She'd been in Jubilee for two weeks, and she was finally feeling comfortable with the prairie town.

But after half an hour of driving the small wagon down country roads that all looked the same, she had to admit that she had no earthly idea where she was.

This land was so flat, she should have been able to see all the way to Omaha. But there were deceptive dips and curves in the earth, and no matter how she looked, or which road she went down, she didn't see anything that looked remotely like a farm.

Finally, in desperation, she stopped the huge horse and climbed up on the seat of the wagon. Big Ole snorted and pawed at the ground, and the ramshackle wagon shimmied. She stood atop the wooden plank bench like a tottering sentinel on the prairie, scanning the horizon for a recognizable sign.

She saw something in the distance, a tiny squarish spot. Carefully she gathered her skirts and prepared to climb down when she realized the faraway spot was moving. It wasn't a farm, but someone else with a wagon. Whoever it was didn't seem to be far away. She'd just wait.

The little spot moved slowly toward her, inching across the landscape. She frowned at it. At this rate, it would be Independence Day before it got to her. Luckily she had her little bag with her. She could make use of this time and record her thoughts so far. Her first story was due in a few days, and she had the perfect angle for it. She took out the pad and pen and began to write. Within minutes her pen was racing across the paper, and she was engrossed in her story.

"Miss Kelly?" Eric's voice spoke right beside her, and her pen scratched a wild line across the sheet.

"You shouldn't sneak up on a body. You almost gave me heart failure!" She put her hand on her chest, and even through the thick cotton weave of her suit, she could feel the pounding.

"I'm sorry." His apology was tinged with amusement, and she glared at him.

"You don't sound sorry."

Big Ole shifted uneasily, and Eric moved quickly to his side. "Shhh, boy," he soothed. "Shhh." He looked at Rose. "I didn't mean to startle you," he said, his hand still protectively on Big Ole's bridle. "But it's not often people just pull over to the side of the road out here and scribble out a few words."

Now that her heart had returned to its normal beating, she remembered her earlier mission. "I wasn't scribbling, I was writing. And I'm out here because I'm lost."

"How could you be—" he began, and then he stopped. "Oh, never mind. Where did you intend to go?"

"I was on my way to Arvid's farm."

"Arvid?" He shook his head in disbelief. "Why would you want to go out there?"

"I'm interviewing him."

"I thought you were interviewing me."

She put the notepad back in her purse. Then she tucked the tiny pen in there, too. With great deliberation, she closed the bag, then faced him. "I tried to, Eric. I really did. I got one thing. One thing."

Eric's extraordinary silence about his past was aggravating her irrationally. She could write the article—and, in fact, she just had—without that information, but not knowing was driving her out of her mind. He was so adamant about not telling her that she was determined he was going to do it.

"Can you direct me to Mr. Frederickson's farm, please?" she asked primly. "I have a few questions for the gentleman." She lifted her chin. "If you won't talk to me, perhaps he will."

Chapter 6

When the land is this vast, we try to tether ourselves in place by creating a web with others. It is not enough to do this and call it done. Our lives always need to be tended as if they were growing things, because they are, in fact, just that.

This wasn't what Eric wanted to hear. He wanted to pick up his ducklings and be on his way back home. But if he led Rose to Arvid's farm, it wouldn't be that simple. They'd end up talking about the day's weather, and then Arvid would take him out to the pond to look at the ducks, and after that they'd take a look at the fields and check on the seedlings, and the next thing he knew, they'd all be sitting around the kitchen table drinking Arvid's Norwegian coffee and eating his cinnamon cookies.

All he wanted were his ducks.

But there was no way around it. He was going to Arvid's, and so was she. The only consolation he could find in the matter was that they'd be in separate wagons on the way out.

He didn't dare leave her alone with Arvid. Who knew what the man would tell Rose? Arvid wasn't the kind of fellow to let a little lack of knowledge stand in his way. He'd have a story of some kind to tell Rose.

"Just follow me," he said, trying not to sound as if he were begrudging her anything.

"I don't want to take you out of your way," she answered, but her relief was clear in her tone. "You could point me in the right direction and—"

He couldn't resist smiling. "Seems to me you were already pointed in the right direction and it didn't do you a bit of good."

She grinned back ruefully. "You know, with a landscape as open as this, you wouldn't think I'd miss something like a tree or a rock or another road." She touched his arm, and his breath caught as he saw again how tiny her hand was. She was such a city woman, so delicate and fragile.

With an effort, he brought himself back to the conversation. "If it's any comfort, you're not far from his farm."

Big Ole snorted impatiently and shook his mane, and Eric nodded at him. "We'd better go before Big Ole takes you back to Jubilee."

Arvid was standing in his yard when they pulled up. "Well, well, well," he said, coming to greet them both. "Two for the price of one, I guess."

"As it turns out, we were both coming out here to see you." Rose leaped out of the wagon before Eric could help her. "But I was lost."

"Lost?" Arvid's eyes twinkled with amusement. "Out here?"

"One of these days," she said, "you'll have signposts all along these roads. Mark my words."

The farmer roared and shook his head. "One of these days a long time from now, maybe. You stay here long enough, it'll be second nature to you, knowing when to turn on these roads."

"I'll just be here six months. And then it's back to Chicago, land of street signs and lampposts."

A knife twisted in Eric's chest. *Six months.* He didn't know if he wanted her to go—or stay. She was changing things in his life, and he didn't like it. He had carefully built a life that was solitary. Jubilee had been the perfect place for him to do that, too. It had allowed him to hide within the life he created for himself. And now in these short two weeks, she had begun to tear down those self-made barriers and force him to think about emotions he'd tucked away long ago.

"Can I pick up the ducklings?" he asked abruptly.

"Sure," Arvid said. "Miss Kelly, you might like to see this."

As they walked toward Arvid's barn, he explained, "Some folks here are raising chickens, but I thought I'd give ducks a try. I'm not sure how it's going to work out, but we'll see. I've got some little fellows set aside for Eric."

The barn still held the morning's coolness, and sunlight filtered through the open door. Bits of dust and straw floated in the air like speckled gold.

Eric heard the ducklings before he saw them. "I've got a box for—" he began, but Rose interrupted him.

"These are the sweetest creatures on the earth," she said, picking one up and cradling it in her hands. "Eric, they'll be wonderful pets."

Eric and Arvid exchanged glances, and Eric cleared his throat. "Uh, Rose, I don't—"

"Just look at this face." She held it close to his chest. "Look at it. What a beautiful little thing God has made. Can I name it? Just this one?"

"Rose—"

"Please?" she wheedled. "I have the perfect name for him. I want to call him Downy."

"Downy the Duck." Arvid's voice sounded suspiciously like he was trying to choke back a laugh, and Eric groaned. He'd give this story half a day before it was all over Jubilee.

"Shhh!" he hissed to Arvid. "You're not making this any easier."

"Making what easier?" Rose's face was soft with love as she kissed the duckling on the head. He'd have to avoid looking into those moss-green eyes if he were ever to have control over his emotions.

Eric sighed. "Nothing. Downy it is."

Rose tapped her fingers on the desk in her room at the Territorial. In the distance, random bangs and snaps told her that boys were shooting off leftover firecrackers. Independence Day had been quite the celebration in Jubilee, complete with a program of music, drama, and oration. She and Linnea had feasted on freshly squeezed lemonade and sampled trays of cookies and cakes and dessert breads.

It was wonderful fodder for her articles. She'd left the big city to find the true America. George would love the angle. It was that ability to tap into the likes of the reading public that had made him such a good editor at the *Tattler*.

She needed to get moving on the articles about Eric, though. She'd go out to his farm bright and early the next day and ask him directly. And if she didn't get good answers from him, she'd move into investigative reporting mode.

There was something she didn't know about him, and it was eating at her not only because as a reporter she was trained to ferret out more information than she'd use in her writing, but also because she had to find out what had carved those two little lines over his nose. Some sorrow, some worry, perhaps even some sin had put those deep etchings there, and if she was going to invest her heart, she wanted to know why.

She rubbed her eyes and leaned back. She must need sleep to be thinking like that. He was the subject of her articles and no more.

As soon as the sun came up the next day, she'd confront him directly.

But opportunity changed her plans.

Matthew was at the desk of the Territorial the next morning, his eyes looking as tired as hers felt. "I came in early," he explained, "since a skunk decided to nest under the steps of my house. It surprised me, and I surprised it, and I'm sure you can smell the result. I've done all I can to get the smell out, and I apologize if I haven't—"

She held up her hand to stop the cascade of words. "Not a problem. You smell fine." It wasn't much of an untruth. He had doused himself with something flowery and strong that did a fairly good job of disguising the remnants of the run-in with the skunk.

"Are you going out, Miss Kelly?" Matthew rubbed his eyes and yawned.

"Soon. I'm going to Eric Johansen's farm."

Matthew smiled. "He's a nice fellow. I'll be looking forward to reading your stories about him."

"Thank you." She leaned in a bit closer, and the skunk odor grew stronger. "Say, I wonder if you can help me."

"I'd be glad to, Miss Kelly. What can I do?"

"I didn't get where Eric came here from. Do you know where he lived before he moved to Jubilee?"

"I'm sorry," Matthew said, "but I don't. Not exactly, that is. East, I suppose. Everybody came from the East, I think."

"Do you have any idea what he did before he got here? Was he a teacher?"

Matthew shook his head. "A teacher? No, I don't think so."

She took a deep breath. "He's a good man, isn't he? I mean, he hasn't been in prison?"

"Prison?" Matthew gaped at her. "What on earth would give you that idea? Prison? No. Not Mr. Johansen. There's not a squarer man in Jubilee than him."

Rose nodded. "I see. That's what I thought. Thank you, Matthew. That's just what I needed to know."

Or not, she thought as she left. She'd come away with basically no more information than she'd started with.

"Miss Kelly!" Mrs. Jenkins waved at her from across the street and hurried to join Rose in front of the Territorial. "What are you doing out so early?" she asked breathlessly.

"I'm going to Eric Johansen's farm."

Mrs. Jenkins beamed at her. "How's that progressing? You must be getting splendid material for your articles from him."

"I am," Rose began and then stopped. She could hear her editor's voice as clearly as if he were speaking in her ear. *Seize the moment, Kelly. Use what's given you, and if it's not given to you, go out and get it and take it. But keep it honest, and keep it clean.* Well, this was honest—and fairly clean. "It's quite interesting, but I'm having trouble getting background from him." She winked conspiratorially at Mrs. Jenkins. "You know how men are. They just will not talk about themselves."

"What do you need to know?"

"Where he lived before he moved to Jubilee. What he did for a living. That kind of thing."

Mrs. Jenkins tilted her head thoughtfully, her white hair catching the early sunshine. "Now isn't that odd? I don't have a clue."

"I'm sure it's all perfectly legitimate," Rose assured her, "but it does make me wonder a bit. After all, it's not like he was a criminal, I'm sure."

It was amazing how many people were out and about at this time of day. Within an hour, Rose had visited with almost everyone she'd met in Jubilee. After Mrs. Jenkins, she saw Arvid, then Linnea, who didn't have much time to talk as she was on her way to the church to check on some new candlesticks, and even the Treases as they opened their store for the day. Each person had the same answer to her questions.

No one knew about Eric Johansen's past.

She'd planted her own kind of seeds during her morning stroll, and if they didn't bear fruit fairly soon—perhaps that was an answer in itself.

Eric walked through his wheat field, appraising the tiny clusters at the end of the stalks. This would be a good yield if the weather held. Of course, hail, rain, drought, even insects could change everything.

And to think this had all come from a bag of tiny seeds. What a miracle!

"How does it look?"

Her voice startled him, and he stood up so quickly that his head spun.

"Good so far. I'm hoping for a bountiful crop, but we still have a ways to go before we can count on the harvest."

The hem of her skirt moved, and a tiny beak peeked out to nab an unsuspecting beetle. "You have company, I see," he commented dryly.

"Company?" she asked blankly.

"The ducks." He pointed at her feet, where one of the ducks was now pecking at her shoelace.

"I must not have shut the gate," she said as she knelt and gathered the ducklings in her arms. "I'll take them back."

There were more than she could hold, and as soon as she captured one, another would wriggle free. "You hold those two," he told her, "and I'll get the rest of them."

"You won't even know I'm there," he thought to himself as one of the ducks veered off under the wheat and he had to leap the row to catch it. *"I'll be a quiet little shadow,"* or whatever it was you said. Ha.

At last they had the ducks safely in their arms and then back in the pen. The creatures were usually all right when he was around, but he liked to keep them in their cage when he was out in the field.

"Downy's quite the leader, isn't he?" Rose asked proudly as Eric latched the ducklings' pen.

"If he were human, he'd be running for governor, I'm sure." Eric stood, and she followed suit. "Are you planning on spending the day out here?"

Rose frowned at him. "Well, that wasn't exactly the most gracious invitation."

He jammed his hands inside his pockets and felt his fingers clench into fists. This was going all wrong. Whenever he was around Rose, his social graces tumbled to rock bottom. He felt like a gawky teenager around the belle of the town.

He summoned all the poise he could muster. "I'm sorry. I didn't mean to be so rude. What did you need from me today? Did you want to learn more about wheat? The operation of the farm? Perhaps a bit about the Homestead Act?"

"No," she said simply. "I want to learn more about you."

"Ah."

"I want to know about your life before Jubilee, where you lived, what you did for a living. Who were your parents, and do you have brothers and sisters? Did you have a dog when you were a boy? What did you read? What were your dreams?"

He took a breath. "My parents are both deceased. I have no brothers or sisters, and I didn't have a dog."

"Tell me more, Eric. Let me know you." She leaned closer, and his breath caught in his throat.

With an effort, he pushed away the thought of taking her in his arms. "There is no more."

She put her hand on his arm. "Eric, are you running away from something?"

He swallowed. "Aren't we all?" he answered lightly. "Now I really have to get back to work."

"Eric. . ." She followed him as he started to walk back to the fields, and he stopped.

Without turning around, he said, "Rose, we made a pact when I said I'd be the subject of your articles. Do you remember the three terms of our agreement?"

"I can't shadow you. I have to respect your privacy. There is no assumption of friendship." Had he imagined it, or had her voice cracked on the last sentence?

"Quit asking about my past. Just quit," he said. "It has nothing to do with my homesteading, and thus nothing to do with you or your articles. Leave it alone. Leave me alone."

He strode into his fields, wondering why he felt as if his world had just crashed down around him—again.

❊

Rose walked through the twilight and looked at the houses in Jubilee. They weren't all that different from the ones in Chicago, she told herself. Inside each one, people lived, people with the same wants and needs as those in the city.

They needed food and water and shelter to keep their bodies alive and healthy. And they needed God to keep their souls alive and healthy. Jubilee wasn't a rough-and-tumble wild town. Quite the contrary—a sense of moral strength was evident in the residents, a trust in a higher power that came through in their everyday lives.

She was changing, too, she realized. She'd lost some of the edge she'd had, and she honestly didn't know if she wanted it back. When she'd held that duckling and it had settled trustingly into her hands, she'd felt something shift inside her—felt it settle and make a home.

Children's laughter floated from one of the houses, and a pang struck her heart. Suddenly she was tired, very tired, of living like a whirlwind in Chicago. She wanted to slow down, to feel earth beneath her feet rather than the sidewalks of the city. There was more to life than the run of parties she covered for the *Tattler*.

Her walk had taken her through the circuit of the small town and brought her back to the center. She was just about to return to the room at the Territorial when Linnea caught up to her.

"Rose," the schoolteacher said breathlessly, "you certainly do walk briskly. I've been trying to catch up with you since the corner."

Her pace hadn't seemed rapid to her, but she was still moving at the speed of the city, where everything went faster. "Sorry," she apologized. "I was thinking. I could use a rest now, though. Let's sit here." She motioned toward the bench across from the church.

"How are you liking Jubilee so far?" Linnea asked when they had seated themselves.

The evening had deepened since Rose had begun her walk, and she looked down the street at the darkening town. "I like it," she said simply at last. "I do."

"It's a splendid place to live, you know," Linnea said. "We chose to live here, and you'll have to excuse us if we're a bit protective of our own."

Rose's head swung around, and she stared at Linnea. "What on earth do you mean? Are you saying that I've done something wrong here?" Her breath stalled in her throat. Quickly she reviewed her activities since arriving. What could she have said or done that would have offended the residents of Jubilee?

"It seems as if almost everyone here is talking about your visit."

Rose struggled to put the words together so they would make sense. What was Linnea talking about?

The icy edge to Linnea's voice struck fear into Rose's heart. She needed the cooperation of the townspeople for her stories to succeed. Had she alienated them already?

Even in the cool of the summer evening, she began to sweat. She needed their help.

Eric lives here, too, she reminded herself. *Rose Kelly, if you've driven him away, you have nothing. Was that why he was so standoffish today? Oh, dear God, help me. Please help.*

She took a deep breath and spoke. Her voice was remarkably steady and strong. "Linnea, what aren't you telling me? What do I need to know that I don't?"

Linnea didn't meet her gaze for a moment, and when she finally faced Rose, her face was filled with pain. "When you arrived in Jubilee, I was at the station. You were so elegant, so exciting, and I thought—I thought you might be my friend." Tears clouded her usually clear eyes. "But I didn't expect that you would do that."

"Do what?" She knew she sounded snappish, but she couldn't help it. If Linnea had a problem, why didn't she just say so? This sashaying around the lamppost was frustrating.

A single tear spilled over and coursed down Linnea's pale cheek. "Under the guise of friendship, you were researching your stories, trying to make us talk about Eric. Every single conversation that we had was directed toward your articles. Did we even matter to you?"

Rose started to speak, but Linnea interrupted her. "And it wasn't just that. You wouldn't stop digging, trying to find something horrible in Eric's past. Even when we said you shouldn't, you kept on. Why can't you just leave him alone?"

"I was not—" Rose began, but even as she spoke, she knew she had done just that. Now that she looked back on what she'd said earlier in the day to each person she'd talked to, the innuendos she'd planted, she realized how manipulative she'd been.

"Did you really think we'd talk behind his back?" Linnea shook her head sadly. "We would never do that. Never."

"I was only trying to find out more about him," Rose protested. "Secondary interviews are an accepted form of newspaper work."

For a moment, Linnea didn't say anything. Then she said with a touch of resignation in her voice, "That may be true in Chicago, but things are different in Jubilee. What you might call 'investigation' is what we'd consider 'prying.' To be honest, people are feeling as if you've taken advantage of their goodwill."

This wasn't the first time someone had accused Rose of snooping to get information, but the charge hadn't bothered her before.

"I'm sorry. I really am." The words were true. She hadn't intended to hurt anyone. "I wanted to fill in the spaces in Eric's history—and there are some major gaps there, you know."

Linnea seemed to relent a bit. "You can't do that."

"I can't?" She tried not to show how those words sparked her interest anew. "Why not?"

The schoolteacher shook her head. "Rose, don't ask."

"I just wonder where he was before he came here. Did he ever tell you?"

"Who knows? It's not like he'd ever say—or we would ever ask."

"Why not?" For the life of her, she'd never understand this town's ability to overlook the past.

"It's just the way we are," Linnea said. "One day, I hope you'll understand."

Rose stood up. She'd respect it, but she'd never understand it.

�֍

Eric herded the ducklings into the cage he'd built for them beside the barn. They were the silliest creatures he'd ever seen. As soon as he thought he had them corralled, one would waddle out, and the others would follow.

He rocked back on his heels and watched the ducks. One of them seemed to be the ringleader. It didn't surprise him that it was the one Rose had named Downy.

How had this woman finagled her way into his life. . .and his heart? He couldn't quite trust her, but more than that, he couldn't quite *not* trust her. It was as if his heart had its own mind.

He thought back to the way her face had softened as she held Downy. He'd known at that moment that she wasn't just a big-city newspaperwoman with hard edges. He saw intelligence compliment her inquisitiveness, and tenderness temper her crustiness. She was quite a woman.

He looked out toward his fields. The moonlight was bright on the newly emerging wheat, and he thought he'd never seen anything as beautiful as this field on this night.

A duckling quacked beside him, and he moved protectively closer to the cage as something rustled in the tall grass next to the barn. He smiled as he remembered Rose holding Downy. The glossy veneer of her big-city ways had vanished when she had the soft duckling in her hands.

Only a city girl would name something destined for the dinner table. Downy nipped his trouser leg through the cage, and Eric chuckled. "Don't worry. You're safe. Thanks to a pushy newspaperwoman from Chicago who can't keep her nose out of my business, you'll live a nice full life here."

He stroked Downy's soft head through the grating of the cage. It was a beautiful night. Nothing on earth could compare to a July night with moonlight spilling across the land.

God had given him his share of problems, his share of suffering, but He'd also given him a full portion of blessings. Tonight his plate was full.

July was the month of beginnings, a time of tender green shoots, of precious ducklings, of strange newspaperwomen who came and tore your life apart.

✄

As Rose went into Redeemer Church, the atmosphere wasn't quite as frosty. People nodded to her, perhaps not as amiably as before, but they were at least recognizing her.

She sat in the front row of the church, her Bible positioned primly on her knees. This morning she'd taken special care with her appearance, and her sleek reddish-gold hair was pulled back into a tight bun with a new white lace bow riding atop it.

Her dress, a pale blue and white windowpane check, was new, having been fashioned just this week by Mrs. Jenkins, who, she'd found out, had sewing talents equal to those she had in the kitchen.

Linnea, who sat at the other end of the pew, nodded briefly to her before turning her eyes back to Reverend Wilton, who was approaching the front of the church. Linnea's eyes looked as red as Rose's felt.

After a mostly sleepless night, she'd come to the decision that she couldn't worry too much about the townspeople mistrusting her. She had asked the questions she'd had to ask. There was no more she could do.

Reverend Wilton began the service, and she opened her Bible to the day's text, which, according to the sign at the side of the sanctuary, was Proverbs 18:4–8. As the minister read the Scripture aloud, she followed along with a growing sense of distress. " 'A fool's mouth is his destruction,'" read Reverend Wilton.

She could feel the congregation's eyes on her, blaming, accusing. And in the back of her mind, she heard her mother's tired voice: *"Rose, dear, watch your words. Take your time. Think before you speak."*

Rose bent her head as the minister led the congregation in silent prayer.

God had given her this impetuous mouth. Could He also give her the power to control it?

Chapter 7

Inside each of us is a big locked room with double-bolted cabinets
and closets where we hide our sins not from others as much as from ourselves.
We may not see those sinful blots on our souls, but they remain there, hidden away
and carefully caged, always hoping for the day when they can wriggle free.

Rose sat in her tidy room at the Territorial, her little note-pad open beside her. She scowled at it and tapped her pen testily. For the most part, the sheets of paper were empty.

She had a story due in the mail by the end of the day, and she was no further along than she'd been when she first arrived.

Where to start? She stood up and paced across the room, the rhythm of her steps helping her direct her unfocused thoughts.

She had many possible angles to take on the story. Mentally she sorted through them, trying to determine which was the best.

George Marshall, her editor at the *Tattler*, had given her some wonderful advice when she'd begun writing for the newspaper. She imagined him standing beside her, clucking in dismay at her skimpy notes. *"Don't know where to start? How about the beginning?"*

She sat down, and slowly, at first, but with increasing speed, she began to tell the tale of her arrival in Jubilee, carefully leaving out her first unexpected meeting with Eric Johansen. This was Jubilee's story.

At last she had it ready. Woven into it were the notes she'd taken so far. She read it through one more time and sat back in her chair, smiling with satisfaction. It was good, and her readers would love it.

She gathered up the story and her little bag and left to send the story.

The small wooden building in the center of the town housed both the telegraph office and the post office. It hummed with activity, and she had to stand in line at the counter.

She wasn't intentionally eavesdropping, but the building was so tiny and crowded that hearing others' conversations was unavoidable. Years of training in the newspaper business had made it nearly impossible for her not to pay attention to those speaking around her.

Two men in work clothes discussed the progress of their respective crops. A woman with two children playing tag around her ankles talked to an older woman about a laundry mishap. An older couple exchanged brief comments about the possibility of rain.

At last it was her turn, and the young man behind the counter, who couldn't have been older than seventeen, put down the mail he was sorting and took the envelope from her. "Chicago, eh?" he asked. "Is this one of those articles I've been hearing so much about?"

All discussions in the room ceased, and an almost-palpable silence fell over the crowd.

Everyone turned and stared at her.

Rose smiled widely at all of them. "Why, yes it is, and I imagine you're all curious about what it says, aren't you?"

The assembled townspeople murmured in assent.

"I'll be delighted to share it with you when it goes into print, which should be soon. My editor at the *Tattler* has promised to send me copies. I hope you'll all be pleased with what I've written."

A slow current of excitement ran through the group, and relief washed through her veins. Perhaps the veil of suspicion had been lifted.

As she turned to leave, she noticed the top envelope of the pile that the mail clerk had been holding. The address brought her up short.

Dr. Eric Johansen.

After that, *Boston Hospital* had been crossed out and *Jubilee, Dakota Territory*, added.

Doctor? Eric was a doctor?

Why would a man leave a medical career in Boston and come to Dakota—and not practice medicine?

And furthermore, why wouldn't he just tell her that?

Eric checked his reflection in the cracked mirror that hung in his bedroom. He looked presentable enough. He must be losing his edge, letting the people at church talk him into this.

A play. And a comic romance, too.

True, he wasn't portraying the lead character, a young swain who, through a series of misunderstandings, ended up courting his loved one's pig.

It could have been worse, he reminded himself. He could have been cast as the pig.

He rode into town, reviewing his lines. He was portraying the next-door neighbor in the play, and although he didn't have many lines, he'd never acted before. He must be out of his mind. That was the only rational explanation.

The play was being staged in the town hall, Jubilee's newest addition. A cluster of people were already milling around the door, waiting for the play to begin. Eric slipped past the group and made it to the back room, where the cast was getting ready.

The cast members were nervously reviewing their lines as if they were opening in New York City. The atmosphere was charged with anticipation.

Eric donned a formal black coat for his part in the play, then wandered through the packed room. Although the play featured only six roles, with the addition of the director, the costumer, and the prompter, the room quickly became overly humid and extremely hot. He ducked outside, welcoming the cool night air.

"You're going to the play, too?" Rose's voice came out of the shadows.

"I'm in the play."

"Ah, a new career for Eric Johansen?"

He froze. Something in her tone made him wonder what she had heard, what she knew—or thought she knew.

"Tonight is my debut and my swan song," he answered lightly. "I suspect after this performance, I won't be called on again to act."

"You never know," she said, moving toward him. "You may have hidden talents."

That did it.

"It's nearly curtain time. I'd better head back inside." Before she could say more, he darted back into the building.

Somehow, in a corner of the busy back room, he found a pocket of solitude. *God, I need Your guidance more than ever. I thought I was getting away from all my mistakes by coming here, but apparently I brought my past with me. And now Rose is here, and without Your help, I'm afraid I might fall in love with her. I can't do that. Help me know what to do. I need You more than ever. I'm lost. . .again.*

✄

The play was charming, Rose thought. It wasn't anything that would have made the dramatic circles in Chicago, but it was entertaining. And while Eric would never be the darling of the Broadway stage, he'd done a respectable job with his role.

"Now don't forget about that concert next week," Mrs. Jenkins said as they left the town hall. "Charlotta Allen is quite the rage in New York City, and we're very lucky to get her to perform here."

Rose had no idea who Charlotta Allen was, and she was fairly sure that she would have come across the name in her work with the *Tattler* if the woman had been famous in New York. Nevertheless, she looked forward to the opportunity to hear her.

The evening had been quite revealing, all in all. Apparently Jubilee had a healthy cultural life. The room had been packed. Matthew was there, as were Arvid and his family, the entire Nielsen clan, and the Treases. Even Reverend Wilton and Linnea were there, sitting next to each other.

Plays, concerts, socials, and parties went on regularly, according to Mrs. Jenkins. Rose had seriously underestimated how well established the town was. It wasn't Chicago, but it was far beyond the two-horse village she'd envisioned.

Eric was silhouetted against the side of the building as he leaped into his wagon. Rose paused only a moment before going to him.

"Eric, you showed a real sense of the theater in there. I'm impressed!"

"Thank you. I'm surprised at how enjoyable it actually was."

"I wanted to ask you before you left—I was hoping I could come out to your farm tomorrow. I promise I won't be a bother. You won't even know I'm there. Might I come out?"

He paused so long that she thought for a moment that he wasn't going to say anything, but finally his response was simple. "Yes."

She found herself smiling to the world at large as she walked the entire way back to the hotel, as she got ready for bed, and even as she picked up her Bible for her evening devotions before sleep.

A day with Eric. The idea was teeming with possibilities.

She opened her Bible and found her favorite verse: *"For where your treasure is, there will your heart be also."* When she couldn't sleep, she would lie awake and sort through her life, trying to determine what her treasure was. Over the years it had gone from being her doll to being her new shoes to being—what would it be now? It was intriguing how her interpretation of that verse had changed during the course of her life as her idea of what her treasure was had evolved.

And maybe, just maybe, she thought as she fell asleep, her heart had changed, too.

Eric splashed cold water on his face. He'd need all his wits about him today.

Rose had said he wouldn't even know she was there. What were the chances of that? Whenever she'd been around him, he'd been painfully aware of her presence.

Last night he could have told her no, he wouldn't be home, but he'd long ago made an agreement with God that he wouldn't lie. Not anymore. He'd already told enough lies for a lifetime, and the last one was the worst. A lie never lived on its own. It had fingers that stretched into every part of his existence.

He'd barely wiped his face dry when he heard the distinctive sound of Big Ole's clopping hooves. "And we're off," he whispered to himself as he went out to meet her.

At least this time she didn't have on those worthless little shoes she'd been wearing before. Instead, sensible brown leather boots poked out from under the hem of her green-flowered skirt.

He was going to clean out the stable today before the sun got too high in the sky. Then he was going to go back into the fields and check on the crops. If there was time, he'd weed his garden and fix the wheel on the wagon that was wobbling.

He had the whole day planned out nicely. Without preamble, he told her the schedule, and she nodded. "Sounds good to me. I can help you, too," she chirped happily as she headed for the stable.

Eric contented himself with rolling his eyes. He could picture how effective she'd be with the day's tasks.

"How's Downy?" she asked as soon as she got to the barn door.

"Growing bigger, but that's what ducks do."

"He's not in his cage." She stopped and frowned at him.

"The duck is all right. He's swimming down in the creek now."

"Do you think it's safe for him to be out of his cage?"

He fought back a laugh. "This is the country, and he's a duck. The ducks go in the cage only at night, and that's only to protect them from predators."

Her forehead crinkled with concern. "I'm not sure that it's enough, but I'll have to trust you."

"I appreciate it," he responded dryly.

Amazingly, she was a tremendous help, and she pitched in fearlessly, even when it meant digging in the dirty straw of the stable. Noon came earlier than he expected, and with it, a problem arose. What would they eat?

"I'm sorry," he began, "but I have to say that I don't have much for us to eat. I usually grab what I can and bring it with me."

"That's not a problem," she said, running her hand over her sweat-stained forehead. "I'm not particular."

Not particular? He thought back to the day he'd met her, how she'd been so impeccably dressed and so very elegantly out of place in Jubilee. Now she was sitting in his barn, scented with the odor of the stable rather than expensive perfume, her calico dress smeared with dirt, and she was beautiful.

He shoved the thought out of his mind. Food. That was what he needed to focus on.

Within minutes, they were sitting on the front step of his home, eating bread and cheese.

"That breeze feels good," she commented as a waft of air lifted a stray lock of hair from the side of her face. "I must look terrible."

He swallowed. "No. Not at all. You look—very nice."

She smiled at him, and he felt as if he were fourteen years old again, awkward and ill at ease around women. "Why, thank you."

The curious ducklings waddled toward them, begging for bread.

For a moment, neither of them spoke as Rose threw bread crumbs for the ducks; then she said, "I don't know much about you."

Every muscle in his body stiffened. "There's not much to know."

"Oh, I'm sure there is. Everybody has a story. If they didn't, I'd be out of a job. I'm interested, for example, in where you lived before you got here."

"I already told you that I wouldn't—"

She waved away his words. "I was horribly pushy that day, and I'm sorry. I realized that I was trying to force you to do something. Now I'd rather that you see on your own how important it is."

He had to step very carefully. He had to stay with his promise to God not to lie. "I thought your story was about homesteading."

"It is. But my readers will want to understand what brought you out here. Was it wanderlust? A desire for a better life? Greed?" Rose leaned toward him. "Can you help me understand?"

"People homestead for many reasons," he said. "Those are probably the prevalent ones."

"And which was yours?"

She was persistent. Either he'd have to answer her question, or he'd have to divert her attention.

"What is yours?" he asked her.

She stopped and stared at him. "My what?"

"Your motivation for coming out here. Why did you do it? Why did you choose me? What do you want?"

"I don't see what this has to do with—"

"I'm trying to show you that there isn't a simple answer, not for you, not for me."

He stood up and tore his bread into shreds, which he tossed toward the ducks. He had to end this conversation.

"Let's get back to work."

Chapter 8

When you feel this open to God, it is tempting to believe that
all is wonderful, all is good, and all can be believed. It is not so.
As much as we wish otherwise, it simply is not so.

Rose groaned as she climbed the stairs to her room at the Territorial. She had never worked so hard. Every muscle in her body screamed for relief. There was nothing she wanted more than a hot bath and sleep.

How did people do this every day? She'd be lucky if she were able to move at all the next day. Eric, on the other hand, seemed tired but invigorated at the end of the day.

He was quite an enigma, this man of the prairie. He had adeptly deflected her attempts to discover information about his past. If he thought this would deter her, though, he was mistaken.

She'd wanted him to answer at least a bit about his life so she could have directed the conversation toward his life as a physician—and why he'd abandoned such a noble career.

Of course, she didn't have to know all that for her series to succeed. But if she could find out, it would make him come alive on paper.

A young woman bearing hot water came into her room. As she filled the small tub in the room—a real luxury in the Territorial, Rose had found out—the maid chattered away. "This must be worlds away from Chicago. What are the stores like? How full are they wearing their skirts now? We don't have much here, but that doesn't mean I have to look like an urchin, at least that's what I tell my ma."

Rose's mind was so exhausted that the talkative young lady's words made little sense. She opted for nods and murmurs at what she hoped were appropriate times.

"I guess there are fancy restaurants in the big city. Have you ever eaten at one? What are they like? Do you go to the theater?"

Rose stifled a yawn. "I don't—"

"You have the most glamorous job ever. Writing the society column must be lots of fun! How did you get your job at the newspaper? I don't think anybody else here had quite as exciting a job. Well, there was an actress, Laura something, but she didn't stay. And Mr. Johansen, of course, but it's mainly that cloud of suspicion, you know, that makes him so mysterious."

"Suspicion?" Suddenly she was wide awake.

The young woman tested the water with her elbow. "There. That should do it."

"You were talking about Eric Johansen?" Rose prompted.

"I was?"

"You said something about a cloud of suspicion."

"Oh, that." She wiped up a spot of water that had dropped on the floor. "I don't know anything for sure, just that he didn't leave wherever he was without some question about something or the other. Something that wasn't too good, if you get my drift, but I don't know what. That's all. Have a good sleep, Miss Kelly."

And with that, Rose was alone—and wide awake.

✷

Eric looked across the field warily. There was no sign of Big Ole anywhere on the horizon. Maybe Rose wasn't coming out again today.

It had been almost two weeks since she'd come out and worked with him. It stunned him to think of it that way, but that's what she had done—worked with him.

He hadn't seen her since then. He hadn't made it to church thanks to a latch on the ducklings' cage that hadn't hooked properly. Sunday morning he'd spent in a torrential downpour trying to corral them from the places they'd chosen to roost.

His worship service had been private and very personal and heavy with thanks to God for keeping the ducklings safe during their nocturnal explorations.

The weekend's rains had kept him indoors, which was in its own way a blessing. One of the things he hadn't expected in farming was how frequently things broke. Reins snapped, bolts got stripped, and wheels cracked.

He'd taken the time of solitude to fix what he could. He'd hammered and patched and nailed until at last he'd accumulated a satisfying pile of repaired items.

He hadn't been able to mend everything, though. His stove was a cranky old thing, and the time had come to replace it with something more reliable. The oven door didn't seal properly, and he tended not to use it during summer since it made the kitchen—and the rest of the house—unbearably warm.

As the days got hotter, he'd find even less reason to cook or bake, but he told himself, as he combed his hair and checked his shirt for spots and stains, that there was no future in delaying the inevitable. He'd need a new stove come winter. He might as well start shopping for it now. No sense in putting it off.

Plus, an annoying little voice told him he might, just might, run into a certain newspaper-woman with hair the color of the sunset and eyes as green as a poplar leaf.

He pushed the notion from his mind. Rose Kelly was nothing to him—and he was nothing to her. He'd seen her type before: the woman who had her goals in sight and would let nothing—and no one—interfere. But more importantly, he'd seen softness in a woman, a woman who. . .

Eric let the thought trail away unfinished. Some areas of the past were totally unproductive to revisit. This was one.

He shoved his hat onto his head, but when he got outside, he took it off again. The recent rains had left the air humid and heavy. By midafternoon, the sun would have baked all the moisture out. It was looking to be a scorcher.

Quite a crowd had gathered outside the general store when he arrived. "What's going on?" he asked one of the children who was standing on tiptoe, trying to peer through the window.

"It's that singing lady," the boy answered, bobbing back and forth in an effort to see inside.

" 'Singing lady'?"

"That woman from New York City. She's singing tonight at the town hall, remember?" The boy craned his neck farther. "Oh, look! There she is. Wait! Here she comes!"

Charlotta Allen glided through the door of the store like a grand ship sailing into port. Feathers plumed from her green sequined hat perched atop hair that was an unnatural shade of blond, and her purple velvet dress was crusted with thick ivory lace. Red boots peeked out from under her hem.

"Wow," the boy breathed in awe, "I can smell her from here."

Eric tried to disguise his laugh with a cough, but he wasn't successful, and at the last moment as his laughter hung in the air, he saw the horrified face of Rose Kelly over the singer's shoulder.

Suddenly his laughter evaporated, and he tried to cover his embarrassment by ducking his head. Some of the townspeople trailed after the singer as she began her promenade to the town hall, while others returned to their business.

Rose stood a moment, clearly torn as to which way to go. Finally she said to him, "For my article," and caught up with the singer.

He entered the store and choked as the smell of the singer's thick perfume assailed him. Freya Trease raised her eyebrows and nodded toward the street. "I'm thinking of boiling some onions to cover that."

The laughter came back, this time unrestrained.

"It's been a pleasure meeting you." Rose nodded at the singer as she began her vocal warm-ups in the small room at the back of the town hall. Walking as rapidly as she could without running, she fled to the door and practically fell outside, taking in great gulps of fresh air.

Eric was standing off to the side, talking to a cluster of people, and he grinned when he saw her. He spoke briefly to the others and came to join Rose.

"Needed a breath of unperfumed air?" he said.

"Desperately. It wouldn't be so bad, except I don't think she's bathed in weeks. There just isn't enough perfume in the world to cover that—although Miss Allen certainly has tried."

He smiled. "It'll be interesting when all of Jubilee crowds in there. It's going to get a bit close, I suspect."

Rose shuddered. Just a few minutes in the store and then in the town hall's back room with Charlotta Allen had been a few minutes too many. She'd had an idea that an interview with the singer would make an interesting sidelight with her articles, but she was more than ready to abandon that angle.

"I can't," she whispered. "I just can't."

"You know," he said, "it's going to be packed in there. They'll probably have to open the doors to keep it fairly cool. We could sit out here and listen."

"What a wonderful idea! There's even a bench there already."

Rose thought back to what the chambermaid had said, about Eric's leaving under "a cloud of suspicion." She hadn't been able to puzzle it out. What could he have done that was so terrible?

And was she safe—working with him at the farm? Sitting with him tonight? They would be within shouting range of the audience if something happened. At his place, she'd have to be especially careful.

After everyone had gone into the building, they sat on the bench. "Do you think they'll miss us?" Rose asked, quite aware of his presence beside her. In contrast to Charlotta Allen, he smelled wonderfully of soap and sun.

"If they do, they'll be jealous that they didn't think of it."

Jealous because they're not sitting next to Eric.

Someone came and propped open the door. "Sorry there aren't any more seats in here, folks. We're plumb full up."

"That's all right," Eric called back. "We'll enjoy it out here."

"Absolutely," Rose added under her breath.

The first notes of the concert spilled out of the hall into the evening air. Rose recognized the piece: It was an aria from *Carmen*. She had heard it performed several times in Chicago, but never quite like this. The notes wobbled and exploded as Miss Allen sang.

"Is it supposed to sound that way?" Eric asked.

"Not exactly," she hedged, trying to be charitable, but the expression on his face stopped her. It was a mixture of disbelief and surprise. "The truth? Not at all."

"Good."

"Good?" She stared at him. "Why would you say that?"

"I was afraid my ears had gone bad."

"They might if you had to listen to this every night." Rose clapped her hand over her mouth. "That was mean. I'm sorry."

"No problem." Eric leaned back and looked at the sky. "No more rain, I guess."

"That would be a nice relief. I spent the weekend in my room at the hotel, working on the articles and even reading a bit." She didn't tell him all she had done—which included a lot of daydreaming about a certain farmer with the brightest blue eyes she'd ever seen.

She needed to change the subject. "Is Downy all right? I worried about him in the rain," she said.

"Rose, he's a duck. He likes being wet."

"I suppose."

The aria crescendoed to a thundering end, and the diva launched right into another operatic selection. At one time, Charlotta Allen might have been a talented soprano, but her voice was past its prime, her range too limited to perform solo works.

The thought that the woman was traveling through small towns in the Dakota Territory, reliant on heavy perfume for hygiene, saddened Rose.

"Do you have a family in Chicago?" Eric asked.

She sat up straight, glad for the interruption of her dreary thoughts. "What an odd question."

"Why is it odd? You've asked me."

"Yes, but I was interviewing you."

"And now I'm interviewing you."

"Fair enough. Yes, I have a family. My parents are still very much a part of my life—and of me. I think I take after my father. He's big and boisterous and opinionated."

"You're not big." Only when he chuckled did she get what he had said.

"Go away." She punched his arm lightly. "Sometimes I wish I were more like my mother, except I couldn't live in the shadow of my father the way she does. Still, she's as quiet and strong as he is loud and strong. I love them both. What about your parents?"

"Are you asking as Rose Kelly, reporter, or Rose Kelly, friend?"

How could she answer that? Was there any way to pour five years of living for the newspaper into one sentence? One paragraph?

"I've been writing for the *Tattler* for five years now," she said. "It's part of who I am. When I'm Rose Kelly, friend, as you put it, I'm also Rose Kelly, reporter. It's difficult, though, with us, since you're not only Eric Johansen, friend. You're also Eric Johansen, subject."

"So can the four of us find happiness together?" he asked lightly.

"Only if you trust me," she answered. "And only if I can trust you."

He reached across the bench and took her hand. "I don't know, Rose. I just don't know."

Rose's emotions tumbled over each other in a chaotic riot. What was happening? Was he saying he couldn't trust her—or she couldn't trust him?

Praying had always settled her soul. That was one thing that Katie Kelly had taught her daughter. Even her father had told her about the importance of prayer, but he put it in more commonplace terms: "When you need help, Rose, my love, go right to the top."

It was good advice.

Dearest God, she prayed, *help me see what I need to see. Help me be what I need to be. Can I trust him? Can I?*

She knew what she wanted the answer to be and why.

Eric Johansen was holding her hand.

Chapter 9

We do not all see with the same eyes. Nor do we hear with the same ears.
A story told again and again loses its truth as it passes through
the mouths of the tellers and the ears of the hearers.

The audience began to stream out of the town hall.

"It's ended," Eric said, torn between happiness that the booming music had stopped and sadness that his time with Rose was almost over.

People walked by them, nodding as they passed. "Well," he said, "maybe it wasn't as bad as we thought. They're smiling."

After Mrs. Jenkins, Linnea, and Reverend Wilton, who were talking in a cluster as they strolled out of the hall, had greeted them cheerfully, he realized why they had all been so jovial. He still had Rose's hand in his.

There was no graceful way out of it. He stood up so suddenly that he nearly knocked the bench over. Rose righted herself—and the bench—and asked, with a upturned grin, "We're leaving?"

"It's late." He cleared his throat. "I'll walk you back to the hotel."

Among the last stragglers coming out of the concert were some of the women from church, who whispered among themselves before approaching the bench. "So nice to see the two of you together. It's a lovely night for romance," Mrs. Jenkins said as she walked by them.

Romance? He'd put up with the church women's match-making efforts, borne them in silence, but this was too much. He knew he should say something, but he couldn't respond. Something dreadful was happening in his throat.

He didn't dare look at Rose. What must she think of him?

"Well." Rose broke the silence. "That was a little more than I expected."

"I'm sorry—"

"No need to apologize for someone else's words," she said briskly. "I'm sure you've done nothing to encourage that notion. Besides," she added with an impish turn to her lips, "maybe she was referring to herself. Is there a Mr. Jenkins? I don't believe I've ever met him."

"There is. He's a quiet sort, doesn't go out of the house much. He's a real bookish fellow and spends much of his time with his personal library. Mr. Jenkins isn't a regular churchgoer, but once in a while, you'll see him there."

"See? Maybe she was inspired by the music to spend some time with her husband."

"You give that concert too much credit. It wasn't really music, and it wasn't much inspiration."

They continued to discuss the evening's entertainment as they strolled back through the town, carefully avoiding any mention of Mrs. Jenkins's comment. The air was gentle, with no hint of the earlier humidity.

Their fingers brushed as they crossed the street in front of the hotel, tempting him to take her hand in his. Instead of inches separating them, though, there was a chasm. He'd overstepped earlier. It wouldn't happen again.

His hand felt empty, and he clenched it tightly against the ache.

At the door of the Territorial, she shifted her little bag from one hand to the other, as if hesitating. "Thank you."

The words took him by surprise. "Thank you? For what?"

She touched his arm and looked him straight in the eyes with those glorious green eyes. "Thank you for sitting with me."

"It was my pleasure," he began, letting his heart soften. From the glow in her expression, she'd enjoyed the evening as much as he had. Maybe, just maybe, this could work out.

"And thank you for working with me on the articles. If you don't mind, I'd like to shadow you some more later this week."

He felt as if she had slugged him in the stomach. So much for the love of a lifetime. He was her subject. How could he keep forgetting that?

"I'm working in the fields. It won't be very exciting."

"I'm not looking for exciting."

Good. Then we're a perfect match, he thought.

"My next article is almost ready," she said. "I just need some background information about you, what made you come out to Jubilee in the first place, and more importantly, what keeps you here." She opened the hotel door. "And don't think you can weasel out of it, Eric Johansen. I always get my story."

With that, she entered the Territorial's lobby, leaving Eric alone on the street with his thoughts.

The moon was hidden, but the stars shone brightly across the prairie. He hadn't decided which he enjoyed more—a moonlit ride home or a starlit ride home. Either way, God provided light for his journey.

How true that was, he mused while Sir Gray, as his horse was now called, navigated the night road to his home. God had always been there, even when the dark minutes had turned into darker hours. God was his light, constantly staying at his side, guiding him.

The light hadn't dimmed. Oh, there had been times when it seemed to have gone behind a cloud, but all he'd had to do was pray those clouds away.

Now, more than ever, he needed a clear light.

He was terribly confused about Rose. Lately she had said things that made him wonder what she knew. If she knew anything, anything at all, he was done for.

She suspected something. He could hear it in her voice, in the questions that seemed innocuous but were, in fact, quite direct.

Caution. Every day of his life required caution, but that was the price he had to pay.

He'd almost let his guard slip this evening. He couldn't risk that. No, not at all. Yet he'd come so close to letting himself relax. He had enjoyed the evening, but was she just trying to get his confidence?

No matter how doggedly Rose pursued her questioning, no matter how her eyes sparkled like liquid emeralds, he had to be on his toes. If she caught him off guard, all he'd worked for here, all he'd built, would come undone.

The stakes were too high to take any chances—even on love.

A shooting star twinkled its way across the Dakota sky, a moving diamond on velvet. It was a reminder of a promise he had made as he left Boston. He could deal with Rose if he broke his promise, but there were certain things a man just didn't do, and going back on his word to the Lord was one of those things.

There was only way to deal with it all. He had promised God that he would never lie again, and the easiest way to do that was to say as little as possible.

He slumped on the wagon seat. Why was it that the easiest way was actually the hardest way?

✻

It was almost as if he were courting her, Rose thought dreamily as she entered the Territorial. When his hand—

"Rose! Rose Kelly!" Rose heard and smelled Charlotta Allen at the same time. If anything, both her voice and her aroma were more powerful than they'd been earlier in the evening.

"Miss Allen, how nice to see you again. Your concert was quite. . ." Rose struggled for a word that would be truthful and yet not hurtful. "Impressive," she settled on at last. "It was quite impressive."

"Thank you very much. I do so enjoy coming to these small frontier burgs to share my gift." Charlotta lifted her substantial chin proudly. "They are so appreciative," she cooed, "of having any sort of art in their lives."

Rose could only nod in silent agreement. "Any sort of art" was precisely correct as a way to describe the diva's singing.

"I'm about to sit down and refresh my throat with a cup of tea." Charlotta motioned grandly toward a small reception room off the lobby. "Would you like to join me for a late-night restorative?"

"Tea would be nice." It did sound good. She was slowly beginning to adjust to the singer's abundance of perfume.

With a great *swoosh* of lace-embellished velvet, Charlotta Allen led Rose to the reception room where the same young chambermaid was setting the table for them.

"Ma'am," she said, with a little curtsy that encompassed both the singer and Rose. Rose couldn't help noticing the way the maid's bright, mink-colored eyes took in every detail of the singer's clothing and hair. She was sure that within a day the young woman would have shared it all with her friends and family.

After they were seated and served with an elegant silver tea service and blue willow china— which Rose suspected did not appear for most guests—Charlotta swirled her tiny silver spoon in the delicate cup and asked with an air of nonchalance, "Who was that dashing young man you were with, dear Rose?"

"Dashing? Oh, you must mean Eric. He's a homesteader here."

"He's quite handsome."

"I suppose he is," Rose answered warily.

"Are you two"—Charlotta swirled her forefinger in the air—"romantically involved?"

"No!" The word shot out of her.

The singer leaned over the table and patted Rose's hand. "Please don't take offense. I'm just such a snoop!"

All of this was leading somewhere. Rose could tell that the singer had something on her mind. All she had to do was be quiet and let Charlotta speak, and eventually she'd learn what the diva's motives were.

"He looks somewhat familiar. More tea?" Charlotta held up the silver teapot.

"Yes, please." *I'll stay here and drink tea until I'm a sloshing mess if necessary,* Rose thought. *I have to find out why she's talking to me. I think it has something to do with Eric.*

"This is amazingly good tea considering where we are, don't you agree?" Charlotta asked.

"Yes, it is."

"You said his name was Eric?"

"Do you recognize him?" Rose had to restrain herself from screaming. This was going so slowly.

"I think so. Is his last name Jorgeson?"

"No. Johansen."

"Ah." Charlotta nodded. "Yes, that's it. Eric Johansen. From Boston."

"You do know him!"

The singer shrugged. "No, I don't. But I've heard of him. Or read about him." Her painted eyebrows met in a deep frown. "Oh my. I can't quite place where I learned this. Isn't it frustrating when you can't recall something like that?"

"Indeed."

"Ah, it's the price I must pay for traveling around the world with my entourage, bringing sunshine and joy into the drab lives of so many."

Rose bit her lip. Hard.

"But we were talking about Mr. Johansen, weren't we, dear?"

Rose nodded.

The diva leaned over the table, so close that her perfume and various scents mingled in an overpowering miasma. "Yes, I know about this Eric Johansen." She ended her pronouncement with a sharp bob of her head.

"And?"

"Well, I am not the kind of person who goes about gossiping and telling tales, but you are such a nice young woman, so kind and sweet, and I don't want anything to happen to you."

Rose's heart flipped painfully. The chambermaid had been right. Tears pressed against her eyelids, and she forced them back. "What. . .what do you know?"

"He murdered someone."

Chapter 10

Perhaps the hardest thing to do is to trust unequivocally. It is also the most dangerous.

Excuse me?" Rose put her cup down so sharply that it rattled in the saucer. She must have heard the singer wrong.

"Oh, silly me, I am such a goose. Look at this. I've made you spill your tea." Charlotta pulled a lace handkerchief from her bosom and mopped ineffectually at the linen tablecloth where a pale brown stain spread.

Rose swallowed. Her throat was terribly dry. "Did you say. . .did you say that Eric. . ." She looked around to make sure they were alone, then whispered the words. "Murdered someone?"

"Yes, dear." Charlotta continued to dab at the spot.

"Are you sure?"

"No, of course I'm not sure. This was awhile ago, you understand, and I only saw his picture in the paper."

"Then you might be recalling someone else." The chamber-maid had said that Eric left Boston under a shadow, but murder! It didn't seem possible. "Yes, I'm sure you're thinking of another person. A name that might sound similar, perhaps?"

The singer stopped her swabbing. "No, I don't think so. It's not the kind of thing I'd forget."

"Who. . .who did he murder?"

"A woman."

Rose's heart seized. Eric, a murderer? Charlotta had to be mixed up. There was no way Eric had murdered anyone.

"You must be mistaken."

The singer waved to the maid who hovered by the door. From the way she was bent toward them, Rose knew the young woman was desperately trying to overhear them, so she clamped her mouth shut when the maid came over.

"Might we have something to eat with our tea?" Charlotta wheedled. She looked at Rose. "An evening of music does take so much out of one."

Rose bit back the reply that rose entirely too easily and merely nodded.

The maid brought them a plate of cookies, and Charlotta poked through them with a pudgy forefinger. "Raisins. They have raisins in them. I do not like raisins. Ah, well." She sighed and chose one anyway and fastidiously picked out each raisin.

Rose waited with waning patience as the diva dissected each cookie. She seemed to have forgotten the subject entirely.

Finally she could bear it no longer. Making sure the maid was well out of earshot, she brought up the matter again. "You were telling me about Eric. You just told me he is a murdering madman."

"Murdering madman? No, dearest, not at all."

Rose was ready to pound her head on the table with frustration, but she fought for control. "But—"

"Oh, I don't think he could be called a madman." The singer shook her head so vehemently that her earrings swung wildly like erratic pendulums under her improbably colored hair. "He's not a madman." She paused and stared at the teapot. "But wouldn't anyone have to be mad to commit murder?" she asked her reflection.

Rose took a deep breath. Her mother had always told her that a lie brought into the sunshine soon evaporated, and she knew what Katie Kelly would advise at the moment. *Bring out the lies. They'll go away, and you'll be left with the truth.* "What happened? Who did he kill, and why?"

"Aren't you quite the little reporter with your questions." The diva's smile was tinged with a touch of evil. "Well, dear, it was quite the story in Boston." Finished at last with the cookies, Charlotta patted her lips with the napkin and placed it on the table. "Of course, there isn't much to tell. He killed one of his patients."

"Killed a patient?" The room spun dangerously around Rose's head, and she gripped the sides of her chair tightly.

"I don't recall the details at all." Charlotta licked her finger-tip and secured the last wayward crumbs on the tablecloth. "Something about a woman. She was a widow, and I think she even had a child or two."

"Why isn't he under arrest?"

Charlotta shrugged her shoulders. "I think he worked something out with the authorities."

Then, as surprisingly as she'd opened the conversation, the singer ended it. She pushed her chair away from the table and stood up. "We travel early tomorrow, so I must bid you good night." She waved her plump hand dismissively and left in a grand flourish.

"Good night," Rose said to the diva's departing back. "Thank you for the tea."

The little maid reappeared and began to clear the table. "I don't think she heard you," she said to Rose.

"No," Rose said, watching as the end of Charlotta's dress vanished up the stairs. She couldn't help but notice that the hem was quite ragged. "No, I don't suppose she did."

She retreated to her room, leaving the young woman to finish cleaning up the remnants of their tea.

As she prepared for bed, she kept turning over in her mind what Charlotta Allen had said. Murder? Could Eric really be guilty of murder?

It didn't seem possible, although certainly she knew that not all murderers were as grotesque on the outside as they were on the inside. Many of them were dangerously charming and used it to their advantage.

Eric didn't seem to fall into either of those categories. Murderer? No, not at all.

But she couldn't dismiss the story out of hand. Some part of it was true; she just didn't know which part. Rose picked up her Bible and found the passage that the minister had used that Sunday. One verse was particularly appropriate: *"The words of a talebearer are as wounds, and they go down into the innermost parts of the belly."*

People's natural predisposition to share their lives through stories had a terrible tendency to lead them into sharing too much. That was, she knew, just a nice way to say that they gossiped.

Rose had covered enough news stories and interviewed enough people to recognize why the singer had felt compelled to tell her the story, even an incomplete one. She'd seen it often— it was the newspaper form of gossip.

George, the editor of the *Tattler*, had his own explanation. He'd shared it with her one night when she'd come back to the paper's offices upset with a source, an elderly man who knew some background information in bits and pieces about a story she'd been pursuing. After four hours of talking to him, she couldn't tell where truth ended and rumor began.

The editor had leaned back in his wooden chair—even in Rose's memory, it creaked—and slowly placed his feet on his cluttered desk and tucked his hands behind his head. *"It's the way some people connect with others,"* he'd said. *"Usually it's the folks who can't make their own relationships work. You know the kind. They don't have friends. Once in a while they have a cat or a dog or even a canary, but that's about as close as they get."*

He'd continued his sensible explanation. Just knowing someone who knew someone made them part of the story in their minds. People's curiosity came partially from caring and partially from nosiness. Either way, he'd pointed out, it was what kept newspapers going.

She sighed. This wasn't good. It was beginning to look like the very trait that made her a success was going to be the thing that brought her world tumbling down around her shoulders.

Rose rubbed her fingers over the gilt letters on her Bible. She was going to need help. Wagonloads of it.

The next morning dawned bright and sunny, and Rose winced as she looked out the window. She hadn't slept at all, and her eyes felt gritty. Throughout the dark hours, she'd gone back and forth in her thoughts, turning her options over and over.

She'd come to an uneasy decision.

Rose picked up her little bag and headed out of the hotel, wincing as the dazzling sun sliced into her reddened eyes. She walked resolutely down the street and turned in at the telegraph office.

Just inside the door, a woman who couldn't have been older than her late teens balanced a child on her hip while listening to a middle-aged woman extol the virtues of her new rug.

"Miss Kelly!" The young mother switched the baby to her other hip. From the relieved expression on her face, Rose suspected the woman was grateful for the break in the conversation.

Rose cooed over the round-faced baby, who gurgled happily in response.

The freckle-faced clerk at the counter was deep in conversation with two older men about the likelihood of a bumper crop. "Excuse me a moment," he said to his companions when he noticed Rose waiting.

The men nodded and stepped aside.

"I'd like to send a telegraph, please," Rose said, laying her tiny purse in front of her. She unlatched it and withdrew a folded sheet of paper. "Send this message to Evelyn Roller at the *Chicago Tattler*."

The clerk opened the sheet of paper and scanned it. "Sorry, Miss Kelly, but I can't quite make this word out. What is this?" His stubby finger pointed to a word.

Rose laughed. "That word is 'researcher.' Evelyn Roller is our researcher at the newspaper. My teachers plagued me endlessly about my dreadful handwriting when I was in school. Can you make out the rest of it?"

The young man squinted at the paper. "Well, to be honest. . ."

Grinning, she took it from him and read it aloud. "To Evelyn Roller, Researcher, *Chicago Tattler*, Chicago, Illinois. Please see what you can find out about Dr. Eric Johansen, formerly of Boston. Charged with murder? When? Who? Thank you, Rose."

A heavy silence fell over the room, and Rose realized with horror what she had just done. The clerk's face was so bloodless that his freckles stood out like splatters of ink. The men stood frozen in place, their hands stopped midmotion.

The baby broke the silence with a wail, and the two women swept out of the building.

"Oh, I'm sorry." Rose's voice cracked. The words were terribly insufficient. "I'm so sorry. I'm sorry."

As she fled the building, she caught a glimpse of Linnea, her hand pressed over her mouth.

She had done some awful things, but nothing as unspeakable as this. She had ruined Eric's life.

Eric scattered grain and watched the ducks race after it. They'd lost their downy fuzz and were now nearly full grown.

What was he going to do with these crazy creatures? He rocked back on his heels and pondered the situation.

How had he gotten saddled with a group of ducks that were supposed to be his self-propagating food supply and that had, instead, turned into very demanding pets? A black-winged insect made the mistake of investigating the strewn grain, and Downy gulped it down.

Maybe he could sell the ducks. Then they'd be off his hands, and the moral quandary about food and pets would be gone.

He snorted. Moral quandaries didn't go away like that. He knew that from experience. He also knew he couldn't run from them. No matter how much he thought he'd taken care of the past, it was forever with him, and now it was finding the most disturbing road back into his life.

Once he would have thought that the world was made up of that which was clearly good and that which was clearly evil, but lately the line between the two was blurring. He'd crossed it once himself and found himself forever stained.

The sound of hooves ended his reflection, and he stood up, groaning a bit as his muscles tried to uncramp. He was getting old.

Big Ole led the wagon right into his farmyard. Rose wasn't even holding on to the reins, he noticed. "You thinking that this horse doesn't need direction?" he asked as he unhitched Big Ole.

Rose patted the huge horse's side. "As if I could tell him anything. It wouldn't matter where I wanted to go. Big Ole decides, and that's where we head off to. For some reason, he seems to think I should be here."

His breath caught in his throat, but then reason took over. Of course she was here. She was observing him for her stories.

She leaned down and scooped up Downy, who promptly nipped her nose. "What are we doing today?" she asked Eric as she rubbed her nose ruefully. "That fellow has quite a bite."

"He just ate a bug."

"Oh, good. Are you comparing my nose to an insect?" Her hands shook a bit as she put the duck back on the ground.

"Are you all right? Did Downy hurt you?"

She stared at Downy as he waddled away in apparent indignation. "I think I offended him by holding him."

"He's the king of the duck yard," Eric answered. "I think he'll recover."

"Will he?" Her voice sounded different, almost as if she were unsure.

"Rose, he's just a duck."

Rose turned to him. Her mossy green eyes pooled with tears. "Eric," she said, "I've done the most hideous thing ever. I don't know what to do."

Eric did the most natural thing he knew. He wrapped his arms around her and held her against him, let her cry out her pain against his shoulder in great gulping sobs until his work shirt was wet with her tears.

His cheek against her hair, he murmured wordless comforts.

"I'm so sorry," she said, her voice muffled against his chest. "I'm so sorry."

"Shhh, shhh. It's going to be fine."

"No, it isn't."

"Shhh." His head turned a bit, and he found himself lightly kissing her sunset-colored hair. He knew it then. He loved her. He would do anything for her. He couldn't stand this anguish she was feeling.

"Shhh, Rose. Shhh, my love."

She pulled back and looked him squarely in the face. "Eric, you can't love me."

"But I do." The freedom the words gave him was astonishing. "I love you, Rose. I love you."

She wrenched free of his grasp. "This is what I have done. I said that you were a murderer—well, I didn't say that exactly, but I said enough so that now everyone will think you're guilty, and to make it worse, I said it at the telegraph office, and now—now, oh, I don't know what will happen now, but you have every right to hate me." The tears began again. "You have every right to hate me as much as I hate myself."

His mouth moved, trying to form words, but none came out.

"Say something," she whispered. "Say something. Don't make me leave in silence."

He turned and walked into the house, his heart shattered on the ground.

413

Chapter 11

In silence we can hear the most clearly.
We must, however, prepare ourselves for what we might hear.

The solitude of the prairie suited Rose's mood. More than anything, she needed to be alone. She dropped the reins and let Big Ole ramble as suited him. Eventually the horse would take her back to Jubilee.

Guilt washed over her like a blood-warm wave. She'd done some imprudent things before, but this was more than that.

She put her face in her hands as if she could blot out her actions. Why, why, why hadn't she thought before she read the telegram aloud?

Or more to the point, why hadn't she just asked Eric?

True, he hadn't been at all open to her inquiries about his past, even the mildest of her questions. And what would he have said to her if she *had* asked him? *"Yes, Rose, I killed someone. Would you like some tea?"*

Still, she should have asked him, shared the story she'd been told, given him the chance.

Perhaps she could blame it on Jubilee. In Chicago, it wouldn't have mattered. There if she'd heard a story like this, she simply would have gone back to the *Tattler* offices, done a bit of research, and had her answer. But here, having to rely on the telegraph for research—

She shook her head. She couldn't justify that train of thought. The problem wasn't the telegraph. It was her rashness.

What had been her strength was now her weakness. She'd turned her impulsive words and her inquisitive nature into her trademark style, a style that had never affected anyone else. But now the consequences were dreadful.

Big Ole slowed at a fork in road, as if asking her which way to take.

"Don't ask me," she said to him. "I seem to have developed a talent for doing exactly the wrong thing."

The horse snorted as if in response and plodded on.

A meadowlark's melody poured across the prairie, a liquid song that held the promise of another summer. Even as the notes caressed Rose's ears, the sound of the grass in the endless Dakota wind was dryer, crisper than it had been when she first arrived.

Autumn was on its way. Her time in Jubilee was more than half over. By Christmas, she'd be back in Chicago, happily making the rounds of holiday parties and not worrying a bit about a man whose life she had destroyed.

A man who'd said he loved her.

The cruel irony struck her. He had held her close, told her he loved her. Those first tender moments of spoken love had been destroyed by her confession.

The wind picked up, and Rose pulled her shawl closer around her shoulders. There was definitely a touch of the season's end in the tendrils that crept in under the edges of the soft wool.

Winter—and then she'd leave. The thought clawed at her. How could she leave Jubilee, leave Eric?

But how could she stay?

Her fingertips toyed with the strap of her tiny purse. She felt so alone, so small on this vast land.

The words she spoke when she first went into Redeemer Church came back to her. She'd told Eric, "God hasn't forgotten me. Why would I forget Him?"

She wasn't alone. Not at all.

Rose knew what she had to do. There on the road between fields and grass, she bowed her head and prayed. *I'm not even sure what to ask for. You know what I need—and what others need. I've caused so much sorrow and suffering. I wish I hadn't done it, and I don't ever want to do it again. Please help me.*

She lifted her head and opened her eyes. Somewhere on the land that stretched into tomorrow was the man she had hurt. The man she loved.

Even the prairie didn't have enough room to hide that fact from her.

A tear dropped onto her purse, blotting a single petal of the embroidered flower with a dark, wet blemish. Maybe she should go back to Chicago and try to forget all that had happened here. She straightened in the wagon, and Big Ole whinnied questioningly at the sudden movement.

That was it. She would return to Chicago and forget about the man with the Dakota sky in his eyes.

Or she could flap her arms and fly to the moon.

Eric sat in front of his house, watching the sunset. He hadn't gone into Jubilee in almost six weeks, not since Rose had made her grand pronouncement in the telegraph office and ruined his life.

September was a gentle month. The days were shorter, and it was time to start thinking about bringing in the potatoes. The wheat was done, harvested when the August sun had baked it to a golden perfection.

Or maybe he'd be best to leave the crop in the ground and simply take his leave. He'd run before. He could do it again.

He could come up with a story to cover his tracks. Not lying, exactly. He could take bits and pieces of the truth and rearrange them into something that would satisfy the wagging tongues and silence the terrible stories.

There was, of course, that pesky problem with his vow to tell the truth. No, he wouldn't lie, no matter what fancy name he put on it.

He could hear a horse coming toward his house, and he stood up, his heart filled with ridiculous hope. Maybe it was Rose come to tell him it was all a mistake, that she loved him and they could—

It was Reverend Wilton. He alighted from his horse with studied caution. "Evening."

"Evening." Eric went out to greet his visitor. This wasn't the first time the minister had come to visit him, and it probably wouldn't be the last. He knew what was on the man's mind.

The minister strolled over to the duck cage. "These fellows have grown mighty big."

"Sure have."

"I believe they're larger than Arvid's. What are you feeding them?"

"I feed them grain, but they get a good share of insects, too."

"Ah. That might be it." The minister continued to study the ducks.

Had simple conversation ever been so. . .not simple? Each exchange seemed to be pulled from the depths of the speakers.

"That one by the corner there, he's fine looking." He was pointing at Downy. "Are you by any chance thinking of selling him?"

"No." As soon as he said it, Eric recognized the folly of it. Of course he should sell Downy. In his mind, that was Rose's duck, and Rose had effectively ended whatever relationship they might have had.

"Are you sure?"

This was his chance, but he said, "The duck's not for sale." Reverend Wilton would think he'd gone around the bend for sure if he'd explained: *Well, you see, I can't have the woman I love, so I'll keep her duck instead.* And maybe he had.

The minister nodded. "To tell the truth, Johansen, I'm not here about the ducks. We haven't seen you in church for quite a while, and I guess we both know why."

Eric swallowed hard. He met Reverend Wilton's gaze squarely. "Yes, sir, we do."

Neither man spoke for a while. Then the minister asked, "Do you want to say anything?"

Eric shoved his hands deep into his pockets as he tried to corral his thoughts. "No."

After another pause, Reverend Wilton said, "Johansen, that's not good enough. I'm sorry, but it's not." He leaned down and pulled a stalk of grass from the ground and bit off the end of it. "I can't think that's the truth, your taking someone's life, but I can't defend you if you won't defend yourself."

Eric's heart pounded, but he spoke slowly and quietly, hoping to deflect more questions. "I haven't asked you to defend me."

Reverend Wilton chewed on the grass stalk a moment, staring out across the fields. At last he spoke. "Murder is a serious charge. I don't care if you were a teacher or a policeman or a pickpocket before you came out here. None of us do. Just as long as you play fair and treat people square. That's the way we live. For all of us, this is our second chance at life, at getting it right."

Eric didn't trust himself to speak. The words probably wouldn't make it past that lump in his throat.

"We've been friends for a long time. I know that you've been fleeing from something in your past, something that's been pulling on your soul so hard that you can't shake it, and I've never asked what it is. My job isn't prying. My job is letting people know that when the burden is too big, they don't have to bear it alone. You know that, don't you?"

Eric nodded.

Reverend Wilton sighed. "I can't feature you as a murdering man, Johansen," the minister continued. "But the townspeople are asking questions, and I think they deserve some answers."

He was right, and Eric knew it. But the bonds of his sworn silence kept him from sharing his past. He lowered his head.

The reverend put his hand on Eric's shoulder. "The people of Jubilee have respected you since you arrived. You're a hardworking man, a Christian man by all accounts, and we're feeling blindsided by this news. All you have to do is explain it to me—even a brief accounting would do—and I can go back to town and reassure the folks that you're exactly what they've always thought. That would clear your name."

Still, Eric stood mute, trapped in his promise.

"I don't have to tell them the story. All they need to know is that everything is all right. That's all."

"There's nothing to tell," Eric muttered, realizing that everything he'd built here in Jubilee was tumbling down around his head like a castle of sand.

Reverend Wilton's lips tightened into a straight line. "Again, Johansen, I can't help you if you won't let me." He got back on his horse, and as he picked up the reins, he turned to Eric. "Even God can't help you if you don't ask Him."

Eric stood motionless as the minister rode away. If only he knew how many times Eric had prayed, how many times he'd fallen to his knees. . . .

And it wasn't that God hadn't answered. No, He had. Loud and clear, God had answered.

❋

Rose stood in the small kitchen of the church. Clouds of steam billowed around as four large pots of potatoes boiled on the stove in preparation for another lefse-making session. The harvest potluck was the next morning

Harvest! Had time ever flown so quickly? Already the first flakes of snow had started. Soon she'd be leaving Jubilee. . .and Eric.

It had been more than two months since she'd exploded his life to smithereens. She hadn't seen him at all. She hadn't dared go out to his farm—she couldn't face him, couldn't stand to see him turn from her as he surely would.

He hadn't been to church, but she'd heard through the Jubilee grapevine that he met with the minister privately.

An unseen hand clutched at her heart as the enormity of what she'd done struck her again.

"Stirring works a bit better if you move the spoon around," Mrs. Jenkins said at her shoulder, and Rose came back to reality with a thump.

"Sorry. I was lost in thought." Rose vigorously swirled the large wooden spoon in each of the pots.

Mrs. Jenkins bobbed her head in response and moved on to supervise a small cluster of women who were examining something very closely.

She'd made an uneasy peace with the people of the church. She'd explained over and over what had happened, how she was simply trying to get to the bottom of a nasty rumor, and after a while, she was accepted back into the fold—tentatively.

If she could disappear inside this billow of steam, she would. As it was, the privacy it afforded her was welcome. The townspeople were pleasant enough toward her, but underlying everything they said or did was a sense of distrust. Even Linnea, who was among the group in the corner, had pulled back from their friendship.

"I made these last night," the schoolteacher told the others. "I found the directions in *Ladies' Home Companion*."

"What are these things?" Mrs. Jenkins asked the women. Rose eavesdropped shamelessly. It was better than returning to her thoughts.

"Napkin rings." Linnea had been carrying a box when she'd come into the church, but she hadn't told Rose what was in it. The box must have held the napkin rings.

A bustle at the door told her someone had arrived.

"Since when does a napkin wear jewelry?" The booming voice belonged to the minister, and Rose turned to watch him, obscured by the steam's pluming fog.

The women greeted Reverend Wilton, who picked up one of the napkin rings and held it in front of his face. "What does this thing do?" he asked.

Linnea took it from him. "I'll show you." She rolled a dish towel and inserted it inside the ring. "You stick the napkin inside the ring, like this." She held out her handiwork.

"Can you tell me why? Oh, I understand. We need to imprison the napkins so they don't escape."

Even without seeing his face, Rose heard the laughter in his voice. But there was something else, an undercurrent of happiness that ran between Linnea and Reverend Wilton.

The answer hit her full force. Linnea and the minister were in love!

How had she missed it? Had Linnea said anything? Or had Rose been too self-absorbed to hear?

She flushed as she remembered when they met for the first time and Linnea mentioned someone in her life. Rose had dropped the subject to begin questioning the teacher about Eric.

There was another disturbance at the door, a scuffle of boots across the wooden floor, and then the minister's voice rang out. "Eric Johansen, don't try to sneak past. I understand these ladies are making your favorite food, and I can't believe you'd walk away from fresh lefse."

Rose quelled a sudden urge to duck under the table. She couldn't see Eric, not now, not in front of everyone.

Quickly she surveyed her options and realized there was only one. She was going to have to stand where she was and make it through the meeting no matter how awful it was going to be.

One lock of copper-colored hair had escaped its bun in the heat of the kitchen, and she tucked it back into place as best she could. Then, with a quick wipe of her palms on her capacious apron, she pasted a smile on her face and stepped away from the steaming potatoes.

"Hello, Eric."

Chapter 12

The air is filled with many things. Insects. Snowflakes.
Words that never should have been spoken. Despite the openness of the prairie,
the air can be just as thick here as it is in the most crowded city.

It wasn't possible for time to stop, to hang suspended in the atmosphere like a thick fog, but that was how it seemed.

Rose's hands clenched into fists, loosened, clenched again. Her cheeks cramped from her artificial smile, and inside, her heart boomeranged around like something gone wild.

Say something, she bid him silently. *Don't turn around and walk away. Please don't do that.*

Eric's gaze was stony. "Hello, Rose."

"How are you doing?" The basics of conversation were the most she could manage.

He didn't answer immediately, as if he were weighing what to say. At last he simply nodded. "Fine."

"And Downy?" She must be out of her mind, worrying about the duck at a time like this.

"He's grown up."

She was suddenly aware that everyone was staring at them, their eyes switching from speaker to speaker as if they were watching a play.

"Well," she said, turning back to the potatoes and stirring them with unnecessary force. "Well."

Behind her, the discussion picked up again.

"I've never known Eric Johansen to pass up lefse fresh off the takke." The voice belonged to Mrs. Jenkins.

"I'm not staying," he answered. "I came in to fix that floorboard again, but I've got to get back to the farm."

"Take some with you. Here, take this package."

Rose turned and saw Mrs. Jenkins press something into Eric's hands. He took it, thanked her, and left as quickly as he'd come.

She handed the spoon to another woman. "The potatoes are almost done. I need a breath of cool air. Do you mind taking over for a while?"

Without waiting for an answer, she rushed from the kitchen into the yard outside the church. The snow had turned to rain, and the wind whipped the heavy droplets against her face. She didn't have a coat on, but the rain-drenched air felt refreshing after the heat of the kitchen.

Eric had unhitched his horse and had one foot in the stirrup.

"Wait!" she called to him. "I want to. . ."

What did she want? She had no idea, just a vague knowledge that he couldn't leave like this with so much unspoken, so much at stake.

He stopped and turned to face her. When she reached his side, he said, "I really don't have anything to say to you."

"Maybe not, but I have things to say to you."

"You've already said enough."

His words struck through her like a lance, and she sagged.

"Eric, I know. I wish I could take it back."

"Well," he said, finishing his mount and grasping the reins, "you can't."

She put her hand on the horse's halter. "Eric, I'm sorry."

"Maybe."

Forgive me, she begged him with her eyes. He studied her face, and for a moment she thought he might soften. But instead he said, so softly that she had to strain to hear him, "I'm done here."

"Done? What do you mean?"

He turned away from her and spoke into the rain. "I'm leaving Jubilee."

She watched him ride away through the rain, his collar turned up against the chill wind, until he was only a speck on the horizon.

How could this have happened? How could she have fallen in love with a murderer?

And now he was leaving her.

Her tears mingled with the raindrops as she stood in front of the church, trying to keep herself together as her world crashed around her.

"Rose?" Linnea spoke behind her. "Rose—"

Rose turned into the outstretched arms of the school-teacher. "I'm sorry, Linnea. I'm so sorry. I made such a mess of everything. It's cost me everything. Eric is leaving, and I don't—" She closed her eyes against the wave of pain. "I don't even have your friendship."

"That's where you're wrong, Rose," Linnea said. "True friendship can survive the greatest storms, and we've been through a wild one. You're my friend, and you always will be."

In the corner of Rose's heart, a little flame of hope flickered.

Eric threw logs into the fireplace to take the chill out of the room. Winter was coming early this year; he could feel it.

At last the kindling caught and began to burn the bark on the underside of the log. Soon enough the log would catch fire, and the small house would be quite warm.

He poked the logs, making sure they were stacked correctly; then he pulled his chair closer. Through the window he could see Downy leading a parade of the other ducks through the downpour, pausing occasionally to nab a surfacing earthworm.

He was going to have to find a home for the ducks. They were too domesticated to leave them here to fend for themselves. Maybe he'd take Reverend Wilton up on his offer to take Downy and the rest of the ducks, too.

Leaving wasn't going to be easy. He'd put down roots here. He'd built this house, farmed this land, made friends.

He picked up his worn Bible and held it in both hands. The words in it had taken him through times of deep despair. He ran his hand over the plain black cover. It was split along the spine, and he thought idly that he should try to repair it.

His first visitor in his new home had been the minister, and Eric would always remember what he'd said. "A good man has a tattered Bible." Well, his Bible was almost in shreds, but somehow Eric didn't feel overly good.

None of this was fair. He didn't deserve what was happening to him. He was caught in the middle of so many webs, all of them based on one horrible day six years ago. He'd done what he'd had to do, and for the rest of his life, his actions would follow him around like an unshakable weight.

He'd never escape his past. All he could ever hope to do was stay one step ahead of it.

He bowed his head and prayed intently. *Dearest Lord, I don't understand why my life will always be ruled by what happened in Boston. I did what I thought I needed to do—You know that—and today, I still think what I did was necessary. But now, here I am, the unforgivable, unable to forgive someone else.*

A log snapped in the fireplace, and he opened his eyes. That was it, after all. He couldn't forgive Rose, and in fact, he didn't know if he should.

He stood and walked around his house. His heart was here on this farm, yet he had to leave. By the end of the week, he would be gone. He had no idea where he was going, just that the time had come again for him to outrun his past.

✳

"No!" Rose stared at Linnea. "You're wrong. No!"

Linnea clasped her friend's hands. "I heard it from the postmaster earlier this morning. He bought Eric's plow. The Fredericksons bought his furniture. Last I heard, he was working out a deal with Mark—Reverend Wilton—about the ducks."

Rose shook her head vehemently.

Worry creased Linnea's forehead. "Rose, you knew that."

"I didn't think he'd leave Jubilee. Not really. And not this soon. I really thought he'd stay and it would all work out when I left to go back to Chicago." She bit her lip. "Oh, none of that's true. That's what I hoped would happen, but of course that's not going to."

"It's more complicated than that. Murder isn't something you just sweep under the rug."

"He can't go." Rose began an uneasy pacing across her hotel room. "He has to stay here."

"Because you're here? Rose, isn't that a bit unfair?"

"There's nothing about this that's fair." Rose sighed. "My mother used to say, 'Least said, soonest mended,' and I'd roll my eyes at her. What did Katie Kelly know, anyway? I make my living saying things. I talk and I write. What did I care about mending anything? Now I know. Do I ever!"

She strode to the window and looked out. "Did he say where he was going?"

"No."

The prairie stretched ahead of her, its land now carved by the harvest, ready to sleep through the winter. In a few weeks she'd be back in Chicago, in her comfortable apartment with fancy restaurants, wonderful shows, extraordinary parties, and a skyline cluttered with buildings.

She could put this behind her, forget the man who had taken her heart, and start again. People did it all the time. That's what the folks in Jubilee had done, after all. They'd left their pasts and begun their lives anew.

Until she'd come into their midst.

Rose strode to the wardrobe and pulled out her coat and hat.

"Where are you going?" Linnea asked.

"To see Eric. I have to do something right while I'm here, and I think this is it."

The schoolteacher tugged at Rose's sleeve. "Rose, I'm not sure about this. It's too cold today. Didn't you feel the bite in the wind? It's not like summer when you could go off—"

Rose spun around and faced her friend. "I'll be fine. You worry too much. But this is something I have to do."

Eric stood in his house. It looked cold and almost sad without the pictures on the wall and the books on the shelves. He'd left his chair and his Bible by the fireplace. Most of the other furniture had been sold or given away.

As soon as the minister came and got the ducks, he could toss the chair in the back of the wagon, put his Bible at his side, and leave.

The sound of a horse and wagon in his yard ended his musings. Reverend Wilton must have come for the ducks.

He threw open the door and stopped. It was Rose. She was trying to do something with Big Ole's harness, and he came to her rescue.

"What are you doing here?" he asked as he fixed the leather straps. He knew he sounded ungracious, but he wanted to. Being impolite was, he told himself, a small exchange for her ruining his life.

Rose didn't speak but went on into his house. He followed her.

"Can I ask what you're doing in my house?"

"It's true, then." She stood in the middle of the nearly empty room. "No books." She touched the empty shelves. "No painting of the battle of Jericho. You're leaving."

"Yes, I am."

"It's what you want to do?"

"I'm not sure I have any choice."

"You do. Of course you do."

"What choice would you have me make, Rose Kelly?"

"You can stay."

"And you can go. Is that it? I stay here, and you go. It works out quite well."

Rose frowned at him. "That's not nice."

"Not nice? Not nice?" He was overcome with the urge to laugh. "Who are you to say that I'm not nice?"

"I told you I'm sorry."

He leaned against the wall and studied the fire that was burning low in the hearth. "Well, that ought to do it, then. You ruin my life, say you're sorry, and we're off to have tea with the Queen? Is it that simple?"

"Might I point out that you ruined your own life?" Rose snapped back at him. "I'm not the one who makes the news. I just report it."

He didn't trust himself to speak for a moment.

His heart had turned to stone, and it hung like a heavy weight in his chest. So this was what love did to people.

He'd never been this close to sharing the story with anyone. Maybe she'd understand, but more likely she'd put it in her newspaper. He couldn't trust her, not with his heart, not with his life.

Instead, he straightened up. "Go. Just go."

She glared at him through narrowed eyes. "You had the chance to be loved, Eric. I'm not sure you've ever known what that means."

"I know what love is."

"Do you know what it means to love someone?"

"Yes."

"And do you know what it means to be loved?"

His answer didn't come so readily. "What I've known of love has nothing to recommend it," he answered at last. "It doesn't seem to be a productive emotion."

"I thought I loved you," she said, "but I never should have let myself do that. You can't escape yourself, and until you do, you will never be able to love."

"Go. Leave. Get out of my house." Anger shook his voice. "Good-bye."

Chapter 13

This is the land of second chances. If we are offered the opportunity to start anew, we must ask ourselves: Will we do it differently? And will we do it better?

Hurt washed over Rose in a hot wave. Tears sprang to her eyes, but she turned away quickly. He was not going to see her cry.

She lifted her chin and walked to the door, her back straight and proud. Silence forged a hardened gap between them that words refused to bridge. The only sound was the whistle of the wind as it blew across the prairie, carrying tiny hard flakes of snow that burned into her cheeks as she prepared the wagon and left the homestead. . .forever.

If he watched her leave, she didn't know it. Pride kept her facing forward, and she got again on the road to Jubilee.

She fought back the tears. This was a love that was destined for failure from the very beginning. She'd been deluding herself to expect that anything could come of it.

Especially, her conscience reminded her, *when you ruined his life.*

The winds increased, and she pulled her scarf farther over her face to protect it from the stinging flakes. The snow became heavier, and she peered from the cave of her scarf, watching the prairie become a swirl of white.

She'd come to Jubilee expecting to make her mark in the newspaper world with these articles, so different from her society-page items. She'd never foreseen that what would happen would be that she'd find the love of her life and then destroy him.

Nor had it ever crossed her mind that she'd lose her heart to man who was a murderer. Or was he?

She still hadn't heard from Evelyn Roller, her research assistant. There was the chance, after all, that Charlotta Allen had gotten the story garbled. She seized on the idea and held it close to her heart.

If that were the situation, it would solve everything. She would announce that she'd been mistaken, she'd gotten wrong information, and it wasn't actually this Eric Johansen who'd killed someone, and within minutes the entire populace of Jubilee would know. In this prairie town, news spread like wildfire through dry grass.

She'd be forgiven, Eric would be forgiven, and she could stay in Jubilee.

Stay in Jubilee. She smiled. It was exactly what she wanted to do. She wanted to stay in Jubilee with Eric—if he would have her.

Maybe an answer had come while she was gone. Suddenly she needed to get back to the telegraph office to see if Evelyn had discovered anything yet.

Big Ole plodded along more slowly as the snow covered the ground. She flapped the reins at him and shouted over the wind, "Let's go!"

The huge horse came to a complete stop, dropping his head against the wind-driven snow. Rose snapped the reins again, and then she saw the problem. Big Ole's harness had come apart.

She got out of the wagon and waded through the rapidly accumulating snow. She took off her gloves and held them in her teeth as she tried to reconnect the metal grommets and the leather straps.

"If I could see what I was doing," she said to Big Ole, who stood patiently, his ears twisted back as he listened to what was going on behind him, "I might be able to do something." But as fast as she could work, the airborne snowflakes landed faster on her eyelashes and her hands and the gear.

She leaned against Big Ole's warm side. "I can't fix it well enough to get us back to Jubilee. We're closer to Eric's house." She led the horse in a U so that they were heading back toward the farm.

For a while she walked with him, guiding him with his bridle until she realized that he'd probably be better off without her assistance.

"Big Ole, I don't know if horses pray, but people do."

She buried her face against his flank. *My life has become one long series of trials, God, and here I am, in trouble again. I shouldn't have gone to Eric's house, and then I shouldn't have left it. Guide us home.* Big Ole neighed softly. *Both of us. If not for me, for Big Ole. He shouldn't have to suffer just because I'm a ninny.*

Rose climbed back into the wagon and dusted the snow off the seat as best she could. "Take me to Eric," she called to the horse. "Take me to the farm."

Big Ole tossed his head and began his slow, ponderous walk, taking them, she hoped, to safety.

✾

Eric paced in front of his fireplace. Rose's words spun around him like bees. She loved him! She'd said she loved him!

He'd been so wrapped up in his own anger that he hadn't let her words penetrate. She loved him!

Stunned by this revelation, he sank into the lone chair in his living room. If she loved him, and he loved her, then maybe, just maybe, their problems could be resolved.

Oh, who was he kidding? He'd just told her to leave.

He'd stood at the window and watched her ride off. She hadn't looked back at all. Once, a patient had told him to turn his face to the future, not to look over his shoulder all the time at the past.

That patient had been the one who had changed his life in so many ways. She was so intricately enlaced in his life that every moment she was there. At night, her pale face, drawn with illness, haunted his dreams. During the day, she trailed his footsteps, asking if he regretted what he had done.

He pushed the memory away. She'd been right. What was in the past were only shadows. He needed to turn his eyes toward the future.

Rose had said she loved him. Then she would understand. He would tell her the truth, tell her what had happened in Boston.

One of the first Bible verses he'd ever memorized as a child came back to him: *"And ye shall know the truth and the truth shall make you free."* He smiled. That was the way he'd learned it, without punctuation or pause, all done in one breath.

He'd tell her—if he got the chance. Somehow they'd work this out.

It was as if a load had been lifted from his shoulders. What was it he'd heard many times? A weight shared was a weight lifted?

If—and he realized how tentative the word was—she agreed to talk to him again, he could stay here in Jubilee. This was where his heart was, not on the road trying to escape the past.

The resurgence of hope was a wonderful thing, he thought wryly as he looked at his nearly empty house, but it often had terrible timing. Well, he mused, perhaps he could get back his furniture and his plow. Knowing the postmaster and Arvid, they'd be willing to return his belongings.

The ducks were still here, including Downy, who'd taken over the farmyard completely. He smiled. A duck, a silly duck, had taken a place in his heart right next to the woman who had named it, and he'd had a harder time making arrangements to part with the ducks than with the household belongings he'd had for years.

The room was growing colder, and when he reached for the poker to stir the logs in the fireplace, the house shook as a fierce gust of wind caught it in its grasp.

In three steps, he crossed to the window. This storm had come out of nowhere, and it was intense. He couldn't see his own wagon in front of his house. The world was white, all white, no matter where he looked.

This wasn't the first blizzard he'd experienced since moving to the Dakota Territory—but it was Rose's first. With horror, he realized she couldn't possibly have made it to Jubilee before the storm struck.

Stupid, stupid! He should have been paying more attention to the weather. He'd lived here long enough to know the signs—a white sky that hung low, the first flakes of snow, and a rising wind. But he'd been too caught up in his own anger to see what was happening around him.

He tried to figure where she'd be right about now. Midway between his house and Jubilee. At the point of no return.

He reached for his coat but stopped. The storm was so fierce that he'd be lost in it, too, if he went out.

The best thing to do with a blizzard was to stay inside. He'd seen enough cases of frostbite to know all too well what exposure would do. If a man was lucky, he lost feeling in his cheeks. If he weren't so lucky, he'd lose his life.

Like all homesteaders out here, he'd quickly learned to anchor a rope to his house near his front door. The rope, the length of the distance from his house to his barn, would be his lifeline in an extended storm. When he'd first arrived, he'd been plied with stories of men who didn't have the rope, or who had but neglected to tie it around their waists when they went out. Once dropped, he was warned, the rope would whip away in the blizzard's gusty winds, and the homesteader would be left to wander in the icy blasts.

He didn't have to worry about his animals.

His horse and the ducks were in the barn, safely insulated against the storm's fury. The ducks liked to get into the horse's stall, probably because of the warmth, he figured, but lately they'd gotten so fat they couldn't squeeze under the gate. Instead, they'd taken to roosting in the loose hay he'd spread in their enclosure, which he'd moved inside when the nights' temperatures had dropped below freezing.

The only one out in the storm was Rose. He squeezed his eyes shut as he remembered what she was wearing: her usual black coat, a large reddish-pink scarf, and thin kidskin leather gloves. He could only imagine what she was wearing on her feet. There probably wasn't a blanket in the wagon—Clanahan was too stingy to provide something like that—and he was sure she hadn't brought one from the hotel.

Would she know what to do? If she got lost and tried to walk somewhere, she'd be disoriented in this storm almost immediately. In a whiteout, when the snow isolated a person totally and obliterated any points of reference, she could be standing right next to the wagon and not see it.

Please, God, lead her back to me.

✼

Big Ole's steps slowed until at last the big horse stopped. Rose climbed out of the wagon, bracing herself against the frigid wind. She clung to the harness and made her way toward him.

Her feet sank into a drift, and she realized with horror what had happened. The wagon was stuck in the snow. She knelt and dug furiously with her hands to free the wheel, but to no avail. All she accomplished was getting her vastly expensive kid leather gloves soaked beyond repair.

She stood up and grimaced as the wind caught her scarf and blew it off her face. She seized the end just as it was vanishing from sight. The wind was too strong to tie the scarf back on, so she stuffed it into her coat. Surely somewhere along the way, there would be some shelter where she could put it back on or at least find a break in the blizzard winds.

Her coat collar raised in a nearly futile effort to keep the snow from being driven into her face, she floundered through the drift to Big Ole. "I don't know how I'm going to do this," she said to him, "but I think I'm going to have to ride you back to Eric's farm. I'm going to unhitch the wagon, and we'll have to leave it here."

She unhitched one side of the harness. "Mr. Clanahan can charge me whatever he wants for this, but the fact is, Big Ole, we're not going anywhere except to heaven if we stay here."

She reached across and tried to detach the other side, but her fingers were too cold and stiff.

Awkwardly she clambered across the tongue of the wagon, talking to Big Ole the entire time. "Just let me unhook you from this side, and we'll be on our way. I have to confess that I've never ridden without a saddle, and I've certainly never ridden any horse as big as you."

The harness had started to slide, and she ducked under Big Ole's belly. "There, I think I've got it now. Just let me get my bag out of the wagon. It's on the seat, just. . ."

The tiny purse was there, but now it was a snow-covered mound. It was close enough to reach if she just stretched. But as she did, her feet lost their traction in the snow, and her body twisted. She felt the sharp pain in her ankle just before her head made contact with the wagon's edge, and then all was black.

�֎

Eric paced the length of his living room. He could cross it in five steps, and he found himself counting them aloud. "*One*, two, *three*, four, *five*, turn. *One*, two, *three*, four, *five*, turn."

She had to be safe. He wouldn't think of anything else. At the very least, she would have found shelter in another homestead. Thinking of anything else was too dire to even consider.

"*One*, two, *three*, four, *five*, turn."

He couldn't stand it. He was driving himself insane. He had to go look for her. It was foolhardy to go out in this storm. He knew that.

But he was a fool.

He sank to his knees and buried his face in his hands. "God, what should I do? Do I go out there and look for her? How will I find her? Please, dearest Lord, I need some guidance, and Rose—Rose needs Your hand to shelter her from this storm. Please keep her safe." He ran out of words. "Please, God. Please."

With renewed wrath, the blizzard shook the house with a mighty roar. He got to his feet and looked out the window at the snowstorm that was keeping him from her.

The world was entirely white. The sky, the ground, the trees, everything was white. There was no way—

For just a moment, the wind subsided. He blinked and leaned closer to the windowpane to make sure.

Yes, there was something out there, a dark shape that moved, just a bit.

Big Ole!

He yelped with happiness.

The horse had more sense than both of them, and he'd brought Rose back to him.

Chapter 14

Winter is a deadly season wearing a beautiful dress of white diamonds.
It is deceptive and demanding. Do not underestimate its beauty—or its power.

Eric threw on his coat, buttoning it crookedly in his attempt to get it on in a hurry. Hat, gloves, scarf—all went on in a blur.

Rose was back!

He picked up the rope that was already anchored to the porch pole and tied it around his waist. He'd try to get both Rose and Big Ole into the barn and out of the storm. The barn was dry and out of the wind and snow. After she'd recuperated a bit, he'd bring her into the house.

The winds flung icy particles right into his skin, but he didn't feel the bite. Nothing was on his mind except one thing, bringing Rose back safely. If something happened to her, he could never forgive himself.

But God had led him to her.

Thank You, dearest God! Thank You! Now please guide me to her. Let me get her and bring her to me. I can't lose her. I can't.

"Rose! I'm coming! Rose!"

The winds picked up again, but he felt safe, tethered as he was to the house. He'd find her and take care of her. Big Ole was swallowed up by the whiteout, but Eric called, and the horse neighed back.

Good. He was headed in the right direction.

"Rose! I'm coming!"

A tug at his waist told him he had reached the end of the rope. "Rose!" Big Ole snorted, and Eric's spirits sank.

The horse must be a good twenty yards away. It was impossible to judge distance in the storm; every sound was distorted. The rope wasn't long enough.

He didn't dare pray on his knees or even shut his eyes. It was too cold. He shook his hands and tromped his feet, keeping the blood running as he prayed out loud. "What do I do now?" he asked God as he rubbed his hands together. "If I take off the rope, I might be lost, too." He rubbed the snow from his eyes. "But if I don't have her, I'm lost anyway. God, be with me. Stay with me."

The image of Rose, earlier in the summer, sitting outside the barn, going through the harness pieces, sprang into his mind. He'd never really finished that project, and right now the bag was still in the barn, filled with—

"Thank You, God!" he shouted as he made his way to the barn.

He looped and knotted the rope around the latch on the barn door. As he dragged the bag to the door, Sir Gray whinnied from the stall behind him.

"Yes, I'm going to make a rope long enough to take me to Jubilee if I need to," he said to the horse as he spread the contents of the bag on the ground.

He ripped off his gloves, blew on his fingers, and rubbed his hands together. "This goes with this. Buckle this. Tie here." The words ran like a murmur from him as he pieced together the parts.

When at last he had a sufficient length, he untied the rope from the door and knotted it to the leather pieces.

"This should work. It has to work." He anchored the free end to his waist, pulled his gloves back on, and ventured out again.

Walking in a whiteout was unsettling. Without visual landmarks to direct him, even one misstep could spell his doom. He could be headed for the stream, or for the barn, or even back to his house.

Wham! Or for Big Ole. He'd walked right into the large horse, and he laughed with relief. "I've never been so glad to see a horse before in my life."

The huge horse was standing by the wagon. "Stay here," he told the horse as he felt his way to the wagon. "It's unhitched," he muttered to himself as he realized that Big Ole was standing next to the wagon, not in front of it. "How odd."

"Rose?" he called. "Rose, I'm here. Where are you?"

There was no answer, and he began to sweat despite the cold.

He came to the wagon and climbed in it. He sprawled over the bench on his stomach and felt under it, hoping to come in contact with her black cloth coat, but she wasn't there.

Then he felt something under his leg. It was something small, and almost immediately he knew what it was.

Rose's bag. He pulled it out of the snow and held it to his cheek. It was all he had of her.

"Rose!" he called, but the wind tore the word out of his mouth, and it vanished into the distance.

With sinking hope, he climbed into the back and searched there. Again, Rose wasn't there.

Could she possibly be under the wagon? He peered underneath it but saw nothing.

The winds broke a bit, and he saw that he wasn't far at all from the barn. Anxiously he scanned the area, hoping to catch a glimpse of a black coat or a reddish-pink scarf or even—he shuddered—a small bump on the ground that hadn't been there before.

There were drifts but nothing else. There was no way to look for her footprints. The wind had already erased his own.

Rose wasn't anywhere in sight. Could she have made it to his barn? The thought buoyed him.

"Come on, boy," he said at last to Big Ole. "Let's check in the barn. Maybe she's there. We'll get you warmed up, too." He grasped the bridle to draw the horse with him, but the horse pulled back in objection.

"What's the matter?" He ran his hands over Big Ole's body. "You don't seem to be injured. Come with me. You can—"

The horse again refused to go.

"Big Ole, move." He pulled with all his might, and the big horse reluctantly moved away. "Get away from the wagon. I don't know why—" The reason Big Ole wouldn't move was right under his feet. Rose was crumpled in the snow beside the wagon, and Big Ole had been standing over her, protecting her from the blizzard.

Eric dropped to her side. Her face was fearfully white, but she was breathing. He scooped her up cautiously and put her across Big Ole's back. "This is precious cargo," he said to the horse. "Let's take her to the barn."

The wind paused, as if catching its breath before another attack, and Eric took advantage of the increased visibility to lead Big Ole and Rose to the haven of the barn. They picked their way through the snow, which was deceptive with its constantly changing patterns. One spot might look flat when actually it was the top of a drift.

Sir Gray greeted them with a gentle whinny. "Yes, it's your old friend, Big Ole. He's a brave horse, so treat him nicely."

With great care, he lifted Rose from Big Ole's broad back and wrapped her in the horse blankets that were draped across the stable's edge. "They don't smell great, but they're warm," he whispered to Rose.

He threw clean hay onto the floor outside the stable and made a bed for her. "I'm sorry," he said as he moved her blanketed form into the hay. "I wish I had better for you, but this is the best I can do right now."

Her gloves were frozen, and he peeled them off and tucked her hands inside the blanket. "That should help. We need to get you some real gloves if you're going to stay in Jubilee."

The words struck his heart like icicles. *If* she stayed in Jubilee. He couldn't think about her not being here.

He began to check her for broken bones, and she moaned in pain when he touched her ankle.

"I've got to do this," he said aloud as he began to remove her boot. Once again she was wearing those absurd little shoes no thicker than a moth's wing. The right shoe wouldn't come off.

"Sorry," he said to her unconscious form, and with a sympathetic wince, he tore the leather apart.

Her ankle was swollen and discolored. His experienced fingers probed tentatively, and at last he covered her foot with the blanket, convinced she had only a bad sprain.

When he saw that she was settled and breathing easily, he swiftly tended to Big Ole, rewarding him with a scoop of oats and draping him with another blanket. "You're quite the hero," he said, rubbing the horse's ears. "Stay here, rest a bit, and I'll take you back tomorrow or whenever we can get through again. But right now, I need to get back to my Rose."

Rose stirred a bit in the bed of hay, and he went to her. Her face and hands were alabaster white and extremely cold. The danger of hypothermia was very real, and as a doctor, he knew that the most effective treatment was to hold her next to him, to share his body heat with hers. Tenderly he picked her up and cradled her in his arms.

He put his lips against her head. Strands of her hair, usually so completely tamed in the strict bun she wore, had escaped their confines, and he smoothed them down.

God, now that I've got her back, let her live.

Taking her away from him now would be unbearably cruel. He clutched her closer and, his words like a litany, asked God one thing: *Let her live. Let her live.*

Outside, the storm abated until only an occasional blast rattled the wooden boards of the barn, while inside a woman slept and a man prayed.

Chapter 15

Trust is the oddest animal on the prairie. It follows us, dogging our footsteps but always lagging back, just out of reach. Coaxing it to us takes patience and endurance.

At last the storm broke entirely. Early blizzards, Eric knew, often ran out of strength quickly, and this one was no exception. It had been ferocious, though, for seven or eight hours, long enough to remind them of the power of snow and wind.

Eric gently moved Rose back to the hay. She murmured slightly but didn't wake up. His legs were asleep, he discovered as he tried to take a few steps. He frowned. This was happening entirely too often.

"You're getting to be an old man, Johansen," he said aloud.

A drift had built up outside the barn, and Eric had to struggle to get the door open. Finally a mighty shove released it far enough for him to slip out.

He gasped at what he saw. The aftermath of a blizzard never failed to awe him. The last rays of the day's sun glimmered across the dazzling white landscape, and Eric had to shield his eyes against the glare. The snow had lost its threat, and now the ground looked like nothing more than wave after wave of powdered diamonds.

Rose's wagon was just on the other side of the barn. It was stopped at an angle, half-buried in a drift. He shuddered as he thought of how close she had come to dying.

She was going to be fine. The swelling on her ankle had diminished greatly. Her pulse and respiration were nearly normal, and except for a few spots on her face and her fingertips, and possibly her toes, she had escaped frostbite.

There was a bruise on her head, too, where she must have hit it. Her unconsciousness, he knew from experience, probably due more to the cold than to the head injury. People caught in extreme cold tended to fall asleep, and they often died from it.

A duck quacked loudly, objecting to something inside the barn, and the others joined in. They'd awaken Rose for sure if he didn't make the cacophony stop.

He raced inside and smiled at what he saw. Rose was propped up, with Downy, at her feet, glaring at her with indignation. "I think I rolled over on him."

Eric shooed the duck away and knelt beside her. He ran his hand over her forehead and picked up her hand, wrapping her wrist with his long fingers.

She smiled, a bit lopsidedly, but it was a smile. "Do I have a fever? Is my pulse all right, Doctor?"

"Was I that obvious?" He let the reference to his past as a doctor slide by. That would be taken care of as soon as she was back on her feet.

Rose looked around and frowned. "What am I doing in your barn?"

"You had an accident, but you're all right."

She shook her head and stopped suddenly, putting her hand to her temple. "Ouch. I shouldn't have done that."

"Hurts?" His trained fingers probed in her hair. "No swellings or cuts except for the abrasion and contusion over your eyebrow."

She grinned. "Scrape and bruise, huh?"

Downy watched the proceedings with diminishing interest, until at last he waddled to her feet and bit the tip of her left shoe.

"You rascal!" Rose chided as Downy left them to join his fellow ducks in an exploration of the snow-covered world outside. "He bit my—Eric! Did you see my ankle? It looks terrible! And where's my shoe?"

"You've got a badly sprained ankle. As for where your shoe is. . ." He held it up and showed her the torn leather. "I couldn't get it off you any other way."

Rose smiled. "That's okay. I don't think I could have worn them again anyway, not after getting them this wet."

"Are you ready to stand?" Eric asked, and she nodded. His heart felt so light that it seemed it could fly. "Let me help you. Don't put your weight on your bad ankle. Lean on me."

Rose's hair was straggling free of its usually tidy bun, and her coat was missing a button. The bright scarf was half tucked in her collar and half hanging free. Yet she was the most beautiful sight he'd ever seen.

"I think I can do it." She took a few tentative steps with his help and stopped. "I'm a bit shaky."

He needed no invitation. He swept her up his arms and carried her to the barn door.

"I was just going to ask if I could lean more on you when I walked," she said with a wink, "but this is good. This is very good."

If he had his way, he'd never let her out of his arms.

Or so he thought. By the time he reached the door of his house, he'd waded through drifts that came up nearly to his waist, he'd stumbled over a limb that was partially buried in the snow, and his hat had fallen off. His nose was running dreadfully, and his fingers were numb.

Yet he would not let his dear burden down for the world. He carried her inside and put her in the rocking chair. The fire had gone out earlier in the day, but the room seemed immediately warmer with her there.

He got a blanket and wrapped it around her. She smiled weakly and shut her eyes. "Nice."

"Let me build a new fire."

The kindling caught immediately, and soon the logs crackled heartily. He made tea for both of them. "Do you want some lefse, too?" he asked. "I have some. Mrs. Jenkins also gave me some stew this morning. I'd nearly forgotten. Stew and lefse sure would hit the spot, don't you think?"

She nodded.

As he prepared their supper, he asked her, "Do you remember what happened?"

"To me?"

He chuckled. "Yes, you goose. How did you end up with Big Ole as your tent out there?"

"I don't recall everything," she said. "The wagon—oh, the harness. Something about the harness."

"Clanahan's cheap harnesses come apart way too often," he growled.

"Yes! That's it! I do remember!" She sat forward, her hands cradling the mug of steaming tea. "But then we got stuck in the snow, and I decided to come back here, and I had to unhook the wagon."

He rocked back on his heels. "Rose, that doesn't make sense. Why would you unhitch the wagon? How were you planning to get here? You weren't going to walk, were you?"

"No," she said. "I was going to ride Big Ole."

He didn't mean to laugh, but the image of her tiny person atop Big Ole's wide back was too much. "You. . .were going to ride Big Ole?" he asked as he fought for control of his laughter.

Her chin lifted proudly. "Yes, I was. What's wrong with that?"

He pressed his lips together tightly and then said, "Nothing. Absolutely nothing. So how far did you get on Big Ole's back?"

"I didn't even get there. I went back to get my bag, and I lost my footing, and—" She paused. "And I think I fell and hit my head."

"And Big Ole came back to stand over you and protect you," he finished softly for her.

Tears pooled in her eyes. "God was certainly watching over me."

He reached across and touched the back of her hand. "He was, indeed."

"How did you find me? You didn't go out in the storm looking for me, did you?" Her forehead wrinkled with concern.

"A bit," he said. "You were just outside the barn—not far away at all."

The creases in her brow deepened.

"The only way I can figure it," Eric said, squeezing her hand, "is that Big Ole was smarter than either you or I, and he started taking you in a circle from the beginning, intending to bring you back here where you'd be safe. And he did. And you are."

She didn't say anything. Instead, she sat in the late afternoon sunlight, her fingers knotting and unknotting as she blinked rapidly.

"I'll attend to the stew," he said quietly. "You just rest."

Rose must have fallen asleep again, for when she woke, the room was bathed in early moonlight.

"Hello, sleepyhead," Eric said. Her eyes adjusted to the diminished light, and she saw that he was sitting in the corner, his legs stretched out in front of him.

"Oh, I'm so sorry. I didn't mean to fall asleep."

"You needed it. How are you feeling?"

"Much better, thank you. My head still aches but not as bad."

"You hungry?"

"Very much."

She watched as he stood and went into the kitchen. When he came out, he had a bowl with a spoon. "Stew from Mrs. Jenkins."

He didn't look like a murderer, she thought as she looked into his clear blue eyes. He couldn't be a killer. He just couldn't be. Not and risk his own life to save her after all she'd done. She wouldn't have blamed him if he'd just left her outside to die.

The stew was wonderful, rich and hearty. "Did you have some?"

"I did."

Neither of them spoke until at last Eric said, "Rose, I owe you an explanation. I hope what I tell you will make you see why I didn't share this with you earlier."

"You don't have to tell me anything," she began, "and—"

He held up one hand. "No. I have to."

"I'll listen."

He stood in front of the fireplace and stared reflectively at the flames. "I was a doctor in Boston. I did pretty well with my practice, and some of the most influential families came to me for medical care."

Rose put the bowl in her lap, the stew untouched, as he continued his story.

"But my favorite patients were those whose lives weren't touched by grandeur or opulence. I treated many who had no way to pay me at all except with their thanks. It was payment enough."

"Eric—"

"One of those patients was a woman, a young mother. Her husband had died in a factory accident before their child was even born, and the woman and her child lived in a grimy apartment in the dirtiest part of town. Yet she kept her rooms and her child and herself cleaner than many of Boston's finest families."

He sighed. "Then one day she got a cold that settled into her lungs. She coughed fiercely, and I begged her to go to the hospital. She wouldn't—she couldn't leave her son alone. He was just a little fellow, barely four."

"There wasn't anyone who could take him, even for a while?" Rose asked.

"It wasn't that. Other family members offered. I offered to watch him myself, but she had a failing. She was proud. No one—not I, not her own mother—could take care of her son the way she could."

"She must have been terrified."

"I think she was. So I did what I could. I left medicine for her. I. . ." His voice broke, and he visibly struggled with the memory before he could speak again. "I left her extra, in case the first doses didn't bring it under control, as often happens. I knew she'd be too proud—and too ashamed that she couldn't pay me—to call me again if she got sick."

He braced his arms on the mantel, his back still to her. "She was sick, so sick. Her fever was out of control, and I know she must have been delirious. Then. . .her son saw the medicine and decided that if one spoon made her feel better, the whole bottle would make her feel really good, and both bottles would cure her entirely."

"Oh no!" Rose breathed, already seeing where this story was going.

"Yes." His head dropped. "The boy gave her all of it, both bottles. She must have been so feverish that she didn't realize what was happening."

"But why would you...? I mean, how did the story...? That's not murder." Her head was starting to spin, partially from the injury, partially from not eating, but mainly from his revelation.

"No, it isn't."

"So why don't you tell the story? The worst thing you did was have a lapse in judgment, but that's only obvious in hindsight."

He turned around and faced her. The moonlight was bright against the snow, and the illumination that came through the uncurtained window outlined his anguish. "I couldn't let a little boy go through life thinking he'd killed his mother, Rose. He had his whole life ahead of him. I couldn't do it. I couldn't."

She held out her hands to him, and he came to her side and knelt. "I lied on the death certificate. I said she'd died from a lung infection, which was, in a roundabout way, the truth. Her family, though, blamed me, and they were right."

"What do you mean?"

"I never should have left her there, that sick, with just the child to watch over her. I shouldn't have left that much medicine. I was wrong, so wrong. I should have insisted she go to the hospital, insisted her son stay with me, something, anything other than what I did."

"No, no," she said. 'You didn't know. How did the murder charge come about, though? I don't understand."

"I was never charged with murder, but there were enough raised eyebrows and innuendos from her relatives to finish off my medical career. Besides, I just didn't have the heart to stay in Boston and pretend to heal people when I'd just killed someone."

"You didn't kill her."

He shrugged. "That's splitting hairs. No one would expect a child that small to know what to do, and she was so desperately ill. That's why I came here, to Jubilee, to start a new life."

"What happened to her son?"

He looked up at her, a knowingly gentle smile on his face. "Only you, Rose, would think to ask that. I'm glad to say that the little boy has found a good home with a couple who wanted a child very badly. They love him very much, and he's doing quite well."

Tears welled in her eyes as she understood. "You did it, didn't you? You found him a home."

"God did that. I was just His hands."

She picked up his hands and held them to her lips. "They're extraordinary hands, Eric. They can deliver a baby or plant a seed."

"Rose," he said, gazing earnestly into her eyes, "you can't tell anyone. What I've told you must stay between us. I promised God that I would always protect that little boy, and I intend to go to my grave keeping my word."

"I won't," she assured him. "It goes to my grave, too."

"Good. And I also will not lie about it. That was part of the promise. I pledged to God that I would tell this one falsehood but never again."

She clasped his hands tightly. "You can trust me. I won't tell anyone. I know that what you've told me tonight is an act of faith. I've done everything in the world to make you not trust me, yet here you're entrusting me with the most important secret you hold."

"There's another secret," he said, his eyes glowing with reflected firelight. "I've fought it every inch of the way, but I won't anymore. Rose, I love you. I think I loved you the moment you stepped off the train and into my heart."

"And you caught me, and you've held me ever since," she finished. "I love you, Eric Johansen. With every ounce of my being, I love you."

Chapter 16

The starlit prairie has no comparison on earth.
Each glowing star is a kiss from our Creator.

The moonlit ride back into Jubilee was spectacular. Eric had put Big Ole in his barn for the evening and had hitched Sir Gray to his sleigh.

Such peace had come over him that he could almost imagine the stars singing. Rose looked at him and smiled, and he realized that the sound wasn't coming from the heavens. He was humming.

"Happy?" she asked, her hand stealing out to touch his arm from under the buffalo robe he'd taken from his own wagon.

"I am." There was no way to share with her the enormity of relief he felt, no longer under the burden of his secret.

"Eric, I'm sorry for what I did."

"I know that," he answered, and it was true. He did know it.

"Are you still leaving Jubilee?" Her voice was small and hesitant.

"I don't want to," he answered, not daring to look at her. He didn't want to move away and abandon all he had built, but he doubted he could ever feel that this was really home again.

He'd sooner have his tongue torn out, though, than say that to her. She clearly felt terrible about her impetuous outburst in the telegraph office, and he was not going to say any more about it than necessary.

"Jubilee fits you like a good coat," she said.

He laughed, and the sound rolled across the prairie night. "I can see why you're a writer."

"Well, it does," she protested, "and I promise that I'll figure out a way to set things right with the folks in town."

He shook his head. "I don't know, Rose. Trust me. I've been over this twelve ways to midnight, and I can't see any way to fix it."

"We Kellys are a stubborn bunch," she said. "Just wait. I'll figure out some way to deal with this."

When they entered the lobby of the Territorial Hotel, Matthew gaped at her. "What happened to you? Are you all right?"

"I'm fine," Rose said. "I had a bit of a problem during the blizzard, but thanks to Eric here, I'm safe and sound."

"You need more rest," Eric warned. "I'll talk to Clanahan about getting Big Ole and the wagon back to him."

He wanted to kiss her good night, but he settled for an awkward pat on her shoulder.

✶

He was right, Rose realized. She did need more rest. She was just about to start to get ready for bed when there was a knock on the door.

She opened it and saw the young chambermaid. "Sorry, ma'am," the maid said, "but I'm to tell you there're two men downstairs in the reception room."

"Two men?"

The maid grinned. "It's just the minister and the doctor. I think they're both checking up on you."

Rose quickly fixed her hair as best she could and limped downstairs to the small room.

The two men stood when she came in.

"We saw Eric, and he told us the story of Big Ole and how he saved you from freezing to death," the doctor said.

"You do know that you're a very lucky young woman," the reverend added. "Blizzards are nothing to be trifled with. God's hand was certainly on you."

"Eric suggested that we come here to visit with you. He's a bit concerned yet about your health, and he wants to make sure you don't have any lingering aftereffects," Dr. Pinkley said. "You look fine to me—a bit worn, perhaps—but we'd all feel more secure if I took a look at the bump on your head, checked your ankle, and made sure you didn't get frostbite."

"I'm not sure exactly why I'm here." The minister peered at her questioningly. "He told us he'd meet us here. Do you know why?"

"Yes." The single word came out in a whisper. "Yes, I think I do. But I can't tell you. I don't know why he said—"

"It's all right, Rose." Eric spoke from the doorway. "I've thought about it, and these two men are not only the safest folks to trust with a secret; they're the only ones who might be able to help us."

He sat next to her, and under the table, she took his hand in hers as he began to tell his story. . . .

✶

The men pushed back their chairs and stood. "I've heard enough," the doctor said. "I'm entirely satisfied that Eric—Dr. Johansen, that is—is not guilty of anything except a heart that is warm and caring."

"I agree," said the minister. "We'll announce that we've investigated and found your reputation to be above reproach. I believe that for most people, the word of a doctor and a man of the cloth will be sufficient to clear your name, Eric."

"How can I thank you both?" Eric asked, shaking each man's hand.

"Well, the pew where the Nielsen family sits has gotten a bit loose," Reverend Wilton said, "and Grethe Nielsen just told me yesterday that they're expecting the eighth little one come spring. I figure that family alone can keep you busy at Redeemer. Pretty soon they'll be occupying two pews."

"And I sure could use some help when I go out of town. Last year I went to visit my sister in Pittsburgh, and some folks here had the nerve to get sick!" The doctor chuckled. "I'd be honored to have you work with me full time or part time, depending on what you prefer."

"You mean depending on whether I can get my plow back," Eric said with a smile. "I sold it to the postmaster when I was planning to leave."

"Oh, he'll sell it back," Reverend Wilton said with a breezy wave. "I'll talk to him if he gives you any trouble."

"Speaking of trouble," the doctor said with a wink to the minister as the two men stood to leave, "what's this I hear about wedding bells for you and a certain schoolteacher?"

"Linnea? Really?" Rose clapped her hands together gleefully.

Reverend Wilton smiled. "Yes, Linnea and I are getting married."

"Wonderful news, Reverend," Eric said, shaking his hand. "Linnea's a good woman."

The three men discussed the merits of marriage, wheat versus oats, and their hopes for a fairly dry winter, and Rose sat back, smiling. This was home. This was where she needed to be, right here in Jubilee, right here with Eric. She began to relax, and soon she had trouble keeping her eyes open.

She yawned, and Eric apologized. "Here I told you to get some rest and kept you up anyway. Go back to your room and get some sleep. I promise no more interruptions!"

She was so exhausted that the long staircase seemed almost endless, even when she was cradled in Eric's protective arms.

"I prescribe sleep," he whispered at her door as his lips brushed her forehead, carefully avoiding the injured part, and she nodded numbly. All she could think of was sleep.

But what she saw when she went into her room woke her up immediately.

There was a white envelope on the table, with a note on the front: *From the telegraph office.* She tore it open with shaking fingers.

Nothing. Best, Evelyn Roller.

Rose sank down on the bed and laughed until she cried. Evelyn, dear Evelyn, who was quite slow, incredibly accurate—and very late.

Eric had given her back her little bag, and although the dyes from the embroidered rose had run together and some of the beading had come off, her tiny notepad and pen were intact.

She sat down and began to write.

> *This is my last article from Jubilee. If there ever was a place that God touched, where He put His fingertip on a plot of land and called it heaven on earth, it is here. The sky and the earth roll on forever, and at the horizon neither sky nor land ends. Instead, they go on farther than the human eye can see, farther than the human mind can comprehend, but not farther than the heart can know.*
>
> *The people here have welcomed me into their fold. Even when I made terrible decisions—and I've made some spectacularly awful ones—they were ready to forgive. I can never thank them enough for that.*
>
> *My mother, the incomparable Katie Kelly, told me time and again when I was growing up that forgiveness is the finest grace, and while I have to admit that at the time I*

thought those were pretty words but empty ones, now I know that what she taught me is true.

I'm tired as I write this. We've had a fierce blizzard, and I almost died in it. But a homesteader risked his life for me to save my own. You've come to know him through these articles. His name is Eric Johansen.

I arrived in Jubilee with a faith in God that was born into my blood by my parents. Every Sunday, Katie and Patrick Kelly marched me into First Church. I know the apostles' names as well as my own brothers'. I can recite the Ten Commandments, the Beatitudes, and the Twenty-third Psalm.

But nothing prepared me for bringing faith, real faith, into my soul like Jubilee did. Like fine, strong metal, it was forged by fire and grows today.

And certainly I wasn't ready for—

She laid down her pen and rubbed her eyes. She was exhausted, but she had to finish. It was almost done. Just one more paragraph. . .

✻

Big Ole had been returned to Clanahan's, and this time the owner gave Rose a smaller horse hooked to a light sleigh. "Now use some common sense," Mr. Clanahan growled when she got into the sleigh, but his words were gentled with concern.

"I'll keep my eye on the weather," she promised him.

The trip to Eric's farm was easy. The cloudless sky was an astonishing blue, and the snow still sparkled in a glittering display of jeweled white.

He emerged from the barn when she arrived. "Dim-witted ducks," he said good-naturedly. "They've gotten into the oats and made quite a mess. You'll never guess which one was the ringleader."

She stood first on one leg, then on the other, like an anxious schoolgirl. She knew she was grinning, but she couldn't stop.

"You've got some news?" he asked. "I'm about ready for a break. Let's go inside, and I'll make us some coffee."

As soon as he joined her at the kitchen table, one of the few pieces of furniture he hadn't sold, she laid the sheets of paper in front of her. "I'm going to burst if I don't tell you," she said. "It's either the best article I've ever written or the worst. Here. You read." She pushed it across the table to him.

She watched his face as he read. He didn't smile, didn't react at all, and her heart contracted. She'd gone too far with it. If only she could reach across and snatch back the words!

It was too telling. Too forward. Too honest.

He laid it down. "Are you serious?"

"Yes. No. Yes, yes, I am. Or not."

A grin toyed around his lips. "As long as you're sure."

She sat up straight, trying to regain the last shreds of her tattered dignity. "I'm sure."

He gave her back the papers. "Would you read me the last paragraph, please? I want to hear it from your lips."

She cleared her throat and began to read:

"I have fallen in love with the Dakota Territory, with the endless blue skies, with the endless wind, with the endless snow. I have also fallen in love with a Dakota homesteader named Eric Johansen. I am here to stay."

Chapter 17

Love is strong. Stronger than a circus weight lifter. Stronger than a jungle tiger.
Stronger than a prairie blizzard. Yet it speaks with a voice softer than a thought—and we hear it.

Linnea fussed with the bouquet of berries and evergreen branches, charmingly tied with a blue and silver streamer that matched the velvet ribbons in Rose's hair. "If you'd waited," she scolded Rose, "you could have had a wildflower bouquet. Getting married in Dakota during the winter limits what I can do."

"This is beautiful," Rose assured her friend. "It looks like Christmas, which it should, since it is. Christmas Eve, that is."

The schoolteacher grinned. "You have such a way with words."

"I'm a bit nervous," Rose confessed. "Does my dress look all right?"

"You look splendid in it. Freya did an amazing job on it, didn't she?" Linnea stood back and studied the ivory lace dress that the shopkeeper had fashioned entirely by hand for Rose. "It looks like a dress you'd find in one of those fancy stores back east, like Macy's."

Rose swirled, letting the material swish around her ankles. "Actually, I saw one like this in Marshall Field's right before I came out here, and Freya managed to figure out what it really looked like from my terrible drawings."

"She's got quite a talent."

"Please tell me that I didn't get any smudges on it. I hadn't planned on it snowing so hard tonight, or I would have brought it over earlier and left it here."

"No, you're perfect. Just perfect."

"I hope so. Everybody's here. Even my brothers." She peeked through the curtain at the back of the room. "Oh no. My father's got Arvid buttonholed about something, or maybe it's the other way around. If my father goes back to Chicago with a duck tucked under his arm, I'll know that Patrick Kelly has finally met his match."

"Rose, honey." Katie Kelly's soft voice spoke to her from the door. "The wedding's going to start soon. Are you ready?"

"Mrs. Kelly, I forgot your corsage!" Linnea pinned an artful concoction of evergreen sprigs and lace onto the soft buttery yellow dress that set off the older woman's gentle gray eyes.

"It's really lovely," Mrs. Kelly said. "Linnea, you are quite a talented young lady. Thank you so much for doing this."

"My pleasure. Let me check on the men and make sure they've all got their boutonnieres on correctly."

When they were alone, Mrs. Kelly took Rose's hands. "Honey, he is the one, isn't he?"

"Yes, Mama, he is."

"Your father and I like him, although you do know that no one on this earth is suitable for you in your father's eyes."

Rose grinned. "Let me guess. He had a talk with Eric."

"Of course he did." The two women shared a knowing smile. "It's a time-honored tradition. He listed all the things Eric is not allowed to do: make you cry, make you sad, make you worry. . . He's got quite an inventory that he went through. He worked on it all the way from Chicago. Whatever the wedding vows don't cover, Papa added it on. He loves you so. We both do."

"I know that, Mama."

"I have something for you."

Katie Kelly leaned down and took a package from under the dressing table that had been set up in a makeshift bride's room. "My mother did this for me, and I want to do it for you."

Inside the tissue wrapping was a pale blue Bible; on the front etched in silver letters were the words *Holy Bible*, and at the bottom, in elegant script, was *Rose Kelly Johansen*.

"It's beautiful, Mama!" Rose breathed.

"Open it, Rose. I've started the heritage page for you."

In Katie Kelly's fine handwriting, the top line had been inscribed: *Rose Kelly m. Eric Johansen, Jubilee, DT, 24 Dec 1879. "Love never fails." 1 Corinthians 13:8.*

"Oh, Mama." Her voice husky as she fought back tears, Rose embraced her mother. "This is perfect. Thank you so much."

Linnea popped her blond head in. "Ready to go, ladies? It's time."

"Any last-minute advice?" Rose asked her mother as she clutched her hands tightly.

"Just this—remember to love him. Keep him close to your heart at all times. And, Rose, honey, if you two pray together, you'll find your path will be easier. But mainly, Rose, love and respect what you two have together."

Rose smiled. "Mama, how could I do anything but that? You and Papa raised me too well."

"Too well?" Katie Kelly hugged her daughter. "I don't know if there's such a thing as that."

"Now!" Linnea whispered. "Here comes Dr. Pinkley to seat you, Mrs. Kelly. As soon as that's done, we're going to have a wedding!"

Somehow Rose got down the aisle, balanced on the strong arm of her father, although she couldn't remember anything except people watching her and the feeling that she was surrounded by smiling faces on every side.

Everyone she had come to know and love in Jubilee was there, all of them wishing her well in her new life.

Eric was waiting for her in front of the altar, looking stylishly elegant in his new black suit. His hair was neatly combed, and he was more handsome than she'd ever seen him. "You're beautiful," he whispered as he took his place beside her.

"Dearly beloved," Reverend Wilton intoned, and with those well-known lines, the ceremony began.

Before she knew it, she'd said, "I do," been kissed by Eric, and was walking down the aisle, her hand in his.

At the end of the aisle, he drew her into his arms. "Well, Mrs. Johansen, how did you like our wedding?"

"I don't know," she confessed. "I was so nervous that the whole thing was a blur. Say," she said, looking up at him teasingly, "you don't suppose we could do it again, do you? I remember saying, 'I do,' but I'm not sure exactly what I agreed to."

"You promised to love me madly for the rest of your life," Eric said. "And make me lefse at least once a week."

"Now that," Rose said, "I can do. Shall we seal it with another kiss?"

"That sounds like a splendid idea." Eric had just bent his head to hers when Patrick Kelly's voice boomed across the church.

"A duck? What would I do with a duck in Chicago? Put it on a leash and walk it in the park?"

✖

News item, Chicago Tattler

Amidst wreaths and candles, Rose Kelly, formerly of Chicago, Illinois, and Eric Johansen, of Jubilee, Dakota Territory, exchanged Christmas Eve wedding vows in Jubilee's Redeemer Church. The former Rose Kelly was an established society page reporter for the Tattler, *recently recognized nationally for a series of articles about homesteading in Dakota. Dr. Johansen is a farmer as well as a physician in Jubilee. We wish the couple great happiness together.*

ABOUT THE AUTHORS

Rosey Dow is a bestselling and award-winning author with more than half a million books sold. Her novel, *Reaping the Whirlwind*, won the Christy Award for excellence in fiction. A former missionary and lifelong mystery buff, Rosey now makes her home in Delaware, where she edits, writes, and speaks full-time. She invites her readers to connect with her on Facebook.

Cathy Marie Hake is a Southern California native. She met her two loves at church: Jesus and her husband, Christopher. An RN, she loved working in oncology as well as teaching Lamaze. Health issues forced her to retire, but God opened new possibilities with writing. Since their children have moved out and are married, Cathy and Chris dote on dogs they rescue from a local shelter. A sentimental pack rat, Cathy enjoys scrapbooking and collecting antiques. "I'm easily distracted during prayer, so I devote certain tasks and chores to specific requests or persons so I can keep faithful in my prayer life." Since her first book in 2000, she's been on multiple bestseller and readers' favorite lists.

Susannah Hayden lives in Colorado and enjoys life in the mountain sunshine with her husband and grown children.

Yvonne Lehman is author of 59 novels and 12 nonfiction books in the Divine Moments series. She founded and directed the Blue Ridge Mountains Christian Writers Conference for 25 years and the Blue Ridge "Autumn in the Mountains" Novelist Retreat for 12 years. She now directs WritingRight – A Mentoring Service for writers. She is General Editor for Candlelight Romance and Guiding Light Women's Fiction with Lighthouse Publishing of the Carolinas. Among her widely-acclaimed books are *Hearts that Survive—A Novel of the Titanic* and *Moments with Billy Graham.* Yvonne lives in the mountains of western North Carolina which provide the setting for many of her novels.

Colleen L. Reece was born and raised in a small western Washington logging town. She learned to read by kerosene lamplight and dreamed of someday writing a book. God has multiplied Colleen's "someday" book into more than 150 titles that have sold six million copies. Colleen was twice voted Heartsong Presents' Favorite Author and later inducted into Heartsong's Hall of Fame. Several of her books have appeared on the CBA Bestseller list.

In first grade, **Janet Spaeth** was asked to write a summary of a story about a family making maple syrup. She wrote all during class, through morning recess, lunch, and afternoon recess, and asked to stay after school. When the teacher pointed out that a summary was supposed to be shorter than the original story, Janet explained that she didn't feel the readers knew the characters well enough, so she was expanding on what was in the first-grade reader. Thus a writer was born. She lives in the Midwest and loves to travel, but to her, the happiest word in the English language is *home.*